Praise for *The Stories of Edith Wharton*:

"A welcome addition to any library."

—*Library Journal*

"No self-respecting Wharton addict should be without this book."
—*Los Angeles Times Book Review*

"Her work is timeless. An excellent choice for inclusion in fiction collections needing representation by this important writer."
—ALA *Booklist*

"Edith Wharton honestly explored the human questions that engaged her imagination, writing 'only for that dispassionate and ironic critic who dwells within the breast.'"
—*St. Louis Post-Dispatch*

The Collected Stories of
EDITH WHARTON

Selected and Introduced by
ANITA BROOKNER

CARROLL & GRAF PUBLISHERS, INC.
NEW YORK

Published by arrangement with Simon & Schuster, London.

First Carroll & Graf hardcover edition 1990
First Carroll & Graf paperback edition 1991
Second hardcover edition 1998

Carroll & Graf Publishers, Inc.
19 West 21st Street
New York, NY 10010

Library of Congress Cataloging-in-Publication Data is available.
ISBN: 0-7867-0523-X

Manufactured in the United States of America

Contents

Introduction

———❦———

Edith Wharton's autobiography, *A Backward Glance*, is a brilliant exercise in both worldliness and concealment. Both of these qualities are completely authentic: no cover-up is intended. For she was both the great lady she so pleasingly describes and that secret inward-looking creature to whom she only briefly alludes. The writing of fiction – and she was tirelessly prolific, combining her work with an extensive social life – proceeds from the hidden self, a self which exists only on the borders of consciousness. Edith Wharton's outer life was spent in the public gaze. She was *mondaine* in every sense of the word, born into a rigidly stratified society of accepted families, married young to a suitable husband, owner of many beautiful houses, and tirelessly available to a host of friends. She was also a great traveller, a great expatriate, and a great worker: indeed her efforts in the First World War earned her a Légion d'Honneur from the French government. As she tells the story, there would not seem to be either the time or the place for a writer of fiction to emerge and to blossom. Indeed the world in which she grew up saw her literary activity as a sort of aberration or solecism, and only one of her numerous relations ever read her books. Her easy sophistication enables her to dismiss this as she seems to have dismissed every other obstacle in her path.

And yet she was that awkward thing, a born writer. When she was a very small child, before she could read or write, she was subject to compulsive episodes of 'making up'. When one of these came upon her she would seize a book, walk up and down, and chant stories of her own invention, turning the pages at intervals which an adult reader might observe. She was even known to abandon a children's tea party when visited by a sudden desire to 'make up'. Perhaps this is not surprising in a child, but then few children go on to write forty books. The same magic impulse that went into the making up episodes seems to have stayed with her throughout her career, for, as she tells it, she never had to search for a theme or a subject, and even the names of her characters arrived of their own accord, sometimes long in advance of the characters themselves.

Those who seek for a sober explanation for these phenomena would no doubt point to the excellence of her education, the sort of education not enjoyed by anyone today. The young Edith Wharton was allowed to read only the finest works in any language. As she spoke French, German, and Italian from an early age she grew up acquainted with the masterpieces of four languages. At the same time she was introduced to the pleasures of Europe, which was to become her second home, in an age when such pleasures had to be pursued over unmade roads and in occasionally dubious hotels. Although she never went to school, she seems to have had the best and kindest of governesses. And of course agreeable company was assured from the start, the society of old New York reinforcing what her own extensive family habitually provided.

This brilliant education had excellent results. A gracious manner and an inspired way with friends might be qualities one would expect from such an upbringing, but in addition to these qualities Edith Wharton had a characteristic which can only be described as zest. She was zestful in the decoration of her houses, zestful in her long and audacious travels, zestful in the delight and enthusiasm which she felt for her work. She seems not to have known fear or discouragement or everyday depression, but perhaps her innate moral and social code forbade her ever to refer to such moods.

That she was aware of the tensions and restrictions of life lived among others is evident in her writing, particularly in her masterpieces, *The House of Mirth, The Custom of the Country, The Reef,* and *The Age of Innocence.* These novels have to do with the doomed attempts to challenge the social code, but at the same time they establish the very real validity of the Dionysiac impulse at work in the challenger. Lily Bart and Undine Spragg are far stronger than those among whom they attempt to establish themselves, just as the exquisite Anna Leath is weaker than the coarse beings to whom it is her lot to be superior. Yet if society wins every time it is a society of vaguely disappointed and disappointing people, idle, rigid, without ambition. Although not as nerveless as the heroes of her great friend Henry James, Edith Wharton's men are no match for her women.

The enormous power of sex – a phenomenon to which no overt reference is made – is apparent in everything she wrote, for Edith Wharton, married very young, liberated herself when she was forty. Sex to her was not merely an affair of the body but the untrammelled enjoyment of the will and of destiny. Throwing off a situation which she might see as stagnant or sterile, she would nevertheless be acutely aware of the conventions that existed to frustrate the free soul. Thus many of her novels, and many more of her stories, have to do with a particularly worrying situation: how to preserve the freedom of an affair within the bounds of marriage, or, alternatively, how to safeguard an affair by turning it into a marriage. For it is seen clearly that without some kind of control, some kind of recognition, no illicitly joined couple will enjoy any kind of society, least of all its own.

Edith Wharton was a writer of stories before she was a novelist. She was an early contributor to Scribner's Magazine, and her first collection, called *The Greater Inclination*, appeared in 1899, to be followed by other volumes at regular intervals, her last appearing in 1937. They are notable for the fact that although her material might vary her style varies not at all. It is consistently even, restrained, well-bred, yet at times audaciously acute. The acuteness is disguised by the beautiful tenor of the narrative, yet she has uncomfortable things to say about men and women. She notes their fundamental incompatibility, yet she is so good-natured that only rarely do relations between the sexes become acrimonious. There may be undertones of tension and tragedy but they will be kept within noble boundaries. Nobility is perhaps her most striking characteristic, and although she is always willing to amuse she is at her finest when she is serious. And when she is serious she stands, as she herself said of another author, 'so nearly among the first'.

The stories in the present volume have been taken from several of her collections, ranging from the sprightliness of 'The Pelican' of 1899 to the pitiless social sketch entitled 'The Last Asset' of 1908, from 'Autres Temps', a study of divorce and its legacy, dating from 1916, to the complex little tragedy, 'Her Son', taken from the 1933 collection, *Human Nature*. I have included one or two ghost stories, a genre in which she was extremely interested throughout her life, although she was perhaps too well balanced ever to bring it completely to life. The reader will encounter the true Edith Wharton in stories such as 'The Reckoning' and 'The Letters', or 'Atrophy', stories in which the desires of the heart are accommodated only with difficulty. Her surprising diversity, her unexpected depths, and her consistent good manners make of her a bewitching writer, one to whom both truth and good manners remain not only attractive but, on payment of a small tribute, permanently available.

ANITA BROOKNER

The Collected Stories of
EDITH WHARTON

The Pelican

SHE was very pretty when I first knew her, with the sweet straight nose and short upper lip of the cameo-brooch divinity, humanized by a dimple that flowered in her cheek whenever anything was said possessing the outward attributes of humor without its intrinsic quality. For the dear lady was providentially deficient in humor: the least hint of the real thing clouded her lovely eye like the hovering shadow of an algebraic problem.

I don't think nature had meant her to be 'intellectual'; but what can a poor thing do, whose husband has died of drink when her baby is hardly six months old, and who finds her coral necklace and her grandfather's edition of the British Dramatists inadequate to the demands of the creditors?

Her mother, the celebrated Irene Astarte Pratt, had written a poem in blank verse on 'The Fall of Man'; one of her aunts was dean of a girls' college; another had translated Euripides – with such a family, the poor child's fate was sealed in advance. The only way of paying her husband's debts and keeping the baby clothed was to be intellectual; and, after some hesitation as to the form her mental activity was to take, it was unanimously decided that she was to give lectures.

They began by being drawing-room lectures. The first time I saw her she was standing by the piano, against the flippant background of Dresden china and photographs, telling a roomful of women preoccupied with their spring bonnets all she thought she knew about Greek art. The ladies assembled to hear her had given me to understand that she was 'doing it for the baby,' and this fact, together with the shortness of her upper lip and the bewildering co-operation of her dimple, disposed me to listen leniently to her dissertation. Happily, at that time Greek art was still, if I may use the phrase, easily handled: it was as simple as walking down a museum gallery lined with pleasant familiar Venuses and Apollos. All the later complications – the archaic and archaistic conundrums; the influences of Assyria and Asia Minor; the conflicting attributions and the wrangles of the erudite – still slumbered in the bosom of the future 'scientific critic.' Greek art in those days

1

began with Phidias and ended with the Apollo Belvedere; and a child could travel from one to the other without danger of losing his way.

Mrs. Amyot had two fatal gifts: a capacious but inaccurate memory, and an extraordinary fluency of speech. There was nothing she did not remember – wrongly; but her halting facts were swathed in so many layers of rhetoric that their infirmities were imperceptible to her friendly critics. Besides, she had been taught Greek by the aunt who had translated Euripides; and the mere sound of the αἰς and οἰς that she now and then not unskillfully let slip (correcting herself, of course, with a start, and indulgently mistranslating the phrase), struck awe to the hearts of ladies whose only 'accomplishment' was French – if you didn't speak too quickly.

I had then but a momentary glimpse of Mrs. Amyot, but a few months later I came upon her again in the New England university town where the celebrated Irene Astarte Pratt lived on the summit of a local Parnassus, with lesser muses and college professors respectfully grouped on the lower ledges of the sacred declivity. Mrs. Amyot, who, after her husband's death, had returned to the maternal roof (even during her father's lifetime the roof had been distinctively maternal); Mrs. Amyot, thanks to her upper lip, her dimple and her Greek, was already ensconced in a snug hollow of the Parnassian slope.

After the lecture was over it happened that I walked home with Mrs. Amyot. From the incensed glances of two or three learned gentlemen who were hovering on the doorstep when we emerged, I inferred that Mrs. Amyot, at that period, did not often walk home alone; but I doubt whether any of my discomfited rivals, whatever his claims to favor, was ever treated to so ravishing a mixture of shyness and self-abandonment, of sham erudition and real teeth and hair, as it was my privilege to enjoy. Even at the opening of her public career Mrs. Amyot had a tender eye for strangers, as possible links with successive centers of culture to which in due course the torch of Greek art might be handed on.

She began by telling me that she had never been so frightened in her life. She knew, of course, how dreadfully learned I was, and when, just as she was going to begin, her hostess had whispered to her that I was in the room, she had felt ready to sink through the floor. Then (with a flying dimple) she had remembered Emerson's line – wasn't it Emerson's? – that beauty is its own excuse for *seeing* and that had made her feel a little more confident, since she was sure that no one *saw* beauty more vividly than she – as a child she used to sit for hours gazing at an Etruscan vase on the bookcase in the library, while her sisters played with their dolls – and if *seeing* beauty was the only excuse one needed for talking about it, why, she was sure I would make allowances and not be *too* critical and sarcastic, especially if, as she thought probable, I had heard of her having lost her poor husband, and how she had to do it for the baby.

Being abundantly assured of my sympathy on these points, she went on to say that she had always wanted so much to consult me about her lectures. Of course, one subject wasn't enough (this view of the limitations of Greek art as a 'subject' gave me a startling idea of the rate at which a successful lecturer might exhaust the universe); she must find others; she had not ventured on any as yet, but she had thought of Tennyson – didn't I *love* Tennyson? She *worshiped* him so that she was sure she could help others to understand him; or what did I think of a 'course' on Raphael or Michelangelo – or on the heroines of Shakespeare? There were some fine steel engravings of Raphael's Madonnas and of the Sistine ceiling in her mother's library, and she had seen Miss Cushman in several Shakespearian roles, so that on these subjects also she felt qualified to speak with authority.

When we reached her mother's door she begged me to come in and talk the matter over; she wanted me to see the baby – she felt as though I should understand her better if I saw the baby – and the dimple flashed through a tear.

The fear of encountering the author of 'The Fall of Man,' combined with the opportune recollection of a dinner engagement, made me evade this appeal with the promise of returning on the morrow. On the morrow, I left too early to redeem my promise; and for several years afterwards I saw no more of Mrs. Amyot.

My calling at that time took me at irregular intervals from one to another of our larger cities, and as Mrs. Amyot was also peripatetic it was inevitable that sooner or later we should cross each other's path. It was therefore without surprise that, one snowy afternoon in Boston, I learned from the lady with whom I chanced to be lunching that, as soon as the meal was over, I was to be taken to hear Mrs. Amyot lecture.

'On Greek art?' I suggested.

'Oh, you've heard her then? No, this is one of the series called "Homes and Haunts of the Poets." Last week we had Wordsworth and the Lake Poets, today we are to have Goethe and Weimar. She is a wonderful creature – all the women of her family are geniuses. You know, of course, that her mother was Irene Astarte Pratt, who wrote a poem on "The Fall of Man": N. P. Willis called her the female Milton of America. One of Mrs. Amyot's aunts has translated Eurip – '

'And is she as pretty as ever?' I irrelevantly interposed.

My hostess looked shocked. 'She is excessively modest and retiring. She says it is actual suffering for her to speak in public. You know she only does it for the baby.'

Punctually at the hour appointed, we took our seats in a lecture hall full of strenuous females in ulsters. Mrs. Amyot was evidently a favorite with these austere sisters, for every corner was crowded, and as we entered a pale usher with an educated mispronunciation was setting forth to several dejected applicants the impossibility of supplying them with seats.

Our own were happily so near the front that when the curtains at the back of the platform parted, and Mrs. Amyot appeared, I was at once able to establish a comparison between the lady placidly dimpling to the applause of her public and the shrinking drawing-room orator of my earlier recollections.

Mrs. Amyot was as pretty as ever, and there was the same curious discrepancy between the freshness of her aspect and the staleness of her theme, but something was gone of the blushing unsteadiness with which she had fired her first random shots at Greek art. It was not that the shots were less uncertain, but that she now had the air of assuming that, for her purpose, the bull's-eye was everywhere, so that there was no need to be flustered in taking aim. This assurance had so facilitated the flow of her eloquence that she seemed to be performing a trick analogous to that of the conjurer who pulls hundreds of yards of white paper out of his mouth. From a large assortment of stock adjectives she chose, with unerring deftness and rapidity, the one that taste and discrimination would most surely have rejected, fitting out her subject with a whole wardrobe of slop-shop epithets irrelevant in cut and size. To the invaluable knack of not disturbing the association of ideas in her audience, she added the gift of what may be called a confidential manner – so that her fluent generalizations about Goethe and his place in literature (the lecture was, of course, manufactured out of Lewes's book) had the flavor of personal experience, of views sympathetically exchanged with her audience on the best way of knitting children's socks, or of putting up preserves for the winter. It was, I am sure, to this personal accent – the moral equivalent of her dimple – that Mrs. Amyot owed her prodigious, her irrational success. It was her art of transposing secondhand ideas into firsthand emotions that so endeared her to her feminine listeners.

To anyone not in search of 'documents' Mrs. Amyot's success was hardly of a kind to make her more interesting, and my curiosity flagged with the growing conviction that the 'suffering' entailed on her by public speaking was at most a retrospective pang. I was sure that she had reached the point of measuring and enjoying her effects, of deliberately manipulating her public; and there must indeed have been a certain exhilaration in attaining results so considerable by means involving so little conscious effort. Mrs. Amyot's art was simply an extension of coquetry: she flirted with her audience.

In this mood of enlightened skepticism I responded but languidly to my hostess' suggestion that I should go with her that evening to see Mrs. Amyot. The aunt who had translated Euripides was at home on

Saturday evenings, and one met 'thoughtful' people there, my hostess explained: it was one of the intellectual centers of Boston. My mood remained distinctly resentful of any connection between Mrs. Amyot and intellectuality, and I declined to go; but the next day I met Mrs. Amyot in the street.

She stopped me reproachfully. She had heard I was in Boston; why had I not come last night? She had been told that I was at her lecture, and it had frightened her – yes, really, almost as much as years ago in Hillbridge. She never *could* get over that stupid shyness, and the whole business was as distasteful to her as ever; but what could she do? There was the baby – he was a big boy now, and boys were *so* expensive! But did I really think she had improved the least little bit? And why wouldn't I come home with her now, and see the boy, and tell her frankly what I had thought of the lecture? She had plenty of flattery – people were *so* kind, and everyone knew that she did it for the baby – but what she felt the need of was criticism, severe, discriminating criticism like mine – oh, she knew that I was dreadfully discriminating!

I went home with her and saw the boy. In the early heat of her Tennyson worship Mrs. Amyot had christened him Lancelot, and he looked it. Perhaps, however, it was his black velvet dress and the exasperating length of his yellow curls, together with the fact of his having been taught to recite Browning to visitors, that raised to fever heat the itching of my palms in his Infant Samuel-like presence. I have since had reason to think that he would have preferred to be called Billy, and to hunt cats with the other boys in the block: his curls and his poetry were simply another outlet for Mrs. Amyot's irrepressible coquetry.

But if Lancelot was not genuine, his mother's love for him was. It justified everything – the lectures *were* for the baby, after all. I had not been ten minutes in the room before I was pledged to help Mrs. Amyot carry out her triumphant fraud. If she wanted to lecture on Plato she should – Plato must take his chance like the rest of us! There was no use, of course, in being 'discriminating.' I preserved sufficient reason to avoid that pitfall, but I suggested 'subjects' and made lists of books for her with a fatuity that became more obvious as time attenuated the remembrance of her smile; I even remember thinking that some men might have cut the knot by marrying her, but I handed over Plato as a hostage and escaped by the afternoon train.

The next time I saw her was in New York, when she had become so fashionable that it was part of the whole duty of woman to be seen at her lectures. The lady who suggested that of course I ought to go and hear Mrs. Amyot, was not very clear about anything except that she was perfectly lovely, and had had a horrid husband, and was doing it to support her boy. The subject of the discourse (I think it was on Ruskin) was clearly of minor importance, not only to my friend, but to the throng of well-dressed and absent-minded ladies who rustled in late, dropped their muffs, and pocketbooks, and undisguisedly lost themselves in the study of each other's apparel. They received Mrs. Amyot with warmth, but she evidently represented a social obligation like going to church, rather than any more personal interest; in fact I suspect that every one of the ladies would have remained away, had they been sure that none of the others were coming.

Whether Mrs. Amyot was disheartened by the lack of sympathy between herself and her hearers, or whether the sport of arousing it had become a task, she certainly imparted her platitudes with less convincing warmth than of old. Her voice had the same confidential inflections, but it was like a voice reproduced by a gramophone; the real woman seemed far away. She had grown stouter without losing her dewy freshness, and her smart gown might have been taken to show either the potentialities of a settled income, or a politic concession to the taste of her hearers. As I listened I reproached myself for ever having suspected her of self-deception in saying that she took no pleasure in her work. I was sure now that she did it only for Lancelot, and judging from the size of her audience and the price of the tickets I concluded that Lancelot must be receiving a liberal education.

I was living in New York that winter, and in the rotation of dinners I found myself one evening at Mrs. Amyot's side. The dimple came out at my greeting as punctually as a cuckoo in a Swiss clock, and I detected the same automatic quality in the tone in which she made her usual pretty demand for advice. She was like a musical box charged with popular airs. They succeeded one another with breathless rapidity, but there was a moment after each when the cylinders scraped and whizzed.

Mrs. Amyot, as I found when I called on her, was living in a sunny flat, with a sitting room of flowers and a tea table that had the air of expecting visitors. She owned that she had been ridiculously successful. It was delightful, of course, on Lancelot's account. Lancelot had been sent to the best school in the country, and if things went well and people didn't tire of his silly mother he was to go to Harvard afterwards. During the next two or three years Mrs. Amyot kept her flat in New York, and radiated art and literature upon the suburbs. I saw her now and then, always stouter, better dressed, more successful and more automatic: she had become a lecturing machine.

I went abroad for a year or two and when I came back she had disappeared. I asked several people about her, but life had closed over her. She had been last heard of as lecturing – still lecturing – but no one seemed to know when or where.

It was in Boston that I found her at last, forlornly swaying to the oscillations of an overhead strap in a crowded trolley car. Her face had so changed that I lost myself in a startled reckoning of the time that had elapsed since our parting. She spoke to me shyly, as though aware of my hurried calculation, and conscious that in five years she ought not to have altered so much as to upset my notion of time. Then she seemed to set it down to her dress, for she nervously gathered her cloak over a gown that asked only to be concealed, and shrank into a seat behind the line of prehensile bipeds blocking the aisle of the car.

It was perhaps because she so obviously avoided me that I felt for the first time that I might be of use to her; and when she left the car I made no excuse for following her.

She said nothing of needing advice and did not ask me to walk home with her, concealing, as we talked, her transparent preoccupations under the guise of a sudden interest in all I had been doing since she had last seen me. Of what concerned her, I learned only that Lancelot was well and that for the present, she was not lecturing – she was tired and her doctor has ordered her to rest. On the doorstep of a shabby house she paused and held out her hand. She had been so glad to see me and perhaps if I were in Boston again – the tired dimple, as it were, bowed me out and closed the door on the conclusion of the phrase.

Two or three weeks later, at my club in New York, I found a letter from her. In it she owned that she was troubled, that of late she had been unsuccessful, and that, if I chanced to be coming back to Boston, and could spare her a little of that invaluable advice which – . A few days later the advice was at her disposal. She told me frankly what had happened. Her public had grown tired of her. She had seen it coming on for some time and was shrewd enough in detecting the causes. She had more rivals than formerly – younger women, she admitted, with a smile that could still afford to be generous – and then her audiences had grown more critical and consequently more exacting. Lecturing – as she understood it – used to be simple enough. You chose your topic – Raphael, Shakespeare, Gothic Architecture, or some such big familiar 'subject' – and read up about it for a week or so at the Athenaeum or the Astor Library, and then told your audience what you had read. Now, it appeared, that simple process was no longer adequate. People had tired of familiar 'subjects'; it was the fashion to be interested in things that one hadn't always known about – natural selection, animal magnetism, sociology and comparative folklore; while, in literature, the demand had become equally difficult to meet, since Matthew Arnold had introduced the habit of studying the 'influence' of one author on another. She had tried lecturing on influences, and had done very well as long as the public was satisfied with the tracing of such obvious influences as that of Turner on Ruskin, of Schiller on Goethe, of Shakespeare on English literature; but such investigations had soon lost all charm for her too-sophisticated audiences, who now demanded either that the influence or the influenced should be quite unknown, or that there should be no perceptible connection between the two. The zest of the performance lay in the measure of ingenuity with which the lecturer established a relation between two people who had probably never heard of each other, much less read each other's work. A pretty Miss Williams with red hair had, for instance, been lecturing with great success on the influence of the Rosicrucians upon the poetry of Keats, while somebody else had given a 'course' on the influence of St. Thomas Aquinas upon Professor Huxley.

Mrs. Amyot, warmed by my participation in her distress, went on to say that the growing demand for evolution was what most troubled her. Her grandfather had been a pillar of the Presbyterian ministry, and the idea of her lecturing on Darwin or Herbert Spencer was deeply shocking to her mother and aunts. In one sense the family had staked its literary as well as its spiritual hopes on the literal inspiration of Genesis: what became of 'The Fall of Man' in the light of modern exegesis?

The upshot of it was that she had ceased to lecture because she could no longer sell tickets enough to pay for the hire of a lecture hall; and as for the managers, they wouldn't look at her. She had tried her luck all through the Eastern States and as far south as Washington; but it was of no use, and unless she could get hold of some new subjects – or, better still, of some new audiences – she must simply go out of the business. That would mean the failure of all she had worked for, since Lancelot would have to leave Harvard. She paused, and wept some of the unbecoming tears that spring from real grief. Lancelot, it appeared, was to be a genius. He had passed his opening examinations brilliantly; he had 'literary gifts'; he had written beautiful poetry, much of which his mother had copied out, in reverentially slanting characters, in a velvet-bound volume which she drew from a locked drawer.

Lancelot's verse struck me as nothing more alarming than growing pains; but it was not to learn this that she had summoned me. What she wanted was to be assured that he was worth working for, an assurance which I managed to convey by the simple stratagem of remarking that the poems reminded me of Swinburne – and so they did, as well as of Browning, Tennyson, Rossetti, and all the other poets who supply young authors with original inspirations.

This point being established, it remained to be decided by what means his mother was, in the French phrase, to pay herself the luxury of a poet. It was clear that this indulgence could be bought only with counterfeit coin, and that the one way of helping Mrs. Amyot was to become a party to the circulation of such currency. My fetish of intellectual integrity went down like a ninepin before the appeal of a woman no longer young and distinctly foolish, but full of those dear contradictions and irrelevancies that will always make flesh and blood prevail against a syllogism. When I took leave of Mrs. Amyot I had promised her a dozen letters to Western universities and had half pledged myself to sketch out a lecture on the reconciliation of science and religion.

In the West she achieved a success which for a year or more embittered my perusal of the morning papers. The fascination that lures the murderer back to the scene of his crime drew my eye to every paragraph celebrating Mrs. Amyot's last brilliant lecture on the influence of something upon somebody; and her own letters – she overwhelmed me with them – spared me no detail of the entertainment given in her honor by the Palimpsest Club of Omaha or of her reception at the university of Leadville. The college professors were especially kind: she assured me that she had never before met with such discriminating sympathy. I winced at the adjective, which cast a sudden light on the vast machinery of fraud that I had set in motion. All over my native land, men of hitherto unblemished integrity were conniving with me in urging their friends to go and hear Mrs. Amyot lecture on the reconciliation of science and religion! My only hope was that, somewhere among the number of my accomplices, Mrs. Amyot might find one who would marry her in the defense of his convictions.

None, apparently, resorted to such heroic measures; for about two years later I was startled by the announcement that Mrs. Amyot was lecturing in Trenton, New Jersey, on modern theosophy in the light of the Vedas. The following week she was at Newark, discussing Schopenhauer in the light of recent psychology. The week after that I was on the deck of an ocean steamer, reconsidering my share in Mrs. Amyot's triumphs with the impartiality with which one views an episode that is being left behind at the rate of twenty knots an hour. After all, I had been helping a mother to educate her son.

The next ten years of my life were spent in Europe, and when I came home the recollection of Mrs. Amyot had become as inoffensive as one of those pathetic ghosts who are said to strive in vain to make themselves visible to the living. I did not even notice the fact that I no longer heard her spoken of; she had dropped like a dead leaf from the bough of memory.

A year or two after my return I was condemned to one of the worst punishments a worker can undergo – an enforced holiday. The doctors who pronounced the inhuman sentence decreed that it should be worked out in the South, and for a whole winter I carried my cough, my thermometer and my idleness from one fashionable orange grove to another. In the vast and melancholy sea of my disoccupation I clutched like a drowning man at any human driftwood within reach. I took a critical and depreciatory interest in the coughs, the thermometers and the idleness of my fellow sufferers; but to the healthy, the occupied, the transient I clung with undiscriminating enthusiasm.

In no other way can I explain, as I look back on it, the importance I attached to the leisurely confidences of a new arrival with a brown beard who, tilted back at my side on a hotel veranda hung with roses, imparted to me one afternoon the simple annals of his past. There was nothing in the tale to kindle the most inflammable imagination, and though the man had a pleasant frank face and a voice differing agreeably from the shrill inflections of our fellow lodgers, it is probable that under different conditions his discursive history of successful business ventures in a Western city would have affected me somewhat in the manner of a lullaby.

Even at the time I was not sure I liked his agreeable voice; it had a self-importance out of keeping with the humdrum nature of his story, as though a breeze engaged in shaking out a tablecloth should have fancied itself inflating a banner. But this criticism may have been a mere mark of my own fastidiousness, for the man seemed a simple fellow, satisfied with his middling fortunes, and already (he was not much past thirty) deep sunk in conjugal content.

He had just started on an anecdote connected with the cutting of his eldest boy's teeth, when a lady I knew, returning from her late drive, paused before us for a moment in the twilight, with the smile which is the feminine equivalent of beads to savages.

'Won't you take a ticket?' she said sweetly.

Of course I would take a ticket – but for what? I ventured to inquire.

'Oh, that's *so* good of you – for the lecture this evening. You needn't go, you know; we're none of us going; most of us have been through it already at Aiken and at Saint Augustine and at Palm Beach. I've given away my tickets to some new people who've just come from the North, and some of us are going to send our maids, just to fill up the room.'

'And may I ask to whom you are going to pay this delicate attention?'

'Oh, I thought you knew – to poor Mrs. Amyot. She's been lecturing all over the South this winter; she's simply *haunted* me ever since I left New York – and we had six weeks of her at Bar Harbor last summer! One has to take tickets, you know, because she's a widow and does it for her son – to pay for his education. She's so plucky and nice about it, and talks about him in such a touching unaffected way, that everybody is sorry for her, and we all simply ruin ourselves in tickets. I do hope that boy's nearly educated!'

'Mrs. Amyot? Mrs. Amyot?' I repeated. 'It she *still* educating her son?'

'Oh, do you know about her? Has she been at it long? There's some comfort in that, for I suppose when the boy's provided for the poor thing will be able to take a rest – and give us one!'

She laughed and held out her hand.

'Here's your ticket. Did you say *tickets* – two? Oh, thanks. Of course you needn't go.'

'But I mean to go. Mrs. Amyot is an old friend of mine.'

'Do you really? That's awfully good of you. Perhaps I'll go too if I can persuade Charlie and the others to come. And I wonder' – in a well-directed aside – 'if your friend – ?'

I telegraphed her under cover of the dusk that my friend was of too recent standing to be drawn into her charitable toils, and she masked her mistake under a rattle of friendly adjurations not to be late, and to be sure to keep a seat for her, as she had quite made up her mind to go even if Charlie and the others wouldn't.

The flutter of her skirts subsided in the distance, and my neighbor, who had half turned away to light a cigar, made no effort to reopen the conversation. At length, fearing he might have overheard the allusion to himself, I ventured to ask if he were going to the lecture that evening.

'Much obliged – I have a ticket,' he said abruptly.

This struck me as in such bad taste that I made no answer; and it was he who spoke next.

'Did I understand you to say that you were an old friend of Mrs. Amyot's?'

'I think I may claim to be, if it is the same Mrs. Amyot I had the pleasure of knowing many years ago. My Mrs. Amyot used to lecture too – '

'To pay for her son's education?'

'I believe so.'

'Well – see you later.'

He got up and walked into the house.

In the hotel drawing room that evening there was but a meager sprinkling of guests, among whom I saw my brown-bearded friend sitting alone on a sofa, with his head against the wall. It could not have been curiosity to see Mrs. Amyot that had impelled him to attend the performance, for it would have been impossible for him, without changing his place, to command the improvised platform at the end of the room. When I looked at him he seemed lost in contemplation of the chandelier.

The lady from whom I had bought my tickets fluttered in late, unattended by Charlie and the others, and assuring me that she would *scream* if we had a lecture on Ibsen – she had heard it three times already that winter. A glance at the program reassured her: it informed us (in the lecturer's own slanting hand) that Mrs. Amyot was to lecture on the Cosmogony.

After a long pause, during which the small audience coughed and moved its chairs and showed signs of regretting that it had come, the door opened, and Mrs. Amyot stepped upon the platform. Ah, poor lady!

Someone said 'Hush!' The coughing and chair shifting subsided, and she began.

It was like looking at one's self early in the morning in a cracked mirror. I had no idea I had grown so old. As for Lancelot, he must have a beard. A beard? The word struck me, and without knowing why I glanced across the room at my bearded friend on the sofa. Oddly enough he was looking at me, with a half-defiant, half-sullen expression; and as our glances crossed, and his fell, the conviction came to me that *he was Lancelot.*

I don't remember a word of the lecture; and yet there was enough of them to have filled a good-sized dictionary. The stream of Mrs. Amyot's eloquence had become a flood: one had the despairing sense that she had sprung a leak, and that until the plumber came there was nothing to be done about it.

The plumber came at length, in the shape of a clock striking ten; my companion, with a sigh of relief, drifted away in search of Charlie and the others; the audience scattered with the precipitation of people who had discharged a duty; and, without surprise, I found the brown-bearded stranger at my elbow.

We stood alone in the bare-floored room, under the flaring chandelier.

'I think you told me this afternoon that you were an old friend of Mrs. Amyot's?' he began awkwardly.

I assented.

'Will you come in and see her?'

'Now? I shall be very glad to, if – '

'She's ready; she's expecting you,' he interposed.

He offered no further explanation, and I followed him in silence. He led me down the long corridor, and pushed open the door of a sitting room.

'Mother,' he said, closing the door after we had entered, 'here's the gentleman who says he used to know you.'

Mrs. Amyot, who sat in an easy chair stirring a cup of bouillon, looked up with a start. She had evidently not seen me in the audience, and her son's description had failed to convey my identity. I saw a frightened look in her eyes; then, like a frost flower on a windowpane, the dimple expanded on her wrinkled cheek, and she held out her hand.

'I'm so glad,' she said, 'so glad!'

She turned to her son, who stood watching us. 'You must have told Lancelot all about me – you've known me so long!'

'I haven't had time to talk to your son – since I knew he was your son,' I explained.

Her brow cleared. 'Then you haven't had time to say anything very dreadful?' she said with a laugh.

'It is he who has been saying dreadful things,' I returned, trying to fall in with her tone.

I saw my mistake. 'What things?' she faltered.

'Making me feel how old I am by telling me about his children.'

'My grandchildren!' she exclaimed with a blush.

'Well, if you choose to put it so.'

She laughed again, vaguely, and was silent. I hesitated a moment and then put out my hand.

'I see you are tired. I shouldn't have ventured to come in at this hour if your son – '

The son stepped between us. 'Yes, I asked him to come,' he said to his mother, in his clear self-assertive voice. 'I haven't told him anything yet; but you've got to – now. That's what I brought him for.'

His mother straightened herself, but I saw her eye waver.

'Lancelot – ' she began.

'Mr. Amyot,' I said, turning to the young men, 'If your mother will let me come back tomorrow, I shall be very glad – '

He struck his hand hard against the table on which he was leaning.

'No, sir! It won't take long, but it's got to be said now.'

He moved nearer to his mother, and I saw his lip twitch under his beard. After all, he was younger and less sure of himself than I had fancied.

'See here, Mother,' he went on, 'there's something here that's got to be cleared up, and as you say this gentleman is an old friend of yours it had better be cleared up in his presence. Maybe he can help explain it – and if he can't, it's got to be explained to *him*.'

Mrs. Amyot's lips moved, but she made no sound. She glanced at me helplessly and sat down. My early inclination to thrash Lancelot was beginning to reassert itself. I took up my hat and moved toward the door.

'Mrs. Amyot is under no obligation to explain anything whatever to me,' I said curtly.

'Well! She's under an obligation to me, then – to explain something in your presence.' He turned to her again. 'Do you know what the people in this hotel are saying? Do you know what he thinks – what they all think? That you're doing this lecturing to support me – to pay for my education! They say you go round telling them so. That's what they buy the tickets for – they do it out of charity. Ask him if it isn't what they say – ask him if they weren't joking about it on the piazza before dinner. The others think I'm a little boy, but he's known you for years, and he must have known how old I was. *He* must have known it wasn't to pay for my education!'

He stood before her with his hands clenched, the veins beating in his temples. She had grown very pale, and her cheeks looked hollow. When she spoke her voice had an odd click in it.

'If – if these ladies and gentlemen have been coming to my lectures out of charity, I see nothing to be ashamed of in that – ' she faltered.

'If they've been coming out of charity to *me*,' he retorted, 'don't you see you've been making me a party to a fraud? Isn't there any shame in that?' His forehead reddened. 'Mother! Can't you see the shame of letting people think I was a deadbeat, who sponged on you for my keep? Let alone making us both the laughingstock of every place you go to!'

'I never did that, Lancelot!'

'Did what?'

'Made you a laughingstock – '

He stepped close to her and caught her wrist.

'Will you look me in the face and swear you never told people you were doing this lecturing business to support me?'

There was a long silence. He dropped her wrists and she lifted a limp handkerchief to her frightened eyes. 'I did do it – to support you – to educate you – ' she sobbed.

'We're not talking about what you did when I was a boy. Everybody who knows me knows I've been a grateful son. Have I ever taken a penny from you since I left college ten years ago?'

'I never said you had! How can you accuse your mother of such wickedness, Lancelot?'

'Have you never told anybody in this hotel – or anywhere else in the last ten years – that you were lecturing to support me? Answer me that!'

'How can you,' she wept, 'before a stranger?'

'Haven't you said such things about *me* to strangers?' he retorted.

'Lancelot!'

'Well – answer me, then. Say you haven't, Mother!' His voice broke unexpectedly and he took her hand with a gentler touch. 'I'll believe anything you tell me,' he said almost humbly.

She mistook his tone and raised her head with a rash clutch at dignity.

'I think you'd better ask this gentleman to excuse you first.'

'No, by God, I won't!' he cried. 'This gentleman says he knows all about you and I mean him to know all about me, too. I don't mean that he or anybody else under this roof shall go on thinking for another twenty-four hours that a cent of their money has ever gone into my pockets since I was old enough to shift for myself. And he shan't leave this room till you've made that clear to him.'

He stepped back as he spoke and put his shoulders against the door.

'My dear young gentleman,' I said politely, 'I shall leave this room exactly when I see fit to do so – and that is now. I have already told you that Mrs. Amyot owes me no explanation of her conduct.'

'But I owe you an explanation of mine – you and everyone who has bought a single one of her lecture tickets. Do you suppose a man who's been through what I went through while that woman was talking to you in the porch before dinner is going to hold his tongue, and not attempt to justify himself? No decent man is going to sit down under that sort of thing. It's enough to ruin his character. If you're my mother's friend, you owe it to me to hear what I've got to say.'

He pulled out his handkerchief and wiped his forehead.

'Good God, Mother!' he burst out suddenly, 'what did you do it for? Haven't you had everything you wanted ever since I was able to pay for it? Haven't I paid you back every cent you spent on me when I was in college? Have I ever gone back on you since I was big enough to work?' He turned to me with a laugh. 'I thought she did it to amuse herself – and because there was such a demand for her lectures. *Such a demand!* That's what she always told me. When we asked her to come out and spend this winter with us in Minneapolis, she wrote back that she couldn't because she had engagements all through the South, and her manager wouldn't let her off. That's the reason why I came all the way on here to see her. We thought she was the most popular lecturer in the United States, my wife and I did! We were awfully proud of it too, I can tell you.' He dropped into a chair, still laughing.

'How can you, Lancelot, how can you!' His mother, forgetful of my presence, was clinging to him with tentative caresses. 'When you didn't need the money any longer I spent it all on the chidlren – you know I did.'

'Yes, on lace christening dresses and life-size rocking horses with real manes! The kind of thing children can't do without.'

'Oh, Lancelot, Lancelot – I loved them so! How can you believe such falsehoods about me?'

'What falsehoods about you?'

'That I ever told anybody such dreadful things?'

He put her back gently, keeping his eyes on hers. 'Did you never tell anybody in this house that you were lecturing to support your son?'

Her hands dropped from his shoulders and she flashed round on me in sudden anger.

'I know what I think of people who call themselves friends and who come between a mother and her son!'

'Oh, Mother, Mother!' he groaned.

I went up to him and laid my hand on his shoulder.

'My dear man,' I said, 'don't you see the uselessness of prolonging this?'

'Yes, I do,' he answered abruptly; and before I could forestall his movement he rose and walked out of the room.

There was a long silence, measured by the lessening reverberations of his footsteps down the wooden floor of the corridor.

When they ceased I approached Mrs. Amyot, who had sunk into her chair. I held out my hand and she took it without a trace of resentment on her ravaged face.

'I sent his wife a sealskin jacket at Christmas!' she said, with the tears running down her cheeks.

The Other Two

WAYTHORN, on the drawing-room hearth, waited for his wife to come down to dinner.

It was their first night under his own roof, and he was surprised at his thrill of boyish agitation. He was not so old, to be sure – his glass gave him little more than the five-and-thirty years to which his wife confessed – but he had fancied himself already in the temperate zone; yet here he was listening for her step with a tender sense of all it symbolized, with some old trail of verse about the garlanded nuptial doorposts floating through his enjoyment of the pleasant room and the good dinner just beyond it.

They had been hastily recalled from their honeymoon by the illness of Lily Haskett, the child of Mrs. Waythorn's first marriage. The little girl, at Waythorn's desire, had been transferred to his house on the day of her mother's wedding, and the doctor, on their arrival, broke the news that she was ill with typhoid, but declared that all the symptoms were favorable. Lily could show twelve years of unblemished health, and the case promised to be a light one. The nurse spoke as reassuringly, and after a moment of alarm Mrs. Waythorn had adjusted herself to the situation. She was very fond of Lily – her affection for the child had perhaps been her decisive charm in Waythorn's eyes – but she had the perfectly balanced nerves which her little girl had inherited, and no woman ever wasted less tissue in unproductive worry. Waythorn was therefore quite prepared to see her come in presently, a little late because of a last look at Lily, but as serene and well-appointed as if her good-night kiss had been laid on the brow of health. Her composure was restful to him; it acted as ballast to his somewhat unstable sensibilities. As he pictured her bending over the child's bed he thought how soothing her presence must be in illness: her very step would prognosticate recovery.

His own life had been a gray one, from temperament rather than circumstance, and he had been drawn to her by the unperturbed gaiety which kept her fresh and elastic at an age when most women's activities are growing either slack or febrile. He knew what was said about her;

16

for, popular as she was, there had always been a faint undercurrent of detraction. When she had appeared in New York, nine or ten years earlier, as the pretty Mrs. Haskett whom Gus Varick had unearthed somewhere – was it in Pittsburg or Utica? – society, while promptly accepting her, had reserved the right to cast a doubt on its own indiscrimination. Inquiry, however, established her undoubted connection with a socially reigning family, and explained her recent divorce as the natural result of a runaway match at seventeen; and as nothing was known of Mr. Haskett it was easy to believe the worst of him.

Alice Haskett's remarriage with Gus Varick was a passport to the set whose recognition she coveted, and for a few years the Varicks were the most popular couple in town. Unfortunately the alliance was brief and stormy, and this time the husband had his champions. Still, even Varick's stanchest supporters admitted that he was not meant for matrimony, and Mrs. Varick's grievances were of a nature to bear the inspection of the New York courts. A New York divorce is in itself a diploma of virtue, and in the semiwidowhood of this second separation Mrs. Varick took on an air of sanctity, and was allowed to confide her wrongs to some of the most scrupulous ears in town. But when it was known that she was to marry Waythorn there was a momentary reaction. Her best friends would have preferred to see her remain in the role of the injured wife, which was as becoming to her as crepe to a rosy complexion. True, a decent time had elapsed, and it was not even suggested that Waythorn had supplanted his predecessor. People shook their heads over him, however, and one grudging friend, to whom he affirmed that he took the step with his eyes open, replied oracularly: 'Yes – and with your ears shut.'

Waythorn could afford to smile at these innuendos. In the Wall Street phrase, he had 'discounted' them. He knew that society has not yet adapted itself to the consequences of divorce, and that till the adaptation takes place every woman who uses the freedom the law accords her must be her own social justification. Waythorn had an amused confidence in his wife's ability to justify herself. His expectations were fulfilled, and before the wedding took place Alice Varick's group had rallied openly to her support. She took it all imperturbably; she had a way of surmounting obstacles without seeming to be aware of them, and Waythorn looked back with wonder at the trivialities over which he had worn his nerves thin. He had the sense of having found refuge in a richer, warmer nature than his own, and his satisfaction, at the moment, was humorously summed up in the thought that his wife, when she had done all she could for Lily, would not be ashamed to come down and enjoy a good dinner.

The anticipation of such enjoyment was not, however, the sentiment expressed by Mrs. Waythorn's charming face when she presently joined him. Though she had put on her most engaging tea gown she had neglected to assume the smile that went with it, and Waythorn thought he had never seen her look so nearly worried.

'What is it?' he asked. 'Is anything wrong with Lily?'

'No; I've just been in and she's still sleeping.' Mrs. Waythorn hesitated. 'But something tiresome has happened.'

He had taken her two hands, and now perceived that he was crushing a paper between them.

'This letter?'

'Yes – Mr. Haskett has written – I mean his lawyer has written.'

Waythorn felt himself flush uncomfortably. He dropped his wife's hands.

'What about?'

'About seeing Lily. You know the courts – '

'Yes, yes,' he interrupted nervously.

Nothing was known about Haskett in New York. He was vaguely supposed to have remained in the outer darkness from which his wife had been rescued, and Waythorn was one of the few who were aware that he had given up his business in Utica and followed her to New York in order to be near his little girl. In the days of his wooing, Waythorn had often met Lily on the doorstep, rosy and smiling, on her way 'to see papa.'

'I am so sorry,' Mrs. Waythorn murmured.

He roused himself. 'What does he want?'

'He wants to see her. You know she goes to him once a week.'

'Well – he doesn't expect her to go to him now, does he?'

'No – he has heard of her illness; but he expects to come here.'

'*Here?*'

Mrs. Waythorn reddened under his gaze. They looked away from each other.

'I'm afraid he has the right. . . . You'll see. . . .' She made a proffer of the letter.

Waythorn moved away with a gesture of refusal. He stood staring about the softly-lighted room, which a moment before had seemed so full of bridal intimacy.

'I'm so sorry,' she repeated. 'If Lily could have been moved – '

'That's out of the question,' he returned impatiently.

'I suppose so.'

Her lip was beginning to tremble, and he felt himself a brute.

'He must come, of course,' he said. 'When is – his day?'

'I'm afraid – tomorrow.'

'Very well. Send a note in the morning.'

The butler entered to announce dinner.

Waythorn turned to his wife. 'Come – you must be tired. It's beastly, but try to forget about it,' he said, drawing her hand through his arm.

'You're so good, dear. I'll try,' she whispered back.

Her face cleared at once, and as she looked at him across the flowers, between the rosy candleshades, he saw her lips waver back into a smile.

'How pretty everything is!' she sighed luxuriously.

He turned to the butler. 'The champagne at once, please. Mrs. Waythorn is tired.'

In a moment or two their eyes met above the sparkling glasses. Her own were quite clear and untroubled: he saw that she had obeyed his injunction and forgotten.

• II •

WAYTHORN, the next morning, went downtown earlier than usual. Haskett was not likely to come till the afternoon, but the instinct of flight drove him forth. He meant to stay away all day – he had thoughts of dining at his club. As his door closed behind him he reflected that before he opened it again it would have admitted another man who had as much right to enter it as himself, and the thought filled him with a physical repugnance.

He caught the elevated at the employees' hour, and found himself crushed between two layers of pendulous humanity. At Eighth Street the man facing him wriggled out, and another took his place. Waythorn glanced up and saw that it was Gus Varick. The men were so close together that it was impossible to ignore the smile of recognition on Varick's handsome overblown face. And after all – why not? They had always been on good terms, and Varick had been divorced before Waythorn's intentions to his wife began. The two exchanged a word on the perennial grievance of the congested trains, and when a seat at their side was miraculously left empty the instinct of self-preservation made Waythorn slip into it after Varick.

The latter drew the stout man's breath of relief. 'Lord – I was beginning to feel like a pressed flower.' He leaned back, looking unconcernedly at Waythorn. 'Sorry to hear that Sellers is knocked out again.'

'Sellers?' echoed Waythorn, starting at his partner's name.

Varick looked surprised. 'You didn't know he was laid up with the gout?'

'No. I've been away – I only got back last night.' Waythorn felt himself reddening in anticipation of the other's smile.

'Ah – yes; to be sure. And Sellers' attack came on two days ago. I'm afraid he's pretty bad. Very awkward for me, as it happens, because he was just putting through a rather important thing for me.'

'Ah?' Waythorn wondered vaguely since when Varick had been dealing in 'important things.' Hitherto he had dabbled only in the shallow pools of speculation, with which Waythorn's office did not usually concern itself.

It occurred to him that Varick might be talking at random, to relieve the strain of their propinquity. That strain was becoming momentarily more apparent to Waythorn, and when, at Cortlandt Street, he caught sight of an acquaintance and had a sudden vision of the picture he and Varick must present to an initiated eye, he jumped up with a muttered excuse.

'I hope you'll find Sellers better,' said Varick civilly, and he stammered back: 'If I can be of any use to you – ' and let the departing crowd sweep him to the platform.

At his office he heard that Sellers was in fact ill with the gout, and would probably not be able to leave the house for some weeks.

'I'm sorry it should have happened so, Mr. Waythorn,' the senior clerk said with affable significance. 'Mr. Sellers was very much upset at the idea of giving you such a lot of extra work just now.'

'Oh, that's no matter,' said Waythorn hastily. He secretly welcomed the pressure of additional business, and was glad to think, when the day's work was over, he would have to call at his partner's on the way home.

He was late for luncheon, and turned in at the nearest restaurant instead of going back to his club. The place was full, and the waiter hurried him to the back of the room to capture the only vacant table. In the cloud of cigar smoke Waythorn did not at once distinguish his neighbors: but presently, looking about him, he saw Varick seated a few feet off. This time, luckily, they were too far apart for conversation, and Varick, who faced another way, had probably not even seen him; but there was an irony in their renewed nearness.

Varick was said to be fond of good living, and as Waythorn sat dispatching his hurried luncheon he looked across half enviously at the other's leisurely degustation of his meal. When Waythorn first saw him he had been helping himself with critical deliberation to a bit of Camembert at the ideal point of liquefaction, and now, the cheese removed, he was just pouring his *café double* from its little two-storied earthen pot. He poured slowly, his ruddy profile bent over the task, and one beringed white hand steadying the lid of the coffeepot; then he stretched his other hand to the decanter of cognac at his elbow, filled a liqueur glass, took a tentative sip, and poured the brandy into his coffe cup.

Waythorn watched him in a kind of fascination. What was he thinking of – only of the flavor of the coffee and the liqueur? Had the morning's meeting left no more trace in his thoughts than on his face? Had his wife so completely passed out of his life that even this odd encounter with her present husband, within a week after her remarriage, was no more than an incident in his day? And as Waythorn mused, another idea struck him: had Haskett ever met Varick as Varick and he had just met? The recollection of Haskett perturbed him, and he rose and left the restaurant, taking a circuitous way out to escape the placid irony of Varick's nod.

It was after seven when Waythorn reached home. He thought the footman who opened the door looked at him oddly.

'How is Miss Lily?' he asked in haste.

'Doing very well, sir. A gentleman – '

'Tell Barlow to put off dinner for half an hour,' Waythorn cut him off, hurrying upstairs.

He went straight to his room and dressed without seeing his wife. When he reached the drawing room she was there, fresh and radiant. Lily's day had been good; the doctor was not coming back that evening.

At dinner Waythorn told her of Sellers' illness and of the resulting complications. She listened sympathetically, adjuring him not to let himself be overworked, and asking vague feminine questions about the routine of the office. Then she gave him the chronicle of Lily's day; quoted the nurse and doctor, and told him who had called to inquire. He had never seen her more serene and unruffled. It struck him, with a curious pang, that she was very happy in being with him, so happy that she found a childish pleasure in rehearsing the trivial incidents of her day.

After dinner they went to the library, and the servant put the coffee and liqueurs on a low table before her and left the room. She looked singularly soft and girlish in her rosy-pale dress, against the dark leather of one of his bachelor armchairs. A day earlier the contrast would have charmed him.

He turned away now, choosing a cigar with affected deliberation.

'Did Haskett come?' he asked, with his back to her.

'Oh, yes – he came.'

'You didn't see him, of course?'

She hesitated a moment. 'I let the nurse see him.'

That was all. There was nothing more to ask. He swung round toward her, applying a match to his cigar. Well, the thing was over for a week, at any rate. He would try not to think of it. She looked up at him, a trifle rosier than usual, with a smile in her eyes.

'Ready for your coffee, dear?'

He leaned against the mantelpiece, watching her as she lifted the coffeepot. The lamplight struck a gleam from her bracelets and tipped her soft hair with brightness. How light and slender she was, and how each gesture flowed into the next! She seemed a creature all compact of harmonies. As the thought of Haskett receded, Waythorn felt himself yielding again to the joy of possessorship. They were his, those white hands with flitting motions, his the light haze of hair, the lips and eyes. . . .

She set down the coffeepot, and reaching for the decanter of cognac, measured off a liqueur glass and poured it into his cup.

Waythorn uttered a sudden exclamation.

'What is the matter?' she said, startled.

'Nothing; only – I don't take cognac in my coffee.'

'Oh, how stupid of me,' she cried.

Their eyes met, and she blushed a sudden agonized red.

• III •

TEN days later, Mr. Sellers, still housebound, asked Waythorn to call on his way downtown.

The senior partner, with his swaddled foot propped up by the fire, greeted his associate with an air of embarrassment.

'I'm sorry, my dear fellow; I've got to ask you to do an awkward thing for me.'

Waythorn waited, and the other went on, after a pause apparently given to the arrangement of his phrases: 'The fact is, when I was knocked out I had just gone into a rather complicated piece of business for – Gus Varick.'

'Well?' said Waythorn, with an attempt to put him at his ease.

'Well – it's this way: Varick came to me the day before my attack. He had evidently had an inside tip from somebody, and had made about a hundred thousand. He came to me for advice, and I suggested his going in with Vanderlyn.'

'Oh, the deuce!' Waythorn exclaimed. He saw in a flash what had happened. The investment was an alluring one, but required negotiation. He listed quietly while Sellers put the case before him, and, the statement ended, he said: 'You think I ought to see Varick?'

'I'm afraid I can't as yet. The doctor is obdurate. And this thing can't wait. I hate to ask you, but no one else in the office knows the ins and outs of it.'

Waythorn stood silent. He did not care a farthing for the success of Varick's venture, but the honor of the office was to be considered, and he could hardly refuse to oblige his partner.

'Very well,' he said, 'I'll do it.'

That afternoon, apprised by telephone, Varick called at the office. Waythorn, waiting in his private room, wondered what the others thought of it. The newspapers, at the time of Mrs. Waythorn's marriage, had acquainted their readers with every detail of her previous matrimonial ventures, and Waythorn could fancy the clerks smiling behind Varick's back as he was ushered in.

Varick bore himself admirably. He was easy without being undignified, and Waythorn was conscious of cutting a much less impressive figure. Varick had no experience of business, and the talk prolonged itself for nearly an hour while Waythorn set forth with scrupulous precision the details of the proposed transaction.

'I'm awfully obliged to you,' Varick said as he rose. 'The fact is I'm not used to having much money to look after, and I don't want to make an ass of myself – ' He smiled, and Waythorn could not help noticing that there was something pleasant about his smile. 'It feels uncommonly queer to have enough cash to pay one's bills. I'd have sold my soul for it a few years ago!'

Waythorn winced at the allusion. He had heard it rumoured that a lack of funds had been one of the determining causes of the Varick separation, but it did not occur to him that Varick's words were intentional. It seemed more likely that the desire to keep clear of embarrassing topics had fatally drawn him into one. Waythorn did not wish to be outdone in civility.

'We'll do the best we can for you,' he said. 'I think this is a good thing you're in.'

'Oh, I'm sure it's immense. It's awfully good of you – ' Varick broke off, embarrassed. 'I suppose the thing's settled now.– but if – '

'If anything happens before Sellers is about, I'll see you again,' said Waythorn quietly. He was glad, in the end, to appear the more self-possessed of the two.

The course of Lily's illness ran smooth, and as the days passed Waythorn grew used to the idea of Haskett's weekly visit. The first time the day came round, he stayed out late, and questioned his wife as to the visit on his return. She replied at once that Haskett had merely seen the nurse downstairs, as the doctor did not wish anyone in the child's sickroom till after the crisis.

The following week Waythorn was again conscious of the recurrence of the day, but had forgotten it by the time he came home to dinner. The crisis of the disease came a few days later, with a rapid decline of fever, and the little girl was pronounced out of danger. In the rejoicing which ensued the thought of Haskett passed out of Waythorn's mind, and one afternoon, letting himself into the house with a latchkey, he went straight to his library without noticing a shabby hat and umbrella in the hall.

In the library he found a small effaced-looking man with a thinnish gray beard sitting on the edge of a chair. The stranger might have been a piano tuner, or one of those mysteriously efficient persons who are summoned in emergencies to adjust some detail of the domestic machinery. He blinked at Waythorn through a pair of gold-rimmed spectacles and said mildly: 'Mr. Waythorn, I presume? I am Lily's father.'

Waythorn flushed. 'Oh – ' he stammered uncomfortably. He broke off, disliking to appear rude. Inwardly he was trying to adjust the actual Haskett to the image of him projected by his wife's reminiscences. Waythorn had been allowed to infer that Alice's first husband was a brute.

'I am sorry to intrude,' said Haskett, with his over-the-counter politeness.

'Don't mention it,' returned Waythorn, collecting himself. 'I suppose the nurse has been told?'

'I presume so. I can wait,' said Haskett. He had a resigned way of speaking, as though life had worn down his natural powers of resistance.

Waythorn stood on the threshold, nervously pulling off his gloves.

'I'm sorry you've been detained. I will send for the nurse,' he said, and as he opened the door he added with an effort: 'I'm glad we can give you a good report of Lily.' He winced as the *we* slipped out, but Haskett seemed not to notice it.

'Thank you, Mr. Waythorn. It's been an anxious time for me.'

'Ah, well, that's past. Soon she'll be able to go to you.' Waythorn nodded and passed out.

In his own room he flung himself down with a groan. He hated the womanish sensibility which made him suffer so acutely from the grotesque chances of life. He had known when he married that his wife's former husbands were both living, and that amid the multiplied contacts of modern existence there were a thousand chances to one that he would run against one or the other, yet he found himself as much disturbed by his brief encounter with Haskett as though the law had not obligingly removed all difficulties in the way of their meeting.

Waythorn sprang up and began to pace the room nervously. He had not suffered half as much from his two meetings with Varick. It was Haskett's presence in his own house that made the situation so intolerable. He stood still, hearing steps in the passage.

'This way, please,' he heard the nurse say. Haskett was being taken upstairs, then: not a corner of the house but was open to him. Waythorn dropped into another chair, staring vaguely ahead of him. On his dressing table stood a photograph of Alice, taken when he had first known her. She was Alice Varick then – how fine and exquisite he had thought her! Those were Varick's pearls about her neck. At Waythorn's instance they had been returned before her marriage. Had Haskett ever given her any trinkets – and what had become of them, Waythorn wondered? He realized suddenly that he knew very little of Haskett's past or present situation; but from the man's appearance and manner of speech he could reconstruct with curious precision the surroundings of Alice's first marriage. And it startled him to think that she had, in the background of her life, a phase of existence so different from anything with which he had connected her. Varick, whatever his faults, was a gentleman, in the conventional, traditional sense of the term: the sense which at that moment seemed, oddly enough, to have most meaning to Waythorn. He and Varick had the same social habits, spoke the same language, understood the same allusions. But this other man . . . it was grotesquely uppermost in Waythorn's mind that Haskett had worn a made-up tie attached with an elastic. Why should that ridiculous detail symbolize the whole man? Waythorn was exasperated by his own paltriness, but the fact of the tie expanded, forced itself on him, became as it were the key to Alice's past. He could see her, as Mrs. Haskett, sitting in a 'front parlor' furnished in plush, with a pianola, and a copy of *Ben Hur* on the center table. He could see her going to the theater with Haskett – or perhaps even to a 'Church Sociable' – she in the 'picture hat' and Haskett in a black frock coat, a little creased, with the made-up tie on an elastic. On the way home they would stop and look at the illuminated shop windows, lingering over the photographs of New York actresses. On Sunday afternoons Haskett would take her for a walk, pushing Lily ahead of them in a white enameled perambulator, and Waythorn had a vision of the people they would stop and talk to. He could fancy how pretty Alice must have looked, in a dress adroitly constructed from the hints of a New York fashion paper, and how she must have looked down on the other women, chafing at her life, and secretly feeling that she belonged in a bigger place.

For the moment his foremost thought was one of wonder at the way in which she had shed the phase of existence which her marriage with Haskett implied. It was as if her whole aspect, every gesture, every inflection, every allusion, were a studied negation of that period of her life. If she had denied being married to Haskett she could hardly have stood more convicted of duplicity than in this obliteration of the self which had been his wife.

Waythorn started up, checking himself in the analysis of her motives. What right had he to create a fantastic effigy of her and then pass judgment on it? She had spoken vaguely of her first marriage as unhappy, had hinted, with becoming reticence, that Haskett had wrought havoc among her young illusions. . . . It was a pity for Waythorn's peace of mind that Haskett's very inoffensiveness shed a new light on the nature of those illusions. A man would rather think that his wife has been brutalized by her first husband than that the process has been reversed.

• IV •

'MR. WAYTHORN, I don't like that French governess of Lily's.'

Haskett, subdued and apologetic, stood before Waythorn in the library, revolving his shabby hat in his hand.

Waythorn, surprised in his armchair over the evening paper, stared back perplexedly at his visitor.

'You'll excuse my asking to see you,' Haskett continued. 'But this is my last visit, and I thought if I could have a word with you it would be a better way than writing to Mrs. Waythorn's lawyer.'

Waythorn rose uneasily. He did not like the French governess either; but that was irrelevant.

'I am not so sure of that,' he returned stiffly; 'but since you wish it I will give your message to – my wife.' He always hesitated over the possessive pronoun in addressing Haskett.

The latter sighed. 'I don't know as that will help much. She didn't like it when I spoke to her.'

Waythorn turned red. 'When did you see her?' he asked.

'Not since the first day I came to see Lily – right after she was taken sick. I remarked to her then that I didn't like the governess.'

Waythorn made no answer. He remembered distinctly that, after that first visit, he had asked his wife if she had seen Haskett. She had lied to him then, but she had respected his wishes since; and the incident cast a curious light on her character. He was sure she would not have seen Haskett that first day if she had divined that Waythorn would object, and the fact that she did not divine it was almost as disagreeable to the latter as the discovery that she had lied to him.

'I don't like the woman,' Haskett was repeating with mild persistency. 'She ain't straight, Mr. Waythorn – she'll teach the child to be underhand. I've noticed a change in Lily – she's too anxious to please – and she don't always tell the truth. She used to be the straightest child, Mr. Waythorn – ' He broke off, his voice a little thick. 'Not but what I want her to have a stylish education,' he ended.

Waythorn was touched. 'I'm sorry, Mr. Haskett; but frankly, I don't quite see what I can do.'

Haskett hesitated. Then he laid his hat on the table, and advanced to the hearthrug, on which Waythorn was standing. There was nothing aggressive in his manner, but he had the solemnity of a timid man resolved on a decisive measure.

'There's just one thing you can do, Mr. Waythorn,' he said. 'You can remind Mrs. Waythorn that, by the decree of the courts, I am entitled to have a voice in Lily's bringing-up.' He paused, and went on more deprecatingly: 'I'm not the kind to talk about enforcing my rights, Mr. Waythorn. I don't know as I think a man is entitled to rights he hasn't known how to hold on to; but this business of the child is different. I've never let go there – and I never mean to.'

The scene left Waythorn deeply shaken. Shamefacedly, in indirect ways, he had been finding out about Haskett; and all that he had learned was favorable. The little man, in order to be near his daughter, had sold

out his share in a profitable business in Utica, and accepted a modest
clerkship in a New York manufacturing house. He boarded in a shabby
street and had few acquaintances. His passion for Lily filled his life.
Waythorn felt that this exploration of Haskett was like groping about
with a dark lantern in his wife's past; but he saw now that there were
recesses his lantern had not explored. He had never inquired into the
exact circumstances of his wife's first matrimonial rupture. On the
surface all had been fair. It was she who had obtained the divorce, and
the court had given her the child. But Waythorn knew how many
ambiguities such a verdict might cover. The mere fact that Haskett
retained a right over his daughter implied an unsuspected compromise.
Waythorn was an idealist. He always refused to recognize unpleasant
contingencies till he found himself confronted with them, and then he
saw them followed by a spectral train of consequences. His next days
were thus haunted, and he determined to try to lay the ghosts by
conjuring them up in his wife's presence.

When he repeated Haskett's request a flame of anger passed over
her face; but she subdued it instantly and spoke with a slight quiver of
outraged motherhood.

'It is very ungentlemanly of him,' she said.

The word grated on Waythorn. 'That is neither here nor there. It's
a bare question of rights.'

She murmured: 'It's not as if he could ever be a help to Lily – '

Waythorn flushed. This was even less to his taste. 'The question is,'
he repeated, 'what authority has he over her?'

She looked downward, twisting herself a little in her seat. 'I am
willing to see him – I thought you objected,' she faltered.

In a flash he understood that she knew the extent of Haskett's claims.
Perhaps it was not the first time she had resisted them.

'My objecting has nothing to do with it,' he said coldly; 'if Haskett
has a right to be consulted you must consult him.'

She burst into tears, and he saw that she expected him to regard
her as a victim.

Haskett did not abuse his rights. Waythorn had felt miserably sure
that he would not. But the governess was dismissed, and from time to
time the little man demanded an interview with Alice. After the first
outburst she accepted the situation with her usual adaptability. Haskett
had once reminded Waythorn of the piano tuner, and Mrs. Waythorn,
after a month or two, appeared to class him with that domestic familiar.
Waythorn could not but respect the father's tenacity. At first he had
tried to cultivate the suspicion that Haskett might be 'up to' something,
that he had an object in securing a foothold in the house. But in his heart
Waythorn was sure of Haskett's single-mindedness; he even guessed in
the latter a mild contempt for such advantages as his relation with the

Waythorns might offer. Haskett's sincerity of purpose made him in vulnerable, and his successor had to accept him as a lien on the property.

Mr. Sellers was sent to Europe to recover from his gout, and Varick's affairs hung on Waythorn's hands. The negotiations were prolonged and complicated; they necessitated frequent conferences between the two men, and the interests of the firm forbade Waythorn's suggesting that his client should transfer his business to another officer.

Varick appeared well in the transaction. In moments of relaxation his coarse streak appeared, and Waythorn dreaded his geniality; but in the office he was concise and clear-headed, with a flattering deference to Waythorn's judgment. Their business relations being so affably established, it would have been absurd for the two men to ignore each other in society. The first time they met in a drawing-room, Varick took up their intercourse in the same easy key, and his hostess' grateful glance obliged Waythorn to respond to it. After that they ran across each other frequently, and one evening at a ball Waythorn, wandering through the remoter rooms, came upon Varick seated beside his wife. She colored a little, and faltered in what she was saying; but Varick nodded to Waythorn without rising, and the latter strolled on.

In the carriage, on the way home, he broke out nervously: 'I didn't know you spoke to Varick.'

Her voice trembled a little. 'It's the first time – he happened to be standing near me; I didn't know what to do. It's so awkward, meeting everywhere – and he said you had been very kind about some business.'

'That's different,' said Waythorn.

She paused a moment. 'I'll do just as you wish,' she returned pliantly. 'I thought it would be less awkward to speak to him when we meet.'

Her pliancy was beginning to sicken him. Had she really no will of her own – no theory about her relation to these men? She had accepted Haskett – did she mean to accept Varick? It was 'less awkward,' as she had said, and her instinct was to evade difficulties or to circumvent them. With sudden vividness Waythorn saw how the instinct had developed. She was 'as easy as an old shoe' – a shoe that too many feet had worn. Her elasticity was the result of tension in too many different directions. Alice Haskett – Alice Varick – Alice Waythorn – she had been each in turn, and had left hanging to each name a little of her privacy, a little of her personality, a little of the inmost self where the unknown god abides.

'Yes – it's better to speak to Varick,' said Waythorn wearily.

• V •

THE winter wore on, and society took advantage of the Waythorn's acceptance of Varick. Harassed hostesses were grateful to them for bridging over a social difficulty, and Mrs. Waythorn was held up as a miracle of good taste. Some experimental spirits could not resist the diversion of throwing Varick and his former wife together, and there were those who thought he found a zest in the propinquity. But Mrs. Waythorn's conduct remained irreproachable. She neither avoided Varick nor sought him out. Even Waythorn could not but admit that she had discovered the solution of the newest social problem.

He had married her without giving much though to that problem. He had fancied that a woman can shed her past like a man. But now he saw that Alice was bound to hers both by the circumstances which forced her into continued relation with it, and by the traces it had left on her nature. With grim irony Waythorn compared himself to a member of a syndicate. He held so many shares in his wife's personality and his predecessors were his partners in the business. If there had been any element of passion in the transaction he would have felt less deteriorated by it. The fact that Alice took her change of husbands like a change of weather reduced the situation to mediocrity. He could have forgiven her for blunders, for excesses; for resisting Haskett, for yielding to Varick; for anything but her acquiescence and her tact. She reminded him of a juggler tossing knives; but the knives were blunt and she knew they would never cut her.

And then, gradually, habit formed a protecting surface for his sensibilities. If he paid for each day's comfort with the small change of his illusions, he grew daily to value the comfort more and set less store upon the coin. He had drifted into a dulling propinquity with Haskett and Varick and he took refuge in the cheap revenge of satirizing the situation. He even began to reckon up the advantages which accrued from it, to ask himself if it were not better to own a third of a wife who knew how to make a man happy than a whole one who had lacked opportunity to acquire the art. For it *was* an art, and made up, like all others, of concessions, eliminations, and embellishments; of lights judiciously thrown and shadows skillfully softened. His wife knew exactly how to manage the lights, and he knew exactly to what training she owed her skill. He even tried to trace the source of his obligations, to discriminate between the influences which had combined to produce his domestic happiness: he perceived that Haskett's commonness had made Alice worship good breeding, while Varick's liberal construction of the marriage bond had taught her to value the conjugal virtues; so that he was directly indebted to his predecessors for the devotion which made his life easy if not inspiring.

From this phase he passed into that of complete acceptance. He

ceased to satirize himself because time dulled the irony of the situation
and the joke lost its humor with its sting. Even the sight of Haskett's
hat on the hall table had ceased to touch the springs of epigram. The
hat was often seen there now, for it had been decided that it was
better for Lily's father to visit her than for the little girl to go to his
boardinghouse. Waythorn, having acquiesced in this arrangement, had
been surprised to find how little difference it made. Haskett was never
obtrusive, and the few visitors who met him on the stairs were unaware
of his identity. Waythorn did not know how often he saw Alice, but
with himself Haskett was seldom in contact.

One afternoon, however, he learned on entering that Lily's father
was waiting to see him. In the library he found Haskett occupying a
chair in his usual provisional way. Waythorn always felt grateful to
him for not leaning back.

'I hope you'll excuse me, Mr. Waythorn,' he said rising. 'I wanted
to see Mrs. Waythorn about Lily, and your man asked me to wait here
till she came in.'

'Of course,' said Waythorn, remembering that a sudden leak had
that morning given over the drawing room to the plumbers.

He opened his cigar case and held it out to his visitor, and Haskett's
acceptance seemed to mark a fresh stage in their intercourse. The spring
evening was chilly, and Waythorn invited his guest to draw up his chair
to the fire. He meant to find an excuse to leave Haskett in a moment;
but he was tired and cold, and after all the little man no longer jarred
on him.

The two were enclosed in the intimacy of their blended cigar smoke
when the door opened and Varick walked into the room. Waythorn
rose abruptly. It was the first time that Varick had come to the house,
and the surprise of seeing him, combined with the singular inopportune-
ness of his arrival, gave a new edge to Waythorn's blunted sensibilities.
He stared at his visitor without speaking.

Varick seemed too preoccupied to notice his host's embarrassment.

'My dear fellow,' he exclaimed in his most expansive tone, 'I must
apologize for tumbling in on you in this way, but I was too late to
catch you downtown, and so I thought – '

He stopped short, catching sight of Haskett, and his sanguine color
deepened to a flush which spread vividly under his scant blond hair.
But in a moment he recovered himself and nodded slightly. Haskett
returned the bow in silence, and Waythorn was still groping for speech
when the footman came in carrying a tea table.

The intrusion offered a welcome vent to Waythorn's nerves. 'What
the deuce are you bringing this here for?' he said sharply.

'I beg your pardon, sir, but the plumbers are still in the drawing
room, and Mrs. Waythorn said she would have tea in the library.' The

footman's perfectly respectful tone implied a reflection on Waythorn's reasonableness.

'Oh, very well,' said the latter resignedly, and the footman proceeded to open the folding tea table and set out its complicated appointments. While this interminable process continued the three men stood motionless, watching it with a fascinated stare, till Waythorn, to break the silence, said to Varick, 'Won't you have a cigar?'

He held out the case he had just tendered to Haskett, and Varick helped himself with a smile. Waythorn looked about for a match, and finding none, proffered a light from his own cigar. Haskett, in the background, held his ground mildly, examining his cigar tip now and then, and stepping forward at the right moment to knock its ash into the fire.

The footman at last withdrew, and Varick immediately began: 'If I could just say half a word to you about this business – '

'Certainly,' stammered Waythorn; 'in the dining room – '

But as he placed his hand on the door it opened from without, and his wife appeared on the threshold.

She came in fresh and smiling, in her street dress and hat, shedding a fragrance from the boa which she loosened in advancing.

'Shall we have tea in here, dear?' she began; and then she caught sight of Varick. Her smiled deepened, veiling a slight tremor of surprise. 'Why, how do you do?' she said with a distinct note of pleasure.

As she shook hands with Varick she saw Haskett standing behind him. Her smile faded for a moment, but she recalled it quickly, with a scarcely perceptible side glance at Waythorn.

'How do you do, Mr. Haskett?' she said, and shook hands with him a shade less cordially.

The three men stood awkwardly before her, till Varick, always the most self-possessed, dashed into an explanatory phrase.

'We – I had to see Waythorn a moment on business,' he stammered, brick-red from chin to nape.

Haskett stepped forward with his air of mild obstinacy. 'I am sorry to intrude; but you appointed five o'clock – ' he directed his resigned glance to the timepiece on the mantel.

She swept aside their embarrassment with a charming gesture of hospitality.

'I'm so sorry – I'm always late; but the afternoon was so lovely.' She stood drawing off her gloves, propitiatory and graceful, diffusing about her a sense of ease and familiarity in which the situation lost its grotesqueness. 'But before talking business,' she added brightly, 'I'm sure everyone wants a cup of tea.'

She dropped into her low chair by the tea table, and the two visitors, as if drawn by her smile, advanced to receive the cups she held out.

She glanced about for Waythorn, and he took the third cup with a laugh.

The Mission of Jane

————— ✦ —————

LETHBURY, SURVEYING his wife across the dinner table, found his transient glance arrested by an indefinable change in her appearance.

'How smart you look! Is that a new gown?' he asked.

Her answering look seemed to deprecate his charging her with the extravagance of wasting a new gown on him, and he now perceived that the change lay deeper than any accident of dress. At the same time, he noticed that she betrayed her consciousness of it by a delicate, almost frightened blush. It was one of the compensations of Mrs. Lethbury's protracted childishness that she still blushed as prettily as at eighteen. Her body had been privileged not to outstrip her mind, and the two, as it seemed to Lethbury, were destined to travel together through an eternity of girlishness.

'I don't know what you mean,' she said.

Since she never did, he always wondered at her bringing this out as a fresh grievance against him; but his wonder was unresentful, and he said good-humoredly: 'You sparkle so that I thought you had on your diamonds.'

She sighed and blushed again.

'It must be,' he continued, 'that you've been to a dressmaker's opening. You're absolutely brimming with illicit enjoyment.'

She stared again, this time at the adjective. His adjectives always embarrassed her; their unintelligibleness savored of impropriety.

'In short,' he summed up, 'you've been doing something that you're thoroughly ashamed of.'

To his surprise she retorted: 'I don't see why I should be ashamed of it!'

Lethbury leaned back with a smile of enjoyment. When there was nothing better going he always liked to listen to her explanations.

'Well – ?' he said.

She was becoming breathless and ejaculatory. 'Of course you'll laugh – you laugh at everything!'

'That rather blunts the point of my derision, doesn't it?' he interjected; but she pushed on without noticing.

32

'It's so easy to laugh at things.'

'Ah,' murmured Lethbury with relish, 'that's Aunt Sophronia's, isn't it?'

Most of his wife's opinions were heirlooms, and he took a quaint pleasure in tracing their descent. She was proud of their age, and saw no reason for discarding them while they were still serviceable. Some, of course, were so fine that she kept them for state occasions, like her great-grandmother's Crown Derby; but from the lady know as Aunt Sophronia she had inherited a stout set of everyday prejudices that were practically as good as new; whereas her husband's, as she noticed, were always having to be replaced. In the early days she had fancied there might be a certain satisfaction in taxing him with the fact; but she had long since been silenced by the reply: 'My dear, I'm not a rich man, but I never use an opinion twice if I can help it.'

She was reduced, therefore, to dwelling on his moral deficiencies; and one of the most obvious of these was his refusal to take things seriously. On this occasion, however, some ulterior purpose kept her from taking up his taunt.

'I'm not in the least ashamed!' she repeated, with the air of shaking a banner to the wind; but the domestic atmosphere being calm, the banner drooped unheroically.

'That,' said Lethbury judicially, 'encourages me to infer that you ought to be, and that, consequently, you've been giving yourself the unusual pleasure of doing something I shouldn't approve of.'

She met this with an almost solemn directness.

'No,' she said. 'You won't approve of it. I've allowed for that.'

'Ah,' he exclaimed, setting down his liqueur glass. 'You've worked out the whole problem, eh?'

'I believe so.'

'That's uncommonly interesting. And what is it?'

She looked at him quietly. 'A baby.'

If it was seldom given her to surprise him, she had attained the distinction for once.

'A baby?'

'Yes.'

'A – human baby?'

'Of course!' she cried, with the virtuous resentment of the woman who has never allowed dogs in the house.

Lethbury's puzzled stare broke into a fresh smile. 'A baby I shan't approve of? Well, in the abstract I don't think much of them, I admit. Is this an abstract baby?'

Again she frowned at the adjective, but she had reached a pitch of exaltation at which such obstacles could not deter her.

'It's the loveliest baby – ' she murmured.

'Ah, then it's concrete. It exists. In this harsh world it draws its breath in pain – '

'It's the healthiest child I ever saw!' she indignantly corrected.

'You've seen it, then?'

Again the accusing blush suffused her. 'Yes – I've seen it.'

'And to whom does this paragon belong?'

And here indeed she confounded him. 'To me – I hope,' she declared.

He pushed his chair back with an articulate murmur. 'To you – ?'

'To *us*,' she corrected.

'Good Lord!' he said. If there had been the least hint of hallucination in her transparent gaze – but no; it was as clear, as shallow, as easily fathomable as when he had first suffered the sharp surprise of striking bottom in it.

It occurred to him that perhaps she was trying to be funny: he knew that there is nothing more cryptic than the humor of the unhumorous.

'Is it a joke?' he faltered.

'Oh, I hope not. I want it so much to be a reality – '

He paused to smile at the limitations of a world in which jokes were not realities, and continued gently: 'But since it is one already – '

'To us, I mean: to you and me. I want – ' her voice wavered, and her eyes with it. 'I have always wanted so dreadfully . . . it has been such a disappointment . . . not to . . .'

'I see,' said Lethbury slowly.

But he had not seen before. It seemed curious now that he had never thought of her taking it in that way, had never surmised any hidden depths beneath her outspread obviousness. He felt as though he had touched a secret spring in her mind.

There was a moment's silence, moist and tremulous on her part, awkward and slightly irritated on his.

'You've been lonely, I suppose?' he began. It was odd, having suddenly to reckon with the stranger who gazed at him out of her trivial eyes.

'At times,' she said.

'I'm sorry.'

'It was not your fault. A man has so many occupations; and women who are clever – or very handsome – I suppose that's an occupation too. Sometimes I've felt that when dinner was ordered I had nothing to do till the next day.'

'Oh,' he groaned.

'It wasn't your fault,' she insisted. 'I never told you – but when I chose that rosebud paper for the front room upstairs, I always thought – '

'Well – ?'

'It would be such a pretty paper – for a baby – to wake up in. That was years ago, of course; but it was rather an expensive paper . . . and it hasn't faded in the least . . .' she broke off incoherently.

'It hasn't faded?'

'No – and so I thought . . . as we don't use the room for anything . . . now that Aunt Sophronia is dead . . . I thought I might . . . you might . . . oh, Julian, if you could only have seen it just waking up in its crib!'

'Seen what – where? You haven't got a baby upstairs?'

'Oh, no – not *yet*,' she said, with her rare laugh – the girlish bubbling of merriment that had seemed one of her chief graces in the early days. It occurred to him that he had not given her enough things to laugh about lately. But then she needed such very elementary things: she was as difficult to amuse as a savage. He concluded that he was not sufficiently simple.

'Alice,' he said almost solemnly, 'what *do* you mean?'

She hesitated a moment: he saw her gather her courage for a supreme effort. Then she said slowly, gravely, as though she were pronouncing a sacramental phrase:

'I'm so lonely without a little child – and I thought perhaps you'd let me adopt one. . . . It's at the hospital . . . its mother is dead . . . and I could . . . pet it, and dress it, and do things for it . . . and it's such a good baby . . . you can ask any of the nurses . . . it would never, *never* bother you by crying. . . .'

• II •

LETHBURY accompanied his wife to the hospital in a mood of chastened wonder. It did not occur to him to oppose her wish. He knew, of course, that he would have to bear the brunt of the situation: the jokes at the club, the inquiries, the explanations. He saw himself in the comic role of the adopted father and welcomed it as an expiation. For in his rapid reconstruction of the past he found himself cutting a shabbier figure than he cared to admit. He had always been intolerant of stupid people, and it was his punishment to be convicted of stupidity. As his mind traversed the years between his marriage and this unexpected assumption of paternity, he saw, in the light of an overheated imagination, many signs of unwonted crassness. It was not that he had ceased to think his wife stupid: she *was* stupid, limited, inflexible; but there was a pathos in the struggles of her swaddled mind, in its blind reachings toward the primal emotions. He had always thought she would have been happier with a child; but he had thought it mechanically, because it had so often been thought before, because it was in the nature of things to think it of every woman, because his wife was so eminently one of a species that she fitted into all the generalizations of the sex.

But he had regarded this generalization as merely typical of the triumph of tradition over experience. Maternity was no doubt the supreme function of primitive woman, the one end to which her whole organism tended; but the law of increasing complexity had operated in both sexes, and he had not seriously supposed that, outside the world of Christmas fiction and anecdotic art, such truisms had any special hold on the feminine imagination. Now he saw that the arts in question were kept alive by the vitality of the sentiments they appealed to.

Lethbury was in fact going through a rapid process of readjustment. His marriage had been a failure, but he had preserved toward his wife the exact fidelity of act that is sometimes supposed to excuse any divagation of feeling; so that, for years, the tie between them had consisted mainly in his abstaining from making love to other women. The abstention had not always been easy, for the world is surprisingly well stocked with the kind of woman one ought to have married but did not; and Lethbury had not escaped the solicitation of such alternatives. His immunity had been purchased at the cost of taking refuge in the somewhat rarefied atmosphere of his perceptions; and his world being thus limited, he had given unusual care to its details, compensating himself for the narrowness of his horizon by the minute finish of his foreground. It was a world of fine shadings and the nicest proportions, where impulse seldom set a blundering foot, and the feast of reason was undisturbed by an intemperate flow of soul. To such a banquet his wife naturally remained uninvited. The diet would have disagreed with her, and she would probably have projected to the other guests. But Lethbury, miscalculating her needs, had hitherto supposed that he had made ample provision for them, and was consequently at liberty to enjoy his own fare without any reproach of mendicancy at his gates. Now he beheld her pressing a starved face against the windows of his life, and in his imaginative reaction he invested her with a pathos borrowed from the sense of his own shortcomings.

In the hospital the imaginative process continued with increasing force. He looked at his wife with new eyes. Formerly she had been to him a mere bundle of negations, a labyrinth of dead walls and bolted doors. There was nothing behind the walls, and the doors led no whither: he had sounded and listened often enough to be sure of that. Now he felt like a traveler who, exploring some ancient ruin, comes on an inner cell, intact amid the general dilapidation, and painted with images which reveal the forgotten uses of the building.

His wife stood by a white crib in one of the wards. In the crib lay a child, a year old, the nurse affirmed, but to Lethbury's eye a mere dateless fragment of humanity projected against a background of conjecture. Over this anonymous particle of life Mrs. Lethbury leaned, such ecstasy reflected in her face as strikes up, in Correggio's 'Nightpiece,' from the child's body to the mother's countenance. It was a light that irradiated and dazzled her. She looked up at an inquiry of Lethbury's, but as their glances met he perceived that she no longer saw him, that he had become as invisible to her as she had long been to him. He had to transfer his question to the nurse.

'What is the child's name?' he asked.

'We call her Jane,' said the nurse.

• III •

LETHBURY, at first, had resisted the idea of a legal adoption; but when he found that his wife could not be brought to regard the child as hers till it had been made so by process of law, he promptly withdrew his objection. On one point only he remained inflexible; and that was the changing of the waif's name. Mrs. Lethbury, almost at once, had expressed a wish to rechristen it: she fluctuated between Muriel and Gladys, deferring the moment of decision like a lady wavering between two bonnets. But Lethbury was unyielding. In the general surrender of his prejudices this one alone held out.

'But Jane is so dreadful,' Mrs. Lethbury protested.

'Well, we don't know that *she* won't be dreadful. She may grow up a Jane.'

His wife exclaimed reproachfully. 'The nurse says she's the loveliest – '

'Don't they always say that?' asked Lethbury patiently. He was prepared to be inexhaustibly patient now that he had reached a firm foothold of opposition.

'It's cruel to call her Jane,' Mrs. Lethbury pleaded.

'It's ridiculous to call her Muriel!'

'The nurse is *sure* she must be a lady's child.'

Lethbury winced: he had tried, all along, to keep his mind off the question of antecedents.

'Well, let her prove it,' he said, with a rising sense of exasperation. He wondered how he could ever have allowed himself to be drawn into such a ridiculous business; for the first time he felt the full irony of it. He had visions of coming home in the afternoon to a house smelling of linseed and paregoric, and of being greeted by a chronic howl as he went upstairs to dress for dinner. He had never been a club man, but he saw himself becoming one now.

The worst of his anticipations were unfulfilled. The baby was surprisingly well and surprisingly quiet. Such infantile remedies as she absorbed were not potent enough to be perceived beyond the nursery; and when Lethbury could be induced to enter that sanctuary, there was nothing to jar his nerves in the mild pink presence of his adopted daughter. Jars there were, indeed: they were probably inevitable in the disturbed routine of the household, but they occurred between Mrs. Lethbury and the nurses, and Jane contributed to them only a placid stare which might have served as a rebuke to the combatants.

In the reaction from his first impulse of atonement, Lethbury noted with sharpened perceptions the effect of the change on his wife's character. He saw already the error of supposing that it could work any transformation in her. It simply magnified her existing qualities. She was like a dried sponge put in water: she expanded, but she did not change her shape. From the standpoint of scientific observation it was curious to see how her stored instincts responded to the pseudo-maternal call. She overflowed with the petty maxims of the occasion. One felt in her the epitome, the consummation, of centuries of animal maternity, so that this little woman, who screamed at a mouse and was nervous about burglars, came to typify the cave mother rending her prey for her young.

It was less easy to regard philosophically the practical effects of her borrowed motherhood. Lethbury found with surprise that she was becoming assertive and definite. She no longer represented the negative side of his life; she showed, indeed, a tendency to inconvenient affirmations. She had gradually expanded her assumption of motherhood till it included his own share in the relation, and he suddenly found himself regarded as the father of Jane. This was a contingency he had not foreseen, and it took all his philosophy to accept it; but there were moments of compensation. For Mrs. Lethbury was undoubtedly happy for the first time in years; and the thought that he had tardily contributed to this end reconciled him to the irony of the means.

At first he was inclined to reproach himself for still viewing the situation from the outside, for remaining a spectator instead of a participant. He had been allured, for a moment, by the vision of severed hands meeting over a cradle, as the whole body of domestic fiction bears witness to their doing; and the fact that no such conjunction took place he could explain only on the ground that it was a borrowed cradle. He did not dislike the little girl. She still remained to him a hypothetical presence, a query rather than a fact; but her nearness was not unpleasant, and there were moments when her tentative utterances, her groping steps, seemed to loosen the dry accretions enveloping his inner self. But even at such moments – moments which he invited and caressed – she did not bring him nearer to his wife. He now perceived that he had made a certain place in his life for Mrs. Lethbury, and that she no longer fitted into it. It was too late to enlarge the space, and so she overflowed and encroached. Lethbury struggled against the sense of submergence. He let down barrier after barrier, yielding privacy after privacy; but his wife's personality continued to dilate. She was no longer herself alone: she was herself and Jane. Gradually, a monstrous fusion of identity, she became herself, himself and Jane; and instead of trying to adapt her to a spare crevice of his character, he found himself carelessly squeezed into the smallest compartment of the domestic economy.

• IV •

HE continued to tell himself that he was satisfied if his wife was happy; and it was not till the child's tenth year that he felt a doubt of her happiness.

Jane had been a preternaturally good child. During the eight years of her adoption she had caused her foster parents no anxiety beyond those connected with the usual succession of youthful diseases. But her unknown progenitors had given her a robust constitution, and she passed unperturbed through measles, chicken pox and whooping cough. If there was any suffering it was endured vicariously by Mrs. Lethbury, whose temperature rose and fell with the patient's, and who could not hear Jane sneeze without visions of a marble angel weeping over a broken column. But though Jane's prompt recoveries continued to belie such premonitions, though her existence continued to move forward on an even keel of good health and good conduct, Mrs. Lethbury's satisfaction showed no corresponding advance. Lethbury, at first, was disposed to add her disappointment to the long list of feminine inconsistencies with which the sententious observer of life builds up his favorable induction; but circumstances presently led him to take a kindlier view of the case.

Hitherto his wife had regarded him as a negligible factor in Jane's evolution. Beyond providing for his adopted daughter, and effacing himself before her, he was not expected to contribute to her well-being. But as time passed he appeared to his wife in a new light. It was he who was to educate Jane. In matters of the intellect, Mrs. Lethbury was the first to declare her deficiencies – to proclaim them, even, with a certain virtuous superiority. She said she did not pretend to be clever, and there was no denying the truth of the assertion. Now, however, she seemed less ready, not to own her limitations, but to glory in them. Confronted with the problem of Jane's instruction she stood in awe of the child.

'I have always been stupid, you know,' she said to Lethbury with a new humility, 'and I'm afraid I shan't know what is best for Jane. I'm sure she has a wonderfully good mind, and I should reproach myself if I didn't give her every opportunity.' She looked at him helplessly. 'You must tell me what ought to be done.'

Lethbury was not unwilling to oblige her. Somewhere in his mental lumber room there rusted a theory of education such as usually lingers among the impedimenta of the childless. He brought this out, refurbished it, and applied it to Jane. At first he thought his wife had not overrated the quality of the child's mind. Jane seemed extraordinarily intelligent. Her precocious definiteness of mind was encouraging to her inexperienced preceptor. She had no difficulty in fixing her attention, and he felt that every fact he imparted was being etched in metal. He helped his wife to engage the best teachers, and for a while continued to take an ex-official interest in his adopted daughter's studies. But gradually his interest waned. Jane's ideas did not increase with her acquisitions. Her young mind remained a mere receptacle of facts: a kind of cold storage from which anything which had been put there could be taken out at a moment's notice, intact but congealed. She developed, moreover, an inordinate pride in the capacity of her mental storehouse, and a tendency to pelt her public with its contents. She was overheard to jeer at her nurse for not knowing when the Saxon Heptarchy had fallen, and she alternately dazzled and depressed Mrs. Lethbury by the wealth of her chronological allusions. She showed no interest in the significance of of the facts she amassed: she simply collected dates as another child might have collected stamps or marbles. To her foster mother she seemed a prodigy of wisdom; but Lethbury saw, with a secret movement of sympathy, how the aptitudes in which Mrs. Lethbury gloried were slowly estranging her from her child.

'She is getting too clever for me,' his wife said to him, after one of Jane's historical flights, 'but I am so glad that she will be a companion to you.'

Lethbury groaned in spirit. He did not look forward to Jane's companionship. She was still a good little girl: but there was something automatic and formal in her goodness, as though it were a kind of moral calisthenics which she went through for the sake of showing her agility. An early consciousness of virtue had moreover constituted her the natural guardian and adviser of her elders. Before she was fifteen she had set about reforming the household. She took Mrs Lethbury in hand first; then she extended her efforts to the servants, with consequences more disastrous to the domestic harmony; and lastly she applied herself to Lethbury. She proved to him by statistics that he smoked too much, and that it was injurious to the optic nerve to read in bed. She took him to task for not going to church more regularly, and pointed out to him the evils of desultory reading. She suggested that a regular course of study encourages mental concentration, and hinted that inconsecutiveness of thought is a sign of approaching age.

To her adopted mother her suggestions were equally pertinent. She instructed Mrs. Lethbury in an improved way of making beef stock, and called her attention to the unhygienic qualities of carpets. She poured out distracting facts about bacilli and vegetable mold, and demonstrated that curtains and picture frames are a hotbed of animal organisms. She learned by heart the nutritive ingredients of the principal articles of diet, and revolutionized the cuisine by an attempt to establish a scientific average between starch and phosphates. Four cooks left during this experiment, and Lethbury fell into the habit of dining at the club.

Once or twice, at the outset, he had tried to check Jane's ardor; but his efforts resulted only in hurting his wife's feelings. Jane remained impervious, and Mrs. Lethbury resented any attempt to protect her from her daughter. Lethbury saw that she was consoled for the sense of her own inferiority by the thought of what Jane's intellectual companionship must be to him; and he tried to keep up the illusion by enduring with what grace he might the blighting edification of Jane's discourse.

• V •

As Jane grew up he sometimes avenged himself by wondering if his wife was still sorry that they had not called her Muriel. Jane was not ugly; she developed, indeed, a kind of categorical prettiness which might have been a projection of her mind. She had a creditable collection of features, but one had to take an inventory of them to find out that she was goodlooking. The fusing grace had been omitted.

Mrs. Lethbury took a pride in her daughter's first steps in the world. She expected Jane to take by her complexion those whom she did not capture by her learning. But Jane's rosy freshness did not work any perceptible ravages. Whether the young men guessed the axioms on her lips and detected the encyclopedia in her eye, or whether they simply found no intrinsic interest in these features, certain it is, that, in spite of her mother's heroic efforts, and of incessant calls on Lethbury's purse, Jane, at the end of her first season, had dropped hopelessly out of the running. A few duller girls found her interesting, and one or two young men came to the house with the object of meeting other young women; but she was rapidly becoming one of the social supernumeraries who are asked out only because they are on people's lists.

The blow was bitter to Mrs. Lethbury; but she consoled herself with the idea that Jane had failed because she was too clever. Jane probably shared this conviction; at all events she betrayed no consciousness of failure. She had developed a pronounced taste for society, and went out, unweariedly and obstinately, winter after winter, while Mrs. Lethbury toiled in her wake, showering attentions on oblivious hostesses. To Lethbury there was something at once tragic and exasperating in the sight of their two figures, the one conciliatory, the other dogged, both pursuing with unabated zeal the elusive prize of popularity. He even began to feel a personal stake in the pursuit, not as it concerned

Jane but as it affected his wife. He saw that the latter was the victim of Jane's disappointment: that Jane was not above the crude satisfaction of 'taking it out' of her mother. Experience checked the impulse to come to his wife's defence; and when his resentment was at its height, Jane disarmed him by giving up the struggle.

Nothing was said to mark her capitulation; but Lethbury noticed that the visiting ceased and that the dressmaker's bills diminished. At the same time Mrs. Lethbury made it known that Jane had taken up charities, and before long Jane's conversation confirmed this announcement. At first Lethbury congratulated himself on the change; but Jane's domesticity soon began to weigh on him. During the day she was sometimes absent on errands of mercy; but in the evening she was always there. At first she and Mrs. Lethbury sat in the drawing room together, and Lethbury smoked in the library; but presently Jane formed the habit of joining him there, and he began to suspect that he was included among the objects of her philanthropy.

Mrs. Lethbury confirmed the suspicion. 'Jane has grown very serious-minded lately,' she said. 'She imagines that she used to neglect you and she is trying to make up for it. Don't discourage her,' she added innocently.

Such a plea delivered Lethbury helpless to his daughter's ministrations; and he found himself measuring the hours he spent with her by the amount of relief they must be affording her mother. There were even moments when he read a furtive gratitude in Mrs. Lethbury's eye.

But Lethbury was no hero, and he had nearly reached the limit of vicarious endurance when something wonderful happened. They never quite knew afterward how it had come about, or who first percevied it; but Mrs. Lethbury one day gave tremulous voice to their discovery.

'Of course,' she said, 'he comes here because of Elise.' The young lady in question, a friend of Jane's, was possessed of attractions which had already been found to explain the presence of masculine visitors.

Lethbury risked a denial. 'I don't think he does,' he declared.

'But Elise is thought very pretty,' Mrs. Lethbury insisted.

'I can't help that,' said Lethbury doggedly.

He saw a faint light in his wife's eyes; but she remarked carelessly: 'Mr. Budd would be a very good match for Elise.'

Lethbury could hardly repress a chuckle: he was so exquisitely aware that she was trying to propitiate the gods.

For a few weeks neither said a word; then Mrs. Lethbury once more reverted to the subject.

'It is a month since Elise went abroad,' she said.

'Is it?'

'And Mr Budd seems to come here just as often – '

'Ah,' said Lethbury with heroic indifference, and his wife hastily changed the subject.

Mr. Winstanley Budd was a young man who suffered from an excess of manner. Politeness gushed from him in the driest season. He was always performing feats of drawing-room chivalry, and the approach of the most unobtrusive female threw him into attitudes which endangered the furniture. His features, being of the cherubic order, did not lend themselves to this role; but there were moments when he appeared to dominate them, to force them into compliance with an aquiline ideal. The range of Mr. Budd's social benevolence made its object hard to distinguish. He spread his cloak so indiscriminately that one could not always interpret the gesture, and Jane's impassive manner had the effect of increasing his demonstrations; she threw him into paroxysms of politeness.

At first he filled the house with his amenities; but gradually it became apparent that his most dazzling effects were directed exclusively to Jane. Lethbury and his wife held their breath and looked away from each other. They pretended not to notice the frequence of Mr. Budd's visits, they struggled against an imprudent inclination to leave the young people too much alone. Their conclusions were the result of indirect observation, for neither of them dared to be caught watching Mr. Budd: they behaved like naturalists on the trail of a rare butterfly.

In his efforts not to notice Mr. Budd, Lethbury centered his attention on Jane; and Jane, at this crucial moment, wrung from him a reluctant admiration. While her parents went about dissembling their emotions, she seemed to have none to conceal. She betrayed neither eagerness nor surprise; so complete was her unconcern that there were moments when Lethbury feared it was obtuseness, when he could hardly help whispering to her that now was the moment to lower the net.

Meanwhile the velocity of Mr. Budd's gyrations increased with the ardor of courtship; his politeness became incandescent, and Jane found herself the center of a pyrotechnical display culminating in the 'set piece' of an offer of marriage.

Mrs. Lethbury imparted the news to her husband one evening after their daughter had gone to bed. The announcement was made and received with an air of detachment, as though both feared to be betrayed into unseemly exultation; but Lethbury, as his wife ended, could not repress the inquiry, 'Have they decided on a day?'

Mrs. Lethbury's superior command of her features enabled her to look shocked. 'What can you be thinking of? He only offered himself at five!'

'Of course – of course – ' stammered Lethbury ' – but nowadays people marry after such short engagements – '

'Engagement!' said his wife solemnly. 'There is no engagement.'

Lethbury dropped his cigar. 'What on earth do you mean?'

'Jane is thinking it over.'

'*Thinking it over?*'

'She has asked for a month before deciding.'

Lethbury sank back with a gasp. Was it genius or was it madness? He felt incompetent to decide; and Mrs. Lethbury's next words showed that she shared his difficulty.

'Of course I don't want to hurry Jane – '

'Of course not,' he acquiesced.

'But I pointed out to her that a young man of Mr. Budd's impulsive temperament might – might easily be discouraged – '

'Yes; and what did she say?'

'She said that if she was worth winning she was worth waiting for.'

• VI •

THE period of Mr. Budd's probation could scarcely have cost him as much mental anguish as it caused his would-be parents-in-law.

Mrs. Lethbury, by various ruses, tried to shorten the ordeal, but Jane remained inexorable; and each morning Lethbury came down to breakfast with the certainty of finding a letter of withdrawl from her discouraged suitor.

When at length the decisive day came, and Mrs. Lethbury, at its close, stole into the library with an air of chastened joy, they stood for a moment without speaking; then Mrs. Lethbury paid a fitting tribute to the proprieties by faltering out: 'It will be dreadful to have to give her up – '

Lethbury could not repress a warning gesture, but even as it escaped him he realized that his wife's grief was genuine.

'Of course, of course,' he said, vainly sounding his own emotional shallows for an answering regret. And yet it was his wife who had suffered most from Jane!

He had fancied that these sufferings would be effaced by the milder atmosphere of their last weeks together; but felicity did not soften Jane. Not for a moment did she relax her dominion: she simply widened it to include the new subject. Mr. Budd found himself under orders with the others; and a new fear assailed Lethbury as he saw Jane assume pre-nuptial control of her betrothed. Lethbury had never felt any strong personal interest in Mr. Budd; but as Jane's prospective husband the young man excited his sympathy. To his surprise he found that Mrs. Lethbury shared the feeling.

'I'm afraid he may find Jane a little exacting,' she said, after an evening dedicated to a stormy discussion of the wedding arrangements. 'She really ought to make some concessions. If he *wants* to be married in a black frock coat instead of a dark grey one – ' She paused and looked doubtfully at Lethbury.

'What can I do about it?' he said.

'You might explain to him – tell him that Jane isn't always – '

Lethbury made an impatient gesture. 'What are you afraid of? His finding her out or his not finding her out?'

Mrs. Lethbury flushed. 'You put it so dreadfully!'

Her husband mused for a moment; then he said with an air of cheerful hypocrisy: 'After all, Budd is old enough to take care of himself.'

But the next day Mrs. Lethbury surprised him. Late in the afternoon she entered the library, so breathless and inarticulate that he scented a catastrophe.

'I've done it!' she cried.

'Done what?'

'Told him.' She nodded toward the door. 'He's just gone. Jane is out, and I had a chance to talk to him alone.'

Lethbury pushed a chair forward and she sank into it.

'What did you tell him? That she is *not* always – '

Mrs. Lethbury lifted a tragic eye. 'No; I told him that she always *is* – '

'Always *is* – ?'

'Yes.'

There was a pause. Lethbury made a call on his hoarded philosophy. He saw Jane suddenly reinstated in her evening seat by the library fire; but an answering chord in him thrilled at his wife's heroism.

'Well – what did he say?'

Mrs. Lethbury's agitation deepened. It was clear that the blow had fallen.

'He . . . he said . . . that we . . . had never understood Jane . . . or appreciated her . . .' The final syllables were lost in her handkerchief, and she left him marveling at the mechanism of woman.

After that, Lethbury faced the future with an undaunted eye. They had done their duty – at least his wife had done hers – and they were reaping the usual harvest of ingratitude with a zest seldom accorded to such reaping. There was a marked change in Mr. Budd's manner, and his increasing coldness sent a genial glow through Lethbury's system. It was easy to bear with Jane in the light of Mr. Budd's disapproval.

There was a good deal to be borne in the last days, and the brunt of it fell on Mrs. Lethbury. Jane marked her transition to the married state by a seasonable but incongruous display of nerves. She became sentimental, hysterical and reluctant. She quarreled with her betrothed and threatened to return the ring. Mrs. Lethbury had to intervene, and Lethbury felt the hovering sword of destiny. But the blow was suspended. Mr. Budd's chivalry was proof against all his bride's caprices and his devotion throve on her cruelty. Lethbury feared that he was too faithful, too enduring, and longed to urge him to vary his tactics. Jane presently reappeared with the ring on her finger, and consented to try on the wedding dress; but her uncertainties, her reactions, were prolonged till the final day.

When it dawned, Lethbury was still in an ecstasy of apprehension. Feeling reasonably sure of the principal actors he had centered his fears on incidental possibilities. The clergyman might have a stroke, or the church might burn down, or there might be something wrong with the license. He did all that was humanly possible to avert such contingencies, but there remained that incalculable factor known as the hand of God. Lethbury seemed to feel it groping for him.

At the altar it almost had him by the nape. Mr. Budd was late; and for five immeasurable minutes Lethbury and Jane faced a churchful of conjecture. Then the bridegroom appeared, flushed but chivalrous, and explaining to his father-in-law under cover of the ritual that he had torn his glove and had to go back for another.

'You'll be losing the ring next,' muttered Lethbury; but Mr. Budd produced this article punctually, and a moment or two later was bearing its wearer captive down the aisle.

At the wedding breakfast Lethbury caught his wife's eye fixed on him in mild disapproval, and understood that his hilarity was exceeding the bounds of fitness. He pulled himself together and tried to subdue his tone; but his jubilation bubbled over like a champagne glass perpetually refilled. The deeper his draughts the higher it rose.

It was at the brim when, in the wake of the dispersing guests, Jane came down in her traveling dress and fell on her mother's neck.

'I can't leave you!' she wailed, and Lethbury felt as suddenly sobered as a man under a shower. But if the bride was reluctant her captor was relentless. Never had Mr. Budd been more dominant, more aquiline. Lethbury's last fears were dissipated as the young man snatched Jane from her mother's bosom and bore her off to the brougham.

The brougham rolled away, the last milliner's girl forsook her post by the awning, the red carpet was folded up, and the house door closed. Lethbury stood alone in the hall with his wife. As he turned toward her, he noticed the look of tired heroism in her eyes, the deepened lines of her face. They reflected his own symptoms too accurately not to appeal to him. The nervous tension had been horrible. He went up to her, and an answering impulse made her lay a hand on his arm. He held it there a moment.

'Let us go off and have a jolly little dinner at a restaurant,' he proposed.

There had been a time when such a suggestion would have surprised her to the verge of disapproval; but now she agreed to it at once.

'Oh, that would be so nice,' she murmured with a great sigh of relief and assuagement.

Jane had fulfilled her mission after all: she had drawn them together at last.

The Reckoning

———— ✥ ————

THE MARRIAGE LAW of the new dispensation will be: *Thou shalt not be unfaithful – to thyself.*'

A discreet murmur of approval filled the studio, and through the haze of cigarette smoke Mrs. Clement Westall, as her husband descended from his improvised platform, saw him merged 'in a congratulatory group of ladies. Westall's informal talks on 'The New Ethics' had drawn about him an eager following of the mentally unemployed – those who, as he had once phrased it, liked to have their brain food cut up for them. The talks had begun by accident. Westall's ideas were known to be 'advanced,' but hitherto their advance had not been in the direction of publicity. He had been, in his wife's opinion, almost pusillanimously careful not to let his personal views endanger his professional standing. Of late, however, he had shown a puzzling tendency to dogmatize, to throw down the gauntlet, to flaunt his private code in the face of society; and the relation of the sexes being a topic always sure of an audience, a few admiring friends had persuaded him to give his after-dinner opinions a larger circulation by summing them up in a series of talks at the Van Sideren studio.

The Herbert Van Siderens were a couple who subsisted, socially, on the fact that they had a studio. Van Sideren's pictures were chiefly valuable as accessories to the *mise en scène* which differentiated his wife's 'afternoons' from the blighting functions held in long New York drawing rooms, and permitted her to offer their friends whiskey and soda instead of tea. Mrs. Van Sideren, for her part, was skilled in making the most of the kind of atmosphere which a lay figure and an easel create; and if at times she found the illusion hard to maintain, and lost courage to the extent of almost wishing that Herbert could paint, she promptly overcame such moments of weakness by calling in some fresh talent, some extraneous re-enforcement of the 'artistic' impression. It was in quest of such aid that she had seized on Westall, coaxing him, somewhat to his wife's surprise, into a flattered participation in her fraud. It was vaguely felt, in the Van Sideren circle, that all the audacities were artistic, and that a teacher who pronounced marriage

47

immoral was somehow as distinguished as a painter who depicted purple grass and a green sky. The Van Sideren set were tired of the conventional color scheme in art and conduct.

Julia Westall had long had her own views on the immorality of marriage; she might indeed have claimed her husband as a disciple. In the early days of their union she had secretly resented his disinclination to proclaim himself a follower of the new creed; had been inclined to tax him with moral cowardice, with a failure to live up to the convictions for which their marriage was supposed to stand. That was in the first burst of propagandism, when, womanlike, she wanted to turn her disobedience into a law. Now she felt differently. She could hardly account for the change, yet being a woman who never allowed her impulses to remain unaccounted for, she tried to do so by saying that she did not care to have the articles of her faith misinterpreted by the vulgar. In this connection, she was beginning to think that almost everyone was vulgar; certainly there were few to whom she would have cared to intrust the defence of so esoteric a doctrine. And it was precisely at this point that Westall, discarding his unspoken principles, had chosen to descend from the heights of privacy, and stand hawking his convictions at the street corner!

It was Una Van Sideren who, on this occasion, unconsciously focused upon herself Mrs. Westall's wandering resentment. In the first place, the girl had no business to be there. It was 'horrid' – Mrs. Westfall found herself slipping back into the old feminine vocabulary – simply 'horrid' to think of a young girl's being allowed to listen to such talk. The fact that Una smoked cigarettes and sipped an occasional cocktail did not in the least tarnish a certain radiant innocency which made her appear the victim, rather than the accomplice, of her parents' vulgarities. Julia Westall felt in a hot helpless way that something ought to be done – that someone ought to speak to the girl's mother. And just then Una glided up.

'Oh, Mrs. Westall, how beautiful it was!' Una fixed her with large limpid eyes. 'You believe it all, I suppose?' she asked with seraphic gravity.

'All – what, my dear child?'

The girl shone on her. 'About the higher life – the freer expansion of the individual – the law of fidelity to one's self,' she glibly recited.

Mrs. Westall, to her own wonder, blushed a deep and burning blush.

'My dear Una,' she said, 'you don't in the least understand what it's all about!'

Miss Van Sideren stared, with a slowly answering blush!' 'Don't you, then?' she murmured.

Mrs. Westall laughed. 'Not always – or altogether! But I should like some tea, please.'

Una led her to the corner where innocent beverages were dispensed. As Julia received her cup she scrutinized the girl more carefully. It was not such a girlish face, after all – definite lines were forming under the rosy haze of youth. She reflected that Una must be six-and-twenty, and wondered why she had not married. A nice stock of ideas she would have as her dowry! If *they* were to be a part of the modern girl's trousseau – .

Mrs. Westall caught herself up with a start. It was as though someone else had been speaking – a stranger who had borrowed her own voice: she felt herself the dupe of some fantastic mental ventriloquism. Concluding suddenly that the room was stifling and Una's tea too sweet, she set down her cup and looked about for Westall: to meet his eyes had long been her refuge from every uncertainty. She met them now, but only, as she felt, in transit; they included her parenthetically in a larger flight. She followed the flight, and it carried her to a corner to which Una had withdrawn – one of the palmy, nooks to which Mrs. Van Sideren attributed the success of her Saturdays. Westall, a moment later, had overtaken his look, and found a place at the girl's side. She bent forward, speaking eagerly; he leaned back, listening, with the depreciatory smile which acted as a filter to flattery, enabling him to swallow the strongest doses without apparent grossness of appetite. Julia winced at her own definition of the smile.

On the way home, in the deserted winter dusk, Westall surprised his wife by a sudden boyish pressure of her arm. 'Did I open their eyes a bit? Did I tell them what you wanted me to?' he asked gaily.

Almost unconsciously, she let her arm slip from his. 'What *I* wanted – ?'

'Why, haven't you – all this time?' She caught the honest wonder of his tone. 'I somehow fancied you'd rather blamed me for not talking more openly before. You almost made me feel, at times, that I was sacrificing principles to expediency.'

She paused a moment over her reply; then she asked quietly: 'What made you decide not to – any longer?'

She felt again the vibration of a faint surprise. 'Why – the wish to please you!' he answered, almost too simply.

'I wish you would not go on, then,' she said abruptly.

He stopped in his quick walk, and she felt his stare through the darkness.

'Not go on – ?'

'Call a hansom, please. I'm tired,' broke from her with a sudden rush of physical weariness.

Instantly his solicitude enveloped her. The room had been infernally hot – and then that confounded cigarette smoke – he had noticed once or twice that she looked pale – she mustn't come to another Saturday. She felt herself yielding, as she always did, to the warm influence of his concern for her, the feminine in her leaning on the man in him with a conscious intensity of abandonment. He put her in the hansom, and her hand stole into his in the darkness. A tear or two rose, and she let them fall. It was so delicious to cry over imaginary troubles!

That evening, after dinner, he surprised her by reverting to the subject of his talk. He combined a man's dislike of uncomfortable questions with an almost feminine skill in eluding them; and she knew that if he returned to the subject he must have some special reason for doing so.

'You seem not to have cared for what I said this afternoon. Did I put the case badly?'

'No – you put it very well.'

'Then what did you mean by saying that you would rather not have me go on with it?'

She glanced at him nervously, her ignorance of his intention deepening her sense of helplessness.

'I don't think I care to hear such things discussed in public.'

'I don't understand you,' he exclaimed. Again the feeling that his surprise was genuine gave an air of obliquity to her own attitude. She was not sure that she understood herself.

'Won't you explain?' he said with a tingle of impatience.

Her eyes wandered about the familiar drawing room which had been the scene of so many of their evening confidences. The shaded lamps, the quiet-colored walls hung with mezzotints, the pale spring flowers scattered here and there in Venice glasses and bowls of old Sèvres, recalled she hardly knew why, the apartment in which the evenings of her first marriage had been passed – a wilderness of rosewood and upholstery, with a picture of a Roman peasant above the mantelpiece, and a Greek slave in statuary marble between the folding doors of the back drawing room. It was a room with which she had never been able to establish any closer relation than that between a traveler and a railway station; and now, as she looked about at the surroundings which stood for her deepest affinities – the room for which she had left that other room – she was startled by the same sense of strangeness and unfamiliarity. The prints, the flowers, the subdued tones of the old porcelain, seemed to typify a superficial refinement which had no relation to the deeper significances of life.

Suddenly she heard her husband repeating his question.

'I don't know that I can explain,' she faltered.

He drew his armchair forward so that he faced her across the hearth. The light of a reading lamp fell on his finely drawn face, which had a kind of surface sensitiveness akin to the surface refinement of its setting.

'Is it that you no longer believe in our ideas?' he asked.

'In our ideas – ?'

'The ideas I am trying to teach. The ideas you and I are supposed to stand for.' He paused a moment. 'The ideas on which our marriage was founded.'

The blood rushed to her face. He had his reasons, then – she was sure now that he had his reasons! In the ten years of their marriage, how often had either of them stopped to consider the ideas on which it was founded? How often does a man dig about the basement of his house to examine its foundations? The foundation is there, of course – the house rests on it – but one lives abovestairs and not in the cellar. It was she, indeed, who in the beginning had insisted on reviewing the situation now and then, on recapitulating the reasons which justified her course, on proclaiming, for time to time, her adherence to the religion of personal independence; but she had long ceased to feel the want of any such ideal standards, and had accepted her marriage as frankly and naturally as though it had been based on the primitive needs of the heart, and required no special sanction to explain or justify it.

'Of course I still believe in our ideas!' she exclaimed.

'Then I repeat that I don't understand. It was part of your theory that the greatest possible publicity should be given to our view of marriage. Have you changed your mind in that respect?'

She hesitated. 'It depends on circumstances – on the public one is addressing. The set of people that the Van Siderens get about them don't care for the truth or falseness of a doctrine. They are attracted simply by its novelty.'

'And yet it was in just such a set of people that you and I met, and learned the truth from each other.'

'That was different.'

'In what way?'

'I was not a young girl, to begin with. It is perfectly unfitting that young girls should be present at – at such times – should hear such things discussed – '

'I thought you considered it one of the deepest social wrongs that such things never *are* discussed before young girls; but that is beside the point, for I don't remember seeing any young girl in my audience today – '

'Except Una Van Sideren!'

He turned slightly and pushed back the lamp at his elbow.

'Oh, Miss Van Sideren – naturally – '

'Why naturally?'

'The daughter of the house – would you have had her sent out with her governess?'

'If I had a daughter I should not allow such things to go on in my house!'

Westall, stroking his moustache, leaned back with a faint smile. 'I fancy Miss Van Sideren is quite capable of taking care of herself.'

'No girl knows how to take care of herself – till it's too late.'

'And yet you would deliberately deny her the surest means of self-defence?'

'What do you call the surest means of self-defence?'

'Some preliminary knowledge of human nature in its relation to the marriage tie.'

She made an impatient gesture. 'How should you like to marry that kind of girl?'

'Immensely – if she were my kind of girl in other respects.'

She took up the argument at another point.

'You are quite mistaken if you think such talk does not affect young girls. Una was in a state of the most absurd exaltation – ' She broke off, wondering why she had spoken.

Westall reopened a magazine which he had laid aside at the beginning of their discussion. 'What you tell me is immensely flattering to my oratorical talent – but I fear you overrate its effect. I can assure you that Miss Van Sideren doesn't have to have her thinking done for her. She's quite capable of doing it herself.'

'You seem very familiar with her mental processes!' flashed unguardedly from his wife.

He looked up quietly from the pages he was cutting.

'I should like to be,' he answered. 'She interests me.'

· II ·

IF there be a distinction in being misunderstood, it was one denied to Julia Westall when she left her first husband. Everyone was ready to excuse and even to defend her. The world she adorned agreed that John Arment was 'impossible,' and hostesses gave a sigh of relief at the thought that it would no longer be necessary to ask him to dine.

There had been no scandal connected with the divorce: neither side had accused the other of the offence euphemistically described as 'statutory'. The Arments had indeed been obliged to transfer their allegiance to a state which recognized desertion as a cause for divorce, and construed the term so liberally that the seeds of desertion were shown to exist in every union. Even Mrs. Arment's second marriage did not make traditional morality stir in its sleep. It was known that she had not met her second husband till after she had parted from the first, and she had, moreover, replaced a rich man by a poor one. Though Clement Westall was acknowledged to be a rising lawyer, it was generally felt that his fortunes would not rise as rapidly as his reputation. The Westalls would probably always have to live quietly and go out to dinner in cabs. Could there be better evidence of Mrs. Arment's complete disinterestedness?

If the reasoning by which her friends justified her course was somewhat cruder and less complex than her own elucidation of the matter, both explanations led to the same conclusion: John Arment was impossible. The only difference was that, to his wife, his impossibility was something deeper than a social disqualification. She had once said, in ironical defence of her marriage, that it had at least preserved her from the necessity of sitting next to him at dinner; but she had not then realized at what cost the immunity was purchased. John Arment was impossible; but the sting of his impossibility lay in the fact that he made it impossible for those about him to be other than himself. By an unconscious process of elimination he had excluded from the world everything of which he did not feel a personal need: had become, as it were, a climate in which only his own requirements survived. This might seem to imply a deliberate selfishness; but there was nothing deliberate about Arment. He was as instinctive as an animal or a child. It was this childish element in his nature which sometimes for a moment unsettled his wife's estimate of him. Was it possible that he was simply undeveloped, that he had delayed, somewhat longer than is usual, the laborious process of growing up? He had the kind of sporadic shrewdness which causes it to be said of a dull man that he is 'no fool'; and it was this quality that his wife found most trying. Even to the naturalist it is annoying to have his deductions disturbed by some unforeseen aberrancy of form or function; and how much more so to the wife whose estimate of herself is inevitably bound up with her judgment of her husband!

Arment's shrewdness did not, indeed, imply any latent intellectual power; it suggested, rather, potentialities of feeling, of suffering, perhaps, in a blind rudimentary way, on which Julia's sensibilities naturally declined to linger. She so fully understood her own reasons for leaving him that she disliked to think they were not as comprehensible to her husband. She was haunted, in her analytic moments, by the look of perplexity, too inarticulate for words, with which he had acquiesced in her explanations.

These moments were rare with her, however. Her marriage had been too concrete a misery to be surveyed philosophically. If she had been unhappy for complex reasons, the unhappiness was as real as though it had been uncomplicated. Soul is more bruisable than flesh, and Julia was wounded in every fiber of her spirit. Her husband's personality seemed to be closing gradually in on her, obscuring the sky and cutting off the air, till she felt herself shut up among the decaying bodies of her starved hopes. A sense of having been decoyed by some world-old conspiracy into this bondage of body and soul filled her with despair. If marriage was the slow lifelong acquittal of a debt contracted in ignorance, then marriage was a crime against human nature. She, for one, would have no share in maintaining the pretense of which she had been a victim: the pretense that a man and a woman, forced into the narrowest of personal relations, must remain there till the end, though they may have outgrown the span of each other's natures as the mature tree outgrows the iron brace about the sapling.

It was in the first heat of her moral indignation that she had met Clement Westall. She had seen at once that he was 'interested,' and had fought off the discovery, dreading any influence that should draw her back into the bondage of conventional relations. To ward off the peril she had, with an almost crude precipitancy, revealed her opinions to him. To her surprise, she found that he shared them. She was attracted by the frankness of a suitor who, while pressing his suit, admitted that he did not believe in marriage. Her worst audacities did not seem to surprise him: he had thought out all that she had felt, and they had reached the same conclusion. People grew at varying rates, and the yoke that was an easy fit for the one might soon become galling to the other. That was what divorce was for: the readjustment of personal relations. As soon as their necessarily transitive nature was recognized they would gain in dignity as well as in harmony. There would be no further need of the ignoble concessions and connivances, the perpetual sacrifice of personal delicacy and moral pride, by means of which imperfect marriages were now held together. Each partner to the contract would be on his mettle, forced to live up to the highest standard of self-development, on pain of losing the other's respect and affection. The low nature could no longer drag the higher down, but must struggle to rise, or remain alone on its inferior level. The only necessary condition to a harmonious marriage was a frank recognition of this truth, and a solemn agreement between the contracting parties to keep faith with themselves, and not to live together for a moment after complete accord had ceased to exist between them. The new adultery was unfaithfulness to self.

It was, as Westall had just reminded her, on this understanding that they had married. The ceremony was an unimportant concession to social prejudice: now that the door of divorce stood open, no marriage need be an imprisonment, and the contract therefore no longer involved any diminution of self-respect. The nature of their attachment placed them so far beyond the reach of such contingencies that it was easy to discuss them with an open mind; and Julia's sense of security made her dwell with a tender insistence on Westall's promise to claim his release when he should cease to love her. The exchange of these vows seemed to make them, in a sense, champions of the new law, pioneers in the forbidden realm of individual freedom: they felt that they had somehow achieved beatitude without martyrdom.

This, as Julia now reviewed the past, she perceived to have been her theoretical attitude toward marriage. It was unconsciously, insidiously, that her ten years of happiness with Westall had developed another conception of the tie; a reversion, rather, to the old instinct of passionate dependency and possessorship that now made her blood revolt at the mere hint of change. Change? Renewal? Was that what they had called it, in their foolish jargon? Destruction, extermination rather – this rending of a myriad fibers interwoven with another's being! Another? But he was not other! He and she were one, one in the mystic sense which alone gave marriage its significance. The new law was not for them, but for the disunited creatures forced into a mockery of union. The gospel she had felt called on to proclaim had no bearing on her own case . . . She sent for the doctor and told him she was sure she needed a nerve tonic.

She took the nerve tonic diligently, but it failed to act as a sedative to her fears. She did not know what she feared; but that made her anxiety the more pervasive. Her husband had not reverted to the subject of his Saturday talks. He was unusually kind and considerate, with a softening of his quick manner, a touch of shyness in his consideration, that sickened her with new fears. She told herself that it was because she looked badly – because he knew about the doctor and the nerve tonic – that he showed this deference to her wishes, this eagerness to screen her from moral drafts; but the explanation simply cleared the way for fresh inferences.

The week passed slowly, vacantly, like a prolonged Sunday. On Saturday the morning post brought a note from Mrs. Van Sideren. Would dear Julia ask Mr. Westall to come half an hour earlier than usual, as there was to be some music after his 'talk'? Westall was just leaving for his office when his wife read the note. She opened the drawing-room door and called him back to deliver the message.

He glanced at the note and tossed it aside. 'What a bore! I shall have to cut my game of racquets. Well, I suppose it can't be helped. Will you write and say it's all right?'

Julia hesitated a moment, her hand stiffening on the chair back against which she leaned.

'You mean to go on with these talks?' she asked.

'I – why not?' he returned; and this time it struck her that his surprise was not quite unfeigned. The perception helped her to find words.

'You said you had started them with the idea of pleasing me – '
'Well?'

'I told you last week that they didn't please me.'

'Last week? – Oh – ' He seemed to make an effort of memory. 'I thought you were nervous then; you sent for the doctor the next day.'

'It was not the doctor I needed; it was your assurance – '

'My assurance?'

Suddenly she felt the floor fail under her. She sank into the chair with a choking throat, her words, her reasons slipping away from her like straws down a whirling flood.

'Clement,' she cried, 'isn't it enough for you to know that I hate it?'

He turned to close the door behind them; then he walked toward her and sat down. 'What is it that you hate?' he asked gently.

She had made a desperate effort to rally her routed argument.

'I can't bear to have you speak as if – as if – our marriage – were like the other kind – the wrong kind. When I heard you there, the other afternoon, before all those inquisitive gossiping people, proclaiming that husbands and wives had a right to leave each other whenever they were tired – or had seen someone else – '

Westall sat motionless, his eyes fixed on a pattern of the carpet.

'You *have* ceased to take this view, then?' he said as she broke off. 'You no longer believe that husbands and wives *are* justified in separating – under such conditions?'

'Under such conditions?' she stammered. 'Yes – I still believe that – but how can we judge for others? What can we know of the circumstances – ?'

He interrupted her. 'I thought it was a fundamental article of our creed that the special circumstances produced by marriage were not to interfere with the full assertion of individual liberty.' He paused a moment. 'I thought that was your reason for leaving Arment.'

She flushed to the forehead. It was not like him to give a personal turn to the argument.

'It was my reason,' she said simply.

'Well, then – why do you refuse to recognize its validity now?'

'I don't – I don't – I only say that one can't judge for others.'

He made an impatient movement. 'This is mere hairsplitting. What you mean is that, the doctrine having served your purpose when you needed it, you now repudiate it.'

'Well,' she exclaimed, flushing again, 'what if I do? What does it matter to us?'

Westall rose from his chair. He was excessively pale, and stood before his wife with something of the formality of a stranger.

'It matters to me,' he said in a low voice, 'because I do *not* repudiate it.'

'Well – ?'

'And because I had intended to invoke it as – '

He paused and drew his breath deeply. She sat silent, almost deafened by her heartbeats.

' –as a complete justification of the course I am about to take.'

Julia remained motionless. 'What course is that?' she asked.

He cleared his throat. 'I mean to claim the fulfilment of your promise.'

For an instant the room wavered and darkened; then she recovered a torturing acuteness of vision. Every detail of her surroundings, pressed upon her: the tick of the clock, the slant of sunlight on the wall, the hardness of the chair arms that she grasped, were a separate wound to each sense.

'My promise – ' she faltered.

'Your part of our mutual agreement to set each other free if one or the other should wish to be released.'

She was silent again. He waited a moment, shifting his position nervously; then he said, with a touch of irritability: 'You acknowledge the agreement?'

The question went through her like a shock. She lifted her head to it proudly. 'I acknowledge the agreement,' she said.

'And – you don't mean to repudiate it?'

A log on the hearth fell forward, and mechanically he advanced and pushed it back.

'No,' she answered slowly, 'I don't mean to repudiate it.'

There was a pause. He remained near the hearth, his elbow resting on the mantelshelf. Close to his hand stood a little cup of jade that he had given her on one of their wedding anniversaries. She wondered vaguely if he noticed it.

'You intend to leave me, then?' she said at length.

His gesture seemed to deprecate the crudeness of the allusion.

'To marry someone else?'

Again his eye and hand protested. She rose and stood before him.

'Why should you be afraid to tell me? Is it Una Van Sideren?'

He was silent.

'I wish you good luck,' she said.

• III •

SHE looked up, finding herself alone. She did not remember when or how he had left the room, or how long afterward she had sat there. The fire still smoldered on the hearth, but the slant of sunlight had left the wall.

Her first conscious thoughts was that she had not broken her word, that she had fulfilled the very letter of their bargain. There had been no crying out, no vain appeal to the past, no attempt at temporizing or evasion. She had marched straight up to the guns.

Now that it was over, she was sickened to find herself alive. She looked about her, trying to recover her hold on reality. Her identity seemed to be slipping from her, as it disappears in a physical swoon. 'This is my room – this is my house,' she heard herself saying. Her room? Her house? She could almost hear the walls laugh back at her.

She stood up, weariness in every bone. The silence of the room frightened her. She remembered, now, having heard the front door close a long time ago: the sound suddenly re-echoed through her brain.

Her husband must have left the house, then – her *husband?* She no longer knew in what terms to think: the simplest phrases had a poisoned edge. She sank back into her chair, overcome by a strange weakness. The clock struck ten – it was only ten o'clock! Suddenly she remembered that she had not ordered dinner . . . or were they dining out that evening? *Dinner – dining out* – the old meaningless phraseology pursued her! She must try to think of herself as she would think of someone else, a someone dissociated from all the familiar routine of the past, whose wants and habits must gradually be learned, as one might spy out the ways of a strange animal. . . .

The clock struck another hour – eleven. She stood up again and walked to the door: she thought she would go upstairs to her room. *Her* room? Again the word derided her. She opened the door, crossed the narrow hall, and walked up the stairs. As she passed, she noticed Westall's sticks and umbrellas: a pair of his gloves lay on the hall table. The same stair carpet mounted between the same walls; the same old French print, and its narrow black frame, faced her on the landing. This visual continuity was intolerable. Within, a gaping chasm; without, the same untroubled and familiar surface. She must get away from it before she could attempt to think. But, once in her room, she sat down on the lounge, a stupor creeping over her. . . .

Gradually her vision cleared. A great deal had happened in the interval – a wild marching and countermarching of emotions, arguments, ideas – a fury of insurgent impulses that fell back spent upon themselves. She had tried, at first, to rally, to organize these chaotic forces. There must be help somewhere, if only she could master the inner tumult. Life could not be broken off short like this, for a whim, a fancy; the law itself would side with her, would defend her. The law? What claim had she upon it? She was the prisoner of her own choice: she had been her own legislator, and she was the predestined victim of the code she had devised. But this was grotesque, intolerable – a mad mistake, for which she could not be held accountable! The law she had despised was still there, might still be invoked . . . invoked, but to what end? Could she ask it to chain Westall to her side? *She* had been allowed to go free when she claimed her freedom – should she show less magnanimity than she had exacted? Magnanimity? The word lashed her with its irony – one does not strike an attitude when one is fighting for life! She would threaten, grovel, cajole . . . she would yield anything to keep her hold on happiness. Ah, but the difficulty lay deeper! The law could not help her – her own apostasy could not help her. She was the victim of the theories she renounced. It was as though some giant machine of her own making had caught her up in its wheels and was grinding her to atoms. . . .

It was afternoon when she found herself out of doors. She walked with an aimless haste, fearing to meet familiar faces. The day was radiant, metallic: one of those searching American days so calculated to reveal the shortcomings of our street-cleaning and the excesses of our architecture. The streets looked bare and hideous; everything stared and glittered. She called a passing hansom, and gave Mrs. Van Sideren's address. She did not know what had led up to the act; but she found herself suddenly resolved to speak, to cry out a warning. It was too late to save herself – but the girl might still be told. The handsom rattled up Fifth Avenue; she sat with her eyes fixed, avoiding recognition. At the Van Siderens' door she sprang out and rang the bell. Action had cleared her brain, and she felt calm and self-possessed. She knew now exactly what she meant to say.

The ladies were both out . . . the parlormaid stood waiting for a card. Julia, with a vague murmur, turned away from the door and lingered a moment on the sidewalk. Then she remembered that she had not paid the cab driver. She drew a dollar from her purse and handed it to him. He touched his hat and drove off, leaving her alone in the long empty street. She wandered away westward, toward strange thoroughfares, where she was not likely to meet acquaintances. The feeling of aimlessness had returned. Once she found herself in the afternoon torrent of Broadway, swept past tawdry shops and flaming theatrical posters, with a succession of meaningless faces gliding by in the opposite direction. . . .

A feeling of faintness reminded her that she had not eaten since morning. She turned into a side street of shabby houses, with rows of ash barrels behind bent area railings. In a basement window she saw the sign 'Ladies' Restaurant': a pie and a dish of doughnuts lay against the dusty pane like petrified food in an ethnological museum. She entered and a young woman with a weak mouth and a brazen eye cleared a table for her near the window. The table was covered with a red-and-white cotton cloth and adorned with a bunch of celery in a thick tumbler and a saltcellar full of grayish lumpy salt. Julia ordered tea, and sat a long time waiting for it. She was glad to be away from the noise and confusion of the streets. The low-ceilinged room was empty, and two or three waitresses with thin pert faces lounged in the background staring at her and whispering together. At last the tea was brought in a discolored metal teapot. Julia poured a cup and drank it hastily. It was black and bitter, but it flowed through her veins like an elixir. She was almost dizzy with exhilaration. Oh, how tired, how unutterably tired she had been!

She drank a second cup, blacker and bitterer, and now her mind was once more working clearly. She felt as vigorous, as decisive, as when she had stood on the Van Siderens' doorstep – but the wish to return there had subsided. She saw now the futility of such an attempt – the humiliation to which it might have exposed her. . . . The pity of it was that she did not know what to do next. The short winter day was fading, and she realized that she could not remain much longer in the restaurant without attracting notice. She paid for her tea and went out into the street. The lamps were alight, and here and there a basement shop cast an oblong of gaslight across the fissured pavement. In the dusk there was something sinister about the aspect of the street, and she hastened back toward Fifth Avenue. She was not used to being out alone at that hour.

At the corner of Fifth Avenue she paused and stood watching the stream of carriages. At last a policeman caught sight of her and signed to her that he would take her across. She had not meant to cross the street, but she obeyed automatically, and presently found herself on the farther corner. There she paused again for a moment; but she fancied the policemen was watching her, and this sent her hastening down the nearest side street. . . . After that she walked a long time, vaguely. . . . Night had fallen, and now and then, through the windows of a passing carriage, she caught the expanse of an evening waistcoat or the shimmer of an opera cloak. . . .

Suddenly she found herself in a familiar street. She stood still a moment, breathing quickly. She had turned the corner without noticing whither it led; but now, a few yards ahead of her, she saw the house in which she had once lived – her first husband's house. The blinds were drawn, and only a faint translucence marked the windows and the transom above the door. As she stood there she heard a step behind her, and a man walked by in the direction of the house. He walked slowly, with a heavy middle-aged gait, his head sunk a little between the shoulders, the red crease of his neck visible above the fur collar of his overcoat. He crossed the street, went up the steps of the house, drew forth a latchkey, and let himself in. . . .

There was no one else in sight. Julia leaned for a long time against the area rail at the corner, her eyes fixed on the front of the house. The feeling of physical weariness had returned, but the strong tea still throbbed in her veins and lit her brain with an unnatural clearness. Presently she heard another step draw near, and moving quickly away, she too crossed the street and mounted the steps of the house. The impulse which had carried her there prolonged itself in a quick pressure of the electric bell – then she felt suddenly weak and tremulous, and grasped the balustrade for support. The door opened and a young footman with a fresh inexperienced face stood on the threshold. Julia knew in an instant that he would admit her.

'I saw Mr. Arment going in just now,' she said. 'Will you ask him to see me for a moment?'

The footman hesitated. 'I think Mr. Arment has gone up to dress for dinner, madam.'

Julia advanced into the hall. 'I am sure he will see me – I will not detain him long,' she said. She spoke quietly, authoritatively, in the tone which a good servant does not mistake. The footman had his hand on the drawing-room door.

'I will tell him, madam. What name, please?'

Julia trembled: she had not thought of that. 'Merely say a lady', she returned carelessly.

The footman wavered and she fancied herself lost; but at that instant the door opened from within and John Arment stepped into the hall. He drew back sharply as he saw her, his florid face turning sallow with the shock; then the blood poured back to it, swelling the veins on his temples and reddening the lobes of his thick ears.

It was long since Julia had seen him, and she was startled at the change in his appearance. He had thickened, coarsened, settled down into the enclosing flesh. But she noted this insensibly: her one conscious thought was that, now she was face to face with him, she must not let him escape till he had heard her. Every pulse in her body throbbed with the urgency of her message.

She went up to him as he drew back. 'I must speak to you,' she said.

Arment hestitated, red and stammering. Julia glanced at the footman, and her look acted as a warning. The instinctive shrinking from a scene predominated over every other impulse, and Arment said slowly: 'Will you come this way?'

He followed her into the drawing room and closed the door. Julia, as she advanced, was vaguely aware that the room at least was unchanged: time had not mitigated its horrors. The contadina still lurched from the chimney breast, and the Greek slave obstructed the threshold of the inner room. The place was alive with memories; they started out from every fold of the yellow satin curtains and glided between the angles of the rosewood furniture. But while some subordinate agency was carrying these impressions to her brain, her whole conscious effort was centered in the act of dominating Arment's will. The fear that he would refuse to hear her mounted like fever to her brain. She felt her purpose melt before it, words and arguments running into each other in the heat of her longing. For a moment her voice failed her, and she imagined herself thrust out before she could speak; but as she was struggling for a word Arment pushed a chair forward, and said quietly: 'You are not well.'

The sound of his voice steadied her. It was neither kind nor unkind – a voice that suspended judgment, rather, awaiting unforeseen developments. She supported herself against the back of the chair and drew a deep breath.

'Shall I send for something?' he continued, with a cold embarrassed politeness.

Julia raised an entreating hand. 'No – no – thank you. I am quite well.'

He paused midway toward the bell, and turned on her. 'Then may I ask – ?'

'Yes,' she interrupted him. 'I came here because I wanted to see you. There is something I must tell you.'

Arment continued to scrutinize her. 'I am surprised at that,' he said. 'I should have supposed that any communication you may wish to make could have been made through our lawyers.'

'Our lawyers!' She burst into a little laugh. 'I don't think they could help me – this time.'

Arment's face took on a barricaded look. 'If there is any question of help – of course – '

It struck her, whimsically, that she had seen that look when some shabby devil called with a subscription book. Perhaps he thought she wanted him to put his name down for so much in sympathy – or even in money. . . . The thought made her laugh again. She saw his look change slowly to perplexity. All his facial changes were slow, and she remembered, suddenly, how it had once diverted her to shift that lumbering scenery with a word. For the first time it struck her that she had been cruel! 'There *is* a question of help,' she said in a softer key; 'you can help me; but only by listening. . . . I want to tell you something. . . .'

Arment's reistance was not yielding. 'Would it not be easier to – write?' he suggested.

She shook her head. 'There is no time to write . . . and it won't take long.' She raised her head and their eyes met. 'My husband has left me,' she said.

'Westall – ?' he stammered, reddening again.

'Yes. This morning. Just as I left you. Because he was tired of me.'

The words, uttered scarcely above a whisper, seemed to dilate to the limit of the room. Arment looked toward the door; then his embarrassed glance returned returned to Julia.

'I am very sorry,' he said awkwardly.

'Thank you,' she murmured.

'But I don't see – '

'No – but you will – in a moment. Won't you listen to me? Please!' Instinctively she had shifted her position, putting herself between him and the door. 'It happened this morning,' she went on in short breathless phrases. 'I never suspected anything – I thought we were – perfectly happy. . . . Suddenly he told me he was tired of me . . . there is a girl he likes better. . . . He has gone to her. . . .' As he spoke, the lurking anguish rose upon her, possessing her once more to the exclusion of every other emotion. Her eyes ached, her throat swelled with it, and two painful tears ran down her face.

Arment's constraint was increasing visibly. 'This – this is very unfortunate,' he began. 'But I should say the law – '

'The law?' she echoed ironically. 'When he asks for his freedom?'

'You are not obliged to give it.'

'You were not obliged to give me mine – but you did.'

He made a protesting gesture.

'You saw that the law couldn't help you – didn't you?' she went on. 'That is what I see now. The law represents material rights – it can't go beyond. If we don't recognize an inner law . . . the obligation that love creates . . . being loved as well as loving . . . there is nothing to prevent our spreading ruin unhindered . . . is there?' She raised her head plaintively, with the look of a bewildered child. 'That is what I see now . . . what I wanted to tell you. He leaves me because he's tired . . . but *I* was not tired; and I don't understand why he is. That's the dreadful part of it – the not understanding: I hadn't realized what it meant. But I've been thinking of it all day, and things have come back to me – things I hadn't noticed . . . when you and I . . .' She moved closer to him, and fixed her eyes on his with the gaze which tries to reach beyond words. 'I see now that *you* didn't understand – did you?'

Their eyes met in a sudden shock of comprehension: a veil seemed to be lifted between them. Arment's lip trembled.

'No,' he said, 'I didn't understand.'

She gave a little cry, almost of triumph. 'I knew it! I knew it! You wondered – you tried to tell me – but no words came. . . . You saw your life falling in ruins . . . the world slipping from you . . . and you couldn't speak or move!'

She sank down on the chair against which she had been leaning. 'Now I know – now I know,' she repeated.

'I am very sorry for you,' she heard Arment stammer.

She looked up quickly. 'That's not what I came for. I don't want you to be sorry. I came to ask you to forgive me . . . for not understanding that *you* didn't understand. . . . That's all I wanted to say.' She rose with a vague sense that the end had come, and put out a groping hand toward the door.

Arment stood motionless. She turned to him with a faint smile.

'You forgive me?'

'There is nothing to forgive – '

'Then you will shake hands for good-bye?' She felt his hand in hers: it was nerveless, reluctant.

'Good-bye,' she repeated. 'I understand now.'

She opened the door and passed out into the hall. As she did so, Arment took an impulsive step forward; but just then the footman, who was evidently alive to his obligations, advanced from the background to let her out. She heard Arment fall back. The footman threw open the door, and she found herself outside in the darkness.

The Last Asset

'THE DEVIL!' Paul Garnett exclaimed as he reread his note; and the dry old gentleman who was at the moment his only neighbor in the modest restaurant they both frequented, remarked with a smile: 'You don't seem particularly disturbed at meeting him.'

Garnett returned the smile. 'I don't know why I apostrophized him, for he's not in the least present – except inasmuch as he may prove to be at the bottom of anything unexpected.'

The old gentleman who, like Garnett, was an American, and spoke in the thin rarefied voice which seems best fitted to emit sententious truths, twisted his lean neck round to cackle out: 'Ah, it's generally a woman who's at the bottom of the unexpected. Not,' he added, leaning forward with deliberation to select a toothpick, 'that that precludes the devil's being there too.'

Garnett uttered the requisite laugh, and his neighbor, pushing back his plate, called out with a perfectly unbending American intonation: 'Gassong! L'addition, silver play.'

His repast, as usual, had been a simple one, and he left only thirty centimes in the plate on which his account was presented; but the waiter, to whom he was evidently a familiar presence, received the tribute with Latin amenity, and hovered helpfully about the table while the old gentleman cut and lighted his cigar.

'Yes,' the latter proceeded, revolving the cigar meditatively between his thin lips, 'they're generally both in the same hole, like the owl and the prairie dog in the natural history books of my youth. I believe it was all a mistake about the owl and the prairie dog, but it isn't about the unexpected. The fact is, the unexpected *is* the devil – the sooner you find that out, the happier you'll be.' He leaned back, tilting his bald head against the blotched mirror behind him, and rambling on with gentle garrulity while Garnett attacked his omelet.

'Get your life down to routine – eliminate surprises. Arrange things so that, when you get up in the morning, you'll know exactly what's going to happen to you during the day – and the next day and the next. I don't say it's funny – it ain't. But it's better than being hit on the

64

head by a brickbat. That's why I always take my meals at this restaurant. I know just how much onion they put in things – if I went to the next place I shouldn't. And I always take the same streets to come here – I've been doing it for ten years now. I know at which crossing to look out – I know what I'm going to see in the shop windows. It saves a lot of wear and tear to know what's coming. For a good many years I never *did* know, from one minute to another, and now I like to think that everything's cut and dried, and nothing unexpected can jump out at me like a tramp from a ditch.'

He paused calmly to knock the ashes from his cigar and Garnett said with a smile: 'Doesn't such a plan of life cut off nearly all the possibilities?'

The old gentleman made a contemptuous motion. 'Possibilities of what? Of being multifariously miserable? There are lots of ways of being miserable, but there's only one way of being comfortable, and that is to stop running round after happiness. If you make up your mind not to be happy there's no reason why you shouldn't have a fairly good time.'

'That was Schopenhauer's idea, I believe,' the young man said, pouring his wine with the smile of youthful incredulity.

'I guess he hadn't the monopoly,' responded his friend. 'Lots of people have found out the secret – the trouble is that so few live up to it.'

He rose from his seat, pushing the table forward, and standing passive while the waiter advanced with his shabby overcoat and umbrella. Then he nodded to Garnett, lifted his hat to the broad-bosomed lady behind the desk, and passed out into the street.

Garnett looked after him with a musing smile. The two had exchanged views on life for two years without so much as knowing each other's names. Garnett was a newspaper correspondent whose work kept him mainly in London, but on his periodic visits to Paris he lodged in a dingy hotel of the Latin quarter, the chief merit of which was its nearness to the cheap and excellent restaurant where the two Americans had made acquaintance. But Garnett's assiduity in frequenting the place arose, in the end, less from the excellence of the food than from the enjoyment of his old friend's conversation. Amid the flashy sophistications of the Parisian life to which Garnett's trade introduced him, the American sage's conversation had the crisp and homely flavor of a native dish – one of the domestic compounds for which the exiled palate is supposed to yearn. It was a mark of the old man's impersonality that, in spite of the interest he inspired, Garnett had never got beyond idly wondering who he might be, where he lived, and what his occupations were. He was presumably a bachelor – a man of family ties, however relaxed, though he might have been as often absent from home, would not have been as regularly present in the same place – and there was about him a boundless desultoriness which renewed Garnett's conviction that there is no one on earth as idle as an American who is not busy. From certain allusions it was plain that he had lived many years in Paris, yet he had not taken the trouble to adapt his tongue to the local inflections, but spoke French with the accent of one who has formed his notion of the language from a phrase book.

The city itself seemed to have made as little impression on him as its speech. He appeared to have no artistic or intellectual curiosities, to remain untouched by the complex appeal of Paris, while preserving, perhaps the more strikingly from his very detachment, that odd American astuteness which seems the fruit of innocence rather than of experience. His nationality revealed itself again in a mild interest in the political problems of his adopted country, though they appeared to preoccupy him only as illustrating the boundless perversity of mankind. The exhibition of human folly never ceased to divert him, and though his examples of it seemed mainly drawn from the columns of one exiguous daily paper, he found there matter for endless variations on his favorite theme. If this monotony of topic did not weary the younger man, it was because he fancied he could detect under it the tragic note of the fixed idea – of some great moral upheaval which had flung his friend stripped and starving on the desert island of the little restaurant where they met. He hardly knew wherein he read this revelation – whether in the shabbiness of the sage's dress, the impersonal courtesy of his manner, or the shade of apprehension which lurked, indescribably, in his guileless yet suspicious eye. There were moments when Garnett could only define him by saying that he looked like a man who had seen a ghost.

• II •

AN apparition almost as startling had come to Garnett himself in the shape of the mauve note handed to him by his *concierge* as he was leaving the hotel for luncheon.

Not that, on the face of it, a missive announcing Mrs. Sam Newell's arrival at Ritz's, and her need of his presence there that day at five, carried any mark of the portentous. It was not her being at Ritz's that surprised him. The fact that she was chronically hard up, and had once or twice lately been so harshly confronted with the consequences as to accept – indeed solicit – a loan of five pounds from him: this circumstance, as Garnett knew, would never be allowed to affect the general tenor of her existence. If one came to Paris, where could one go but to Ritz's? Did he see her in some grubby hole across the river? Or in a family *pension* near the Place de l'Etoile? There was no affectation in her tendency to gravitate toward what was costliest and most conspicuous. In doing so she obeyed one of the profoundest instincts of her nature, and it was another instinct which taught her to gratify the first at any cost, even to that of dipping into the pocket of an impecunious journalist. It was a part of her strength – and of her charm, too – that she did such things naturally, openly, without any of the grimaces of dissimulation or compunction.

Her recourse to Garnett had of course marked a specially low ebb in her fortunes. Save in moments of exceptional dearth she had richer sources of supply; and he was nearly sure that by running over the 'society column' of the Paris *Herald* he should find an explanation, not perhaps of her presence at Ritz's, but of her means of subsistence there. What perplexed him was not the financial but the social aspect of the case. When Mrs. Newell had left London in July she had told him that, between Cowes and Scotland, she and Hermy were provided for till the middle of October: after that, as she put it, they would have to look about. Why, then, when she had in her hand the opportunity of living for three months at the expense of the British aristocracy, did she rush off to Paris at heaven knew whose expense in the beginning of September? She was not a woman to act incoherently; if she made mistakes they were not of that kind. Garnett felt sure she would never willingly relax her hold on her distinguished friends – was it possible that it was they who had somewhat violently let go of her?

As Garnett reviewed the situation he began to see that his possibility had for some time been latent in it. He had felt that something might happen at any moment – and was not this the something he had obscurely foreseen? Mrs. Newell really moved too fast: her position was as perilous as that of an invading army without a base of supplies. She used up everything too quickly – friends, credit, influence, forbearance. It was so easy for her to acquire all these – what a pity she had never learned to keep them! He himself, for instance – the most insignificant of her acquisitions – was beginning to feel like a squeezed sponge at the mere thought of her; and it was this sense of exhaustion, of the inability to provide more, either materially or morally, which had provoked his exclamation on opening her note. From the first days of their acquaintance her prodigality had amazed him, but he had believed it to be surpassed by the infinity of her resources. If she exhausted old supplies she always had new ones to replace them. When one set of people began to find her impossible, another was always beginning to find her indispensable. Yes – but there were limits – there were only so many sets of people, at least in her classification, and when she came to an end of them, what then? Was this flight to Paris a sign that she had come to an end – was she going to try Paris because London had failed her? The time of year precluded such a conjecture. Mrs. Newell's Paris was nonexistent in September. The town was a

desert of gaping trippers – he could as soon think of her seeking social
restoration at Margate.

For a moment it occurred to him that she might have come over
to renew her wardrobe; but he knew her dates too well to dwell long
on this. It was in April and December that she visited the dressmakers:
before December, he had heard her explain, one got nothing but 'the
American fashions.' Mrs. Newell's scorn of all things American was
somewhat illogically coupled with the determination to use her own
Americanism to the utmost as a means of social advance. She had found
out long ago that, on certain lines, it paid in London to be American,
and she had manufactured for herself a personality independent of
geographical or social demarcations, and presenting that remarkable
blend of plantation dialect, Bowery slang and hyperbolic statement,
which expresses the British idea of an unadulterated Americanism. Mrs.
Newell, for all her talents, was not by nature either humorous or
hyperbolic, and there were times when it would doubtless have been a
relief to her to be as stolid as some of the persons whose dullness it
was her fate to enliven. It was perhaps the need of relaxing which had
drawn her into her odd intimacy with Garnett, with whom she did not
have to be either scrupulously English or artificially American, since
the impression she made on him was of no more consequence than that
which she produced on her footman. Garnett was aware that he owed
his success to his insignificance, but the fact affected him only as adding
one more element to his knowledge of Mrs. Newell's character. He
was as ready to sacrifice his personal vanity in such a cause as he had
been, at the outset of their acquaintance, to sacrifice his professional
pride to the opportunity of knowing her.

When he had accepted the position of 'London correspondent' (with
an occasional side glance at Paris) to the New York *Searchlight*, he
had not understood that his work was to include the obligation of
'interviewing': indeed, had the possibility presented itself in advance,
he would have met it by packing his valise and returning to the drudgery
of his assistant editorship in New York. But when, after three months
in Europe, he received a letter from his chief, suggesting that he should
enliven the Sunday *Searchlight* by a series of 'Talks with Smart Americans in London' (beginning say, with Mrs. Sam Newell), the change
of focus already enabled him to view the proposal without passion. For
his life on the edge of the great world caldron of art, politics and
pleasure – of that high-spiced brew which is nowhere else so subtly
and variously compounded – had bred in him an eagerness to taste of
the heady mixture. He knew he should never have the full spoon at his
lips, but he recalled the peasant girl in one of Browning's plays, who
boasts of having eaten polenta cut with a knife which has carved an
ortolan. Might not Mrs. Newell, who had so successfully cut a way

into the dense and succulent mass of English society, serve as the knife to season his polenta?

He had expected, as the result of the interview, to which she promptly, almost eagerly, agreed, no more than the glimpse of brightly-lit vistas which a waiting messenger may catch through open doors; but instead he had found himself drawn at once into the inner sanctuary, not of London society, but of Mrs. Newell's relation to it. She had been candidly charmed by the idea of the interview: it struck him that she was conscious of the need of being freshened up. Her appearance was brilliantly fresh, with the inveterate freshness of the toilet table; her paint was as impenetrable as armor. But her personality was a little tarnished: she was in want of social renovation. She had been doing and saying the same things for too long a time. London, Cowes, Hamburg, Scotland, Monte Carlo – that had been the round since Hermy was a baby. Hermy was her daughter, Miss Hermione Newell, who was called in presently to be shown off to the interviewer and add a paragraph to the celebration of her mother's charms.

Miss Newell's appearance was so full of an unassisted freshness that for a moment Garnett made the mistake of fancying that she could fill a paragraph of her own. But he soon found that her vague personality was merely tributary to her parent's; that her youth and grace were, in some mysterious way, her mother's rather than her own. She smiled obediently on Garnett, but could contribute little beyond her smile, and the general sweetness of her presence, to the picture of Mrs. Newell's existence that it was the young man's business to draw. And presently he found that she had left the room without his noticing it.

He learned in time that this unnoticeableness was the most conspicuous thing about her. Burning at best with a mild light, she became invisible in the glare of her mother's personality. It was in fact only as a product of her environment that poor Hermione struck the imagination. With the smartest woman in London as her guide and example she had never developed a taste for dress, and with opportunities for enlightenment from which Garnett's fancy recoiled she remained simple, unsuspicious and tender, with an inclination to good works and afternoon church, a taste for the society of dull girls, and a clinging fidelity to old governesses and retired nursemaids. Mrs. Newell, whose boast it was that she looked facts in the face, frankly owned that she had not been able to make anything of Hermione. 'If she has a role I haven't discovered it,' she confessed to Garnett. 'I've tried everything, but she doesn't fit in anywhere.'

Mrs. Newell spoke as if her daughter were a piece of furniture acquired without due reflection, and for which no suitable place could be found. She got, of course, what she could out of Hermione, who wrote her notes, ran her errands, saw tiresome people for her, and occupied an intermediate office between that of lady's maid and secretary; but such small returns on her investment were not what Mrs. Newell had counted on. What was the use of producing and educating a handsome daughter if she did not, in some more positive way, contribute to her parent's advancement?

• III •

'IT's about Hermy,' Mrs. Newell said, rising from the heap of embroidered cushions which formed the background of her afternoon repose.

Her sitting room at Ritz's was full of warmth and fragrance. Long-stemmed roses filled the vases on the chimney piece, in which a fire sparkled with that effect of luxury which fires produce when the weather is not cold enough to justify them. On the writing table, among notes and cards, and signed photographs of celebrities, Mrs. Newell's gold inkstand, her jeweled pen holder, her heavily monogrammed dispatch box, gave back from their expensive surfaces the glint of the flame, which sought out and magnified the orient of the pearls among the lady's laces and found a mirror in the pink polish of her fingertips. It was just such a scene as a little September fire, lit for show and not for warmth, would delight to dwell on and pick out in all its opulent details; and even Garnett, inured to Mrs. Newell's capacity for extracting manna from the desert, reflected that she must have found new fields to glean.

'It's about Hermy,' she repeated, making room for him at her side, 'I had to see you at once. We came over yesterday from London.'

Garnett, seating himself, continued his leisurely survey of the room. In the blaze of Mrs. Newell's refulgence Hermione, as usual, faded out of sight, and he hardly noticed her mother's allusion.

'I've never seen you more resplendent,' he remarked.

She received the tribute with complacency. 'The rooms are not bad, are they? We came over with the Woolsey Hubbards (you've heard of them, of course? – they're from Detroit), and really they do things very decently. Their motor met us at Boulogne, and the courier always wires ahead to have the rooms filled with flowers. This salon is really a part of their suite, I simply couldn't have afforded it myself.'

She delivered these facts in a high decisive voice, which had a note like the clink of her many bracelets and the rattle of her ringed hands against the enameled cigarette case that she held out to Garnett after helping herself from its contents.

'You are always meeting such charming people,' said the young man with mild irony; and, reverting to her first remark, he bethought himself to add: 'I hope Miss Hermione is not ill?'

'Ill? She was never ill in her life,' exclaimed Mrs. Newell, as though her daughter had been accused of an indelicacy.

'It was only that you said you had come over on her account.'

'So I have. Hermione is to be married.'

Mrs. Newell brought out the words impressively, drawing back to observe their effect on her visitor. It was such that he received them with a long silent stare, which finally passed into a cry of wonder. 'Married? For heaven's sake, to whom?'

Mrs. Newell continued to regard him with a smile so serene and victorious that he saw she took his somewhat unseemly astonishment as a merited tribute to her genius. Presently she extended a glittering hand and took a sheet of notepaper from the blotter.

'You can have that put in tomorrow's *Herald*, she said.

Garnett, receiving the paper, read in Hermione's own finished hand: 'A marriage has been arranged, and will shortly take place, between the Comte Louis du Trayas, son of the Marquis du Trayas de la Baume, and Miss Hermione Newell, daughter of Samuel C. Newell, Esq., of Elmira, N. Y. Comte Louis du Trayas belongs to one of the oldest and most distinguished families in France, and is equally well connected in England, being the nephew of Lord Saint Priscoe and a cousin of the Countess of Morningfield, whom he frequently visits at Adham and Portlow.'

The perusal of this document filled Garnett with such deepening wonder that he could not, for the moment, even do justice to the strangeness of its being written out for publication in the bride's own hand. Hermione a bride! Hermione a future countess! Hermione on the brink of a marriage which would give her not only a great 'situation' in the Parisian world but a footing in some of the best houses in England! Regardless of its unflattering implications, Garnett prolonged his stare of amazement till Mrs. Newell somewhat sharply exclaimed – 'Well, didn't I always tell you she'd marry a Frenchman?'

Garnett, in spite of himself, smiled at this revised version of his hostess's frequent assertion that Hermione was too goody-goody to take in England, but that with her little dowdy air she might very well 'go off' in the Faubourg if only a *dot* could be raked up – and the recollection flashed a new light on the versatility of Mrs. Newell's genius.

'But how did you do it – ?' was on the tip of his tongue; and he had barely time to give the query the more conventional turn of: 'How did it happen?'

'Oh, we were up at Glaish with the Edmund Fitzarthurs. Lady Edmund is a sort of cousin of the Morningfields', who have a shooting lodge near Glaish – a place called Portlow – and young Trayas was there with them. Lady Edmund, who is a dear, drove Hermy over to Portlow, and the thing was done in no time. He simply fell over head and ears in love with her. You know Hermy is really very handsome in her peculiar way. I don't think you've ever appreciated her,' Mrs. Newell summed up with a note of reproach.

'I've appreciated her, I assure you; but one somehow didn't think of her marrying – so soon.'

'Soon? She's three and twenty; but you've no imagination,' said Mrs. Newell; and Garnett inwardly admitted that he had not enough to soar to the heights of her invention. For the marriage, of course, was her invention, a superlative stroke of business in which he was sure the principal parties had all been passive agents in which everyone, from the bankrupt and disreputable Fitzarthurs to the rich and immaculate Morningfields, had by some mysterious sleight of hand been made to fit into Mrs. Newell's designs. But it was not enough for Garnett to marvel at her work – he wanted to understand it, to take it apart, to find out how the trick had been done. It was true that Mrs. Newell had always said Hermy might go off in the Faubourg if she had a *dot* – but even Mrs. Newell's juggling could harldy conjure up a *dot:* such feats as she was able to perform in this line were usually made to serve her own urgent necessities. And besides, who was likely to take sufficient interest in Hermione to supply her with the means of marrying a French nobleman? The flowers ordered in advance by the Woolsey Hubbards' courier made Garnett wonder if that accomplished functionary had also wired over to have Miss Newell's settlements drawn up. But of all the comments hovering on his lips the only one he could decently formulate was the remark that he supposed Mrs. Newell and her daughter had come over to see the young man's family and make the final arrangements.

'Oh, they're made – everything's settled,' said Mrs. Newell, looking him squarely in the eye. 'You're wondering, of course, about the *dot* – Frenchmen never go off their heads to the extent of forgetting *that;* or at least their parents don't allow them to.'

Garnett murmured a vague assent, and she went on without the least appearance of resenting his curiosity: 'It all came about so fortunately. Only fancy, just the week they met I got a little legacy from an aunt in Elmira – a good soul I hadn't seen or heard of for years. I suppose I ought to have put on mourning for her, by the way, but it would have eaten up a good bit of the legacy, and I really needed it all for poor Hermy. Oh, it's not a fortune, you understand – but the young man is madly in love, and has always had his own way, so after a lot of correspondence it's been arranged. They saw Hermy this morning, and they're enchanted.'

'And the marriage takes place very soon?'

'Yes, in a few weeks, here. His mother is an invalid and couldn't have gone to England. Besides, the French don't travel. And as Hermy has become a Catholic – '

'Already?'

Mrs. Newell stared. 'It doesn't take long. And it suits Hermy exactly – she can go to church so much oftener. So I thought,' Mrs. Newell concluded with dignity, 'that a wedding at Saint Philippe du Roule would be the most suitable thing at this season.'

'Dear me,' said Garnett, 'I am left breathless – I can't catch up with you. I suppose even the day is fixed, though Miss Hermione doesn't mention it,' and he indicated the official announcement in his hand.

Mrs. Newell laughed. 'Hermy had to write that herself, poor dear, because my scrawl's too hideous – but I dictated it. No, the day's not fixed – that's why I sent for you.' There was a splendid directness about Mrs. Newell. It would never have occurred to her to pretend to Garnett that she had summoned him for the pleasure of his company.

'You've sent for me – to fix the day?' he inquired humorously.

'To remove the last obstacle to its being fixed.'

'I? What kind of an obstacle could I have the least effect on?'

Mrs. Newell met his banter with a look which quelled it. 'I want you to find her father.'

'Her father? Miss Hermione's – ?'

'My husband, of course. I suppose you know he's living.'

Garnett blushed at his own clumsiness. 'I – yes – that is, I really knew nothing – ' he stammered, feeling that each word added to it. If Hermione was unnoticeable, Mr. Newell had always been invisible. The young man had never so much as given him a thought, and it was awkward to come on him so suddenly at a turn of the talk.

'Well, he is – living here in Paris,' said Mrs. Newell, with a note of asperity which seemed to imply that her friend might have taken the trouble to post himself on this point.

'In Paris? But in that case isn't it quite simple – ?'

'To find him? I dare say it won't be difficult, though he's rather mysterious. But the point is that I can't go to him – and that if I write to him he won't answer.'

'Ah,' said Garnett thoughtfully.

'And so you've got to find him for me, and tell him.'

'Tell him what?'

'That he must come to the wedding – that we must show ourselves together at church and afterward in the sacristy.'

She delivered the behest in her sharp imperative key, the tone of the born commander. But for once Garnett ventured to question her orders.

'And supposing he won't come?'

'He must if he cares for his daughter's happiness. She can't be married without him.'

'Can't be married?'

'The French are like that – especially the old families. I was given to understand at once that my husband must appear – if only to establish the fact that we're not divorced.'

'Ah – you're *not*, then?' escaped from Garnett.

'Mercy no! Divorce is stupid. They don't like it in Europe. And in this case it would have been the end of Hermy's marriage. They wouldn't think of letting their son marry the child of divorced parents.'

'How fortunate, then – '

'Yes: but I always think of such things beforehand. And of course I've told them that my husband will be present.'

'You think he will consent?'

'No; not at first; but you must make him. You must tell him how sweet Hermione is – and you must see Louis, and be able to describe their happiness. You must dine here tonight – he's coming. We're all dining with the Hubbards, and they expect you. They've given Hermy some very good diamonds – though I should have preferred a check, as she'll be horribly poor. But I think Kate Hubbard means to do something about the trousseau – Hermy is at Paquin's with her now. You've no idea how delightful all our friends have been. Ah, here is one of them now,' she broke off smiling, as the door opening to admit, without preliminary announcement, a gentleman so glossy and ancient, with such a fixed unnatural freshness of smile and eye, that he gave Garnett the effect of having been embalmed and then enameled. It needed not the exotic-looking ribbon in the visitor's buttonhole, nor Mr. Newell's introduction of him as her friend Baron Schenkelderff, to assure Garnett of his connection with a race as ancient as his appearance.

Baron Schenkelderff greeted his hostess with paternal playfulness, and the young man with an ease which might have been acquired on the Stock Exchange and in the dressing rooms of 'leading ladies.' He spoke a faultless colorless English, from which one felt he might pass with equal mastery to half a dozen other languages. He inquired patronizingly for the excellent Hubbards, asked his hostess if she did not mean to give him a drop of tea and a cigarette, remarked that he need not ask if Hermione was still closeted with the dressmaker, and, on the waiter's coming in answer to his ring, ordered the tea himself, and added a request for *fine champagne*. It was not the first time that Garnett had seen such minor liberties taken in Mrs. Newell's drawing room, but they had hitherto been taken by persons who had at least the superiority of knowing what they were permitting themselves, whereas the young man felt almost sure that Baron Schenkelderff's manner was the most distinguished he could achieve; and this deepened the disgust with which, as the minutes passed, he yielded to the conviction that the Baron was Mrs. Newell's 'aunt'.

• IV •

GARNETT had always foreseen that Mrs. Newell might someday ask him to do something he should greatly dislike. He had never gone so far as to conjecture what it might be, but had simply felt that if he allowed his acquaintance with her to pass from spectatorship to participation he must be prepared to find himself, at any moment, in a queer situation.

The moment had come; and he was relieved to find that he could meet it by refusing her request. He had not always been sure that she would leave him this alternative. She had a way of involving people in her complications without their being aware of it; and Garnett had pictured himself in holes so tight that there might not be room for a wriggle. Happily in this case he could still move freely. Nothing compelled him to act as an intermediary between Mrs. Newell and her husband, and it was preposterous to suppose that, even in a life of such perpetual upheaval as hers, there were no roots which struck deeper than her casual intimacy with himself. She had simply laid hands on him because he happened to be within reach, and he would put himself out of reach by leaving for London on the morrow.

Having thus inwardly asserted his independence, he felt free to let his fancy dwell on the strangeness of the situation. He had always supposed that Mrs. Newell, in her flight through life, must have thrown a good many victims to the wolves, and had assumed that Mr. Newell had been among the number. That he had been dropped overboard at an early stage in the lady's career seemed probable from the fact that neither his wife nor his daughter ever mentioned him. Mrs. Newell was incapable of reticence, and if her husband had still been an active element in her life he would certainly have figured in her conversation. Garnett, if he thought of the matter at all, had concluded that divorce must long since have elminated Mr. Newell; but he now saw how he had underrated his friend's faculty for using up the waste material of life. She had always struck him as the most extravagant of women, yet it turned out that by a miracle of thrift she had for years kept a superfluous husband on the chance that he might someday be useful. The day had come, and Mr. Newell was to be called from his obscurity. Garnett wondered what had become of him in the interval, and in what shape he would respond to the evocation. The fact that his wife feared he might not respond to it at all seemed to show that his exile was voluntary, or had at least come to appear preferable to other alternatives; but if that were the case it was curious he should not have taken legal means to free himself. He could hardly have had his wife's motives for wishing to maintain the vague tie between them; but conjecture lost itself in trying to picture what his point of view was likely to be, and Garnett, on his way to the Hubbards' dinner that evening, could not help regretting that circumstances denied him the opportunity of meeting so enigmatic a person. The young man's knowledge of Mrs. Newell's methods made him feel that her husband might be an interesting study. This, however, did not affect his resolve to keep clear of the business. He entered the Hubbards' dining room with the firm intention of refusing to execute Mrs. Newell's commission, and if he changed his mind in the course of the evening it was not owing to that lady's persuasions.

Garnett's curiosity as to the Hubbards' share in Hermione's marriage was appeased before he had been five minutes at their table.

Mrs. Woolsey Hubbard was an expansive blonde, whose ample but disciplined outline seemed the result of a well-matched struggle between her cook and her corset maker. She talked a great deal of what was appropriate in dress and conduct, and seemed to regard Mrs. Newell as a final arbiter on both points. To do or to wear anything inappropriate would have been extremely mortifying to Mrs. Hubbard, and she was evidently resolved, at the price of eternal vigilance, to prove her familiarity with what she frequently referred to as 'the right thing.' Mr. Hubbard appeared to have no such preoccupations. Garnett, if called on to describe him, would have done so by saying that he was the American who always pays. The young man, in the course of his foreign wanderings, had come across many fellow citizens of Mr. Hubbard's type in the most diverse company and surroundings; and wherever they were to be found, they always had their hands in their pockets. Mr. Hubbard's standard of gentility was the extent of a man's capacity to 'foot the bill'; and as no one but an occasional compatriot cared to dispute the privilege with him he seldom had reason to doubt his social superiority.

Garnett, nevertheless, did not believe that this lavish pair were, as Mrs. Newell would have phrased it, 'putting up' Hermione's *dot*. They would go very far in diamonds but they would hang back from securities. Their readiness to pay was indefinably mingled with a dread of being expected to, and their prodigalities would take flight at the first hint of coercion. Mrs. Newell, who had had a good deal of experience in managing this type of millionaire, could be trusted not to arouse their susceptibilities, and Garnett was therefore certain that the chimerical legacy had been extracted from other pockets. There were none in view but those of Baron Schenkelderff, who, seated at Mrs. Hubbard's right, with a new order in his buttonhole, and a fresh glaze upon his features, enchanted that lady by his careless references to crowned heads and his condescending approval of the champagne. Garnett was more than ever certain that it was the Baron who was paying; and it was this conviction which made him suddenly resolve that, at any cost, Hermione's marriage must take place. He had felt no special interest in the marriage except as one more proof of Mrs. Newell's extraordinary capacity; but now it appealed to him from the girl's own standpoint. For he saw, with a touch of compunction, that in the mephitic air of her surroundings a love story of miraculous freshness had flowered. He had only to intercept the glances which the young couple exchanged to find himself transported to the candid region of romance. It was evident that Hermione adored and was adored; that the lovers believed in each other and in everyone about them, and that even the legacy of the defunct aunt had not been too great a strain on their faith in human nature.

His first glance at the Comte Louis du Trayas showed Garnett that, by some marvel of fitness, Hermione had happened on a kindred nature. If the young man's long mild features and shortsighted glance revealed no special force of character, they showed a benevolence and simplicity as incorruptible as her own, and declared that their possessor, whatever his failings, would never imperil the illusions she had so wondrously preserved. The fact that the girl took her good fortune naturally, and did not regard herself as suddenly snatched from the jaws of death, added poignancy to the situation; for if she missed this way of escape, and was thrown back on her former life, the day of discovery could not be long deferred. It made Garnett shiver to think of her growing old between her mother and Schenkelderff, or such successors of the Baron's as might probably attend on Mrs. Newell's waning fortunes; for it was clear to him that the Baron marked the first stage in his friend's decline. When Garnett took leave that evening he had promised Mrs. Newell that he would try to find her husband.

• V •

If Mr. Newell read in the papers the announcement of his daughter's marriage it did not cause him to lift the veil of seclusion in which his wife represented him as shrouded.

A round of the American banks in Paris failed to give Garnett his address, and it was only in chance talk with one of the young secretaries of the Embassy that he was put on Mr. Newell's track. The secretary's father, it appeared, had known the Newells some twenty years earlier. He had had business relations with Mr. Newell, who was then a man of property, with factories or something of the kind, the narrator thought, somewhere in western New York. There had been at this period, for Mrs. Newell, a phase of large hospitality and showy carriages in Washington and at Narragansett. Then her husband had had reverses, had lost heavily in Wall Street, and had finally drifted abroad and disappeared from sight. The young man did not know at what point in his financial decline Mr. Newell had parted company with his wife and daughter; 'though you may bet your hat,' he philosophically concluded, 'that the old girl hung on as long as there were any pickings.' He did not himself know Mr. Newell's address, but opined that it might be extracted from a certain official of the Consulate, if Garnett could give a sufficiently good reason for the request; and here in fact Mrs. Newell's emissary learned that her husband was to be found in an obscure street of the Luxembourg quarter.

In order to be near the scene of action, Garnett went to breakfast at his usual haunt, determined to dispatch his business as early in the day as politeness allowed. The headwaiter welcomed him to a table near that of the transatlantic sage, who sat in his customary corner, his head tilted back against the blistered mirror at an angle suggesting that in a freer civilization his feet would have sought the same level. He greeted Garnett affably and the two exchanged their usual generalizations on life till the sage rose to go; whereupon it occurred to Garnett to accompany him. His friend took the offer in good part, merely remarking that he was going to the Luxembourg Gardens, where it was his invariable habit, on good days, to feed the sparrows with the remains of his breakfast roll; and Garnett replied that, as it happened, his own business lay in the same direction.

'Perhaps, by the way,' he added, 'you can tell me how to find the rue Panonceaux, where I must go presently. I thought I knew this quarter fairly well, but I have never heard of it.'

His companion came to a halt on the narrow pavement, to the confusion of the dense and desultory traffic which flows through the old streets of the Latin quarter. He fixed his mild eye on Garnett and gave a twist to the cigar which lingered in the corner of his mouth.

'The rue Panonceaux? It *is* an out-of-the-way hole, but I can tell you how to find it,' he answered.

He made no motion to do so, however, but continued to bend on the young man the full force of his interrogative gaze; then he added: 'Would you mind telling me your object in going there?'

Garnett looked at him with surprise: a question so unblushingly personal was strangely out of keeping with his friend's usual attitude of detachment. Before he could reply, however, the other had continued: 'Do you happen to be in search of Samuel C. Newell?'

'Why, yes, I am,' said Garnett with a start of conjecture.

His companion uttered a sigh. 'I supposed so,' he said resignedly; 'and in that case,' he added, 'we may as well have the matter out in the Luxembourg.'

Garnett had halted before him with deepening astonishment. 'But you don't mean to tell me – ?' he stammered.

The little man made a motion of assent. 'I am Samuel C. Newell,' he said; 'and if you have no objection, I prefer not to break through my habit of feeding the sparrows. We are five minutes late as it is.'

He quickened his pace without awaiting a reply from Garnett, who walked beside him in unsubdued wonder till they reached the

Luxembourg Gardens, where Mr. Newell, making for one of the less frequented alleys, seated himself on a bench and drew the fragment of a roll from his pocket. His coming was evidently expected, for a shower of little dusky bodies at once descended on him, and the gravel fluttered with battling beaks and wings as he distributed his dole.

It was not till the ground was white with crumbs, and the first frenzy of his pensioners appeased, that he turned to Garnett and said: 'I presume, sir, that you come from my wife.'

Garnett colored with embarrassment: the more simply the old man took his mission the more complicated it appeared to himself.

'From your wife – and from Miss Newell,' he said at length. 'You have perhaps heard that your daughter is to be married.'

'Oh, yes – I read the *Herald* pretty faithfully,' said Miss Newell's parent, shaking out another handful of crumbs.

Garnett cleared his throat. 'Then you have no doubt thought it natural that, under the circumstances, they should wish to communicate with you.'

The sage continued to fix his attention on the sparrows. 'My wife,' he remarked, 'might have written to me.'

'Mrs. Newell was afraid she might not hear from you in reply.'

'In reply? Why should she? I suppose she merely wishes to announce the marriage. She knows I have no money left to buy wedding presents,' said Mr. Newell astonishingly.

Garnett felt his color deepen: he had a vague sense of standing as the representative of something guilty and enormous, with which he had rashly identified himself.

'I don't think you understand,' he said. 'Mrs. Newell and your daughter have asked me to see you because they're anxious that you should consent to appear at the wedding.'

Mr. Newell, at this, ceased to give his attention to the birds, and turned a compassionate gaze on Garnett.

'My dear sir – I don't know your name – ' he remarked, 'would you mind telling me how long you've been acquainted with Mrs. Newell?' And without waiting for an answer he added: 'If you wait long enough she will ask you to do some very disagreeable things for her.'

This echo of his own thoughts gave Garnett a twinge of discomfort, but he made shift to answer good-humoredly: 'If you refer to my present errand, I must tell you that I don't find it disagreeable to do anything which may be of service to Miss Hermione.'

Mr. Newell fumbled in his pocket, as though searching unavailingly for another morsel of bread; then he said: 'From her point of view I shall not be the most important person at the ceremony.'

Garnett smiled. 'That is hardly a reason – ' he began; but he was checked by the brevity of tone with which his companion replied: 'I am not aware that I am called upon to give you my reasons.'

'You are certainly not,' the young man rejoined, 'except in so far as you are willing to consider me as the messenger of your wife and daughter.'

'Oh, I accept your credentials,' said the other with his dry smile; 'What I don't recognize is their right to send a message.'

This reduced Garnett to silence, and after a moment's pause, Mr. Newell drew his watch from his pocket.

'I am sorry to cut the conversation short, but my days are mapped out with a certain regularity, and this is the hour for my nap.' He rose as he spoke and held out his hand with a glint of melancholy humor in his small clear eyes.

'You dismiss me, then? I am to take back a refusal?' the young man exclaimed.

'My dear sir, those ladies have got on very well without me for a number of years: I imagine they can put through this wedding without my help.'

'You're mistaken, then; if it were not for that I shouldn't have undertaken this errand.'

Mr. Newell paused as he was turning away. 'Not for what?' he inquired.

'The fact that, as it happens, the wedding can't be put through without your help.'

Mr. Newell's thin lips formed a noiseless whistle. 'They've got to have my consent, have they? Well, is he a good young man?'

'The bridegroom?' Garnett echoed in surprise. 'I hear the best accounts of him – and Miss Newell is very much in love.'

Her parent met this with an odd smile. 'Well, then, I give my consent – it's all I've got left to give,' he added philosophically.

Garnett hesitated. 'But if you consent – if you approve – why do you refuse your daughter's request?'

Mr. Newell looked at him a moment. 'Ask Mrs. Newell!' he said. And as Garnett was again silent, he turned away with a slight gesture of leave-taking.

But in an instant the young man was at his side. 'I will not ask your reasons, sir,' he said, 'but I will give you mine for being here. Miss Newell cannot be married unless you are present at the ceremony. The young man's parents know that she has a father living, and they give their consent only on condition that he appears at her marriage. I believe it is customary in old French families – '

'Old French families be damned!' said Mr. Newell, 'She had better marry an American.' And he made a more decided motion to free himself from Garnett's importunities.

But his resistance only strengthened the young man's. The more unpleasant the latter's task became, the more unwilling he grew to see his efforts end in failure. During the three days which had been consumed in his quest it had become clear to him that the bridegroom's parents, having been surprised to a reluctant consent, were but too ready to withdraw it on the plea of Mr. Newell's nonappearance. Mrs. Newell, on the last edge of tension, had confided to Garnett that the Morningfields were 'being nasty'; and he could picture the whole powerful clan, on both sides of the Channel, arrayed in a common resolve to exclude poor Hermione from their ranks. The very inequality of the contest stirred in his blood, and made him vow that in this case, at least, the sins of the parents should not be visited on the children. In his talk with the young secretary he had obtained certain glimpses of Baron Schenkelderff's past that fortified this resolve. The Baron, at one time a familiar figure in a much-observed London set, had been mixed up in an ugly money-lending business ending in suicide, which had excluded him from the society most accessible to his race. His alliance with Mrs. Newell was doubtless a desperate attempt at rehabilitation, a forlorn hope on both sides, but likely to be an enduring tie because it represented, to both partners, their last chance of escape from social extinction. That Hermione's marriage was a mere stake in their game did not in the least affect Garnett's view of its urgency. If on their part it was a sordid speculation, to her it had the freshness of the first wooing. If it made of her a mere pawn in their hands, it would put her, so Garnett hoped, beyond further risk of such base uses; and to achieve this had become a necessity to him.

The sense that, if he lost sight of Mr. Newell, the latter might not easily be found again, nerved Garnett to hold his ground in spite of the resistance he encountered; and he tried to put the full force of his plea into the tone with which he cried: 'Ah, you don't know your daughter!'

• VI •

MRS. NEWELL, that afternoon, met him on the threshold of her sitting room with a 'Well?' of pent-up anxiety.

In the room itself, Baron Schenkelderff sat with crossed legs and head thrown back, in an attitude which he did not see fit to alter at the young man's approach.

Garnett hesitated; but it was not the summariness of the Baron's greeting which he resented.

'You've found him?' Mrs. Newell exclaimed.

'Yes; but – '

She followed his glance and answered it with a slight shrug. 'I can't take you into my room, because there's a dressmaker there, and she won't go because she's waiting to be paid. Schenkelderff,' she exclaimed, 'you're not wanted; please go and look out of the window.'

The Baron rose, and, lighting a cigarette, laughingly retired to the embrasure. Mrs. Newell flung herself down and signed to Garnett to take a seat by her side.

'Well – you've found him? You've talked with him?'

'Yes; I've talked with him – for an hour.'

She made an impatient movement. 'That's too long! Does he refuse?'

'He doesn't consent.'

'Then you mean – ?'

'He wants time to think it over.'

'Time? There *is* no time – did you tell him so?'

'I told him so; but you must remember that he has plenty. He has taken twenty-four hours.'

Mrs. Newell groaned. 'Oh, that's too much. When he thinks things over he always refuses.'

'Well, he would have refused at once if I had not agreed to the delay.'

She rose nervously from her seat and pressed her hands to her forehead. 'It's too hard, after all I've done! The trousseau is ordered – think how disgraceful! You must have managed him badly; I'll go and see him myself.'

The Baron, at this, turned abruptly from his study of the Place Vendome.

'My dear creature, for heaven's sake don't spoil everything!' he exclaimed.

Mrs. Newell colored furiously. 'What's the meaning of that brilliant speech?'

'I was merely putting myself in the place of a man on whom you have ceased to smile.'

He picked up his hat and stick, nodded knowingly to Garnett, and walked towards the door with an air of creaking jauntiness.

But on the threshold Mrs. Newell waylaid him.

'Don't go – I must speak to you,' she said, following him into the antechamber; and Garnett remembered the dressmaker who was not to be dislodged from her bedroom.

In a moment Mrs. Newell returned, with a small flat packet which she vainly sought to dissemble in an inaccessible pocket.

'He makes everything too odious!' she exclaimed; but whether she referred to her husband or the Baron it was left to Garnett to decide.

She sat silent, nervously twisting her cigarette case between her fingers, while her visitor rehearsed the details of his conversaiton with Mr. Newell. He did not indeed tell her the arguments he had used to shake her husband's resolve, since in his eloquent sketch of Hermione's situation there had perforce entered hints unflattering to her mother;

but he gave the impression that his hearer had in the end been moved, and for that reason had consented to defer his refusal.

'Ah, it's not that – it's to prolong our misery!' Mrs. Newell exclaimed; and after a moment she added drearily: 'He's been waiting for such an opportunity for years.'

It seemed needless for Garnett to protract his visit, and he took leave with the promise to report at once the result of his final talk with Mr. Newell. But as he was passing through the antechamber a side door opened and Hermione stood before him. Her face was flushed and shaken out of its usual repose, and he saw at once that she had been waiting for him.

'Mr. Garnett!' she said in a whisper.

He paused, considering her with surprise: he had never supposed her capable of such emotion as her voice and eyes revealed.

'I want to speak to you; we are quite safe here. Mamma is with the dressmaker,' she explained, closing the door behind her, while Garnett laid aside his hat and stick.

'I am at your service,' he said.

'You have seen my father? Mamma told me that you were to see him today,' the girl went on, standing close to him in order that she might not have to raise her voice.

'Yes; I've seen him,' Garnett replied with increasing wonder. Hermione had never before mentioned her father to him, and it was by a slight stretch of veracity that he had included her name in her mother's plea to Mr. Newell. He had supposed her to be either unconscious of the transaction, or else too much engrossed in her own happiness to give it a thought; and he had forgiven her the last alternative in consideration of the abnormal character of her filial relations. But he now saw that he must readjust his view of her.

'You went to ask him to come to the wedding: I know about it,' Hermione continued. 'Of course it's the custom – people will think it odd if he does not come.' She paused, and then asked: 'Does he consent?'

'No; he has not yet consented.'

'Ah, I thought so when I saw Mamma just now!'

'But he hasn't quite refused – he has promised to think it over.'

'But he hated it – he hated the idea?'

Garnett hesitated. 'It seemed to arouse painful associations.'

'Ah, it would – it would!' she exclaimed.

He was astonished at the passion of her accent; astonished still more at the tone with which she went on, laying her hand on his arm: 'Mr. Garnett, he must not be asked – he has been asked too often to do things that he hated!'

Garnett looked at the girl with a shock of awe. What abysses of knowledge did her purity hide?'

'But, my dear Miss Hermione – ' he began.

'I know what you are going to say,' she interrupted him. 'It is necessary that he should be present at the marriage, or the du Trayas will break it off. They don't want it very much, at any rate,' she added with a strange candor, 'and they'll not be sorry, perhaps – for of course Louis would have to obey them.'

'So I explained to your father,' Garnett assured her.

'Yes – yes; I knew you would put it to him. But that makes no difference. He must not be forced to come unwillingly.'

'But if he sees the point – after all, no one can force him!'

'No; but if it's painful to him – if it reminds him too much. . . . Oh, Mr. Garnett, I was not a child when he left us. . . . I was old enough to see . . . to see how it must hurt him even now to be reminded. Peace was all he asked for, and I want him to be left in peace!'

Garnett paused in deep embarrassment. 'My dear child, there is no need to remind you that your own future – '

She had a gesture that recalled her mother. 'My future must take care of itself; he must not be made to see us!' she said imperatively. And as Garnett remained silent she went on: 'I have always hoped he didn't hate me, but he would hate me now if he were forced to see me.'

'Not if he could see you at this moment!'

She lifted her face with swimming eyes.

'Well, go to him, then; tell him what I've said to you!'

Garnett continued to stand before her, deeply struck. 'It might be the best thing,' he reflected inwardly; but he did not give utterance to the thought. He merely put out his hand, holding Hermione's in a long pressure.

'I will do whatever you wish,' he replied.

'You understand that I'm in earnest?' she urged.

'I'm quite sure of it.'

'Then I want you to repeat to him what I've said – I want him to be left undisturbed. I don't want him ever to hear of us again!'

The next day, at the appointed hour, Garnett resorted to the Luxembourg Gardens, which Mr. Newell had named as a meeting place in preference to his own lodgings. It was clear he did not wish to admit the young man any farther into his privacy than the occasion required, and the extreme shabbiness of his dress hinted that pride might be the cause of his reluctance.

Garnett found him feeding the sparrows, but he desisted at the young man's approach, and said at once: 'You won't thank me for bringing you all this distance.'

'If that means that you're going to send me away with a refusal, I have come to spare you the necessity,' Garnett answered.

Mr. Newell turned on him a glance of undisguised wonder, in which a tinge of disappointment might almost have been detected.

'Ah – they've got no use for me, after all?' he said ironically.

Garnett, in reply, related without comment his conversation with Hermione, and the message with which she had charged him. He remembered her words exactly and repeated them without modification, heedless of what they implied or revealed.

Mr. Newell listened with an immovable face, occasionally casting a crumb to his flock. When Garnett ended he asked: 'Does her mother know of this?'

'Assuredly not!' cried Garnett with a movement of disgust.

'You must pardon me; but Mrs. Newell is a very ingenious woman.' Mr. Newell shook out his remaining crumbs and turned thoughtfully toward Garnett.

'You believe it's quite clear to Hermione that these people will use my refusal as a pretext for backing out of the marriage?'

'Perfectly clear – she told me so herself.'

'Doesn't she consider the young man rather chickenhearted?'

'No; he has already put up a big fight for her, and you know the French look at these things differently. He's only twenty-three, and his marrying against his parents' approval is in itself an act of heroism.'

'Yes; I believe they look at it that way,' Mr. Newell assented. He rose and picked up the half-smoked cigar which he had laid on the bench beside him.

'What do they wear at these French weddings, anyhow? A dress suit, isn't it?' he asked.

The question was such a surprise to Garnett that for the moment he could only stammer out – 'You consent then? I may go and tell her?'

'You may tell my girl – yes.' He gave a vague laugh and added: 'One way or another, my wife always get what she wants.'

• VII •

MR. NEWELL'S consent brought with it no accompanying concessions. In the first flush of success Garnett had pictured himself as bringing together the father and daughter, and hovering in an attitude of benediction over a family group in which Mrs. Newell did not very distinctly figure.

But Mr. Newell's conditions were inflexible. He would 'see the thing through' for his daughter's sake; but he stipulated that in the meantime there should be no meetings or further communications of any kind. He agreed to be ready when Garnett called for him, at the appointed hour on the wedding day; but until then he begged to be left alone. To this decision he adhered immovably, and when Garnett

conveyed it to Hermione she accepted it with a deep look of understanding. As for Mrs. Newell she was too much engrossed in the
nuptial preparations to give her husband another thought. She had
gained her point, she had disarmed her foes, and in the first flush of
success she had no time to remember by what means her victory had
been won. Even Garnett's services received little recognition, unless he
found them sufficiently compensated by the new look in Hermione's
eyes.

The principal figures in Mrs. Newell's foreground were the Woolsey
Hubbards and Baron Schenkelderff. With these she was in hourly
consultation, and Mrs. Hubbard went about aureoled with the importance of her close connection with an 'aristocratic marriage,' and dazzled
by the Baron's familiarity with the intricacies of the Almanach de
Gotha. In his society and Mrs. Newell's, Mrs. Hubbard evidently felt
that she had penetrated to the sacred precincts where 'the right thing'
flourished in its native soil. As for Hermione, her look of happiness
had returned, but with an undertint of melancholy, visible perhaps only
to Garnett, but to him always hauntingly present. Outwardly she sank
back into her passive self, resigned to serve as the brilliant lay figure
on which Mrs. Newell hung the trophies of conquest. Preparations for
the wedding were zealously pressed. Mrs. Newell knew the danger of
giving people time to think things over, and her fears about her husband
being allayed, she began to dread a new attempt at evasion on the part
of the bridegroom's family.

'The sooner it's over the sounder I shall sleep!' she declared to
Garnett; and all the mitigations of art could not conceal the fact that
she was desperately in need of that restorative. There were movements,
indeed, when he was sorrier for her than for her husband or her
daughter; so black and unfathomable appeared the abyss into which she
must slip back if she lost her hold on this last spar of safety.

But she did not lose her hold; his own experience, as well as her
husband's declaration, might have told him that she always got what
she wanted. How much she had wanted this particular thing was shown
by the way in which, on the last day, when all peril was over, she
bloomed out in renovated splendor. It gave Garnett a shivering sense
of the ugliness of the alternative which had confronted her.

The day came; the showy coupé provided by Mrs. Newell presented
itself punctually at Garnett's door, and the young man entered it and
drove to the rue Panonceaux. It was a little melancholy back street,
with lean old houses sweating rust and damp, and glimpses of pit-like
gardens, black and sunless, between walls bristling with iron spikes.
On the narrow pavement a blind man pottered along led by a red-eyed
poodle: a little farther on a disheveled woman sat grinding coffee on
the threshold of a *buvette*. The bridal carriage stopped before one of
the doorways, with a clatter of hoofs and harness which drew the

neighborhood to its windows, and Garnett started to mount the ill-smelling stairs to the fourth floor, on which he learned from the *concierge* that Mr. Newell lodged. But halfway up he met the latter descending and they turned and went down together.

Hermione's parent wore his usual imperturbable look, and his eye seemed as full as ever of generalizations on human folly; but there was something oddly shrunken and submerged in his appearance, as though he had grown smaller or his clothes larger. And on the last hypothesis Garnett paused – for it became evident to him that Mr. Newell had hired his dress suit.

Seated at the young man's side on the satin cushions, he remained silent while the carriage rolled smoothly and rapidly through the network of streets leading to the Boulevard Saint-Germain; only once he remarked, glancing at the elaborate fittings of the coupé: 'Is this Mrs. Newell's carriage?'

'I believe so – yes,' Garnett assented, with the guilty sense that in defining that lady's possessions it was impossible not to trespass on those of her friends.

Mr. Newell made no further comment, but presently requested his companion to rehearse to him once more the exact duties which were to devolve on him during the coming ceremony. Having mastered these he remained silent, fixing a dry speculative eye on the panorama of the brilliant streets, till the carriage drew up at the entrance of Saint Philippe du Roule.

With the same air of composure he followed his guide through the mob of spectators, and up the crimson velvet steps, at the head of which, but for a word from Garnett, a formidable Suisse, glittering with cocked hat and mace, would have checked the advance of the small crumpled figure so oddly out of keeping with the magnificence of the bridal party. The French fashion prescribing that the family *cortège* shall follow the bride to the altar, the vestibule of the church was thronged with the participators in the coming procession; but if Mr. Newell felt any nervousness at his sudden projection into this unfamiliar group, nothing in his look or manner betrayed it. He stood beside Garnett till a white-favored carriage, dashing up to the church with superlative glitter of highly groomed horseflesh, and silver-plated harness, deposited the snowy apparition of the bride, supported by her mother; then, as Hermione entered the vestibule, he went forward quietly to meet her.

The girl wrapped in the haze of her bridal veil, and a little confused, perhaps, by the anticipation of the meeting, paused a moment, as if in doubt, before the small oddly-clad figure which blocked her path – a horrible moment to Garnett, who felt a pang of misery at this satire on the infallibility of the filial instinct. He longed to make some sign, to break in some way the pause of uncertainty; but before he could

move he saw Mrs. Newell give her daughter a sharp push, he saw a
blush of compunction flood Hermione's face, and the girl, throwing
back her veil, bent her tall head and flung her arms about her father.

Mr. Newell emerged unshaken from the embrace: it seemed to have
no effect beyond giving an odder twist to his tie. He stood beside his
daughter till the church doors were thrown open; then, at a sign from
the verger, he gave her his arm, and the strange couple with the long
train of fashion and finery behind them, started on their march to the
altar.

Garnett had already slipped into the church and secured a post of
vantage which gave him a side view over the assemblage. The building
was thronged – Mrs. Newell had attained her ambition and given
Hermione a smart wedding. Garnett's eye traveled curiously from one
group to another – from the numerous representatives of the bridegroom's family, all stamped with the same air of somewhat dowdy
distinction, the air of having had their thinking done for them for so
long that they could no longer perform the act individually, and the
heterogeneous company of Mrs. Newell's friends, who presented, on
the opposite side of the nave, every variety of individual conviction in
dress and conduct. Of the two groups that latter was decidedly the
more interesting to Garnett, who observed that it comprised not only
such recent acquisitions as the Woolsey Hubbards and the Baron, but
also sundry more important figures which of late had faded to the verge
of Mrs. Newell's horizon. Hermione's marriage had drawn them back,
had once more made her mother a social entity, had in short already
accomplished the object for which it had been planned and executed.

And as he looked about him Garnett saw that all the other actors
in the show faded into insignificance beside the dominant figure of Mrs.
Newell, became mere marionettes pulled hither and thither by the
hidden wires of her intention. One and all they were there to serve her
ends and accomplish her purpose: Schenkelderff and the Hubbards to
pay for the show, the bride and bridegroom to seal and symbolize her
social rehabilitation, Garnett himself as the humble instrument adjusting
the different parts of the complicated machinery, and her husband,
finally, as the last stake in her game, the last asset on which she could
draw to rebuild her fallen fortunes. At the thought Garnett was filled
with a deep disgust for what the scene signified, and for his own share
in it. He had been her tool and dupe like the others; if he imagined that
he was serving Hermione, it was for her mother's ends that he had
worked. What right had he to sentimentalize a marriage founded on
such base connivances, and how could he have imagined that in so
doing he was acting a disinterested part?

While these thoughts were passing through his mind the ceremony
had already begun, and the principal personages in the drama were
ranged before him in the row of crimson velvet chairs which fills the

foreground of a Catholic marriage. Through the glow of lights and the perfumed haze about the altar, Garnett's eyes rested on the central figures of the group, and gradually the others disappeared from his view and his mind. After all, neither Mrs. Newell's schemes nor his own share in them could ever unsanctify Hermione's marriage. It was one more testimony to life's indefatigable renewals, to nature's secret of drawing fragrance from corruption; and as his eyes turned from the girl's illuminated presence to the resigned and stoical figure sunk in the adjoining chair, it occurred to him that he had perhaps worked better than he knew in placing them, if only for a moment, side by side.

The Letters

Up the hill from the station at St. Cloud, Lizzie West climbed in the cold spring sunshine. As she breasted the incline, she noticed the first waves of wisteria over courtyard railings and the highlights of new foliage against the walls of ivy-matted gardens; and she thought again, as she had thought a hundred times before, that she had never seen so beautiful a spring.

She was on her way to Deerings' house in a street near the hilltop, and every step was dear and familiar to her. She went there five times a week to teach little Juliet Deering, the daughter of Mr. Vincent Deering, the distinguished American artist. Juliet had been her pupil for two years, and day after day, during that time, Lizzie West had mounted the hill in all weathers; sometimes with her umbrella bent against the rain, sometimes with her frail cotton parasol unfurled beneath a fiery sun, sometimes with the snow soaking through her boots or a bitter wind piercing her thin jacket, sometimes with the dust whirling about her and bleaching the flowers of the poor little hat that *had* to 'carry her through' till next summer

At first the ascent had seemed tedious enough, as dull as the trudge to her other lessons. Lizzie was not a heaven-sent teacher; she had no born zeal for her calling, and though she dealt kindly and dutifully with her pupils, she did not fly to them on winged feet. But one day something had happened to change the face of life, and since then the climb to the Deering house had seemed like a dream flight up a heavenly stairway.

Her heart beat faster as she remembered it – no longer in a tumult of fright and self-reproach, but softly, happily, as if brooding over a possession that none could take from her.

It was on a day of the previous October that she had stopped, after Juliet's lesson, to ask if she might speak to Juliet's papa. One had always to apply to Mr. Deering if there was anything to be said about the lessons. Mrs. Deering lay on her lounge upstairs, reading relays of dog-eared novels, the choice of which she left to the cook and the nurse, who were always fetching them for her from the *cabinet de lecture;* and it was understood in the house that she was not to be 'bothered' about Juliet. Mr. Deering's interest in his daughter was fitful rather than consecutive; but at least he was approachable, and listened sympathetically, if a little absently, stroking his long fair mustache, while Lizzie stated her difficulty or put in her plea for maps or copybooks.

'Yes, yes – of course – whatever you think right,' he would always assent, sometimes drawing a five-franc piece from his pocket, and laying it carelessly on the table, or oftener saying, with his charming smile: 'Get what you please, and just put it on your account, you know.'

But this time Lizzie had not come to ask for maps or copybooks, or even to hint, in crimson misery – as once, poor soul, she had had to do – that Mr. Deering had overlooked her last little account – had probably not noticed that she had left it, some two months earlier, on a corner of his littered writing table. That hour had been bad enough, though he had done his best to carry it off gallantly and gaily; but this was infinitely worse. For she had come to complain of her pupil; to say that, much as she loved little Juliet, it was useless, unless Mr. Deering could 'do something,' to go on with the lessons.

'It wouldn't be honest – I should be robbing you; I'm not sure that I haven't already,' she half laughed, through mounting tears, as she put her case. Little Juliet would not work, would not obey. Her poor little drifting existence floated aimlessly between the kitchen and the *lingerie*, and all the groping tendrils of her curiosity were fastened about the life of the backstairs.

It was the same kind of curiosity that Mrs. Deering, overheard in her drug-scented room, lavished on her dog-eared novels and on the 'society notes' of the morning paper; but since Juliet's horizon was not yet wide enough to embrace these loftier objects, her interest was centered in the anecdotes that Céleste and Suzanne brought back from the market and the library. That these were not always of an edifying nature the child's artless prattle too often betrayed; but unhappily they occupied her fancy to the complete exclusion of such nourishing items as dates and dynasties, and the sources of the principal European rivers.

At length the crisis became so acute that poor Lizzie felt herself bound to resign her charge or ask Mr. Deering's intervention; and for Juliet's sake she chose the harder alternative. It *was* hard to speak to him not only because one hated to confess one's failure, and hated still more to ascribe it to such vulgar causes, but because one blushed to bring them to the notice of a spirit engaged with higher things. Mr. Deering was very busy at that moment: he had a new picture 'on.' And Lizzie entered the studio with a flutter of one profanely intruding on some sacred rite; she almost heard the rustle of retreating wings as she approached.

And then – and then – how differently it had all turned out! Perhaps it wouldn't have, if she hadn't been such a goose – she who so seldom cried, so prided herself on a stoic control of her little twittering cageful of 'feelings.' But if she had cried, it was because he had looked at her so kindly, and because she had nevertheless felt him so pained and shamed by what she said. The pain, of course, lay for both in the implication behind her words – in the one word she left unspoken. If little Juliet was as she was, it was because of the mother upstairs – the mother who had given the child her frivolous impulses, and grudged her the care that might have corrected them. The case so obviously revolved in its own vicious circle that when Mr. Deering had murmured, 'Of course if my wife were not an invalid,' they both turned with a spring to the flagrant 'bad example' of Céleste and Suzanne, fastening on that with a mutual insistence that ended in his crying out: 'All the more, then, how can you leave her to them?'

'But if I do her no good?' Lizzie wailed; and it was then that, when he took her hand and assured her gently, 'But you do, you do!' – it was then that, in the traditional phrase, she 'broke down,' and her poor little protest quivered off into tears.

'You do *me* good, at any rate – you make the house seem less like a desert,' she heard him say; and the next moment she felt herself drawn to him, and they kissed each other through her weeping.

They kissed each other – there was the new fact. One does not, if one is a poor little teacher living in Mme. Clopin's Pension Suisse at Passy, and if one has pretty brown hair and eyes that reach out trustfully to other eyes – one does not, under these common but defenceless conditions, arrive at the age of twenty-five without being now and then kissed – waylaid once by a noisy student between two doors, surprised once by one's grey-bearded professor as one bent over the 'theme' he was correcting – but these episodes, if they tarnish the surface, do not reach the heart: it is not the kiss endured, but the kiss returned, that lives. And Lizzie West's first kiss was for Vincent Deering.

As she drew back from it, something new awoke in her – something deeper than the fright and the shame, and the penitent thought of Mrs. Deering. A sleeping germ of life thrilled and unfolded, and started out to seek the sun.

She might have felt differently, perhaps – the shame and penitence might have prevailed – had she not known him so kind and tender, and guessed him so baffled, poor and disappointed. She knew the failure of his married life, and she divined a corresponding failure in his artistic career. Lizzie, who had made her own faltering snatch at the same laurels, brought her thwarted proficiency to bear on the question of his pictures, which she judged to be remarkable, but suspected of having somehow failed to affirm their merit publicly. She understood that he had tasted an earlier moment of success: a *mention*, a medal, something official and tangible; then the tide of publicity had somehow set the other way, and left him stranded in a noble isolation. It was incredible that any one so naturally eminent and exceptional should have been subject to the same vulgar necessities that governed her own life, should have known poverty and obscurity and indifference. But she gathered that this had been the case, and felt that it formed the miraculous link between them. For through what medium less revealing than that of shared misfortune would he ever have perceived so inconspicuous an object as herself? And she recalled now how gently his eyes had rested on her from the first – the grey eyes that might have seemed mocking if they had not seemed so gentle.

She remembered how kindly he had met her the first day, when Mrs. Deering's inevitable headache had prevented her receiving the new teacher. Insensibly he had led Lizzie to talk of herself and his questions had at once revealed his interest in the little stranded compatriot doomed to earn a precarious living so far from her native shore. Sweet as the moment of unburdening had been, she wondered afterward what had determined it: how she, so shy and sequestered, had found herself letting slip her whole poverty-stricken story, even to the avowal of the ineffectual 'artistic' tendencies that had drawn her to Paris, and had then left her there to the dry task of tuition. She wondered at first, but she understood now; she understood everything after he had kissed her. It was simply because he was as kind as he was great.

She thought of this now as she mounted the hill in the spring sunshine, and she thought of all that had happened since. The intervening months, as she looked back at them, were merged in a vast golden haze, through which here and there rose the outline of a shining island. The haze was the general enveloping sense of his love, and the shining islands were the days they had spent together. They had never kissed again under his own roof. Lizzie's professional honor had a keen edge, but she had been spared the necessity of making him feel it. It was of the essence of her fatality that he always 'understood' when his failing to do so might have imperiled his hold on her.

But her Thursdays and Sundays were free, and it soon became a habit to give them to him. She knew, for her peace of mind, only too much about pictures, and galleries and churches had been the one outlet from the greyness of her personal conditions. For poetry, too, and the other imaginative forms of literature, she had always felt more than she had hitherto had occasion to betray; and now all these folded sympathies shot out their tendrils to the light. Mr. Deering knew how to express with unmatched clearness the thoughts that trembled in her mind: to talk with him was to soar up into the azure on the outspread wings of his intelligence, and look down, dizzily yet clearly, on all the wonders and glories of the world. She was a little ashamed, sometimes, to find how few definite impressions brought back so fast when he was near, and his smile made his words seem like a long quiver of light. Afterward, in quieter hours, fragments of their talk emerged in her memory with wondrous precision, every syllable as minutely chiseled as some of the delicate objects in crystal or ivory that he pointed out in the museums they frequented. It was always a puzzle to Lizzie that some of their hours should be so blurred and others so vivid.

She was reliving all these memories with unusual distinctness, because it was a fortnight since she had seen her friend. Mrs. Deering, some six weeks previously, had gone to visit a relative at St. Raphael; and, after she had been a month absent, her husband and the little girl had joined her. Lizzie's adieux to Deering had been made on a rainy afternoon in the damp corridors of the Aquarium at the Trocadéro. She could not receive him at her own *pension*. That a teacher should be visited by the father of a pupil, especially when that father was still, as Madame Clopin said, *si bien*, was against that lady's austere Helvetian code. And from Deering's first tentative hint of another solution Lizzie had recoiled in a wild flurry of all her scruples. He took her 'No, no, *no!*' as he took all her twists and turns of conscience, with eyes half tender and half mocking, and an instant acquiescence which was the finest homage to the 'lady' she felt he divined and honored in her.

So they continued to meet in museums and galleries, or to extend, on fine days, their explorations to the suburbs, where now and then, in the solitude of grove or garden, the kiss renewed itself, fleeting, isolated, or prolonged in a shy pressure of the hand. But on the day of his leave-taking the rain kept them under cover; and as they threaded the subterranean windings of the Aquarium, and Lizzie gazed unseeingly at the grotesque faces glaring at her through walls of glass, she felt like a drowned wretch at the bottom of the sea, with all her sunlit memories rolling over her like the waves of its surface.

'You'll never see him again – never see him again,' the waves boomed in her ears through his last words; and when she had said goodbye to him at the corner, and had scrambled, wet and shivering, into the Passy omnibus, its grinding wheels took up the derisive burden – 'Never see him, never see him again.'

All that was only two weeks ago, and here she was, as happy as a lark, mounting the hill to his door in the fresh spring sunshine! So weak a heart did not deserve such a radiant fate; and Lizzie said to herself that she would never again distrust her star.

• II •

THE cracked bell tinkled sweetly through her heart as she stood listening for Juliet's feet. Juliet, anticipating the laggard Suzanne, almost always opened the door for her governess, not from any eagerness to hasten the hour of her studies, but from the irrepressible desire to see what was going on in the street. But doubtless on this occasion some unusually absorbing incident had detained the child belowstairs; for Lizzie, after vainly waiting for a step, had to give the bell a second twitch. Even a third produced no response, and Lizzie, full of dawning fears, drew back to look up at the house. She saw that the studio shutters stood wide, and then noticed, without surprise, that Mrs. Deering's were still unopened. No doubt Mrs. Deering was resting after the fatigue of the journey. Instinctively Lizzie's eyes turned again to the studio window; and as she looked, she saw Deering approach it. He caught sight of her, and an instant later was at the door. He lookd paler than usual, and she noticed that he wore a black coat.

'I rang and rang – where is Juliet?' she asked.

He looked at her gravely; then, without answering, he led her down the passage to the studio, and closed the door when she had entered.

'My wife is dead – she died suddenly ten days ago. Didn't you see it in the papers?' he said.

Lizzie, with a cry, sank down on the rickety divan propped against the wall. She seldom saw a newspaper, since she could not afford one for her own perusal, and those supplied to the Pension Clopin were usually in the hands of its more privileged lodgers till long after the hour when she set out on her morning round.

'No; I didn't see it,' she stammered.

Deering was silent. He stood twisting an unlit cigarette in his hand, and looking down at her with a gaze that was both constrained and hesitating.

She, too, felt the constraint of the situation, the impossibility of finding words which, after what had passed between them, should seem neither false nor heartless: and at last she exclaimed, standing up: 'Poor little Juliet! Can't I go to her?'

'Juliet is not here. I left her at St. Raphaël with the relations with whom my wife was staying.'

'Oh,' Lizzie murmured, feeling vaguely that this added to the difficulty of the moment. How differently she had pictured their meeting! 'I'm so – so sorry for her!' she faltered.

Deering made no reply, but, turning on his heel, walked the length of the studio and halted before the picture on the easel. It was the landscape he had begun the previous autumn, with the intention of sending it to the Salon that spring. But it was still unfinished – seemed, indeed, hardly more advanced than on the fateful October day when Lizzie, standing before it for the first time, had confessed her inability to deal with Juliet. Perhaps the same thought struck its creator, for he broke into a dry laugh and turned from the easel with a shrug.

Under his protracted silence Lizzie roused herself to the fact that, since her pupil was absent, there was no reason for her remaining any longer; and as Deering approached her she rose and said with an effort: 'I'll go, then. You'll send for me when she comes back?'

Deering still hesitated, tormenting the cigarette between his fingers. 'She's not coming back – not at present.'

Lizzie heard him with a drop of the heart. Was everything to be changed in their lives? Of course; how could she have dreamed it would be otherwise? She could only stupidly repeat: 'Not coming back? Not this spring?'

'Probably not, since our friends are so good as to keep her. The fact is, I've got to go to America. My wife left a little property, a few pennies, that I must go and see to – for the child.'

Lizzie stood before him, a cold knife in her breast. 'I see – I see,' she reiterated, feeling all the while that she strained her eyes into utter blackness.

'It's a nuisance, having to pull up stakes,' he went on, with a fretful glance about the studio.

She lifted her eyes to his face. 'Shall you be gone long?' she took courage to ask.

'There again – I can't tell. It's all so mixed up.' He met her look for an incredibly long strange moment. 'I hate to go!' he murmured abruptly.

Lizzie felt a rush of moisture to her lashes, and the familiar wave of weakness at her heart. She raised her hand to her face with an instinctive gesture, and as she did so he held out his arms.

'Come here, Lizzie!' he said.

And she went – went with a sweet wild throb of liberation, with the sense that at last the house was his, that *she* was his, if he wanted her; that never again would that silent presence in the room above constrain and shame her rapture.

He pushed back her veil and covered her face with kisses. 'Don't cry, you little goose!' he said.

• III •

THAT they must see each other before his departure, in some place less exposed than their usual haunts, was as clear to Lizzie as it appeared to be to Deering. His expressing the wish seemed, indeed, the sweetest testimony to the quality of his feeling, since, in the first weeks of the most perfunctory widowerhood, a man of his stamp is presumed to abstain from light adventures. If, then, he wished so much to be quietly and gravely with her, it could be only for reasons she did not call by name, but of which she felt the sacred tremor in her heart; and it would have seemed to her vain and vulgar to put forward, at such a moment, the conventional objections with which such little exposed existences defend the treasure of their freshness.

In such a mood as this one may descend from the Passy omnibus at the corner of the Pont de la Concorde (she had not let him fetch her in a cab) with a sense of dedication almost solemn, and may advance to meet one's fate, in the shape of a gentleman of melancholy elegance, with an auto taxi at his call, as one has advanced to the altar steps in some girlish bridal vision.

Even the experienced waiter ushering them into an upper room of the quiet restaurant on the Seine could hardly have supposed their quest for privacy to be based on the familiar motive, so soberly did Deering give his orders, while his companion sat small and grave at his side. She did not, indeed, mean to let her distress obscure their hour together: she was already learning that Deering shrank from sadness. He should see that she had courage and gaiety to face their coming separation, and yet give herself meanwhile to this completer nearness; but she waited, as always for him to strike the opening note.

Looking back at it later, she wondered at the sweetness of the hour. Her heart was unversed in happiness, but he had found the tone to lull her fears, and make her trust her fate for any golden wonder. Deepest of all, he gave her the sense of something tacit and established between them, as if his tenderness were a habit of the heart hardly needing the support of outward proof.

Such proof as he offered came, therefore, as a kind of crowning luxury, the flowering of a profoundly rooted sentiment; and here again the instinctive reserves and defences would have seemed to vulgarize what his confidence ennobled. But if all the tender casuistries of her heart were at his service, he took no grave advantage of them. Even when they sat alone after dinner, with the lights of the river trembling through their one low window, and the rumor of Paris enclosing them in a heart of silence, he seemed, as much as herself, under the spell of hallowing influences. She felt it most of all as she yielded to the arm he presently put about her, to the long caress he laid on her lips and eyes: not a word or gesture missed the note of quiet understanding, or cast a doubt, in retrospect, on the pact they sealed with their last look.

That pact, as she reviewed it through a sleepless night, seemed to have consisted mainly, on his part, in pleadings for full and frequent news of her, on hers in the promise that it should be given as often as he wrote to ask it. She did not wish to show too much eagerness, too great a desire to affirm and define her hold on him. Her life had given her a certain acquaintance with the arts of defence: girls in her situation were supposed to know them all, and to use them as occasion called. But Lizzie's very need of them had intensified her disdain. Just because she was so poor, and had always, materially, so to count her change and calculate her margin, she would at least know the joy of emotional prodigality, and give her heart as recklessly as the rich their millions. She was sure now that Deering loved her, and if he had seized the occasion of their farewell to give her some definitely worded sign of his feeling – if, more plainly, he had asked her to marry him – his doing so would have seemed less a proof of his sincerity than of his suspecting in her the need of such a warrant. That he had abstained seemed to show that he trusted her as she trusted him, and that they were one most of all in this complete security of understanding.

She had tried to make him guess all this in the chariness of her promise to write. She would write; of course she would. But he would be busy, preoccupied, on the move: it was for him to let her know when he wished a word, to spare her the embarrassment of ill-timed intrusions.

'Intrusions?' He had smiled the word away. 'You can't well intrude, my darling, on a heart where you're already established to the complete exclusion of other lodgers.' And then, taking her hands, and looking up from them into her happy dizzy eyes: 'You don't know much about being in love, do you, Lizzie?' he laughingly ended.

It seemed easy enough to reject this imputation in a kiss; but she wondered afterward if she had not deserved it. Was she really cold and conventional, and did other women give more richly and recklessly? She found that it was possible to turn about every one of her reserves and delicacies so that they looked like selfish scruples and petty pruderies, and at this game she came in time to exhaust all the resources of casuistry.

Meanwhile the first days after Deering's departure wore a soft refracted light like the radiance lingering after sunset. *He*, at any rate, was taxable with no reserves, no calculations, and his letters of farewell, from train and steamer, filled her with long murmurs and echoes of his presence. How he loved her, how he loved her – and how he knew how to tell her so!

She was not sure of possessing the same gift. Unused to the expression of personal emotion, she wavered between the impulse to pour out all she felt and the fear lest her extravagance should amuse or even bore him. She never lost the sense that what was to her the central crisis of experience must be a mere episode in a life so predestined as his to romantic incidents. All that she felt and said would be subjected to the test of comparison with what others had already given him: from all quarters of the globe she saw passionate missives winging their way toward Deering, for whom her poor little swallow flight of devotion could certainly not make a summer. But such moments were succeeded by others in which she raised her head and dared affirm no woman had ever loved him just as she had, and that none, therefore, had probably found just such things to say to him. And this conviction strengthened the other less solidly based belief that *he* also, for the same reason, had found new accents to express his tenderness, and that the three letters she wore all day in her shabby blouse, and hid all night beneath her pillow, not only surpassed in beauty, but differed in quality from, all he had ever penned for other eyes.

They gave her, at any rate, during the weeks that she wore them on her heart, sensations more complex and delicate than Deering's actual presence had ever produced. To be with him was always like breasting a bright rough sea that blinded while it buoyed her; but his letters formed a still pool of contemplation, above which she could bend, and see the reflection of the sky, and the myriad movements of the life that flitted and gleamed below the surface. The wealth of this hidden life – that was what most surprised her! She had had no inkling of it, but had kept on along the narrow track of habit, like a traveler climbing a road in a fog, and suddenly finding himself on a sunlit crag between leagues of sky and dizzy depths of valley. And the odd thing was that all the people about her – the whole world of the Passy pension – seemed plodding along the same dull path, preoccupied with the pebbles underfoot, and unaware of the glory beyond the fog!

There were hours of exultation, when she longed to cry out to them what one saw from the summit – and hours of abasement, when she asked herself why *her* feet had been guided there, while others, no doubt as worthy, stumbled and blundered in obscurity. She felt, in particular, an urgent pity for the two or three other girls at Mme. Clopin's – girls older, duller, less alive than she, and by that very token more thrown upon her sympathy. Would they ever know? Had they ever known? Those were the questions that haunted her as she crossed her companions on the stairs, faced them at the dinner table, and listened to their poor pining talk in the dimly lit slippery-seated *salon*. One of the girls was Swiss, another English; a third, Andora Macy, was a young lady from the Southern States who was studying French with the ultimate object of imparting it to the inmates of a girls' school at Macon, Georgia.

Andora Macy was pale, faded, immature. She had a drooping accent, and a manner which fluctuated between arch audacity and fits of panicky hauteur. She yearned to be admired, and feared to be insulted; and yet seemed wistfully conscious that she was destined to miss both these extremes of sensation, or to enjoy them only in the experiences of her more privileged friends.

It was perhaps for this reason that she took a tender interest in Lizzie, who had shrunk from her at first, as the depressing image of her own probable future, but to whom she now suddenly became an object of sentimental pity.

• IV •

MISS MACY'S room was next to Miss West's, and the Southerner's knock often appealed to Lizzie's hospitality when Mme. Clopin's early curfew had driven her boarders from the *salon*. It sounded thus one evening, just as Lizzie, tired from an unusually long day of tuition, was in the act of removing her dress. She was in too indulgent a mood to withhold her 'Come in,' and as Miss Macy crossed the threshold, Lizzie felt that Vincent Deering's first letter – the letter from the train – had slipped from her bosom to the floor.

Miss Macy, as promptly aware, darted forward to recover it. Lizzie stooped also, instinctively jealous of her touch; but the visitor reached the letter first, and as she seized it, Lizzie knew that she had seen whence it fell, and was weaving round the incident a rapid web of romance.

Lizzie blushed with annoyance. 'It's too stupid, having no pockets! If one gets a letter as one is going out in the morning, one has to carry it in one's blouse all day.'

Miss Macy looked at her fondly. 'It's warm from your heart!' she breathed, reluctantly yielding up the missive.

Lizzie laughed, for she knew it was the letter that had warmed her heart. Poor Andora Macy! *She* would never know. Her bleak bosom would never take fire from such a contact. Lizzie looked at her with kind eyes, chafing at the injustice of fate.

The next evening, on her return home, she found her friend hovering in the entrance hall.

'I thought you'd like me to put this in your own hand,' Andora whispered significantly, pressing a letter upon Lizzie. 'I couldn't *bear* to see it lying on the table with the others.'

It was Deering's letter from the steamer. Lizzie blushed to the forehead, but without resenting Andora's divination. She could not have breathed a word of her bliss, but she was not sorry to have it guessed, and pity for Andora's destitution yielded to the pleasure of using it as a mirror for her own abundance.

Deering wrote again on reaching New York, a long fond dissatisfied letter, vague in its indication to his own projects, specific in the expression of his love. Lizzie brooded over every syllable till they formed the undercurrent of all her waking thoughts, and murmured through her midnight dreams; but she would have been happier if they had shed some definite light on the future.

That would come, no doubt, when he had had time to look about and got his bearings. She counted up the days that must elapse before she received his next letter, and stole down early to peep at the papers, and learn when the next American mail was due. At length the happy date arrived, and she hurried distractedly through the day's work, trying to conceal her impatience by the endearments she bestowed upon her pupils. It was easier, in her present mood, to kiss them than to keep them at their grammars.

That evening, on Mme. Clopin's threshold, her heart beat so wildly that she had to lean a moment against the doorpost before entering. But on the hall table, where the letters lay, there was none for her.

She went over them with an impatient hand, her heart dropping down and down, as she had sometimes fallen down on endless stairway in a dream – the very same stairway up which she had seemed to fly when she climbed the long hill to Deering's door. Then it struck her that Andora might have found and secreted her letter, and with a spring she was on the actual stairs, and rattling Miss Macy's door handle.

'You've a letter for me, haven't you?' she panted.

Miss Macy enclosed her in attenuated arms. 'Oh, darling, did you expect another?'

'Do give it to me!' Lizzie pleaded with eager eyes.

'But I haven't any! There hasn't been a sign of a letter for you.'

'I know there is. There *must* be,' Lizzie cried, stamping her foot.

'But, dearest, I've *watched* for you, and there's been nothing.'

Day after day, for the ensuing weeks, the same scene re-enacted itself with endless variations. Lizzie, after the first sharp spasm of disappointment, made no effort to conceal her anxiety from Miss Macy, and the fond Andora was charged to keep a vigilant eye upon the postman's coming and to spy on the *bonne* for possible negligence or perfidy. But these elaborate precautions remained fruitless, and no letter from Deering came.

During the first fortnight of silence, Lizzie exhausted all the ingenuities of explanation. She marveled afterward at the reasons she had found for Deering's silence: there were moments when she almost argued herself into thinking it more natural than his continuing to write. There was only one reason which her intelligence rejected; and that was the possibility that he had forgotten her, that the whole episode had faded from his mind like a breath from a mirror. From that she resolutely averted her thoughts, conscious that if she suffered herself to contemplate it, the motive power of life would fail, and she would no longer understand why she rose in the morning and lay down at night.

If she had had leisure to indulge her anguish she might have been unable to keep such speculations at bay. But she had to be up and working: the *blanchisseuse* had to be paid, and Mme. Clopin's weekly bill, and all the little 'extras' that even her frugal habits had to reckon with. And in the depths of her thought dwelt the dogging fear of illness and incapacity, goading her to work while she could. She hardly remembered the time when she had been without that fear; it was second nature now, and it kept her on her feet when other incentives might have failed. In the blankness of her misery she felt no dread of death; but the horror of being ill and 'dependent' was in her blood.

In the first weeks of silence she wrote again and again to Deering, entreating him for a word, for a mere sign of life. From the first she had shrunk from seeming to assert any claim on his future, yet in her bewilderment she now charged herself with having been too possessive, too exacting in her tone. She told herself that his fastidiousness shrank from any but a 'light touch,' and that hers had not been light enough. She should have kept to the character of the 'little friend,' the artless consciousness in which tormented genius may find an escape from its complexities; and instead, she had dramatized their relation, exaggerated her own part in it, presumed, forsooth, to share the front of the stage with him, instead of being content to serve as scenery or chorus.

But though, to herself, she admitted, and even insisted on, the episodical nature of the experience, on the fact that for Deering it could be no more than in incident, she was still convinced that his sentiment for her, however fugitive, had been genuine.

His had not been the attitude of the unscrupulous male seeking a vulgar 'advantage.' For a moment he had really needed her, and if he was silent now, it was perhaps because he feared that she had mistaken the nature of the need, and built vain hopes on its possible duration.

It was of the essence of Lizzie's devotion that it sought, instinctively, the larger freedom of its object; she could not conceive of love under any form of exaction or compulsion. To make this clear to Deering became an overwhelming need, and in a last short letter she explicitly freed him from whatever sentimental obligation its predecessors might have seemed to impose. In this communication she playfully accused herself of having unwittingly sentimentalized their relation, affecting, in self-defence, a retrospective astuteness, a sense of the impermanence of the tenderer sentiments, that almost put Deering in the position of having mistaken coquetry for surrender. And she ended, gracefully, with a plea for the continuance of the friendly regard which she had 'always understood' to be the basis of their sympathy. The document, when completed, seemed to her worthy of what she conceived to be Deering's conception of a woman of the world – and she found a spectral satisfaction in the thought of making her final appearance before him in this distinguished character. But she was never destined to learn what effect the appearance produced; for the letter, like those it sought to excuse, remained unanswered.

• V •

THE fresh spring sunshine which had so often attended Lizzie West on her dusty climb up the hill of St. Cloud, beamed on her, some two years later in a scene and a situation of altered import.

Its rays, filtered through the horse chestnuts of the Champs Elysées, shone on the graveled circle about Laurent's restaurant; and Miss West, seated at a table within that privileged space, presented to the light a hat much better able to sustain its scrutiny than those which had shaded the brow of Juliet Deering's instructions.

Her dress was in keeping with the hat, and both belonged to a situation rife with such possibilities as the act of a leisurely luncheon at Laurent's in the opening week of the Salon. Her companions, of both sexes, confirmed this impression by an appropriateness of attire and an case of manner implying the largest range of selection between the forms of Parisian idleness; and even Andora Macy, seated opposite, as in the place of co-hostess or companion, reflected, in coy greys and mauves, the festal note of the occasion.

This note reverberated persistently in the ears of a solitary gentleman straining for glimpses of the group from a table wedged in the remotest corner of the garden; but to Miss West herself the occurrence did not rise above the usual. For nearly a year she had been acquiring the habit of such situations, and the act of offering a luncheon at Laurent's to her cousins, the Harvey Mearses of Providence, and their friend Mr. Jackson Benn, produced in her no emotion beyond the languid glow which Mr. Benn's presence was beginning to impart to such scenes.

'It's frightful, the way you've got used to it,' Andora Macy had wailed, in the first days of her friend's transfigured fortunes, when Lizzie West had waked one morning to find herself among the heirs of an ancient miserly cousin whose testamentary dispositions had formed, since her earliest childhood, the subject of pleasantry and conjecture in her own improvident family. Old Hezron Mears had never given any sign of life to the luckless Wests; had perhaps hardly been conscious of including them in the carefully drawn will which, following the old American convention, scrupulously divided his millions among his kin. It was by a mere genealogical accident that Lizzie, falling just within the golden circle, found herself possessed of a pittance sufficient to release her from the prospect of a long grey future in Mme. Clopin's *pension*.

The release had seemed wonderful at first; yet she presently found that it had destroyed her former world without giving her a new one. On the ruins of the old *pension* life bloomed the only flower that had ever sweetened her path; and beyond the sense of present ease, and the removal of anxiety for the future, her reconstructed existence blossomed with no compensating joys. She had hoped great things from the oppor-

tunity to rest, to travel, to look about her, above all, in various artful
feminine ways, to be 'nice' to the companions of her less privileged
state; but such widenings of scope left her, as it were, but the more
conscious of the empty margin of personal life beyond them. It was
not till she woke to the leisure of her new days that she had the full
sense of what was gone from them.

Their very emptiness made her strain to pack them with transient
sensations: she was like the possessor of an unfurnished house, with
random furniture and bric-a-brac perpetually pouring in 'on approval.'
It was in this experimental character that Mr. Jackson Benn had fixed
her attention, and the languid effort of her imagination to adjust him
to her taste was seconded by the fond complicity of Andora, and by
the smiling approval of her cousins. Lizzie did not discourage these
attempts: she suffered serenely Andora's allusions to Mr. Benn's infatu-
ation, and Mrs. Mears's boasts of his business standing. All the better
if they could drape his narrow square-shouldered frame and round
unwinking countenance in the trailing mists of sentiment: Lizzie looked
and listened, not unhopeful of the miracle.

'I never saw anything like the way these Frenchmen stare! Doesn't
it make you nervous, Lizzie?' Mrs. Mears broke out suddenly, ruffling
her feather boa about an outraged bosom. Mrs. Mears was still in that
stage of development when her countrywomen taste to the full the peril
of being exposed to the gaze of the licentious Gaul.

Lizzie roused herself from the contemplation of Mr. Benn's round
baby cheeks and the square blue jaw resting on his perpendicular collar.
'Is someone staring at me?' she asked.

'Don't turn round, whatever you do! There – just over there,
between the rhododendrons – the tall blond man alone at that table.
Really, Harvey, I think you ought to speak to the headwaiter, or
something, though I suppose in one of these places they'd only laugh
at you,' Mrs. Mears shudderingly concluded.

Her husband, as if inclining to this probability, continued the undisturbed dissection of his chicken wing, but Mr. Benn, perhaps conscious
that his situation demanded a more punctilious attitude, sternly revolved
upon the parapet of his high collar in the direction of Mrs. Mears's
glance.

'What, that fellow all alone over there? Why, *he's* not French; he's
an American,' he then proclaimed with a perceptible relaxing of the
muscles.

'Oh!' murmured Mrs. Mears, as perceptibly disappointed, and Mr.
Benn continued: 'He came over on the steamer with me. He's some
kind of an artist – a fellow named Deering. He was staring at *me*, I
guess: wondering whether I was going to remember him. Why, how
d' 'e do? How are you? Why, yes, of course; with pleasure – my friends,

Mrs. Harvey Mears – Mr. Mears; my friends, Miss Macy and Miss West.'

'I have the pleasure of knowing Miss West,' said Vincent Deering with a smile.

• VI •

EVEN through his smile Lizzie had seen, in the first moment, how changed he was; and the impression of the change deepened to the point of pain when, a few days later, in reply to his brief note, she granted him a private hour.

That the first sight of his writing – the first answer to her letters – should have come, after three long years, in the shape of this impersonal line, too curt to be called humble, yet revealing a consciousness of the past in the studied avoidance of its language! As she read, her mind flashed back over what she had dreamed his letters would be, over the exquisite answers she had composed above his name. There was nothing exquisite in the lines before her; but dormant nerves began to throb again at the mere touch of the paper he had touched, and she threw the note into the fire before she dared to reply to it.

Now that he was actually before her again, he became, as usual, the one live spot in her consciousness. Once more her tormented self sank back passive and numb, but now with all its power of suffering mysteriously transferred to the presence, so known yet so unknown, at the opposite corner of her hearth. She was still Lizzie West, and he was still Vincent Deering; but the Styx rolled between them, and she saw his face through its fog. It was his face, really, rather than his words, that told her, as she furtively studied it, the tale of failure and discouragement which had so blurred its handsome lines. She kept, afterward, no precise memory of the details of his narrative: the pain it evidently cost him to impart it was so much the sharpest fact in her new vision of him. Confusedly, however, she gathered that on reaching America he had found his wife's small property gravely impaired; and that, while lingering on to secure what remained of it, he had contrived to sell a picture or two, and had even known a moment of success, during which he received orders and set up a studio. Then the tide had ebbed, his work had remained on his hands, and a tedious illness, with its miserable sequel of debt, soon wiped out his advantage. There followed a period of eclipse, during which she inferred that he had tried his hand at diverse means of livelihood, accepting employment from a fashionable house decorator, designing wallpapers, illustrating magazine articles, and acting for a time – she dimly understood – as the social tout of a new hotel desirous of advertising its restaurant. These disjointed facts were strung on a slender thread of personal allusions –

references to friends who had been kind (jealously, she guessed them to be women), and to enemies who had schemed against him. But, true to his tradition of 'correctness,' he carefully avoided the mention of names, and left her imagination to grope dimly through a crowded world in which there seemed little room for her small shy presence.

As she listened, her private grievance vanished beneath the sense of his unhappiness. Nothing he had said explained or excused his conduct to her; but he had suffered, he had been lonely, had been humiliated, and she felt, with a fierce maternal rage, that there was no possible justification for any scheme of things in which such facts were possible. She could not have said why: she simply knew that it hurt too much to see him hurt.

Gradually it came to her that her absence of resentment was due to her having so definitely settled her own future. She was glad she had decided – as she now felt she had – to marry Jackson Benn, if only for the sense of detachment it gave her in dealing with Vincent Deering. Her personal safety insured her the requisite impartiality, and justified her in lingering as long as she chose over the last lines of a chapter to which her own act had fixed the close. Any lingering hesitations as to the finality of this decision were dispelled by the need of making it known to Deering: and when her visitor paused in his reminiscences to say, with a sigh, 'But many things have happened to you too,' the words did not so much evoke the sense of her altered fortunes as the image of the suitor to whom she was about to entrust them.

'Yes, many things; it's three years,' she answered.

Deering sat leaning forward, in his sad exiled elegance, his eyes gently bent on hers; and at his side she saw the form of Mr. Jackson Benn, with shoulders preternaturally squared by the cut of his tight black coat, and a tall shiny collar sustaining his baby cheeks and hard blue chin. Then the vision faded as Deering began to speak.

'Three years,' he repeated musingly. 'I've so often wondered what they'd brought you.'

She lifted her head with a blush, and the terrified wish that he should not – at the cost of all his notions of correctness – lapse into the blunder of becoming 'personal.'

'You've wondered?' she smiled back bravely.

'Do you suppose I haven't?' His look dwelt on her. 'Yes, I dare say that *was* what you thought of me.'

She had her answer pat – 'Why, frankly, you know, I *didn't* think of you at all.' But the mounting tide of her memories swept it indignantly away. If it was his correctness to ignore, it could never be hers to disavow!

'*Was* that what you thought of me?' she heard him repeat in a tone of sad insistence; and at that, with a lift of her head, she resolutely answered: 'How could I know what to think? I had no word from you.'

If she had expected, and perhaps almost hoped, that this answer would create a difficulty for him, the gaze of quiet fortitude with which he met it proved that she had underestimated his resources.

'No, you had no word. I kept my vow,' he said.

'You vow?'

'That you *shouldn't* have a word – not a syllable. Oh, I kept it through everything!'

Lizzie's heart was sounding in her ears the old confused rumor of the sea of life, but through it she desperately tried to distinguish the still small voice of reason.

'What was your vow? Why shouldn't I have had a syllable from you?'

He sat motionless, still holding her with a look so gentle that it almost seemed forgiving.

Then, abruptly, he rose, and crossing the space between them, sat down in a chair at her side. The movement might have implied a forgetfulness of changed conditions, and Lizzie, as if thus viewing it, drew slightly back; but he appeared not to notice her recoil, and his eyes, at last leaving her face, slowly and approvingly made the round of the small bright drawing room. 'This is charming. Yes, things *have* changed for you,' he said.

A moment before, she had prayed that he might be spared the error of a vain return upon the past. It was as if all her retrospective tenderness, dreading to see him at such a disadvantage, rose up to protect him from it. But his evasiveness exasperated her, and suddenly she felt the desire to hold him fast, face to face with his own words.

Before she could repeat her question, however, he had met her with another.

'You *did* think of me, then? Why are you afraid to tell me that you did?'

The unexpectedness of the challenge wrung a cry from her. 'Didn't my letters tell you so enough?'

'Ah – your letters – ' Keeping her gaze on his with unrelenting fixity, she could detect in him no confusion, not the least quiver of a nerve. He only gazed back at her more sadly.

'They went everywhere with me – your letters,' he said.

'Yet you never answered them.' At last the accusation trembled to her lips.

'Yet I never answered them.'

'Did you ever so much as read them, I wonder?'

All the demons of self-torture were up in her now, and she loosed them on him as if to escape from their rage.

Deering hardly seemed to hear her question. He merely shifted his attitude, leaning a little nearer to her, but without attempting, by the least gesture, to remind her of the privileges which such nearness had once implied.

'There were beautiful, wonderful things in them,' he said, smiling.

She felt herself stiffen under his smile. 'You've waited three years to tell me so!'

He looked at her with grave surprise. 'And do you resent my telling you, even now?'

His parries were incredible. They left her with a sense of thrusting at emptiness, and a desperate, almost vindictive desire to drive him against the wall and pin him there.

'No. Only I wonder you should take the trouble to tell me, when at the time – '

And now, with a sudden turn, he gave her the final surprise of meeting her squarely on her own ground.

'When at the time, I didn't? But how *could* I – at the time?'

'Why couldn't you? You've not yet told me.'

He gave her again his look of disarming patience. 'Do I need to? Hasn't my whole wretched story told you?'

'Told me why you never answered my letters?'

'Yes – since I could only answer them in one way: by protesting my love and my longing.'

There was a pause, of resigned expectancy on his part, on hers of a wild, confused reconstruction of her shattered past. 'You mean, then, that you didn't write because – '

'Because I found, when I reached America, that I was a pauper: that my wife's money was gone, and that what I could earn – I've so little gift that way! – was barely enough to keep Juliet clothed and educated. It was as if an iron door had been locked and barred between us.'

Lizzie felt herself driven back, panting, on the last defences of her incredulity. 'You might at least have told me – have explained. Do you think I shouldn't have understood?'

He did not hesitate. 'You would have understood. It wasn't that.'

'What was it then?' she quavered.

'It's wonderful you shouldn't see! Simply that I couldn't write you *that*. Anything else – not *that*!'

'And so you preferred to let me suffer?'

There was a shade of reproach in his eyes. 'I suffered too,' he said.

It was his first direct appeal to her compassion, and for a moment it nearly unsettled the delicate poise of her sympathies, and sent them trembling in the direction of scorn and irony. But even as the impulse rose it was stayed by another sensation. Once again, as so often in the past, she became aware of a fact which, in his absence, she always failed to reckon with; the fact of the deep irreducible difference between his image in her mind and his actual self – the mysterious alteration in her judgment produced by the inflections of his voice, the look of his eyes, the whole complex pressure of his personality. She had phrased it once, self-reproachfully, by saying to herself that she 'never could remember him – ' so completely did the sight of him supersede the counterfeit about which her fancy wove its perpetual wonders. Bright and breathing as that counterfeit was, it became a figment of the mind at the touch of his presence, and on this occasion the immediate result was to cause her to feel his possible unhappiness with an intensity beside which her private injury paled.

'I suffered horribly,' he repeated, 'and all the more that I couldn't make a sign, couldn't cry out my misery. There was only one escape from it all – to hold my tongue, and pray that you might hate me.'

The blood rushed to Lizzie's forehead. 'Hate you – you prayed that I might hate you?'

He rose from his seat, and moving closer, lifted her hand in his. 'Yes, because your letters showed me that if you didn't, you'd be unhappier still.'

Her hand lay motionless, with the warmth of his flowing through it, and her thoughts, too – her poor fluttering stormy thoughts – felt themselves suddenly penetrated by the same soft current of communion.

'And I meant to keep my resolve,' he went on, slowly releasing his clasp. 'I meant to keep it even after the random stream of things swept me back here, in your way; but when I saw you the other day I felt that what had been possible at a distance was impossible now that we were near each other. How could I see you, and let you hate me?'

He had moved away, but not to resume his seat. He merely paused at a little distance, his hand resting on a chair back, in the transient attitude that precedes departure.

Lizzie's heart contracted. He was going, then, and this was his farewell. He was going, and she could find no word to detain him but the senseless stammer: 'I never hated you.'

He considered her with a faint smile. 'It's not necessary, at any rate, that you should do so now. Time and circumstances have made me so harmless – that's exactly why I've dared to venture back. And I wanted to tell you how I rejoice in your good fortune. It's the only obstacle between us that I can't bring myself to wish away.'

Lizzie sat silent, spellbound, as she listened, by the sudden evocation of Mr. Jackson Benn. He stood there again, between herself and Deering, perpendicular and reproachful, but less solid and sharply outlined than before, with a look in his small hard eyes that desperately wailed for re-embodiment.

Deering was continuing his farewell speech. 'You're rich now – you're free. You will marry.' She saw him holding out his hand.

'It's not true that I'm engaged!' she broke out. They were the last words she had meant to utter; they were hardly related to her conscious thoughts; but she felt her whole will gathered up in the irrepressible impulse to repudiate and fling away from her forever the spectral claim of Mr. Jackson Benn.

• VII •

IT was the firm conviction of Andora Macy that every object in the Vincent Deerings' charming little house at Neuilly had been expressly designed for the Deerings' son to play with.

The house was full of pretty things, some not obviously applicable to the purpose; but Miss Macy's casuistry was equal to the baby's appetite, and the baby's mother was no match for them in the art of defending her possessions. There were moments, in fact, when she almost fell in with Andora's summary division of her works of art into articles safe or unsafe for the baby to lick, or resisted it only to the extent of occasionally substituting some less precious, or less perishable, object for the particular fragility on which her son's desire was fixed. And it was with this intention that, on a certain spring morning – which wore the added luster of being the baby's second birthday – she had murmured, with her mouth in his curls, and one hand holding a bit of Chelsea above his clutch: 'Wouldn't he rather have that beautiful shiny thing in Aunt Andora's hand?'

The two friends were together in Lizzie's morning room – the room she had chosen, on acquiring the house, because, when she sat there, she could hear Deering's step as he paced up and down before his easel in the studio she had built for him. His step had been less regularly audible than she had hoped, for, after three years of wedded bliss, he had somehow failed to settle down to the great work which was to result from that state; but even when she did not hear him she knew that he was there, above her head, stretched out on the old divan from St. Cloud, and smoking countless cigarettes while he skimmed the morning papers; and the sense of his nearness had not yet lost its first keen edge of wonder.

Lizzie herself, on the day in question, was engaged in a more arduous task than the study of the morning's news. She had never unlearned the habit of orderly activity, and the trait she least understood in her husband's character was his way of letting the loose ends of life hang as they would. She had been disposed to ascribe this to the chronic incoherence of his first *ménage;* but now she knew that, though he basked under her beneficent rule, he would never feel any impulse to further its work. He liked to see things fall into place about him at a wave of her wand; but his enjoyment of her household magic in no way diminished his smiling irresponsibility, and it was with one of its least amiable consequences that his wife and her friend were now dealing.

Before them stood two travel-worn trunks and a distended portmanteau, which had shed their heterogeneous contents over Lizzie's rosy carpet. They represented the hostages left by her husband on his somewhat precipitate departure from a New York boardinghouse, and redeemed by her on her learning, in a curt letter from his landlady, that the latter was not disposed to regard them as an equivalent for the arrears of Deering's board.

Lizzie had not been shocked by the discovery that her husband had left America in debt. She had too sad an acquaintance with the economic strain to see any humiliation in such accidents; but it offended her sense of order that he should not have liquidated his obligation in the three years since their marriage. He took her remonstrance with his usual good humor, and left her to forward the liberating draft, though her delicacy had provided him with a bank account which assured his personal independence. Lizzie had discharged the duty without repugnance, since she knew that his delegating it to her was the result of his indolence and not of any design on her exchequer. Deering was not dazzled by money; his altered fortunes had tempted him to no excesses: he was simply too lazy to draw the check, as he had been too lazy to remember the debt it canceled.

'No, dear! No!' Lizzie lifted the Chelsea higher. 'Can't you find something for him, Andora, among that rubbish over there? Where's the beaded bag you had in your hand? I don't think it could hurt him to lick that.'

Miss Macy, bag in hand, rose from her knees, and stumbled across the room through the frayed garments and old studio properties. Before the group of mother and son she fell into a rapturous attitude.

'Do look at him reach for it, the tyrant! Isn't he just like the young Napoleon?'

Lizzie laughed and swung her son in air. 'Dangle it before him, Andora. If you let him have it too quickly, he won't care for it. He's just like any man, I think.'

Andora slowly lowered the bag till the heir of the Deerings closed his masterful fist upon it. 'There – my Chelsea's safe!' Lizzie smiled, setting her boy on the floor, and watching him stagger away with his booty.

Andora stood beside her, watching too. 'Do you know where the bag came from, Lizzie?'

Mrs. Deering, bent above a pile of discollared shirts, shook an inattentive head. 'I never saw such wicked washing! There isn't one that's fit to mend. The bag? No: I've not the least idea.'

Andora surveyed her incredulously. 'Doesn't it make you utterly miserable to think that some woman may have made it for him?'

Lizzie, still bowed in scrutiny above the shirts, broke into a laugh. 'Really, Andora, really! Six, seven, nine; no, there isn't even a dozen. There isn't a whole dozen of *anything*. I don't see how men live alone.'

Andora broodingly pursued her theme. 'Do you mean to tell me it doesn't make you jealous to handle these things of his that other women may have given him?'

Lizzie shook her head again, and, straightening herself with a smile, tossed a bundle in her friend's direction. 'No, I don't feel jealous. Here, count these socks for me, like a darling.'

Andora moaned 'Don't you feel *anything at all?*' as the socks landed in her hollow bosom; but Lizzie, intent upon her task, tranquilly continued to unfold and sort. She felt a great deal as she did so, but her feelings were too deep and delicate for the simplifying processes of speech. She only knew that each article she drew from the trunks sent through her the long tremor of Deering's touch. It was part of her wonderful new life that everything belonging to him contained an infinitesimal fraction of himself – a fraction becoming visible in the warmth of her love as certain secret elements become visible in rare intensities of temperature. And in the case of the objects before her, poor shabby witnesses of his days of failure, what they gave out acquired a special poignancy from its contrast to his present cherished state. His shirts were all in round dozens now, and washed as carefully as old lace. As for his socks, she knew the pattern of every pair, and would have liked to see the washerwoman who dared to mislay one, or bring it home with the colors 'run'! And in these homely tokens of his well-being she saw the symbol of what her tenderness had brought him. He was safe in it, encompassed by it, morally and materially, and she defied the embattled powers of malice to reach him through the armor of her love. Such feelings, however, were not communicable, even had one desired to express them: they were no more to be distinguished from the sense of life itself than bees from the lime blossoms in which they murmur.

'Oh, do *look* at him, Lizzie! He's found out how to open the bag!'

Lizzie lifted her head to look a moment at her son, throned on a heap of studio rubbish, with Andora before him on adoring knees. She thought vaguely 'Poor Andora!' and then resumed the discouraged inspection of a buttonless white waistcoat. The next sound she was conscious of was an excited exclamation from her friend.

'Why, Lizzie, do you know what he used the bag for? To keep your letters in!'

Lizzie looked up more quickly. She was aware that Andora's pronoun had changed its object, and was now applied to Deering. And it struck her as odd, and slightly disagreeable, that a letter of hers should be found among the rubbish abandoned in her husband's New York lodgings.

'How funny! Give it to me, please.'

'Give it to Aunt Andora, darling! Here – look inside, and see what else a big, big boy can find there! Yes, here's another! Why, why – '

Lizzie rose with a shade of impatience and crossed the floor to the romping group beside the other trunk.

'What is it? Give me the letters, please.' As she spoke, she suddenly recalled the day when, in Mme. Clopin's *pension*, she had addressed a similar behest to Andora Macy.

Andora lifted to her a *look* of startled conjecture. 'Why, this one's never been opened! Do you suppose that awful woman could have kept it from him?'

Lizzie laughed. Andora's imaginings were really puerile! 'What awful woman? His landlady? Don't be such a goose, Andora. How can it have been kept back from him, when we've found it among his things?'

'Yes; but then why was it never opened?'

Andora held out the letter, and Lizzie took it. The writing was hers; the envelope bore the Passy postmark; and it was unopened. She looked at it with a sharp drop of the heart.

'Why, so are the others – all unopened!' Andora threw out on a rising note; but Lizzie, stooping over, checked her.

'Give them to me, please.'

'Oh, Lizzie, Lizzie – ' Andora, on her knees, held back the packet, her pale face paler with anger and compassion. 'Lizzie, they're the letters I used to post for you – the letters he never answered! *Look!*'

'Give them back to me, please.' Lizzie possessed herself of the letters.

The two women faced each other, Andora still kneeling, Lizzie motionless before her. The blood had rushed to her face, humming in her ears, and forcing itself into the veins of her temples. Then it ebbed, and she felt cold and weak.

'It must have been some plot – some conspiracy,' Andora cried, so fired by the ecstasy of invention that for the moment she seemed lost to all but the aesthetic aspect of the case.

Lizzie averted her eyes with an effort, and they rested on the boy, who sat at her feet placidly sucking the tassels of the bag. His mother stooped and extracted them from his rosy mouth, which a cry of wrath immediately filled. She lifted him in her arms, and for the first time no current of life ran from his body into hers. He felt heavy and clumsy, like some other woman's child; and his screams annoyed her.

'Take him away, please, Andora.'

'Oh, Lizzie, Lizzie!' Andora wailed.

Lizzie held out the child, and Andora, struggling to her feet, received him.

'I know just how you feel,' she gasped, above the baby's head.

Lizzie, in some dark hollow of herself, heard the faint echo of a laugh. Andora always thought she knew how people felt!

'Tell Marthe to take him with her when she fetches Juliet home from school.'

'Yes, yes.' Andora gloated on her. 'If you'd only give way, my darling!'

The baby, howling, dived over Andora's shoulder for the bag.

'Oh, *take* him!' his mother ordered.

Andora, from the door, cried out: 'I'll be back at once. Remember, love, you're not alone!'

But Lizzie insisted, 'Go with them – I wish you to go with them,' in the tone to which Miss Macy had never learned the answer.

The door closed on her reproachful back, and Lizzie stood alone. She looked about the disordered room, which offered a dreary image of the havoc of her life. An hour or two ago, everything about her had been so exquisitely ordered, without and within: her thoughts and her emotions had all been outspread before her like jewels laid away symmetrically in a collector's cabinet. Now they had been tossed down helter-skelter among the rubbish there on the floor, and had themselves turned to rubbish like the rest. Yes, there lay her life at her feet, among all that tarnished trash.

She picked up her letters, ten in all, and examined the flaps of the envelopes. Not one had been opened – not one. As she looked, every word she had written fluttered to life, and every feeling prompting it sent a tremor through her. With vertiginous speed and microscopic distinctness of vision she was reliving that whole period of her life, stripping bare again the ruin over which the drift of three happy years had fallen.

She laughed at Andora's notion of a conspiracy – of the letters having been 'kept back.' She required no extraneous aid in deciphering the mystery: her three years' experience of Deering shed on it all the light she needed. And yet a moment before she had believed herself to be perfectly happy! Now it was the worst part of her pain that it did not really surprise her.

She knew so well how it must have happened. The letters had reached him when he was busy, occupied with something else, and had been put aside to be read at some future time – a time which never came. Perhaps on the steamer, even, he had met 'someone else' – the 'someone' who lurks, veiled and ominous, in the background of every woman's thoughts about her lover. Or perhaps he had been merely forgetful. She knew now that the sensations which he seemed to feel most intensely left no reverberations in his memory – that he did not relive either his pleasures or his pains. She needed no better proof than the lightness of his conduct toward his daughter. He seemed to have taken it for granted that Juliet would remain indefinitely with the friends who had received her after her mother's death, and it was at Lizzie's suggestion that the little girl was brought home and that they had established themselves at Neuilly to be near her school. But Juliet once with them, he became the model of a tender father, and Lizzie wondered that he had not felt the child's absence, since he seemed so affectionately aware of her presence.

Lizzie had noted all this in Juliet's case, but had taken for granted that her own was different; that she formed, for Deering, the exception which every woman secretly supposes herself to form in the experience of the man she loves. She had learned by this time that she could not modify his habits; but she imagined that she had deepened his sensibilities, had furnished him with an 'ideal' – angelic function! And she now saw that the fact of her letters – her unanswered letters – having on his own assurance, 'meant so much' to him, had been the basis on which this beautiful fabric was reared.

There they lay now, the letters, precisely as when they had left her hands. He had not had time to read them; and there had been a moment in her past when that discovery would have been to her the sharpest pang imaginable. She had traveled far beyond that point. She could have forgiven him now for having forgotten her; but she could never forgive him for having deceived her.

She sat down, and looked again about the room. Suddenly she heard his step overhead, and her heart contracted. She was afraid that he was coming down to her. She sprang up and bolted the door; then she dropped into the nearest chair, tremulous and exhausted, as if the act had required an immense effort. A moment later she heard him on the stairs, and her tremor broke into a fit of shaking. 'I loathe you – I loathe you!' she cried.

She listened apprehensively for his touch on the handle of the door. He would come in, humming a tune, to ask some idle question and lay a caress on her hair. But no, the door was bolted; she was safe. She continued to listen, and the step passed on. He had not been coming to her, then. He must have gone downstairs to fetch something – another newspaper, perhaps. He seemed to read little else, and she sometimes wondered when he had found time to store the material that used to serve for their famous 'literary' talks. The wonder shot through her again, barbed with a sneer. At that moment it seemed to her that everything he had ever done and been was a lie.

She heard the house door close, and started up. Was he going out? It was not his habit to leave the house in the morning.

She crossed the room to the window, and saw him walking, with a quick decided step, between the lilacs to the gate. What could have called him forth at that unusual hour? It was odd that he should not have told her. The fact that she thought it odd suddenly showed her how closely their lives were interwoven. She had become a habit to him, and he was fond of his habits. But to her it was as if a stranger had opened the gate and gone out. She wondered what he would feel if he knew that she felt *that*.

'In a hour he will know,' she said to herself, with a kind of fierce exultation; and immediately she began to dramatize the scene. As soon as he came in she meant to call him up to her room and hand him the letters without a word. For a moment she gloated on the picture; then her imagination recoiled. She was humiliated by the thought of humiliating him. She wanted to keep his image intact; she would not see him.

He had lied to her about her letters – had lied to her when he found it to his interest to regain her favor. Yes, there was the point to hold fast. He had sought her out when he learned that she was rich. Perhaps he had come back from America on purpose to marry her; no doubt he had come back on purpose. It was incredible that she had not seen this at the time. She turned sick at the thought of her fatuity and of the grossness of his arts. Well, the event proved that they were all he needed. . . . But why had he gone out at such an hour? She was irritated to find herself still preoccupied by his comings and goings.

Turning from the window, she sat down again. She wondered what she meant to do next. . . . No, she would not show him the letters; she would simply leave them on his table and go away. She would leave the house with her boy and Andora. It was a relief to feel a definite plan forming itself in her mind – something that her uprooted thoughts could fasten on. She would go away, of course; and meanwhile, in order not to see him, she would feign a headache, and remain in her room till after luncheon. Then she and Andora would pack a few things, and fly with the child while he was dawdling about upstairs in the studio. When one's house fell, one fled from the ruins: nothing could be simpler, more inevitable.

Her thoughts were checked by the impossibility of picturing what would happen next. Try as she would, she could not see herself and the child away from Deering. But that, of course, was because of her nervous weakness. She had youth, money, energy: all the trumps were on her side. It was much more difficult to imagine what would become of Deering. He was do dependent on her, and they had been so happy together! It struck her as illogical and even immoral, and yet she knew he had been happy with her. It never happened like that in novels: happiness 'built on a lie' always crumbled, burying the presumptuous architect beneath its ruins. According to the laws of fiction, Deering, having deceived her once, would inevitably have gone on deceiving her. Yet she knew he had not gone on deceiving her. . . .

She tried again to picture her new life. Her friends, of course, would rally about her. But the prospect left her cold; she did not want them to rally. She wanted only one thing – the life she had been living before she had given her baby the embroidered bag to play with. Oh, why had she given him the bag? She had been so happy, they had all been so happy! Every nerve in her clamored for her lost happiness, angrily, irrationally, as the boy had clamored for his bag! It was horrible to know too much; there was always blood in the foundations. Parents 'kept things' from children – protected them from all the dark secrets of pain and evil. And was any life livable unless it were thus protected? Could anyone look in the Medusa's face and live?

But why should she leave the house, since it was hers? Here, with her boy and Andora, she could still make for herself the semblance of a life. It was Deering who would have to go; he would understand that as soon as he saw the letters.

She saw him going – leaving the house as he had left it just now. She saw the gate closing on him for the last time. Now her vision was acute enough: she saw him as distinctly as if he were in the room. Ah, he would not like returning to the old life of privations and expedients! And yet she knew he would not plead with her.

Suddenly a new thought seized her. What if Andora had rushed to him with the tale of the discovery of the letters – with the 'Fly, you are discovered!' of romantic fiction? What if he *had* left her for good? It would not be unlike him, after all. For all his sweetness he was always evasive and inscrutable. He might have said to himself that he would forestall her action, and place himself at once on the defensive. It might be that she *had* seen him out of the gate for the last time.

She looked about the room again, as if the thought had given it a new aspect. Yes, this alone could explain her husband's going out. It was past twelve o'clock, their usual luncheon hour, and he was scrupulously punctual at meals, and gently reproachful if she kept him waiting. Only some unwanted event could have caused him to leave the house at such an hour and with such marks of haste. Well, perhaps it was better that Andora should have spoken. She mistrusted her own courage; she almost hoped the deed had been done for her. Yet her next sensation was one of confused resentment. She said to herself, 'Why has Andora interfered?' She felt baffled and angry, as though her prey had escaped her. If Deering had been in the house she would have gone to him instantly and overwhelmed him with her scorn. But he had gone out, and she did not know where he had gone, and oddly mingled with her anger against him was the latent instinct of vigilance, the solicitude of the woman accustomed to watch over the man she loves. It would be strange never to feel that solicitude again, never to hear him say, with his hand on her hair: 'You foolish child, were you worried? Am I late?'

The sense of his touch was so real that she stiffened herself against it, flinging back her head as if to throw off his hand. The mere thought of his caress was hateful; yet she felt it in all her veins. Yes, she felt it, but with horror and repugnance. It was something she wanted to escape from, and the fact of struggling against it was what made its hold so strong. It was as though her mind were sounding her body to make sure of its allegiance, spying on it for any secret movement of revolt. . . .

To escape from the sensation, she rose and went again to the window. No one was in sight. But presently the gate began to swing back, and her heart gave a leap – she knew not whether up or down. A moment later the gate opened to admit a perambulator, propelled by the nurse and flanked by Juliet and Andora. Lizzie's eyes rested on the familiar group as if she had never seen it before, and she stood motionless, instead of flying down to meet the children.

Suddenly there was a step on the stairs, and she heard Andora's knock. She unbolted the door, and was strained to her friend's emaciated bosom.

'My darling!' Miss Macy cried. 'Remember you have your child – and me!'

Lizzie loosened herself. She looked at Andora with a feeling of estrangement which she could not explain.

'Have you spoken to my husband?' she asked, drawing coldly back.

'Spoken to him? No.' Andora stared at her, surprised.

'Then you haven't met him since he went out?'

'No, my love. Is he out? I haven't met him.'

Lizzie sat down with a confused sense of relief, which welled up to her throat and made speech difficult.

Suddenly light seemed to come to Andora. 'I understand, dearest. You don't feel able to see him yourself. You want me to go to him for you.' She looked eagerly about her, scenting the battle. 'You're right, darling. As soon as he comes in, I'll go to him. The sooner we get it over, the better.'

She followed Lizzie, who had turned restlessly back to the window. As they stood there, the gate moved again, and Deering entered.

'There he is now!' Lizzie felt Andora's excited clutch upon her arm. 'Where are the letters? I will go down at once. You allow me to speak for you? You trust my woman's heart? Oh, believe me, darling,' Miss Macy panted, 'I shall know exactly what to say to him!'

'What to say to him?' Lizzie absently repeated.

As her husband advanced up the path she had a sudden vision of their three years together. Those years were her whole life; everything before them had been colorless and unconscious, like the blind life of the plant before it reaches the surface of the soil. The years had not been exactly what she had dreamed; but if they had taken away certain illusions they had left richer realities in their stead. She understood now that she had gradually adjusted herself to the new image of her husband as he was, as he would always be. He was not the hero of her dreams, but he was the man she loved, and who had loved her. For she saw now, in this last wide flash of pity and initiation, that, as a comely marble may be made out of worthless scraps of mortar, glass, and pebbles, so out of mean mixed substances may be fashioned a love that will bear the stress of life.

More urgently, she felt the pressure of Miss Macy's hand.

'I shall hand him the letters without a word. You may rely, love, on my sense of dignity. I know everything you're feeling at this moment!'

Deering had reached the doorstep. Lizzie watched him in silence till he disappeared under the projecting roof of the porch; then she turned and looked almost compassionately at her friend.

'Oh, poor Andora, you don't know anything – you don't know anything at all!' she said.

Autres Temps . . .

MRS. LIDCOTE, as the huge menacing mass of New York defined itself far off across the waters, shrank back into her corner of the deck and sat listening with a kind of unreasoning terror to the steady onward drive of the screws.

She had set out on the voyage quietly enough – in what she called her 'reasonable' mood – but the week at sea had given her too much time to think of things and had left her too long alone with the past.

When she was alone, it was always the past that occupied her. She couldn't get away from it, and she didn't any longer care to. During her long years of exile she had made her terms with it, had learned to accept the fact that it would always be there, huge, obstructing, encumbering, bigger and more dominant than anything the future could ever conjure up. And, at any rate, she was sure of it, she understood it, knew how to reckon with it; she had learned to screen and manage and protect it as one does an afflicted member of one's family.

There had never been any danger of her being allowed to forget the past. It looked out at her from the face of every acquaintance, it appeared suddenly in the eyes of strangers when a word enlightened them: 'Yes, *the* Mrs. Lidcote, don't you know?' It had sprung at her the first day out, when, across the dining room, from the captain's table, she had seen Mrs. Lorin Boulger's revolving eyeglass pause and the eye behind it grow as blank as a dropped blind. The next day, of course, the captain had asked: 'You know your ambassadress, Mrs. Boulger?' and she had replied that, No, she seldom left Florence, and hadn't been to Rome for more than a day since the Boulgers had been sent to Italy. She was so used to these phrases that it cost her no effort to repeat them. And the captain had promptly changed the subject.

No, she didn't, as a rule, mind the past, because she was used to it and understood it. It was a great concrete fact in her path that she had to walk around every time she moved in any direction. But now, in the light of the unhappy event that had summoned her from Italy, – the sudden unanticipated news of her daughter's divorce from Horace Pursh and remarriage with Wilbour Barkley – the past, her own poor miserable past, started up at her with eyes of accusation, became, to her disordered fancy, like the afflicted relative suddenly breaking away from nurses and keepers and publicly parading the horror and misery she had, all the long years, so patiently screened and secluded.

Yes, there it had stood before her through the agitated weeks since the news had come – during her interminable journey from India, where Leila's letter had overtaken her, and the feverish halt in her apartment in Florence, where she had had to stop and gather up her possessions for a fresh start – there it had stood grinning at her with a new balefulness which seemed to say: 'Oh, but you've got to look at me *now*, because I'm not only your own past but Leila's present.'

Certainly it was a master stroke of those arch-ironists of the shears and spindle to duplicate her own story in her daughter's. Mrs. Lidcote had always somewhat grimly fancied that, having so signally failed to be of use to Leila in other ways, she would at least serve her as a warning. She had even abstained from defending herself, from making the best of her case, had stoically refused to plead extenuating circumstances, lest Leila's impulsive sympathy should lead to deductions that might react disastrously on her own life. And now that very thing had happened, and Mrs. Lidcote could hear the whole of New York saying with one voice: 'Yes, Leila's done just what her mother did. With such an example what could you expect?'

Yet if she had been an example, poor woman, she had been an awful one; she had been, she would have supposed, of more use as a deterrent than a hundred blameless mothers as incentives. For how could anyone who had seen anything of her life in the last eighteen years have had the courage to repeat so disastrous an experiment?

Well, logic in such cases didn't count, example didn't count, nothing probably counted but having the same impulses in the blood; and that was the dark inheritance she had bestowed upon her daughter. Leila hadn't consciously copied her; she had simply 'taken after' her, had been a projection of her own long-past rebellion.

Mrs. Lidcote had deplored, when she started, that the 'Utopia' was a slow steamer, and would take eight full days to bring her to her unhappy daughter; but now, as the moment of reunion approached, she would willingly have turned the boat about and fled back to the high seas. It was not only because she felt still so unprepared to face what New York had in store for her, but because she needed more time to dispose of what the 'Utopia' had already given her. The past was bad enough, but the present and future were worse, because they were less comprehensible, and because, as she grew older, surprises and inconsequences troubled her more than the worst certainties.

There was Mrs. Boulger, for instance. In the light, or rather the darkness, of new developments, it might really be that Mrs. Boulger had not meant to cut her, but had simply failed to recognize her.

Mrs. Lidcote had arrived at this hypothesis simply by listening to the conversation of the persons sitting next to her on deck – two lively young women with the latest Paris hats on their heads and the latest New York ideas in them. These ladies, as to whom it would have been impossible for a person with Mrs. Lidcote's old-fashioned categories to determine whether they were married or unmarried, 'nice' or 'horrid,' or any one or other of the definite things which young women, in her youth and her society, were conveniently assumed to be, had revealed a familiarity with the world of New York that, again according to Mrs. Lidcote's traditions, should have implied a recognized place in it. But in the present fluid state of manners what did anything imply except what their hats implied – that no one could tell what was coming next?

They seemed, at any rate, to frequent a group of idle and opulent people who executed the same gestures and revolved on the same pivots as Mrs. Lidcote's daughter and her friends: their Coras, Matties and Mabels seemed at any moment likely to reveal familiar patronymics, and once one of the speakers, summing up a discussion of which Mrs. Lidcote had missed the beginning, had affirmed with headlong confidence: 'Leila? Oh, *Leila's* all right.'

Could it be *her* Leila, the mother had wondered, with a sharp thrill of apprehension? If only they would mention surnames! But their talk leaped elliptically from allusion to allusion, their unfinished sentences dangled over bottomless pits of conjecture, and they gave their bewildered hearer the impression not so much of talking only of their intimates, as of being intimate with everyone alive.

Her old friend Franklin Ide could have told her, perhaps; but here was the last day of the voyage, and she hadn't yet found courage to ask him. Great as had been the joy of discovering his name on the passenger list and seeing his friendly bearded face in the throng against the taffrail at Cherbourg, she had as yet said nothing to him except, when they had met: 'Of course I'm going out to Leila.'

She had said nothing to Franklin Ide because she had always instinctively shrunk from taking him into her confidence. She was sure he felt sorry for her, sorrier perhaps than anyone had ever felt; but he had always paid her the supreme tribute of not showing it. His attitude allowed her to imagine that compassion was not the basis of his feeling for her, and it was part of her joy in his friendship that it was the one relation seemingly unconditioned by her state, the only one in which she could think and feel and behave like any other woman.

Now, however, as the problem of New York loomed nearer, she began to regret that she had not spoken, had not at least questioned him about the hints she had gathered on the way. He did not know the two ladies next to her, he did not even, as it chanced, know Mrs. Lorin Boulger; but he knew New York, and New York was the sphinx whose riddle she must read or perish.

Almost as the thought passed through her mind his stooping shoulders and grizzled head detached themselves against the blaze of light in the west, and he sauntered down the empty deck and dropped into the chair at her side.

'You're expecting the Barkleys to meet you, I suppose?' he asked.

It was the first time she had heard any one pronounce her daughter's new name, and it occurred to her that her friend, who was shy and inarticulate, had been trying to say it all the way over and had at last shot it out at her only because he felt it must be now or never.

'I don't know. I cabled, of course. But I believe she's at – they're at – *his* place somewhere.'

'Oh, Barkley's; yes, near Lenox, isn't it? But she's sure to come to town to meet you.'

He said it so easily and naturally that her own constraint was relieved, and suddenly, before she knew what she meant to do, she had burst out: 'She may dislike the idea of seeing people.'

Ide, whose absent shortsighted gaze had been fixed on the slowly gliding water, turned in his seat to stare at his companion.

'Who? Leila?' he said with an incredulous laugh.

Mrs. Lidcote flushed to her faded hair and grew pale again. 'It took *me* a long time – to get used to it,' she said.

His look grew gently commiserating. 'I think you'll find' – he paused for a word – 'that things are different now – altogether easier.'

'That's what I've been wondering – ever since we started.' She was determined now to speak. She moved nearer, so that their arms touched, and she could drop her voice to a murmur. 'You see, it all came on me in a flash. My going off to India and Siam on that long trip kept me away from letters for weeks at a time; and she didn't want to tell me beforehand – oh, I understand *that*, poor child! You know how good she's always been to me; how she's tried to spare me. And she knew, of course, what a state of horror I'd be in. She knew I'd rush off to her at once and try to stop it. So she never gave me a hint of anything, and she even managed to muzzle Susy Suffern – you know Susy is the one of the family who keeps me informed about things at home. I don't yet see how she prevented Susy's telling me; but she did. And her first letter, the one I got up at Bangkok, simply said the thing was over – the divorce, I mean – and that the very next day she'd – well, I suppose there was no use waiting; and *he* seems to have behaved as well as possible, to have wanted to marry her as much as – '

'Who? Barkley?' he helped her out. 'I should say so! Why what do you suppose – ' He interrupted himself. 'He'll be devoted to her, I assure you.'

'Oh, of course; I'm sure he will. He's written me – really beautifully. But it's a terrible strain on a man's devotion. I'm not sure that Leila realizes – '

Ide sounded again his little reassuring laugh. 'I'm not sure that you realize, *They're* all right.'

It was the very phrase that the young lady in the next seat had applied to the unknown 'Leila,' and its recurrence on Ide's lips flushed Mrs. Lidcote with fresh courage.

'I wish I knew just what you mean. The two young women next to me – the ones with the wonderful hats – have been talking in the same way.'

'What? About Leila?'

'About *a* Leila; I fancied it might be mine. And about society in general. All their friends seem to be divorced; some of them seem to announce their engagements before they get their decree. One of them – *her* name was Mabel – as far as I could make out, her husband found out that she meant to divorce him by noticing that she wore a new engagement ring.'

'Well, you see Leila did everything "regularly," as the French say,' Ide rejoined.

'Yes; but are these people in society? The people my neighbors talk about?'

He shrugged his shoulders. 'It would take an arbitration commission a good many sittings to define the boundaries of society nowadays. But at any rate they're in New York; and I assure you you're *not*; you're farther and farther from it.'

'But I've been back there several times to see Leila.' She hesitated and looked away from him. Then she brought out slowly: 'And I've never noticed – the least change – in – in my own case – '

'Oh,' he sounded deprecatingly, and she trembled with the fear of having gone too far. But the hour was past when such scruples could restrain her. She must know where she was and where Leila was. 'Mrs. Boulger still cuts me,' she brought out with an embarrassed laugh.

'Are you sure? You've probably cut *her;* if not now, at least in the past. And in a cut if you're not first you're nowhere. That's what keeps up so many quarrels.'

The word roused Mrs. Lidcote to a renewed sense of realities. 'But the Purshes,' she said – 'the Purshes are so strong! There are so many of them, and they all back each other up, just as my husband's family did. I know what it means to have a clan against one. They're stronger than any number of separate friends. The Purshes will *never* forgive Leila for leaving Horace. Why, his mother opposed his marrying her because of – of me. She tried to get Leila to promise that she wouldn't see me when they went to Europe on their honeymoon. And now she'll say it was my example.'

Her companion, vaguely stroking his beard, mused a moment upon this; then he asked, with seeming irrelevance, 'What did Leila say when you wrote that you were coming?'

'She said it wasn't the least necessary, but that I'd better come, because it was the only way to convince me that it wasn't.'

'Well, then, that proves she's not afraid of the Purshes.'

She breathed a long sigh of remembrance. 'Oh, just at first, you know – one never is.'

He laid his hand on hers with a gesture of intelligence and pity. 'You'll see, you'll see,' he said.

A shadow lengthened down the deck before them, and a steward stood there, proffering a Marconigram.

'Oh, now I shall know!' she exclaimed.

She tore the message open, and then let it fall on her knees, dropping her hands on it in silence.

Ide's inquiry roused her: 'It's all right?'

'Oh, quite right. Perfectly. She can't come; but she's sending Susy Suffern. She says Susy will explain.' After another silence she added, with a sudden gush of bitterness: 'As if I needed any explanation!'

She felt Ide's hesitating glance upon her. 'She's in the country?'

'Yes. "Prevented last moment. Longing for you, expecting you. Love from both." Don't you *see*, the poor darling, that she couldn't face it?'

'No, I don't.' He waited. 'Do you mean to go to her immediately?'

'It will be too late to catch a train this evening; but I shall take the first tomorrow morning.' She considered a moment. 'Perhaps it's better. I need a talk with Susy first. She's to meet me at the dock, and I'll take her straight back to the hotel with me.'

As she developed this plan, she had the sense that Ide was still thoughtfully, even gravely, considering her. When she ceased, he remained silent a moment; then he said almost ceremoniously: 'If your talk with Miss Suffern doesn't last too late, may I come and see you when it's over? I shall be dining at my club, and I'll call you up at about ten, if I may. I'm off to Chicago on business tomorrow morning, and it would be a satisfaction to know, before I start, that your cousin's been able to reassure you, as I know she will.'

He spoke with a shy deliberateness that, even to Mrs. Lidcote's troubled perceptions, sounded a long-silenced note of feeling. Perhaps the breaking down of the barrier of reticence between them had released unsuspected emotions in both. The tone of his appeal moved her curiously and loosened the tight strain of her fears.

'Oh, yes, come – do come,' she said, rising. The huge threat of New York was imminent now, dwarfing, under long reaches of embattled masonry, the great deck she stood on and all the little specks of life it carried. One of them, drifting nearer, took the shape of her maid, followed by luggage-laden stewards, and signing to her that it was time to go below. As they descended to the main deck, the throng swept her against Mrs. Lorin Boulger's shoulder, and she heard the ambassadress call out to someone, over the vexed sea of hats: 'So sorry! I should have been delighted, but I've promised to spend Sunday with some friends at Lenox.'

• II •

SUSY SUFFERN's explanation did not end till after ten o'clock, and she had just gone when Franklin Ide, who, complying with an old New York tradition, had caused himself to be preceded by a long white box of roses, was shown into Mrs. Lidcote's sitting room.

He came forward with his shy half-humorous smile and, taking her hand, looked at her for a moment without speaking.

'It's all right,' he then pronounced.

Mrs. Lidcote returned his smile. 'It's extraordinary. Everything's changed. Even Susy has changed; and you know the extent to which Susy used to represent the old New York. There's no old New York left, it seems. She talked in the most amazing way. She snaps her fingers at the Purshes. She told me – *me*, that every woman had a right to happiness and that self-expression was the highest duty. She accused me of misunderstanding Leila; she said my point of view was conventional! She was bursting with pride at having been in the secret, and wearing a brooch that Wilbur Barkley'd given her!'

Franklin Ide had seated himself in the armchair she had pushed forward for him under the electric chandelier. He threw back his head and laughed. 'What did I tell you?'

'Yes; but I can't believe that Susy's not mistaken. Poor dear, she has the habit of lost causes; and she may feel that, having stuck to me, she can do no less than stick to Leila.'

'But she didn't – did she – openly defy the world for you? She didn't snap her fingers at the Lidcotes?'

Mrs. Lidcote shook her head, still smiling. 'No. It was enough to defy *my* family. It was doubtful at one time if they would tolerate her seeing me, and she almost had to disinfect herself after each visit. I believe that at first my sister-in-law wouldn't let the girls come down when Susy dined with her.'

'Well, isn't your cousin's present attitude the best possible proof that times have changed?'

'Yes, yes; I know.' She leaned forward from her sofa-corner, fixing her eyes on his thin kindly face, which gleamed on her indistinctly through her tears. 'If it's true, it's – it's dazzling. She says Leila's perfectly happy. It's as if an angel had gone about lifting gravestones, and the buried people walked again, and the living didn't shrink from them.'

'That's about it,' he assented.

She drew a deep breath, and sat looking away from him down the long perspective of lamp-fringed streets over which her windows hung.

'I can understand how happy you must be,' he began at length.

She turned to him impetuously. 'Yes, yes; I'm happy. But I'm lonely, too – lonelier than ever. I didn't take up much room in the world before; but now – where is there a corner for me? Oh, since I've begun to confess myself, why shouldn't I go on? Telling you this lifts a gravestone from *me!* You see, before this, Leila needed me. She was unhappy, and I knew it, and though we hardly ever talked of it I felt that, in a way, the thought that I'd been through the same thing, and down to the dregs of it, helped her. And her needing me helped *me.* And when the news of her marriage came my first thought was that now she'd need me more than ever, that she'd have no one but me to turn to. Yes, under all my distress there was a fierce joy in that. It was so new and wonderful to feel again that there was one person who wouldn't be able to get on without me! And now what you and Susy tell me seems to have taken my child from me; and just at first that's all I can feel.'

'Of course it's all you feel.' He looked at her musingly. 'Why didn't Leila come to meet you?'

'That was really my fault. You see, I'd cabled that I was not sure of being able to get off on the 'Utopia,' and apparently my second cable was delayed, and when she received it she'd already asked some people over Sunday – one or two of her old friends, Susy says. I'm so glad they should have wanted to go to her at once; but naturally I'd rather have been alone with her.'

'You still mean to go, then?'

'Oh, I must. Susy wanted to drag me off to Ridgefield with her over Sunday, and Leila sent me word that of course I might go if I wanted to, and that I was not to think of her; but I know how disappointed she would be. Susy said she was afraid I might be upset at her having people to stay, and that, if I minded, she wouldn't urge me to come. But if *they* don't mind, why should I? And of course, if they're willing to go to Leila it must mean – '

'Of course. I'm glad you recognize that,' Franklin Ide exclaimed abruptly. He stood up and went over to her, taking her head with one of his quick gestures. 'There's something I want to say to you,' he began – .

The next morning, in the train, through all the other contending thoughts in Mrs. Lidcote's mind there ran the warm undercurrent of what Franklin Ide had wanted to say to her.

He had wanted, she knew, to say it once before, when, nearly eight years earlier, the hazard of meeting at the end of a rainy autumn in a deserted Swiss hotel had thrown them for a fortnight into unwonted propinquity. They had walked and talked together, borrowed each other's books and newspapers, spent the long chill evenings over the fire in the dim lamplight of her little pitch-pine sitting room; and she had been wonderfully comforted by his presence, and hard frozen places in her had melted, and she had known that she would be desperately sorry when he went. And then, just at the end, in his odd indirect way, he had let her see that it rested with her to have him stay. She could still relive the sleepless night she had given to that discovery. It was preposterous, of course, to think of repaying his devotion by accepting such a sacrifice; but how find reasons to convince him? She could not bear to let him think her less touched, less inclined to him than she was: the generosity of his love deserved that she should repay it with the truth. Yet how let him see what she felt, and yet refuse what he offered? How confess to him what had been on her lips when he made the offer: 'I've seen what it did to one man; and there must never, never be another'? The tacit ignoring of her past had been the element in which their friendship lived, and she could not suddenly, to him of all men, begin to talk of herself like a guilty woman in a play. Somehow, in the end, she had managed it, had averted a direct explanation, had made him understand that her life was over, that she existed only for her daughter, and that a more definite word from him would have been almost a breach of delicacy. She was so used to behaving as if her life were over! And, at any rate, he had taken her hint, and she had been able to spare her sensitiveness and his. The next year, when he came to Florence to see her, they met again in the old friendly way; and that till now had continued to be the tenor of their intimacy.

And now, suddenly and unexpectedly, he had brought up the question again, directly this time, and in such a form that she could not evade it: putting the renewal of his plea, after so long an interval, on the ground that, on her own showing, her chief argument against it no longer existed.

'You tell me Leila's happy. If she's happy, she doesn't need you—need you, that is, in the same way as before. You wanted, I know, to be always in reach, always free and available if she should suddenly call you to her or take refuge with you. I understood that – I respected it. I didn't urge my case because I saw it was useless. You couldn't, I understand well enough, have felt free to take such happiness as life with me might give you while she was unhappy, and, as you imagined, with no hope of release. Even then I didn't feel as you did about it; I understood better the trend of things here. But ten years ago the change hadn't really come; and I had no way of convincing you that it was coming. Still, I always fancied that Leila might not think her case was closed, and so I chose to think that ours wasn't either. Let me go on thinking so, at any rate, till you've seen her, and confirmed with your own eyes what Susy Suffern tells you.'

• III •

ALL through what Susy Suffern told and retold her during their four
hours' flight to the hills this plea of Ide's kept coming back to Mrs.
Lidcote. She did not yet know what she felt as to its bearing on her
own fate, but it was something on which her confused thoughts could
stay themselves amid the welter of new impressions, and she was
inexpressibly glad that he had said what he had, and said it at that
particular moment. It helped her to hold fast to her identity in the rush
of strange names and new categories that her cousin's talk poured out
on her.

With the progress of the journey Miss Suffern's communications
grew more and more amazing. She was like a cicerone preparing the
mind of an inexperienced traveler for the marvels about to burst on it.

'You won't know Leila. She's had her pearls reset. Sargent's to paint
her. Oh, and I was to tell you that she hopes you won't mind being
the least bit squeezed over Sunday. The house was built by Wilbour's
father, you know, and it's rather old-fashioned – only ten spare
bedrooms. Of course that's small for what they mean to do, and she'll
show you the new plans they've had made. Their idea is to keep the
present house as a wing. She told me to explain – she's so dreadfully
sorry not to be able to give you a sitting room just at first. They're
thinking of Egypt for next winter, unless, of course, Wilbour gets his
appointment. Oh, didn't she write you about that? Why, he wants
Rome, you know – the second secretaryship. Or, rather, he wanted
England; but Leila insisted that if they went abroad she must be near
you. And of course, what she says is law. Oh, they quite hope they'll
get it. You see Horace's uncle is in the Cabinet – one of the assistant
secretaries – and I believe he has a good deal of pull – '

'Horace's uncle? You mean Wilbour's, I suppose,' Mrs. Lidcote
interjected, with a gasp of which a fraction was given to Miss Suffern's
flippant use of the language.

'Wilbour's? No, I don't. I mean Horace's. There's no bad feeling
between them, I assure you. Since Horace's engagement was announced
– you didn't know Horace was engaged? Why, he's marrying one of
Bishop Thorbury's girls: the red-haired one who wrote the novel that
everyone's talking about. *This Flesh of Mine*. They're to be married in
the cathedral. Of course Horace *can*, because it was Leila who – but,
as I say, there's not the *least* feeling, and Horace wrote himself to his
uncle about Wilbour.'

Mrs. Lidcote's thoughts fled back to what she had said to Ide the
day before on the deck of the 'Utopia.' 'I didn't take up much room
before, but now where is there a corner for me?' Where indeed in this
crowded, topsy-turvy world, with its headlong changes and helter-
skelter readjustments, its new tolerances and indifferences and accom-

modations, was there room for a character fashioned by slower sterner processes and a life broken under their inexorable pressure? And then, in a flash, she viewed the chaos from a new angle, and order seemed to move upon the void. If the old processes were changed, her case was changed with them; she, too, was a part of the general readjustment, a tiny fragment of the new pattern worked out in bolder freer harmonies. Since her daughter had no penalty to pay, was not she herself released by the same stroke? The rich arrears of youth and joy were gone; but was there not time enough left to accumulate new stores of happiness? That, of course, was what Franklin Ide had felt and had meant her to feel. He had seen at once what the change in her daughter's situation would make in her view of her own. It was almost – wondrously enough! – as if Leila's folly had been the means of vindicating hers.

Everything else for the moment faded for Mrs. Lidcote in the glow of her daughter's embrace. It was unnatural, it was almost terrifying, to find herself standing on a strange threshold, under an unknown roof, in a big hall of pictures, flowers, firelight, and hurrying servants, and in this spacious unfamiliar confusion to discover Leila, bareheaded, laughing, authoritative, with a strange young man jovially echoing her welcome and transmitting her orders; but once Mrs. Lidcote had her child on her breast, and her child's 'It's all right, you old darling!' in her ears, every other feeling was lost in the deep sense of well-being that only Leila's hug could give.

The sense was still with her, warming her veins and pleasantly fluttering her heart, as she went up to her room after luncheon. A little constrained by the presence of visitors, and not altogether sorry to defer for a few hours the 'long talk' with her daughter for which she somehow felt herself tremulously unready, she had withdrawn, on the plea of fatigue, to the bright luxurious bedroom into which Leila had again and again apologized for having been obliged to squeeze her. The room was bigger and finer than any in her small apartment in Florence; but it was not the standard of affluence implied in her daughter's tone about it that chiefly struck her, nor yet the finish and complexity of its appointments. It was the look it shared with the rest of the house, and with the perspective of the gardens beneath its windows, of being part of an 'establishment' – of something solid, avowed, founded on sacraments and precedents and principles. There was nothing about the place, or about Leila and Wilbour, that suggested either passion or peril: their relation seemed as comfortable as their furniture and as respectable as their balance at the bank.

This was, in the whole confusing experience, the thing that confused Mrs. Lidcote most, that gave her at once the deepest feeling of security for Leila and the strongest sense of apprehension for herself. Yes, there was something oppressive in the completeness and compactness of

Leila's well-being. Ide had been right: her daughter did not need her. Leila, with her first embrace, had unconsciously attested the fact in the same phrase as Ide himself and as the two young women with the hats. 'It's all right, you old darling!' she had said: and her mother sat alone, trying to fit herself into the new scheme of things which such a certainty betokened.

Her first distinct feeling was one of irrational resentment. If such a change was to come, why had it not come sooner? Here was she, a woman not yet old, who had paid with the best years of her life for the theft of the happiness that her daughter's contemporaries were taking as their due. There was no sense, no sequence, in it. She had had what she wanted, but she had to pay too much for it. She had had to pay the last bitterest price of learning that love has a price: that it is worth so much and no more. She had known the anguish of watching the man she loved discover this first, and of reading the discovery in his eyes. It was a part of her history that she had not trusted herself to think of for a long time past: she always took a big turn about that haunted corner. But now, at the sight of the young man downstairs, so openly and jovially Leila's, she was overwhelmed at the senseless waste of her own adventure, and wrung with the irony of perceiving that the success or failure of the deepest human experiences may hang on a matter of chronology.

Then gradually the thought of Ide returned to her. 'I chose to think that our case wasn't closed,' he had said. She had been deeply touched by that. To everyone else her case had been closed so long! *Finis* was scrawled all over her. But here was one man who had believed and waited, and what if what he believed in and waited for were coming true? If Leila's 'all right' should really foreshadow hers?

As yet, of course, it was impossible to tell. She had fancied, indeed, when she entered the drawing room before luncheon, that a too-sudden hush had fallen on the assembled group of Leila's friends, on the slender vociferous young women and the lounging golf-stockinged young men. They had all received her politely, with the kind of petrified politeness that may be either a tribute to age or a protest at laxity; but to them, of course, she must be an old woman because she was Leila's mother, and in a society so dominated by youth the mere presence of maturity was a constraint.

One of the young girls, however, had presently emerged from the group, and, attaching herself to Mrs. Lidcote, had listened to her with a blue gaze of admiration which gave the older woman a sudden happy consciousness of her long-forgotten social graces. It was agreeable to find herself attracting this young Charlotte Wynn, whose mother had been among her closest friends, and in whom something of the soberness and softness of the earlier manners had survived. But the little colloquy, broken up by the announcement of luncheon, could of course result in nothing more definite than this reminiscent emotion.

No, she could not yet tell how her own case was to be fitted into the new order of things; but there were more people – 'older people' Leila had put it – arriving by the afternoon train, and that evening at dinner she would doubtless be able to judge. She began to wonder nervously who the newcomers might be. Probably she would be spared the embarrassment of finding old acquaintances among them; but it was odd that her daughter had mentioned no names.

Leila had proposed that, later in the afternoon, Wilbour should take her mother for a drive: she said she wanted them to have a 'nice, quiet talk.' But Mrs. Lidcote wished her talk with Leila to come first, and had, moreover, at luncheon, caught stray allusions to an impending tennis match in which her son-in-law was engaged. Her fatigue had been a sufficient pretext for declining the drive, and she had begged Leila to think of her as peacefully resting in her room till such time as they could snatch their quiet moment.

'Before tea, then, you duck!' Leila with a last kiss had decided; and presently Mrs. Lidcote, through her open window, had heard the fresh loud voices of her daughter's visitors chiming across the gardens from the tennis court.

• IV •

LEILA had come and gone, and they had had their talk. It had not lasted as long as Mrs. Lidcote wished, for in the middle of it Leila had been summoned to the telephone to receive an important message from town, and had sent word to her mother that she couldn't come back just then, as one of the young ladies had been called away unexpectedly and arrangements had to be made for her departure. But the mother and daughter had had almost an hour together, and Mrs. Lidcote was happy. She had never seen Leila so tender, so solicitous. The only thing that troubled her was the very excess of this solicitude, the exaggerated expression of her daughter's annoyance that their first moments together should have been marred by the presence of strangers.

'Not strangers to me, darling, since they're friends of yours,' her mother had assured her.

'Yes; but I know your feeling, you queer wild mother. I know how you've always hated people.' (*Hated people!* Had Leila forgotten why?) 'And that's why I told Susy that if you preferred to go with her to Ridgefield on Sunday I should perfectly understand, and patiently wait for our good hug. But you didn't really mind them at luncheon, did you, dearest?'

Mrs. Lidcote, at that, had suddenly thrown a startled look at her daughter. 'I don't mind things of that kind any longer,' she had simply answered.

'But that doesn't console me for having exposed you to the bother of it, for having let you come here when I ought to have *ordered* you off to Ridgefield with Susy. If Susy hadn't been stupid she'd have made you go there with her. I hate to think of you up here all alone.'

Again Mrs. Lidcote tried to read something more than a rather obtuse devotion in her daughter's radiant gaze. 'I'm glad to have had a rest this afternoon, dear; and later – '

'Oh, yes, later, when all this fuss is over, we'll more than make up for it, shan't we, you precious darling?' And at this point Leila had been summoned to the telephone, leaving Mrs. Lidcote to her conjectures.

These were still floating before her in cloudy uncertainty when Miss Suffern tapped at the door.

'You've come to take me down to tea? I'd forgotten how late it was', Mrs. Lidcote exclaimed.

Miss Suffern, a plump peering little woman, with prim hair and a conciliatory smile, nervously adjusted the pendent bugles of her elaborate black dress. Miss Suffern was always in mourning, and always commemorating the demise of distant relatives by wearing the discarded wardrobe of their next of kin. 'It isn't *exactly* mourning,' she would say; 'but it's the only stitch of black poor Julia had – and of course George was only my mother's step-cousin.'

As she came forward Mrs. Lidcote found herself humorously wondering whether she were mourning Horace Pursh's divorce in one of his mother's old black satins.

'Oh, *did* you mean to go down for tea?' Susy Suffern peered at her, a little fluttered. 'Leila sent me up to keep you company. She thought it would be cozier for you to stay here. She was afraid you were feeling rather tired.'

'I was; but I've had the whole afternoon to rest in. And this wonderful sofa to help me.'

'Leila told me to tell you that she'd rush up for a minute before dinner, after everybody had arrived; but the train is always dreadfully late. She's in despair at not giving you a sitting room; she wanted to know if I thought you really minded.'

'Of course I don't mind. It's not like Leila to think I should.' Mrs. Lidcote drew aside to make way for the housemaid, who appeared in the doorway bearing a table spread with a bewildering variety of tea cakes.

'Leila saw to it herself,' Miss Suffern murmured as the door closed. 'Her one idea is that you should feel happy here.'

It struck Mrs. Lidcote as one more mark of the subverted state of things that her daughter's solicitude should find expression in the multiplicity of sandwiches and the piping hotness of muffins; but then everything that had happened since her arrival seemed to increase her confusion.

The note of a motor horn down the drive gave another turn to her thoughts. 'Are those the new arrivals already?' she asked.

'Oh, dear, no; they won't be here till after seven.' Miss Suffern craned her head from the window to catch a glimpse of the motor. 'It must be Charlotte leaving.'

'Was it the little Wynn girl who was called away in a hurry? I hope it's not on account of illness.'

'Oh, no; I believe there was some mistake about dates. Her mother telephoned her that she was expected at the Stepleys, at Fishkill, and she had to be rushed over to Albany to catch a train.'

Mrs. Lidcote meditated. 'I'm sorry. She's a charming young thing. I hoped I should have another talk with her this evening after dinner.'

'Yes; it's too bad.' Miss Sufern's gaze grew vague. 'You *do* look tired, you know,' she continued, seating herself at the tea table and preparing to dispense its delicacies. 'You must go straight back to your sofa and let me wait on you. The excitement has told on you more than you think, and you mustn't fight against it any longer. Just stay quietly up here and let yourself go. You'll have Leila to yourself on Monday.'

Mrs. Lidcote received the teacup which her cousin proffered, but showed no other disposition to obey her injunctions. For a moment she stirred her tea in silence; then she asked: 'Is it your idea that I should stay quietly up here till Monday?'

Miss Suffern set down her cup with a gesture so sudden that it endangered an adjacent plate of scones. When she had assured herself of the safety of the scones she looked up with a fluttered laugh. 'Perhaps, dear, by tomorrow you'll be feeling differently. The air here, you know – '

'Yes, I know.' Mrs. Lidcote bent forward to help herself to a scone. 'Who's arriving this evening?' she asked.

Miss Suffern frowned and peered. 'You know my wretched head for names. Leila told me – but there are so many – '

'So many? She didn't tell me she expected a big party.'

'Oh, not big: but rather outside of her little group. And of course, as it's the first time, she's a little excited at having the older set.'

'The older set? Our contemporaries, you mean?'

'Why – yes.' Miss Suffern paused as if to gather herself up for a leap. 'The Ashton Gileses,' she brought out.

'The Aston Gileses? Really? I shall be glad to see Mary Giles again. It must be eighteen years,' said Mrs. Lidcote steadily.

'Yes,' Miss Suffern gasped, precipitately refilling her cup.

'The Ashton Gileses; and who else?'

'Well, the Sam Fresbies. But the most important person, of course, is Mrs. Lorin Boulger.'

'Mrs. Boulger? Leila didn't tell me she was coming.'

'Didn't she? I suppose she forgot everything when she saw you. But the party was got up for Mrs. Boulger. You see, it's very important that she should – well, take a fancy to Leila and Wilbour; his being appointed to Rome virtually depends on it. And you know Leila insists on Rome in order to be near you. So she asked Mary Giles, who's intimate with the Boulgers, if the visit couldn't possibly be arranged; and Mary's cable caught Mrs. Boulger at Cherbourg. She's to be only a fortnight in America; and getting her to come directly here was rather a triumph.'

'Yes; I see it was,' said Mrs. Lidcote.

'You know, she's rather – rather fussy; and Mary was a little doubtful if – '

'If she would, on account of Leila?' Mrs. Lidcote murmured.

'Well, yes. In her official position. But luckily she's a friend of the Barkleys. And finding the Gileses and Fresbies here will make it all right. The times have changed!' Susy Suffern indulgently summed up.

Mrs. Lidcote smiled. 'Yes; a few years ago it would have seemed improbable that I should ever again be dining with Mary Giles and Harriet Fresbie and Mrs. Lorin Boulger.'

Miss Suffern did not at the moment seem disposed to enlarge upon this theme; and after an interval of silence Mrs. Lidcote suddenly resumed: 'Do they know I'm here, by the way?'

The effect of her question was to produce in Miss Suffern an exaggerated access of peering and frowning. She twitched the tea things about, fingered her bugles, and, looking at the clock, exclaimed amazedly: 'Mercy! Is it seven already?'

'Not that it can make any difference, I suppose,' Mrs. Lidcote continued. 'But did Leila tell them I was coming?'

Miss Suffern looked at her with pain. 'Why, you don't suppose, dearest, that Leila would do anything – '

Mrs. Lidcote went on: 'For, of course, it's of the first importance, as you say, that Mrs. Lorin Boulger should be favorably impressed, in order that Wilbour may have the best possible chance of getting Rome.'

'I *told* Leila you'd feel that, dear. You see, it's actually on *your* account – so that they may get a post near you – that Leila invited Mrs. Boulger.'

'Yes, I see that.' Mrs. Lidcote, abruptly rising from her seat, turned her eyes to the clock. 'But, as you say, it's getting late. Oughtn't we to dress for dinner?'

Miss Suffern, at the suggestion, stood up also, an agitated hand among her bugles. 'I do wish I could persuade you to stay up here this evening. I'm sure Leila'd be happier if you would. Really, you're much too tired to come down.'

'What nonsense, Susy!' Mrs. Lidcote spoke with a sudden sharpness, her hand stretched to the bell. 'When do we dine? At half-past eight? Then I must really send you packing. At my age it takes time to dress.'

Miss Suffern, thus projected toward the threshold, lingered there to repeat: 'Leila'll never forgive herself if you make an effort you're not up to.' But Mrs. Lidcote smiled on her without answering, and the icy light-wave propelled her through the door.

• V •

MRS. LIDCOTE, though she had made the gesture of ringing for her maid, had not done so.

When the door closed, she continued to stand motionless in the middle of her soft spacious room. The fire which had been kindled at twilight danced on the brightness of silver and mirrors and sober gilding; and the sofa toward which she had been urged by Miss Suffern heaped up its cushions in inviting proximity to a table laden with new books and papers. She could not recall having ever been more luxuriously housed, or having ever had so strange a sense of being out alone, under the night, in a wind-beaten plain. She sat down by the fire and thought.

A knock on the door made her lift her head, and she saw her daughter on the threshold. The intricate ordering of Leila's fair hair and the flying folds of her dressing gown showed that she had interrupted her dressing to hasten to her mother; but once in the room she paused a moment, smiling uncertainly, as though she had forgotten the object of her haste.

Mrs. Lidcote rose to her feet. 'Time to dress, dearest? Don't scold! I shan't be late.

'To dress?' Leila stood before her with a puzzled look. 'Why, I thought, dear – I mean, I hoped you'd decided just to stay here quietly and rest.'

Her mother smiled. 'But I've been resting all the afternoon!'

'Yes, but – you know you *do* look tired. And when Susy told me just now that you meant to make the effort – '

'You came to stop me?'

'I came to tell you that you needn't feel in the least obliged – '

'Of course. I understand that.'

There was a pause during which Leila, vaguely averting herself from her mother's scrutiny, drifted toward the dressing table and began to disturb the symmetry of the brushes and bottles laid out on it. 'Do your visitors know that I'm here?' Mrs. Lidcote suddenly went on.

'Do they – of course – why, naturally,' Leila rejoined, absorbed in trying to turn the stopper of a salts bottle.

'Then won't they think it odd if I don't appear?'

'Oh, not in the least, dearest. I assure you they'll *all* understand.' Leila laid down the bottle and turned back to her mother, her face alight with reassurance.

Mrs. Lidcote stood motionless, her head erect, her smiling eyes on her daughter's. 'Will they think it odd if I *do?*'

Leila stopped short, her lips half parted to reply. As she paused, the color stole over her bare neck, swept up to her throat, and burst into flame in her cheeks. Thence it sent its devastating crimson up to her very temples, to the lobes of her ears, to the edges of her eyelids, beating all over her in fiery waves, as if fanned by some imperceptible wind.

Mrs. Lidcote silently watched the conflagration; then she turned away her eyes with a slight laugh. 'I only meant that I was afraid it might upset the arrangement of your dinner table if I didn't come down. If you can assure me that it won't, I believe I'll take you at your word and go back to this irresistible sofa.' She paused, as if waiting for her daughter to speak; then she held out her arms. 'Run off and dress, dearest; and don't have me on your mind.' She clasped Leila close, pressing a long kiss on the last afterglow of her subsiding blush. 'I do feel the least bit overdone, and if it won't inconvenience you to have me drop out of things, I believe I'll basely take to my bed and stay there till your party scatters. And now run off, or you'll be late; and make my excuses to them all.'

• VI •

THE Barkleys' visitors had dispersed, and Mrs. Lidcote, completely restored by her two days' rest, found herself, on the following Monday, alone with her children and Miss Suffern.

There was a note of jubilation in the air, for the party had 'gone off' so extraordinarily well, and so completely, at it appeared, to the satisfaction of Mrs. Lorin Boulger, that Wilbour's early appointment to Rome was almost to be counted on. So certain did this seem that the prospect of a prompt reunion mitigated the distress with which Leila learned of her mother's decision to return almost immediately to Italy. No one understood this decision; it seemed to Leila absolutely unintelligible that Mrs. Lidcote should not stay on with them till their own fate was fixed, and Wilbour echoed her astonishment.

'Why shouldn't you, as Leila says, wait here till we can all pack up and go together?'

Mrs. Lidcote smiled her gratitude with her refusal. 'After all, it's not yet sure that you'll be packing up.'

'Oh, you ought to have seen Wilbour with Mrs. Boulger,' Leila triumphed.

'No, you ought to have seen Leila with her,' Leila's husband exulted.

Miss Suffern enthusiastically appended: 'I *do* think inviting Harriet Fresbie was a stroke of genius!'

'Oh, we'll be with you soon,' Leila laughed. 'So soon that it's really foolish to separate.'

But Mrs. Lidcote held out with the quiet firmness which her daughter knew it was useless to oppose. After her long months in India, it was really imperative, she declared, that she should get back to Florence and see what was happening to her little place there; and she had been so comfortable on the 'Utopia' that she had a fancy to return by the same ship. There was nothing for it, therefore, but to acquiesce in her decision and keep her with them till the afternoon before the day of the 'Utopia's' sailing. This arrangement fitted in with certain projects which, during her two days' seclusion, Mrs. Lidcote had silently matured. It had become to her of the first importance to get away as soon as she could, and the little place in Florence, which held her past in every fold of its curtains and between every page of its books, seemed now to her the one spot where that past would be endurable to look upon.

She was not unhappy during the intervening days. The sight of Leila's well-being, the sense of Leila's tenderness, were, after all, what she had come for; and of these she had had full measure. Leila had never been happier or more tender; and the contemplation of her bliss, and the enjoyment of her affection, were an absorbing occupation for her mother. But they were also a sharp strain on certain overtightened chords, and Mrs. Lidcote, when at last she found herself alone in the New York hotel to which she had returned the night before embarking, had the feeling that she had just escaped with her life from the clutch of a giant hand.

She had refused to let her daughter come to town with her; she had even rejected Susy Suffern's company. She wanted no viaticum but that of her own thoughts; and she let these come to her without shrinking from them as she sat in the same high-hung sitting room in which, just a week before, she and Franklin Ide had had their memorable talk.

She had promised her friend to let him hear from her, but she had not kept her promise. She knew that he had probably come back from Chicago, and that if he learned of her sudden decision to return to Italy it would be impossible for her not to see him before sailing; and as she wished above all things not to see him she had kept silent, intending to send him a letter from the steamer.

There was no reason why she should wait till then to write it. The actual moment was more favorable, and the task, though not agreeable, would at least bridge over an hour of her lonely evening. She went up to the writing table, drew out a sheet of paper and began to write his name. And as she did so, the door opened and he came in.

The words she met him with were the last she could have imagined herself saying when they had parted. 'How in the world did you know that I was here?'

He caught her meaning in a flash. 'You didn't want me to, then?' He stood looking at her. 'I suppose I ought to have taken your silence as meaning that. But I happened to meet Mrs. Wynn, who is stopping here, and she asked me to dine with her and Charlotte, and Charlotte's young man. They told me they'd seen you arriving this afternoon, and I couldn't help coming up.'

There was a pause between them, which Mrs. Lidcote at last surprisingly broke with the exclamation: 'Ah, she *did* recognize me, then!'

'Recognize you?' he stared. 'Why – '

'Oh, I saw she did, though she never moved an eyelid. I saw it by Charlotte's blush. The child has the prettiest blush. I saw that her mother wouldn't let her speak to me.'

Ide put down his hat with an impatient laugh. 'Hasn't Leila cured you of your delusions?'

She looked at him intently. 'Then you don't think Margaret Wynn meant to cut me?'

'I think your ideas are absurd.'

She paused for a perceptible moment without taking this up; then she said, at a tangent: 'I'm sailing tomorrow early. I meant to write to you – there's the letter I'd begun.'

Ide followed her gesture, and then turned his eyes back to her face. 'You didn't mean to see me, then, or even to let me know that you were going till you'd left?'

'I felt it would be easier to explain to you in a letter – '

'What in God's name is there to explain?' She made no reply, and he pressed on: 'It can't be that you're worried about Leila, for Charlotte Wynn told me she'd been there last week, and there was a big party arriving when she left: Fresbies and Gileses, and Mrs. Lorin Boulger – all the board of examiners! If Leila has passed *that*, she's got her degree.'

Mrs. Lidcote had dropped down into a corner of the sofa where she had sat during their talk of the week before. 'I was stupid,' she began abruptly. 'I ought to have gone to Ridgefield with Susy. I didn't see till afterward that I was expected to.'

'You were expected to?'

'Yes. Oh, it wasn't Leila's fault. She suffered – poor darling; she was distracted. But she'd asked her party before she knew I was arriving.'

'Oh, as to that – ' Ide drew a deep breath of relief. 'I can understand that it must have been a disappointment not to have you to herself just at first. But, after all, you were among old friends or their children: the Gileses and Fresbies – and little Charlotte Wynn.' He paused a moment before the last name, and scrutinized her hesitatingly. 'Even if they came at the wrong time, you must have been glad to see them all at Leila's.'

She gave him back his look with a faint smile. 'I didn't see them.'

'You didn't see them?'

'No. That is, excepting little Charlotte Wynn. That child is exquisite. We had a talk before luncheon the day I arrived. But when her mother found out that I was staying in the house she telephoned her to leave immediately, and so I didn't see her again.'

The color rushed to Ide's sallow face. 'I don't know where you get such ideas!'

She pursued, as if she had not heard him: 'Oh, and I saw Mary Giles for a minute too. Susy Suffern brought her up to my room the last evening, after dinner, when all the others were at bridge. She meant it kindly – but it wasn't much use.'

'But what were you doing in your room in the evening after dinner?'

'Why, you see, when I found out my mistake in coming, – how embarrassing it was for Leila, I mean – I simply told her I was very tired, and preferred to stay upstairs till the party was over.'

Ide, with a groan, struck his hand against the arm of his chair. 'I wonder how much of all this you simply imagined!'

'I didn't imagine the fact of Harriet Fresbie's not even asking if she might see me when she knew I was in the house. Nor of Mary Giles's getting Susy, at the eleventh hour, to smuggle her up to my room when the others wouldn't know where she'd gone; nor poor Leila's ghastly fear lest Mrs. Lorin Boulger, for whom the party was given, should guess I was in the house, and prevent her husband's giving Wilbour the second secretaryship because she'd been obliged to spend a night under the same roof with his mother-in-law!'

Ide continued to drum on his chair arm with exasperated fingers. 'You don't *know* that any of the acts you describe are due to the causes you suppose.'

Mrs. Lidcote paused before replying, as if honestly trying to measure the weight of this argument. Then she said in a low tone: 'I know that Leila was in an agony lest I should come down to dinner the first night. And it was for me she was afraid, not for herself. Leila is never afraid for herself.'

'But the conclusions you draw are simply preposterous. There are narrow-minded women everywhere, but the women who were at Leila's knew perfectly well that their going there would give her a sort of social sanction, and if they were willing that she should have it, why on earth should they want to withhold it from you?'

'That's what I told myself a week ago, in this very room, after my first talk with Susy Suffern.' She lifted a misty smile to his anxious eyes. 'That's why I listened to what you said to me the same evening, and why your arguments half-convinced me, and made me think that what had been possible for Leila might not be impossible for me. If the new dispensation had come, why not for me as well as for the others? I can't tell you the flight my imagination took!'

Franklin Ide rose from his seat and crossed the room to a chair near her sofa corner. 'All I cared about was that it seemed – for the moment – to be carrying you toward me,' he said.

'I cared about that, too. That's why I meant to go away without seeing you.' They gave each other grave look for look. 'Because, you see, I was mistaken,' she went on. 'We were both mistaken. You say it's preposterous that the women who didn't object to accepting Leila's hospitality should have objected to meeting me under her roof. And so it is; but I begin to understand why. It's simply that society is much too busy to revise its own judgments. Probably no one in the house with me stopped to consider that my case and Leila's were identical. They only remembered that I'd done something which, at the time I did it, was condemned by society. My case had been passed on and classified: I'm the woman who has been cut for nearly twenty years. The older people have half-forgotten why, and the younger ones have never really known: it's simply become a tradition to cut me. And traditions that have lost their meaning are the hardest of all to destroy.'

Ide sat motionless while she spoke. As she ended, he stood up with a short laugh and walked across the room to the window. Outside, the immense black prospect of New York, strung with its myriad lines of light, stretched away into the smoky edges of the night. He showed it to her with a gesture.

'What do you suppose such words as you've been using – "society," "tradition," and the rest – mean to all the life out there?'

She came and stood by him in the window. 'Less than nothing, of course. But you and I are not out there. We're shut up in a little tight round of habit and association, just as we're shut up in this room. Remember, I thought I'd got out of it once; but what really happened was that the other people went out, and left me in the same little room. The only difference was that I was there alone. Oh, I've made it habitable now, I'm used to it; but I've lost any illusions I may have had as to an angel's opening the door.'

Ide again laughed impatiently. 'Well, if the door won't open, why not let another prisoner in? At least it would be less of a solitude – '

She turned from the dark window back into the vividly lighted room.

'It would be more of a prison. You forget that I know all about that. We're all imprisoned, of course – all of us middling people, who don't carry our freedom in our brains. But we've accommodated ourselves to our different cells, and if we're moved suddenly into the new ones we're likely to find a stone wall where we thought there was thin air, and to knock ourselves senseless against it. I saw a man do that once.'

Ide, leaning with folded arms against the window frame, watched her in silence as she moved restlessly about the room, gathering together some scattered books and tossing a handful of torn letters into the paper basket. When she ceased, he rejoined: 'All you say is based on preconceived theories. Why didn't you put them to the test by coming down to meet your old friends? Don't you see the inference they would naturally draw from your hiding yourself when they arrived? It looked as though you were afraid of them – or as though you hadn't forgiven them. Either way, you put them in the wrong instead of waiting to let them put you in the right. If Leila had buried herself in a desert do you suppose society would have gone to fetch her out? You say you were afraid for Leila and that she was afraid for you. Don't you see what all these complications of feeling mean? Simply that you were too nervous at the moment to let things happen naturally, just as you're too nervous now to judge them rationally.' He paused and turned her eyes to her face. 'Don't try to just yet. Give yourself a little more time. Give *me* a little more time. I've always known it would take time.'

He moved nearer, and she let him have her hand. With the grave kindness of his face so close above her she felt like a child roused out of frightened dreams and finding a light in the room.

'Perhaps you're right – ' she heard herself begin; then something within her clutched her back, and her hand fell away from him.

'I know I'm right: trust me,' he urged. 'We'll talk of this in Florence soon.'

She stood before him, feeling with despair his kindness, his patience and his unreality. Everything he said seemed like a painted gauze let down between herself and the real facts of life; and a sudden desire seized her to tear the gauze into shreds.

She drew back and looked at him with a smile of superficial reassurance. 'You *are* right – about not talking any longer now. I'm nervous and tired, and it would do no good. I brood over things too much. As you say, I must try not to shrink from people'. She turned away and glanced at the clock. 'Why, it's only ten! If I send you off I shall begin to brood again; and if you stay we shall go on talking about the same thing. Why shouldn't we go down and see Margaret Wynn for half an hour?'

She spoke lightly and rapidly, her brilliant eyes on his face. As she watched him, she saw it change, as if her smile had thrown a too vivid light upon it.

'Oh, no – not tonight!' he exclaimed.

'Not tonight? Why, what other night have I, when I'm off at dawn?

Besides, I want to show you at once that I mean to be more sensible –
that I'm not going to be afraid of people any more. And I should really
like another glimpse of little Charlotte.' He stood before her, his hand
in his beard, with the gesture he had in moments of perplexity. 'Come!'
she ordered him gaily, turning to the door.

He followed her and laid his hand on her arm. 'Don't you think –
hadn't you better let me go first and see? They told me they'd had a
tiring day at the dressmaker's. I dare say they have gone to bed.'

'But you said they'd a young man of Charlotte's dining with them.
Surely he wouldn't have left by ten? At any rate, I'll go down with
you and see. It takes so long if one sends a servant first.' She put him
gently aside, and then paused as a new thought struck her. 'Or wait,
my maid's in the next room. I'll tell her to go and ask if Margaret will
receive me. Yes, that's much the best way.'

She turned back and went toward the door that led to her bedroom;
but before she could open it she felt Ide's quick touch again.

'I believe – I remember now – Charlotte's young man was
suggesting that they should all go out – to a music hall or something
of the sort. I'm sure – I'm positively sure that you won't find them.'

Her hand dropped from the door, his dropped from her arm, and
as they drew back and faced each other she saw the blood rise slowly
through his sallow skin, redden his neck and ears, encroach upon the
edges of his beard, and settle in dull patches under his kind troubled
eyes. She had seen the same blush on another face, and the same impulse
of compassion she had then felt made her turn her gaze away again.

A knock on the door broke the silence, and a porter put his head
into the room.

'It's only just to know how many pieces there'll be to go down to
the steamer in the morning.'

With the words she felt that the veil of painted gauze was torn in
tatters, and that she was moving again among the grim edges of reality.

'Oh, dear,' she exclaimed, 'I never *can* remember! Wait a minute; I
shall have to ask my maid.'

She opened her bedroom door and called out: 'Annette!'

The Long Run

The shade of those our days that had no tongue.

IT WAS LAST WINTER, after a twelve years' absence from New York, that I saw again, at one of the Jim Cumnors' dinners, my old friend Halston Merrick.

The Cumnors' house is one of the few where, even after such a lapse of time, one can be sure of finding familiar faces and picking up old threads; where for a moment one can abandon one's self to the illusion that New York humanity is a shade less unstable than its bricks and mortar. And that evening in particular I remember feeling that there could be no pleasanter way of re-entering the confused and careless world to which I was returning than through the quiet softly-lit dining room in which Mrs. Cumnor, with a characteristic sense of my needing to be broken in gradually, had contrived to assemble so many friendly faces.

I was glad to see them all, including the three or four I did not know, or failed to recognize, that had no difficulty in passing as in the tradition and of the group; but I was most of all glad – as I rather wonderingly found – to set eyes again on Halston Merrick.

He and I had been at Harvard together, for one thing, and had shared there curiosities and ardors a little outside the current tendencies: had, on the whole, been more critical than our comrades, and less amenable to the accepted. Then, for the next following years, Merrick had been a vivid and promising figure in young American life. Handsome, careless, and free, he had wandered and tasted and compared. After leaving Harvard he had spent two years at Oxford; then he had accepted a private secretaryship to our Ambassador in England, and had come back from this adventure with a fresh curiosity about public affairs at home, and the conviction that men of his kind should play a larger part in them. This led, first, to his running for a State Senatorship which he failed to get, and ultimately to a few months of intelligent activity in a municipal office. Soon after being deprived of this post by

144

a change of party he had published a small volume of delicate verse, and, a year later, an odd uneven brilliant book on Municipal Government. After that one hardly knew where to look for his next appearance; but chance rather disappointingly solved the problem by killing off his father and placing Halston at the head of the Merrick Iron Foundry at Yonkers.

His friends had gathered that, whenever this regrettable contingency should occur, he meant to dispose of the business and continue his life of free experiment. As often happens in just such cases, however, it was not the moment for a sale, and Merrick had to take over the management of the foundry. Some two years later he had a chance to free himself; but when it came he did not choose to take it. This tame sequel to an inspiriting start was disappointing to some of us, and I was among those disposed to regret Merrick's drop to the level of the prosperous. Then I went away to a big engineering job in China, and from there to Africa, and spent the next twelve years out of sight and sound of New York doings.

During that long interval I heard of no new phase in Merrick's evolution, but this did not surprise me, as I had never expected from him actions resonant enough to cross the globe. All I knew – and this did surprise me – was that he had not married, and that he was still in the iron business. All through those years, however, I never ceased to wish, in certain situations and at certain turns of thought, that Merrick were in reach, that I could tell this or that to Merrick. I had never, in the interval, found any one with just his quickness of perception and just his sureness of response.

After dinner, therefore, we irresistibly drew together. In Mrs. Cumnor's big easy drawing room cigars were allowed, and there was no break in the communion of the sexes; and, this being the case, I ought to have sought a seat beside one of the ladies among whom we were allowed to remain. But, as had generally happened of old when Merrick was in sight, I found myself steering straight for him past all minor ports of call.

There had been no time, before dinner, for more than the barest expression of satisfaction at meeting, and our seats had been at opposite ends of the longish table, so that we got our first real look at each other in the secluded corner to which Mrs. Cumnor's vigilance now directed us.

Merrick was still handsome in his stooping tawny way: handsomer perhaps, with thinnish hair and more lines in his face, than in the young excess of his good looks. He was very glad to see me and conveyed his gladness by the same charming smile; but as soon as we began to talk I felt a change. It was not merely the change that years and experience and altered values bring. There was something more fundamental the matter with Merrick, something dreadful, unforeseen, unaccountable: Merrick had grown conventional and dull.

In the glow of his frank pleasure in seeing me I was ashamed to analyze the nature of the change; but presently our talk began to flag – fancy a talk with Merrick flagging! – and self-deception became impossible as I watched myself handing out platitudes with the gesture of the salesman offering something to a purchaser 'equally good.' The worst of it was that Merrick – Merrick, who had once felt everything! – didn't seem to feel the lack of spontaneity in my remarks, but hung on them with a harrowing faith in the resuscitating power of our past. It was as if he hugged the empty vessel of our friendship without perceiving that the last drop of its essence was dry.

But after all, I am exaggerating. Through my surprise and disappointment I felt a certain sense of well-being in the mere physical presence of my old friend. I liked looking at the way his dark hair waved away from the forehead, at the tautness of his dry brown cheek, the thoughtful backward tilt of his head, the way his brown eyes mused upon the scene through lowered lids. All the past was in his way of looking and sitting, and I wanted to stay near him, and felt that he wanted me to stay; but the devil of it was that neither of us knew what to talk about.

It was this difficulty which caused me, after a while, since I could not follow Merrick's talk, to follow his eyes in their roaming circuit of the room.

At the moment when our glances joined, his had paused on a lady seated at some distance from our corner. Immersed, at first, in the satisfaction of finding myself again with Merrick, I had been only half aware of this lady, as of one of the few persons present whom I did not know, or had failed to remember. There was nothing in her appearance to challenge my attention or to excite my curiosity, and I don't suppose I should have looked at her again if I had not noticed that my friend was doing so.

She was a woman of about forty-seven, with fair faded hair and a young figure. Her gray dress was handsome but ineffective, and her pale and rather serious face wore a small unvarying smile which might have been pinned on with her ornaments. She was one of the women in whom increasing years show rather what they have taken than what they have bestowed, and only on looking closely did one see that what they had taken must have been good of its kind.

Phil Cumnor and another man were talking to her, and the very intensity of the attention she bestowed on them betrayed the straining of rebellious thoughts. She never let her eyes stray or her smile drop; and at the proper moment I saw she was ready with the proper sentiment.

The party, like most of those that Mrs. Cumnor gathered about her, was not composed of exceptional beings. The people of the old vanished New York set were not exceptional: they were mostly cut on the same convenient and unobtrusive pattern; but they were often exceedingly 'nice.' And this obsolete quality marked every look and gesture of the lady I was scrutinizing.

While these reflections were passing through my mind I was aware that Merrick's eyes rested still on her. I took a cross-section of his look and found in it neither surprise nor absorption, but only a certain sober pleasure just about at the emotional level of the rest of the room. If he continued to look at her, his expression seemed to say, it was only because, all things considered, there were fewer reasons for looking at anybody else.

This made me wonder what were the reasons for looking at *her;* and as a first step toward enlightenment I said: 'I'm sure I've seen the lady over there in gray – '

Merrick detached his eyes and turned them on me with a wondering look.

'Seen her? You know her.' He waited. '*Don't* you know her? It's Mrs. Reardon.'

I wondered that he should wonder, for I could not remember, in the Cumnor group or elsewhere, having known anyone of the name he mentioned.

'But perhaps,' he continued, 'you hadn't heard of her marriage? You knew her as Mrs. Trant.'

I gave him back his stare. 'Not Mrs. Philip Trant?'

'Yes; Mrs. Philip Trant.'

'Not Paulina?'

'Yes – Paulina,' he said, with a just perceptible delay before the name.

In my surprise I continued to stare at him. He averted his eyes from mine after a moment, and I saw that they had strayed back to her. 'You find her so changed?' he asked.

Something in his voice acted as a warning signal, and I tried to reduce my astonishment to less unbecoming proportions. 'I don't find that she looks much older.'

'No. Only different?' he suggested, as if there were nothing new to him in my perplexity.

'Yes – awfully different.'

'I suppose we're all awfully different. To you, I mean – coming from so far?'

'I recognized all the rest of you,' I said, hesitating. 'And she used to be the one who stood out most.'

There was a flash, a wave, a stir of something deep down in his eyes. 'Yes,' he said. '*That's* the difference.'

'I see it is. She – she looks worn down. Soft but blurred, like the figures in that tapestry behind her.'

He glanced at her again, as if to test the exactness of my analogy.

'Life wears everybody down,' he said.

'Yes – except those it makes more distinct. They're the rare ones, of course; but she *was* rare.'

He stood up suddenly, looking old and tired. 'I believe I'll be off. I wish you'd come down to my place for Sunday. . . . No, don't shake hands – I want to slide away unawares.'

He had backed away to the threshold and was turning the noiseless doorknob. Even Mrs. Cumnor's doorknobs had tact and didn't tell.

'Of course I'll come,' I promised warmly. In the last ten minutes he had begun to interest me again.

'All right. Good-bye.' Half through the door he paused to add: '*She* remembers you. You ought to speak to her.'

'I'm going to. But tell me a little more.' I thought I saw a shade of constraint on his face, and did not add as I had meant to: 'Tell me – because she interests me – what wore her down?' Instead, I asked: 'How soon after Trant's death did she remarry?'

He seemed to make an effort of memory. 'It was seven years ago, I think.'

'And is Reardon here tonight?'

'Yes; over there, talking to Mrs. Cumnor.'

I looked across the broken groupings and saw a large glossy man with straw-colored hair and red face, whose shirt and shoes and complexion seemed all to have received a coat of the same expensive varnish.

As I looked there was a drop in the talk about us, and I heard Mr. Reardon pronounce in a big booming voice: 'What I say is: what's the good of disturbing things? Thank the Lord, I'm content with what I've got!'

'Is *that* her husband? What's he like?'

'Oh, the best fellow in the world,' said Merrick, going.

• II •

MERRICK had a little place at Riverdale, where he went occasionally to be near the Iron Works, and where he hid his weekends when the world was too much with him.

Here, on the following Saturday afternoon I found him awaiting me in a pleasant setting of books and prints and faded parental furniture.

We dined late, and smoked and talked afterward in his book-walled study till the terrier on the hearthrug stood up and yawned for bed. When we took the hint and moved toward the staircase I felt, not that

I had found the old Merrick again, but that I was on his track, had come across traces of his passage here and there in the thick jungle that had grown up between us. But I had a feeling that when I finally came on the man himself he might be dead. . . .

As we started upstairs he turned back with one of his abrupt shy movements, and walked into the study.

'Wait a bit!' he called to me.

I waited, and he came out in a moment carrying a limp folio.

'It's typewritten. Will you take a look at it? I've been trying to get to work again,' he explained, thrusting the manuscript into my hand.

'What? Poetry, I hope?' I exclaimed.

He shook his head with a gleam of derision. 'No – just general considerations. The fruit of fifty years of inexperience.'

He showed me to my room and said good night.

The following afternoon we took a long walk inland, across the hills, and I said to Merrick what I could of his book. Unluckily there wasn't much to say. The essays were judicious, polished and cultivated; but they lacked the freshness and audacity of his youthful work. I tried to conceal my opinion behind the usual generalizations, but he broke through these feints with a quick thrust to the heart of my meaning.

'It's worn down – blurred? Like the figures in the Cumnors' tapestry?'

I hesitated. 'It's a little too damned resigned,' I said.

'Ah,' he exclaimed, 'so am I. Resigned.' He switched the bare brambles by the roadside. 'A man can't serve two masters.'

'You mean business and literature?'

'No; I mean theory and instinct. The gray tree and the green. You've got to choose which fruit you'll try; and you don't know till afterward which of the two has the dead core.'

'How can anybody be sure that only one of them has?'

'I'm sure,' said Merrick sharply.

We turned back to the subject of his essays, and I was astonished at the detachment with which he criticized and demolished them. Little by little, as we talked, his old perspective, his old standards came back to him; but with the difference that they no longer seemed like functions of his mind but merely like attitudes assumed or dropped at will. He could still, with an effort, put himself at the angle from which he had formerly seen things; but it was with the effort of a man climbing mountains after a sedentary life in the plain.

I tried to cut the talk short, but he kept coming back to it with nervous insistence, forcing me into the last retrenchments of hypocrisy, and anticipating the verdict I held back. I perceived that a great deal – immensely more than I could see a reason for – had hung for him on my opinion of his book.

Then, as suddenly, his insistence dropped and, as if ashamed of having forced himself so long on my attention, he began to talk rapidly and uninterestingly of other things.

We were alone again that evening, and after dinner, wishing to efface the impression of the afternoon, and above all to show that I wanted him to talk about himself, I reverted to his work. 'You must need an outlet of that sort. When a man's once had it in him, as you have – and when other things begin to dwindle – '

He laughed. 'Your theory is that a man ought to be able to return to the Muse as he comes back to his wife after he's ceased to interest other women?'

'No; as he comes back to his wife after the day's work is done.' A new thought came to me as I looked at him. 'You ought to have had one,' I added.

He laughed again. 'A wife, you mean? So that there'd have been someone waiting for me even if the Muse decamped?' He went on after a pause: 'I've a notion that the kind of woman worth coming back to wouldn't be much more patient than the Muse. But as it happens I never tried – because, for fear they'd chuck me, I put them both out of doors together.'

He turned his head and looked past me with a queer expression at the low-paneled door at my back. 'Out of that very door they went – the two of 'em, on a rainy night like this: and one stopped and looked back, to see if I wasn't going to call her – and I didn't – and so they both went.'

• III •

'The Muse?' (said Merrick, refilling my glass and stooping to pat the terrier as he went back to his chair) 'Well, you've met the Muse in the little volume of sonnets you used to like; and you've met the woman too, and you used to like *her;* though you didn't know her when you saw her the other evening. . . .

'No, I won't ask you how she struck you when you talked to her: I know. She struck you like that stuff I gave you to read last night. She's conformed – I've conformed – the mills have caught us and ground us: ground us, oh, exceedingly small!

'But you remember what she was, and that's the reason why I'm telling you this now. . . .

'You may recall that after my father's death I tried to sell the Works. I was impatient to free myself from anything that would keep me tied to New York. I don't dislike my trade, and I've made, in the end, a fairly good thing of it; but industrialism was not, at that time, in the line of my tastes, and I know now that it wasn't what I was meant for.

Above all, I wanted to get away, to see new places and rub up against different ideas. I had reached a time of life – the top of the first hill, so to speak – where the distance draws one, and everything in the foreground seems tame and stale. I was sick to death of the particular set of conformities I had grown up among; sick of being a pleasant popular young man with a long line of dinners on my list, and the dead certainty of meeting the same people, or their prototypes, at all of them.

'Well – I failed to sell the Works, and that increased my discontent. I went through moods of cold unsociability, alternating with sudden flushes of curiosity, when I gloated over stray scraps of talk overheard in railway stations and omnibuses, when strange faces that I passed in the street tantalized me with fugitive promises. I wanted to be among things that were unexpected and unknown; and it seemed to me that nobody about me understood in the least what I felt, but that somewhere just out of reach there was someone who *did*, and whom I must find or despair. . . .

'It was just then that, one evening, I saw Mrs. Trant for the first time.

'Yes: I know – you wonder what I mean. I'd known her, of course, as a girl; I'd met her several times after her marriage; and I'd lately been thrown with her, quite intimately and continuously, during a succession of country-house visits. But I had never, as it happened, really *seen* her. . . .

'It was at a dinner at the Cumnors'; and there she was, in front of the very tapestry we saw her against the other evening, with people about her, and her face turned from me, and nothing noticeable or different in her dress or manner; and suddenly she stood out for me against the familiar unimportant background, and for the first time I saw a meaning in the stale phrase of a picture's walking out of its frame. For, after all, most people *are* just that to us: pictures, furniture, the inanimate accessories of our little island area of sensation. And then sometimes one of these graven images moves and throws out live filaments toward us, and the line they make draws us across the world as the moon track seems to draw a boat across the water. . . .

'There she stood; and as this queer sensation came over me I felt that she was looking steadily at me, that her eyes were voluntarily, consciously resting on me with the weight of the very question I was asking.

'I went over and joined her, and she turned and walked with me into the music room. Earlier in the evening someone had been singing, and there were low lights there, and a few couples still sitting in those confidential corners of which Mrs. Cumnor has the art; but we were under no illusion as to the nature of these presences. We knew that they were just painted in, and that the whole of life was in us two, flowing back and forward between us. We talked, of course; we had the attitudes, even the words, of the others: I remember her telling me her plans for the spring and asking me politely about mine! As if there were the least sense in plans, now that this thing had happened!

'When we went back into the drawing room I had said nothing to her that I might not have said to any other woman of the party; but when we shook hands I knew we should meet the next day – and the next. . . .

'That's the way, I take it, that Nature has arranged the beginning of the great enduring loves; and likewise of the little epidermal flurries. And how is a man to know where he is going?

'From the first my feeling for Paulina Trant seemed to me a grave business; but then the Enemy is given to producing that illusion. Many a man – I'm talking of the kind with imagination – has thought he was seeking a soul when all he wanted was a closer view of its tenement. And I tried – honestly tried – to make myself think I was in the latter case. Because, in the first place, I didn't, just then, want a big disturbing influence in my life; and because I didn't want to be a dupe; and because Paulina Trant was not, according to hearsay, the kind of woman for whom it was worth-while to bring up the big batteries. . . .

'But my resistance was only half-hearted. What I really felt – *all* I really felt – was the flood of joy that comes of heightened emotion. She had given me that, and I wanted her to give it to me again. That's as near as I've ever come to analyzing my state in the beginning.

'I knew her story, as no doubt you know it: the current version, I mean. She had been poor and fond of enjoyment, and she had married that pompous stick Philip Trant because she needed a home, and perhaps also because she wanted a little luxury. Queer how we sneer at women for wanting the thing that gives them half their attraction!

'People shook their heads over the marriage, and divided, prematurely, into Philip's partisans and hers: for no one thought it would work. And they were almost disappointed when, after all, it did. She and her wooden consort seemed to get on well enough. There was a ripple, at one time, over her friendship with young Jim Dalham, who was always with her during a summer at Newport and an autumn in Italy; then the talk died out, and she and Trant were seen together, as before, on terms of apparent good fellowship.

'This was the more surprising because, from the first, Paulina had never made the least attempt to change her tone or subdue her colors. In the gray Trant atmosphere she flashed with prismatic fires. She smoked, she talked subversively, she did as she liked and went where she chose, and danced over the Trant prejudices and the Trant principles as if they'd been a ballroom floor; and all without apparent offence to her solemn husband and his cloud of cousins. I believe her frankness and directness struck them dumb. She moved like a kind of primitive

Una through the virtuous rout, and never got a finger mark on her freshness.

'One of the finest things about her was the fact that she never, for an instant, used her situation as a means of enhancing her attraction. With a husband like Trant it would have been so easy! He was a man who always saw the small sides of big things. He thought most of life compressible into a set of bylaws and the rest unmentionable; and with his stiff frock-coated and tall-hatted mind, instinctively distrustful of intelligences in another dress, with his arbitrary classification of whatever he didn't understand into "the kind of thing I don't approve of," "the kind of thing that isn't done," and – deepest depth of all – "the kind of thing I'd rather not discuss," he lived in bondage to a shadowy moral etiquette of which the complex rites and awful penalties had cast an abiding gloom upon his manner.

'A woman like his wife couldn't have asked a better foil; yet I'm sure she never consciously used his dullness to relieve her brilliancy. She may have felt that the case spoke for itself. But I believe her reserve was rather due to a lively sense of justice, and to the rare habit (you said she was rare) of looking at facts as they are, without any throwing of sentimental limelights. She knew Trant could no more help being Trant than she could help being herself – and there was an end of it. I've never known a woman who "made up" so little mentally. . . .

'Perhaps her very reserve, the fierceness of her implicit rejection of sympathy, exposed her the more to – well, to what happened when we met. She said afterward that it was like having been shut up for months in the hold of a ship, and coming suddenly on deck on a day that was all flying blue and silver. . . .

'I won't try to tell you what she was. It's easier to tell you what her friendship made of me; and I can do that best by adopting her metaphor of the ship. Haven't you, sometimes, at the moment of starting on a journey, some glorious plunge into the unknown, been tripped up by the thought: "If only one hadn't to come back"? Well, with her one had the sense that one would never have to come back; that the magic ship would always carry one farther. And what an air one breathed on it! And, oh, the wind, and the islands, and the sunsets!

'I said just now "her friendship"; and I used the word advisedly. Love is deeper than friendship, but friendship is a good deal wider. The beauty of our relation was that it included both dimensions. Our thoughts met as naturally as our eyes: it was almost as if we loved each other because we liked each other. The quality of a love may be tested by the amount of friendship it contains, and in our case there was no dividing line between loving and liking, no disproportion between them, no barrier against which desire beat in vain or from which thought fell back unsatisfied. Ours was a robust passion that could give an open-eyed account of itself, and not a beautiful madness shrinking away from the proof. . . .

'For the first months friendship sufficed us, or rather gave us so much by the way that we were in no hurry to reach what we knew it was leading to. But we were moving there nevertheless, and one day we found ourselves on the borders. It came about through a sudden decision of Trant's to start on a long tour with his wife. We had never foreseen that: he seemed rooted in his New York habits and convinced that the whole social and financial machinery of the metropolis would cease to function if he did not keep an eye on it through the columns of his morning paper, and pronounce judgment on it in the afternoon at his club. But something new had happened to him: he caught a cold, which was followed by a touch of pleurisy, and instantly he perceived the intense interest and importance which ill-health may add to life. He took the fullest advantage of it. A discerning doctor recommended travel in a warm climate; and suddenly, the morning paper, the afternoon club, Fifth Avenue, Wall Street, all the complex phenomena of the metropolis, faded into insignificance, and the rest of the terrestrial globe, from being a mere geographical hypothesis, useful in enabling one to determine the latitude of New York, acquired reality and magnitude as a factor in the convalescence of Mr. Philip Trant.

'His wife was absorbed in preparations for the journey. To move him was like mobilizing an army, and weeks before the date set for their departure it was almost as if she were already gone.

'This foretaste of separation showed us what we were to each other. Yet I was letting her go – and there was no help for it, no way of preventing it. Resistance was as useless as the vain struggles in a nightmare. She was Trant's and not mine: part of his luggage when he traveled as she was part of his household furniture when he stayed at home. . . .

'The day she told me that their passages were taken – it was on a November afternoon, in her drawing room in town – I turned away from her and, going to the window, stood looking out at the torrent of traffic interminably pouring down Fifth Avenue. I watched the senseless machinery of life revolving in the rain and mud, and tried to picture myself performing my small function in it after she had gone from me.

' "It can't be – it can't be!" I exclaimed.

' "What can't be?"

'I came back into the room and sat down by her. "This – this – " I hadn't any words. "Two weeks!" I said. "What's two weeks?"

'She answered, vaguely, something about their thinking of Spain for the spring – .

' "Two weeks – two weeks!" I repeated. "And the months we've lost – the days that belonged to us!"

' "Yes," she said, "I'm thankful it's settled."

'Our words seemed irrelevant, haphazard. It was as if each were answering a secret voice, and not what the other was saying.

' "Don't you *feel* anything at all?" I remember bursting out at her. As I asked it the tears were streaming down her face. I felt angry with her, and was almost glad to note that her lids were red and that she didn't cry becomingly. I can't express my sensation to you except by saying that she seemed part of life's huge league against me. And suddenly I thought of an afternoon we had spent together in the country, on a ferny hillside, when we had sat under a beech tree, and her hand had lain palm upward in the moss, close to mine, and I had watched a little black and red beetle creeping over it. . . .

'The bell rang, and we heard the voice of a visitor and the click of an umbrella in the umbrella stand.

'She rose to go into the inner drawing room, and I caught her suddenly by the wrist. "You understand," I said, "that we can't go on like this?"

' "I understand," she answered, and moved away to meet her visitor. As I went out I heard her saying in the other room: "Yes, we're really off on the twelfth."

• IV •

'I WROTE her a long letter that night, and waited two days for a reply.

'On the third day I had a brief line saying that she was going to spend Sunday with some friends who had a place near Riverdale, and that she would arrange to see me while she was there. That was all.

'It was on a Saturday that I received the note and I came out here the same night. The next morning was rainy, and I was in despair, for I had counted on her asking me to take her for a drive or a long walk. It was hopeless to try to say what I had to say to her in the drawing room of a crowded country house. And only eleven days were left!

'I stayed indoors all the morning, fearing to go out lest she should telephone me. But no sign came, and I grew more and more restless and anxious. She was too free and frank for coquetry, but her silence and evasiveness made me feel that, for some reason, she did not wish to hear what she knew I meant to say. Could it be that she was, after all, more conventional, less genuine, than I had thought? I went again and again over the whole maddening round of conjecture; but the only conclusion I could rest in was that, if she loved me as I loved her, she would be as determined as I was to let no obstacle come between us during the days that were left.

'The luncheon hour came and passed, and there was no word from her. I had ordered my trap to be ready, so that I might drive over as soon as she summoned me; but the hours dragged on, the early twilight came, and I sat here in this very chair, or measured up and down, up and down, the length of this very rug – and still there was no message and no letter.

'It had grown quite dark, and I had ordered away, impatiently, the servant who came in with the lamps: I couldn't *bear* any definite sign that the day was over! And I was standing there on the rug, staring at the door, and noticing a bad crack in its panel, when I heard the sound of wheels on the gravel. A word at last, no doubt – a line to explain. . . . I didn't seem to care much for her reasons, and I stood where I was and continued to stare at the door. And suddenly it opened and she came in.

'The servant followed her with a light, and then went out and closed the door. Her face looked pale in lamplight, but her voice was as clear as a bell.

' "Well," she said, "you see I've come."

'I started toward her with hands outstretched. "You've come – you've come!" I stammered.

'Yes; it was like her to come in that way – without dissimulation or explanation or excuse. It was like her, if she gave at all, to give not furtively or in haste, but openly, deliberately, without stinting the measure or counting the cost. But her quietness and serenity disconcerted me. She did not look like a woman who has yielded impetuously to an uncontrollable impulse. There was something almost solemn in her face.

'The effect of it stole over me as I looked at her, suddenly subduing the huge flush of gratified longing.

' "You're here, here, here!" I kept repeating, like a child singing over a happy word.

' "You said," she continued, in her grave clear voice, "that we couldn't go on as we were – "

' "Ah, it's divine of you!" I held out my arms to her.

'She didn't draw back from them, but her faint smile said, "Wait," and lifting her hands she took the pins from her hat, and laid the hat on the table.

'As I saw her dear head bare in the lamplight, with the thick hair waving away from the parting, I forgot everything but the bliss and wonder of her being here – here, in my house, on my hearth – that fourth rose from the corner of the rug is the exact spot where she was standing. . . .

'I drew her to the fire, and made her sit down in the chair you're in, and knelt down by her, and hid my face on her knees. She put her hand on my head, and I was happy to the depths of my soul.

' "Oh, I forgot – " she exclaimed suddenly. I lifted my head and our eyes met. Hers were smiling.

'She reached out her hand, opened the little bag she had tossed down with her hat, and drew a small object from it. "I left my trunk at the station. Here's the check. Can you send for it?" she asked.

'Her trunk – she wanted me to send for her trunk! Oh, yes – I see your smile, your "lucky man!" Only, you see, I didn't love her in that way. I knew she couldn't come to my house without running a big risk of discovery, and my tenderness for her, my impulse to shield her, was stronger, even then, than vanity or desire. Judged from the point of view of those emotions I fell terribly short of my part. I hadn't any of the proper feelings. Such an act of romantic folly was so unlike her that it almost irritated me, and I found myself desperately wondering how I could get her to reconsider her plan without – well, without seeming to want her to.

'It's not the way a novel hero feels; it's probably not the way a man in real life ought to have felt. But it's the way I felt – and she saw it.

'She put her hands on my shoulders and looked at me with deep, deep eyes. "Then you didn't expect me to stay?" she asked.

'I caught her hands and pressed them to me, stammering out that I hadn't dared to dream. . . .

' "You thought I'd come – just for an hour?"

' "How could I dare think more? I adore you, you know, for what you've done! But it would be known if you – if you stayed on. My servants – everybody about here knows you. I've no right to expose you to the risk." She made no answer, and I went on tenderly: "Give me, if you will, the next few hours: there's a train that will get you to town by midnight. And then we'll arrange something – in town – where it's safer for you – more easily managed. . . . It's beautiful, it's heavenly of you to have come; but I love you too much – I must take care of you and think for you – '

'I don't suppose it ever took me so long to say so few words, and though they were profoundly sincere they sounded unutterably shallow, irrelevant and grotesque. She made no effort to help me out, but sat silent, listening, with her meditative smile. "It's my duty, dearest, as a man," I rambled on. "The more I love you the more I'm bound – "

' "Yes; but you don't understand," she interrupted.

'She rose as she spoke, and I got up also, and we stood and looked at each other.

' "I haven't come for a night; if you want me I've come for always," she said.

'Here again, if I give you an honest account of my feelings I shall write myself down as the poor-spirited creature I suppose I am. There wasn't, I swear, at the moment, a grain of selfishness, of personal reluctance, in my feeling. I worshiped every hair of her head – when we were together I was happy, when I was away from her something was gone from every good thing; but I had always looked on our love for each other, our possible relation to each other, as such situations are looked on in what is called society. I had supposed her, for all her freedom and originality, to be just as tacitly subservient to that view as I was: ready to take what she wanted on the terms on which society concedes such taking, and to pay for it by the usual restrictions, concealments and hypocrisies. In short, I supposed that she would "play the game" – look out for her own safety, and expect me to look out for it. It sounds cheap enough, put that way – but it's the rule we live under, all of us. And the amazement of finding her suddenly outside of it, oblivious of it, unconscious of it, left me, for an awful minute, stammering at her like a graceless dolt. . . . Perhaps it wasn't even a minute; but in it she had gone the whole round of my thoughts.

' "It's raining," she said, very low. "I suppose you can telephone for a trap?"

'There was no irony or resentment in her voice. She walked slowly across the room and paused before the Brangwyn etching over there. "That's a good impression. *Will* you telephone, please?" she repeated.

'I found my voice again, and with it the power of movement. I followed her and dropped at her feet. "You can't go like this!" I cried.

'She looked down on me from heights and heights. "I can't stay like this," she answered.

'I stood up and we faced each other like antagonists. "You don't know," I accused her passionately, "in the least what you're asking me to ask of you!"

' "Yes, I do; *everything*," she breathed.

' "And it's got to be that or nothing?"

' "Oh, on both sides," she reminded me.

' "*Not* on both sides. It's not fair. That's why – "

' "Why you won't?"

' "Why I cannot – may not!"

' "Why you'll take a night and not a life?"

'The taunt, for a woman usually so sure of her aim, fell so short of the mark that its only effect was to increase my conviction of her helplessness. The very intensity of my longing for her made me tremble where she was fearless. I had to protect her first, and think of my own attitude afterward.

'She was too discerning not to see this too. Her face softened, grew inexpressibly appealing, and she dropped again into that chair you're in, leaned forward, and looked up with her grave smile.

' "You think I'm beside myself – raving? (You're not thinking of yourself, I know.) I'm not: I never was saner. Since I've known you I've often thought this might happen. This thing between us isn't an ordinary thing. If it had been we shouldn't, all these months, have drifted. We should have wanted to skip to the last page – and then throw down the book. We shouldn't have felt we could *trust* the future as we did. We were in no hurry because we knew we shouldn't get tired; and when two people feel that about each other they must live together – or part. I don't see what else they can do. A little trip along the coast won't answer. It's the high seas – or else tied up to Lethe wharf. And I'm for the high seas, my dear!"

'Think of sitting here – here, in this room, in this chair – and listening to that, and seeing the light on her hair, and hearing the sound of her voice! I don't suppose there ever was a scene just like it. . . .

'She was astounding – inexhaustible; through all my anguish of resistance I found a kind of fierce joy in following her. It was lucidity at white heat: the last sublimation of passion. She might have been an angel arguing a point in the empyrean if she hadn't been, so completely, a woman pleading for her life. . . .

'Her life: that was the thing at stake! She couldn't do with less of it than she was capable of; and a woman's life is inextricably part of the man's she cares for.

'That was why, she argued, she couldn't accept the usual solution: couldn't enter into the only relation that society tolerates between people situated like ourselves. Yes: she knew all the arguments on *that* side: didn't I suppose she'd been over them and over them? She knew (for hadn't she often said it of others?) what is said of the woman who, by throwing in her lot with her lover's, binds him to a lifelong duty which has the irksomeness without the dignity of marriage. Oh, she could talk on that side with the best of them: only she asked me to consider the other – the side of the man and woman who love each other deeply and completely enough to want their lives enlarged, and not diminished, by their love. What, in such a case – she reasoned – must be the inevitable effect of concealing, denying, disowning, the central fact, the motive power of one's existence? She asked me to picture the course of such a love: first working as a fever in the blood, distorting and deflecting everything, making all other interests insipid, all other duties irksome, and then, as the acknowledged claims of life regained their hold, gradually dying – the poor starved passion! – for want of the wholesome necessary food of common living and doings, yet leaving life impoverished by the loss of all it might have been.

' "I'm not talking, dear – " I see her now, leaning toward me with shining eyes: "I'm not talking of the people who haven't enough to fill their days, and to whom a little mystery, a little maneuvering, gives an illusion of importance that they can't afford to miss; I'm talking of you and me, with all our tastes and curiosities and activities; and I ask you what our love would become if we had to keep it apart from our lives, like a pretty useless animal that we went to peep at and feed with sweetmeats through its cage?"

'I won't, my dear fellow, go into the other side of our strange duel: the arguments I used were those that most men in my situation would have felt bound to use, and that most women in Paulina's accept instinctively, without even formulating them. The exceptionalness, the significance, of the case lay wholly in the fact that she had formulated them all and then rejected them. . . .

'There was one point I didn't, of course, touch on; and that was the popular conviction (which I confess I shared) that when a man and a woman agree to defy the world together the man really sacrifices much more than the woman. I was not even conscious of thinking of this at the time, though it may have lurked somewhere in the shadow of my scruples for her; but she dragged it out into the daylight and held me face to face with it.

' "Remember, I'm not attempting to lay down any general rule," she insisted; "I'm not theorizing about Man and Woman, I'm talking about you and me. How do I know what's best for the woman in the next house? Very likely she'll bolt when it would have been better for her to stay at home. And it's the same with the man: he'll probably do the wrong thing. It's generally the weak heads that commit follies, when it's the strong ones that ought to: and my point is that you and I are both strong enough to behave like fools if we want to. . . .

' "Take you own case first – because, in spite of the sentimentalists, it's the man who stands to lose most. You'll have to give up the Iron Works: which you don't much care about – because it won't be particularly agreeable for us to live in New York: which you don't care much about either. But you won't be sacrificing what is called 'a career.' You made up your mind long ago that your best chance of self-development, and consequently of general usefulness, lay in thinking rather than doing; and, when we first met, you were already planning to sell out your business, and travel and write. Well! Those ambitions are of a kind that won't be harmed by your dropping out of your social setting. On the contrary, such work as you want to do ought to gain by it, because you'll be brought nearer to life-as-it-is, in contrast to life-as-a-visiting-list. . . ."

'She threw back her head with a sudden laugh. "And the joy of not having any more visits to make! I wonder if you've ever thought of *that?* Just at first, I mean; for society's getting so deplorably lax that, little by little, it will edge up to us – you'll see! I don't want to idealize the situation, dearest, and I won't conceal from you that in time we shall be called on. But, oh, the fun we shall have had in the interval! And then, for the first time we shall be able to dictate our own terms, one of which will be that no bores need apply. Think of being cured of all one's chronic bores! We shall feel as jolly as people do after a successful operation."

'I don't know why this nonsense sticks in my mind when some of the graver things we said are less distinct. Perhaps it's because of a certain iridescent quality of feeling that made gaiety seem like sunshine through a shower. . . .

' "You ask me to think of myself?" she went on. "But the beauty of our being together will be that, for the first time, I shall dare to! Now I have to think of all the tedious trifles I can pack the days with, because I'm afraid – I'm afraid – to hear the voice of the real me, down below, in the windowless underground hole where I keep her. . . .

' "Remember again, please, it's not Woman, it's Paulina Trant, I'm talking of. The woman in the next house may have all sorts of reasons – honest reasons – for staying there. There may be some one there who needs her badly: for whom the light would go out if she went. Whereas to Philip I've been simply – well, what New York was before he decided to travel: the most important thing in life till he made up his mind to leave it; and now merely the starting place of several lines of steamers. Oh, I didn't have to love you to know that! I only had to live with *him*. . . . If he lost his eyeglasses he'd think it was the fault of the eyeglasses; he'd really feel that the eyeglasses had been careless. And he'd be convinced that no others would suit him quite as well. But at the optician's he'd probably be told that he needed something a little different, and after that he'd feel that the old eyeglasses had never suited him at all, and that *that* was their fault too. . . ."

'At one moment – but I don't recall when – I remember she stood up with one of her quick movements, and came toward me, holding out her arms. "Oh, my dear, I'm pleading for my life; do you suppose I shall ever want for arguments?" she cried. . . .

'After that, for a bit, nothing much remains with me except a sense of darkness and of conflict. The one spot of daylight in my whirling brain was the conviction that I couldn't – whatever happened – profit by the sudden impulse she had acted on, and allow her to take, in a moment of passion, a decision that was to shape her whole life. I couldn't so much as lift my little finger to keep her with me then, unless I were prepared to accept for her as well as for myself the full consequences of the future she had planned for us. . . .

'Well – there's the point: I wasn't. I felt in her – poor fatuous idiot that I was! – that lack of objective imagination which had always seemed to me to account, at least in part, for many of the so-called heroic qualities in women. When their feelings are involved they simply can't look ahead. Her unfaltering logic notwithstanding, I felt this about Paulina as I listened. She had a specious air of knowing where she was going, but she didn't. She seemed the genius of logic and understanding, but the demon of illusion spoke through her lips. . . .

'I said just now that I hadn't, at the outset, given my own side of the case a thought. It would have been truer to say that I hadn't given it a *separate* thought. But I couldn't think of her without seeing myself as a factor – the chief factor – in her problem, and without recognizing that whatever the experiment made of me, it must fatally, in the end, make of her. If I couldn't carry the thing through she must break down with me: we should have to throw our separate selves into the melting pot of this mad adventure, and be "one" in a terrible indissoluble completeness of which marriage is only an imperfect counterpart. . . .

'There could be no better proof of her extraordinary power over me, and of the way she had managed to clear the air of sentimental illusion, than the fact that I presently found myself putting this before her with a merciless precision of touch.

' "If we love each other enough to do a thing like this, we must love each other enough to see just what it is we're going to do."

'So I invited her to the dissecting table, and I see now the fearless eye with which she approached the cadaver. "For that's what it is, you know," she flashed out at me, at the end of my long demonstration. "It's a dead body, like all the instances and examples and hypothetical cases that ever were! What do you expect to learn from *that?* The first great anatomist was the man who stuck his knife in a heart that was beating; and the only way to find out what doing a thing will be like is to do it!"

'She looked away from me suddenly, as if she were fixing her eyes on some vision on the outer rim of consciousness. "No: there's one other way," she exclaimed; "and that is, *not* to do it! To abstain and refrain; and then see what we become, or what we don't become, in the long run, and to draw our inferences. That's the game that almost everybody about us is playing, I suppose; there's hardly one of the dull people one meets at dinner who hasn't had, just once, the chance of a berth on a ship that was off for the Happy Isles, and hasn't refused it for fear of sticking on a sandbank!

' "I'm doing my best, you know," she continued, "to see the sequel as you see it, as you believe it's your duty to me to see it. I know the instances you're thinking of: the listless couples wearing out their lives in shabby watering places, and hanging on the favour of hotel acquaintances; or the proud quarreling wretches shut up alone in a fine house because they're too good for the only society they can get, and trying to cheat their boredom by squabbling with their tradesmen and spying on their servants. No doubt there are such cases; but I don't recognize either of us in those dismal figures. Why, to do it would be to admit that our life, yours and mine, is in the people about us and not in ourselves; that we're parasites and not self-sustaining creatures; and that the lives we're leading now are so brilliant, full and satisfying that what we should have to give up would surpass even the blessedness of being together!"

'At that stage, I confess, the solid ground of my resistance began to give way under me. It was not that my convictions were shaken, but that she had swept me into a world whose laws were difficult, where one could reach out in directions that the slave of gravity hasn't pictured. But at the same time my opposition hardened from reason into instinct. I knew it was her voice, and not her logic, that was unsettling me. I knew that if she'd written out her thesis and sent it to me by post I should have made short work of it; and again the part of me which I called by all the finest names: my chivalry, my unselfishness, my superior masculine experience, cried out with one voice. "You can't let a woman use her graces to her own undoing – you can't, for her own sake, let her eyes convince you when her reasons don't!"

'And then, abruptly, and for the first time, a doubt entered me: a doubt of her perfect moral honesty. I don't know how else to describe my feeling that she wasn't playing fair, that in coming to my house, in throwing herself at my head (I called things by their names), she had perhaps not so much obeyed an irresistible impulse as deeply, deliberately reckoned on the dissolvent effect of her generosity, her rashness and her beauty. . . .

'From the moment that this mean doubt raised its head in me I was once more the creature of all the conventional scruples: I was repeating, before the looking glass of my self-consciousness, all the stereotyped gestures of the "man of honor." . . . Oh, the sorry figure I must have cut! You'll understand my dropping the curtain on it as quickly as I can. . . .

'Yet I remember, as I made my point, being struck by its impressiveness. I was suffering and enjoying my own suffering. I told her that, whatever step we decided to take, I owed it to her to insist on its being taken soberly, deliberately –

'("No: it's 'advisedly,' isn't it? Oh, I was thinking of the Marriage Service," she interposed with a faint laugh.)

' –That if I accepted, there, on the spot, her headlong beautiful gift of herself, I should feel I had taken an unfair advantage of her, an advantage which she would be justified in reproaching me with afterward; that I was not afraid to tell her this because she was intelligent enough to know that my scruples were the surest proof of the quality of my love; that I refused to owe my happiness to an unconsidered impulse; that we must see each other again, in her own house, in less agitating circumstances, when she had had time to reflect on my words, to study her heart and look into the future. . . .

'The factitious exhilaration produced by uttering these beautiful sentiments did not last very long, as you may imagine. It fell, little by little, under her quiet gaze, a gaze in which there was neither contempt nor irony nor wounded pride, but only a tender wistfulness of interrogation; and I think the acutest point in my suffering was reached when she said, as I ended: "Oh; yes, of course I understand."

' "If only you hadn't come to me here!" I blurted out in the torture of my soul.

'She was on the threshold when I said it, and she turned and laid her hand gently on mine. "There was no other way," she said; and at the moment it seemed to me like some hackneyed phrase in a novel that she had used without any sense of its meaning.

'I don't remember what I answered or what more we either of us said. At the end a desperate longing to take her in my arms and keep her with me swept aside everything else, and I went up to her, pleading, stammering, urging I don't know what. . . . But she held me back with a quiet look, and went. I had ordered the carriage, as she asked me to; and my last definite recollection is of watching her drive off in the rain. . . .

'I had her promise that she would see me, two days later, at her house in town, and that we should then have what I called "a decisive talk"; but I don't think that even at the moment I was the dupe of my phrase. I knew, and she knew, that the end had come. . . .

• V •

'IT was about that time (Merrick went on after a long pause) that I definitely decided not to sell the Works, but to stick to my job and conform my life to it.

'I can't describe to you the rage of conformity that possessed me. Poetry, ideas – all the picture-making processed stopped. A kind of dull self-discipline seemed to me the only exercise worthy of a reflecting mind. I *had* to justify my great refusal, and I tried to do it by plunging myself up to the eyes into the very conditions I had been instinctively struggling to get away from. The only possible consolation would have been to find in a life of business routine and social submission such moral compensations as may reward the citizen if they fail the man; but to attain to these I should have had to accept the old delusion that the social and the individual man are two. Now, on the contrary, I found soon enough that I couldn't get one part of my machinery to work effectively while another wanted feeding: and that in rejecting what had seemed to me a negation of action I had made all my action negative.

'The best solution, of course, would have been to fall in love with another woman; but it was long before I could bring myself to wish that this might happen to me. . . . Then, at length, I suddenly and violently desired it; and as such impulses are seldom without some kind of imperfect issue I contrived, a year or two later, to work myself up into the wished-for state. . . . She was a woman in society, and with all the awe of that institution that Paulina lacked. Our relation was consequently one of those unavowed affairs in which triviality is the only alternative to tragedy. Luckily we had, on both sides, risked only as much as prudent people stake in a drawing-room game; and when the match was over I take it that we came out fairly even.

'My gain, at all events, was of an unexpected kind. The adventure had served only to make me understand Paulina's abhorrence of such experiments, and at every turn of the slight intrigue I had felt how exasperating and belittling such a relation was bound to be between two people who, had they been free, would have mated openly. And so from a brief phase of imperfect forgetting I was driven back to a deeper and more understanding remembrance. . . .

'This second incarnation of Paulina was one of the strangest episodes of the whole strange experience. Things she had said during our extraordinary talk, things I had hardly heard at the time, came back to me with singular vividness and a fuller meaning. I hadn't any longer the cold consolation of believing in my own perspicacity: I saw that her insight had been deeper and keener than mine.

'I remember, in particular, starting up in bed one sleepless night as there flashed into my head the meaning of her last words: "There was no other way; the phrase I had half-smiled at at the time, as a parrot-like echo of the novel heroine's stock farewell. I had never, up to that moment, wholly understood why Paulina had come to my house that night. I had never been able to make that particular act – which could hardly, in the light of her subsequent conduct, be dismissed as a blind surge of passion – square with my conception of her character. She was at once the most spontaneous and the steadiest-minded woman I had ever known, and the last to wish to owe any advantage to surprise, to unpreparedness, to any play on the spring of sex. The better I came, retrospectively, to know her, the more sure I was of this, and the less intelligible her act appeared. And then, suddenly, after a night of hungry restless thinking, the flash of enlightenment came. She had come to my house, had brought her trunk with her, had thrown herself at my head with all possible violence and publicity, in order to give me a pretext, a loophole, an honorable excuse, for doing and saying – why, precisely what I had said and done!

'As the idea came to me it was as if some ironic hand had touched an electric button, and all my fatuous phrases had leapt out on me in fire.

'Of course she had known all along just the kind of thing I should say if I didn't at once open my arms to her; and to save my pride, my dignity, my conception of the figure I was cutting in her eyes, she had recklessly and magnificently provided me with the decentest pretext a man could have for doing a pusillanimous thing. . . .

'With that discovery the whole case took a different aspect. It hurt less to think of Paulina – and yet it hurt more. The tinge of bitterness, of doubt, in my thoughts of her had had a tonic quality. It was harder to go on persuading myself that I had done right as, bit by bit, my theories crumbled under the test of time. Yet, after all, as she herself had said, one could judge of results only in the long run. . . .

'The Trants stayed away for two years; and about a year after they got back, you may remember, Trant was killed in a railway accident. You know Fate's way of untying a knot after everybody has given up tugging at it!

'Well – there I was, completely justified: all my weaknesses turned into merits! I had "saved" a weak woman from herself, I had kept her to the path of duty, I had spared her the humiliation of scandal and the misery of self-reproach; and now I had only to put our my hand and take my reward.

'I had avoided Paulina since her return, and she had made no effort to see me. But after Trant's death I wrote her a few lines, to which she sent a friendly answer, and when a decent interval had elapsed, and I asked if I might call on her, she answered at once that she would see me.

'I went to her house with the fixed intention of asking her to marry me – and I left it without having done so. Why? I don't know that I can tell you. Perhaps you would have had to sit there opposite her, knowing what I did and feeling as I did, to understand why. She was kind, she was compassionate – I could see she didn't want to make it hard for me. Perhaps she even wanted to make it easy. But there, between us, was the memory of the gesture I hadn't made, forever parodying the one I was attempting! There wasn't a word I could think of that hadn't an echo in it of words of hers I had been deaf to; there wasn't an appeal I could make that didn't mock the appeal I had rejected. I sat there and talked of her husband's death, of her plans, of my sympathy; and I knew she understood; and knowing that, in a way, made it harder. . . . The doorbell rang and the footman came in to ask if she would receive other visitors. She looked at me a moment and said "Yes," and I got up and shook hands and went away.

'A few days later she sailed for Europe, and the next time we met she had married Reardon. . . .'

• VI •

IT was long past midnight, and the terrier's hints became imperious.

Merrick rose from his chair, pushed back a fallen log and put up the fender. He walked across the room and stared a moment at the Brangwyn etching before which Paulina Trant had paused at a memorable turn of their talk. Then he came back and laid his hand on my shoulder.

'She summed it all up, you know, when she said that one way of finding out whether a risk is worth taking is *not* to take it, and then to see what one becomes in the long run, and draw one's inferences. The long run – well, we've run it, she and I. I know what I've become, but that's nothing to the misery of knowing what she's become. She had to have some kind of life, and she married Reardon. Reardon's a very good fellow in his way; but the worst of it is that it's not her way. . . .

'No: the worst of it is that now she and I meet as friends. We dine at the same houses, we talk about the same people, we play bridge together, and I lend her books. And sometimes Reardon slaps me on the back and says: "Come in and dine with us, old man! What you want is to be cheered up!" And I go and dine with them, and he tells me how jolly comfortable she makes him, and what an ass I am not to marry; and she presses on me a second helping of *poulet Maryland*, and I smoke one of Reardon's cigars, and at half-past ten I get into my overcoat, and walk back alone to my rooms. . . .'

After Holbein

———————❦———————

ANSON WARLEY had had his moments of being a rather remarkable man; but they were only intermittent; they recurred at ever-lengthening intervals; and between times he was a small poor creature, chattering with cold inside, in spite of his agreeable and even distinguished exterior.

He had always been perfectly aware of these two sides of himself (which, even in the privacy of his own mind, he contemptuously refused to dub a dual personality); and as the rather remarkable man could take fairly good care of himself, most of Warley's attention was devoted to ministering to the poor wretch who took longer and longer turns at bearing his name, and was more and more insistent in accepting the invitations which New York, for over thirty years, had tirelessly poured out on him. It was in the interest of this lonely fidgety unemployed self that Warley, in his younger days, had frequented the gaudiest restaurants and the most glittering Palace Hotels of two hemispheres, subscribed to the most advanced literary and artistic reviews, bought the pictures of the young painters who were being the most vehemently discussed, missed few of the showiest first nights in New York, London or Paris, sought the company of the men and women – especially the women – most conspicuous in fashion, scandal, or any other form of social notoriety, and thus tried to warm the shivering soul within him at all the passing bonfires of success.

The original Anson Warley had begun by staying at home in his little flat, with his books and his thoughts, when the other poor creature went forth; but gradually – he hardly knew when or how – he had slipped into the way of going too, till finally he made the bitter discovery that he and the creature had become one, except on the increasingly rare occasions when, detaching himself from all casual contingencies, he mounted to the lofty watershed which fed the sources of his scorn. The view from there was vast and glorious, the air was icy but exhilarating; but soon he began to find the place too lonely, and too difficult to get to, especially as the lesser Anson not only refused to go up with him but began to sneer, at first ever so faintly, then with increasing insolence, at this affectation of a taste for the heights.

'What's the use of scrambling up there, anyhow? I could understand it if you brought down anything worth-while – a poem or a picture of your own. But just climbing and staring: what does it lead to? Fellows with the creative gift have got to have their occasional Sinaïs; I can see that. But for a mere looker-on like you, isn't that sort of thing rather a pose? You talk awfully well – brilliantly, even (oh, my dear fellow, no false modesty between you and *me*, please!) But who the devil is there to listen to you, up there among the glaciers? And sometimes, when you come down, I notice that you're rather – well, heavy and tongue-tied. Look out, or they'll stop asking us to dine! And sitting at home every evening – brr! Look here, by the way; if you've got nothing better for tonight, come along with me to Chrissy Torrance's – or the Bob Briggses' – or Princess Kate's; anywhere where there's lots of racket and sparkle, places that people go to in Rollses, and that are smart and hot and overcrowded, and you have to pay a lot – in one way or another – to get in.'

Once and again, it is true, Warley still dodged his double and slipped off on a tour to remote uncomfortable places, where there were churches or pictures to be seen, or shut himself up at home for a good bout of reading, or just, in sheer disgust at his companion's platitude, spent an evening with people who were doing or thinking real things. This happened seldomer than of old, however, and more clandestinely; so that at last he used to sneak away to spend two or three days with an archaeologically-minded friend, or an evening with a quiet scholar, as furtively as if he were stealing to a lover's tryst; which, as lovers' trysts were now always kept in the limelight, was after all a fair exchange. But he always felt rather apologetic to the other Warley about these escapades – and, if the truth were known, rather bored and restless before they were over. And in the back of his mind there lurked an increasing dread of missing something hot and noisy and overcrowded when he went off to one of his mountain tops. 'After all, that highbrow business has been awfully overdone – now hasn't it?' the little Warley would insinuate, rummaging for his pearl studs, and consulting his flat evening watch as nervously as if it were a railway timetable. 'If only we haven't missed something really jolly by all this backing and filling. . . .'

'Oh, you poor creature, you! Always afraid of being left out, aren't you? Well – just for once, to humor you, and because I happen to be feeling rather stale myself. But only to think of a sane man's wanting to go to places just because they're hot and smart and overcrowded!' And off they would dash together. . . .

• II •

ALL that was long ago. It was years now since there had been two distinct Anson Warleys. The lesser one had made away with the other, done him softly to death without shedding of blood; and only a few people suspected (and they no longer cared) that the pale white-haired man, with the small slim figure, the ironic smile and the perfect evening clothes, whom New York still indefatigably invited, was nothing less than a murderer.

Anson Warley – Anson Warley! No party was complete without Anson Warley. He no longer went abroad now; too stiff in the joints; and there had been two or three slight attacks of dizziness. . . . Nothing to speak of, nothing to think of, even; but somehow one dug one's self into one's comfortable quarters, and felt less and less like moving out of them, except to motor down to Long Island for weekends, or to Newport for a few visits in summer. A trip to the Hot Springs, to get rid of the stiffness, had not helped much, and the ageing Anson Warley (who really, otherwise, felt as young as ever) had developed a growing dislike for the promiscuities of hotel life and the monotony of hotel food.

Yes; he was growing more fastidious as he grew older. A good sign, he thought. Fastidious not only about food and comfort but about people also. It was still a privilege, a distinction, to have him to dine. His old friends were faithful, and the new people fought for him, and often failed to get him; to do so they had to offer very special inducements in the way of cuisine, conversation or beauty. Young beauty; yes, that would do it. He did like to sit and watch a lovely face, and call laughter into lovely eyes. But no dull dinners for *him*, not even if they fed you off gold. As to that he was as firm as the other Warley, the distant aloof one with whom he had – er, well, parted company, oh, quite amicably, a good many years ago. . . .

On the whole, since that parting, life had been much easier and pleasanter; and by the time the little Warley was sixty-three he found himself looking forward with equanimity to an eternity of New York dinners.

Oh, but only at the right houses – always at the right houses; that was understood! The right people – the right setting – the right wines. . . . He smiled a little over his perennial enjoyment of them; said 'Nonsense, Filmore,' to his devoted tiresome manservant, who was beginning to hint that really, every night, sir, and sometimes a dance afterward, was too much, especially when you kept at it for months on end; and Dr. –

'Oh, damn your doctors!' Warley snapped. He was seldom ill-tempered; he knew it was foolish and upsetting to lose one's self-control. But Filmore began to be a nuisance, nagging him, preaching at him. As if he himself wasn't the best judge. . . .

Besides, he chose his company. He'd stay at home any time rather than risk a boring evening. Damned rot, what Filmore had said about his going out every night. Not like poor old Mrs. Jaspar, for instance . . . he smiled self-approvingly as he evoked her tottering image. 'That's the kind of fool Filmore takes me for,' he chuckled, his good humor restored by an analogy that was so much to his advantage.

Poor old Evelina Jaspar! In his youth, and even in his prime, she had been New York's chief entertainer – 'leading hostess,' the newspapers called her. Her big house in Fifth Avenue had been an entertaining machine. She had lived, breathed, invested and reinvested her millions, to no other end. At first her pretext had been that she had to marry her daughters and amuse her sons; but when sons and daughters had married and left her she had seemed hardly aware of it; she had just gone on entertaining. Hundreds, no thousands of dinners (on gold plate, of course, and with orchids, and all the delicacies that were out of season), had been served in that vast pompous dining room, which one had only to close one's eyes to transform into a railway buffet for millionaires, at a big junction, before the invention of restaurant trains. . . .

Warley closed his eyes, and did so picture it. He lost himself in amused computation of the annual number of guests, of saddles of mutton, of legs of lamb, of terrapin, canvas backs, magnums of champagne and pyramids of hothouse fruit that must have passed through that room in the last forty years.

And even now, he thought – hadn't one of old Evelina's nieces told him the other day, half bantering, half shivering at the avowal, that the poor old lady, who was gently dying of softening of the brain, still imagined herself to be New York's leading hostess, still sent out invitations (which of course were never delivered), still ordered terrapin, champagne and orchids, and still came down every evening to her great shrouded drawing rooms, with her tiara askew on her purple wig, to receive a stream of imaginary guests?

Rubbish, of course – a macabre pleasantry of the extravagant Nelly Pierce, who had always had her joke at Aunt Evelina's expense. . . . But Warley could not help smiling at the thought that those dull monotonous dinners were still going on in their hostess's clouded imagination. Poor old Evelina, he thought! In a way she was right. There was really no reason why that kind of standardized entertaining should ever cease; a performance so undiscriminating, so undifferentiated, that one could almost imagine, in the hostess' tired brain, all the dinners she had ever given merging into one Gargantuan pyramid of food and drink, with the same faces, perpetually the same faces, gathered stolidly about the same gold plate.

Thank heaven, Anson Warley had never conceived of social values in terms of mass and volume. It was years since he had dined at Mrs. Jaspar's. He even felt that he was not above reproach in that respect. Two or three times, in the past, he had accepted her invitations (always sent out weeks ahead), and then chucked her at the eleventh hour for something more amusing. Finally, to avoid such risks, he had made it a rule always to refuse her dinners. He had even – he remembered – been rather funny about it once, when someone had told him that Mrs. Jaspar couldn't understand . . . was a little hurt . . . said it couldn't be true that he always had another engagement the nights she asked him. . . . 'True? Is the truth what she wants? All right! Then the next time I get a "Mrs. Jaspar requests the pleasure" I'll answer it with a "Mr. Warley declines the boredom." Think she'll understand that, eh?' And the phrase became a catchword in his little set that winter. ' "Mr. Warley declines the boredom" – good, good, *good!*' 'Dear Anson, I do hope you won't decline the boredom of coming to lunch next Sunday to meet the new Hindu Yoghi' – or the new saxophone soloist, or that genius of a mulatto boy who plays Negro spirituals on a toothbrush; and so on and so on. He only hoped poor old Evelina never heard of it. . . .

'Certainly I shall *not* stay at home tonight – why, what's wrong with me?' he snapped, swinging round on Filmore.

The valet's long face grew longer. His way of answering such questions was always to pull out his face; it was his only means of putting any expression into it. He turned away into the bedroom, and Warley sat alone by his library fire. . . . Now what did the man see that was wrong with him, he wondered? He had felt a little confusion that morning, when he was doing his daily sprint around the Park (his exercise was reduced to that!); but it had been only a passing flurry, of which Filmore could of course know nothing. And as soon as it was over his mind had seemed more lucid, his eye keener, than ever; as sometimes (he reflected) the electric light in his library lamps would blaze up too brightly after a break in the current, and he would say to himself, wincing a little at the sudden glare on the page he was reading: 'That means that it'll go out again in a minute.'

Yes; his mind, at that moment, had been quite piercingly clear and perceptive; his eye had passed with a renovating glitter over every detail of the daily scene. He stood still for a minute under the leafless trees of the Mall, and looking about him with the sudden insight of age, understood that he had reached the time of life when Alps and cathedrals became as transient as flowers.

Everything was fleeting, fleeting . . . yes, that was what had given him the vertigo. The doctors, poor fools, called it the stomach, or high blood pressure; but it was only the dizzy plunge of the sands in the hour glass, the everlasting plunge that emptied one of heart and bowels, like the drop of an elevator from the top floor of a skyscraper.

Certainly, after that moment of revelation, he had felt a little more tired than usual for the rest of the day; the light had flagged in his mind as it sometimes did in his lamps. At Chrissy Torrance's, where he had lunched, they had accused him of being silent, his hostess had said that he looked pale; but he had retorted with a joke, and thrown himself into the talk with a feverish loquacity. It was the only thing to do; for he could not tell all these people at the lunch table that very morning he had arrived at the turn in the path from which mountains look as transient as flowers – and that one after another they would all arrive there too.

He leaned his head back and closed his eyes, but not in sleep. He did not feel sleepy, but keyed up and alert. In the next room he heard Filmore reluctantly, protestingly, laying out his evening clothes. . . . He had no fear about the dinner tonight; a quiet intimate little affair at an old friend's house. Just two or three congenial men, and Elfmann, the pianist (who would probably play), and that lovely Elfrida Flight. The fact that people asked him to dine to meet Elfrida Flight seemed to prove pretty conclusively that he was still in the running! He chuckled softly at Filmore's pessimism, and thought: 'Well, after all, I suppose no man seems young to his valet. . . . Time to dress very soon,' he thought; and luxuriously postponed getting up out of his chair. . . .

• III •

'SHE's worse than usual tonight,' said the day nurse, laying down the evening paper as her colleague joined her. 'Absolutely determined to have her jewels out.'

The night nurse, fresh from a long sleep and an afternoon at the movies with a gentleman friend, threw down her fancy bag, tossed off her hat and rumpled up her hair before old Mrs. Jaspar's tall toilet mirror. 'Oh, I'll settle that – don't you worry,' she said brightly.

'Don't you fret her, though, Miss Cress,' said the other, getting wearily out of her chair. 'We're very well off here, take it as a whole, and I don't want her pressure rushed up for nothing.'

Miss Cress, still looking at herself in the glass, smiled reassuringly at Miss Dunn's pale reflection behind her. She and Miss Dunn got on very well together, and knew on which side their bread was buttered. But at the end of the day Miss Dunn was always fagged out and fearing the worst. The patient wasn't as hard to handle as all that. Just let her ring for her old maid, old Lavinia, and say: 'My sapphire velvet tonight, with the diamond stars' – and Lavinia would know exactly how to manage her.

Miss Dunn had put on her hat and coat, and crammed her knitting, and the newspaper, into her bag, which, unlike Miss Cress's, was capacious and shabby; but she still loitered undecided on the threshold. 'I could stay with you till ten as easy as not. . . .' She looked almost reluctantly about the big high-studded dressing room (everything in the house was high-studded), with its rich dusky carpet and curtains, and its monumental dressing table draped with lace and laden with gold-backed brushes and combs, gold-stoppered toilet bottles, and all the charming paraphernalia of beauty at her glass. Old Lavinia even renewed every morning the roses and carnations in the slim crystal vases between the powder boxes and the nail polishers. Since the family had shut down the hothouses at the uninhabited country place on the Hudson, Miss Cress suspected that old Lavinia bought these flowers out of her own pocket.

'Cold out tonight?' queried Miss Dunn from the door.

'Fierce . . . reg'lar blizzard at the corners. Say, shall I lend you my fur scarf?' Miss Cress, pleased with the memory of her afternoon (they'd be engaged soon, she thought), and with the drowsy prospect of an evening in a deep armchair near the warm gleam of the dressing-room fire, was disposed to kindliness toward that poor thin Dunn girl, who supported her mother, and her brother's idiot twins. And she wanted Miss Dunn to notice her new fur.

'My! Isn't it too lovely? No, not for worlds, thank you. . . .' Her hand on the doorknob, Miss Dunn repeated: 'Don't you cross her now,' and was gone.

Lavinia's bell rang furiously, twice; then the door between the dressing room and Mrs. Jaspar's bedroom opened, and Mrs. Jaspar herself emerged.

'Lavinia!' she called, in a high irritated voice; then, seeing the nurse, who had slipped into her print dress and starched cap, she added in a lower tone: 'Oh, Miss Lemoine, good evening.' Her first nurse, it appeared, had been called Miss Lemoine; and she gave the same name to all the others, quite unaware that there had been any changes in the staff.

'I heard talking, and carriages driving up. Have people begun to arrive?' she asked nervously. 'Where is Lavinia? I still have my jewels to put on.'

She stood before the nurse, the same petrifying apparition which always, at this hour, struck Miss Cress to silence. Mrs. Jaspar was tall; she had been broad; and her bones remained impressive though the flesh had withered on them. Lavinia had encased her, as usual, in her low-necked purple velvet dress, nipped in at the waist in the old-fashioned way, expanding in voluminous folds about the hips and flowing in a long train over the darker velvet of the carpet. Mrs. Jaspar's swollen feet could no longer be pushed into the high-heeled satin slippers which went with the dress; but her skirts were so long and spreading that, by taking short steps, she managed (so Lavinia daily assured her) entirely to conceal the broad round tips of her black orthopedic shoes.

'Your jewels, Mrs. Jaspar? Why, you've got them on,' said Miss Cress brightly.

Mrs. Jaspar turned her porphyry-tinted face to Miss Cress, and looked at her with a glassy incredulous gaze. Her eyes, Miss Cress thought, were the worst. . . . She lifted one old hand, veined and knobbed as a raised map, to her elaborate purple-black wig, groped among the puffs and curls and undulations (queer, Miss Cress thought, that it never occurred to her to look into the glass), and after an interval affirmed: 'You must be mistaken, my dear. Don't you think you ought to have your eyes examined?'

The door opened again, and a very old woman, so old as to make Mrs. Jaspar appear almost young, hobbled in with sidelong steps. 'Excuse me, madam. I was downstairs when the bell rang.'

Lavinia had probably always been small and slight; now, beside her towering mistress, she looked a mere feather, a straw. Everything about her had dried, contracted, been volatilized into nothingness, except her watchful gray eyes, in which intelligence and comprehension burned like two fixed stars. 'Do excuse me, madam,' she repeated.

Mrs. Jaspar looked at her despairingly. 'I hear carriages driving up. And Miss Lemoine says I have my jewels on; and I know I haven't.'

'With that lovely necklace!' Miss Cress ejaculated.

Mrs. Jaspar's twisted hand rose again, this time to her denuded shoulders, which were as stark and barren as the rock from which the hand might have been broken. She felt and felt, and tears rose in her eyes. . . .

'Why do you lie to me?' she burst out passionately.

Lavinia softly intervened. 'Miss Lemoine meant how lovely you'll be when you get the necklace on, madam.'

'Diamonds, diamonds,' said Mrs. Jaspar with an awful smile.

'Of course, madam.'

Mrs. Jaspar sat down at the dressing table, and Lavinia, with eager random hands, began to adjust the *point de Venise* about her mistress' shoulders, and to repair the havoc wrought in the purple-black wig by its wearer's gropings for her tiara.

'Now you do look lovely, madam,' she sighed.

Mrs. Jaspar was on her feet again, stiff but incredibly active. ('Like a cat she is,' Miss Cress used to relate.) 'I do hear carriages – or is it an automobile? The Magraws, I know, have one of those new-fangled automobiles. And now I hear the front door opening. Quick, Lavinia! My fan, my gloves, my handkerchief . . . how often have I got to tell you? I used to have a *perfect* maid – '

Lavinia's eyes brimmed. 'That was me, madam,' she said, bending to straighten out the folds of the long purple-velvet train. ('To watch the two of 'em,' Miss Cress used to tell a circle of appreciative friends, 'is a lot better than any circus.')

Mrs. Jaspar paid no attention. She twitched the train out of Lavinia's vacillating hold, swept to the door, and then paused there as if stopped by a jerk of her constricted muscles. 'Oh, but my diamonds – you cruel woman, you! You're letting me down without my diamonds!' Her ruined face puckered up in a grimace like a new-born baby's, and she began to sob despairingly. 'Everybody . . . every . . . body's . . . against me . . .' she wept in her powerless misery.

Lavinia helped herself to her feet and tottered across the floor. It was almost more than she could bear to see her mistress in distress. 'Madam, madam – if you'll just wait till they're got out of the safe,' she entreated.

The woman she saw before her, the woman she was entreating and consoling, was not the old petrified Mrs. Jaspar with porphyry face and wig awry whom Miss Cress stood watching with a smile, but a young proud creature, commanding and splendid in her Paris gown of amber *moiré*, who, years ago, had burst into just such furious sobs because, as she was sweeping down to receive her guests, the doctor had told her that little Grace, with whom she had been playing all the afternoon, had a diphtheritic throat, and no one must be allowed to enter. 'Everybody's against me, everybody . . .' she sobbed in her fury; and the young Lavinia, stricken by such Olympian anger, had stood speechless, longing to comfort her, and secretly indignant with little Grace and the doctor. . . .

'If you'll just wait, madam, while I go down and ask Munson to open the safe. There's no one come yet, I do assure you. . . .'

Munson was the old butler, the only person who knew the combination of the safe in Mrs. Jaspar's bedroom. Lavinia had once known it too, but now she was no longer able to remember it. The worst of it was that she feared lest Munson, who had been spending the day in the Bronx, might not have returned. Munson was growing old too, and he did sometimes forget about these dinner parties of Mrs. Jaspar's, and then the stupid footman, George, had to announce the names; and you couldn't be sure that Mrs. Jaspar wouldn't notice Munson's absence, and be excited and angry. These dinner party nights were killing old Lavinia, and she did so want to keep alive; she wanted to live long enough to wait on Mrs. Jaspar to the last.

She disappeared, and Miss Cress poked up the fire, and persuaded Mrs. Jaspar to sit down in an armchair and 'tell her who was coming.' It always amused Mrs. Jaspar to say over the long list of her guests' names, and generally she remembered them fairly well, for they were always the same – the last people, Lavinia and Munson said, who had dined at the house, on the very night before her stroke. With recovered complacency she began, counting over one after another on her ring-laden fingers: 'The Italian Ambassador, the Bishop, Mr. and Mrs. Torrington Bligh, Mr. and Mrs. Fred Amesworth, Mr. and Mrs. Mitchell Magraw, Mr. and Mrs. Torrington Bligh. . . .' ('You've said them before,' Miss Cress interpolated, getting out her fancy knitting – a necktie for her friend – and beginning to count the stitches.) And Mrs. Jaspar, distressed and bewildered by the interruption, had to repeat over and over: 'Torrington Bligh, Torrington Bligh,' till the connection was re-established, and she went on again swimmingly with 'Mr. and Mrs. Fred Amesworth, Mr. and Mrs. Mitchell Magraw, Miss Laura Ladew, Mr. Harold Ladew, Mr. and Mrs. Benjamin Bronx, Mr. and Mrs. Torrington Bl – no, I mean, Mr. Anson Warley. Yes, Mr. Anson Warley; that's it,' she ended complacently.

Miss Cress smiled and interrupted her counting. 'No, that's *not* it.'

'What do you mean, my dear – not it?'

'Mr. Anson Warley. He's not coming.'

Mrs. Jaspar's jaw fell, and she stared at the nurse's coldly smiling face. 'Not coming?'

'No. He's not coming. He's not on the list.' (That old list! As if Miss Cress didn't know it by heart! Everybody in the house did, except the booby, George, who heard it reeled off every other night by Munson, and who was always stumbling over the names, and having to refer to the written paper.)

'Not on the list?' Mrs. Jaspar gasped.

Miss Cress shook her pretty head.

Signs of uneasiness gathered on Mrs. Jaspar's face and her lip began to tremble. It always amused Miss Cress to give her these little jolts, though she knew Miss Dunn and the doctors didn't approve of her doing so. She knew also that it was against her own interests, and she did try to bear in mind Miss Dunn's oft-repeated admonition about not sending up the patient's blood pressure; but when she was in high spirits, as she was tonight (they would certainly be engaged), it was irresistible to get a rise out of the old lady. And she thought it funny, this new figure unexpectedly appearing among those time-worn guests. ('I wonder what the rest of 'em 'll say to him,' she giggled inwardly.)

'No; he's not on the list.' Mrs. Jaspar, after pondering deeply, announced the fact with an air of recovered composure.

'That's what I told you,' snapped Miss Cress.

'He's not on the list; but he promised me to come. I saw him yesterday,' continued Mrs. Jaspar, mysteriously.

'You *saw* him – where?'

She considered. 'Last night, at the Fred Amesworths' dance.'

'Ah,' said Miss Cress, with a little shiver; for she knew that Mrs. Amesworth was dead, and she was the intimate friend of the trained nurse who was keeping alive, by dint of *piqûres* and high frequency, the inarticulate and inanimate Mr. Amesworth. 'It's funny,' she remarked to Mrs. Jaspar, 'that you'd never invited Mr. Warley before.'

'No, I hadn't; not for a long time. I believe he felt I'd neglected him; for he came up to me last night, and said he was so sorry he hadn't been able to call. It seems he's been ill, poor fellow. Not as young as he was! So of course I invited him. He was very much gratified.'

Mrs. Jaspar smiled at the remembrance of her little triumph; but Miss Cress's attention had wandered, as it always did when the patient became docile and reasonable. She thought: 'Where's old Lavinia? I bet she can't find Munson.' And she got up and crossed the floor to look into Mrs. Jaspar's bedroom, where the safe was.

There an astonishing sight met her. Munson, as she had expected, was nowhere visible; but Lavinia, on her knees before the safe, was in the act of opening it herself, her twitching hand slowly moving about the mysterious dial.

'Why, I thought you'd forgotten the combination!' Miss Cress exclaimed.

Lavinia turned a startled face over her shoulder. 'So I had, Miss. But I've managed to remember it, thank God. I *had* to, you see, because Munson's forgot to come home.'

'Oh,' said the nurse incredulously ('Old fox,' she thought, 'I wonder why she's always pretended she'd forgotten it.') For Miss Cress did not know that the age of miracles is not yet past.

Joyous, trembling, her cheeks wet with grateful tears, the little old woman was on her feet again, clutching to her breast the diamond stars, the necklace of solitaires, the tiara, the earrings. One by one she spread them out on the velvet-lined tray in which they always used to be carried from the safe to the dressing room; then, with rambling fingers, she managed to lock the safe again, and put the keys in the drawer where they belonged, while Miss Cress continued to stare at her in amazement. 'I don't believe the old witch is as shaky as she makes out,' was her reflection as Lavinia passed her, bearing the jewels to the dressing room where Mrs. Jaspar, lost in pleasant memories, was still computing: 'The Italian Ambassador, the Bishop, the Torrington Blighs, the Mitchell Magraws, the Fred Amesworths. . . .'

Mrs. Jaspar was allowed to go down to the drawing room alone on dinner party evenings because it would have mortified her too much to receive her guests with a maid or a nurse at her elbow; but Miss Cress and Lavinia always leaned over the stair rail to watch her descent, and make sure it was accomplished in safety.

'She do look lovely yet, when all her diamonds is on,' Lavinia sighed, her purblind eyes bedewed with memories, as the bedizened wig and purple velvet disappeared at the last bend of the stairs. Miss

Cress, with a shrug, turned back to the fire and picked up her knitting, while Lavinia set about the slow ritual of tidying up her mistress' room. From below they heard the sound of George's stentorian monologue: 'Mr. and Mrs. Torrington Bligh, Mr. and Mrs. Mitchell Magraw . . . Mr. Ladew, Miss Laura Ladew. . . .'

• IV •

ANSON WARLEY, who had always prided himself on his equable temper, was conscious of being on edge that evening. But it was an irritability which did not frighten him (in spite of what those doctors always said about the importance of keeping calm) because he knew it was due merely to the unusual lucidity of his mind. He was in fact feeling uncommonly well, his brain clear and all his perceptions so alert that he could positively hear the thoughts passing through his manservant's mind on the other side of the door, as Filmore grudgingly laid out the evening clothes.

Smiling at the man's obstinacy, he thought: 'I shall have to tell them tonight that Filmore thinks I'm no longer fit to go into society.' It was always pleasant to hear the incredulous laugh with which his younger friends received any allusion to his supposed senility. 'What, *you?* Well, that's a good one!' And he thought it was, himself.

And then, the moment he was in his bedroom, dressing, the sight of Filmore made him lose his temper again. 'No; *not* those studs, confound it. The black onyx ones – haven't I told you a hundred times? Lost them, I suppose? Sent them to the wash again in a soiled shirt? That it?' He laughed nervously, and sitting down before his dressing table began to brush back his hair in short angry strokes.

'Above all,' he shouted out suddenly, 'don't stand there staring at me as if you were watching to see exactly at what minute to telephone for the undertaker!'

'The under – ? Oh, sir!' gasped Filmore.

'The – the – damn it, are you *deaf* too? Who said undertaker? I said *taxi;* can't you hear what I say?'

'You want me to call a taxi, sir?'

'No; I don't. I've already told you so. I'm going to walk.' Warley straightened his tie, rose and held out his arms toward his dress coat.

'It's bitter cold, sir; better let me call a taxi all the same.'

Warley gave a short laugh. 'Out with it, now! What you'd really like to suggest is that I should telephone to say I can't dine out. You'd scramble me some eggs instead, eh?'

'I wish you would stay in, sir. There's eggs in the house.'

'My overcoat,' snapped Warley.

'Or else let me call a taxi; now do, sir.'

Warley slipped his arms into his overcoat, tapped his chest to see if his watch (the thin evening watch) and his notecase were in their proper pockets, turned back to put a dash of lavender on his handkerchief, and walked with stiff quick steps toward the front door of his flat.

Filmore, abashed, preceded him to ring for the lift; and then, as it quivered upward through the long shaft, said again: 'It's a bitter cold night, sir; and you've had a good deal of exercise today.'

Warley leveled a contemptuous glance at him. 'Dare say that's why I'm feeling so fit,' he retorted as he entered the lift.

It *was* bitter cold; the icy air hit him in the chest when he stepped out of the overheated building, and he halted on the doorstep and took a long breath. 'Filmore's missed his vocation; ought to be nurse to a paralytic,' he thought. 'He'd love to have to wheel me about in a chair.'

After the first shock of the biting air he began to find it exhilarating, and walked along at a good pace, dragging one leg ever so little after the other. (The *masseur* had promised him that he'd soon be rid of that stiffness.) Yes – decidedly a fellow like himself ought to have a younger valet; a more cheerful one, anyhow. He felt like a young'un himself this evening; as he turned into Fifth Avenue he rather wished he could meet someone he knew, some man who'd say afterward at his club: 'Warley? Why, I saw him sprinting up Fifth Avenue the other night like a two-year-old; that night it was four or five below. . . .' He needed a good counter-irritant for Filmore's gloom. 'Always have young people about you,' he thought as he walked along; and at the words his mind turned to Elfrida Flight, next to whom he would soon be sitting in a warm pleasantly lit dining room – *where?*

It came as abruptly as that: the gap in his memory. He pulled up at it as if his advance had been checked by a chasm in the pavement at his feet. Where the dickens was he going to dine? And with whom was he going to dine? God! But things didn't happen in that way; a sound strong man didn't suddenly have to stop in the middle of the street and ask himself where he was going to dine. . . .

'Perfect in mind, body and understanding.' The old legal phrase bobbed up inconsequently into his thoughts. Less than two minutes ago he had answered in every particular to that description; what was he now? He put his hand to his forehead, which was bursting; then he lifted his hat and let the cold air blow for a while over his overheated temples. It was queer, how hot he'd got, walking. Fact was, he'd been sprinting along at a damned good pace. In future he must try to remember not to hurry. . . . Hang it – one more thing to remember! . . . Well, but what was all the fuss about? Of course, as people got older their memories were subject to these momentary lapses; he'd noticed if often enough among his contemporaries. And, brisk and alert though he still was, it wouldn't do to imagine himself totally exempt from human ills. . . .

Where was it he was dining? Why, somewhere farther up Fifth Avenue; he was perfectly sure of that. With that lovely . . . that lovely. . . . No; better not make any effort for the moment. Just keep calm, and stroll slowly along. When he came to the right street corner of course he'd spot it; and then everything would be perfectly clear again. He walked on, more deliberately, trying to empty his mind of all thoughts. 'Above all,' he said to himself, 'don't worry.'

He tried to beguile his nervousness by thinking of amusing things. 'Decline the boredom – ' He thought he might get off that joke tonight. 'Mrs. Jaspar requests the pleasure – Mr. Warley declines the boredom.' Not so bad, really; and he had an idea he'd never told it to the people . . . what in hell *was* their name?..the people he was on his way to dine with . . . *Mrs. Jaspar requests the pleasure*. Poor old Mrs. Jaspar; again it occurred to him that he hadn't always been very civil to her in old times. When everybody's running after a fellow it's pardonable now and then to chuck a boring dinner at the last minute; but all the same, as one grew older one understood better how an unintentional slight of that sort might cause offense, cause even pain. And he hated to cause people pain. . . . He thought perhaps he'd better call on Mrs. Jaspar some afternoon. She'd be surprised! Or ring her up, poor old girl, and propose himself, just informally, for dinner. One dull evening wouldn't kill him – and how pleased she'd be! Yes – he thought decidedly . . . when he got to be her age, he could imagine how much he'd like it if somebody still in the running should ring him up unexpectedly and say –

He stopped, and looked up, slowly, wonderingly, at the wide illuminated façade of the house he was approaching. Queer coincidence – it was the Jaspar house. And all lit up; for a dinner evidently. And that was queerer yet; almost uncanny; for here he was, in front of the door, as the clock struck a quarter past eight; and of course – he remembered it quite clearly now – it was just here, it was with Mrs. Jaspar, that he was dining . . . Those little lapses of memory never lasted more than a second or two. How right he'd been not to let himself worry. He pressed his hand on the doorbell.

'God,' he thought, as the double doors swung open, 'but it's good to get in out of the cold.'

• V •

IN that hushed sonorous house the sound of the doorbell was as loud to the two women upstairs as if it had been rung in the next room.

Miss Cress raised her head in surprise, and Lavinia dropped Mrs. Jaspar's other false set (the more comfortable one) with a clatter on the marble washstand. She stumbled across the dressing room, and hastened out to the landing. With Munson absent, there was no knowing how George might muddle things. . . .

Miss Cress joined her. 'Who is it?' she whispered excitedly. Below, they heard the sound of a hat and a walking stick being laid down on the big marble-topped table in the hall, and then George's stentorian drone: 'Mr. Anson Warley.'

'It is – it *is!* I can see him – a gentleman in evening clothes,' Miss Cress whispered, hanging over the stair rail.

'Good gracious – mercy me! And Munson not here! Oh, whatever, whatever shall we do?' Lavinia was trembling so violently that she had to clutch the stair rail to prevent herself from falling. Miss Cress thought, with her cold lucidity: 'She's a good deal sicker than the old woman.'

'What shall we do, Miss Cress? That fool of a George – he's showing him in! Who could have thought it?' Miss Cress knew the images that were whirling through Lavinia's brain: the vision of Mrs. Jaspar's having another stroke at the sight of this mysterious intruder, of Mr. Anson Warley's seeing her there, in her impotence and her abasement, of the family's being summoned, and rushing in to exclaim, to question, to be horrified and furious – and all because poor old Munson's memory was going, like his mistress', like Lavinia's, and because he had forgotten that it was one of the *dinner nights.* Oh, misery! . . . The tears were running down Lavinia's cheeks, and Miss Cress knew she was thinking: 'If the daughters send him off – and they will – where's he going to, old and deaf as he is, and all his people dead? Oh, if only he can hold on till she dies, and get his pension. . . .'

Lavinia recovered herself with one of her supreme efforts. 'Miss Cress, we must go down at once, at once! Something dreadful's going to happen. . . .' She began to totter toward the little velvet-lined lift in the corner of the landing.

Miss Cress took pity on her. 'Come along,' she said. 'But nothing dreadful's going to happen. You'll see.'

'Oh, thank you, Miss Cress. But the shock – the awful shock to her – of seeing that strange gentleman walk in.'

'Not a bit of it.' Miss Cress laughed as she stepped into the lift. 'He's not a stranger. She's expecting him.'

'Expecting him? Expecting Mr. Warley?'

'Sure she is. She told me so just now. She says she invited him yesterday.'

'But, Miss Cress, what are you thinking of? Invite him – how? When you know she can't write nor telephone?'

'Well, she says she saw him; she saw him last night at a dance.'

'Oh, God,' murmured Lavinia, covering her eyes with her hands.

'At a dance at the Fred Amesworths' – that's what she said,' Miss

Cress pursued, feeling the same little shiver run down her back as when Mrs. Jaspar had made the statement to her.

'The Amesworths – oh, not the Amesworths?' Lavinia echoed, shivering too. She dropped her hands from her face, and followed Miss Cress out of the lift. Her expression had become less anguished, and the nurse wondered why. In reality, she was thinking, in a sort of dreary beatitude: 'But if she's suddenly got as much worse as this, she'll go before me, after all, my poor lady, and I'll be able to see to it that she's properly laid out and dressed, and nobody but Lavinia's hands'll touch her.'

'You'll see – if she was expecting him, as she says, it won't give her a shock, anyhow. Only, how did *he* know?' Miss Cress whispered, with an acuter renewal of her shiver. She followed Lavinia with muffled steps down the passage to the pantry, and from there the two women stole into the dining room, and placed themselves noiselessly at its farther end, behind the tall Coromandel screen through the cracks of which they could peep into the empty room.

The long table was set, as Mrs. Jaspar always insisted that it should be on these occasions; but old Munson not having returned, the gold plate (which his mistress also insisted on) had not been got out, and all down the table, as Lavinia saw with horror, George had laid the coarse blue-and-white plates from the servants' hall. The electric wall lights were on, and the candles lit in the branching Sèvres candelabra – so much at least had been done. But the flowers in the great central dish of Rose Dubarry porcelain, and in the smaller dishes which accompanied it – the flowers, oh shame, had been forgotten! They were no longer real flowers; the family had long since suppressed that expense; and no wonder, for Mrs. Jaspar always insisted on orchids. But Grace, the youngest daughter, who was the kindest, had hit on the clever device of arranging three beautiful clusters of artificial orchids and maidenhair, which had only to be lifted from their shelf in the pantry and set in the dishes – only, of course, that imbecile footman had forgotten, or had not known where to find them. And, oh, horror, realizing his oversight too late, no doubt, to appeal to Lavinia, he had taken some old newspapers and bunched them up into something that he probably thought resembled a bouquet, and crammed one into each of the priceless Rose Dubarry dishes.

Lavinia clutched at Miss Cress's arm. 'Oh, look – look what he's done; I shall die of the shame of it. . . . Oh, Miss, hadn't we better slip around to the drawing room and try to coax my poor lady upstairs again, afore she ever notices?'

Miss Cress, peering through the crack of the screen, could hardly suppress a giggle. For at that moment the double doors of the dining room were thrown open, and George, shuffling about in a baggy livery inherited from a long-departed predecessor of more commanding build, bawled out in his loud singsong: 'Dinner is served, madam.'

'Oh, it's too late,' moaned Lavinia. Miss Cress signed to her to keep silent, and the two watchers glued their eyes to their respective cracks of the screen.

What they saw, far off down the vista of empty drawing rooms, and after an interval during which (as Lavinia knew) the imaginary guests were supposed to file in and take their seats, was the entrance, at the end of the ghostly cortège, of a very old woman, still tall and towering, on the arm of a man somewhat smaller than herself, with a fixed smile on a darkly pink face, and a slim erect figure clad in perfect evening clothes, who advanced with short measured steps, profiting (Miss Cress noticed) by the support of the arm he was supposed to sustain. 'Well – I never!' was the nurse's inward comment.

The couple continued to advance, with rigid smiles and eyes staring straight ahead. Neither turned to the other, neither spoke. All their attention was concentrated on the immense, the almost unachievable effort of reaching that point, halfway down the long dinner table, opposite the big Dubarry dish, where George was drawing back a gilt armchair for Mrs. Jaspar. At last they reached it, and Mrs. Jaspar seated herself, and waved a stony hand to Mr. Warley. 'On my right.' He gave a little bow, like the bend of a jointed doll, and with infinite precaution let himself down into his chair. Beads of perspiration were standing on his forehead, and Miss Cress saw him draw out his handkerchief and wipe them stealthily away. He then turned his head somewhat stiffly toward his hostess.

'Beautiful flowers,' he said, with great precision and perfect gravity, waving his hand toward the bunched-up newspaper in the bowl of Sèvres.

Mrs. Jaspar received the tribute with complacency. 'So glad . . . orchids . . . from High Lawn . . . every morning,' she simpered.

'Marvelous,' Mr. Warley completed.

'I always say to the Bishop . . . ,' Mrs. Jaspar continued.

'Ha – of course,' Mr. Warley warmly assented.

'Not that I don't think . . .'

'Ha – rather!'

George had reappeared from the pantry with a blue crockery dish of mashed potatoes. This he handed in turn to one after another of the imaginary guests, and finally presented to Mrs. Jaspar and her right-hand neighbor.

They both helped themselves cautiously, and Mrs. Jaspar addressed an arch smile to Mr. Warley. ''Nother month – no more oysters.'

'Ha – no more!'

George, with a bottle of Apollinaris wrapped in a napkin, was saying to each guest in turn: 'Perrier-Jouet, '95.' (He had picked that up, thought Miss Cress, from hearing old Munson repeat it so often.)

'Hang it – well, then just a sip,' murmured Mr. Warley.

'Old times,' bantered Mrs. Jaspar; and the two turned to each other and bowed their heads and touched glasses.

'I often tell Mrs. Amesworth . . . ,' Mrs. Jaspar continued, bending to an imaginary presence across the table.

'Ha – *ha!*' Mr. Warley approved.

George reappeared and slowly encircled the table with a dish of spinach. After the spinach the Apollinaris also went the rounds again, announced successively as Château Lafite, '74, and 'the old Newbold Madeira.' Each time that George approached his glass, Mr. Warley made a feint of lifting a defensive hand, and then smiled and yielded. 'Might as well – hanged for a sheep . . . ,' he remarked gaily; and Mrs. Jaspar giggled.

Finally a dish of Malaga grapes and apples was handed. Mrs. Jaspar, now growing perceptibly languid, and nodding with more and more effort at Mr. Warley's pleasantries, transferred a bunch of grapes to her plate, but nibbled only two or three. 'Tired,' she said suddenly, in a whimper like a child's; and she rose, lifting herself up by the arms of her chair, and leaning over to catch the eye of an invisible lady, presumably Mrs. Amesworth, seated opposite to her. Mr. Warley was on his feet too, supporting himself by resting one hand on the table in a jaunty attitude. Mrs. Jaspar waved to him to be reseated. 'Join us – after cigars,' she smilingly ordained; and with a great and concentrated effort he bowed to her as she passed toward the double doors which George was throwing open. Slowly, majestically, the purple-velvet train disappeared down the long enfilade of illuminated rooms, and the last door closed behind her.

'Well, I do believe she's enjoyed it!' chuckled Miss Cress, taking Lavinia by the arm to help her back to the hall. Lavinia, for weeping, could not answer.

• VI •

ANSON WARLEY found himself in the hall again, getting into his fur-lined overcoat. He remembered suddenly thinking that the rooms had been intensely overheated, and that all the other guests had talked very loud and laughed inordinately. 'Very good talk though, I must say,' he had to acknowledge.

In the hall, as he got his arms into his coat (rather a job, too, after that Perrier-Jouet) he remembered saying to somebody (perhaps it was to the old butler): 'Slipping off early – going on; 'nother engagement,' and thinking to himself the while that when he got out into the fresh air again he would certainly remember where the other engagement was. He smiled a little while the servant, who seemed a clumsy fellow, fumbled with the fastening of the door. 'And Filmore, who thought I wasn't even well enough to dine out! Damned ass! What would he say if he knew I was going on?'

The door opened, and with an immense sense of exhilaration Mr. Warley issued forth from the house and drew in a first deep breath of night air. He heard the door closed and bolted behind him, and continued to stand motionless on the step, expanding his chest, and drinking in the icy draught.

"Spose it's about the last house where they give you Perrier-Jouet, '95,' he thought; and then: 'Never heard better talk either. . . .'

He smiled again with satisfaction at the memory of the wine and the wit. Then he took a step forward, to where a moment before the pavement had been – and where now there was nothing.

Atrophy

NORA FRENWAY settled down furtively in her corner of the Pullman and, as the express plunged out of the Grand Central Station, wondered at herself for being where she was. The porter came along. 'Ticket?' 'Westover.' She had instinctively lowered her voice and glanced about her. But neither the porter nor her nearest neighbors – fortunately none of them known to her – seemed in the least surprised or interested by the statement that she was traveling to Westover.

Yet what an earth-shaking announcement it was! Not that she cared, now; not that anything mattered except the one overwhelming fact which had convulsed her life, hurled her out of her easy velvet-lined rut, and flung her thus naked to the public scrutiny. . . . Cautiously, again, she glanced about her to make doubly sure that there was no one, absolutely no one, in that Pullman whom she knew by sight.

Her life had been so carefully guarded, so inwardly conventional in a world where all the outer conventions were tottering, that no one had ever known she had a lover. No one – of that she was absolutely sure. All the circumstances of the case had made it necessary that she should conceal her real life – her only real life – from everyone about her; from her half-invalid irascible husband, his prying envious sisters, and the terrible monumental old chieftainess, her mother-in-law, before whom all the family quailed and humbugged and fibbed and fawned.

What nonsense to pretend that nowadays, even in big cities, in the world's greatest social centers, the severe old-fashioned standards had given place to tolerance, laxity and ease! You took up the morning paper, and you read of girl bandits, movie star divorces, 'hold-ups' at balls, murder and suicide and elopement, and a general welter of disjointed disconnected impulses and appetites; then you turned your eyes onto your own daily life, and found yourself as cribbed and cabined, as beset by vigilant family eyes, observant friends, all sorts of embodied standards, as any white muslin novel heroine of the sixties!

In a different way, of course. To the casual eye Mrs. Frenway herself might have seemed as free as any of the young married women of her group. Poker playing, smoking, cocktail drinking, dancing, painting,

187

short skirts, bobbed hair and the rest – when had these been denied to her? If by any outward sign she had differed too markedly from her kind – lengthened her skirts, refused to play for money, let her hair grow, or ceased to make up – her husband would have been the first to notice it, and to say: 'Are you ill? What's the matter? How queer you look! What's the sense of making yourself conspicuous?' For he and his kind had adopted all the old inhibitions and sanctions, blindly transferring them to a new ritual, as the receptive Romans did when strange gods were brought into their temples. . . .

The train had escaped from the ugly fringes of the city, and the soft spring landscape was gliding past her: glimpses of green lawns, budding hedges, pretty irregular roofs, and miles and miles of alluring tarred roads slipping away into mystery. How often she had dreamed of dashing off down an unknown road with Christopher!

Not that she was a woman to be awed by the conventions. She knew she wasn't. She had always taken their measure, smiled at them – and conformed. On account of poor George Frenway, to begin with. Her husband, in a sense, was a man to be pitied; his weak health, his bad temper, his unsatisfied vanity, all made him a rather forlornly comic figure. But it was chiefly on account of the two children that she had always resisted the temptation to do anything reckless. The least self-betrayal would have been the end of everything. Too many eyes were watching her, and her husband's family was so strong, so united – when there was anybody for them to hate – and at all times so influential, that she would have been defeated at every point, and her husband would have kept the children.

At the mere thought she felt herself on the brink of an abyss. 'The children are my religion,' she had once said to herself; and she had no other.

Yet here she was on her way to Westover. . . . Oh, what did it matter now? That was the worst of it – it was too late for anything between her and Christopher to matter! She was sure he was dying. The way in which his cousin, Gladys Brincker, had blurted it out the day before at Kate Salmer's dance: 'You didn't know – poor Kit? Thought you and he were such pals! Yes; awfully bad, I'm afraid. Return of the old trouble! I know there've been two consultations – they had Knowlton down. They say there's not much hope; and nobody but that forlorn frightened Jane mounting guard. . . .'

Poor Christopher! His sister Jane Aldis, Nora suspected, forlorn and frightened as she was, had played in his life a part nearly as dominant as Frenway and the children in Nora's. Loyally, Christopher always pretended that she didn't; talked of her indulgently as 'poor Jenny.' But didn't she, Nora, always think of her husband as 'poor George'? Jane Aldis, of course, was much less self-assertive, less demanding, than George Frenway; but perhaps for that very reason she would appeal all the more to a man's compassion. And somehow, under her unobtrusive air, Nora had – on the rare occasions when they met – imagined that Miss Aldis was watching and drawing her inferences. But then Nora always felt, where Christopher was concerned, as if her breast were a pane of glass through which her trembling palpitating heart could be seen as plainly as holy viscera in a reliquary. Her sober after-thought was that Jane Aldis was just a dowdy self-effacing old maid whose life was filled to the brim by looking after the Westover place for her brother, and seeing that the fires were lit and the rooms full of flowers when he brought down his friends for a weekend.

Ah, how often he had said to Nora: 'If I could have you to myself for a weekend at Westover' – quite as if it were the easiest thing imaginable, as far as his arrangements were concerned! And they had even pretended to discuss how it could be done. But somehow she fancied he said it because he knew that the plan, for her, was about as feasible as a weekend in the moon. And in reality her only visits to Westover had been made in the company of her husband, and that of other friends, two or three times, at the beginning. . . . For after that she wouldn't. It was three years now since she had been there.

Gladys Brincker, in speaking of Christopher's illness, had looked at Nora queerly, as though suspecting something. But no – what nonsense! No one had ever suspected Nora Frenway. Didn't she know what her friends said of her? 'Nora? No more temperament than a lamp post. Always buried in her books. . . . Never very attractive to men, in spite of her looks.' Hadn't she said that of other women, who perhaps, in secret, like herself . . . ?

The train was slowing down as it approached a station. She sat up with a jerk and looked at her wrist watch. It was half-past two, the station was Ockham; the next would be Westover. In less than an hour she would be under his roof, Jane Aldis would be receiving her in that low paneled room full of books, and she would be saying – what would she be saying?

She had gone over their conversation so often that she knew not only her own part in it but Miss Aldis's by heart. The first moments would of course be painful, difficult; but then a great wave of emotion, breaking down the barriers between the two anxious women, would fling them together. She wouldn't have to say much, to explain; Miss Aldis would just take her by the hand and lead her upstairs to the room.

That room! She shut her eyes, and remembered other rooms where she and he had been together in their joy and their strength. . . . No, not that; she must not think of that now. For the man she had met in those other rooms was dying; the man she was going to was some one so different from that other man that it was like a profanation to associate their images. . . . And yet the man she was going to was her own Christopher, the one who had lived in her soul: and how his soul

must be needing hers, now that it hung alone on the dark brink! As if
anything else mattered at such a moment! She neither thought nor cared
what Jane Aldis might say or suspect; she wouldn't have cared if the
Pullman had been full of prying acquaintances, of if George and all
George's family had got in at that last station.

She wouldn't have cared a fig for any of them. Yet at the same
moment she remembered having felt glad that her old governess, whom
she used to go and see twice a year, lived at Ockham – so that if George
did begin to ask questions, she could always say: 'Yes, I went to see
poor old Fräulein; she's absolutely crippled now. I shall have to give
her a Bath chair. Could you get me a catalogue of prices?' There wasn't
a precaution she hadn't thought of – and now she was ready to scatter
them all to the winds. . . .

Westover – *Junction!*

She started up and pushed her way out of the train. All the people
seemed to be obstructing her, putting bags and suitcases in her way.
And the express stopped for only two minutes. Suppose she should be
carried on to Albany?

Westover Junction was a growing place, and she was fairly sure
there would be a taxi at the station. There was one – she just managed
to get to it ahead of a traveling man with a sample case and a new
straw hat. As she opened the door a smell of damp hay and bad tobacco
greeted her. She sprang in and gasped: 'To Oakfield. You know? Mr.
Aldis's place near Westover.'

• II •

IT began exactly as she had expected. A surprised parlormaid – why
surprised? – showed her into the low paneled room that was so full of
his presence, his books, his pipes, his terrier dozing on the shabby rug.
The parlormaid said she would go and see if Miss Aldis could come
down. Nora wanted to ask if she were with her brother – and how he
was. But she found herself unable to speak the words. She was afraid
her voice might tremble. And why should she question the parlormaid,
when in a moment, she hoped, she was to see Miss Aldis?

The woman moved away with a hushed step – the step which
denotes illness in the house. She did not immediately return, and the
interval of waiting in that room, so strange yet so intimately known,
was a new torture to Nora. It was unlike anything she had imagined.
The writing table with his scattered pens and letters was more than she
could bear. His dog looked at her amicably from the hearth, but made
no advances; and though she longed to stroke him, to let her hand rest
where Christopher's had rested, she dared not for fear he should bark
and disturb the peculiar hush of that dumb watchful house. She stood

in the window and looked out at the budding shrubs and the bulbs pushing up through the swollen earth.

'This way, please.'

Her heart gave a plunge. Was the woman actually taking her upstairs to his room? Her eyes filled, she felt herself swept forward on a great wave of passion and anguish. . . . But she was only being led across the hall into a stiff lifeless drawing room – the kind that bachelors get an upholsterer to do for them, and then turn their backs on forever. The chairs and sofas looked at her with an undisguised hostility, and then resumed the moping expression common to furniture in unfrequented rooms. Even the spring sun slanting in through the windows on the pale marquetry of a useless table seemed to bring no heat or light with it.

The rush of emotion subsided, leaving in Nora a sense of emptiness and apprehension. Supposing Jane Aldis should look at her with the cold eyes of this resentful room? She began to wish she had been friendlier and more cordial to Jane Aldis in the past. In her intense desire to conceal from everyone the tie between herself and Christopher she had avoided all show of interest in his family; and perhaps, as she now saw, excited curiosity by her very affectation of indifference.

No doubt it would have been more politic to establish an intimacy with Jane Aldis; and today, how much easier and more natural her position would have been! Instead of groping about – as she was again doing – for an explanation of her visit, she could have said: 'My dear, I came to see if there was anything in the world I could do to help you.'

She heard a hesitating step in the hall – a hushed step like the parlormaid's – and saw Miss Aldis pause near the half-open door. How old she had grown since their last meeting! Her hair, untidily pinned up, was gray and lanky. Her eyelids, always reddish, were swollen and heavy, her face sallow with anxiety and fatigue. It was odd to have feared so defenseless an adversary. Nora, for an instant, had the impression that Miss Aldis had wavered in the hall to catch a glimpse of her, take the measure of the situation. But perhaps she had only stopped to push back a strand of hair as she passed in front of a mirror.

'Mrs. Frenway – how good of you!' She spoke in a cool detached voice, as if her real self were elsewhere and she were simply an automaton wound up to repeat the familiar forms of hospitality. 'Do sit down,' she said.

She pushed forward one of the sulky armchairs, and Nora seated herself stiffly, her handbag clutched on her knee, in the self-conscious attitude of a country caller.

'I came – '

'So good of you,' Miss Aldis repeated. 'I had no idea you were in this part of the world. Not the slightest.'

Was it a lead she was giving? Or did she know everything, and wish to extend to her visitor the decent shelter of a pretext? Or was she really so stupid –

'You're staying with the Brinckers, I suppose. Or the Northrups? I remember the last time you came to lunch here you motored over with Mr. Frenway from Northrups'. That must have been two years ago, wasn't it?' She put the question with an almost sprightly show of interest.

'No – three years,' said Nora, mechanically.

'Was it? As long ago as that? Yes – you're right. That was the year we moved the big fern-leaved beech. I remember Mr. Frenway was interested in tree moving, and I took him out to show him where the tree had come from. He *is* interested in tree moving, isn't he?'

'Oh, yes; very much.'

'We had those wonderful experts down to do it. "Tree doctors," they call themselves. They have special appliances, you know. The tree is growing better than it did before they moved it. But I suppose you've done a great deal of transplanting on Long Island.'

'Yes. My husband does a good deal of transplanting.'

'So you've come over from the Northrups'? I didn't even know they were down at Maybrook yet. I see so few people.'

'No; not from the Northrups'.'

'Oh – the Brinckers'? Hal Brincker was here yesterday, but he didn't tell me you were staying there.'

Nora hesitated. 'No. The fact is, I have an old governess who lives at Ockham. I go to see her sometimes. And so I came on to Westover –' She paused, and Miss Aldis interrogated brightly: 'Yes?' as if prompting her in a lesson she was repeating.

'Because I saw Gladys Brincker the other day, and she told me that your brother was ill.'

'Oh.' Miss Aldis gave the syllable its full weight, and set a full stop after it. Her eyebrows went up, as if in a faint surprise. The silent room seemed to close in on the two speakers, listening. A resuscitated fly buzzed against the sunny windowpane. 'Yes; he's ill,' she conceded at length.

'I'm so sorry; I . . . he has been . . . such a friend of ours . . . so long. . . .'

'Yes; I've often heard him speak of you and Mr. Frenway.' Another full stop sealed this announcement. ('No, she knows nothing,' Nora thought.) 'I remember his telling me that he thought a great deal of Mr. Frenway's advice about moving trees. But then you see our soil is so different from yours. I suppose Mr. Frenway has had your soil analyzed?'

'Yes; I think he has.'

'Christopher's always been a great gardener.'

'I hope he's not – not very ill? Gladys seemed to be afraid – '

'Illness is always something to be afraid of, isn't it?'

'But you're not – I mean, not anxious . . . not seriously?'

'It's so kind of you to ask. The doctors seem to think there's no particular change since yesterday.'

'And yesterday?'

'Well, yesterday they seemed to think there might be.'

'A change, you mean?'

'Well, yes.'

'A change – I hope for the better?'

'They said they weren't sure; they couldn't say.'

The fly's buzzing had become so insistent in the still room that it seemed to be going on inside of Nora's head, and in the confusion of sound she found it more and more difficult to regain a lead in the conversation. And the minutes were slipping by, and upstairs the man she loved was lying. It was absurd and lamentable to make a pretense of keeping up this twaddle. She would cut through it, no matter how.

'I suppose you've had – a consultation?'

'Oh, yes; Dr. Knowlton's been down twice.'

'And what does he – '

'Well; he seems to agree with the others.'

There was another pause, and then Miss Aldis glanced out of the window. 'Why, who's that driving up?' she inquired. 'Oh, it's your taxi, I suppose, coming up the drive.'

'Yes. I got out at the gate.' She dared not add: 'For fear the noise might disturb him.'

'I hope you had no difficulty in finding a taxi at the Junction?'

'Oh, no; I had no difficulty.'

'I think it was so kind of you to come – not even knowing whether you'd find a carriage to bring you out all this way. And I know how busy you are. There's always so much going on in town, isn't there, even at this time of year?'

'Yes; I suppose so. But your brother – '

'Oh, of course my brother won't be up to any sort of gaiety; not for a long time.'

'A long time; no. But you do hope – '

'I think everybody about a sick bed ought to hope, don't you?'

'Yes; but I mean – '

Nora stood up suddenly, her brain whirling. Was it possible that she and that woman had sat thus facing each other for half an hour, piling up this conversational rubbish, while upstairs, out of sight, the truth, the meaning of their two lives hung on the frail thread of one man's intermittent pulse? She could not imagine why she felt so powerless and baffled. What had a woman who was young and handsome and beloved to fear from a dowdy and insignificant old maid? Why, the antagonism that these very graces and superiorities would create in the other's breast, especially if she knew they were all spent in charming the being on whom her life depended. Weak in herself, but powerful from her circumstances, she stood at bay on the ruins of all that Nora had ever loved. 'How she must hate me – and I never thought of it,' mused Nora, who had imagined that she had thought of everything where her relation to her lover was concerned. Well, it was too late now to remedy her omission; but at least she must assert herself, must say something to save the precious minutes that remained and break through the stifling web of platitudes which her enemy's tremulous hand was weaving around her.

'Miss Aldis – I must tell you – I came to see – '

'How he was? So very friendly of you. He would appreciate it, I know. Christopher is so devoted to his friends.'

'But you'll – you'll tell him that I – '

'Of course. That you came on purpose to ask about him. As soon as he's a little bit stronger.'

'But I mean – now?'

'Tell him now that you called to inquire? How good of you to think of that too! Perhaps tomorrow morning, if he's feeling a little bit brighter – '

Nora felt her lips drying as if a hot wind had parched them. They would hardly move. 'But now – now – today.' Her voice sank to a whisper as she added: 'Isn't he conscious?'

'Oh, yes; he's conscious; he's perfectly conscious.' Miss Aldis emphasized this with another of her long pauses. 'He shall certainly be told that you called.' Suddenly she too got up from her seat and moved toward the window. 'I must seem dreadfully inhospitable, not even offering you a cup of tea. But the fact is, perhaps I ought to tell you – if you're thinking of getting back to Ockham this afternoon there's only one train that stops at the Junction after three o'clock.' She pulled out an old-fashioned enameled watch with a wreath of roses about the dial, and turned almost apologetically to Mrs. Frenway. 'You ought to be at the station by four o'clock at the latest; and with one of those old Junction taxis. . . . I'm so sorry; I know I must appear to be driving you away.' A wan smile drew up her pale lips.

Nora knew just how long the drive from Westover Junction had taken, and understood that she was being delicately dismissed. Dismissed from life – from hope – even from the dear anguish of filling her eyes for the last time with the face which was the one face in the world to her! ('But then she does know everything,' she thought.)

'I mustn't make you miss your train, you know.'

'Miss Aldis, is he – has he seen anyone?' Nora hazarded in a painful whisper.

'Seen anyone? Well, there've been all the doctors – five of them!

And then the nurses. Oh, but you mean friends, of course. Naturally.'
She seemed to reflect. 'Hal Brincker, yes; he saw our cousin Hal
yesterday – but not for very long.'

Hal Brincker! Nora knew what Christopher thought of his Brincker
cousins – blighting bores, one and all of them, he always said. And in
the extremity of his illness the one person privileged to see him had
been – Hal Brincker! Nora's eyes filled; she had to turn them away for
a moment from Miss Aldis's timid inexorable face.

'But today?' she finally brought out.

'No. Today he hasn't seen anyone; not yet.' The two women stood
and looked at each other; then Miss Aldis glanced uncertainly about
the room. 'But couldn't I – Yes, I ought at least to have asked you if
you won't have a cup of tea. So stupid of me! There might still be
time. I never take tea myself.' Once more she referred anxiously to her
watch. 'The water is sure to be boiling, because the nurse's tea is just
being taken up. If you'll excuse me a moment I'll go and see.'

'Oh, no; no!' Nora drew in a quick sob. 'How can you? . . . I mean,
I don't want any. . . .'

Miss Aldis looked relieved. 'Then I shall be quite sure that you
won't reach the station too late.' She waited again, and then held out
a long stony hand. 'So kind – I shall never forget your kindness.
Coming all this way, when you might so easily have telephoned from
town. Do please tell Mr. Frenway how I appreciated it. You will
remember to tell him, won't you? He sent me such an interesting
collection of pamphlets about tree moving. I should like him to know
how much I feel his kindness in letting you come.' She paused again,
and pulled in her lips so that they became a narrow thread, a mere line
drawn across her face by a ruler. 'But, no; I won't trouble you; I'll
write to thank him myself.' Her hand ran out to an electric bell on the
nearest table. It shrilled through the silence, and the parlormaid
appeared with a stagelike promptness.

'The taxi, please? Mrs. Frenway's taxi.'

The room became silent again. Nora thought: 'Yes; she knows
everything.' Miss Aldis peeped for the third time at her watch, and
then uttered a slight unmeaning laugh. The bluebottle banged against
the window, and once more it seemed to Nora that its sonorities were
reverberating inside her head. They were deafeningly mingled there
with the explosion of the taxi's reluctant starting-up and its convulsed
halt at the front door. The driver sounded his horn as if to summon
her. 'He's afraid too that you'll be late!' Miss Aldis smiled.

The smooth slippery floor of the hall seemed to Nora to extend
away in front of her for miles. At its far end she saw a little tunnel of
light, a miniature maid, a toy taxi. Somehow she managed to travel
the distance that separated her from them, though her bones ached with
weariness, and at every step she seemed to be lifting a leaden weight.

The taxi was close to her now, its door was open, she was getting in. The same smell of damp hay and bad tobacco greeted her. She saw her hostess standing on the threshold. 'To the Junction, driver – back to the Junction,' she heard Miss Aldis say. The taxi began to roll toward the gate. As it moved away Nora heard Miss Aldis calling: 'I'll be sure to write and thank Mr. Frenway.'

Pomegranate Seed

CHARLOTTE ASHBY paused on her doorstep. Dark had descended on the brilliancy of the March afternoon, and the grinding rasping street life of the city was at its highest. She turned her back on it, standing for a moment in the old-fashioned, marble-flagged vestibule before she inserted her key in the lock. The sash curtains drawn across the panes of the inner door softened the light within to a warm blur through which no details showed. It was the hour when, in the first months of her marriage to Kenneth Ashby, she had most liked to return to that quiet house in a street long since deserted by business and fashion. The contrast between the soulless roar of New York, its devouring blaze of lights, the oppression of its congested traffic, congested houses, lives, minds and this veiled sanctuary she called home, always stirred her profoundly. In the very heart of the hurricane she had found her tiny islet – or thought she had. And now, in the last months, everything was changed, and she always wavered on the doorstep and had to force herself to enter.

While she stood there she called up the scene within: the hall hung with old prints, the ladder-like stairs, and on the left her husband's long shabby library, full of books and pipes and worn armchairs inviting to meditation. How she had loved that room! Then, upstairs, her own drawing room, in which, since the death of Kenneth's first wife, neither furniture nor hangings had been changed, because there had never been money enough, but which Charlotte had made her own by moving furniture about and adding more books, another lamp, a table for the new reviews. Even on the occasion of her only visit to the first Mrs. Ashby – a distant, self-centered woman, whom she had known very slightly – she had looked about her with an innocent envy, feeling it to be exactly the drawing room she would have liked for herself; and now for more than a year it had been hers to deal with as she chose – the room to which she hastened back at dusk on winter days, where she sat reading by the fire, or answering notes at the pleasant roomy desk, or going over her step-children's copybooks, till she heard her husband's step.

Sometimes friends dropped in; sometimes – oftener – she was alone; and she liked that best, since it was another way of being with Kenneth, thinking over what he had said when they parted in the morning, imagining what he would say when he sprang up the stairs, found her by herself and caught her to him.

Now, instead of this, she thought of one thing only – the letter she might or might not find on the hall table. Until she had made sure whether or not it was there, her mind had no room for anything else. The letter was always the same – a square gravish envelope with 'Kenneth Ashby, Esquire,' written on it in bold but faint characters. From the first it had struck Charlotte as peculiar that anyone who wrote such a firm hand should trace the letters so lightly; the address was always written as though there were not enough ink in the pen, or the writer's wrist were too weak to bear upon it. Another curious thing was that, in spite of its masculine curves, the writing was so visibly feminine. Some hands are sexless, some masculine, at first glance; the writing on the gray envelope, for all its strength and assurance, was without doubt a woman's. The envelope never bore anything but the recipient's name; no stamp, no address. The letter was presumably delivered by hand – but by whose? No doubt it was slipped into the letter box, whence the parlormaid, when she closed the shutters and lit the lights, probably extracted it. At any rate, it was always in the evening, after dark, that Charlotte saw it lying there. She thought of the letter in the singular, as 'it,' because, though there had been several since her marriage – seven, to be exact – they were so alike in appearance that they had become merged in one another in her mind, become one letter, become 'it.'

The first had come the day after their return from their honeymoon – a journey prolonged to the West Indies, from which they had returned to New York after an absence of more than two months. Re-entering the house with her husband, late on that first evening – they had dined at his mother's – she had seen, alone on the hall table, the gray envelope. Her eye fell on it before Kenneth's, and her first thought was: 'Why, I've seen that writing before'; but where she could not recall. The memory was just definite enough for her to identify the script whenever it looked up at her faintly from the same pale envelope; but on that first day she would have thought no more of the letter if, when her husband's glance lit on it, she had not chanced to be looking at him. It all happened in a flash – his seeing the letter, putting out his hand for it, raising it to his shortsighted eyes to decipher the faint writing, and then abruptly withdrawing the arm he had slipped through Charlotte's, and moving away to the hanging light, his back turned to her. She had waited – waited for a sound, an exclamation; waited for him to open the letter; but he had slipped it into his pocket without a word and followed her into the library. And there they had sat down by the fire and lit their cigarettes, and he had remained silent, his head thrown back broodingly against the armchair, his eyes fixed on the hearth, and presently had passed his hand over his forehead and said: 'Wasn't it unusually hot at my mother's tonight? I've got a splitting head. Mind if I take myself off to bed?'

That was the first time. Since then Charlotte had never been present when he had received the letter. It usually came before he got home from his office, and she had to go upstairs and leave it lying there. But even if she had not seen it, she would have known it had come by the change in his face when he joined her – which, on those evenings, he seldom did before they met for dinner. Evidently, whatever the letter contained, he wanted to be by himself to deal with it; and when he reappeared he looked years older, looked emptied of life and courage, and hardly conscious of her presence. Sometimes he was silent for the rest of the evening; and if he spoke, it was usually to hint some criticism of her household arrangements, suggest some change in the domestic administration, to ask, a little nervously, if she didn't think Joyce's nursery governess was rather young and flighty, or if she herself always saw to it that Peter – whose throat was delicate – was properly wrapped up when he went to school. At such times Charlotte would remember the friendly warnings she had received when she became engaged to Kenneth Ashby: 'Marrying a heartbroken widower! Isn't that rather risky? You know Elsie Ashby absolutely dominated him'; and how she had jokingly replied: 'He may be glad of a little liberty for a change.' And in this respect she had been right. She had needed no one to tell her, during the first months, that her husband was perfectly happy with her. When they came back from their protracted honeymoon the same friends said: 'What have you done to Kenneth? He looks twenty years younger'; and this time she answered with careless joy: 'I suppose I've got him out of his groove.'

But what she noticed after the gray letters began to come was not so much his nervous tentative faultfinding – which always seemed to be uttered against his will – as the look in his eyes when he joined her after receiving one of the letters. The look was not unloving, not even indifferent; it was the look of a man who had been so far away from ordinary events that when he returns to familiar things they seem strange. She minded that more than the faultfinding.

Though she had been sure from the first that the handwriting on the gray envelope was a woman's, it was long before she associated the mysterious letters with any sentimental secret. She was too sure of her husband's love, too confident of filling his life, for such an idea to occur to her. It seemed far more likely that the letters – which certainly did not appear to cause him any sentimental pleasure – were addressed to the busy lawyer than to the private person. Probably they were from some tiresome client – women, he had often told her, were nearly always tiresome as clients – who did not want her letters opened by his secretary and therefore had them carried to his house. Yes; but in that case the unknown female must be unusually troublesome, judging from the effect her letters produced. Then again, though his professional discretion was exemplary, it was odd that he had never uttered an impatient comment, never remarked to Charlotte, in a moment of expansion, that there was a nuisance of a woman who kept badgering him about a case that had gone against her. He had made more than one semiconfidence of the kind – of course without giving names or details; but concerning this mysterious correspondent his lips were sealed.

There was another possibility: what is euphemistically called an 'old entanglement.' Charlotte Ashby was a sophisticated woman. She had few illusions about the intricacies of the human heart; she knew that there were often old entanglements. But when she had married Kenneth Ashby, her friends, instead of hinting at such a possibility, had said: 'You've got your work cut out for you. Marrying a Don Juan is a sinecure to it. Kenneth's never looked at another woman since he first saw Elsie Corder. During all the years of their marriage he was more like an unhappy lover than a comfortably contented husband. He'll never let you move an armchair or change the place of a lamp; and whatever you venture to do, he'll mentally compare with what Elsie would have done in your place.'

Except for an occasional nervous mistrust as to her ability to manage the children – a mistrust gradually dispelled by her good humor and the children's obvious fondness for her – none of these forebodings had come true. The desolate widower, of whom his nearest friends said that only his absorbing professional interests had kept him from suicide after his first wife's death, had fallen in love, two years later, with Charlotte Gorse, and after an impetuous wooing had married her and carried her off on a tropical honeymoon. And ever since he had been as tender and lover-like as during those first radiant weeks. Before asking her to marry him he had spoken to her frankly of his great love for his first wife and his despair after her sudden death; but even then he had assumed no stricken attitude, or implied that life offered no possibility of renewal. He had been perfectly simple and natural, and had confessed to Charlotte that from the beginning he had hoped the future held new gifts for him. And when, after their marriage, they returned to the house where his twelve years with his first wife had been spent, he had told Charlotte at once that he was sorry he couldn't afford to do the place over for her, but that he knew every woman had her own views about furniture and all sorts of household arrangements a man would never notice, and had begged her to make any changes she saw fit without bothering to consult him. As a result, she made as few as possible; but his way of beginning their new life in the old setting was so frank and unembarrassed that it put her immediately at her ease, and she was almost sorry to find that the portrait of Elsie Ashby, which used to hang over the desk in his library, had been transferred in their absence to the children's nursery. Knowing herself to be the indirect cause of this banishment, she spoke of it to her husband; but he answered: 'Oh, I thought they ought to grow up with her looking down on them.' The answer moved Charlotte, and satisfied her; and as time went by she had to confess that she felt more at home in her house, more at ease and in confidence with her husband, since that long coldly beautiful face on the library wall no longer followed her with guarded eyes. It was as if Kenneth's love had penetrated to the secret she hardly acknowledged to her own heart – her passionate need to feel herself the sovereign even of his past.

With all this stored-up happiness to sustain her, it was curious that she had lately found herself yielding to a nervous apprehension. But there the apprehension was; and on this particular afternoon – perhaps because she was more tired than usual, or because of the trouble of finding a new cook or, for some other ridiculously trivial reason, moral or physical – she found herself unable to react against the feeling. Latchkey in hand, she looked back down the silent street to the whirl and illumination of the great thoroughfare beyond, and up at the sky already aflare with the city's nocturnal life. 'Outside there,' she thought, 'skyscrapers, advertisements, telephones, wireless, airplanes, movies, motors, and all the rest of the twentieth century; and on the other side of the door something I can't explain, can't relate to them. Something as old as the world, as mysterious as life. . . . Nonsense! What am I worrying about. There hasn't been a letter for three months now – not since the day we came back from the country after Christmas. . . . Queer that they always seem to come after our holidays! . . . Why should I imagine there's going to be one tonight!'

No reason why, but that was the worst of it – one of the worst! – that there were days when she would stand there cold and shivering with the premonition of something inexplicable, intolerable, to be faced on the other side of the curtained panes; and when she opened the door and went in, there would be nothing; and on other days when she felt the same premonitory chill, it was justified by the sight of the gray envelope. So that ever since the last had come she had taken to feeling cold and premonitory every evening, because she never opened the door without thinking the letter might be there.

Well, she'd had enough of it: that was certain. She couldn't go on like that. If her husband turned white and had a headache on the days when the letter came, he seemed to recover afterwards; but she couldn't. With her the strain had become chronic, and the reason was not far to seek. Her husband knew from whom the letter came and what was in it; he was prepared beforehand for whatever he had to deal with, and master of the situation, however bad; whereas she was shut out on the dark with her conjectures.

'I can't stand it! I can't stand it another day!' she exclaimed aloud, as she put her key in the lock. She turned the key and went in; and there, on the table, lay the letter.

• II •

SHE was almost glad of the sight. It seemed to justify everything, to put a seal of definiteness on the whole blurred business. A letter for her husband; a letter from a woman – no doubt another vulgar case of 'old entanglement.' What a fool she had been ever to doubt it, to rack her brains for less obvious explanations! She took up the envelope with a steady contemptuous hand, looked closely at the faint letters, held it against the light and just discerned the outline of the folded sheet within. She knew that now she would have no peace till she found out what was written on that sheet.

Her husband had not come in; he seldom got back from his office before half-past six or seven, and it was not yet six. She would have time to take the letter up to the drawing room, hold it over the tea kettle which at that hour always simmered by the fire in expectation of her return, solve the mystery and replace the letter where she had found it. No one would be the wiser, and her gnawing uncertainty would be over. The alternative, of course, was to question her husband; but to do that seemed even more difficult. She weighed the letter between thumb and finger, looked at it again under the light, started up the stairs with the envelope – and came down again and laid it on the table.

'No, I evidently can't,' she said, disappointed.

What should she do, then. She couldn't go up alone to that warm welcoming room, pour out her tea, look over her correspondence, glance at a book or review – not with that letter lying below and the knowledge that in a little while her husband would come in, open it and turn into the library alone, as he always did on the days when the gray envelope came.

Suddenly she decided. She would wait in the library and see for herself; see what happened between him and the letter when they thought themselves unobserved. She wondered the idea had never occurred to her before. By leaving the door ajar, and sitting in the corner behind it, she could watch him unseen. . . . Well, then, she would watch him! She drew a chair into the corner, sat down, her eyes on the crack, and waited.

As far as she could remember, it was the first time she had ever tried to surprise another person's secret, but she was conscious of no compunction. She simply felt as if she were fighting her way through a stifling fog that she must at all cost get out of.

At length she heard Kenneth's latchkey and jumped up. The impulse to rush out and meet him had nearly made her forget why she was there: but she remembered in time and sat down again. From her post she covered the whole range of his movements – saw him enter the hall, draw the key from the door and take off his hat and overcoat. Then he turned to throw his gloves on the hall table, and at that moment he saw the envelope. The light was full on his face, and what Charlotte first noted there was a look of surprise. Evidently he had not expected the letter – had not thought of the possibility of its being there that day. But though he had not expected it, now that he saw it he knew well enough what it contained. He did not open it immediately, but stood motionless, the color slowly ebbing from his face. Apparently he could not make up his mind to touch it; but at length he put out his hand, opened the envelope, and moved with it to the light. In doing so he turned his back on Charlotte, and she saw only his bent head and slightly stooping shoulders. Apparently all the writing was on one page, for he did not turn the sheet but continued to stare at it for so long that he must have reread it a dozen times – or so it seemed to the woman breathlessly watching him. At length she saw him move; he raised the letter still closer to his eyes, as though he had not fully deciphered it. Then he lowered his head, and she saw his lips touch the sheet.

'Kenneth!' she exclaimed, and went on out into the hall.

The letter clutched in his hand, her husband turned and looked at her. 'Where were you?' he said, in a low bewildered voice, like a man waked out of his sleep.

'In the library, waiting for you.' She tried to steady her voice: 'What's the matter! What's in that letter? You look ghastly.'

Her agitation seemed to calm him, and he instantly put the envelope into his pocket with a slight laugh. 'Ghastly? I'm sorry. I've had a hard day in the office – one or two complicated cases. I look dog-tired, I suppose.'

'You didn't look tired when you came in. It was only when you opened that letter – '

He had followed her into the library, and they stood gazing at each other. Charlotte noticed how quickly he had regained his self-control; his profession had trained him to rapid mastery of face and voice. She saw at once that she would be at a disadvantage in any attempt to surprise his secret, but at the same moment she lost all desire to maneuver, to trick him into betraying anything he wanted to conceal. Her wish was still to penetrate the mystery, but only that she might help him to bear the burden it implied. 'Even if it *is* another woman,' she thought.

'Kenneth,' she said, her heart beating excitedly, 'I waited here on purpose to see you come in. I wanted to watch you while you opened that letter.'

His face, which had paled, turned to dark red; then it paled again. 'That letter? Why especially that letter?'

'Because I've noticed that whenever one of those letters comes it seems to have such a strange effect on you.'

A line of anger she had never seen before came out between his eyes, and she said to herself: 'The upper part of his face is too narrow; this is the first time I ever noticed it.'

She heard him continue, in the cool and faintly ironic tone of the prosecuting lawyer making a point: 'Ah, so you're in the habit of watching people open their letters when they don't know you're there?'

'Not in the habit. I never did such a thing before. But I had to find out what she writes to you, at regular intervals, in those gray envelopes.'

He weighed this for a moment; then: 'The intervals have not been regular,' he said.

'Oh, I dare say you've kept a better account of the dates than I have,' she retorted, her magnanimity vanishing at his tone. 'All I know is that every time that woman writes to you – '

'Why do you assume it's a woman?'

'It's a woman's writing. Do you deny it?'

He smiled. 'No, I don't deny it. I asked only because the writing is generally supposed to look more like a man's.'

Charlotte passed this over impatiently. 'And this woman – what does she write to you about?'

Again he seemed to consider a moment. 'About business.'

'Legal business?'

'In a way, yes. Business in general.'

'You look after her affairs for her?'

'Yes.'

'You've looked after them for a long time?'

'Yes. A very long time.'

'Kenneth, dearest, won't you tell me who she is?'

'No, I can't.' He paused, and brought out, as if with a certain hesitation: 'Professional secrecy.'

The blood rushed from Charlotte's heart to her temples. 'Don't say that – don't!'

'Why not?'

'Because I saw you kiss the letter.'

The effect of the words was so disconcerting that she instantly repented having spoken them. Her husband, who had submitted to her cross-questioning with a sort of contemptuous composure, as though he were humoring an unreasonable child, turned on her a face of terror and distress. For a minute he seemed unable to speak; then, collecting himself, with an effort, he stammered out: 'The writing is very faint; you must have seen me holding the letter close to my eyes to try to deciper it.'

'No; I saw you kissing it.' He was silent. 'Didn't I see you kissing it?'

He sank back into indifference. 'Perhaps.'

'Kenneth! You stand there and say that – to me?'

'What possible difference can it make to you? The letter is on business, as I told you. Do you suppose I'd lie about it? The writer is a very old friend whom I haven't seen for a long time.'

'Men don't kiss business letters, even from women who are very old friends, unless they have been their lovers, and still regret them.'

He shrugged his shoulders slightly and turned away, as if he considered the discussion at an end and were faintly disgusted at the turn it had taken.

'Kenneth!' Charlotte moved toward him and caught hold of his arm.

He paused with a look of weariness and laid his hand over hers. 'Won't you believe me?' he asked gently.

'How can I? I've watched these letters come to you – for months now they've been coming. Ever since we came back from the West Indies – one of them greeted me the very day we arrived. And after each one of them I see their mysterious effect on you, I see you disturbed, unhappy, as if someone were trying to estrange you from me.'

'No dear; not that. Never!'

She drew back and looked at him with passionate entreaty. 'Well, then, prove it to me, darling. It's so easy!'

He forced a smile. 'It's not easy to prove anything to a woman who's once taken an idea into her head.'

'You've only got to show me the letter.'

His hand slipped from hers and he drew back and shook his head.

'You won't?'

'I can't.'

'Then the woman who wrote it is your mistress.'

'No, dear. No.'

'Not now, perhaps. I suppose she's trying to get you back, and you're struggling, out of pity for me. My poor Kenneth.'

'I swear to you she never was my mistress.'

Charlotte felt the tears rushing to her eyes. 'Ah, that's worse, then – that's hopeless! The prudent ones are the kind that keep their hold on a man. We all know that.' She lifted her hands and hid her face in them.

Her husband remained silent; he offered neither consolation nor denial, and at length, wiping away her tears, she raised her eyes almost timidly to his.

'Kenneth, think! We've been married such a short time. Imagine what you're making me suffer. You say you can't show me this letter. You refuse even to explain it.'

'I've told you the letter is on business. I will swear to that too.'

'A man will swear to anything to screen a woman. If you want me to believe you, at least tell me her name. If you'll do that, I promise you I won't ask to see the letter.'

There was a long interval of suspense, during which she felt her heart beating against her ribs in quick admonitory knocks, as if warning her of the danger she was incurring.

'I can't,' he said at length.

'Not even her name?'

'No.'

'You can't tell me anything more?'

'No.'

Again a pause; this time they seemed both to have reached the end of their arguments and to be helplessly facing each other across a baffling waste of incomprehension.

Charlotte stood breathing rapidly, her hands against her breast. She felt as if she had run a hard race and missed the goal. She had meant to move her husband and had succeeded only in irritating him; and this error of reckoning seemed to change him into a stranger, a mysterious incomprehensible being whom no argument or entreaty of hers could reach. The curious thing was that she was aware in him of no hostility or even impatience, but only of a remoteness, an inaccessibility, far more difficult to overcome. She felt herself excluded, ignored, blotted out of his life. But after a moment or two, looking at him more calmly, she saw that he was suffering as much as she was. His distant guarded face was drawn with pain; the coming of the gray envelope, though it always cast a shadow, had never marked him as deeply as this discussion with his wife.

Charlotte took heart; perhaps, after all, she had not spent her last shaft. She drew nearer and once more laid her hand on his arm. 'Poor Kenneth! If you knew how sorry I am for you – '

She thought he winced slightly at this expression of sympathy, but he took her hand and pressed it.

'I can think of nothing worse than to be incapable of loving long,' she continued, 'to feel the beauty of a great love and to be too unstable to bear its burden.'

He turned on her a look of wistful reproach. 'Oh, don't say that of me. Unstable!'

She felt herself at last on the right tack, and her voice trembled with excitement as she went on: 'Then what about me and this other woman? Haven't you already forgotten Elsie twice within a year?'

She seldom pronounced his first wife's name; it did not come naturally to her tongue. She flung it out now as if she were flinging some dangerous explosive into the open space between them, and drew back a step, waiting to hear the mine go off.

Her husband did not move; his expression grew sadder, but showed no resentment. 'I have never forgotten Elsie,' he said.

Charlotte could not repress a faint laugh. 'Then, you poor dear, between the three of us – '

'There are not – ' he began; and then broke off and put his hand to his forehead.

'Not what?'

'I'm sorry; I don't believe I know what I'm saying. I've got a blinding headache.' He looked wan and furrowed enough for the statement to be true, but she was exasperated by his evasion.

'Ah, yes; the gray envelope headache!'

She saw the surprise in his eyes. 'I'd forgotten how closely I've been watched,' he said coldly. 'If you'll excuse me, I think I'll go up and try an hour in the dark, to see if I can get rid of this neuralgia.'

She wavered; then she said, with desperate resolution: 'I'm sorry your head aches. But before you go I want to say that sooner or later this question must be settled between us. Someone is trying to separate us, and I don't care what it costs me to find out who it is.' She looked him steadily in the eyes. 'If it costs me your love, I don't care! If I can't have your confidence I don't want anything from you.'

He still looked at her wistfully. 'Give me time.'

'Time for what? It's only a word to say.'

'Time to show you that you haven't lost my love or my confidence.'

'Well, I'm waiting.'

He turned toward the door, and then glanced back hesitatingly. 'Oh, do wait, my love,' he said, and went out of the room.

She heard his tired step on the stairs and the closing of his bedroom door above. Then she dropped into a chair and buried her face in her folded arms. Her first movement was one of compunction, she seemed to herself to have been hard, unhuman, unimaginative. 'Think of telling him that I didn't care if my insistence cost me his love! The lying rubbish!' She started up to follow him and unsay the meaningless words. But she was checked by a reflection. He had had his way, after all; he had eluded all attacks on his secret, and now he was shut up alone in his room, reading that other woman's letter.

• III •

SHE was still reflecting on this when the surprised parlormaid came in and found her. No, Charlotte said, she wasn't going to dress for dinner; Mr. Ashby didn't want to dine. He was very tired and had gone up to his room to rest; later she would have something brought on a tray to the drawing room. She mounted the stairs to her bedroom. Her dinner dress was lying on the bed, and at the sight the quiet routine of her daily life took hold of her and she began to feel as if the strange talk she had just had with her husband must have taken place in another world, between two beings who were not Charlotte Gorse and Kenneth Ashby, but phantoms projected by her fevered imagination. She recalled the year since her marriage – her husband's constant devotion; his persistent, almost too insistent tenderness; the feeling he had given her at times of being too eagerly dependent on her, too searchingly close to her; as if there were not air enough between her soul and his. It seemed preposterous, as she recalled all this, that a few moments ago she should have been accusing him of an intrigue with another woman! But, then, what –

Again she was moved by the impulse to go up to him, beg his pardon and try to laugh away the misunderstanding. But she was restrained by the fear of forcing herself upon his privacy. He was troubled and unhappy, oppressed by some grief or fear; and he had shown her that he wanted to fight out his battle alone. It would be wiser, as well as more generous, to respect his wish. Only, how strange, how unbearable, to be there, in the next room to his, and feel herself at the other end of the world! In her nervous agitation she almost regretted not having had the courage to open the letter and put it back on the hall table before he came in. At least she would have known what his secret was, and the bogy might have been laid. For she was beginning now to think of the mystery as something conscious, malevolent: a secret persecution before which he quailed, yet from which he could not free himself. Once or twice in his evasive eyes she thought she had detected a desire for help, an impulse of confession, instantly restrained and suppressed. It was as if he felt she could have helped him if she had known, and yet had been unable to tell her!

There flashed through her mind the idea of going to his mother. She was very fond of old Mrs. Ashby, a firm-fleshed clear-eyed old lady, with an astringent bluntness of speech which responded to the forthright and simple in Charlotte's own nature. There had been a tacit bond between them ever since the day when Mrs. Ashby Senior, coming to lunch for the first time with her new daughter-in-law, had been received by Charlotte downstairs in the library, and glancing up at the empty wall above her son's desk, had remarked laconically: 'Elsie gone, eh?' adding, at Charlotte's murmured explanation: 'Nonsense. Don't have her back. Two's company.' Charlotte, at this reading of her thoughts, could hardly refrain from exchanging a smile of complicity with her mother-in-law; and it seemed to her now that Mrs. Ashby's almost uncanny directness might pierce to the core of this new mystery. But here again she hesitated, for the idea almost suggested a betrayal. What right had she to call in anyone, even so close a relation, to surprise a secret which her husband was trying to keep from her? 'Perhaps, by and by, he'll talk to his mother of his own accord,' she thought, and then ended: 'But what does it matter? He and I must settle it between us.'

She was still brooding over the problem when there was a knock on the door and her husband came in. He was dressed for dinner and seemed surprised to see her sitting there, with her evening dress lying unheeded on the bed.

'Aren't you coming down?'

'I thought you were not well and had gone to bed,' she faltered.

He forced a smile. 'I'm not particularly well, but we'd better go down.' His face, though still drawn, looked calmer than when he had fled upstairs an hour earlier.

'There it is; he knows what's in the letter and has fought his battle out again, whatever it is,' she reflected, 'while I'm still in darkness.' She rang and gave a hurried order that dinner should be served as soon as possible – just a short meal, whatever could be got ready quickly, as both she and Mr. Ashby were rather tired and not very hungry.

Dinner was announced, and they sat down to it. At first neither seemed able to find a word to say; then Ashby began to make conversation with an assumption of ease that was more oppressive than his silence. 'How tired he is! How terribly overtired!' Charlotte said to herself, pursuing her own thoughts while he rambled on about municipal politics, aviation, an exhibition of modern French painting, the health of an old aunt and the installing of the automatic telephone. 'Good heavens, how tired he is!'

When they dined alone they usually went into the library after dinner, and Charlotte curled herself up on the divan with her knitting while he settled down in his armchair under the lamp and lit a pipe. But this evening, by tacit agreement, they avoided the room in which their strange talk had taken place, and went up to Charlotte's drawing room.

They sat down near the fire, and Charlotte said: 'Your pipe?' after he had put down his hardly tasted coffee.

He shook his head. 'No, not tonight.'

'You must go to bed early; you look terribly tired. I'm sure they overwork you at the office.'

'I suppose we all overwork at times.'

She rose and stood before him with sudden resolution. 'Well, I'm not going to have you use up your strength slaving in that way. It's absurd. I can see you're ill.' She bent over him and laid her hand on his forehead. 'My poor old Kenneth. Prepare to be taken away soon on a long holiday.'

He looked up at her, startled. 'A holiday?'

'Certainly. Didn't you know I was going to carry you off at Easter? We're going to start in a fortnight on a month's voyage to somewhere or other. On any one of the big cruising steamers.' She paused and bent closer, touching his forehead with her lips. 'I'm tired, too, Kenneth.'

He seemed to pay no heed to her last words, but sat, his hands on his knees, his head drawn back a little from her caress, and looked up at her with a stare of apprehension. 'Again? My dear, we can't; I can't possibly go away.'

'I don't know why you say "again," Kenneth; we haven't taken a real holiday this year.'

'At Christmas we spend a week with the children in the country.'

'Yes, but this time I mean away from the children, from servants, from the house. From everything that's familiar and fatiguing. Your mother will love to have Joyce and Peter with her.'

He frowned and slowly shook his head. 'No, dear; I can't leave them with my mother.'

'Why, Kenneth, how absurd! She adores them. You didn't hesitate to leave them with her for over two months when we went to the West Indies.'

He drew a deep breath and stood up uneasily. 'That was different.'

'Different? Why?'

'I mean, at that time I didn't realize – ' He broke off as if to choose his words and then went on: 'My mother adores the children, as you say. But she isn't always very judicious. Grandmothers always spoil children. And sometimes she talks before them without thinking.' He turned to his wife with an almost pitiful gesture of entreaty. 'Don't ask me to, dear.'

Charlotte mused. It was true that the elder Mrs. Ashby had a fearless tongue, but she was the last woman in the world to say or hint anything before her grandchildren at which the most scrupulous parent could take offense. Charlotte looked at her husband in perplexity.

'I don't understand.'

He continued to turn on her the same troubled and entreating gaze. 'Don't try to,' he muttered.

'Not try to?'

'Not now – not yet.' He put up his hands and pressed them against his temples. 'Can't you see that there's no use in insisting? I can't go away, no matter how much I might want to.'

Charlotte still scrutinized him gravely. 'The question is, *do* you want to?'

He returned her gaze for a moment; then his lips began to tremble, and he said, hardly above his breath. 'I want – anything you want.'

'And yet – '

'Don't ask me. I can't leave – I can't!'

'You mean that you can't go away out of reach of those letters!'

Her husband had been standing before her in an uneasy half-hesitating attitude, now he turned abruptly away and walked once or twice up and down the length of the room, his head bent, his eyes fixed on the carpet.

Charlotte felt her resentfulness rising with her fears. 'It's that,' she persisted. 'Why not admit it? You can't live without them.'

He continued his troubled pacing of the room; then he stopped short, dropped into a chair and covered his face with his hands. From the shaking of his shoulders, Charlotte saw that he was weeping. She had never seen a man cry, except her father after her mother's death, when she was a little girl, and she remembered still how the sight had frightened her. She was frightened now; she felt that her husband was being dragged away from her into some mysterious bondage, and that she must use up her last atom of strength in the struggle for his freedom, and for hers.

'Kenneth – Kenneth!' she pleaded, kneeling down beside him. 'Won't you listen to me? Won't you try to see what I'm suffering? I'm not unreasonable, darling, really not. I don't suppose I should ever have noticed the letters if it hadn't been for their effect on you. It's not my way to pry into other people's affairs; and even if the effect had been different – yes, yes, listen to me – if I'd seen that the letters made you happy, that you were watching eagerly for them, counting the days, between their coming, that you wanted them, that they gave you something I haven't known how to give – why, Kenneth, I don't say I shouldn't have suffered from that, too; but it would have been in a different way, and I should have had the courage to hide what I felt, and the hope that someday you'd come to feel about me as you did about the writer of the letters. But what I can't bear is to see how you dread them, how they make you suffer, and yet how you can't live without them and won't go away lest you should miss one during your absence. Or perhaps,' she added, her voice breaking into a cry of accusation – 'perhaps it's because she's actually forbidden you to leave. Kenneth, you must answer me! Is that the reason? Is it because she's forbidden you that you won't go away with me?'

She continued to kneel at his side, and raising her hands, she drew his gently down. She was ashamed of her persistence, ashamed of uncovering that baffled disordered face, yet resolved that no such scruples should arrest her. His eyes were lowered, the muscles of his face quivered; she was making him suffer even more than she suffered herself. Yet this no longer restrained her.

'Kenneth, is it that? She won't let us go away together?'

Still he did not speak or turn his eyes to her; and a sense of defeat swept over her. After all, she thought, the struggle was a losing one. 'You needn't answer. I see I'm right,' she said.

Suddenly, as she rose, he turned and drew her down again. His hands caught hers and pressed them so tightly that she felt her rings cutting into her flesh. There was something frightened, convulsive in his hold; it was the clutch of a man who felt himself slipping over a precipice. He was staring up at her now as if salvation lay in the face she bent above him. 'Of course we'll go away together. We'll go wherever you want,' he said in a low confused voice; and putting his arm about her, he drew her close and pressed his lips on hers.

• IV •

CHARLOTTE had said to herself: 'I shall sleep tonight,' but instead she sat before her fire into the small hours, listening for any sound that came from her husband's room. But he, at any rate, seemed to be resting after the tumult of the evening. Once or twice she stole to the door and in the faint light that came in from the street through his open window she saw him stretched out in heavy sleep – the sleep of weakness and exhaustion. 'He's ill,' she thought – 'he's undoubtedly ill. And it's not overwork; it's this mysterious persecution.'

She drew a breath of relief. She had fought through the weary fight and the victory was hers – at least for the moment. If only they could have started at once – started for anywhere! She knew it would be useless to ask him to leave before the holidays; and meanwhile the secret influence – as to which she was still so completely in the dark – would continue to work against her, and she would have to renew the struggle day after day till they started on their journey. But after that everything would be different. If once she could get her husband away under other skies, and all to herself, she never doubted her power to release him from the evil spell he was under. Lulled to quiet by the thought, she too slept at last.

When she woke, it was long past her usual hour, and she sat up in bed surprised and vexed at having overslept herself. She always liked to be down to share her husband's breakfast by the library fire; but a glance at the clock made it clear that he must have started long since for his office. To make sure, she jumped out of bed and went into his room, but it was empty. No doubt he had looked in on her before leaving, seen that she still slept, and gone downstairs without disturbing her; and their relations were sufficiently lover-like for her to regret having missed their morning hour.

She rang and asked if Mr. Ashby had already gone. Yes, nearly an hour ago, the maid said. He had given orders that Mrs. Ashby should not be waked and that the children should not come to her till she sent for them. . . . Yes, he had gone up to the nursery himself to give the order. All this sounded usual enough, and Charlotte hardly knew why she asked: 'And did Mr. Ashby leave no other message?'

Yes, the maid said, he did; she was so sorry she'd forgotten. He'd told her, just as he was leaving to say to Mrs. Ashby that he was going to see about their passages, and would she please be ready to sail tomorrow?

Charlotte echoed the woman's 'Tomorrow,' and sat staring at her incredulously. 'Tomorrow – you're sure he said to sail tomorrow?'

'Oh, ever so sure, ma'am. I don't know how I could have forgotten to mention it.'

'Well, it doesn't matter. Draw my bath, please.' Charlotte sprang up, dashed through her dressing, and caught herself singing at her image in the glass as she sat brushing her hair. It made her feel young again to have scored such a victory. The other woman vanished to a speck on the horizon, as this one, who ruled the foreground, smiled back at the reflection of her lips and eyes. He loved her, then – he loved her as passionately as ever. He had divined what she had suffered, had understood that their happiness depended on their getting away at once, and finding each other again after yesterday's desperate groping in the fog. The nature of the influence that had come between them did not much matter to Charlotte now; she had faced the phantom and dispelled it. 'Courage – that's the secret! If only people who are in love weren't always so afraid of risking their happiness by looking it in the eyes.' As she brushed back her light abundant hair it waved electrically above her head, like the palms of victory. Ah, well, some women knew how to manage men, and some didn't – and only the fair – she gaily para-phrased – deserve the brave! Certainly she was looking very pretty.

The morning danced along like a cockleshell on a bright sea – such a sea as they would soon be speeding over. She ordered a particularly good dinner, saw the children off to their classes, had her trunks brought down, consulted with the maid about getting out summer clothes – for of course they would be heading for heat and sunshine – and wondered if she oughtn't to take Kenneth's flannel suits out of camphor. 'But how absurd,' she reflected, 'that I don't yet know where we're going!' She looked at the clock, saw that it was close on noon, and decided to call him up at his office. There was a slight delay; then she heard his secretary's voice saying that Mr. Ashby had looked in for a moment early, and left again almost immediately. . . . Oh, very well; Charlotte would ring up later. How soon was he likely to be back? The secretary answered that she couldn't tell; all they knew in the office was that when he left he had said he was in a hurry because he had to go out of town.

Out of town! Charlotte hung up the receiver and sat blankly gazing into new darkness. Why had he gone out of town? And where had he gone? And of all days, why should he have chosen the eve of their suddenly planned departure? She felt a faint shiver of apprehension. Of course he had gone to see that woman – no doubt to get her permission to leave. He was as completely in bondage as that; and Charlotte had been fatuous enough to see the palms of victory on her forehead. She burst into a laugh and, walking across the room, sat down again before her mirror. What a different face she saw! The smile on her pale lips seemed to mock the rosy vision of the other Charlotte. But gradually her color crept back. After all, she had a right to claim the victory, since her husband was doing what she wanted, not what the other woman exacted of him. It was natural enough, in view of his abrupt decision to leave the next day, that he should have arrangements to make, business matters to wind up; it was not even necessary to suppose that his mysterious trip was a visit to the writer of the letters. He might simply have gone to see a client who lived out of town. Of course they would not tell Charlotte at the office; the secretary had hesitated before imparting even such meager information as the fact of Mr. Ashby's absence. Meanwhile she would go on with her joyful preparation, content to learn later in the day to what particular island of the blest she was to be carried.

The hours wore on, or rather were swept forward on a rush of eager preparations. At last the entrance of the maid who came to draw the curtains roused Charlotte from her labors, and she saw to her surprise that the clock marked five. And she did not yet know where they were going the next day! She rang up her husband's office and was told that Mr. Ashby had not been there since the early morning. She asked for his partner, but the partner could add nothing to her information, for he himself, his suburban train having been behind time, had reached the office after Ashby had come and gone. Charlotte stood perplexed; then she decided to telephone to her mother-in-law. Of course Kenneth, on the eve of a month's absence, must have gone to see his mother. The mere fact that the children – in spite of his vague objections – would certainly have to be left with old Mrs. Ashby, made it obvious that he would have all sorts of matters to decide with her. At another time Charlotte might have felt a little hurt at being excluded from their conference, but nothing mattered now that she had won the day, that her husband was still hers and not another woman's. Gaily she called up Mrs. Ashby, heard her friendly voice, and began: 'Well, did Kenneth's news surprise you? What do you think of our elopement?'

Almost instantly, before Mrs. Ashby could answer, Charlotte knew what her reply would be, Mrs. Ashby had not seen her son, she had had no word from him and did not know what her daughter-in-law meant. Charlotte stood silent in the intensity of her surprise. 'But then, where *has* he been?' she thought. Then, recovering herself, she explained their sudden decision to Mrs. Ashby, and in doing so, gradually regained her own self-confidence, her conviction that nothing could ever again come between Kenneth and herself. Mrs. Ashby took the news calmly and approvingly. She too, had thought that Kenneth looked worried and over-tired, and she agreed with her daughter-in-law that in such cases change was the surest remedy. 'I'm always so glad when he gets away. Elsie hated traveling; she was always finding pretexts to prevent his going anywhere. With you, thank goodness, it's different.' Nor was Mrs. Ashby surprised at his not having had time to let her know of his departure. He must have been in a rush from the moment the decision was taken; but no doubt he'd drop in before dinner. Five minutes' talk was really all they needed. 'I hope you'll gradually cure Kenneth of his mania for going over and over a question that could be settled in a dozen words. He never used to be like that, and if he carried the habit into his professional work he'd soon lose all his clients. . . . Yes, do come in for a minute, dear, if you have time; no doubt he'll turn up while you're here.' The tonic ring of Mrs. Ashby's voice echoed on reassuringly in the silent room while Charlotte continued her preparations.

Toward seven the telephone rang, and she darted to it. Now she would know! But it was only from the conscientious secretary, to say that Mr. Ashby hadn't been back, or sent any word, and before the office closed she thought she ought to let Mrs. Ashby know. 'Oh, that's all right. Thanks a lot!' Charlotte called out cheerfully, and hung up the receiver with a trembling hand. But perhaps by this time, she reflected, he was at his mother's. She shut her drawers and cupboards, put on her hat and coat and called up to the nursery that she was going out for a minute to see the children's grandmother.

Mrs. Ashby lived nearby, and during her brief walk through the cold spring dusk Charlotte imagined that every advancing figure was her husband's. But she did not meet him on the way, and when she entered the house she found her mother-in-law alone. Kenneth had neither telephoned nor come. Old Mrs. Ashby sat by her bright fire, her knitting needles flashing steadily through her active old hands, and her mere bodily presence gave reassurance to Charlotte. Yes, it was certainly odd that Kenneth had gone off for the whole day without letting any of them know; but, after all, it was to be expected. A busy lawyer held so many threads in his hands that any sudden change of plan would oblige him to make all sorts of unforeseen arrangements and adjustments. He might have gone to see some client in the suburbs and been detained there; his mother remembered his telling her that he had charge of the legal business of a queer old recluse somewhere in New Jersey, who was immensely rich but too mean to have a telephone. Very likely Kenneth had been stranded there.

But Charlotte felt her nervousness gaining on her. When Mrs. Ashby asked her at what hour they were sailing the next day and she had to say she didn't know – that Kenneth had simply sent her word he was going to take their passages – the uttering of the words again brought home to her the strangeness of the situation. Even Mrs. Ashby conceded that it was odd; but she immediately added that it only showed what a rush he was in.

'But, mother, it's nearly eight o'clock! He must realize that I've got to know when we're starting tomorrow.'

'Oh, the boat probably doesn't sail till evening. Sometimes they have to wait till midnight for the tide. Kenneth's probably counting on that. After all, he has a level head.'

Charlotte stood up. 'It's not that. Something has happened to him.'

Mrs. Ashby took off her spectacles and rolled up her knitting. 'If you begin to let yourself imagine things – '

'Aren't you in the least anxious?'

'I never am till I have to be. I wish you'd ring for dinner, my dear. You'll stay and dine? He's sure to drop in here on his way home.'

Charlotte called up her own house. No, the maid said, Mr. Ashby hadn't come in and hadn't telephoned. She would tell him as soon as he came that Mrs. Ashby was dining at his mother's. Charlotte followed her mother-in-law into the dining room and sat with parched throat before her empty plate, while Mrs. Ashby dealt calmly and efficiently with a short but carefully prepared repast. 'You'd better eat something, child, or you'll be as bad as Kenneth. . . . Yes, a little more asparagus, please, Jane.'

She insisted on Charlotte's drinking a glass of sherry and nibbling a bit of toast; then they returned to the drawing room, where the fire had been made up, and the cushions in Mrs. Ashby's armchair shaken out and smoothed. How safe and familiar it all looked; and out there, somewhere in the uncertainty and mystery of the night, lurked the answer to the two women's conjectures, like an indistinguishable figure prowling on the threshold.

At last Charlotte got up and said: 'I'd better go back. At this hour Kenneth will certainly go straight home.'

Mrs. Ashby smiled indulgently. 'It's not very late, my dear. It doesn't take two sparrows long to dine.'

'It's after nine.' Charlotte bent down to kiss her. 'The fact is, I can't keep still.'

Mrs. Ashby pushed aside her work and rested her two hands on the arms of her chair. 'I'm going with you,' she said, helping herself up.

Charlotte protested that it was too late, that it was not necessary, that she would call up as soon as Kenneth came in, but Mrs. Ashby had already rung for her maid. She was slightly lame, and stood resting on her stick while her wraps were brought. 'If Mr. Kenneth turns up, tell him he'll find me at his own house,' she instructed the maid as the two women got into the taxi which had been summoned. During the short drive Charlotte gave thanks that she was not returning home alone. There was something warm and substantial in the mere fact of

Mrs. Ashby's nearness, something that corresponded with the clearness of her eyes and the texture of her fresh firm complexion. As the taxi drew up she laid her hand encouragingly on Charlotte's. 'You'll see; there'll be a message.'

The door opened at Charlotte's ring and the two entered. Charlotte's heart beat excitedly; the stimulus of her mother-in-law's confidence was beginning to flow through her veins.

'You'll see – you'll see,' Mrs. Ashby repeated.

The maid who opened the door said no, Mr. Ashby had not come in, and there had been no message from him.

'You're sure the telephone's not out of order?' his mother suggested; and the maid said, well it certainly wasn't half an hour ago; but she'd just go and ring up to make sure. She disappeared, and Charlotte turned to take off her hat and cloak. As she did so her eyes lit on the hall table, and there lay a gray envelope, her husband's name faintly traced on it. 'Oh!' she cried out, suddenly aware that for the first time in months she had entered her house without wondering if one of the gray letters would be there.

'What is it, my dear?' Mrs. Ashby asked with a glance of surprise.

Charlotte did not answer. She took up the envelope and stood staring at it as if she could force her gaze to penetrate to what was within. Then an idea occurred to her. She turned and held out the envelope to her mother-in-law.

'Do you know that writing?' she asked.

Mrs. Ashby took the letter. She had to feel with her other hand for her eyeglasses, and when she had adjusted them she lifted the envelope to the light. 'Why!' she exclaimed, and then stopped. Charlotte noticed that the letter shook in her usually firm hand. 'But this is addressed to Kenneth,' Mrs. Ashby said at length, in a low voice. Her tone seemed to imply that she felt her daughter-in-law's question to be slightly indiscreet.

'Yes, but no matter,' Charlotte spoke with sudden decision. 'I want to know – do you know the writing?'

Mrs. Ashby handed back the letter. 'No,' she said distinctly.

The two women had turned into the library. Charlotte switched on the electric light and shut the door. She still held the envelope in her hand.

'I'm going to open it,' she announced.

She caught her mother-in-law's startled glance. 'But, dearest – a letter not addressed to you? My dear, you can't!'

'As if I cared about that – now!' She continued to look intently at Mrs. Ashby. 'This letter may tell me where Kenneth is.'

Mrs. Ashby's glossy bloom was effaced by a quick pallor; her firm cheeks seemed to shrink and wither. 'Why should it? What makes you believe – It can't possibly – '

Charlotte held her eyes steadily on that altered face. 'Ah, then you *do* know the writing?' she flashed back.

'Know the writing? How should I? With all my son's correspondents. . . . What I do know is – ' Mrs. Ashby broke off and looked at her daughter-in-law entreatingly, almost timidly.

Charlotte caught her by the wrist. 'Mother! What do you know? Tell me! You must!'

'That I don't believe any good ever came of a woman's opening her husband's letters behind his back.'

The words sounded to Charlotte's irritated ears as flat as a phrase culled from a book of moral axioms. She laughed impatiently and dropped her mother-in-law's wrist. 'Is that all? No good can come of this letter, opened or unopened. I know that well enough. But whatever ill comes, I mean to find out what's in it.' Her hands had been trembling as they held the envelope, but now they grew firm, and her voice also. She still gazed intently at Mrs. Ashby. 'This is the ninth letter addressed in the same hand that has come for Kenneth since we've been married. Always these same gray envelopes. I've kept count of them because after each one he has been like a man who has had some dreadful shock. It takes him hours to shake off their effect. I've told him so, I've told him I must know from whom they come, because I can see they're killing him. He won't answer my questions; he says he can't tell me anything about the letters, but last night he promised to go away with me to get away from them.'

Mrs. Ashby, with shaking steps, had gone to one of the armchairs and sat down in it, her head drooping forward on her breast. 'Ah,' she murmured.

'So now you understand – '

'Did he tell you it was to get away from them?'

'He said, to get away – to get away. He was sobbing so that he could hardly speak. But I told him I knew that was why.'

'And what did he say?'

'He took me in his arms and said he'd go wherever I wanted.'

'Ah, thank God!' said Mrs. Ashby. There was a silence, during which she continued to sit with bowed head, and eyes averted from her daughter-in-law. At last she looked up and spoke. 'Are you sure there have been as many as nine?'

'Perfectly. This is the ninth. I've kept count.'

'And he has absolutely refused to explain?'

'Absolutely.'

Mrs. Ashby spoke through pale contracted lips. 'When did they begin to come? Do you remember?'

Charlotte laughed again. 'Remember? The first one came the night we got back from our honeymoon.'

'All that time?' Mrs. Ashby lifted her head and spoke with sudden energy. 'Then – yes, open it.'

The words were so unexpected that Charlotte felt the blood in her temples, and her hands began to tremble again. She tried to slip her finger under the flap of the envelope, but it was so tightly stuck that she had to hunt on her husband's writing table for his ivory letter opener. As she pushed about the familiar objects his own hands had so lately touched, they sent through her the icy chill emanating from the little personal effects of someone newly dead. In the deep silence of the room the tearing of the paper as she slit the envelope sounded like a human cry. She drew out the sheet and carried it to the lamp.

'Well?' Mrs. Ashby asked below her breath.

Charlotte did not move or answer. She was bending over the page with wrinkled brows, holding it nearer and nearer to the light. Her sight must be blurred, or else dazzled by the reflection of the lamplight on the smooth surface of the paper, for, strain her eyes as she would, she could discern only a few faint strokes, so faint and faltering as to be nearly undecipherable.

'I can't make it out,' she said.

'What do you mean, dear?'

'The writing's so indistinct. . . . Wait.'

She went back to the table and, sitting down close to Kenneth's reading lamp, slipped the letter under a magnifying glass. All this time she was aware that her mother-in-law was watching her intently.

'Well?' Mrs. Ashby breathed.

'Well, it's no clearer. I can't read it.'

'You mean the paper is an absolute blank?'

'No, not quite. There is writing on it. I can make out something like "mine" – oh, and "come". It might be "come." '

Mrs. Ashby stood up abruptly. Her face was even paler than before. She advanced to the table and, resting her two hands on it, drew a deep breath. 'Let me see,' she said, as if forcing herself to a hateful effort.

Charlotte felt the contagion of her whiteness. 'She knows,' she thought. She pushed the letter across the table. Her mother-in-law lowered her head over it in silence, but without touching it with her pale wrinkled hands.

Charlotte stood watching her as she herself, when she had tried to read the letter, had been watched by Mrs. Ashby. The latter fumbled for her glasses, held them to her eyes, and bent still closer to the outspread page, in order, as it seemed, to avoid touching it. The light of the lamp fell directly on her old face, and Charlotte reflected what depths of the unknown may lurk under the clearest and most candid lineaments. She had never seen her mother-in-law's features express any but simple and sound emotions – cordiality, amusement, a kindly sympathy; now and again a flash of wholesome anger. Now they seemed to wear a look of fear and hatred, of incredulous dismay and almost cringing defiance. It was as if the spirits warring within her had distorted her face to their own likeness. At length she raised her head. 'I can't – I can't,' she said in a voice of childish distress.

'You can't make it out either?'

She shook her head, and Charlotte saw two tears roll down her cheeks.

'Familiar as the writing is to you?' Charlotte insisted with twitching lips.

Mrs. Ashby did not take up the challenge. 'I can make out nothing – nothing.'

'But you do know the writing?'

Mrs. Ashby lifted her head timidly; her anxious eyes stole with a glance of apprehension around the quiet familiar room. 'How can I tell? I was startled at first. . . .'

'Startled by the resemblance?'

'Well, I thought – '

'You'd better say it out, mother! You knew at once it was her writing?'

'Oh, wait, my dear – wait.'

'Wait for what?'

Mrs. Ashby looked up; her eyes, traveling slowly past Charlotte, were lifted to the blank wall behind her son's writing table.

Charlotte, following the glance, burst into a shrill laugh of accusation. 'I needn't wait any longer! You've answered me now! You're looking straight at the wall where her picture used to hang.'

Mrs. Ashby lifted her hand with a murmur of warning. 'Sh-h.'

'Oh, you needn't imagine that anything can ever frighten me again!' Charlotte cried.

Her mother-in-law still leaned against the table. Her lips moved plaintively. 'But we're going mad – we're both going mad. We both know such things are impossible.'

Her daughter-in-law looked at her with a pitying stare. 'I've known for a long time now that everything was possible.'

'Even this?'

'Yes, exactly this.'

'But this letter – after all, there's nothing in this letter – '

'Perhaps there would be to him. How can I tell? I remember his saying to me once that if you were used to a handwriting the faintest stroke of it became legible. Now I see what he meant. He *was* used to it.'

'But the few strokes that I can make out are so pale. No one could possibly read that letter.'

Charlotte laughed again. 'I suppose everything's pale about a ghost,' she said stridently.

'Oh, my child – my child – don't say it!'

'Why shouldn't I say it, when even the bare walls cry it out? What difference does it make if her letters are illegible to you and me? If even you can see her face on that blank wall, why shouldn't he read her writing on this blank paper? Don't you see that she's everywhere in this house, and the closer to him because to everyone else she's become invisible?' Charlotte dropped into a chair and covered her face with her hands. A turmoil of sobbing shook her from head to foot. At length a touch on her shoulder made her look up, and she saw her mother-in-law bending over her. Mrs. Ashby's face seemed to have grown still smaller and more wasted, but it had resumed its usual quiet look. Through all her tossing anguish, Charlotte felt the impact of that resolute spirit.

'Tomorrow – tomorrow. You'll see. There'll be some explanation tomorrow.'

Charlotte cut her short. 'An explanation? Who's going to give it, I wonder?'

Mrs. Ashby drew back and straightened herself heroically. 'Kenneth himself will,' she cried out in a strong voice. Charlotte said nothing and the old woman went on: 'But meanwhile we must act; we must notify the police. Now, without a moment's delay. We must do everything – everything.'

Charlotte stood up slowly and stiffly; her joints felt as cramped as an old woman's. 'Exactly as if we thought it could do any good to do anything?'

Resolutely Mrs. Ashby cried: 'Yes!' and Charlotte went up to the telephone and unhooked the receiver.

Her Son

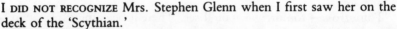

I DID NOT RECOGNIZE Mrs. Stephen Glenn when I first saw her on the deck of the 'Scythian.'

The voyage was more than half over, and we were counting on Cherbourg within forty-eight hours, when she appeared on deck and sat down beside me. She was as handsome as ever, and not a day older-looking than when we had last met – toward the end of the war, in 1917 it must have been, not long before her only son, the aviator, was killed. Yet now, five years later, I was looking at her as if she were a stranger. Why? Not, certainly, because of her white hair. She had had the American woman's frequent luck of acquiring it while the face beneath was still fresh, and a dozen years earlier, when we used to meet at dinners, at the Opera, that silver diadem already crowned her. Now, looking more closely, I saw that the face beneath was still untouched; what then had so altered her? Perhaps it was the faint line of anxiety between her dark strongly-drawn eyebrows; or the setting of the eyes themselves, those somber starlit eyes which seemed to have sunk deeper into their lids, and showed like glimpses of night through the arch of a cavern. But what a gloomy image to apply to eyes as tender as Catherine Glenn's! Yet it was immediately suggested by the look of the lady in deep mourning who had settled herself beside me, and now turned to say: 'So you don't know me, Mr. Norcutt – Catherine Glenn?'

The fact was flagrant. I acknowledged it, and added: 'But why didn't I? I can't imagine. Do you mind my saying that I believe it's because you're even more beautiful now than when I last saw you?'

She replied with perfect simplicity: 'No, I don't mind – because I ought to be; that is, if there's any meaning in anything.'

'Any meaning – ?'

She seemed to hesitate; she had never been a woman who found words easily. 'Any meaning in life. You see, since we've met I've lost everything: my son, my husband.' She bent her head slightly, as though the words she pronounced were holy. Then she added, with the air of striving for more scrupulous accuracy: 'Or, at least, almost everything.'

The 'almost' puzzled me. Mrs. Glenn, as far as I knew, had had no

222

child but the son she had lost in the war; and the old uncle who had brought her up had died years earlier. I wondered if, in thus qualifying her loneliness, she alluded to the consolations of religion.

I murmured that I knew of her double mourning; and she surprised me still further by saying: 'Yes; I saw you at my husband's funeral. I've always wanted to thank you for being there.'

'But of course I was there.'

She continued: 'I noticed all of Stephen's friends who came. I was very grateful to them, and especially to the young ones.' (This was meant for me.) 'You see,' she added, 'a funeral is – is a very great comfort.'

Again I looked surprise.

'My son – my son Philip – ' (why should she think it necessary to mention his name, since he was her only child?) ' – my son Philip's funeral took place just where his airplane fell. A little village in the Somme; his father and I went there immediately after the Armistice. One of our army chaplains read the service. The people from the village were there – they were so kind to us. But there was no one else – no personal friends; at that time only the nearest relations could get passes. Our boy would have wished it. . . . he would have wanted to stay where he fell. But it's not the same as feeling one's friends about one, as I did at my husband's funeral.'

While she spoke she kept her eyes intently, almost embarrassingly, on mine. It had never occurred to me that Mrs. Stephen Glenn was the kind of woman who would attach any particular importance to the list of names at her husband's funeral. She had always seemed aloof and abstracted, shut off from the world behind the high walls of a happy domesticity. But on adding this new indication of character to the fragments of information I had gathered concerning her first appearance in New York, and to the vague impression she used to produce on me when we met, I began to see that lists of names were probably just what she would care about. And then I asked myself what I really knew of her. Very little, I perceived; but no doubt just as much as she wished me to. For, as I sat there, listening to her voice, and catching unguarded glimpses of her crepe-shadowed profile, I began to suspect that what had seemed in her a rather dull simplicity might be the vigilance of a secretive person; or perhaps of a person who had a secret. There is a world of difference between them, for the secretive person is seldom interesting and seldom has a secret; but I felt inclined – though nothing I knew of her justified it – to put her in the other class.

I began to think over the years of our intermittent acquaintance – it had never been more, for I had known the Glenns well. She had appeared in New York when I was a very young man, in the nineties, as a beautiful girl from Kentucky or Alabama – a niece of old Colonel Reamer's. Left an orphan, and penniless, when she was still almost a child, she had been passed about from one reluctant relation to another, and had finally (the legend ran) gone on the stage, and followed a strolling company across the continent. The manager had deserted his troupe in some far-off state, and Colonel Reamer, fatuous, impecunious, and no doubt perplexed as to how to deal with the situation, had yet faced it manfully, and shaking off his bachelor selfishness had taken the girl into his house. Such a past, though it looks dove-colored now, seemed hectic in the nineties, and gave a touch of romance and mystery to the beautiful Catherine Reamer, who appeared so aloof and distinguished, yet had been snatched out of such promiscuities and perils.

Colonel Reamer was a ridiculous old man: everything about him was ridiculous – his 'toupee' (probably the last in existence), his vague military title, his anecdotes about southern chivalry, and duels between other gentlemen with military titles and civilian pursuits, and all the obsolete swagger of a character dropped out of Martin Chuzzlewit. He was the notorious bore of New York; tolerated only because he was old Mrs. So-and-so's second cousin, because he was poor, because he was kindly – and because, out of his poverty, he had managed, with a smile and a gay gesture, to shelter and clothe his starving niece. Old Reamer, I recalled, had always had a passion for lists of names; for seeing his own appear in the society column of the morning papers, for giving you those of the people he had dined with, or been unable to dine with because already bespoken by others even more important. The young people called him 'Old Previous-Engagement,' because he was so anxious to have you know that, if you hadn't met him at some particular party, it was because he had been previously engaged at another.

Perhaps, I thought, it was from her uncle that Mrs. Glenn had learned to attach such importance to names, to lists of names, to the presence of certain people on certain occasions, to a social suitability which could give a consecration even to death. The profile at my side, so marble-pure, so marble-sad, did not suggest such preoccupation, neither did the deep entreating gaze she bent on me; yet many details fitted into the theory.

Her very marriage to Stephen Glenn seemed to confirm it. I thought back, and began to reconstruct Stephen Glenn. He was considerably older than myself, and had been a familiar figure in my earliest New York; a man who was a permanent ornament to society, who looked precisely as he ought, spoke, behaved, received his friends, filled his space on the social stage, exactly as his world expected him to. While he was still a young man, old ladies in perplexity over some social problem (there were many in those draconian days) would consult Stephen Glenn as if he had been one of the Ancients of the community. Yet there was nothing precociously old or dry about him. He was one of the handsomest men of his day; a good shot, a leader of cotillions. He practiced at the bar, and became a member of a reputed legal firm chiefly occupied with the management of old ponderous New York estates. In process of time the old ladies who had consulted him about social questions began to ask his advice about investments; and on this point he was considered equally reliable. Only one cloud shadowed his early life. He had married a distant cousin, an effaced sort of woman who bore him no children, and presently (on that account, it was said) fell into suicidal melancholia; so that for a good many years Stephen Glenn's handsome and once hospitable house must have been a grim place to go home to. But at last she died, and after a decent interval the widower married Miss Reamer. No one was greatly surprised. It had been observed that the handsome Stephen Glenn and the beautiful Catherine Reamer were drawn to each other; and though the old ladies thought he might have done better, some of the more caustic remarked that he could hardly have done differently, after having made Colonel Reamer's niece so 'conspicuous.' The attentions of a married man, especially of one unhappily married, and virtually separated from his wife, were regarded in those days as likely to endanger a young lady's future. Catherine Reamer, however, rose above these hints as she had above the perils of her theatrical venture. One had only to look at her to see that, in that smooth marble surface there was no crack in which detraction could take root.

Stephen Glenn's house was opened again, and the couple began to entertain in a quiet way. It was thought natural that Glenn should want to put a little life into the house which had so long been a sort of tomb; but though the Glenn dinners were as good as the most carefully chosen food and wine could make them, neither of the pair had the gifts which make hospitality a success, and by the time I knew them, the younger set had come to regard dining with them as somewhat of a bore. Stephen Glenn was still handsone, his wife still beautiful, perhaps more beautiful than ever; but the apathy of prosperity seemed to have settled down on them, and they wore their beauty and affability like expensive clothes put on for the occasion. There was something static, unchanging in their appearance, as there was in their affability, their conversation, the menus of their carefully planned dinners, the studied arrangement of the drawing room furniture. They had a little boy, born after a year of marriage, and they were devoted parents, given to lengthy anecdotes about their son's doings and sayings; but one could not imagine their tumbling about with him on the nursery floor. Someone said they must go to bed with their crowns on, like the kings and queens on packs of cards; and gradually, from being thought distinguished and impressive, they came to be regarded as wooden, pompous and slightly absurd. But the old ladies still spoke of Stephen Glenn as a man who had done his family credit, and his wife began to acquire his figurehead attributes, and to be consulted, as he was, about the minuter social problems. And all the while – I thought as I looked back – there seemed to have been no one in their lives with whom they were really intimate. . . .

Then, of a sudden, they again became interesting. It was when their only son was killed, attacked alone in mid-sky by a German air squadron. Young Phil Glenn was the first American aviator to fall; and when the news came people saw that the Mr.-and-Mrs. Glenn they had known was a mere façade, and that behind it were a passionate father and mother, crushed, rebellious, agonizing, but determined to face their loss dauntlessly, though they should die of it.

Stephen Glenn did die of it, barely two years later. The doctors ascribed his death to a specific disease; but everybody who knew him knew better. 'It was the loss of the boy,' they said; and added: 'It's terrible to have only one child.'

Since her husband's funeral I had not seen Mrs. Glenn; I had completely ceased to think of her. And now, on my way to take up a post at the American Consulate in Paris, I found myself sitting beside her and remembering these things. 'Poor creatures – it's as if two marble busts had been knocked off their pedestals and smashed,' I thought, recalling the faces of husband and wife after the boy's death; 'and she's been smashed twice, poor woman. . . . Yet she says it has made her more beautiful. . . .' Again I lost myself in conjecture.

• II •

I was told that a lady in deep mourning wanted to see me on urgent business, and I looked out of my private den at the Paris Consulate into the room hung with maps and Presidents, where visitors were sifted out before being passed on to the Vice-consul or the Chief.

The lady was Mrs. Stephen Glenn.

Six or seven months had passed since our meeting on the 'Scythian,' and I had again forgotten her very existence. She was not a person who stuck in one's mind; and once more I wondered why, for in her statuesque weeds she looked nobler, more striking than ever. She glanced at the people awaiting their turn under the maps and the Presidents, and asked in a low tone if she could see me privately.

I was free at the moment, and I led her into my office and banished the typist.

Mrs. Glenn seemed disturbed by the signs of activity about me. 'I'm afraid we shall be interrupted. I wanted to speak to you alone,' she said.

I assured her we were not likely to be disturbed if she could put what she had to say in a few words –

'Ah, but that's just what I can't do. What I have to say can't be put in a few words.' She fixed her splendid nocturnal eyes on me, and I read in them a distress so deep that I dared not suggest postponement.

I said I would do all I could to prevent our being interrupted, and in reply she just sat silent, and looked at me, as if after all she had nothing further to communicate. The telephone clicked, and I rang for my secretary to take the message; then one of the clerks came in with papers for my signature. I said: 'I'd better sign and get it over,' and she sat motionless, her head slightly bent, as if secretly relieved by the delay. The clerk went off, I shut the door again, and when we were alone she lifted her head and spoke. 'Mr. Norcutt,' she asked, 'have you ever had a child?'

I replied with a smile that I was not married. She murmured: 'I'm sorry – excuse me,' and looked down again at her black-gloved hands, which were clasped about a black bag richly embroidered with dull jet. Everything about her was as finished, as costly, as studied, as if she were a young beauty going forth in her joy; yet she looked like a heartbroken woman.

She began again: 'My reason for coming is that I've promised to help a friend, a poor woman who's lost all trace of her son – her only surviving son – and is hunting for him.' She paused, though my expectant silence seemed to encourage her to continue. 'It's a very sad case; I must try to explain. Long ago, as a girl, my friend fell in love with a married man – a man unhappily married.' She moistened her lips, which had become parched and colorless. 'You mustn't judge them too severely. . . . He had great nobility of character – the highest standards – but the situation was too cruel. His wife was insane; at that time there was no legal release in such cases. If you were married to a lunatic only death could free you. It was a most unhappy affair – the poor girl pitied her friend profoundly. Their little boy. . . .' Suddenly she stood up with a proud and noble movement and leaned to me across the desk. 'I am that woman,' she said.

She straightened herself and stood there, trembling, erect, like a swathed figure of woe on an illustrious grave. I thought: 'What this inexpressive woman was meant to express is grief – ' and marveled at the wastefulness of Nature. But suddenly she dropped back into her chair, bowed her face against the desk, and burst into sobs. Her sobs were not violent; they were soft, low, almost rhythmical, with lengthening intervals between, like the last drops of rain after a long downpour; and I said to myself: 'She's cried so much that this must be the very end.'

She opened the jet bag, took out a delicate handkerchief, and dried her eyes. Then she turned to me again. 'It's the first time I've ever spoken of this . . . to any human being except one.'

I laid my hand on hers. 'It was no use – my pretending,' she went on, as if appealing to me for justification.

'Is it ever? And why should you, with an old friend?' I rejoined, attempting to comfort her.

'Ah, but I've had to – for so many years, to be silent has become my second nature.' She paused, and then continued in a softer tone: 'My baby was so beautiful . . . do you know, Mr. Norcutt, I'm sure I should know him anywhere. . . . Just two years and one month older than my second boy, Philip . . . the one you know.' Again she hesitated, and then, in a warmer burst of confidence, and scarcely above a whisper: 'We christened the eldest Stephen. We knew it was dangerous: it might give a clue – but I felt I must give him his father's name, the name I loved best. . . . It was all I could keep of my baby. And Stephen understood; he consented. . . .'

I sat and stared at her. What! This child of hers that she was telling me of was the child of Stephen Glenn? The two had had a child two years before the birth of their lawful son Philip? And consequently nearly a year before their marriage? I listened in a stupor, trying to reconstruct in my mind the image of a new, of another, Stephen Glenn, of the suffering reckless man behind the varnished image familiar to me. Now and then I murmured: 'Yes . . . yes . . .' just to help her to go on.

'Of course it was impossible to keep the baby with me. Think – at my uncle's! My poor uncle . . . he would have died of it. . . .'

'And so you died instead?'

I had found the right word; her eyes filled again, and she stretched her hands to mine. 'Ah, you've understood! Thank you. Yes; I died.' She added: 'Even when Philip was born I didn't come to life again – not wholly. Because there was always Stevie . . . part of me belonged to Stevie forever.'

'But when you and Glenn were able to marry, why – ?'

She hung her head, and the blood rose to her worn temples. 'Ah, why? . . . Listen; you mustn't blame my husband. Try to remember what life was thirty years ago in New York. He had his professional standing to consider. A woman with a shadow on her was damned. . . . I couldn't discredit Stephen. . . . We knew *positively* that our baby was in the best of hands. . . .'

'You never saw him again?'

She shook her head. 'It was part of the agreement – with the persons who took him. They wanted to imagine he was their own. We knew we were fortunate . . . to find such a safe home, so entirely beyond suspicion . . . we had to accept the conditions.' She looked up with a faint flicker of reassurance in her eyes. 'In a way it no longer makes any difference to me – the interval. It seems like yesterday. I know he's been well cared for, and I should recognize him anywhere. No child ever had such eyes. . . .' She fumbled in her bag, drew out a small morocco case, opened it, and showed me the miniature of a baby a few

months old. 'I managed, with the greatest difficulty, to get a photograph of him – and this was done from it. Beautiful? Yes. I shall be
able to identify him anywhere. . . . It's only twenty-seven years. . . .'

• III •

OUR talk was prolonged, the next day, at the quiet hotel where Mrs.
Glenn was staying; but it led – it could lead – to nothing definite.

The unhappy woman could only repeat and amplify the strange
confession stammered out at the Consulate. As soon as her child was
born it had been entrusted with the utmost secrecy to a rich childless
couple, who at once adopted it, and disappeared forever. Disappeared,
that is, in the sense that (as I guessed) Stephen Glenn was as determined
as they were that the child's parents should never hear of them again.
Poor Catherine had been very ill at her baby's birth. Tortured by the
need of concealment, of taking up her usual life at her uncle's as quickly
as possible, of explaining her brief absence in such a way as to avert
suspicion, she had lived in a blur of fear and suffering, and by the time
she was herself again the child was gone, and the adoption irrevocable.
Thereafter, I gathered, Glenn made it clear that he wished to avoid the
subject, and she learned very little about the couple who had taken her
child except that they were of good standing, and came from somewhere in Pennsylvania. They had gone to Europe almost immediately,
it appeared, and no more was heard of them. Mrs. Glenn understood
that Mr. Brown (their name was Brown) was a painter, and that they
went first to Italy, then to Spain – unless it was the other way round.
Stephen Glenn, it seemed, had heard of them through an old governess
of his sister's, a family confidante, who was the sole recipient of poor
Catherine's secret. Soon afterwards the governess died, and with her
disappeared the last trace of the mysterious couple; for it was not going
to be easy to wander about Europe looking for a Mr. and Mrs. Brown
who had gone to Italy or Spain with a baby twenty-seven years ago.
But that was what Mrs. Glenn meant to do. She had a fair amount of
money, she was desperately lonely, she had no aim or interest or
occupation or duty – except to find the child she had lost.

What she wanted was some sort of official recommendation to our
consuls in Italy and Spain, accompanied by a private letter hinting at
the nature of her errand. I took these papers to her and when I did so
I tried to point out the difficulties and risks of her quest, and suggested
that she ought to be accompanied by someone who could advise her –
hadn't she a man of business, or a relation, a cousin, a nephew? No,
she said; there was no one; but for that matter she needed no one. If
necessary she could apply to the police, or employ private detectives;
and any American consul to whom she appealed would know how to

advise her. 'In any case,' she added, 'I couldn't be mistaken – I should always recognize him. He was the very image of his father. And if there were any possibility of my being in doubt, I have the miniature, and photographs of his father as a young man.'

She drew out the little morocco case and offered it again for my contemplation. The vague presentment of a child a few months old – and by its help she expected to identify a man of nearly thirty!

Apparently she had no clue beyond the fact that, all those years ago, the adoptive parents were rumored to have sojourned in Europe. She was starting for Italy because she thought she remembered that they were said to have gone there first – in itself a curious argument. Wherever there was an American consul she meant to apply to him. First at Genoa; then Milan; then Florence, Rome and Naples. In one or the other of these cities she would surely discover some one who could remember the passage there of an American couple named Brown with the most beautiful baby boy in the world. Even the long arm of coincidence could not have scattered so widely over southern Europe American couples of the name of Brown, with a matchlessly beautiful baby called Stephen.

Mrs. Glenn set forth in a mood of almost mystical exaltation. She promised that I should hear from her as soon as she had anything definite to communicate: 'which means that you *will* hear – and soon!' she concluded with a happy laugh. But six months passed without my receiving any direct news, though I was kept on her track by a succession of letters addressed to my chief by various consuls who wrote to say that a Mrs. Stehpen Glenn had called with a letter of recommendation, but that unluckily it had been impossible to give her any assistance 'as she had absolutely no data to go upon.' Alas poor lady –

And, then, one day, about eight months after her departure, there was a telegram. 'Found my boy. Unspeakably happy. Long to see you.' It was signed Catherine Glenn, and dated from a mountain cure in Switzerland.

• IV •

THAT summer, when the time came for my vacation, it was raining in Paris even harder than it had rained all the preceding winter, and I decided to make a dash for the sun.

I had read in the papers that the French Riviera was suffering from a six months' drought; and though I didn't half believe it, I took the next train for the south. I got out at Les Calanques, a small bathing place between Marseilles and Toulon, where there was a fairish hotel, and pine woods to walk in, and there, that very day, I saw seated on the beach the majestic figure of Mrs. Stephen Glenn. The first thing that struck me was that she had at last discarded her weeds. She wore a thin white dress, and a wide brimmed hat of russet straw shaded the fine oval of her face. She saw me at once, and springing up advanced across the beach with a light step. The sun, striking on her hat brim, cast a warm shadow on her face; and in that semishade it glowed with recovered youth. 'Dear Mr. Norcutt! How wonderful! Is it really you? I've been meaning to write for weeks; but I think happiness has made me lazy and my days are so full,' she declared with a joyous smile.

I looked at her with increased admiration. At the Consulate, I remembered, I had said to myself that grief was what Nature had meant her features to express; but that was only because I had never seen her happy. No; even when her husband and her son Philip were alive, and the circle of her well-being seemed unbroken, I had never seen her look as she looked now. And I understood that, during all those years, the unsatisfied longing for her eldest child, the shame at her own cowardice in disowning and deserting him, and perhaps her secret contempt for her husband for having abetted (or more probably exacted) that desertion, must have been eating into her soul, deeper, far deeper, than satisfied affections could reach. Now everything in her was satisfied; I could see it.

'How happy you look!' I exclaimed.

'But of course.' She took it as simply as she had my former remark on her heightened beauty; and I perceived that what had illumined her face when we met on the steamer was not sorrow but the dawn of hope. Even then she had felt certain that she was going to find her boy; now she had found him and was transfigured. I sat down beside her on the sands. 'And now tell me how the incredible thing happened.'

She shook her head. 'Not incredible – inevitable. When one has lived for more than half a life with one object in view it's bound to become a reality. I *had* to find Stevie; and I found him.' She smiled with the inward brooding smile of a Madonna – an image of the eternal mother who, when she speaks of her children in old age, still feels them at the breast.

Of details as I made out there were few; or perhaps she was too confused with happiness to give them. She had hunted up and down Italy for her Mr. and Mrs. Brown, and then suddenly, at Alassio, just as she was beginning to give up hope, and had decided (in a less sanguine mood) to start for Spain, the miracle had happened. Falling into talk, on her last evening, with a lady in the hotel lounge, she had alluded vaguely – she couldn't say why – to the object of her quest; and the lady, snatching the miniature from her, and bursting into tears, had identified the portrait as her adopted child's, and herself as the long-sought Mrs. Brown. Papers had been produced, dates compared, all to Mrs. Glenn's complete satisfaction. There could be no doubt that she had found her Stevie (thank heaven, they had kept the name!); and the only shadow on her joy was the discovery that he was lying ill, menaced with tuberculosis, at some Swiss mountain cure. Or rather, that was part of another sadness; of the unfortunate fact that his adopted parents had lost nearly all their money just as he was leaving school, and hadn't been able to do much for him in the way of medical attention or mountain air – the very things he needed as he was growing up. Instead, since he had a passion for painting, they had allowed him to live in Paris, rather miserably, in the Latin Quarter, and work all day in one of those big schools – Julian's wasn't it? The very worst thing for a boy whose lungs were slightly affected; and this last year he had had to give up, and spend several months in a cheap hole in Switzerland. Mrs. Glenn joined him there at once – ah, that meeting! – and as soon as she had seen him, and talked with the doctors, she became convinced that all that was needed to ensure his recovery was comfort, care and freedom from anxiety. His lungs, the doctors assured her, were all right again; and he had such a passion for the sea that after a few weeks in a good hotel at Montana he had persuaded Mrs. Glenn to come with him to the Mediterranean. But she was firmly resolved on carrying him back to Switzerland for another winter, no matter how much he objected; and Mr. and Mrs. Brown agreed that she was absolutely right –

'Ah; there's still a Mr. Brown?'

'Oh, yes.' She smiled at me absently, her whole mind on Stevie. 'You'll see them both – they're here with us. I invited them for a few weeks, poor souls. I can't altogether separate them from Stevie – not yet.' (It was clear that eventually she hoped to.)

No, I assented; I supposed she couldn't; and just then she exclaimed: 'Ah, there's my boy!' and I saw a tall stooping young man approaching us with the listless step of convalescence. As he came nearer I felt that I was going to like him a good deal better than I had expected – though I don't know why I had doubted his likeableness before knowing him. At any rate, I was taken at once by the look of his dark-lashed eyes, deep set in a long thin face which I suspected of being too pale under the carefully acquired sunburn. The eyes were friendly, humorous, ironical; I liked a little less the rather hard lines of the mouth, until his smile relaxed them into boyishness. His body, lank and loose-jointed, was too thin for his suit of light striped flannel, and the untidy dark hair tumbling over his forehead adhered to his temples as if they were perpetually damp. Yes, he looked ill, this young Glenn.

I remembered wondering, when Mrs. Glenn told me her story, why it had not occurred to her that her oldest son had probably joined the American forces and might have remained on the field with his junior. Apparently this tragic possibility had never troubled her. She seemed to have forgotten that there had ever been a war, and that a son of her own, with thousands of young Americans of his generation, had lost his life in it. And now it looked as though she had been gifted with a kind of prescience. The war did not last long enough for America to be called on to give her weaklings, as Europe had, and it was clear that Stephen Glenn, with his narrow shoulders and hectic cheekbones, could never have been wanted for active service. I suspected him of having been ill for longer than his mother knew.

Mrs. Glenn shone on him as he dropped down beside us. 'This is an old friend, Stephen, a very dear friend of your father's.' She added, extravagantly, that but for me she and her son might never have found each other. I protested: 'How absurd,' and young Glenn, stretching out his long limbs against the sandbank, and crossing his arms behind his head, turned on me a glance of rather weary good humor. 'Better give me a longer trial, my dear, before you thank him.'

Mrs. Glenn laughed contentedly, and continued, her eyes on her son: 'I was telling him that Mr. and Mrs. Brown are with us.'

'Ah, yes – ' said Stephen indifferently. I was inclined to like him a little less for his undisguised indifference. Ought he to have allowed his poor and unlucky foster parents to be so soon superseded by this beautiful and opulent new mother? But, after all, I mused, I had not yet seen the Browns, and though I had begun to suspect, from Catherine's tone as well as from Stephen's, that they both felt the presence of that couple to be vaguely oppressive, I decided that I must wait before drawing any conclusions. And then suddenly Mrs. Glenn said, in a tone of what I can only describe as icy cordiality: 'Ah, here they come now. They must have hurried back on purpose – '

• V •

MR. and Mrs. Brown advanced across the beach. Mrs. Brown led the way; she walked with a light springing step, and if I had been struck by Mrs. Glenn's recovered youthfulness, her co-mother, at a little distance, seemed to me positively girlish. She was smaller and much slighter than Mrs. Glen, and looked so much younger that I had a moment's doubt as to the possibility of her having, twenty-seven years earlier been of legal age to adopt a baby. Certainly she and Mr. Brown must have had exceptional reasons for concluding so early that heaven was not likely to bless their union. I had to admit, when Mrs. Brown came up, that I had overrated her juvenility. Slim, active and girlish she remained; but the freshness of her face was largely due to artifice, and the golden glints in her chestnut hair were a thought too golden. Still, she was a very pretty woman, with the alert cosmopolitan air of one who had acquired her elegance in places where the very best counterfeits are found. It will be seen that my first impression was none too favorable; but for all I knew of Mrs. Brown it might turn out that she had made the best of meager opportunities. She met my name with a conquering smile, said: 'Ah, yes – dear Mr. Norcutt. Mrs. Glenn has told us all we owe you' – and at the 'we' I detected a faint shadow on Mrs. Glenn's brow. Was it only maternal jealousy that provoked it? I suspected an even deeper antagonism. The women were so different, so diametrically opposed to each other in appearance, dress, manner, and the inherited standards, that if they had met as strangers it would have been hard for them to find a common ground of understanding; and the fact of that ground being furnished by Stephen hardly seemed to ease the situation.

'Well, what's the matter with taking some notice of little me?' piped a small dry man dressed in too-smart flannels, and wearing a too-white Panama which he removed with an elaborate flourish.

'Oh, of course! My husband – Mr. Norcutt.' Mrs. Brown laid a jeweled hand on Stephen's recumbent shoulder. 'Steve, you rude boy, you ought to have introduced your dad.' As she pressed his shoulder I noticed that her long oval nails were freshly lacquered with the last new shade of coral, and that the forefinger was darkly yellowed with nicotine. This familiar color scheme struck me at the moment as peculiarly distasteful.

Stephen vouchsafed no answer, and Mr. Brown remarked to me sardonically. 'You know you won't lose your money or your morals in this secluded spot.'

Mrs. Brown flashed a quick glance at him. 'Don't be so silly! It's much better for Steve to be in a quiet place where he can just sleep and eat and bask. His mother and I are going to be firm with him about that – aren't we, dearest?' She transferred her lacquered talons to Mrs. Glenn's shoulder, and the latter, with a just perceptible shrinking, replied gaily: 'As long as we can hold out against him!'

'Oh, this is the very place I was pining for,' said Stephen placidly. ('Gosh – *pining!*' Mr. Brown interpolated.) Stephen tilted his hat forward over his sunburnt nose with the drawn nostrils, crossed his arms under his thin neck, and closed his eyes. Mrs. Brown bent over Mrs. Glenn with one of her quick gestures. 'Darling – before we go in to lunch do let me fluff you out a little: so.' With a flashing hand she loosened the soft white waves under Mrs. Glenn's spreading hat brim. 'There – that's better; isn't it, Mr. Norcutt?'

Mrs. Glenn's face was a curious sight. The smile she had forced gave place to a marble rigidity; the old statuesqueness which had melted to flesh and blood stiffened her features again. 'Thank you . . . I'm afraid I never think. . . .'

'No, you never do; that's the trouble!' Mrs. Brown shot an arch glance at me. 'With her looks, oughtn't she to think? But perhaps it's lucky for the rest of us poor women she didn't – eh, Stevie?'

The color rushed to Mrs. Glenn's face; she was going to retort; to snub the dreadful woman. But the new softness had returned, and she merely lifted a warning finger. 'Oh, don't, please . . . speak to him. Can't you see that he's fallen asleep?'

O great King Solomon, I thought – and bowed my soul before the mystery.

I spent a fortnight at Les Calanques, and every day my perplexity deepened. The most conversible member of the little group was undoubtedly Stephen. Mrs. Glenn was as she had always been; beautiful, benevolent and inarticulate. When she sat on the beach beside the dozing Stephen, in her flowing dress, her large white umbrella tilted to shelter him, she reminded me of a carven angel spreading broad wings above a tomb (I could never look at her without being reminded of statuary); and to converse with a marble angel so engaged can never have been easy. But I was perhaps not wrong in suspecting that her smiling silence concealed a reluctance to talk about the Browns. Like many perfectly unegotistical women Catherine Glenn had no subject of conversation except her own affairs; and these at present so visibly hinged on the Browns that it was easy to see why silence was simpler.

Mrs. Brown, I may as well confess, bored me acutely. She was a perfect specimen of the middle-aged flapper, with layers and layers of hard-headed feminine craft under her romping ways. All this I suffered from chiefly because I knew it was making Mrs. Glenn suffer. But after all it was thanks to Mrs. Brown that she had found her son; Mrs. Brown had brought up Stephen, had made him (one was obliged to suppose) the whimsical dreamy charming creature he was; and again and again, when Mrs. Brown outdid herself in girlish archness or middle-aged craft, Mrs. Glenn's wounded eyes said to mine: 'Look at Stephen, isn't that enough?'

Certainly it was enough, enough even to excuse Mr. Brown's jocular allusions and arid anecdotes, his boredom at Les Calanques, and the too-liberal potations in which he drowned it. Mr. Brown, I may add, was not half as trying as his wife. For the first two or three days I was mildly diverted by his contempt for the quiet watering place in which his women had confined him, and his lordly conception of the life of pleasure, as exemplified by intimacy with the headwaiters of gilt-edged restaurants and the lavishing of large sums on horse racing and cards. 'Damn it, Norcutt, I'm not used to being mewed up in this kind of place. Perhaps it's different with you – all depends on a man's standards, don't it? Now before I lost my money – ' and so on. The odd thing was that, though this loss of fortune played a large part in the conversation of both husband and wife, I never somehow believed in it – I mean in the existence of the fortune. I hinted as much one day to Mrs. Glenn, but she only opened her noble eyes reproachfully, as if

I had implied that it discredited the Browns to dream of a fortune they had never had. 'They tell me Stephen was brought up with every luxury. And besides – their own tastes seem rather expensive, don't they?' she argued gently.

'That's the very reason.'

'The reason – ?'

'The only people I know who are totally without expensive tastes are the overwhelmingly wealthy. You see it when you visit palaces. They sleep on camp beds and live on boiled potatoes.'

Mrs. Glenn smiled. 'Stevie wouldn't have liked that.'

Stephen smiled also when I alluded to these past splendors. 'It must have been before I cut my first teeth. I know Boy's always talking about it; but I've got to take it on faith, just as you have.'

'Boy – ?'

'Didn't you know? He's always called "Boy." Boydon Brown – abbreviated by friends and family to "Boy." The Boy Browns. Suits them, doesn't it?'

It did; but I was sure that it suited him to say so.

'And you've always addressed your adopted father in that informal style?'

'Lord, yes; nobody's formal with Boy except headwaiters. They bow down to him; I don't know why. He's got the manner. I haven't. When I go to a restaurant they always give me the worst table and the stupidest waiter.' He leaned back against the sandbank and blinked contentedly seaward. 'Got a cigarette?'

'You know you oughtn't to smoke,' I protested.

'I know; but I do.' He held out a lean hand with prominent knuckles. 'As long as Kit's not about.' He called the marble angel, his mother, 'Kit'! And yet I was not offended – I let him do it, just as I let him have one of my cigarettes. If 'Boy' had a way with headwaiters his adopted son undoubtedly had one with lesser beings; his smile, his faint hoarse laugh would have made me do his will even if his talk had not conquered me. We sat for hours on the sands, discussing and dreaming; not always undisturbed, for Mrs. Brown had a tiresome way of hovering and 'listening in', as she archly called it – ('I don't want Stevie to depreciate his poor ex-mamma to you.' she explained one day); and whenever Mrs. Brown (who, even at Les Calanques, had contrived to create a social round for herself) was bathing, dancing, playing bridge, or being waved, massaged or manicured, the other mother, assuring herself from an upper window that the coast was clear, would descend in her gentle majesty and turn our sandbank into a throne by sitting on it. But now and then Stephen and I had a half hour to ourselves and then I tried to lead his talk to the past.

He seemed willing enough that I should, but uninterested, and unable to recover many details. 'I never can remember things that don't matter – and so far nothing about me has mattered,' he said with a humorous melancholy. 'I mean, not till I struck mother Kit.'

He had vague recollections of continental travels as a little boy; had afterward been at a private school in Switzerland; had tried to pass himself off as a Canadian volunteer in 1915, and in 1917 to enlist in the American army, but had failed in each case – one had only to look at him to see why. The war over, he had worked for a time at Julian's and then broken down; and after that it had been a hard row to hoe till mother Kit came along. By George, but he'd never forget what she'd done for him – never!

'Well, it's a way mothers have with their sons,' I remarked.

He flushed under his bronze tanning, and said simply: 'Yes – only you see I didn't know.'

His view of the Browns, while not unkindly, was so detached that I suspected him of regarding his own mother with the same objectivity; but when we spoke of her there was a different note in his voice. 'I didn't know' – it was a new experience to him to be really mothered. As a type, however, she clearly puzzled him. He was too sensitive to class her (as the Browns obviously did) as a simple-minded woman to whom nothing had ever happened: but he could not conceive what sort of thing could happen to a woman of her kind. I gathered that she had explained the strange episode of his adoption by telling him that at the time of his birth she had been 'secretly married' – poor Catherine! – to his father, but that 'family circumstances' had made it needful to conceal his existence till the marriage could be announced; by which time he had vanished with his adopted parents. I guessed how it must have puzzled Stephen to adapt his interpretation of this ingenuous tale to what, in the light of Mrs. Glenn's character, he could make out of her past. Of obvious explanations there were plenty; but evidently none fitted into his vision of her. For a moment (I could see) he had suspected a sentimental lie, a tender past, between Mrs. Glenn and myself; but this his quick perceptions soon discarded, and he apparently resigned himself to regarding her as inscrutably proud and incorrigibly perfect. 'I'd like to paint her some day – if ever I'm fit to,' he said; and I wondered whether his scruples applied to his moral or artistic inadequacy.

At the doctor's orders he had dropped his painting altogether since his last breakdown; but it was manifestly the one thing he cared for, and perhaps the only reason he had for wanting to get well. 'When you've dropped to a certain level, it's so damnably easy to keep on till you're altogether down and out. So much easier than dragging up hill again. But I do want to get well enough to paint mother Kit. She's a subject.'

One day it rained, and he was confined to the house. I went up to sit with him, and he got out some of his sketches and studies. Instantly he was transformed from an amiably mocking dilettante into an absorbed and passionate professional. 'This is the only life I've ever had. All the rest – !' He made a grimace that turned his thin face into a death's-head. 'Cinders!'

The studies were brilliant – there was no doubt of that. The question was – the eternal question – what would they turn into when he was well enough to finish them? For the moment the problem did not present itself and I could praise and encourage him in all sincerity. My words brought a glow into his face, but also, as it turned out, sent up his temperature. Mrs. Glenn reproached me mildly; she begged me not to let him get excited about his pictures. I promised not to, and reassured on that point she asked if I didn't think he had talent – real talent? 'Very great talent, yes,' I assured her, and she burst into tears – not of grief or agitation, but of a deep unwelling joy. 'Oh, what have I done to deserve it all – to deserve such happiness? Yet I always knew if I could find him he'd make me happy!' She caught both my hands, and pressed her wet cheek on mine. That was one of her unclouded hours.

There were others not so radiant. I could see that the Browns were straining at the leash. With the seductions of Juan-les-Pins and Antibes in the offing, why, their frequent allusions implied, must they remain marooned at Les Calanques? Of course, for one thing, Mrs. Brown admitted she hadn't the clothes to show herself on a smart *plage*. Though so few were worn they had to come from the big dressmakers; and the latter's charges, everybody knew, were in inverse ration to the amount of material used. 'So that to be really naked is ruinous.' she concluded, laughing; and I saw the narrowing of Catherine's lips. As for Mr. Brown, he added morosely that if a man couldn't take a hand at baccarat, or offer his friends something decent to eat and drink, it was better to vegetate at Les Calanques, and be done with it. Only, when a fellow'd been used to having plenty of money. . . .

I saw at once what had happened. Mrs. Glenn, whose material wants did not extend beyond the best plumbing and expensive clothes (and the latter were made to do for three seasons), did not fully understand the Brown's aspirations. Her fortune, though adequate, was not large, and she had settled on Stephen's adoptive parents an allowance which, converted into francs, made a generous showing. It was obvious, however, that what they hoped was to get more money. There had been debts in the background, perhaps; who knew but the handsome Stephen had had his share of them? One day I suggested discreetly to Mrs. Glenn that if she wished to be alone with her son she might offer the Browns a trip to Juan-les-Pins, or some such center of gaiety. But I pointed out that the precedent might be dangerous, and advised her first to consult Stephen. 'I suspect he's as anxious to have them go as you are,' I said recklessly; and her flush of pleasure rewarded me. 'Oh, you mustn't say that,' she reproved me, laughing, and added that she would think over my advice, I am not sure if she did consult Stephen, but she offered the Browns a holiday, and they accepted it without false pride.

• VI •

AFTER my departure from Les Calanques I had no news of Mrs. Glenn till she returned to Paris in October. Then she begged me to call at the hotel where I had previously seen her, and where she was now staying with Stephen – and the Browns.

She suggested, rather mysteriously, my dining with her on a particular evening, when, as she put it, 'everybody' would be out; and when I arrived she explained that Stephen had gone to the country for the week-end, with some old comrades from Julian's, and that the Browns were dining at a smart nightclub in Montmartre. 'So we'll have a quiet time all by ourselves.' She added that Steve was so much better that he was trying his best to persuade her to spend the winter in Paris, and let him get back to his painting, but in spite of the good news I thought she looked worn and dissatisfied.

I was surprised to find the Browns still with her, and told her so.

'Well, you see, it's difficult,' she returned with a troubled frown. 'They love Stephen so much that they won't give him up; and how can I blame them? What are my rights, compared to theirs?'

Finding this hard to answer, I put another question 'Did you enjoy your quiet time with Stephen while they were in Juan-les-Pins?'

'Oh, they didn't go; at least Mrs. Brown didn't – Chrissy she likes me to call her,' Mrs. Glenn corrected herself hurriedly. 'She couldn't bear to leave Stephen.'

'So she sacrificed Juan-les-Pins, and that handsome check?'

'Not the check; she kept that. Boy went,' Mrs. Glenn added apologetically. Boy and Chrissy – it had come to that! I looked away from my old friend's troubled face before putting my next question. 'And Stephen – ?'

'Well, I can't exactly tell how he feels. But I sometimes think he'd like to be alone with me.' A passing radiance smoothed away her frown. 'He's hinted that, if we decide to stay here, they might be tempted by winter sports, and go to the Engadine later.'

'So that they would have the benefit of the high air instead of Stephen?' She coloured a little, looked down, and then smiled at me. 'What can I do?'

I resolved to sound Stephen on his adopted parents. The present situation would have to be put an end to somehow; but it had puzzling elements. Why had Mrs. Brown refused to go to Juan-les-Pins? Was it, as I had suspected, because there were debts, and more pressing uses for the money? Or was it that she was so much attached to her adopted son as to be jealous of his mother's influence? This was far more to be feared; but it did not seem to fit in with what I knew of Mrs. Brown. The trouble was that what I knew was so little. Mrs. Brown, though in one way so intelligble, was in another as cryptic to me as Catherine Glenn was to Stephen. The surface was transparent enough; but what did the blur beneath conceal? Troubled waters, or just a mud flat? My only hope was to try to get Stephen to tell me.

Stephen had hired a studio – against his doctor's advice, I gathered – and spent most of his hours there, in the company of his old group of painting friends. Mrs. Glenn had been there once or twice, but in spite of his being so sweet and dear to her she had felt herself in the way – as she undoubtedly was. 'I can't keep up with their talk, you know,' she explained. With whose talk could she, poor angel?

I suggested that, for the few weeks of their Paris sojourn, it would be kinder to let Stephen have his fling; and she agreed. Afterward, in the mountains, he could recuperate, youth had such powers of self-healing. But I urged her to insist on his spending another winter in the Engadine; not at one of the big fashionable places –

She interrupted me. 'I'm afraid Boy and Chrissy wouldn't like – '

'Oh, for God's sake; can't you give Boy and Chrissy another check, and send them off to Egypt, or to Monte Carlo?'

She hesitated. 'I could try; but I don't believe she'd go. Not without Stevie.'

'And what does Stevie say?'

'What can he say? She brought him up. She was there – all the years when I'd failed him.'

It was unanswerable, and I felt the uselessness of any advice I could give. The situation could be changed only by some internal readjustment. Still, out of pity for the poor mother, I determined to try a word with Stephen. She gave me the address of his studio, and the next day I went there.

It was in a smart-looking modern building in the Montparnasse quarter; lofty, well-lit and well-warmed. What a contrast to his earlier environment! I climbed to his door, rang the bell and waited. There were sounds of moving about within, but as no one came I rang again; and finally Stephen opened the door. His face lit up pleasantly when he saw me. 'Oh, it's you, my dear fellow!' But I caught a hint of constraint in his voice.

'I'm not in the way? Don't mind throwing me out if I am.'

'I've got a sitter – ' he began, visibly hesitating.

'Oh, in that case – '

'No, no; it's only – the fact is, it's Chrissy. I was trying to do a study of her – '

He led me across the passage and into the studio. It was large and flooded with light. Divans against the walls; big oak tables; shaded lamps, a couple of tall screens. From behind one of them emerged Mrs. Brown, hatless, and slim, in a pale summer-like frock, her chestnut hair becomingly tossed about her eyes. 'Dear Mr. Norcutt. So glad you turned up! I was getting such a stiff neck – Stephen's merciless.'

'May I see the result?' I asked; and 'Oh, no,' she protested in mock terror, 'it's too frightful – it really is. I think he thought he was doing a *nature morte* – lemons and a bottle of beer, or something!'

'It's not fit for inspection,' Stephen agreed.

The room was spacious, and not overcrowded. Glancing about, I could see only one easel with a painting on it. Stephen went up and turned the canvas face inward, with the familiar gesture of the artist who does not wish to challenge attention. But before he did so I had remarked that the painting was neither a portrait of Mrs. Brown nor a still-life. It was a rather brilliant three-quarter sketch of a woman's naked back and hips. A model, no doubt – but why did he wish to conceal it?

'I'm so glad you came.' Mrs. Brown repeated, smiling intensely. I stood still, hoping she was about to go; but she dropped down on one of the divans, tossing back her tumbled curls. 'He works too hard, you know; I wish you'd tell him so. Steve, come here and stretch out,' she commanded, indicating the other end of the divan. 'You ought to take a good nap.'

The hint was so obvious that I said: 'In that case I'd better come another time.'

'No, no; wait till I give you a cocktail. We all need cocktails. Where's the shaker, darling?' Mrs. Brown was on her feet again, alert and gay. She dived behind the screen which had previously concealed her, and reappeared with the necessary appliances. 'Bring up that little table, Mr. Norcutt, please. Oh I know – dear Kit doesn't approve of cocktails; and she's right. But look at him – dead-beat! If he will slave at his painting, what's he to do? I was scolding him about it when you came in.'

The shaker danced in her flashing hands, and in a trice she was holding a glass out to me, and another to Stephen, who had obediently flung himself down on the divan. As he took the glass she bent and laid her lips on his damp hair. 'You bad boy, you!'

I looked at Stephen. 'You ought to get out of this, and start straight off for Switzerland,' I admonished him.

'Oh, hell,' he groaned. 'Can't you get Kit to drop all that?'

Mrs. Brown made an impatient gesture. 'Isn't he too foolish? Of course he ought to go away. He looks like nothing on earth. But his only idea of Switzerland is one of those awful places we used to have to go to because they were cheap, where there's nothing to do in the

evening but to sit with clergyman's wives looking at stereopticon views
of glaciers. I tell him he'll love St. Moritz. There's a thrill there every
minute.'

Stephen closed his eyes and sank his head back in the cushions
without speaking. His face was drawn and weary; I was startled at the
change in him since we had parted at Les Calanques.

Mrs. Brown, following my glance, met it with warning brows and
a finger on her painted lips. It was like a parody of Mrs. Glenn's
maternal gesture, and I perceived that it meant. 'Can't you see that he's
falling asleep? Do be tactful and slip out without disturbing him.'

What could I do but obey? A moment later the studio door had
closed on me, and I was going down the long flights of stairs. The
worst of it was that I was not at all sure that Stephen was really asleep.

• VII •

THE next morning I received a telephone call from Stephen asking me
to lunch. We met at a quiet restaurant near his studio, and when, after
an admirably-chosen meal, we settled down to coffe and cigars, he said
carelessly: 'Sorry you got thrown out that way yesterday.'

'Oh, well – I saw you were tired, and I didn't want to interfere
with your nap.'

He looked down moodily at his plate. 'Tired – yes, I'm tired. But
I didn't want a nap. I merely simulated slumber to try and make Chrissy
shut up.'

'Ah – ' I said.

He shot a quick glance at me, almost resentfully, I thought. Then
he went on: 'There are times when aimless talk nearly kills me. I
wonder,' he broke out suddenly, 'If you can realize what it feels like
for a man who's never – I mean for an orphan – suddenly to find
himself with two mothers?'

I said I could see it might be arduous.

'Arduous! It's literally asphyxiating.' He frowned, and then smiled
whimsically. 'When I need all the fresh air I can get!'

'My dear fellow – what you need first of all is to get away from
cities and studios.'

His frown deepened. 'I know; I know all that. Only, you see – well,
to begin with, before I turn up my toes I want to do something for
mother Kit.'

'Do something?'

'Something to show her that I was – was worth all this fuss.' He
paused, and turned his coffee spoon absently between his long twitching
fingers.

I shrugged. 'Whatever you do, she'll always think that. Mothers do.'

He murmured after me slowly: 'Mothers – '

'What she wants you to do now is to get well,' I insisted.

'Yes; I know; I'm pledged to get well. But somehow that bargain doesn't satisfy me. If I don't get well I want to leave something behind me that'll make her think: "If he'd lived a little longer he'd have pulled it off".'

'If you left a gallery of masterpieces it wouldn't help her much.'

His face clouded, and he looked at me wistfully. 'What the devil else can I do?'

'Go to Switzerland, and let yourself be bored there for a whole winter. Then you can come back and paint, and enjoy your success instead of having the enjoyment done for you by your heirs.'

'Oh, what a large order – ' he sighed, and drew out his cigarettes.

For a moment we were both silent; then he raised his eyes and looked straight at me. 'Supposing I don't get well, there's another thing . . .' He hesitated a moment. 'Do you happen to know if my mother has made her will?'

I imagine my look must have surprised him, for he hurried on: 'It's only this: if I should drop out – you can never tell – there are Chrissy and Boy, poor, helpless devils. I can't forget what they've been to me . . . done for me . . . though sometimes I daresay I seem ungrateful . . .'

I listened to his embarrassed phrases with an embarrassment at least as great. 'You may be sure your mother won't forget either,' I said.

'No; I suppose not. Of course not. Only sometimes – you can see for yourself that things are a little breezy. . . . They feel that perhaps she doesn't always remember for how many years . . .' He brought the words out as though he were reciting a lesson. 'I can't forget it . . . of course,' he added, painfully.

I glanced at my watch, and stood up. I wanted to spare him the evident effort of going on. 'Mr. and Mrs. Brown's tastes don't always agree with your mother's. That's evident. If you could persuade them to go off somewhere – or to lead more independent lives when they're with her – mightn't that help?'

He cast a despairing glance at me. 'Lord – I wish you'd try! But you see they're anxious – anxious about their future. . . .'

'I'm sure they needn't be,' I answered shortly, more and more impatient to make an end.

His face lit up with a suddenness that hurt me. 'Oh, well . . . it's sure to be all right if you say so. Of course you know.'

'I know your mother,' I said, holding out my hand for good-bye.

• VIII •

SHORTLY after my lunch with Stephen Glenn I was unexpectedly
detached from my job in Paris and sent on a special mission to the
other side of the world. I was sorry to bid good-bye to Mrs. Glenn,
but relieved to be rid of the thankless task of acting as her counselor.
Not that she herself was not thankful, poor soul; but the situation
abounded in problems, to not one of which could I find a solution; and
I was embarrassed by her simple faith in my ability to do so. 'Get rid
of the Browns; pension them off,' I could only repeat; but since my
talk with Stephen I had little hope of his mother's acting on this suggestion. 'You'll probably all end up together in St. Moritz,' I prophesied;
and a few months later a belated Paris *Herald*, overtaking me in my
remote corner of the globe, informed me that among the guests of the
new Ice Palace Hotel at St. Moritz were Mrs. Glenn of New York, Mr.
Stephen Glenn, and Mr. and Mrs. Boydon Brown. From succeeding
numbers of the same sheet I learned that Mr. and Mrs. Boydon Brown
were among those entertaining on the opening night of the new
Restaurant des Glaciers, that the Boydon Brown cup for the most original
costume at the Annual Fancy Ball of the Skiers' Club had been won
by Miss Thora Dacy (costume designed by the well-known artist,
Stephen Glenn), and that Mr. Boydon Brown had been one of the
stewards of the dinner given to the participants in the ice hockey match
between the St. Moritz and Suvretta teams. And on such items I was
obliged to nourish my memory of my friends, for no direct news came
to me from any of them.

When I bade Mrs. Glenn good-bye I had told her that I had hopes
of a post in the State Department at the close of my temporary mission,
and she said, a little wistfully; 'How wonderful if we could meet next
year in America! As soon as Stephen is strong enough I want him to
come back and live with me in his father's house.' This seemed a natural
wish; and it struck me that it might be the means of effecting a break
with the Browns. But Mrs. Glenn shook her head. 'Chrissy says a
winter in New York would amuse them both tremendously.'

I was not so sure that it would amuse Stephen, and therefore did
not base much hope on the plan. The one thing Stephen wanted was
to get back to Paris and paint: it would presumably be his mother's lot
to settle down there when his health permitted.

I heard nothing more until I got back to Washington the following
spring; then I had a line from Stephen. The winter in the Engadine had
been a deadly bore, but had really done him good, and his mother was
just leaving for Paris to look for an apartment. She meant to take one
on a long lease, and have the furniture of the New York house sent
out – it would be jolly getting it arranged. As for him, the doctors said
he was well enough to go on with his painting and, as I knew, it was

the one thing he cared for; so I might cast off all anxiety about the family. That was all – and perhaps I should have obeyed if Mrs. Glenn had also written. But no word, no message even, came from her; and as she always wrote when there was good news to give, her silence troubled me.

It was in the course of the same summer, during a visit to Bar Harbor, that one evening, dining with a friend, I found myself next to a slight pale girl with large gray eyes, who suddenly turned them on me reproachfully. 'Then you don't know me? I'm Thora.'

I looked my perplexity, and she added: 'Aren't you Steve Glenn's great friend? He's always talking of you.' My memory struggled with a tangle of oddments, from which I finally extricated the phrase in the *Herald* about Miss Thora Dacy and the fancy-dress ball at St. Moritz. 'You're the young lady who won the Boydon Brown prize in a costume designed by the well-known artist, Mr. Stephen Glenn!'

Her charming face fell. 'If you know me only through that newspaper rubbish. . . . I had an idea the well-known artist might have told you about me.'

'He's not much of a correspondent.'

'No; but I thought – '

'Why won't you tell me yourself instead?'

Dinner was over, and the company had moved out to a wide, starlit verandah looking seaward. I found a corner for two, and installed myself there with my new friend, who was also Stephen's. 'I like him awfully – don't you?' she began at once. I liked her way of saying it; I liked her direct gaze; I found myself thinking: 'But this may turn out to be the solution!' For I felt sure that, if circumstances ever gave her the right to take part in the coming struggle over Stephen, Thora Dacy would be on the side of the angels.

As if she had guessed my thought she continued: 'And I do love Mrs. Glenn too – don't you?'

I assured her that I did, and she added: 'And Steve loves her – I'm sure he does!'

'Well, if he didn't – !' I exclaimed indignantly.

'That's the way I feel; he ought to. Only, you see, Mrs. Brown – the Browns adopted him when he was a baby, didn't they, and brought him up as if he'd been their own child? I suppose they must know him better than any of us do; and Mrs. Brown says he can't help feeling bitter about – I don't know all the circumstances, but his mother did desert him soon after he was born, didn't she? And if it hadn't been for the Browns – '

'The Browns – the Browns! It's a pity they don't leave it to other people to proclaim their merits! And I don't believe Stephen does feel as they'd like you to think. If he does, he ought to be kicked. If – if complicated family reasons obliged Mrs. Glenn to separate herself from him when he was a baby, the way she mourned for him all those years, and her devotion since they've come together again, have atoned a thousand-fold for that old unhappiness; and no one knows it better than Stephen.'

The girl received this without protesting. 'I'm so glad – so glad.' There was a new vibration in her voice; she looked up gravely. 'I've always *wanted* to love Mrs. Glenn the best.'

'Well, you'd better; especially if you love Stephen.'

'Oh, I do love him,' she said simply. 'But of course I understand his feeling as he does about the Browns.'

I hesitated, not knowing how I ought to answer the question I detected under this; but at length I said: 'Stephen, at any rate, must feel that Mrs. Brown has no business to insinuate anything against his mother. He ought to put a stop to that.' She met the suggestion with a sigh, and stood up to join another group. 'Thora Dacy may yet save us!' I thought, as my gaze followed her light figure across the room.

I had half a mind to write of that meeting to Stephen or to his mother; but the weeks passed while I procrastinated, and one day I received a note from Stephen. He wrote (with many messages from Mrs. Glenn) to give me their new address, and to tell me that he was hard at work at his painting, and doing a 'promising portrait of mother Kit.' He signed himself my affectionate Steve, and added underneath: 'So glad you've come across little Thora. She took a most tremendous shine to you. Do please be nice to her; she's a dear child. But don't encourage any illusions about me, please; marrying's not in my program.' 'So that's that,' I thought, and tore the letter up rather impatiently. I wondered if Thora Dacy already knew that her illusions were not to be encouraged.

• IX •

THE months went by, and I heard no more from my friends. Summer came round again, and with it the date of my six weeks' holiday, which I purposed to take that year in Europe. Two years had passed since I had last seen Mrs. Glenn, and during that time I had received only two or three brief notes from her, thanking me for Christmas wishes, or telling me that Stephen was certainly better, though he would take no care of himself. But several months had passed since the date of her last report.

I had meant to spend my vacation in a trip in south-western France, and on the way over I decided to invite Stephen Glenn to join me. I therefore made direct for Paris, and the next morning rang him up at Mrs. Glenn's. Mrs. Brown's voice met me in reply, informing me that Stephen was no longer living with his mother. 'Read the riot act to us all a few months ago – said he wanted to be independent. You know his fads. Dear Catherine was foolishly upset. As I said to her . . . yes, I'll give you his address; but poor Steve's not well just now . . . Oh, go on a trip with you? No; I'm afraid there's no chance of that. The truth is, he told us he didn't want to be bothered – rather warned us off the premises; even poor old Boy; and you know he adores Boy. I haven't seen him myself for several days. But you can try . . . Oh, of course you can try . . . No; I'm afraid you can't see Catherine either – not just at present. She's been ill too – feverish; worrying about her naughty Steve, I suspect. I'm mounting guard for a few days, and not letting her see anybody till her temperature goes down. And would you do me a favor? Don't write – don't let her know you're here. Not for a day or two, I mean. . . . She'd be so distressed at not being able to see you. . . .'

She rang off, and left me to draw my own conclusions.

They were not of the pleasantest. I was perplexed by the apparent sequestration of both my friends, still more so by the disquieting mystery of Mrs. Glenn's remaining with the Brown's while Stephen had left them. Why had she not followed her son? Was it because she had not been allowed to? I conjectured that Mrs. Brown, knowing I was likely to put these questions to the persons concerned, was maneuvering to prevent my seeing them. If she could maneuver, so could I; but for the moment I had to consider what line to take. The fact of her givin me Stephen's address made me suspect that she had taken measures to prevent my seeing him; and if that were so there was not much use in making the attempt. And Mrs. Glenn was in bed, and 'feverish', and not to be told of my arrival. . . .

After a day's pondering I reflected that telegrams sometimes penetrate where letters fail to, and decided to telegraph to Stephen. No reply came, but the following afternoon, as I was leaving my hotel a taxi drove up and Mrs. Glenn descended from it. She was dressed in black, with many hanging scarves and veils, as if she either feared the air or the searching eyes of someone who might be interested in her movements. But for her white hair and heavy stooping lines she might have suggested the furtive figure of a young woman stealing to her lover. But when I looked at her the analogy seemed a profanation.

To women of Catherine Glenn's ripe beauty thinness gives a sudden look of age; and the face she raised among her thrown-back veils was emaciated. Illness and anxiety had scarred her as years and weather scar some beautiful still image on a church front. She took my hand, and I led her into the empty reading-room. 'You've been ill!' I said.

'Not very; just a bad cold.' It was characteristic that while she looked at me with grave beseeching eyes her words were trivial, ordinary. 'Chrissy's so devoted – takes such care of me. She was afraid to have me go out. The weather's so unsettled, isn't it? But really I'm all right; and as it cleared this morning I just ran off for a minute to see you.' The entreaty in her eyes became a prayer. 'Only don't tell her, will you? Dear Steve's been ill too – did you know? And so I just slipped out while Chrissy went to see him. She sees him nearly every day, and brings me the news.' She gave a sigh and added, hardly above a whisper: 'He sent me your address. She doesn't know.'

I listened with a sense of vague oppression. Why this mystery, this watching, these evasions? Was it because Steve was not allowed to write to me that he had smuggled my address to his mother? Mystery clung about us in damp fog-like coils, like the scarves and veils about Mrs. Glenn's thin body. But I knew that I must let my visitor tell her tale in her own way; and, of course, when it was told, most of the mystery subsisted, for she was in it, enveloped in it, blinded by it. I gathered, however, that Stephen had been very unhappy. He had met at St. Moritz a girl whom he wanted to marry: Thora Dacy – ah, I'd heard of her, I'd met her? Mrs. Glenn's face lit up. She had thought the child lovely; she had known the family in Washington – excellent people; she had been so happy in the prospect of Stephen's happiness. And then something had happened . . . she didn't know, she had an idea that Chrissy hadn't liked the girl. The reason Stephen gave was that in his state of health he oughtn't to marry; but at the time he'd been perfectly well – the doctors had assured his mother that his lungs were sound, and that there was no such scruples, still less why Chrissy should have encouraged them. For Chrissy had also put it on the ground of health; she had approved his decision. And since then he had been unsettled irritable, difficult – oh, very difficult. Two or three months ago the state of tension in which they had all been living had reached a climax; Mrs. Glenn couldn't say how or why – it was still obscure to her. But she suspected that Stephen had quarreled with the Browns. They had patched it up now, they saw each other; but for a time there had certainly been something wrong. And suddenly Stephen had left the apartment, and moved into a wretched studio in a shabby quarter. The only reason he gave for leaving was that he had too many mothers – that was a joke, of course, Mrs. Glenn explained . . . but her eyes filled as she said it.

Poor mother – and, alas, poor Stephen! All the sympathy I could spare from the mother went to the son. He had behaved harshly, cruelly, no doubt; the young do; but under what provocation! I understood his saying that he had too many mothers; and I suspected that what he had tried for – and failed to achieve – was a break with the Browns. Trust Chrissy to baffle that attempt, I thought bitterly; she had obviously deflected the dispute, and made the consequences fall upon his mother. And at bottom everything was unchanged.

Unchanged – except for that thickening of the fog. At the moment it was almost as impenetrable to me as to Mrs. Glenn. Certain things

I could understand that she could not: for instance, why Stephen had left home. I could guess that the atmosphere had become unbreathable. But if so, it was certainly Mrs. Brown's doing, and what interest had she in sowing discord between Stephen and his mother? With a shock of apprehension my mind reverted to Stephen's enquiry about his mother's will. It had offended me at the time; now it frightened me. If I was right in suspecting that he had tried to break with his adopted parents – over the question of the will, no doubt, or at any rate over their general selfishness and rapacity – then his attempt had failed, since he and the Browns were still on good terms, and the only result of the dispute had been to separate him from his mother. At the thought my indignation burned afresh. 'I mean to see Stephen,' I declared, looking resolutely at Mrs. Glenn.

'But he's not well enough, I'm afraid; he told me to send you his love, and to say that perhaps when you come back – '

'Ah, you've seen him, then?'

She shook her head. 'No; he telegraphed me this morning. He doesn't even write any longer.' Her eyes filled, and she looked away from me.

He too used the telegraph! It gave me more to think about than poor Mrs. Glenn could know. I continued to look at her. 'Don't you want to send him a telegram in return? You could write it here, and give it to me,' I suggested. She hesitated, seemed half to assent, and then stood up abruptly.

'No; I'd better not. Chrissy takes my messages. If I telegraphed she might wonder – she might be hurt – '

'Yes; I see.'

'But I must be off; I've stayed too long.' She cast a nervous glance at her watch. 'When you come back . . .' she repeated.

When we reached the door of the hotel rain was falling, and I drew her back into the vestibule while the porter went to call a taxi. 'Why haven't you your own motor?' I asked.

'Oh, Chrissy wanted the motor. She had to go to see Stevie – and of course she didn't know I should be going out. You won't tell her, will you?' Mrs. Glenn cried back to me as the door of the taxi closed on her.

The taxi drove off, and I was standing on the pavement looking after it when a handsomely appointed private motor glided up to the hotel. The chauffeur sprang down, and I recognized him as the man who had driven Mrs. Glenn when we had been together at Les Calanques. I was therefore not surprised to see Mrs. Brown, golden haired and slim, descending under his unfurled umbrella. She held a note in her hand, and looked at me with a start of surprise. 'What luck! I was going to try to find out when you were likely to be in – and here you are! Concierges are always so secretive that I'd written as well.' She held the envelope up with her brilliant smile. 'Am I butting in? Or may I come and have a talk?'

I led her to the reading room which Mrs. Glenn had so lately left, and suggested a cup of tea which I had forgotten to offer to her predecessor.

She made a gay grimace. 'Tea? Oh, no – thanks. Perhaps we might go round presently to the Nouveau Luxe grill for a cocktail. But it's rather early yet; there's nobody there at this hour. And I want to talk to you about Stevie.'

She settled herself in Mrs. Glenn's corner, and as she sat there, slender and alert in her perfectly-cut dark coat and skirt, with her silver fox slung at the exact fashion plate angle, I felt the irony of these two women succeeding each other in the same seat to talk to me on the same subject. Mrs. Brown groped in her bag for a jade cigarette case, and lifted her smiling eyes to mine. 'Catherine's just been here, hasn't she? I passed her in a taxi at the corner,' she remarked lightly.

'She's been here; yes. I scolded her for not being in her own motor.' I rejoined, with an attempt at the same tone.

Mrs. Brown laughed. 'I knew you would! But I'd taken the motor on purpose to prevent her going out. She has a very bad cold, as I told you; and the doctor has absolutely forbidden – '

'Then why didn't you let me go to see her?'

'Because the doctor forbids her to see visitors. I told you that too. Didn't you notice how hoarse she is?'

I felt my anger rising. 'I noticed how unhappy she is,' I said bluntly.

'Oh, unhappy – why is she unhappy? If I were in her place I should just lie back and enjoy life,' said Mrs. Brown, with a sort of cold impatience.

'She's unhappy about Stephen.'

Mrs. Brown looked at me quickly. 'She came here to tell you so, I suppose? Well – he *has* behaved badly.'

'Why did you let him?'

She laughed again, this time ironically. 'Let him? Ah, you believe in that legend? The legend that I do what I like with Stephen.' She bent her head to light another cigarette. 'He's behaved just as badly to me, my good man – and to Boy. And *we* don't go about complaining!'

'Why should you, when you see him every day?'

At this she bridled, with a flitting smile. 'Can I help it – if it's me he wants?'

'Yes, I believe you can,' I said resolutely.

'Oh, thanks! I suppose I ought to take that as a compliment.'

'Take it as you like. Why don't you make Stephen see his mother?'

'Dear Mr. Norcutt, if I had any influence over Stephen, do you suppose I'd let him quarrel with his bread and butter? To put it on utilitarian grounds, why should I?' She lifted her clear shallow eyes and looked straight into mine – and I found no answer. There was something impenetrable to me beneath that shallowness.

'But why did Stephen leave his mother?' I persisted.

She shrugged, and looked down at her rings, among which I fancied I saw a new one, a dark luminous stone in claws of platinum. She caught my glance. 'You're admiring my brown diamond? A beauty, isn't it? Dear Catherine gave it to me for Christmas. The angel! Do you suppose I wouldn't do anything to spare her all this misery? I wish I could tell you why Stephen left her. Perhaps . . . perhaps because she *is* such an angel . . . Young men – you understand? She was always wrapping him up, lying awake to listen for his latchkey. . . . Steve's rather a Bohemian; suddenly he struck – that's all I know.'

I saw at once that this contained a shred of truth wrapped round an impenetrable lie; and I saw also that to tell that lie had not been Mrs. Brown's main object. She had come for a still deeper reason, and I could only wait for her to reveal it.

She glanced up reproachfully. 'How hard you are on me – always! From the very first day – don't I know? And never more than now. Don't you suppose I can guess what you're thinking? You're accusing me of trying to prevent your seeing Catherine; and in reality I came here to ask you to see her – to beg you to – as soon as she's well enough. If you'd only trusted me, instead of persuading her to slip off on the sly and come here in this awful weather. . . .'

It was on the tip of my tongue to declare that I was guiltless of such perfidy; but it occurred to me that my visitor might be trying to find out how Mrs. Glenn had known I was in Paris, and I decided to say nothing.

'At any rate, if she's no worse I'm sure she could see you tomorrow. Why not come and dine? I'll carry Boy off to a restaurant, and you and she can have a cozy evening together, like old times. You'd like that, wouldn't you?' Mrs. Brown's face was veiled with a retrospective emotion: I saw that, less acute than Stephen, she still believed in a sentimental past between myself and Catherine Glenn. 'She must have been one of the loveliest creatures that ever lived – wasn't she? Even now no one can come up to her. You don't know how I wish she liked me better; that she had more confidence in me. If she had, she'd know that I love Stephen as much as she does – perhaps more. For so many years he was mine, all mine! But it's all so difficult – at this moment, for instance. . . .' She paused, jerked her silver fox back into place, and gave me a prolonged view of meditative lashes. At last she said: 'Perhaps you don't know that Steve's final folly has been to refuse his allowance. He returned the last check to Catherine with a dreadful letter.'

'Dreadful? How?'

'Telling her he was old enough to shift for himself – that he refused to sell his independence any longer, perfect madness.'

'Atrocious cruelty – '

'Yes; that too. I told him so. But do you realize the result?' The lashes, suddenly lifted, gave me the full appeal of wide, transparent eyes. 'Steve's starving – voluntarily starving himself. Or would be, if Boy and I hadn't scraped together our last pennies. . . .'

'If independence is what he wants, why should he take your pennies when he won't take his mother's?'

'Ah – there's the point. He will.' She looked down again, fretting her rings. 'Ill as he is, how could he live if he didn't take somebody's pennies? If I could sell my brown diamond without Catherine's missing it I'd have done it long ago, and you need never have known of all this. But she's so sensitive – and she notices everything. She literally spies on me. I'm at my wits' end. If you'd only help me!'

'How in the world can I?'

'You're the only person who can. If you'd persuade her, as long as this queer mood of Stephen's lasts, to draw his monthly check in my name, I'd see that he gets it – and that he uses it. He would, you know, if he thought it came from Boy and me.'

I looked at her quickly. 'That's why you want me to see her. To get her to give you her son's allowance?'

Her lips parted as if she were about to return an irritated answer; but she twisted them into a smile. 'If you like to describe it in that way – I can't help your putting an unkind interpretation on whatever I do. I was prepared for that when I came here.' She turned her bright inclement face on me. 'If you think I enjoy humiliating myself! After all, it's not so much for Stephen that I ask it as for his mother. Have you thought of that? If she knew that in his crazy pride he was depriving himself of the most necessary things, wouldn't she do anything on earth to prevent it? She's his *real* mother. . . . I'm nothing. . . .'

'You're everything, if he sees you and listens to you.'

She received this with the air of secret triumph that met every allusion to her power over Stephen. Was she right, I wondered, in saying that she loved him even more than his mother did? 'Everything?' she murmured deprecatingly. 'It's you who are everything, who can help us all. What can I do?'

I pondered a moment, and then said, 'You can let me see Stephen.'

The color rushed up under her powder. 'Much good that would do – if I could! But I'm afraid you'll find his door barricaded.'

'That's a pity,' I said coldly.

'It's very foolish of him,' she assented.

Our conversation had reached a deadlock, and I saw that she was distinctly disappointed – perhaps even more than I was. I suspected that while I could afford to wait for a solution she could not.

'Of course, if Catherine is willing to sit by and see the boy starve' – she began.

'What else can she do? Shall we go over to the Nouveau Luxe bar and study the problem from the cocktail angle?' I suggested.

Mrs. Brown's delicately penciled brows gathered over her transparent eyes. 'You're laughing at me – and at Steve. It's rather heartless of you, you know,' she said, making a movement to rise from the deep armchair in which I had installed her. Her movements, as always, were quick and smooth; she got up and sat down with the ease of youth. But her face startled me – it had suddenly shrunk and withered, so that the glitter of cosmetics hung before it like a veil. A pang of compunction shot through me. I felt that it *was* heartless to make her look like that. I could no longer endure the part I was playing. 'I'll – see what I can do to arrange things,' I stammered. 'If only she's not too servile,' I thought, feeling that my next move hung on the way in which she received my reassurance.

She stood up with a quick smile. 'Ogre!' she just breathed, her lashes dancing. She was laughing at me under her breath – the one thing she could have done just then without offending me. 'Come; we *do* need refreshment, don't we?' She slipped her arm through mine as we crossed the lounge and emerged on the wet pavement.

• X •

THE cozy evening with which Mrs. Brown had tempted me was not productive of much enlightenment. I found Catherine Glenn tired and pale, but happy at my coming, with a sort of furtive schoolgirl happiness which suggested the same secret apprehension as I had seen in Mrs. Brown's face when she found I would not help her to capture Stephen's allowance. I had already perceived my mistake in letting Mrs. Brown see this, and during our cocktail epilogue at the Nouveau Luxe had tried to restore her confidence; but her distrust had been aroused, and in spite of her recovered good humor I felt that I should not be allowed to see Stephen.

In this respect poor Mrs. Glenn could not help me. She could only repeat the lesson which had evidently been drilled into her. 'Why should I deny what's so evident – and so natural? When Stevie's ill and unhappy it's not to me he turns. During so many years he knew nothing of me, never even suspected my existence; and all the while *they* were there, watching over him, loving him, slaving for him. If he concealed his real feelings now it might be only on account of the – the financial inducements; and I like to think my boy's too proud for that. If you see him, you'll tell him so, won't you? You'll tell him that, unhappy as he's making me, mistaken as he is, I enter into his feelings as – as only his mother can.' She broke down, and hid her face from me.

When she regained her composure she rose and went over to the writing table. From the blotting book she drew an envelope. 'I've drawn this check in your name – it may be easier for you to get Stevie to accept a few bank notes than a check. You must try to persuade him – tell him his behavior is making the Browns just as unhappy as it is me, and that he has no right to be cruel to them, at any rate.' She lifted her head and looked into my eyes heroically.

I went home perplexed, and pondering on my next move; but (not wholly to my surprise) the question was settled for me the following morning by a telephone call from Mrs. Brown. Her voice rang out cheerfully.

'Good news! I've had a talk with Steve's doctor – on the sly, of course. Steve would kill me if he knew! The doctor says he's really better; you can see him today if you'll promise to stay only a few minutes. Of course I must first persuade Steve himself, the silly boy. You can't think what a savage mood he's in. But I'm sure I can bring him round – he's so fond of you. Only before that I want to see you myself – ' ('Of course,' I commented inwardly, feeling that here at last was the gist of the communication.) 'Can I come presently – before you go out? All right; I'll turn up in an hour.'

Within the hour she was at my hotel; but before her arrival I had decided on my course, and she on her side had probably guessed what it would be. Our first phrases, however, were noncommital. As we exchanged them I saw that Mrs. Brown's self-confidence was weakening, and this incited me to prolong the exchange. Stephen's doctor, she assured me, was most encouraging; one lung only was affected, and that slightly; his recovery now depended on careful nursing, good food, cheerful company – all the things of which, in his foolish obstinacy, he had chosen to deprive himself. She paused, expectant –

'And if Mrs. Glenn handed over his allowance to you, you could ensure his accepting what he's too obstinate to take from his mother?'

Under her carefully prepared complexion the blood rushed to her temples. 'I always knew you were Steve's best friend!' She looked away quickly, as if to hide the triumph in her eyes.

'Well, if I am, he's first got to recognize it by seeing me.'

'Of course – of course!' She corrected her impetuosity. 'I'll do all I can. . . .'

'That's a great deal, as we know,' Under their lowered lashes her eyes followed my movements as I turned my coat back to reach an inner pocket. She pressed her lips tight to control their twitching. 'There, then!' I said.

'Oh, you angel, you! I should never have dared to ask Catherine,' she stammered with a faint laugh as the bank notes passed from my hand to her bag.

'Mrs. Glenn understood – she always understands.'

'She understands when *you* ask,' Mrs. Brown insinuated, flashing her lifted gaze on mine. The sense of what was in the bag had already given her a draught of courage, and she added quickly: 'Of course I needn't warn you not to speak of all this to Steve. If he knew of our talk it would wreck everything.'

'I can see that,' I remarked, and she dropped her lids again, as though I had caught her in a blunder.

'Well, I must go; I'll tell him his best friend's coming. . . . I'll reason with him. . . .' she murmured, trying to disguise her embarrassment in emotion. I saw her to the door, and into Mrs. Glenn's motor, from the interior of which she called back: 'You know you're going to make Catherine as happy as I am.'

Stephen Glenn's new habitation was in a narrow and unsavory street, and the building itself contrasted mournfully with the quarters in which he had last received me. As I climbed the greasy stairs I felt as much perplexed as ever. I could not yet see why Stephen's quarrel with Mrs. Glenn should, even partially, have included the Browns, nor, if it had, why he should be willing to accept from their depleted purse the funds he was too proud to receive from his mother. It gave me a feeling of uneasy excitement to know that behind the door at which I stood the answer to these problems awaited me.

No one answered my knock, so I opened the door and went in. The studio was empty, but from the room beyond Stephen's voice called out irritably: 'Who is it?' and then, in answer to my name: 'Oh, Norcutt – come in.'

Stephen Glenn lay in bed, in a small room with a window opening on a dimly-lit inner courtyard. The room was bare and untidy, the bedclothes were tumbled, and he looked at me with the sick man's instinctive resentfulness at any intrusion on his lonely pain. 'Above all,' the look seemed to say, 'don't try to be kind.'

Seeing that moral pillow smoothing would be resented I sat down beside him without any comment on the dismalness of the scene, or on his own aspect, much as it disquietened me.

'Well, old man – ' I began, wondering how to go on; but he cut short my hesitation. 'I've been wanting to see you for ever so long,' he said.

In my surprise I had nearly replied: 'That's not what I'd been told' – but, resolved to go warily, I rejoined with a sham gaiety. 'Well, here I am!'

Stephen gave me the remote look which the sick turn on those arch aliens, the healthy. 'Only,' he pursued, 'I was afraid if you did come you'd begin and lecture me; and I couldn't stand that – I can't stand anything. I'm *raw!*' he burst out.

'You might have known me better than to think I'd lecture you.'

'Oh, I don't know. Naturally the one person you care about in all this is – mother Kit.'

'Your mother,' I interposed.

He raised his eyebrows with the familiar ironic movement; then they drew together again over his sunken eyes. 'I wanted to wait till I was up to discussing things. I wanted to get this fever out of me.'

'You don't look feverish now.'

'No; they've brought it down. But I'm down with it. I'm very low,' he said, with a sort of chill impartiality, as though speaking of someone whose disabilities did not greatly move him. I replied that the best way for him to pull himself up again was to get out of his present quarters and let himself be nursed and looked after.

'Oh, don't argue!' he interrupted.

'Argue – ?'

'You're going to tell me to go back to – to my mother. To let her fatten me up. Well, it's no use. I won't take another dollar from her – not one.'

I met this in silence, and after a moment perceived that my silence irritated him more than any attempt at argument. I did not want to irritate him, and I began: 'Then why don't you go off again with the Browns? There's nothing you can do that your mother won't understand – '

'And suffer from!' he interjected.

'Oh, as to suffering – she's seasoned.'

He bent his slow feverish stare on me. 'So am I.'

'Well, at any rate, you can spare her by going off at once into good air, and trying your level best to get well. You know as well as I do that nothing else matters to her. She'll be glad to have you go away with the Browns – I'll answer for that.'

He gave a short laugh, so harsh and disenchanted that I suddenly felt he was right: to laugh like that he must be suffering as much as his mother. I laid my hand on his thin wrist. 'Old man – '

He jerked away. 'No, no. Go away with the Browns? I'd rather be dead. I'd rather hang on here till I *am* dead.'

The outburst was so unexpected that I sat in silent perplexity. Mrs. Brown had told the truth, then, when she said he hated them too? Yet he saw them, he accepted their money. . . . The darkness deepened as I peered into it.

Stephen lay with half-closed lids, and I saw that whatever enlightenment he had to give would have to be forced from him. The perception made me take a sudden resolve.

'When one is physically down and out one *is* raw, as you say: one hates everybody. I know you don't really feel like that about the Browns; but if they've got on your nerves, and you want to go off by

yourself, you might at least accept the money they're ready to give
you – '

He raised himself on his elbow with an ironical stare. 'Money? They
borrow money; they don't give it.'

'Ah – ' I thought; but aloud I continued: 'They're prepared to give
it now. Mrs. Brown tells me – '

He lifted his hand with a gesture that cut me short; then he leaned
back, and drew a painful breath or two. Beads of moisture came out
on his forehead. 'If she told you that, it means she's got more out of
Kit. Or out of Kit through *you* – is that it?' he brought out roughly.

His clairvoyance frightened me almost as much as his physical
distress – and the one seemed, somehow, a function of the other, as
though the wearing down of his flesh had made other people's diapha-
nous to him, and he could see through it to their hearts. 'Stephen – ' I
began imploringly.

Again his lifted hand checked me. 'No, wait.' He breathed hard
again and shut his eyes. Then he opened them and looked into mine.
'There's only one way out of this.'

'For you to be reasonable.'

'Call it that if you like. I've got to see mother Kit – and without
their knowing it.'

My perplexity grew, and my agitation with it. Could it be that the
end of the Browns was in sight? I tried to remember that my first
business was to avoid communicating my agitation to Stephen. In a
tone that I did my best to keep steady I said: 'Nothing could make
your mother happier. You're all she lives for.'

'She'll have to find something else soon.'

'No, no. Only let her come, and she'll make you well. Mothers
work miracles – '

His inscrutable gaze rested on mine. 'So they say. Only, you see,
she's not my mother.'

He spoke so quietly, in such a low detached tone, that at first the
words carried no meaning to me. If he had been excited I should have
suspected fever, delirium; but voice and eyes were clear. 'Now you
understand,' he added.

I sat beside him stupidly, speechless, unable to think. 'I don't understand anything,' I stammered. Such a possibility as his words suggested
had never once occurred to me. Yet he wasn't delirious, he wasn't
raving – it was I whose brain was reeling as if in fever.

'Well, I'm not the long-lost child. The Browns are not *her* Browns.
It's all a lie and an imposture. We faked it up between us, Chrissy and
I did – her simplicity made it so cruelly easy for us. Boy didn't have
much to do with it; poor old Boy! He just sat back and took his
share. . . . *Now* you do see,' he repeated, in the cold explanatory tone
in which he might have set forth someone else's shortcomings.

My mind was still a blur while he poured out, in broken sentences, the details of the conspiracy – the sordid tale of a trio of society adventurers come to the end of their resources, and suddenly clutching at this unheard-of chance of rescue, affluence, peace. But gradually, as I listened, the glare of horror with which he was blinding me turned into a strangely clear and penetrating light, forcing its way into obscure crannies, elucidating the incomprehensible, picking out one by one the links that bound together his framents of face. I saw – but what I was my gaze shrank from.

'Well,' I heard him say, between his difficult breaths, 'now do you begin to believe me?'

'I don't know. I can't tell. Why on earth,' I broke out, suddenly relieved at the idea, 'should you want to see your mother if this isn't all a ghastly invention?'

'To tell her what I've just told you – make a clean breast of it. Can't you see?'

'If that's the reason, I see you want to kill her – that's all.'

He grew paler under his paleness. 'Norcutt, I can't go on like this; I've got to tell her. I want to do it at once. I thought I could keep up the lie a little longer – let things go on drifting – but I can't. I held out because I wanted to get well first, and paint her picture – leave her that to be proud of, anyhow! Now that's all over, and there's nothing left but the naked shame. . . .' He opened his eyes and fixed them again on mine. 'I want you to bring her here today – without *their* knowing it. You've got to manage it somehow. It'll be the first decent thing I've done in years.'

'It will be the most unpardonable,' I interrupted angrily. 'The time's past for trying to square your own conscience. What you've got to do now is to go on lying to her – you've got to get well, if only to go on lying to her!'

A thin smile flickered over his face. 'I can't get well.'

'That's as it may be. You can spare her, anyhow.'

'By letting things go on like this?' He lay for a long time silent; then his lips drew up in a queer grimace. 'It'll be horrible enough to be a sort of expiation – '

'It's the only one.'

'It's the worst.'

He sank back wearily. I saw that fatigue had silenced him, and wondered if I ought to steal away. My presence could not but be agitating; yet in his present state it seemed almost as dangerous to leave him as to stay. I saw a flask of brandy on the table, a glass beside it. I poured out some brandy and held it to his lips. He emptied the glass slowly, and as his head fell back I heard him say: 'Before I knew her I thought I could pull it off. . . . But, you see, her sweetness. . . .'

'If she heard you say that it would make up for everything.'

'Even for what I've just told you?'

'Even for that. For God's sake hold your tongue, and just let her come here and nurse you.'

He made no answer, but under his lids I saw a tear or two.

'Let her come – let her come,' I pleaded, taking his dying hand in mine.

• XI •

NATURE does not seem to care for dramatic climaxes. Instead of allowing Stephen to die at once, his secret on his lips, she laid on him the harsher task of living though weary weeks, and keeping back the truth till the end.

As a result of my visit, he consented, the next day, to be carried back in an ambulance to Mrs. Glenn's; and when I saw their meeting it seemed to me that ties of blood were frail compared to what drew those two together. After she had fallen on her knees at his bedside, and drawn his head to her breast, I was almost sure he would not speak; and he did not.

I was able to stay with Mrs. Glenn till Stephen died, then I had to hurry back to my post in Washington. When I took leave of her she told me that she was following on the next steamer with Stephen's body. She wished her son to have a New York funeral, a funeral like his father's, at which all their old friends could be present. 'Not like poor Phil's, you know – ' and I recalled the importance she had attached to the presence of her husband's friends at his funeral. 'It's something to remember afterwards,' she said, with dry eyes. 'And it will be their only way of knowing my Stephen. . . .' It was of course impossible to exclude Mr. and Mrs. Brown from these melancholy rites; and accordingly they sailed with her.

If Stephen had recovered she had meant, as I knew, to reopen her New York house; but now that was not to be thought of. She sold the house, and all it contained, and a few weeks later sailed once more for Paris – again with the Browns.

I had resolved after Stephen's death – when the first shock was over – to do what I could toward relieving her of the Browns' presence. Though I could not tell her the truth about them, I might perhaps help her to effect some transaction which would relieve her of their company. But I soon saw that this was out of the question; and the reason deepened my perplexity. It was simply that the Browns – or at least Mrs. Brown – had become Mrs. Glenn's chief consolation in her sorrow. The two women, so incessantly at odds while Stephen lived were now joined in a common desolation. It seemed like profaning Catherine Glenn's grief to compare Mrs. Brown's to it; yet, in the first weeks after Stephen's death, I had to admit that Mrs. Brown mourned him as genuinely, as inconsolably, as his supposed mother. Indeed, it would be nearer the truth to say that Mrs. Brown's grief was more hopeless and rebellious than the other's. After all, as Mrs. Glenn said, it was much worse for Chrissy. 'She had so little compared to me; and she gave as much, I suppose. Think what I had that she's never known; those precious months of waiting for him, when he was part of me when we were one body and one soul. And then, years afterwards, when I was searching for him, and knowing all the while I should find him; and after that, our perfect life together – our perfect understanding. All that – there's all that left to me! And what did she have? Why, when she shows me his little socks and shoes (she's kept them all so carefully) they're *my* baby's socks and shoes, not hers – and I know she's thinking of it when we cry over them. I see now that I've been unjust to her . . . and cruel . . . For he *did* love me best; and that ought to have made me kinder – '

Yes; I had to recognize that Mrs. Brown's grief was as genuine as her rival's, that she suffered more bleakly and bitterly. Every turn to the strange story had been improbable and incalculable, and this new freak of fate was the most unexpected. But since it brought a softening to my poor friend's affliction, and offered a new pretext for her self-devotion, I could only hold my tongue and be thankful that the Browns were at last serving some humaner purpose.

The next time I returned to Paris the strange trio were still together, and still living in Mrs. Glenn's apartment. Its walls were now hung with Stephen's paintings and sketches – among them many unfinished attempts at a portrait of Mrs. Glenn – and the one mother seemed as eager as the other to tell me that a well-known collector of modern art had been so struck by their quality that there was already some talk of a posthumous exhibition. Mrs. Brown triumphed peculiarly in the affair. It was she who had brought the collector to see the pictures, she who had always known that Stephen had genius; it was with the Browns' meager pennies that he had been able to carry on his studies at Julian's, long before Mrs. Glenn had appeared. 'Catherine doesn't pretend to know much about art. Do you, my dear? But, as I tell her, when you're a picture yourself you don't have to bother about other people's pictures. There – your hat's crooked again! Just let me straighten it, darling – ' I saw Mrs. Glenn wince a little, as she had winced the day at Les Calanques when Mrs. Brown, with an arch side glance at me, had given a more artful twist to her friend's white hair.

It was evident that time, in drying up the source which had nourished the two women's sympathy, had revived their fundamental antagonism. It was equally clear, however, that Mrs. Brown was making every effort to keep on good terms with Mrs. Glenn. That substantial benefits thereby accrued to her I had no doubt; but at least she kept up in Catherine's mind the illusion of the tie between them.

Mrs. Brown had certainly sorrowed for Stephen as profoundly as a woman of her kind could sorrow; more profoundly, indeed, than I had thought possible. Even now, when she spoke of him, her metallic voice broke, her metallic mask softened. On the rare occasions when I found myself alone with her (and I had an idea she saw to it that they were rare), she spoke so tenderly of Stephen, so affectionately of Mrs. Glenn that I could only suppose she knew nothing of my last talk with the poor fellow. If she had, she would almost certainly have tried to ensure my silence; unless, as I sometimes imagined, a supreme art led her to feign unawareness. But, as always when I speculated on Mrs. Brown, I ended up against a blank wall.

The exhibition of Stephen's pictures took place, and caused (I learned from Mrs. Glenn) a little flutter in the inner circle of connoisseurs. Mrs. Glenn deluged me with newspaper rhapsodies which she doubtless never imagined had been bought. But presently, as a result of the show, a new difference arose between the two women. The pictures had been sufficiently remarked for several purchasers to present themselves, and their offers were so handsome that Mrs. Brown thought they should be accepted. After all, Stephen would have regarded the sale of the pictures as the best proof of his success, if they remained hidden away at Mrs. Glenn's, she, who had the custody of his name, was obviously dooming it to obscurity. Nevertheless she persisted in refusing. If selling her darling's pictures was the price of glory, then she must cherish his genius in secret. Could anyone imagine that she would ever part with a single stroke of his brush? She was his mother; no one else had a voice in the matter. I divined that the struggle between herself and Mrs. Brown had been not only sharp but prolonged, and marked by a painful interchange of taunts. 'If it hadn't been for me,' Mrs. Brown argued, 'the pictures would never have existed'; and 'If it hadn't been for me,' the other retorted, 'my Stephen would never have existed.' It ended – as I had foreseen – in the adoptive parents accepting from Mrs. Glenn a sum equivalent to the value at which they estimated the pictures. The quarrel quieted down, and a few months later Mrs. Glenn was remorsefully accusing herself of having been too hard on Chrissy.

So the months passed. With their passage news came to me more rarely; but I gathered from Mrs. Glenn's infrequent letters that she had been ill, and from her almost illegible writing that her poor hands were stiffening with rheumatism. Finally, a year later, a letter announced that the doctors had warned her against spending her winters in the damp climate of Paris, and that the apartment had been disposed of, and its contents (including, of course, Stephen's pictures) transported to a villa at Nice. The Browns had found the villa and managed the translation – with their usual kindness. After that there was a long silence.

It was not until over two years later that I returned to Europe; and as my short holiday was taken in winter and I meant to spend it in Italy, I took steamer directly to Villefranche. I had not announced my visit to Mrs. Glenn, I was not sure till the last moment of being able to get off; but that was not the chief cause of my silence. Though relations between the incongruous trio seemed to have become harmonious, it was not without apprehension that I had seen Mrs. Glenn leave New York with the Browns. She was old, she was tired and stricken; how long would it be before she became a burden to her beneficiaries? This was what I wanted to find out without giving them time to prepare themselves or their companion for my visit. Mrs. Glenn had written that she wished very particularly to see me, and had begged me to let her know if there were a chance of my coming abroad; but though this increased my anxiety it strengthened my resolve to arrive unannounced, and I merely replied that she could count on seeing me as soon as I was able to get away.

Though some months had since gone by I was fairly sure of finding her still at Nice, for in the newspapers I had bought on landing I had lit on several allusions to Mrs. and Mrs. Boydon Brown. Apparently the couple had an active press agent, for an attentive world was daily supplied with a minute description of Mrs. 'Boy' Brown's casino toilets, the value of the golf and pigeon-shooting cups offered by Mr. 'Boy' Brown to various fashionable sporting clubs, and the names of the titled guests whom they entertained at the local 'Lidos' and 'Jardins Fleuris.' I wondered how much the chronicling of these events was costing Mrs. Glenn, but reminded myself that it was part of the price she had to pay for the hours of communion over Stephen's little socks. At any rate it proved that my old friend was still in the neighbourhood; and the next day I set out to find her.

I waited till the afternoon, on the chance of her being alone at the hour when mundane affairs were most likely to engage the Browns; but when my taxi driver had brought me to the address I had given him I found a locked garden gate and a shuttered house. The sudden fear of some new calamity seized me. My first thought was that Mrs. Glenn must have died; yet if her death had occurred before my sailing I could hardly have failed to hear of it, and if it was more recent I must have seen it announced in the papers I had read since landing. Besides, if the Browns had so lately lost their benefactress they would hardly have played such a part in the social chronicles I had been studying. There was no particular reason why a change of address should portend tragedy; and when at length a reluctant portress appeared in answer to my ringing she said, yes, if it was the Americans I was after, I was right: they had moved away a week ago. Moved – and where to? She shrugged and declared she didn't know; but probably not far, she thought, with the old white-haired lady so ill and helpless.

'Ill and helpless – then why did they move?'

She shrugged again. 'When people don't pay their rent, they have to move don't they? When they don't even settle with the butcher and baker before they go, or with the laundress who was fool enough to do their washing – and it's I who speak to you, Monsieur!'

This was worse than I had imagined. I produced a bank note, and in return the victimized concierge admitted that she had secured the fugitive's new address – though they were naturally not anxious to have it known. As I had surmised, they had taken refuge within the kindly bounds of the principality of Monaco; and the taxi carried me to a small shabby hotel in one of the steep streets above the Casino. I could imagine nothing less in harmony with Catherine Glenn or her condition than to be ill and unhappy in such a place. My only consolation was that now perhaps there might be an end to the disastrous adventure. 'After all,' I thought, as I looked up at the cheerless front of the hotel, 'if the catastrophe has come the Browns can't have any reason for hanging on to her.'

A red-faced lady with a false front and false teeth emerged from the back office to receive me.

Madame Glenn – Madame Brown? Oh, yes; they were staying at the hotel – they were both upstairs now, she believed. Perhaps Monsieur was the gentleman that Madame Brown was expecting? She had left word that if he came he was to go up without being announced.

I was inspired to say that I was that gentleman; at which the landlady rejoined that she was sorry the lift was out of order, but that I would find the ladies at number 5 on the third floor. Before she had finished I was halfway up.

A few steps down an unventilated corridor brought me to number 5; but I did not have to knock, for the door was ajar – perhaps in expectation of the other gentleman. I pushed it open, and entered a small plushy sitting room, with faded mimosa in ornate vases, newspapers and cigarette ends scattered on the dirty carpet, and a bronzed-over plaster Bayadère posturing before the mantelpiece mirror. If my first glance took such sharp note of these details it is because they seemed almost as much out of keeping with Catherine Glenn as the table laden with gin and bitters, empty cocktail glasses and disks of sodden lemon.

It was not the first time it had occurred to me that I was partly responsible for Mrs. Glenn's unhappy situation. The growing sense of that responsiblity had been one of my reasons for trying to keep an eye on her, for wanting her to feel that in case of need she could count on me. But on the whole my conscience had not been oppressed. The impulse which had made me exact from Stephen the promise never to undeceive her had necessarily governed my own conduct. I had only to recall Catherine Glenn as I had first known her to feel sure that, after all, her life had been richer and deeper than if she had spent it, childless and purposeless, in the solemn upholstery of her New York house. I had had nothing to do with her starting on her strange quest; but I was certain that in what had followed she had so far found more happiness than sorrow.

But now? As I stood in that wretched tawdry room I wondered if I had not laid too heavy a burden on my conscience in keeping the truth from her. Suddenly I said to myself: 'The time has come – whatever happens I must get her away from these people.' But then I remembered how Stephen's death had drawn the two ill-sorted women together, and wondered if to destroy that tie would not now be the crowning cruelty.

I was still uneasily deliberating when I heard a voice behind the door opposite the one by which I had entered. The room beyond must have been darkened, for I had not noticed before that this door was also partly open. 'Well, have you had your nap?' a woman's voice said irritably. 'Is there something you want before I go out? I told you that the man who's going to arrange for the loan is coming for me. He'll be here in a minute.' The voice was Mrs. Brown's, but so sharpened and altered that at first I had not known it. 'This is how she speaks when she thinks there's no one listening,' I thought.

I caught an indistinct murmur in reply; then the rattle of drawnback curtain rings; then Mrs. Brown continuing: 'Well, you may as well sign the letter now. Here it is – you've only got to write your name. . . . Your glasses? I don't know where your glasses are – you're always dropping your things about. I'm sorry, I can't keep a maid to wait on you – but there's nothing in this letter you need be afraid of. I've told you before that it's only a formality. Boy's told you so too, hasn't he? I don't suppose you mean to suggest that we're trying to do you out of your money, do you? We've got to have enough to keep going. Here, let me hold your hand while you sign. My hand's shaky too . . . it's all this beastly worry. . . . Don't you imagine you're the only person who's had a bad time of it. . . . Why, what's the matter? Why are you pushing me away – ?'

Till now I had stood motionless, unabashed by the fact that I was eavesdropping. I was ready enough to stoop to that if there was no other way of getting at the truth. But at the question: 'Why are you pushing me away?' I knocked hurriedly at the door of the inner room.

There was a silence after my knock. 'There he is! You'll have to sign now,' I heard Mrs. Brown exclaim; and I opened the door and went in. The room was a bedroom; like the other, it was untidy and shabby. I noticed a stack of canvases, framed and unframed, piled up against the wall. In an armchair near the window Mrs. Glenn was seated. She was wrapped in some sort of dark dressing gown, and a lace cap covered her white hair. The face that looked out from it had still the same carven beauty; but its texture had dwindled from marble to worn ivory. Her body too had shrunk, so that, low in her chair, under her loose garments, she seemed to have turned into a little broken doll. Mrs. Brown on the contrary, perhaps by contrast, appeared large and almost towering. At first glance I was more startled by the change in her appearance than in Mrs. Glenn's. The latter had merely followed more quickly than I had hoped she would, the natural decline of the years; whereas Mrs. Brown seemed like another woman. It was not only that she had grown stout and heavy, or that her complexion had coarsened so noticeably under the skillful make-up. In spite of her good clothes and studied coiffure there was something haphazard and untidy in her appearance. Her hat, I noticed, had slipped a little sideways on her smartly waved head, her bright shallow eyes looked blurred and red, and she held herself with a sort of vacillating erectness. Gradually the incredible fact was borne in on me; Mrs. Brown had been drinking.

'Why, where on earth – ?' she broke out, bewildered, as my identity dawned on her. She put up a hand to straighten her hat, and in doing so dragged it over too far on the other side.

'I beg your pardon. I was told to come to number 5, and as there was no one in the sitting room I knocked on this door.'

'Oh, you knocked? I didn't hear you knock,' said Mrs. Brown suspiciously; but I had no ears for her, for my old friend had also recognized me, and was holding out her trembling hands. 'I knew you'd come – I said you'd come!' she cried out to me.

Mrs. Brown laughed. 'Well, you've said he would often enough. But it's taken some time for it to come true.'

'I knew you'd come,' Mrs. Glenn repeated, and I felt her hand pass tremblingly over my hair as I stooped to kiss her.

'Lovers' meeting!' Mrs. Brown tossed at us with an unsteady gaiety; then she leaned against the door, and stood looking on ironically. 'You didn't expect to find us in this palatial abode, did you?'

'No. I went to the villa first.'

Mrs. Glenn's eyes dwelt on me softly. I sat down beside her, and she put her hand in mine. Her withered fingers trembled incessantly.

'Perhaps,' Mrs. Brown went on, 'if you'd come sooner you might have arranged things so that we could have stayed there. I'm powerless – I can't do anything with her. The fact that for years I looked after the child she deserted weighs nothing with her. She doesn't seem to think she owes us anything.'

Mrs. Glenn listened in silence, without looking at her accuser. She kept her large sunken eyes fixed on mine. 'There's no money left,' she said when the other ended.

'No money! No money! That's always the tune nowadays. There

was always plenty of money for her precious – money for all his whims and fancies, for journeys, for motors, for doctors, for – well, what's the use of going on? But not that there's nobody left but Boy and me, who slaved for her darling for years, who spent our last penny on him when his mother'd forgotten his existence – now there's nothing left! Now she can't afford anything; now she won't even pay her own bills; now she'd sooner starve herself to death than let us have what she owes us. . . .'

'My dear – my dear.' Mrs. Glenn murmured, her eyes still on mine.

'Oh, don't "my dear" me,' Mrs. Brown retorted passionately. 'What you mean is: "How can you talk like that before him?" I suppose you think I wish he hadn't come. Well, you never were more mistaken, I'm glad he's here; I'm glad he's found out where you're living, and how you're living. Only this time I mean him to hear our side of the story instead of only yours.'

Mrs. Glenn pressed my hand in her twitching fingers. 'She wants me to sign a paper. I don't understand.'

'You don't understand? Didn't Boy explain it to you? You said you understood then.' Mrs. Brown turned to me with a shrug. 'These whims and capers . . . all I want is money enough to pay the bills. . . . so that we're not turned out of this hole too. . . .'

'There is no money,' Mrs. Glenn softly reiterated.

My heart stood sill. The scene must at all costs be ended, yet I could think of no way of silencing the angry woman. At length I said: 'If you'll leave me for a little while with Mrs. Glenn perhaps she'll be able to tell me – '

'How's she to tell you what she says she doesn't understand herself? If I leave her with you all she'll tell you is lies about us – I found that out long ago.' Mrs. Brown took a few steps in my direction, and then, catching at the window curtain, looked at me with a foolish laugh. 'Not that I'm pining for her society. I have a good deal of it in the long run. But you'll excuse me for saying that, as far as this matter is concerned, it's entirely between Mrs. Glenn and me.'

I tightened my hold on Mrs. Glenn's hand, and sat looking at Mrs. Brown in the hope that a silent exchange of glances might lead farther than the vain bandying of arguments. For a moment she seemed dominated; I began to think she had read in my eyes the warning I had tried to put there. If there was any money left I might be able to get it from Catherine after her own attempts had failed; that was what I was trying to remind her of, and what she understood my looks were saying. Once before I had done the trick; supposing she were to trust me to try again? I saw that she wavered; but her brain was not alert, as it had been on that other occasion. She continued to stare at me through a blur of drink and anger; I could see her thoughts clutching uneasily at my suggestion and then losing their hold on it. 'Oh, we all know you think you're God Almighty!' she broke out with a contemptuous toss.

'I think I could help you if I could have a quiet talk with Mrs. Glenn.'

'Well, you can have your quiet talk.' She looked about her, and pulling up a chair plumped down into it heavily. 'I'd love to hear what you've got to say to each other,' she declared.

Mrs. Glenn's hand began to shake again. She turned her head toward Mrs. Brown. 'My dear, I should like to see my friend alone.'

'I should like! I should like! I daresay you would. It's always been what *you'd* like – but now it's going to be what I choose. And I choose to assist at the conversation between Mrs. Glenn and Mr. Norcutt, instead of letting them quietly say horrors about me behind my back.'

'Oh, Chrissy – ' my old friend murmured; then she turned to me and said, 'You'd better come back another day.'

Mrs. Brown looked at me with a sort of feeble cunning. 'Oh, you needn't send him away, I've told you my friend's coming – he'll be here in a minute. If you'll sign that letter I'll take it to the bank with him, and Mr. Norcutt can stay here and tell you all the news. Now wouldn't that be nice and cozy?' she concluded coaxingly.

Looking into Mrs. Glenn's pale frightened face I was on the point of saying: 'Well, sign it then, whatever it is – anything to get her to go.' But Mrs. Glenn straightened her drooping shoulders and repeated softly: 'I can't sign it.'

A flush rose to Mrs. Brown's forehead. 'You can't? That's final, is it?' She turned to me. 'It's all money she owed us, mind you – money we've advanced to her – in one way or another. Every penny of it. And now she sits there and says she won't pay us!'

Mrs. Glenn, twisting her fingers into mine, gave a barely audible laugh. 'Now he's here I'm safe,' she said.

The crimson of Mrs. Brown's face darkened to purple. Her lower lip trembled and I saw she was struggling for words that her dimmed brain could not supply. 'God Almighty – you think he's God Almighty!' She evidently felt the inadequacy of this, for she stood up suddenly, and coming close to Mrs. Glenn's armchair, stood looking down on her in impotent anger. 'Well, I'll show you – ' She turned to me, moved by another impulse. 'You know well enough you could make her sign if you chose to.'

My eyes and Mrs. Brown's met again. Hers were saying: 'It's your last chance – it's *her* last chance. I warn you – ' and mine replying: 'Nonsense, you can't frighten us, you can't even frighten *her* while I'm here. And if she doesn't want to sign you shan't force her to. I have something up my sleeve that would shut you up in five seconds if you knew.'

She kept her thick stare on mine till I felt as if my silent signal must have penetrated it. But she said nothing, and at last I exclaimed: 'You know well enough the risk you're running – '

Perhaps I had better not have spoken. But that dumb dialogue was getting on my nerves. If she wouldn't see, it was time to make her –

Ah, she saw now – she saw fast enough! My words seemed to have cleared the last fumes from her brain. She gave me back my look with one almost as steady; then she laughed.

'The risk I'm running? Oh, that's it, is it? That's the pull you thought you had over me? Well I'm glad you know – and I'm glad to tell you that I've known all along that you knew. I'm sick and tired of all the humbug – if she won't sign I'm going to tell her everything myself. So now the cards are on the table, and you can take your choice. It's up to you. The risk's on your side now!'

The unaccountable woman – drunkenly incoherent a moment ago, and now hitting the nail on the head with such fiendish precision! I sat silent, meditating her hideous challenge without knowing how to meet it. And then I became aware that a quiver had passed over Mrs. Glenn's face, which had become smaller and more ivory-yellow than before. She leaned towards me as if Mrs. Brown, who stood close above us, could not hear what we were saying.

'What is it she means to tell me? I don't care unless it's something bad about Stevie. And it couldn't be that, could it? How does she know? No one can come between a son and his mother.'

Mrs. Brown gave one of her sudden laughs. 'A son and his mother? I daresay not! Only I'm just about fed up with having you think you're his mother.'

It was the one thing I had not foreseen – that she would possess herself of my threat and turn it against me. The risk was too deadly; and so no doubt she would have felt if she had been in a state to measure it. She was not; and there lay the peril.

Mrs. Glenn sat quite still after the other's outcry, and I hoped it had blown past her like some mere rag of rhetoric. Then I saw that the meaning of the words had reached her, but without carrying conviction. She glanced at me with the flicker of a smile. 'Now she says I'm not his mother – !' It's her last round of ammunition; but don't be afraid – it won't make me sign, the smile seemed to whisper to me.

Mrs. Brown caught the unspoken whisper, and her exasperation rushed to meet it. 'You don't believe me? I knew you wouldn't! Well, ask your friend here; ask Mr. Norcutt; you always believe everything he says. He's known the truth for ever so long – long before Stephen died he knew he wasn't your son.'

I jumped up, as if to put myself between my friends and some bodily harm: but she held fast to my hand with her clinging twitching fingers. 'As if she knew what it is to have a son! All those long months when he's one with you. . . . *Mothers* know,' she said.

'Mothers, yes! I don't say you didn't have a son and desert him. I say that son wasn't Stephen. Don't you suppose I know? Sometimes I've wanted to laugh in your face at the way you went on about him . . . Sometimes I used to have to rush out of the room, just to have my laugh out by myself. . . .'

Mrs. Brown stopped with a gasp, as if the fury of the outburst had shaken her back to soberness, and she saw for the first time what she had done. Mrs. Glenn sat with her head bowed; her hand had grown cold in mine. I looked at Mrs. Brown and said: 'Now won't you leave us? I suppose there's nothing left to say.'

She blinked at me through her heavy lids; I saw she was wavering. But at the same moment Mrs. Glenn's clutch tightened; she drew me down to her, and looked at me out of her deep eyes. 'What does she mean when she says you knew about Stevie?'

I pressed her hand without answering. All my mind was concentrated on the effort of silencing my antagonist and getting her out of the room. Mrs. Brown leaned in the window frame and looked down on us. I could see that she was dismayed at what she had said, and yet exultant; and my business was to work on the dismay before the exultation mastered it. But Mrs. Glenn still held me down; her eyes seemed to be forcing their gaze into me. 'Is it true?' she asked almost inaudibly.

'True?' Mrs. Brown burst out. 'Ask him to swear to you it's not true – see what he looks like then! He was in the conspiracy, you old simpleton.'

Mrs. Glenn's head straightened itself again on her weak neck: her face wore a singular majesty. 'You were my friend – ' she appealed to me.

'I've always been your friend.'

'Then I don't have to believe her.'

Mrs. Brown seemed to have been gathering herself up for a last onslaught. She saw that I was afraid to try to force her from the room, and the discovery gave her a sense of hazy triumph, as if all that was left to her was to defy me. 'Tell her I'm lying – why don't you tell her I'm lying?' she taunted me.

I knelt down by my old friend and put my arm about her. 'Will you come away with me now – at once? I'll take you wherever you want to go. . . . I'll look after you. . . . I'll always look after you.'

Mrs. Glenn's eyes grew wider. She seemed to weigh my words till their sense penetrated her; then she said, in the same low voice: 'It is true, then?'

'Come away with me; come away with me,' I repeated.

I felt her trying to rise; but her feet failed under her and she sank back. 'Yes, take me away from her,' she said.

Mrs. Brown laughed. 'Oh, that's it, is it? "Come away from that

bad woman, and I'll explain everything, and make it all right" . . .
Why don't you adopt *him* instead of Steve? I dare say that's what he's
been after all the time. That's the reason he was so determined we
shouldn't have your money. . . .' She drew back, and pointed to the
door. 'You can go with him – who's to prevent you? I couldn't if I
wanted to. I see now it's for him we've been nursing your precious
millions. . . . Well, go with him, and he'll tell you the whole
story. . . .' A strange secretive smile stole over her face. 'All except
one bit . . . there's one bit he doesn't know; but *you're* going to know
it now.'

She stepped nearer, and I held up my hand; but she hurried on, her
eyes on Mrs. Glenn. 'What he doesn't know is why we fixed the thing
up. Steve wasn't my adopted son any more than he was your real one.
Adopted son, indeed! How old do you suppose I am? He was my lover.
There – do you understand? My lover! That's why we faked up that
ridiculous adoption story, and all the rest of it – because he was desperately ill, and down and out, and we hadn't a penny, the three of us,
and I had to have money for him, and didn't care how I got it, didn't
care for anything on earth but seeing him well again, and happy.' She
stopped and drew a panting breath. 'There – I'd rather have told you
that than have your money. I'd rather you should know what Steve
was to me than think any longer that you owned him. . . .'

I was still kneeling by Mrs. Glenn, my arm about her. Once I felt
her heart give a great shake; then it seemed to stop altogether. Her eyes
were no longer turned to me, but fixed in a wide stare on Mrs. Brown.
A tremor convulsed her face; then, to my amazement, it was smoothed
into an expression of childish serenity, and a faint smile, half playful,
half ironic, stole over it.

She raised her hand and pointed tremulously to the other's
disordered headgear. 'My dear – your hat's crooked,' she said.

For a moment I was bewildered; then I saw that, very gently, she
was at last returning the taunt that Mrs. Brown had so often addressed
to her. The shot fired, she leaned back against me with the satisfied
sigh of a child; and immediately I understood that Mrs. Brown's blow
had gone wide. A pitiful fate had darkened Catherine Glenn's intelligence at the exact moment when to see clearly would have been the
final anguish.

Mrs. Brown understood too. She stood looking at us doubtfully;
then she said in a tone of feeble defiance: 'Well, I had to tell her.'

She turned and went out of the room, and I continued to kneel by
Mrs. Glenn. Her eyes had gradually clouded, and I doubted if she still
knew me; but her lips nursed their soft smile, and I saw that she must
have been waiting for years to launch that little shaft at her enemy.

Charm Incorporated

'JIM! I'm afraid . . . I'm dreadfully afraid. . . .'

James Targatt's wife knelt by his armchair, the dark hair flung off her forehead, her dark eyes large with tears as they yearned up at him throught those incredibly long lashes.

'Afraid? Why – what's the matter?' he retorted, annoyed at being disturbed in the slow process of digesting the dinner he had just eaten at Nadeja's last new restaurant – a Ukrainian one this time. For they went to a different restaurant every night, usually, at Nadeja's instigation, hunting out the most exotic that New York at the high tide of its prosperity had to offer. 'That sturgeon stewed in cream – ' he thought wearily. 'Well, what is it?'

'It's Boris, darling. I'm afraid Boris is going to marry a film star. That Halma Hoboe, you know . . . she's the greatest of them all. . . .' By this time the tears were running down Nadeja's cheeks. Targatt averted his mind from the sturgeon long enough to wonder if he would ever begin to understand his wife, much less his wife's family.

'Halma Hoboe? Well, why on earth shouldn't he? Has she got her divorce from the last man all right?'

'Yes, of course.' Nadeja was still weeping. 'But I thought perhaps you'd mind Boris's leaving us. He will have to stay out at Hollywood now, he says. And I shall miss my brother so dreadfully. Hollywood's very far from New York – no? We shall miss Boris, shan't we, James?'

'Yes, yes. Of course. Great boy, Boris! Funny to be related to a movie star. "My sister-in-law, Halma Hoboe." Well, as long as he couldn't succeed on the screen himself – ' said Targatt, suddenly sounding a latent relief, which came to the surface a moment later. 'She'll have to pay his bills now,' he muttered, too low for his wife to hear. He reached out for a second cigar, let his head sink back comfortably against the chair cushions, and thought to himself: 'Well, perhaps the luck's turning. . . .' For it was the first time, in the eight years of his marriage to Nadeja, that any information imparted to him concerning her family had not immediately led up to his having to draw another check.

• II •

JAMES TARGATT had always been on his guard against any form of
sentimental weakness; yet now, as he looked back on his life, he began
to wonder if one occasion on which he had been false to this principle
might not turn out to be his best stroke of business.

He had not had much difficulty in guarding himself against
marriage. He had never felt an abstract yearning for fatherhood, or
believed that to marry an old-fashioned affectionate girl, who hated
society, and wanted to stay home and darn and scrub, would really
help an ambitious man in his career. He thought it was probably
cheaper in the end to have your darning and scrubbing done for you by
professionals, even if they came from one of those extortionate valeting
establishments that before the depression, used to charge a dollar a
minute for such services. And eventually he found a stranded German
widow who came to him on starvation wages, fed him well and inex-
pensively, and kept the flat looking as fresh and shiny as a racing yacht.
So there was no earthly obligation for him to marry; and when he
suddenly did so, no question of expediency had entered into the
arrangement.

He supposed afterward that what had happened to him was what
people called falling in love. He had never allowed for that either, and
even now he was not sure if it was the right name for the knock-down
blow dealt to him by his first sight of Nadeja. Her name told you her
part of the story clearly enough. She came straight out of that struggling
mass of indistinguishable human misery that Targatt called 'Wardrift.'
One day – he still wondered how, for he was fiercely on his guard
against such intrusions – she had forced her way into his office, and
tried to sell him (of all things!) a picture painted by her brother Serge.
They were all starving, she said; and very likely it was true. But that
had not greatly moved him. He had heard the same statement made
too often by too many people, and it was too painfully connected in
his mind with a dreaded and rapidly increasing form of highway
robbery called 'Appeals.' Besides, Targatt's imagination was not
particularly active, and as he was always sure of a good meal himself,
it never much disturbed him to be told that others were not. So he
couldn't to this day have told you how it came about that he bought
Serge's picture on the spot, and married Nadeja a few weeks afterward.
He had been knocked on the head – sandbagged; a regular hold-up.
That was the only way to describe it.

Nadeja made no attempt to darn or scrub for him – which was
perhaps just as well, as he liked his comforts. On the contrary, she
made friends at once with the German widow, and burdened that
industrious woman with the additional care of her own wardrobe,
which was negligible before her marriage, but increased rapidly after

she became Mrs. Targatt. There was a second servant's room above the flat, and Targatt rather reluctantly proposed that they should get in a girl to help Hilda; but Nadeja said, no, she didn't believe Hilda would care for that; and the room would do so nicely for Paul, her younger brother, the one who was studying to be a violinist.

Targatt hated music, and suffered acutely (for a New Yorker) from persistently recurring noises; but Paul, a nice boy, also with long-lashed eyes, moved into the room next to Hilda's and practised the violin all day and most of the night. The room was directly over that which Targatt now shared with Nadeja – and of which all but the space occupied by his shaving stand had by this time become her exclusive property. But he bore with Paul's noise, and it was Hilda who struck. She said she loved music that gave her *Heimweh*, but this kind only kept her awake; and to Targatt's horror she announced her intention of leaving at the end of the month.

It was the biggest blow he had ever had since he had once – and only once – been on the wrong side of the market. He had no time to hunt for another servant, and was sure Nadeja would not know how to find one. Nadeja, when he broke the news to her, acquiesced in this view of her incapacity. 'But why do we want a servant? I could never see,' she said. 'And Hilda's room would do very nicely for my sister Olga, who is learning to be a singer. She and Paul could practice together – '

'Oh, Lord,' Targatt interjected.

'And we could all go out to restaurants; a different one every night: it's much more fun, isn't it? And there are people who come in and clean – no? Hilda was a robber – I didn't want to tell you, but . . .'

Within a week the young Olga, whose eyelashes were even longer than Paul's, was settled in the second servant's room, and within a month Targatt had installed a grand piano in his own drawing room, (where it took up all the space left by Nadeja's divan), so that Nadeja could accompany Olga when Paul was not available.

• III •

TARGATT had never, till that moment, thought much about Nadeja's family. He understood that his father-in-law had been a Court dignitary of high standing, with immense landed estates and armies of slaves – no, he believed they didn't have slaves, or serfs, or whatever they called them, any longer in those outlandish countries east or south of Russia. Targatt was not strong on geography. He did not own an atlas, and had never yet had time to go to the Public Library and look up his father-in-law's native heath. In fact, he had never had time to read, or to think consecutively on any subject but money-making; he knew only that old man Kouradjine had been a big swell in some country in which the Bolsheviks had confiscated everybody's property, and where the women (and the young men too) apparently all had long eyelashes. But that was all part of a vanished fairy tale; at present the old man was only Number So-much on one Near East Relief list, while Paul and Olga and the rest of them (Targatt wasn't sure even yet how many there were) figured on similar lists, though on a more modest scale, since they were supposedly capable of earning their own living. But were they capable of it, and was there any living for them to earn? That was what Targatt in the course of time began to ask himself.

Targatt was not a particularly sociable man; but in his bachelor days, he had fancied inviting a friend to dine now and then, chiefly to have the shine of his mahogany table marveled at, and Hilda's *Wienerschnitzel* praised. This was all over now. His meals were all taken in restaurants – a different one each time; and they were usually shared with Paul, Olga, Serge (the painter) and the divorced sister, Katinka, who had three children and a refugee lover, Dmitri.

At first this state of affairs was very uncomfortable, and even painful, for Targatt; but since it seemed inevitable he adjusted himself to it, and buried his private cares in an increased business activity.

His activity was, in fact, tripled by the fact that it was no longer restricted to his own personal affairs, but came more and more to include such efforts as organizing an exhibition of Serge's pictures, finding the funds for Paul's violin tuition, trying to make it worth somebody's while to engage Olga for a concert tour, pushing Katinka into a saleswoman's job at a fashionable dressmaker's, and persuading a friend in a bank to recommend Dmitri as interpreter to foreign clients. All this was difficult enough, and if Targatt had not been sustained by Nadeja's dogged optimism his courage might have failed him; but the crowning problem was how to deal with the youngest brother, Boris, who was just seventeen, and had the longest eyelashes of all. Boris was too old to be sent to school, too young to be put into a banker's or broker's office, and too smilingly irresponsible to hold the job for twenty-four hours if it had been offered to him. Targatt, for three years after his marriage, had had only the vaguest ideas of Boris's existence, for he was not among the first American consignment of the family. But suddenly he drifted in alone, from Odessa or Athens, and joined the rest of the party at the restaurant. By this time the Near East Relief Funds were mostly being wound up, and in spite of all Targatt's efforts it was impossible to get financial aid for Boris, so for the first months he just lolled in a pleasant aimless way on Nadeja's divan; and as he was very particular about the quality of his cigarettes, and consumed a large supply daily, Targatt for the first time began to regard one of Nadeja's family with a certain faint hostility.

Boris might have been less of a trial if, by the time he came, Targatt had been able to get the rest of the family on their legs; but, however often he repeated this attempt, they invariably toppled over on him. Serge could not sell his pictures, Paul could not get an engagement in an orchestra, Olga had given up singing for dancing, so that her tuition had to begin all over again; and to think of Dmitri and Katinka, and Katinka's three children, was not conducive to repose at the end of a hard day in Wall Street.

Yet in spite of everything Targatt had never really been able to remain angry for more than a few moments with any member of the Kouradjine group. For some years this did not particularly strike him; he was given neither to self-analysis nor the dissection of others, except where business dealings were involved. He had been taught, almost in the nursery, to discern, and deal with, the motives determining a given course in business; but he knew no more of human nature's other mainsprings than if the nursery were still his habitat. He was vaguely conscious that Nadeja was aware of this, and that it caused her a faint amusement. Once, when they had been dining with one of his business friends, and the latter's wife, an ogling bore, had led the talk to the shopworn question of how far mothers ought to enlighten their little girls on – well you know . . . just *how much* ought they to be taught? That was the delicate point, Mrs. Targatt, wasn't it? – Nadeja, thus cornered, had met the question with a gaze of genuine bewilderment. 'Taught? Do you have to be *taught?* I think it is Nature who will tell them – no? But myself I should first teach dressmaking and cooking,' she said with her shadowy smile. And now, reviewing the Kouradjine case, Targatt suddenly thought. 'But that's it! Nature *does* teach the Kouradjines. It's a gift like a tenor voice. The thing is to know how to make the best use of it – ' and he fell to musing on this newly discovered attribute. It was – what? Charm? Heaven forbid! The very word made his flesh creep with memories of weary picnics and wearier dinners where, with pink food in fluted papers, the discussion of 'What is Charm?' had formed the staple diet. 'I'd run a mile from a woman with charm; and so would most men,' Targatt thought with a retrospective shudder. And he tried, for the first time, to make a conscious inventory of Nadeja's attributes.

She was not beautiful; he was certain of that. He was not good at seeing people, really seeing them, even when they were just before his eyes, much less at visualizing them in absence. When Nadeja was away all he could ever evoke of her was a pleasant blur. But he wasn't such a blind bat as not to know when a woman was beautiful. Beauty, however, was made to look at, not to live with; he had never wanted to marry a beautiful woman. And Nadeja wasn't clever, either; not in talk, that is. (And that, he mused, was certainly one of her qualities.) With regard to the other social gifts, so-called: cards, for instance? Well, he knew she and Katinka were not above fishing out an old pack and telling their fortunes, when they thought he wasn't noticing; but anything as scientific as bridge frightened her, and she had the good sense not to try to learn. So much for society; and as for the home – well, she could hardly be called a good housekeeper, he supposed. But remembering his mother, who had been accounted a paragon in that line, he gave thanks for this deficiency of Nadeja's also. Finally he said to himself: 'I seem to like her for all the things she is *not*.' This was not satisfactory; but he could do no better. 'Well, somehow, she fits into the cracks,' he concluded; and inadequate as this also sounded, he felt it might turn out to be a clue to the Kouradjines. Yes, they certainly fitted in; squeezing you a little, overlapping you a good deal, but never – and there was the point – sticking into you like the proverbial thorn, or crowding you uncomfortably, or for any reason making you wish they weren't there.

This fact, of which he had been dimly conscious from the first, arrested his attention now because he had a sudden glimpse of its business possibilities. Little Boris had only had to borrow a hundred dollars of him for the trip to Hollywood, and behold little Boris was already affianced to the world's leading movie star! In the light of this surprising event Targatt suddenly recalled that Katinka, not long before, had asked him if he wouldn't give Dmitri, who had not been a success at the bank, a letter recommending him for some sort of employment in the office of a widowed millionaire who was the highest light on Targatt's business horizon. Targatt had received the suggestion without enthusiasm. 'Your sister's crazy,' he said to Nadeja. 'How can I recommend that fellow to a man like Bellamy? Has he ever had any business training?'

'Well, we know Mr. Bellamy's looking for a bookkeeper, because he asked you if you knew of one,' said Nadeja.

'Yes; but what are Dmitri's qualifications? Does he know anything whatever about bookkeeping?'

'No; not yet. But he says perhaps he could buy a little book about it.'

'Oh, Lord – ' Targatt groaned.

'Even so, you don't think you could recommend him, darling?'

'No; I couldn't, I'm afraid.'

Nadeja did not insist; she never insisted. 'I've found out a new restaurant, where they make much better blinys. Shall I tell them all to meet us there tonight at half-past eight?' she suggested.

Now, in the light of Boris's news, Targatt began to think this conversation over. Dmitri was an irredeemable fool; but Katinka – what about giving the letter for old Bellamy to Katinka? Targatt didn't see exactly how he could word it; but he had an idea that Nadeja would tell him. Those were the ways in which she was really clever. A few days later he asked: 'Has Dmitri got a job yet?'

She looked at him in surprise. 'No, as you couldn't recommend him he didn't buy the book.'

'Oh, damn the book. . . . See here, Nadeja; supposing I were to give Katinka a letter for old Bellamy?'

He had made the suggestion with some embarrassment, half expecting that he would have to explain. But not to Nadeja. 'Oh, darling, you always think of the right thing,' she answered, kissing him; and as he had foreseen she told him just how to word the letter.

'And I will lend her my silver fox to wear,' she added. Certainly the social education of the Kouradjines had been far more comprehensive than Targatt's.

Katinka went to see Mr. Bellamy, and when she returned she reported favourably on the visit. Nothing was as yet decided about Dmitri, as she had been obliged to confess that he had had no training as an accountant; but Mr. Bellamy had been very kind, and had invited her to come to his house some afternoon to see his pictures.

From this visit also Katinka came back well-pleased, though she seemed not to have accomplished anything further with regard to Dmitri. She had, however, been invited by Mr. Bellamy to dine and go to a play; and a few weeks afterward she said to Targatt and Nadeja: 'I think I will live with Mr. Bellamy. He has an empty flat that I could have, and he would furnish it beautifully.'

Though Targatt prided himself on an unprejudiced mind he winced slightly at this suggestion. It seemed cruel to Dmitri, and decidedly uncomfortable as far as Targatt and Nadeja were concerned.

'But, Katinka, if Bellamy's so gone on you, he ought to marry you,' he said severely.

Katinka nodded her assent. 'Certainly he ought. And I think he will, after I have lived with him a few months.'

This upset every single theory of Targatt's with regard to his own sex. 'But, my poor girl – if you go and live with a man first like . . . like any woman he could have for money, why on earth should he want to marry you afterward?'

Katinka looked at him calmly. Her eyelashes were not as long as Nadeja's, but her eyes were as full of wisdom. 'Habit,' she said simply, and in an instant Targatt's conventional world was in fragments at his feet. Who knew better than he did that if you once had the Kouradjine habit you couldn't be cured of it? He said nothing more, and sat back to watch what happened to Mr. Bellamy.

• IV •

MR. BELLAMY did not offer Dmitri a position as bookkeeper; but soon after his marriage to Katinka he took him into his house as social secretary. Targatt had a first movement of surprise and disapproval, but he saw that Nadeja did not share it. 'That's very nice,' she said. 'I was sure Katinka would not desert Dmitri. And Mr. Bellamy is so generous. He is going to adopt Katinka's three children.'

But it must not be thought that the fortunes of all the Kouradjines ran as smoothly. For a brief moment Targatt had imagined that the infatuated Bellamy was going to assume the charge of the whole tribe; but Wall Street was beginning to be uneasy, and Mr. Bellamy restricted his hospitality to Katinka's children and Dmitri, and, like many of the very rich, manifested no interest in those whose misfortunes did not immediately interfere with his own comfort. Thus vanished even the dream of a shared responsibility, and Targatt saw himself facing a business outlook decidedly less dazzling, and with a still considerable number of Kouradjines to provide for. Olga, in particular, was a cause of some anxiety. She was less adaptable, less suited to fitting into cracks, than the others, and her various experiments in song and dance had all broken down for lack of perseverance. But she was (at least so Nadeja thought) by far the best-looking of the family; and finally Targatt decided to pay for her journey to Hollywood, in the hope that Boris would put her in the way of becoming a screen star. This suggestion, however, was met by a telegram from Boris ominously dated from Reno: 'Don't send Olga am divorcing Halma.'

For the first time since his marriage Targatt felt really discouraged. Were there perhaps too many Kouradjines, and might the Kouradjine habit after all be beginning to wear thin? The family were all greatly perturbed by Boris's news, and when – after the brief interval required to institute and complete divorce proceedings against his film star – Boris left Reno and turned up in New York, his air of unperturbed good humor was felt to be unsuitable to the occasion. Nadeja, always hopeful, interpreted it as meaning that he was going to marry another and even richer star; but Boris said God forbid, and no more Hollywood for him. Katinka and Bellamy did not invite him to come and stay, and the upshot of it was that his bed was made up on the Targatts' drawing-room divan, while he shared the bathroom with Targatt and Nadeja.

Things dragged on in this way for some weeks, till one day Nadeja came privately to her husband. 'He has got three millions,' she whispered with wide eyes. 'Only yesterday was he sure. The check has come. Do you think, darling, she ought to have allowed him more?'

Targatt did not think so; he was inarticulate over Boris's achievement. 'What's he going to do with it?' he gasped.

'Well, I think first he will invest it, and then he will go to the Lido. There is a young girl there, I believe, that he is in love with. I knew Boris would not divorce for nothing. He is going there to meet her.'

Targatt could not disguise an impulse of indignation. Before investing his millions, was Boris not going to do anything for his family? Nadeja said she had thought of that too; but Boris said he had invested the money that morning, and of course there would be no interest coming in till the next quarter. And meanwhile he was so much in love that he had taken his passage for the following day on the 'Berengaria'. Targatt thought that only natural, didn't he?

Targatt swallowed his ire, and said, yes, he supposed it was natural enough. After all, if the boy had found a young girl he could really love and respect, and if he had the money to marry her and settle down, no one could blame him for rushing off to press his suit. And Boris rushed.

But meanwhile the elimination of two Kouradjines had not had the hoped-for effect of reducing the total number of the tribe. On the contrary, that total had risen; for suddenly three new members had appeared. One was an elderly and completely ruined Princess (a distant cousin, Nadeja explained) with whom old Kouradjine had decided to contract a tardy alliance, now that the rest of the family were provided for. 'He could do no less,' Katinka and Nadeja mysteriously agreed.) And the other, and more sensational, newcomers were two beautiful young creatures, known respectively to the tribe as Nick and Mouna, but whose difficulties at the passport office made it seem that there were legal doubts as to their remaining names. These difficulties, through Targatt's efforts, were finally overcome and, snatched from the jaws of Ellis Island, Nick and Mouna joyfully joined the party at another new restaurant, 'The Transcaucasian,' which Nadeja had recently discovered.

Targatt's immensely enlarged experience of human affairs left him in a little doubt as to the parentage of Nick and Mouna, and when Nadeja whispered to him one night (through the tumult of Boris's late bath next door): 'You see, poor Papa felt he could no longer fail to provide for them,' Targatt did not dream of asking why.

. But he now had no less than seven Kouradjines more or less dependent on him, and the next night he sat up late and did some figuring and thinking. Even to Nadeja he could not explain in blunt language the result of this vigil; but he said to her the following day: 'What's become of that flat of Bellamy's that Katinka lived in before – '

'Why, he gave the lease to Katinka as a wedding present; but it seems that people are no more as rich as they were, and as it's such a very handsome flat, and the rent is high, the tenants can no longer afford to keep it – '

'Well,' said Targatt with sudden resolution, 'tell your sister if she'll make a twenty-five per cent cut on the rent I'll take over the balance of the lease.'

Nadeja gasped. 'Oh, James, you are an angel! But what do you think you could then do with it?'

Targatt threw back his shoulders. 'Live in it,' he recklessly declared.

• V •

IT was the first time (except when he had married Nadeja) that he had even been reckless; and there was no denying that he enjoyed the sensation. But he had not acted wholly for the sake of enjoyment; he had an ulterior idea. What that idea was he did not choose to communicate to anyone at present. He merely asked Katinka, who, under the tuition of Mr. Bellamy's experienced butler, had developed some rudimentary ideas of housekeeping, to provide Nadeja with proper servants, and try to teach her how to use them; and he then announced to Nadeja that he had made up his mind to do a little entertaining. He and Nadeja had already made a few fashionable acquaintances at the Bellamys', and these they proceeded to invite to the new flat, and to feed with exotic food, and stimulate with abstruse cocktails. At these dinners Targatt's new friends met the younger and lovelier of the Kouradjines: Paul, Olga, Nick and Mouna, and they always went away charmed with the encounter.

Considerable expense was involved by this new way of life; and still more when Nadeja, at Targatt's instigation, invited Olga, Nick and Mouna to come and live with them. Nadeja was overcome with gratitude at this suggestion; but her gratitude, like all her other emotions, was so exquisitely modulated that it fell on Targatt like the gentle dew from heaven, merely fostering in him a new growth of tenderness. But still Targatt did not explain himself. He had his idea, and knowing that Nadeja would not bother him with questions he sat back quietly and waited, though Wall Street was growing more and more unsettled, and there had been no further news of Boris, and Paul and Olga were still without a job.

The Targatts' little dinners, and Nadeja's exclusive cocktail parties, began to be the rage in a set far above the Bellamys'. There were almost always one or two charming young Kouradjines present; but they were now so sought after in smartest Park Avenue and gayest Long Island that Targatt and Nadeja had to make sure of securing their presence beforehand, so there was never any danger of there being too many on the floor at once.

On the contrary, there were occasions when they all simultaneously failed to appear; and on one of these evenings, Targatt, conscious that the party had not 'come off,' was about to vent his irritation against the absent Serge, when Nadeja said gently: 'I'm sorry Serge didn't tell you. But I think he was married today to Mrs. Leeper.'

'Mrs. Leeper? Not the Dazzle Tooth Paste woman he met at the Bellamys', who wanted him to decorate her ballroom?'

'Yes; but I think she did not after all want him to decorate her ballroom. And so she has married him instead.'

A year earlier Targatt would have had no word but an uncomprehending groan. But since then his education had proceeded by leaps and bounds, and now he simply said: 'I see – ' and turned back to his breakfast with a secret smile. He had received Serge's tailor's bill the day before, and had been rehearsing half the night what he was going to say to Serge when they met. But now he merely remarked: 'That woman has a two million dollar income,' and thought to himself that the experiment with the flat was turning out better than he could have imagined. If Serge could be disposed of so easily there was no cause to despair of Paul or Olga. 'Hasn't Mrs. Leeper a nephew?' he asked Nadeja; who, as if she had read his thought, replied regretfully: 'Yes, but I'm afraid he's married.'

'Oh, well – send Boris to talk to him!' Targatt jeered; and Nadeja, who never laughed, smiled a little and replied: 'Boris too will soon be married.' She handed her husband the morning papers, which he had not yet had time to examine, and he read, in glowing headlines, the announcement of the marriage in London of Prince Boris Kouradjine, son of Prince Peter Kouradjine, hereditary sovereign of Daghestan, and Chamberlain at the court of his late Imperial Majesty the Czar Nicholas, to Miss Mamie Guggins of Rapid Rise, Oklahoma. 'Boris has a little exaggerated our father's rank,' Nadeja commented; but Targatt said thoughtfully: 'No one can exaggerate the Guggins' fortune.' And Nadeja gave a quiet sigh.

It must not be supposed that this rise in the fortunes of the Kouradjines was of any direct benefit to Targatt. He had never expected that, or even hoped it. No Kouradjine had ever suggested making any return for the sums expended by Targatt in vainly educating and profitably dressing his irresistible in-laws; nor had Targatt's staggering restaurant bills been reduced by any offer of participation. Only the old Princess (as it was convenient, with so many young ones about, to call her when she was out of hearing) had said tearfully, on her wedding day: 'Believe me, my good James, what you have done for us all will not be forgotten when we return to Daghestan.' And she spoke with such genuine emotion, the tears were so softening to her tired magnificent eyes, that Targatt, at the moment, felt himself repaid.

Other and more substantial returns he did draw from his alliance with the Kouradjines; and it was the prospect of these which had governed his conduct. From the day when it had occurred to him to send Katinka to intercede with Mr. Bellamy, Targatt had never once swerved from his purpose. And slowly but surely he was beginning to reap his reward.

Mr. Bellamy, for instance, had not seen his way to providing for the younger Kouradjines; but he was ready enough to let Targatt in on the ground floor of one of those lucrative deals usually reserved for the already wealthy. Mrs. Leeper, in her turn, gave him the chance to buy a big block of Dazzle Tooth Paste shares on exceptional terms; and as fashion and finance became aware of the younger Kouradjines, and fell under their spell, Targatt's opportunities for making quick turnovers became almost limitless. And now a pleasant glow stole down his spine at the thought that all previous Kouradjine alliances paled before the staggering wealth of Boris's bride. 'Boris really does owe me a good turn,' he mused; but he had no expectation that it would be done with Boris's knowledge. The new Princess Boris was indeed induced to hand over her discarded wardrobe to Olga and Mouna, and Boris presented cigarette cases to his brothers and brother-in-law; but here his prodigalities ended. Targatt, however, was not troubled; for years he had longed to meet the great Mr. Guggins, and here he was, actually related to that gentleman's only child!

Mr. Guggins, when under the influence of domestic happiness or alcohol, was almost as emotional as the Kouradjines. On his return to New York, after the parting from his only child, he was met on the dock by Targatt and Nadeja, who suggested his coming to dine that night at a jolly new restaurant with all the other Kouradjines; and Mrs. Guggins was so much drawn to the old Princess, to whom she confided how difficult it was to get reliable window washers at Rapid Rise, that the next day Targatt, as he would have put it, had the old man in his pocket. Mr. Guggins stayed a week in New York, and when he departed Targatt knew enough about the Guggins industries to make some very useful reinvestments; and Mrs. Guggins carried off Olga as her social secretary.

• VI •

STIMULATED by these successive achievements Targatt's tardily developed imagination was growing like an Indian juggler's tree. He no longer saw any limits to what might be done with the Kouradjines. He had already found a post for the old Prince as New York representative of a leading firm of Paris picture dealers, Paul and Nick were professional dancers at fashionable nightclubs, and for the moment only Mouna, the lovely but difficult, remained on Targatt's mind and his payroll.

It was the first time in his life that Targatt had tasted the fruits of ease, and he found them surprisingly palatable. He was no longer young, it took him more time than of old to get around a golf course, and he occasionally caught himself telling his good stories twice over to the same listener. But life was at once exciting and peaceful, and he had to own that his interests had been immensely enlarged. All that, of course, he owed in the first instance to Nadeja. Poor Nadeja – she was not as young as she had been, either. She was still slender and supple, but there were little lines in the corners of her eyes, and a certain droop of the mouth. Others might not notice these symptoms, Targatt thought; but they had not escaped *him*. For Targett, once so unseeing in the presence of beauty, had now become an adept in appraising human flesh-and-blood, and smiled knowingly when his new friends commended Mouna's young charms, or inclined the balance in favor of the more finished Olga. There was nothing anyone could tell him now about the relative 'values' of the Kouradjines: he had them tabulated as if they were vintage wines, and it was a comfort to him to reflect that Nadeja was, after all, the one whose market value was least considerable. It was sheer luck – a part of his miraculous Kouradjine luck – that his choice had fallen on the one Kouradjine about whom there was never likely to be the least fuss or scandal; and after an exciting day in Wall Street, or a fatiguing struggle to extricate Paul or Mouna from some fresh scrape, he would sink back with satisfaction into his own unruffled domesticity.

There came a day, however, when he began to feel that the contrast between his wife and her sisters was too much to Nadeja's disadvantage. Was it because the others had smarter clothes – or, like Katinka, finer jewels? Poor Nadeja, he reflected, had never had any jewels since her engagement ring; and that was a shabby affair. Was it possible, Targatt conjectured, that as middle age approached she was growing dowdy, and needed the adventitious enhancements of dressmaker and beauty doctor? Half-sheepishly he suggested that she oughtn't to let herself be outdone by Katinka, who was two or three years her senior; and he reinforced the suggestion by a diamond chain from Cartier's and a good-humored hint that she might try Mrs. Bellamy's dressmaker.

Nadeja received the jewel with due raptures, and appeared at their next dinner in a gown which was favorably noticed by everyone present. Katinka said: 'Well, at last poor Nadeja is really *dressed*,' and Mouna sulked visibly, and remarked to her brother-in-law: 'If you want the right people to ask me about you might let me get a few clothes at Nadeja's place.'

All this was as it should be, and Targatt's satisfaction increased as he watched his wife's returning bloom. It seemed funny to him that, even on a sensible woman like Nadeja, clothes and jewels should act as a tonic; but then the Kouradjines *were* funny, and heaven knew Targatt had no reason to begrudge them any of their little fancies – especially now that Olga's engagement to Mrs. Guggins' brother (representative of the Guggins interests in London and Paris) had been officially announced. When the news came, Targatt gave his wife a pair of emerald earrings, and suggested that they should take their summer holiday in Paris.

It was the same winter that New York was thrown into a flutter by the announcement that the famous portrait painter, Axel Svengaart, was coming over to 'do' a chosen half-dozen sitters. Svengaart had

never been to New York before, had always sworn that anybody who
wanted to be painted by him must come to his studio at Oslo; but it
suddenly struck him that the American background might give a fresh
quality to his work, and after painting one lady getting out of her car
in front of her husband's motorworks, and Mrs. Guggins against the
background of a spouting oil well at Rapid Rise, he appeared in New
York to organize a show of these sensational canvases. New York was
ringing with the originality and audacity of this new experiment. After
expecting to be 'done' in the traditional setting of the Gothic library or
the Quattrocento *salon*, it was incredibly exciting to be portrayed literally surrounded by the acknowledged sources of one's wealth; and the
wife of a fabulously rich plumber was nearly persuaded to be done
stepping out of her bath, in a luxury bathroom fitted with the latest
ablutionary appliances.

Fresh from these achievements, Axel Svengaart carried his Viking
head and Parisian monocle from one New York drawing room to
another, gazing, appraising – even, though rarely, praising – but absolutely refusing to take another order, or to postpone by a single day the
date of his sailing. 'I've got it all here,' he said, touching first his brow
and then his pocket; and the dealer who acted as his impresario let it
be understood that even the most exaggerated offers would be rejected.

Targatt had, of course, met the great man. In old days he would
have been uncomfortably awed by the encounter; but now he could
joke easily about the Gugginses, and even ask Svengaart if he had not
been struck by his sister-in-law, who was Mrs. Guggins' social
secretary, and was about to marry Mr. Guggins's Paris representative.

'Ah – the lovely Kouradjine; yes. She made us some delicious
blinys,' Svengaart nodded approvingly; but Targatt saw with surprise
that as a painter he was uninterested in Olga's plastic possibilities.

'Ah, well, I suppose you've had enough of us – I hear you're off
this week.'

The painter dropped his monocle. 'Yes, I've had enough.' It was
after dinner, at the Bellamys', and abruptly he seated himself on the
sofa at Targatt's side. 'I don't like your frozen food,' he pursued.
'There's only one thing that would make me put off my sailing.' He
readjusted his monocle and looked straight at Targatt. 'If you'll give
me the chance to paint Mrs. Targatt – oh, for that I'd wait another
month.'

Targatt stared at him, too surprised to answer. Nadeja – the great
man wanted to paint Nadeja! The idea aroused so many conflicting
considerations that his reply, when it came, was a stammer. 'Why
really . . . this is a surprise . . . a great honor, of course. . . .' A vision
of Svengaart's price for a mere head thrust itself hideously before his
eyes. Svengaart, seeing him as it were encircled by millionaires, probably took him for a very rich man – was perhaps maneuvering to

extract an extra big offer from him. For what other inducement could there be to paint Nadeja? Targatt turned the question with a joke. 'I suspect you're confusing me with my brother-in-law Bellamy. He ought to have persuaded you to paint his wife. But I'm afraid my means wouldn't allow. . . .'

The other interrupted him with an irritated gesture. 'Please – my dear sir. I can never be "persuaded" to do a portrait. And in the case of Mrs. Targatt I had no idea of selling you her picture. If I paint her, it would be for myself.'

Targatt's stare widened. 'For yourself? You mean – you'd paint the picture just to keep it?' He gave an embarrassed laugh. 'Nadeja would be enormously flattered, of course. But, between ourselves, would you mind telling me why you want to do her?'

Svengaart stood up with a faint laugh. 'Because she's the only really paintable woman I've seen here. The lines are incomparable for a full-length. And I can't tell you how I should enjoy the change.'

Targatt continued to stare. Murmurs of appreciation issued from his parched lips. He remembered now that Svengaart's charge for a three-quarter-length was fifteen thousand dollars. And he wanted to do Nadeja full length for nothing! Only – Targatt remined himself – the brute wanted to keep the picture. So where was the good? It would only make Nadeja needlessly conspicuous; and to give all those sittings for nothing . . . well, it looked like sharp practice, somehow. . . .

'Of course, as I say, my wife would be immensely flattered; only she's very busy – her family, social obligations and so on; I really can't say. . . .'

Svengaart smiled. 'In the course of a portrait I usually make a good many studies; some almost as finished as the final picture. If Mrs. Targatt cared to accept one – '

Targatt flushed to the roots of his thinning hair. A Svengaart study over the drawing-room mantelpiece! ('Yes – nice thing of Nadeja, isn't it? You'd know a Svengaart anywhere . . . it was his own idea; he insisted on doing her. . . .')

Nadeja was just lifting a pile of music from the top of the grand piano. She was going to accompany Mouna, who had taken to singing. As she stood with lifted arms, profiled against the faint hues of the tapestried wall, the painter exclaimed: 'There – there! I have it! Don't you see now why I want to do her?'

But Targatt, for the moment, could not speak. Secretly he thought Nadeja looked much as usual – only perhaps a little more tired; she had complained of a headache that morning. But his courage rose to the occasion. 'Ah, my wife's famous "lines", eh? Well, well, I can't promise – you'd better come over and try to persuade her yourself.'

He was so dizzy with it that as he led Svengaart toward the piano the Bellamys' parquet floor felt like glass under his unsteady feet.

• VII •

TARGATT's rapture was acute but short-lived. Nadeja 'done' by Axel Svengaart – he had measured the extent of it in a flash. He had stood aside and watched her with a deep smile of satisfaction while the light of wonder rose in her eyes; when she turned them on him for approval he had nodded his assent. Of course she must sit to the great man, his glance signaled back. He saw that Svengaart was amused at her having to ask her husband's permission; but this only intensified Targatt's satisfaction. They'd see, damn it, if his wife could be ordered about like a professional model! Perhaps the best moment was when, the next day, she said timidly: 'But, Jim, have you thought about the price?' and he answered, his hands in his pockets, an easy smile on his lips: 'There's no price to think about. He's doing you for the sake of your beautiful "lines". And we're to have a replica, free gratis. Did you know you had beautiful lines, old Nad?'

She looked at him gravely for a moment. 'I hadn't thought about them for a long time,' she said.

Targatt laughed and tapped her on the shoulder. What a child she was! But afterward it struck him that she had not been particularly surprised by the painter's request. Perhaps she had always known she was paintable, as Svengaart called it. Perhaps – and here he felt a little chill run over him – perhaps Svengaart had spoken to her already, had come to an understanding with her before making his request to Targatt. The idea made Targatt surprisingly uncomfortable, and he reflected that it was the first occasion in their married life when he had suspected Nadeja of even the most innocent duplicity. And this, if it were true, could hardly be regarded as wholly innocent. . . .

Targatt shook the thought off impatiently. He was behaving like the fellow in Pagliacci. Really this associating with foreigners might end in turning a plain businessman into an opera singer! It was the day of the first sitting, and as he started for his office he called back gaily to Nadeja: 'Well, so long! And don't let that fellow turn your head.'

He could not get much out of Nadeja about the sittings. It was not that she seemed secretive; but she was never very good at reporting small talk, and things that happened outside of the family circle, even if they happened to herself, always seemed of secondary interest to her. And meanwhile the sittings went on and on. In spite of his free style Svengaart was a slow worker; and he seemed to find Nadeja a difficult subject. Targatt began to brood over the situation: some people thought the fellow handsome, in the lean greyhound style; and he had an easy cosmopolitan way – the European manner. It was what Nadeja was used to; would she suddenly feel that she had missed something during all these years? Targatt turned cold at the thought. It had never before occurred to him what a humdrum figure he was. The contemplation of his face in the shaving glass became so distasteful to him that he averted his eyes, and nearly cut his throat in consequence. Nothing of the greyhound style about him – or the Viking either.

Slowly, as these thoughts revolved in his mind, he began to feel that he, who had had everything from Nadeja, had given her little or nothing in return. What he had done for her people weighed as nothing in this revaluation of their past. The point was: what sort of a life had he given Nadeja? And the answer: no life at all! She had spent her best years looking after other people; he could not remember that she had ever asserted a claim or resented an oversight. And yet she was neither dull nor insipid: she was simply Nadeja – a creature endlessly tolerant, totally unprejudiced, sublimely generous and unselfish.

Well – it would be funny, Targatt thought, with a twist of almost physical pain, if nobody else had been struck by such unusual qualities. If it had taken him over ten years to find them out, others might have been less blind. He had never noticed her 'lines', for instance; yet that painter fellow, the moment he'd clapped eyes on her – !

Targatt sat in his study, twisting about restlessly in his chair. Where *was* Nadeja, he wondered? The winter dusk had fallen, and painters do not work without daylight. The day's sitting must be over – and yet she had not come back. Usually she was always there to greet him on his return from the office. She had taught him to enjoy his afternoon tea, with a tiny caviar sandwich and a slice of lemon, and the samovar was already murmuring by the fire. When she went to see any of her family she always called up to say if she would be late; but the maid said there had been no message from her.

Targatt got up and walked the floor impatiently; then he sat down again, lit a cigarette, and threw it away. Nadeja, he remembered, had not been in the least shocked when Katinka had decided to live with Mr. Bellamy; she had merely wondered if the step were expedient, and had finally agreed with Katinka that it was. Nor had Boris's matrimonial maneuvers seemed to offend her. She was entirely destitute of moral indignation; this painful reality was now borne in on Targatt for the first time. Cruelty shocked her; but otherwise she seemed to think that people should do as they pleased. Yet, all the while, had she ever done what *she* pleased? There was the torturing enigma! She seemed to allow such latitude to others, yet to ask so little for herself.

Well, but didn't the psychologist fellows say that there was an hour in every woman's life – every self-sacrificing woman's – when the claims of her suppressed self suddenly asserted themselves, body and soul, and she forgot everything else, all her duties, ties, responsibilities? Targatt broke off with a bitter laugh. What did 'duties, ties, responsibilities' mean to Nadeja? No more than to any of the other Kouradjines. Their vocabulary had no parallels with his. He felt a sudden overwhelming loneliness, as if all these years he had been married to a changeling, an opalescent creature swimming up out of the sea. . . .

No, she couldn't be at the studio any longer; or if she were, it wasn't to sit for her portrait. Curse the portrait, he thought – why had he ever consented to her sitting to Svengaart? Sheer cupidity; the snobbish ambition to own a Svengaart, the glee of getting one for nothing. The more he proceeded with this self-investigation the less he cared for the figure he cut. But however poor a part he had played so far, he wasn't going to add to it the role of the duped husband. . . .

'Damn it, I'll go round there myself and see,' he muttered, squaring his shoulders, and walking resolutely across the room to the door. But as he reached the entrance hall the faint click of a latchkey greeted him; and sweeter music he had never heard. Nadeja stood in the doorway, pale but smiling. 'Jim – you were not going out again?'

He gave a sheepish laugh. 'Do you know what time it is? I was getting scared.'

'Scared for me?' She smiled again. 'Dear me, yes! It's nearly dinner time, isn't it?'

He followed her into the drawing room and shut the door. He felt like a husband in an old-fashioned problem play; and in a moment he had spoken like one. 'Nad, where've you come from?' he broke out abruptly.

'Why, the studio. It was my last sitting.'

'People don't sit for their portraits in the dark.'

He saw a faint surprise in her eyes as she bent to the samovar. 'No; I was not sitting all the time. Not for the last hour or more, I suppose.'

She spoke as quietly as usual, yet he thought he caught a tremor of resentment in her voice. Against himself – or against the painter? But how he was letting his imagination run away with him! He sat down in his accustomed armchair, took the cup of tea she held out. He was determined to behave like a reasonable being, yet never had reason appeared to him so unrelated to reality. 'Ah, well – I suppose you two had a lot of things to talk about. You rather fancy Svengaart, don't you?'

'Oh, yes; I like him very much. Do you know,' she asked earnestly, 'How much he has made during his visit to America? It was of course in confidence that he told me. Two-hundred thousand dollars. And he was rich before.'

She spoke so solemnly that Targatt burst into a vague laugh. 'Well, what of it? I don't know that it showed much taste to brag to you about the way he skins his sitters. But it shows he didn't make much of a sacrifice in painting you for nothing,' he said irritably.

'No; I said to him he might have done you too.'

'*Me?*' Targatt's laugh redoubled. 'Well, what did he say to that?'

'Oh, he laughed as you are now laughing,' Nadeja rejoined. 'But he says he will never marry – never.'

Targatt put down his cup with a rattle. '*Never marry?* What the devil are you talking about? Who cares whether he marries, anyhow?' he gasped with a dry throat.

'I do,' said Nadeja.

There was a silence. Nadeja was lifting her teacup to her lips, and something in the calm free movement reminded him of Svengaart's outburst when he had seen her lift the pile of music. For the first time in his life Targatt seemed to himself to be looking at her; and he wondered if it would also be the last. He cleared his throat and tried to speak, to say something immense, magnanimous. 'Well, if – '

'No; it's useless. He will hear nothing. I said to him: You will never anywhere find such a *plastik* as Mouna's. . . .'

'*Mouna's?*'

She turned to him with a slight shrug. 'Oh, my poor Jim, are you quite blind? Haven't you seen how we have all been trying to make him want to marry Mouna? It will be almost my first failure, I think,' she concluded with a half-apologetic sigh.

Targatt rested his chin on his hands and looked up at her. She looked tired, certainly, and older; too tired and old for any one still well under forty. And Mouna – why in God's name should she be persecuting this man to marry Mouna? It was indecent, it was shocking, it was unbelievable. . . . Yet not for a moment did he doubt the truth of what she said.

'Mouna?' he could only repeat stupidly.

'Well, you see, darling, we're all a little anxious about Mouna. And I was so glad when Svengaart asked to paint me, because I thought: Now's my opportunity. But no, it was not to be.'

Targatt drew a deep breath. He seemed to be inhaling some life-giving element, and it was with the most superficial severity that he said: 'I don't fancy this idea of your throwing your sister at men's heads.'

'No, it was no use,' Nadeja sighed, with her usual complete unawareness of any moral rebuke in his comment.

Targatt stood up uneasily. 'He wouldn't have her at any price?'

She shook her head sadly. 'Foolish man!'

Targatt went up to her and took her abruptly by the wrist. 'Look at me, Nadeja – straight. Did he refuse her because he wanted *you?*'

She gave her light lift of the shoulders, and the rare color flitted across her pale cheeks. 'Isn't it always the way of men? What they can't get – '

'Ah; so he's been making love to you all this time, has he?'

'But of course not, James. What he wished was to marry me. That is something quite different, is it not?'

'Yes. I see.'

Targatt had released her wrist and turned away. He walked once or twice up and down the length of the room, no more knowing where he was than a man dropped blindfolded onto a new planet. He knew what he wanted to do and to say; the words he had made up his mind to speak stood out in letters of fire against the choking blackness. 'You must feel yourself free – ' Five words, and so easy to speak! 'Perfectly free – perfectly free,' a voice kept crying within him. It was the least he could do, if he were ever to hold up his head again; but when he opened his mouth to speak not a sound came. At last he halted before Nadeja again, his face working like a frightened child's.

'Nad – what would you like best in the world to do? If you'll tell me I – I want you to do it!' he stammered. And with hands of ice he waited.

Nadeja looked at him with a slowly growing surprise. She had turned very pale again.

'Even if,' he continued, half choking, 'you understand, Nad, even if – '

She continued to look at him in her grave maternal way. 'Is this true, what you are now saying?' she asked very low. Targatt nodded.

A little smile wavered over her lips. 'Well, darling, if only I could have got Mouna safely married, I should have said: Don't you think that now at last we could afford to have a baby?'

All Souls'

QUEER AND INEXPLICABLE as the business was, on the surface it appeared fairly simple – at the time, at least; but with the passing of years, and owing to there not having been a single witness of what happened except Sara Clayburn herself, the stories about it have become so exaggerated, and often so ridiculously inaccurate, that it seems necessary that someone connected with the affair, though not actually present – I repeat that when it happened my cousin was (or thought she was) quite alone in her house – should record the few facts actually known.

In those days I was often at Whitegates (as the place had always been called) – I was there, in fact, not long before, and almost immediately after, the strange happenings of those thirty-six hours. Jim Clayburn and his widow were both my cousins, and because of that, and of my intimacy with them, both families think I am more likely than anybody else to be able to get at the facts, as far as they can be called facts, and as anybody can get at them. So I have written down, as clearly as I could, the gist of the various talks I had with cousin Sara, when she could be got to talk – it wasn't often – about what occurred during that mysterious weekend.

I read the other day in a book by a fashionable essayist that ghosts went out when electric light came in. What nonsense! The writer, though he is fond of dabbling, in a literary way, in the supernatural, hasn't even reached the threshold of his subject. As between turreted castles patrolled by headless victims with clanking chains, and the comfortable suburban house with a refrigerator and central heating where you feel, as soon as you're in it, *that there's something wrong*, give me the latter for sending a chill down the spine! And, by the way, haven't you noticed that it's generally not the high-strung and imaginative who see ghosts, but the calm matter-of-fact people who don't believe in them, and are sure they wouldn't mind if they did see one? Well, that was the case with Sara Clayburn and her house. The house, in spite of its age – it was built, I believe, about 1780 – was open, airy, high-ceilinged, with electricity, central heating and all the modern appliances: and its mistress was – well, very much like her house. And, anyhow, this isn't exactly a ghost story and I've dragged in the analogy only as a way of showing you what kind of woman my cousin was, and how unlikely it would have seemed that what happened at Whitegates should have happened just there – or to her.

When Jim Clayburn died the family all thought that, as the couple had no children, his widow would give up Whitegates and move either to New York or Boston – for being of good Colonial stock, with many relatives and friends, she would have found a place ready for her in either. But Sally Clayburn seldom did what other people expected, and in this case she did exactly the contrary; she stayed at Whitegates.

'What, turn my back on the old house – tear up all the family roots, and go and hang myself up in a bird-cage flat in one of those new skyscrapers in Lexington Avenue, with a bunch of chickweed and a cuttlefish to replace my good Connecticut mutton? No, thank you. Here I belong, and here I stay till my executors hand the place over to Jim's next-of-kin – that stupid fat Presley boy. . . . Well, don't let's talk about him. But I tell you what – I'll keep him out of here as long as I can.' And she did – for being still in the early fifties when her husband died, and a muscular, resolute figure of a woman, she was more than a match for the fat Presley boy, and attended his funeral a few years ago, in correct mourning, with a faint smile under her veil.

Whitegates was a pleasant hospitable-looking house, on a height overlooking the stately windings of the Connecticut River; but it was five or six miles from Norrington, the nearest town, and its situation would certainly have seemed remote and lonely to modern servants. Luckily, however, Sara Clayburn had inherited from her mother-in-law two or three old stand-bys who seemed as much a part of the family tradition as the roof they lived under; and I never heard of her having any trouble in her domestic arrangements.

The house, in Colonial days, had been foursquare, with four spacious rooms on the ground floor, an oak-floored hall dividing them, the usual kitchen extension at the back, and a good attic under the roof. But Jim's grandparents, when interest in the 'Colonial' began to revive, in the early eighties, had added two wings, at right angles to the south front, so that the old 'circle' before the front door became a grassy court, enclosed on three sides, with a big elm in the middle. Thus the house was turned into a roomy dwelling, in which the last three generations of Clayburns had exercised a large hospitality; but the architect had respected the character of the old house, and the enlargement made it more comfortable without lessening its simplicity. There was a lot of land about it, and Jim Clayburn, like his father before him, farmed it, not without profit, and played a considerable and respected part in state politics. The Clayburns were always spoken of as a 'good influence' in the county, and the townspeople were glad when they learned that Sara did not mean to desert the place – 'though it must be lonesome, winters, living all alone up there atop of that hill' – they remarked as the days shortened, and the first snow began to pile up under the quadruple row of elms along the common.

Well, if I've given you a sufficiently clear idea of Whitegates and the Clayburns – who shared with their old house a sort of reassuring orderliness and dignity – I'll efface myself, and tell the tale, not in my cousin's words, for they were too confused and fragmentary, but as I built it up gradually out of her half-avowals and nervous reticences. If the thing happened at all – and I must leave you to judge of that – I think it must have happened in this way. . . .

• I •

THE morning had been bitter, with a driving sleet – though it was only the last day of October – but after lunch a watery sun showed for a while through banked-up woolly clouds, and tempted Sara Clayburn out. She was an energetic walker, and given, at that season, to tramping three or four miles along the valley road, and coming back by way of Shaker's wood. She had made her usual round, and was following the main drive to the house when she overtook a plainly-dressed woman walking in the same direction. If the scene had not been so lonely – the way to Whitegates at the end of an autumn day was not a frequented one – Mrs. Clayburn might not have paid any attention to the woman, for she was in no way noticeable; but when she caught up with the intruder my cousin was surprised to find that she was a stranger – for the mistress of Whitegates prided herself on knowing, at least by sight, most of her country neighbors. It was almost dark, and the woman's face was hardly visible, but Mrs. Clayburn told me she recalled her as middle-aged, plain and rather pale.

Mrs. Clayburn greeted her, and then added: 'You're going to the house?'

'Yes, ma'am,' the woman answered, in a voice that the Connecticut Valley in old days would have called 'foreign,' but that would have been unnoticed by ears used to the modern multiplicity of tongues. 'No, I couldn't say where she came from,' Sara always said. 'What struck me as queer was that I didn't know her.'

She asked the woman, politely, what she wanted, and the woman answered: 'Only to see one of the girls.' The answer was natural enough, and Mrs. Clayburn nodded and turned off from the drive to the lower part of the gardens, so that she saw no more of the visitor then or afterward. And, in fact, a half hour later something happened which put the stranger entirely out of her mind. The brisk and light-footed Mrs. Clayburn, as she approached the house, slipped on a frozen puddle, turned her ankle and lay suddenly helpless.

Price, the butler, and Agnes, the dour old Scottish maid whom Sara had inherited from her mother-in-law, of course knew exactly what to do. In no time they had their mistress stretched out on a lounge, and Dr. Selgrove had been called up from Norrington. When he arrived, he ordered Mrs. Clayburn to bed, did the necessary examining and bandaging, and shook his head over her ankle, which he feared was fractured. He thought, however, that if she would swear not to get up, or even shift the position of her leg, he could spare her the discomfort of putting it in plaster. Mrs. Clayburn agreed, the more promptly as the doctor warned her that any rash movement would prolong her immobility. Her quick imperious nature made the prospect trying, and she was annoyed with herself for having been so clumsy. But the mischief was done, and she immediately thought what an opportunity she would have for going over her accounts and catching up with her correspondence. So she settled down resignedly in her bed.

'And you won't miss much, you know, if you have to stay there a few days. It's beginning to snow, and it looks as if we were in for a good spell of it,' the doctor remarked, glancing through the window as he gathered up his implements. 'Well, we don't often get snow here as early as this; but winter's got to begin sometime,' he concluded philosophically. At the door he stopped to add: 'You don't want me to send up a nurse from Norrington? Not to nurse you, you know; there's nothing much to do till I see you again. But this is a pretty lonely place when the snow begins, and I thought maybe – '

Sara Clayburn laughed. 'Lonely? With my old servants? You forget how many winters I've spent here alone with them. Two of them were with me in my mother-in-law's time.'

'That's so,' Dr. Selgrove agreed. 'You're a good deal luckier than most people, that way. Well, let me see; this is Saturday. We'll have to let the inflammation go down before we can X-ray you. Monday morning, first thing, I'll be here with the X-ray man. If you want me sooner, call me up,' And he was gone.

• II •

THE foot at first, had not been very painful; but toward the small hours Mrs. Clayburn began to suffer. She was a bad patient, like most healthy and active people. Not being used to pain she did not know how to bear it, and the hours of wakefulness and immobility seemed endless. Agnes, before leaving her, had made everything as comfortable as possible. She had put a jug of lemonade within reach, and had even (Mrs. Clayburn thought it odd afterward) insisted on bringing in a tray with sandwiches and a thermos of tea. 'In case you're hungry in the night, madam.'

'Thank you; but I'm never hungry in the night. And I certainly shan't be tonight – only thirsty. I think I'm feverish.'

'Well, there's the lemonade, madam.'

'That will do. Take the other things away, please.' (Sara had always hated the sight of unwanted food 'messing about' in her room.)

'Very well, madam. Only you might – '

'Please take it away,' Mrs. Clayburn repeated irritably.

'Very good, madam.' But as Agnes went out, her mistress heard her set the tray down softly on a table behind the screen which shut off the door.

'Obstinate old goose!' she thought, rather touched by the old woman's insistence.

Sleep, once it had gone, would not return, and the long black hours moved more and more slowly. How late the dawn came in November! 'If only I could move my leg,' she grumbled.

She lay still and strained her ears for the first steps of the servants. Whitegates was an early house, its mistress setting the example; it would surely not be long now before one of the women came. She was tempted to ring for Agnes, but refrained. The woman had been up late, and this was Sunday morning, when the household was always allowed a little extra time. Mrs. Clayburn reflected restlessly: 'I was a fool not to let her leave the tea beside the bed, as she wanted to. I wonder if I could get up and get it?' But she remembered the doctor's warning, and dared not move. Anything rather than risk prolonging her imprisonment. . . .

Ah, there was the stable clock striking. How loud it sounded in the snowy stillness! One-two-three-four-five. . . .

What? Only five? Three hours and a quarter more before she could hope to hear the door handle turned. . . . After a while she dozed off again, uncomfortably.

Another sound aroused her. Again the stable clock. She listened. But the room was still in deep darkness, and only six strokes fell. . . . She thought of reciting something to put her to sleep, but she seldom read poetry, and being naturally a good sleeper, she could not remember any of the usual devices against insomnia. The whole of her leg felt like lead now. The bandages had grown terribly tight – her ankle must have swollen. . . . She lay staring at the dark windows, watching for the first glimmer of dawn. At last she saw a pale filter of daylight through the shutters. One by one the objects between the bed and the window recovered first their outline, then their bulk, and seemed to be stealthily regrouping themselves, after goodness knows what secret displacements during the night. Who that has lived in an old house could possibly believe that the furniture in it stays still all night? Mrs. Clayburn almost fancied she saw one little slender-legged table slipping hastily back into its place.

'It knows Agnes is coming, and it's afraid,' she thought whimsically. Her bad night must have made her imaginative for such nonsense as that about the furniture had never occurred to her before. . . .

At length, after hours more, as it seemed, the stable clock struck eight. Only another quarter of an hour. She watched the hand moving slowly across the face of the little clock beside her bed . . . ten minutes . . . five . . . only five! Agnes was as punctual as destiny . . . in two minutes now she would come. The two minutes passed, and she did not come. Poor Agnes – she had looked pale and tired the night before. She had overslept herself, no doubt – or perhaps she felt ill, and would send the housemaid to replace her. Mrs. Clayburn waited.

She waited half an hour; then she reached up to the bell at the head of the bed. Poor old Agnes – her mistress felt guilty about waking her. But Agnes did not appear – and after a considerable interval Mrs. Clayburn, now with a certain impatience, rang again. She rang once; twice; three times – but still no one came.

Once more she waited; then she said to herself: 'There must be something wrong with the electricity.' Well – she could find out by switching on the bed lamp at her elbow (how admirably the room was equipped with every practical appliance!). She switched it on – but no light came. Electric current cut off; and it was Sunday, and nothing could be done about it till the next morning. Unless it turned out to be just a burnt-out fuse, which Price could remedy. Well, in a moment now some one would surely come to her door.

It was nine o'clock before she admitted to herself that something uncommonly strange must have happened in the house. She began to feel a nervous apprehension; but she was not the woman to encourage it. If only she had had the telephone put in her room, instead of out on the landing! She measured mentally the distance to be traveled, remembered Dr. Selgrove's admonition, and wondered if her broken ankle would carry her there. She dreaded the prospect of being put in plaster, but she had to get to the telephone, whatever happened.

She wrapped herself in her dressing gown, found a walking stick, and, resting heavily on it, dragged herself to the door. In her bedroom the careful Agnes had closed and fastened the shutters, so that it was not much lighter there than at dawn; but outside in the corridor the cold whiteness of the snowy morning seemed almost reassuring. Mysterious things – dreadful things – were associated with darkness; and here was the wholesome prosaic daylight come again to banish them. Mrs. Clayburn looked about her and listened. Silence. A deep nocturnal silence in that day-lit house, in which five people were presumably coming and going about their work. It was certainly strange. . . . She looked out of the window, hoping to see someone crossing the court or coming along the drive. But no one was in sight, and the snow seemed to have the place to itself: a quiet steady snow. It was still falling, with a business-like regularity, muffling the outer world in layers on layers of thick white velvet, and intensifying the silence within. A noiseless world – were people so sure that absence of noise was what they wanted? Let them first try a lonely country house in a November snowstorm!

She dragged herself along the passage to the telephone. When she unhooked the receiver she noticed that her hand trembled.

She rang up the pantry – no answer. She rang again. Silence – more silence! It seemed to be piling itself up like the snow on the roof and in the gutters. Silence. How many people that she knew had any idea what silence was – and how loud it sounded when you really listened to it?

Again she waited: then she rang up 'Central.' No answer. She tried three times. After that she tried the pantry again. . . . The telephone was cut off, then; like the electric current. Who was at work downstairs, isolating her thus from the world? Her heart began to hammer. Luckily there was a chair near the telephone, and she sat down to recover her strength – or was it her courage?

Agnes and the housemaid slept in the nearest wing. She would certainly get as far as that when she had pulled herself together. Had she the courage – ? Yes, of course she had. She had always been uregarded as a plucky woman; and had so regarded herself. But this silence –

It occurred to her that by looking from the window of a neighboring bathroom she could see the kitchen chimney. There ought to be smoke coming from it at that hour; and if there were she thought she would be less afraid to go on. She got as far as the bathroom and looking through the window saw that no smoke came from the chimney. Her sense of loneliness grew more acute. Whatever had happened below-stairs must have happened before the morning's work had begun. The cook had not had time to light the fire, the other servants had not yet begun their round. She sank down on the nearest chair, struggling against her fears. What next would she discover if she carried on her investigations?

The pain in her ankle made progress difficult; but she was aware of it now only as an obstacle to haste. No matter what it cost her in physical suffering, she must find out what was happening belowstairs – or had happened. But first she would go to the maid's room. And if that were empty – well, somehow she would have to get herself downstairs.

She limped along the passage, and on the way steadied herself by resting her hand on a radiator. It was stone-cold. Yet in that well-ordered house in winter the central heating, though damped down at night, was never allowed to go out, and by eight in the morning a mellow warmth pervaded the rooms. The icy chill of the pipes startled her. It was the chauffeur who looked after the heating – so he too was involved in the mystery, whatever it was, as well as the house servants. But this only deepened the problem.

• III •

AT Agnes's door Mrs. Clayburn paused and knocked. She expected no answer, and there was none. She opened the door and went in. The room was dark and very cold. She went to the window and flung back the shutters; then she looked slowly around, vaguely apprehensive of what she might see. The room was empty but what frightened her was not so much its emptiness as its air of scrupulous and undisturbed order. There was no sign of anyone having lately dressed in it – or undressed the night before. And the bed had not been slept in.

Mrs. Clayburn leaned against the wall for a moment; then she crossed the floor and opened the cupboard. That was where Agnes kept her dresses; and the dresses were there, neatly hanging in a row. On the shelf above were Agnes's few and unfashionable hats, rearrangements of her mistress's old ones. Mrs. Clayburn, who knew them all, looked at the shelf, and saw that one was missing. And so was also the warm winter coat she had given to Agnes the previous winter.

The woman was out, then; had gone out, no doubt, the night before, since the bed was unslept in, the dressing and washing appliances untouched. Agnes, who never·set foot out of the house after dark, who despised the movies as much as she did the wireless, and could never be persuaded that a little innocent amusement was a necessary element in life, had deserted the house on a snowy winter night, while her mistress lay upstairs, suffering and helpless! Why had she gone, and where had she gone? When she was undressing Mrs. Clayburn the night before, taking her orders, trying to make her more comfortable, was she already planning this mysterious nocturnal escape? Or had something – the mysterious and dreadful Something for the clue of which Mrs. Clayburn was still groping – occurred later in the evening, sending the maid downstairs and out of doors into the bitter night? Perhaps one of the men at the garage – where the chauffeur and gardener lived – had been suddenly taken ill, and someone had run up to the house for Agnes. Yes – that must be the explanation. . . . Yet how much it left unexplained.

Next to Agnes's room was the linen room; beyond that was the housemaid's door. Mrs. Clayburn went to it and knocked. 'Mary!' No one answered, and she went in. The room was in the same immaculate order as her maid's, and here too the bed was unslept in, and there were no signs of dressing or undressing. The two women had no doubt gone out together – gone where?

More and more the cold unanswering silence of the house weighed down on Mrs. Clayburn. She had never thought of it as a big house, but now, in this snowy winter light, it seemed immense, and full of ominous corners around which one dared not look.

Beyond the housemaid's room were the back stairs. It was the nearest way down, and every step that Mrs. Clayburn took was increasingly painful; but she decided to walk slowly back, the whole length of the passage, and go down by the front stairs. She did not know why she did this; but she felt that at the moment she was past reasoning, and had better obey her instinct.

More than once she had explored the ground floor alone in the small hours, in search of unwonted midnight noises; but now it was not the idea of noises that frightened her, but that inexorable and hostile silence, the sense that the house had retained in full daylight its nocturnal mystery, and was watching her as she was watching it; that in entering those empty orderly rooms she might be disturbing some unseen confabulation on which beings of flesh-and-blood had better not intrude.

The broad oak stairs were beautifully polished, and so slippery that she had to cling to the rail and let herself down tread by tread. And as she descended, the silence descended with her – heavier, denser, more absolute. She seemed to feel its steps just behind her, softly keeping time with hers. It had a quality she had never been aware of in any other silence, as though it were not merely an absence of sound, a thin barrier between the ear and the surging murmur of life just beyond, but an impenetrable substance made out of the world-wide cessation of all life and all movement.

Yes, that was what laid a chill on her: the feeling that there was no limit to this silence, no outer margin, nothing beyond it. By this time she had reached the foot of the stairs and was limping across the hall to the drawing room. Whatever she found there, she was sure, would be mute and lifeless; but what would it be? The bodies of her dead servants, mown down by some homicidal maniac? And what if it were her turn next – if he were waiting for her behind the heavy curtains of the room she was about to enter? Well, she must find out – she must face whatever lay in wait. Not impelled by bravery – the last drop of courage had oozed out of her – but because anything, anything was better than to remain shut up in that snowbound house without knowing whether she was alone in it or not, 'I must find that out, I must find that out,' she repeated to herself in a sort of meaningless sing-song.

The cold outer light flooded the drawing room. The shutters had not been closed, nor the curtains drawn. She looked about her. The room was empty, and every chair in its usual place. Her armchair was pushed up by the chimney, and the cold hearth was piled with the ashes of the fire at which she had warmed herself before starting on her ill-fated walk. Even her empty coffee cup stood on a table near the armchair. It was evident that the servants had not been in the room since she had left it the day before after luncheon. And suddenly the conviction entered into her that, as she found the drawing room, so she would find the rest of the house; cold, orderly – and empty. She would find nothing, she would find no one. She no longer felt any dread of ordinary human dangers lurking in those dumb spaces ahead of her. She knew she was utterly alone under her own roof. She sat down to rest her aching ankle, and looked slowly about her.

There were the other rooms to be visited, and she was determined to go through them all – but she knew in advance that they would give no answer to her question. She knew it, seemingly, from the quality of the silence which enveloped her. There was no break, no thinnest crack in it anywhere. It had the cold continuity of the snow which was still falling steadily outside.

She had no idea how long she waited before nerving herself to continue her inspection. She no longer felt the pain in her ankle, but was only conscious that she must not bear her weight on it, and therefore moved very slowly, supporting herself on each piece of furniture in her path. On the ground floor no shutter had been closed, no curtain drawn, and she progressed without difficulty from room to room: the library, her morning room, the dining room. In each of them, every piece of furniture was in its usual place. In the dining room, the table had been laid for her dinner of the previous evening, and the candelabra, with candles unlit, stood reflected in the dark mahogany. She was not the kind of woman to nibble a poached egg on a tray when she was alone, but always came down to the dining room, and had what she called a civilized meal.

The back premises remained to be visited. From the dining room she entered the pantry, and there too everything was in irreproachable order. She opened the door and looked down the back passage with its neat linoleum floor covering. The deep silence accompanied her; she still felt it moving watchfully at her side, as though she were its prisoner and it might throw itself upon her if she attempted to escape. She limped on toward the kitchen. That of course would be empty too, and immaculate. But she must see it.

She leaned a minute in the embrasure of a window in the passage. 'It's like the "Mary Celeste" – a "Mary Celeste" on *terra firma*,' she thought, recalling the unsolved sea mystery of her childhood. 'No one ever knew what happened on board the "Mary Celeste." And perhaps no one will ever know what has happened here. Even I shan't know.'

At the thought her latent fear seemed to take on a new quality. It was like an icy liquid running through every vein, and lying in a pool about her heart. She understood now that she had never before known what fear was, and that most of the people she had met had probably never known either. For this sensation was something quite different. . . .

It absorbed her so completely that she was not aware how long she remained leaning there. But suddenly a new impulse pushed her forward, and she walked on toward the scullery. She went there first because there was a service slide in the wall, through which she might peep into the kitchen without being seen; and some indefinable instinct told her that the kitchen held the clue to the mystery. She still felt strongly that whatever had happened in the house must have its source and center in the kitchen.

In the scullery, as she had expected, everything was clean and tidy. Whatever had happened, no one in the house appeared to have been taken by surprise; there was nowhere any sign of confusion or disorder, 'It looks as if they'd known beforehand, and put everything straight,' she thought. She glanced at the wall facing the door, and saw that the slide was open. And then, as she was approaching it, the silence was broken. A voice was speaking in the kitchen – a man's voice, low but emphatic, and which she had never heard before.

She stood still, cold with fear. But this fear was again a different one. Her previous terrors had been speculative, conjectural, a ghostly emanation of the surrounding silence. This was a plain everyday dread of evildoers. Oh, God, why had she not remembered her husband's revolver, which ever since his death had lain in a drawer in her room?

She turned to retreat across the smooth slippery floor but halfway her stick slipped from her, and crashed down on the tiles. The noise seemed to echo on and on through the emptiness, and she stood still, aghast. Now that she had betrayed her presence, flight was useless. Whoever was beyond the kitchen door would be upon her in a second. . . .

But to her astonishment the voice went on speaking. It was as though neither the speaker nor his listeners had heard her. The invisible stranger spoke so low that she could not make out what he was saying, but the tone was passionately earnest, almost threatening. The next moment she realized that he was speaking in a foreign language, a language unknown to her. Once more her terror was surmounted by the urgent desire to know what was going on, so close to her yet unseen. She crept to the slide, peered cautiously through into the kitchen, and saw that it was as orderly and empty as the other rooms. But in the middle of the carefully scoured table stood a portable wireless, and the voice she heard came out of it. . . .

She must have fainted then, she supposed; at any rate she felt so weak and dizzy that her memory of what next happened remained indistinct. But in the course of time she groped her way back to the pantry, and there found a bottle of spirits – brandy or whisky, she could not remember which. She found a glass, poured herself a stiff drink, and while it was flushing through her veins, managed, she never knew with how many shuddering delays, to drag herself through the deserted ground floor, up the stairs, and down the corridor to her own room. There, apparently, she fell across the threshold, again unconscious. . . .

When she came to, she remembered, her first care had been to lock herself in; then to recover her husband's revolver. It was not loaded, but she found some cartridges, and succeeded in loading it. Then she remembered that Agnes, on leaving her the evening before, had refused to carry away the tray with the tea and sandwiches, and she fell on them with a sudden hunger. She recalled also noticing that a flask of brandy had been put beside the thermos, and being vaguely surprised. Agnes's departure, then, had been deliberately planned, and she had known that her mistress, who never touched spirits, might have need of a stimulant before she returned. Mrs. Clayburn poured some of the brandy into her tea, and swallowed it greedily.

After that (she told me later) she remembered that she had managed to start a fire in her grate, and after warming herself, had got back into her bed, piling on it all the coverings she could find. The afternoon passed in a haze of pain, out of which there emerged now and then a dim shape of fear – the fear that she might lie there alone and untended till she died of cold, and of the terror of her solitude. For she was sure by this time that the house was empty – completely empty, from garret to cellar. She knew it was so, she could not tell why; but again she felt that it must be because of the peculiar quality of the silence – the silence which had dogged her steps wherever she went, and was now folded down on her like a pall. She was sure that the nearness of any other human being, however dumb and secret, would have made a faint crack in the texture of that silence, flawed it as a sheet of glass is flawed by a pebble thrown against it. . . .

• IV •

'Is that easier?' the doctor asked, lifting himself from bending over her ankle. He shook his head disapprovingly. 'Looks to me as if you'd disobeyed orders – eh? Been moving about, haven't you? And I guess Dr. Selgrove told you to keep quiet till he saw you again, didn't he?'

The speaker was a stranger, whom Mrs. Clayburn knew only by name. Her own doctor had been called away that morning to the bedside of an old patient in Baltimore, and had asked this young man, who was beginning to be known at Norrington, to replace him. The newcomer was shy, and somewhat familiar, as the shy often are, and Mrs. Clayburn decided that she did not much like him. But before she could convey this by the tone of her reply (and she was past mistress of the shades of disapproval) she heard Agnes speaking – yes, Agnes, the same, the usual Agnes, standing behind the doctor, neat and stern-looking as ever. 'Mrs. Clayburn must have got up and walked about in the night instead of ringing for me, as she'd ought to,' Agnes intervened severely.

This was too much! In spite of the pain, which was now exquisite, Mrs. Clayburn laughed. 'Ringing for you? How could I, with the electricity cut off?'

'The electricity cut off?' Agnes's surprise was masterly. 'Why, when was it cut off?' She pressed her finger on the bell beside the bed, and the call tinkled through the quiet room. 'I tried that bell before I left you last night, madam, because if there'd been anything wrong with it I'd have come and slept in the dressing room sooner than leave you here alone.'

Mrs. Clayburn lay speechless, staring up at her. 'Last night? But last night I was all alone in the house.'

Agnes's firm features did not alter. She folded her hands resignedly across her trim apron. 'Perhaps the pain's made you a little confused, madam.' She looked at the doctor, who nodded.

'The pain in your foot must have been pretty bad,' he said.

'It was,' Mrs. Clayburn replied. 'But it was nothing to the horror of being left alone in this empty house since the day before yesterday, with the heat and the electricity cut off, and the telephone not working.'

The doctor was looking at her in evident wonder. Agnes's sallow face flushed slightly, but only as if in indignation at an unjust charge. 'But, madam, I made up your fire with my own hands last night – and look, it's smoldering still. I was getting ready to start it again just now, when the doctor came.'

'That's so. She was down on her knees before it,' the doctor corroborated.

Again Mrs. Clayburn laughed. Ingeniously as the tissue of lies was being woven about her, she felt she could still break through it. 'I made up the fire myself yesterday – there was no one else to do it,' she said, addressing the doctor, but keeping her eyes on her maid. 'I got up twice to put on more coal, because the house was like a sepulcher. The central heating must have been out since Saturday afternoon.'

At this incredible statement Agnes's face expressed only a polite distress: but the new doctor was evidently embarrassed at being drawn

into an unintelligible controversy with which he had no time to deal.
He said he had brought the X-ray photographer with him, but that the
ankle was too much swollen to be photographed at present. He asked
Mrs. Clayburn to excuse his haste, as he had all Dr. Selgrove's patients
to visit besides his own, and promised to come back that evening to
decide whether she could be X-rayed then, and whether, as he evidently
feared, the ankle would have to be put in plaster. Then, handing his
prescriptions to Agnes, he departed.

Mrs. Clayburn spent a feverish and suffering day. She did not feel
well enough to carry on the discussion with Agnes; she did not ask to
see the other servants. She grew drowsy, and understood that her mind
was confused with fever. Agnes and the housemaid waited on her as
attentively as usual, and by the time the doctor returned in the evening
her temperature had fallen; but she decided not to speak of what was
on her mind until Dr. Selgrove reappeared. He was to be back the
following evening; and the new doctor preferred to wait for him before
deciding to put the ankle in plaster – though he feared this was now
inevitable.

• V •

THAT afternoon Mrs. Clayburn had me summoned by telephone, and
I arrived at Whitegates the following day. My cousin, who looked pale
and nervous, merely pointed to her foot, which had been put in plaster,
and thanked me for coming to keep her company. She explained that
Dr. Selgrove had been taken suddenly ill in Baltimore, and would not
be back for several days, but that the young man who replaced him
seemed fairly competent. She made no allusion to the strange incidents
I have set down, but I felt at once that she had received a shock which
her accident, however painful, could not explain.

Finally, one evening, she told me the story of her strange weekend,
as it had presented itself to her unusually clear and accurate mind, and
as I have recorded it above. She did not tell me this till several weeks
after my arrival; but she was still upstairs at the time, and obliged to
divide her days between her bed and a lounge. During those endless
intervening weeks, she told me, she had thought the whole matter
over: and though the events of the mysterious thirty-six hours were
still vivid to her, they had already lost something of their haunting
terror, and she had finally decided not to reopen the question with
Agnes, or to touch on it in speaking to the other servants. Dr. Selgrove's
illness had been not only serious but prolonged. He had not yet
returned, and it was reported that as soon as he was well enough he
would go on a West Indian cruise, and not resume his practice at
Norrington till the spring. Dr. Selgrove, as my cousin was perfectly

aware, was the only person who could prove that thirty-six hours had elapsed between his visit and that of his successor; and the latter, a shy young man, burdened by the heavy additional practice suddenly thrown on his shoulders, told me (when I risked a little private talk with him) that in the haste of Dr. Selgrove's departure the only instructions he had given about Mrs. Clayburn were summed up in the brief memorandum: 'Broken ankle. Have X-rayed.'

Knowing my cousin's authoritative character, I was surprised at her decision not to speak to the servants of what had happened; but on thinking it over I concluded she was right. They were all exactly as they had been before that unexplained episode: efficient, devoted, respectful and respectable. She was dependent on them and felt at home with them, and she evidently preferred to put the whole matter out of her mind, as far as she could. She was absolutely certain that something strange had happened in her house, and I was more than ever convinced that she had received a shock which the accident of a broken ankle was not sufficient to account for; but in the end I agreed that nothing was to be gained by cross-questioning the servants or the new doctor.

I was at Whitegates off and on that winter and during the following summer, and when I went home to New York for good early in October I left my cousin in her old health and spirits. Dr. Selgrove had been ordered to Switzerland for the summer, and this further postponement of his return to his practice seemed to have put the happenings of the strange weekend out of her mind. Her life was going on as peacefully and normally as usual, and I left her without anxiety, and indeed without a thought of the mystery, which was now nearly a year old.

I was living then in a small flat in New York by myself, and I had hardly settled into it when, very late one evening – on the last day of October – I heard my bell ring. As it was my maid's evening out, and I was alone, I went to the door myself, and on the threshold, to my amazement, I saw Sara Clayburn. She was wrapped in a fur cloak, with a hat drawn down over her forehead, and a face so pale and haggard that I saw something dreadful must have happened to her. 'Sara,' I gasped, not knowing what I was saying, 'where in the world have you come from at this hour?'

'From Whitegates. I missed the last train and came by car.' She came in and sat down on the bench near the door. I saw that she could hardly stand, and sat down beside her, putting my arm about her. 'For heaven's sake, tell me what's happened.'

She looked at me without seeming to see me. 'I telephoned to Nixon's and hired a car. It took me five hours and a quarter to get here.' She looked about her. 'Can you take me in for the night? I've left my luggage downstairs.'

'For as many nights as you like. But you look so ill – '

She shook her head. 'No; I'm not ill. I'm only frightened – deathly frightened,' she repeated in a whisper.

Her voice was so strange, and the hands I was pressing between mine were so cold, that I drew her to her feet and led her straight to my little guest room. My flat was in an old-fashioned building, not many stories high, and I was on more human terms with the staff than is possible in one of the modern Babels. I telephoned down to have my cousin's bags brought up, and meanwhile I filled a hot water bottle, warmed the bed, and got her into it as quickly as I could. I had never seen her as unquestioning and submissive, and that alarmed me even more than her pallor. She was not the woman to let herself be undressed and put to bed like a baby; but she submitted without a word, as though aware that she had reached the end of her tether.

'It's good to be here,' she said in a quieter tone, as I tucked her up and smoothed the pillows. 'Don't leave me yet, will you – not just yet.'

'I'm not going to leave you for more than a minute – just to get you a cup of tea,' I reassured her; and she lay still. I left the door open, so that she could hear me stirring about in the little pantry across the passage, and when I brought her the tea she swallowed it gratefully, and a little color came into her face. I sat with her in silence for some time; but at last she began: 'You see it's exactly a year – '

I should have preferred to have her put off till the next morning whatever she had to tell me; but I saw from her burning eyes that she was determined to rid her mind of what was burdening it, and that until she had done so it would be useless to proffer the sleeping draft I had ready.

'A year since what?' I asked stupidly, not yet associating her precipitate arrival with the mysterious occurrences of the previous year at Whitegates.

She looked at me in surprise. 'A year since I met that woman. Don't you remember – the strange woman who was coming up the drive the afternoon when I broke my ankle? I didn't think of it at the time, but it was on All Souls' eve that I met her.'

Yes, I said, I remembered that it was.

'Well – and this is All Souls' eve, isn't it? I'm not as good as you are on Church dates, but I thought it was.'

'Yes. This is All Souls' eve.'

'I thought so. . . . Well, this afternoon I went out for my usual walk. I'd been writing letters, and paying bills, and didn't start till late; not till it was nearly dusk. But it was a lovely clear evening. And as I got near the gate, there was the woman coming in – the same woman . . . going toward the house. . . .'

I pressed my cousin's hand, which was hot and feverish now. 'If it was dusk, could you be perfectly sure it was the same woman?' I asked.

'Oh, perfectly sure, the evening was so clear. I knew her and she knew me; and I could see she was angry at meeting me. I stopped her and asked: "Where are you going?" just as I had asked her last year. And she said, in the same queer half-foreign voice: "Only to see one of the girls", as she had before. Then I felt angry all of a sudden, and I said: "You shan't set foot in my house again. Do you hear me? I order you to leave." And she laughed; yes, she laughed – very low, but distinctly. By that time it had got quite dark, as if a sudden storm was sweeping up over the sky, so that though she was so near me I could hardly see her. We were standing by the clump of hemlocks at the turn of the drive, and as I went up to her, furious at her impertinence, she passed behind the hemlocks, and when I followed her she wasn't there. . . . No; I swear to you she wasn't there. . . . And in the darkness I hurried back to the house, afraid that she would slip by me and get there first. And the queer thing was that as I reached the door the black cloud vanished, and there was the transparent twilight again. In the house everything seemed as usual, and the servants were busy about their work; but I couldn't get it out of my head that the woman, under the shadow of that cloud, had somehow got there before me.' She paused for breath, and began again. 'In the hall I stopped at the telephone and rang up Nixon, and told him to send me a car at once to go to New York, with a man he knew to drive me. And Nixon came with the car himself. . . .'

Her head sank back on the pillow and she looked at me like a frightened child. 'It was good of Nixon,' she said.

'Yes; it was very good of him. But when they saw you leaving – the servants, I mean. . . .'

'Yes. Well, when I got upstairs to my room I rang for Agnes. She came, looking just as cool and quiet as usual. And when I told her I was starting for New York in half an hour – I said it was on account of a sudden business call – well, then her presence of mind failed her for the first time. She forgot to look surprised, she even forgot to make an objection – and you know what an objector Agnes is. And as I watched her I could see a little secret spark of relief in her eyes, though she was so on her guard. And she just said: "Very well, madam," and asked me what I wanted to take with me. Just as if I were in the habit of dashing off to New York after dark on an autumn night to meet a business engagement! No, she made a mistake not to show any surprise – and not even to ask me why I didn't take my own car. And her losing her head in that way frightened me more than anything else. For I saw she was so thankful I was going that she hardly dared speak, for fear she should betray herself, or I should change my mind.'

After that Mrs. Clayburn lay a long while silent, breathing less unrestfully; and at last she closed her eyes, as though she felt more at ease now that she had spoken, and wanted to sleep. As I got up quietly to leave her, she turned her head a little and murmured: 'I shall never go back to Whitegates again.' Then she shut her eyes and I saw that she was falling asleep.

I have set down above, I hope without omitting anything essential, the record of my cousin's strange experience as she told it to me. Of what happened at Whitegates that is all I can personally vouch for. The rest – and of course there is a rest – is pure conjecture; and I give it only as such.

My cousin's maid, Agnes, was from the isle of Skye, and the Hebrides, as everyone knows, are full of the supernatural – whether in the shape of ghostly presences, or the almost ghostlier sense of unseen watchers peopling the long nights of those stormy solitudes. My cousin, at any rate, always regarded Agnes as the – perhaps unconscious, at any rate irresponsible – channel through which communications from the other side of the veil reached the submissive household at White-gates. Though Agnes had been with Mrs. Clayburn for a long time without any peculiar incident revealing this affinity with the unknown forces, the power to communicate with them may all the while have been latent in the woman, only awaiting a kindred touch; and that touch may have been given by the unknown visitor whom my cousin, two years in succession, had met coming up the drive at Whitegates on the eve of All Souls'. Certainly the date bears out my hypothesis; for I suppose that, even in this unimaginative age, a few people still remember that All Souls' eve is the night when the dead can walk – and when, by the same token, other spirits, piteous or malevolent, are also freed from the restrictions which secure the earth to the living on the other days of the year.

If the recurrence of this date is more than a coincidence – and for my part I think it is – then I take it that the strange woman who twice came up the drive at Whitegates on All Souls' eve was either a 'fetch,' or else, more probably, and more alarmingly, a living woman inhabited by a witch. The history of witchcraft, as is well known, abounds in such cases, and such a messenger might well have been delegated by the powers who rule in these matters to summon Agnes and her fellow servants to a midnight 'Coven' in some neighboring solitude. To learn what happens at Covens, and the reason of the irresistible fascination they exercise over the timorous and superstitious, one need only address oneself to the immense body of literature dealing with these mysterious rites. Anyone who has once felt the faintest curiosity to assist at a Coven apparently soon finds the curiosity increase to desire, the desire to an uncontrollable longing, which, when the opportunity presents itself, breaks down all inhibitions; for those who have once taken part in a Coven will move heaven and earth to take part again.

★

Such is my – conjectural – explanation of the strange happenings at Whitegates. My cousin always said she could not believe that incidents which might fit into the desolate landscape of the Hebrides could occur in the cheerful and populous Connecticut Valley; but if she did not believe, she at least feared – such moral paradoxes are not uncommon – and though she insisted that there must be some natural explanation of the mystery, she never returned to investigate it.

'No, no,' she said with a little shiver, whenever I touched on the subject of her going back to Whitegates, 'I don't want ever to risk seeing that woman again. . . .' And she never went back.

The Lamp of Psyche

DELIA CORBETT was too happy; her happiness frightened her. Not on theological grounds, however; she was sure that people had a right to be happy; but she was equally sure that it was a right seldom recognized by destiny. And her happiness almost touched the confines of pain – it bordered on that sharp ecstasy which she had known, through one sleepless night after another, when what had now become a reality had haunted her as an unattainable longing.

Delia Corbett was not in the habit of using what the French call *gros mots* in the rendering of her own emotions; she took herself, as a rule, rather flippantly, with a dash of contemptuous pity. But she felt that she had now entered upon a phase of existence wherein it became her to pay herself an almost reverential regard. Love had set his golden crown upon her forehead, and the awe of the office allotted her subdued her doubting heart. To her had been given the one portion denied to all other women on earth, the immense, the unapproachable privilege of becoming Laurence Corbett's wife.

Here she burst out laughing at the sound of her own thoughts, and rising from her seat walked across the drawing room and looked at herself in the mirror above the mantelpiece. She was past thirty and had never been very pretty; but she knew herself to be capable of loving her husband better and pleasing him longer than any other woman in the world. She was not afraid of rivals; he and she had seen each other's souls.

She turned away, smiling carelessly at her insignificant reflection, and went back to her armchair near the balcony. The room in which she sat was very beautiful; it pleased Corbett to make all his surroundings beautiful. It was the drawing room of his hotel in

Paris, and the balcony near which his wife sat overlooked a small bosky garden framed in ivied walls, with a mouldering terra-cotta statue in the center of its cup-shaped lawn. They had now been married some two months and, after traveling for several weeks, had both desired to return to Paris; Corbett because he was really happier there than elsewhere, Delia because she passionately longed to enter as a wife the house where she had so often come and gone as a guest. How she used to find herself dreaming in the midst of one of Corbett's delightful dinners (to which she and her husband were continually being summoned) of a day when she might sit at the same table, but facing its master, a day when no carriage should wait to whirl her away from the brightly lit porte-cochère, and when, after the guests had gone, he and she should be left alone in his library and she might sit down beside him and put her hand in his! The high-minded reader may infer from this that I am presenting him, in the person of Delia Corbett, with a heroine whom he would not like his wife to meet; but how many of us could face each other in the calm consciousness of moral rectitude if our inmost desire were not hidden under a convenient garb of lawful observance?

Delia Corbett, as Delia Benson, had been a very good wife to her first husband; some people (Corbett among them) had even thought her laxly tolerant of 'poor Benson's' weaknesses. But then she knew her own; and it is admitted that nothing goes so far toward making us blink the foibles of others as the wish to have them extend a like mercy to ourselves. Not that Delia's foibles were of a tangible nature; they belonged to the order which escapes analysis by the coarse process of our social standards. Perhaps their very immateriality, the consciousness that she could never be brought to book for them before any human tribunal, made her the more restive under their weight; for she was of a nature to prefer buying her happiness to stealing it. But her rising scruples were perpetually being allayed by some fresh indiscretion of Benson's, to which she submitted with an undeviating amiability which flung her into the opposite extreme of wondering if she didn't really influence him to do wrong – if she mightn't help him to do better. All these psychological subtleties exerted, however, no influence over her conduct which, since the day of her marriage, had been a model of delicate circumspection. It was only necessary to look at Benson to see that the most eager reformer could have done little to improve him. In the first place he must have encountered the initial difficulty, most disheartening to reformers, of making his neophyte distinguish between right and wrong. Undoubtedly it was within the measure even of Benson's primitive perceptions to recognize that some actions were permissible and others were not; but his sole means of classifying them was to try both, and then deny having committed those of which his wife disapproved. Delia had once owned a poodle who greatly desired to sleep on a white fur rug which she destined to other uses. She and the poodle disagreed on the subject, and the latter, though submitting to her authority (when reinforced by a whip), could never be made to see the justice of her demand, and consequently (as the rug frequently revealed) never missed an opportunity of evading it when her back was turned. Her husband often reminded her of the poodle, and, not having a whip or its moral equivalent to control him with, she had long since resigned herself to seeing him smudge the whiteness of her early illusions. The worst of it was that her resignation was such a cheap virtue. She had to be perpetually rousing herself to a sense of Benson's enormities; through the ever-lengthening perspective of her indifference they looked as small as the details of a landscape seen through the wrong end of a telescope. Now and then she tried to remind herself that she had married him for love; but she was well aware that the sentiment she had once entertained for him had nothing in common with the state of mind which the words now represent to her; and this naturally diminished the force of the argument. She had married him at nineteen, because he had beautiful blue eyes and always wore a gardenia in his coat; really, as far as she could remember, these considerations had been the determining factors in her choice. Delia as a child (her parents were since dead) had been a much-indulged daughter, with a liberal allowance of pocket-money, and permission to spend it unquestioned and unadvised. Subsequently, she used sometimes to look, in a critical humor, at the various articles which she had purchased in her teens; futile chains and lockets, valueless china knickknacks, and poor engravings of sentimental pictures. These, as a chastisement to her taste, she religiously preserved; and they often made her think of Benson. No one, she could not but reflect, would have blamed her if, with the acquirement of a fuller discrimination, she had thrown them all out of the window and replaced them by some object of permanent merit; but she was expected not only to keep Benson for life, but to conceal the fact that her taste had long since discarded him.

It could hardly be expected that a woman who reasoned so dispassionately about her mistakes should attempt to deceive herself about her preferences. Corbett personified all those finer amenities of mind and manners which may convert the mere act of being into a beneficent career; to Delia he seemed the most admirable man she had ever met, and she would have thought it disloyal to her best aspirations not to admire him. But she did not attempt to palliate her warmer feeling under the mask of a plausible esteem; she knew that she loved him, and scorned to disavow that also. So well, however, did she keep her secret that Corbett himself never suspected it, until her husband's death freed her from the obligation of concealment. Then, indeed, she gloried in its confession; and after two years of widowhood, and more than two months of marriage, she was still under the spell of that moment of exquisite avowal.

She was reliving it now, as she often did in the rare hours which separated her from her husband; when presently she heard his step on the stairs, and started up with the blush of eighteen. As she walked across the room to meet him she asked herself perversely (she was given to such obliqueness of self-scrutiny) if to a dispassionate eye he would appear as complete, as supremely well-equipped as she beheld him, or if she walked in a cloud of delusion, dense as the god-concealing mist of Homer. But whenever she put this question to herself, Corbett's appearance instantly relegated it to the limbo of solved enigmas; he was so obviously admirable that she wondered that people didn't stop her in the street to attest her good fortune.

As he came forward now, his renewal of satisfaction was so strong in her that she felt an impulse to seize him and assure herself of his reality; he was so perilously like the phantasms of joy which had mocked her dissatisfied past. But his coat sleeve was convincingly tangible; and, pinching it, she felt the muscles beneath.

'What – all alone?' he said, smiling back her welcome.

'No, I wasn't – I was with you!' she exclaimed; then fearing to appear fatuous, added, with a slight shrug, 'Don't be alarmed – it won't last.'

'That's what frightens me,' he answered, gravely.

'Precisely,' she laughed; 'and I shall take good care not to reassure you!'

They stood face to face for a moment, reading in each other's eyes the completeness of their communion; then he broke the silence by saying, 'By the way, I'd forgotten; here's a letter for you.'

She took it unregardingly, her eyes still deep in his; but as her glance turned to the envelope she uttered a note of pleasure.

'Oh, now nice – it's from your only rival!'

'Your Aunt Mary?'

She nodded. 'I haven't heard from her in a month – and I'm afraid I haven't written to her either. You don't know how many beneficent intentions of mine you divert from their proper channels.'

'But your Aunt Mary has had you all your life – I've only had you two months,' he objected.

Delia was still contemplating the letter with a smile. 'Dear thing!' she murmured. 'I wonder when I shall see her?'

'Write and ask her to come and spend the winter with us.'

'What – and leave Boston, and her kindergartens, and associated charities, and symphony concerts, and debating clubs? You don't know Aunt Mary!'

'No, I don't. It seems so incongruous that you should adore such a bundle of pedantries.'

'I forgive that, because you've never seen her. How I wish you could!'

He stood looking down at her with the all-promising smile of the happy lover. 'Well, if she won't come to us we'll go to her.'

'Laurence – and leave this!'

'It will keep – we'll come back to it. My dear girl, don't beam so; you make me feel as if you hadn't been happy until now.'

'No – but it's your thinking of it!'

'I'll do more than think; I'll act; I'll take you to Boston to see your Aunt Mary.'

'Oh, Laurence, you'd hate doing it.'

'Not doing it together.'

She laid her hand for a moment on his. 'What a difference that does make in things!' she said, as she broke the seal of the letter.

'Well, I'll leave you to commune with Aunt Mary. When you've done, come and find me in the library.'

Delia sat down joyfully to the perusal of her letter, but as her eye traveled over the closely-written pages her gratified expression turned to one of growing concern; and presently, thrusting it back into the envelope, she followed her husband to the library. It was a charming room and singularly indicative, to her fancy, of its occupant's character; the expanse of harmonious bindings, the fruity bloom of Renaissance bronzes, and the imprisoned sunlight of two or three old pictures fitly epitomizing the delicate ramifications of her husband's taste. But now her glance lingered less appreciatively than usual on the warm tones and fine lines which formed so expressive a background for Corbett's fastidious figure.

'Aunt Mary has been ill – I'm afraid she's been seriously ill,' she announced as he rose to receive her. 'She fell in coming downstairs from one of her tenement house inspections, and it brought on water on the knee. She's been laid up ever since – some three or four weeks now. I'm afraid it's rather bad at her age; and I don't know how she will resign herself to keeping quiet.'

'I'm very sorry,' said Corbett, sympathetically; 'but water on knee isn't dangerous, you know.'

'No – but the doctor says she mustn't go out for weeks and weeks; and that will drive her mad. She'll think the universe has come to a standstill.'

'She'll find it hasn't,' suggested Corbett, with a smile which took the edge from his comment.

'Ah, but such discoveries hurt – especially if one makes them late in life!'

Corbett stood looking affectionately at his wife.

'How long is it,' he asked, 'since you have seen your Aunt Mary?'

'I think it must be two years. Yes, just two years; you know I went home on business after – ' She stopped; they never alluded to her first marriage.

Corbett took her hand. 'Well,' he declared, glancing rather wistfully at the Paris Bordone above the mantelpiece, 'we'll sail next month and pay her a little visit.'

• II •

CORBETT was really making an immense concession in going to America at that season; he disliked the prospect at all times, but just as his hotel in Paris had reopened its luxurious arms to him for the winter, the thought of departure was peculiarly distasteful. Delia knew it, and winced under the enormity of the sacrifice which he had imposed upon himself; but he bore the burden so lightly, and so smilingly derided her impulse to magnify the heroism of his conduct, that she gradually yielded to the undisturbed enjoyment of her anticipations. She was really very glad to be returning to Boston as Corbett's wife; her occasional appearances there as Mrs. Benson had been so eminently unsatisfactory to herself and her relatives that she naturally desired to efface them by so triumphal a re-entry. She had passed so great a part of her own life in Europe that she viewed with a secret leniency Corbett's indifference to his native land; but though she did not mind his not caring for his country she was intensely anxious that his country should care for him. He was a New Yorker, and entirely unknown, save by name, to her little circle of friends and relatives in Boston; but she reflected, with tranquil satisfaction, that, if he were cosmopolitan enough for Fifth Avenue, he was also cultured enough for Beacon Street. She was not so confident of his being altruistic enough for Aunt Mary; but Aunt Mary's appreciations covered so wide a range that there seemed small doubt of his coming under the head of one of her manifold enthusiasms.

Altogether Delia's anticipations grew steadily rosier with the approach to Sandy Hook; and to her confident eye the Statue of Liberty, as they passed under it in the red brilliance of a winter sunrise, seemed to look down upon Corbett with her Aunt Mary's most approving smile.

Delia's Aunt Mary – known from the Back Bay to the South End as Mrs. Mason Hayne – had been the chief formative influence of her niece's youth. Delia, after the death of her parents, had even spent two years under Mrs. Hayne's roof, in direct contrast with all her apostolic ardors, her inflammatory zeal for righteousness in everything from baking powder to municipal government; and though the girl never felt any inclination to interpret her aunt's influence in action, it was potent in modifying her judgment of herself and others. Her parents had been incurably frivolous, Mrs.

Hayne was incurably serious, and Delia, by some unconscious powers of selection, tended to frivolity of conduct, corrected by seriousness of thought. She would have shrunk from the life of unadorned activity, the unsmiling pursuit of Purposes with a capital letter, to which Mrs. Hayne's energies were dedicated; but it lent relief to her enjoyment of the purposeless to measure her own conduct by her aunt's utilitarian standards. This curious sympathy with aims so at variance with her own ideals would hardly have been possible to Delia had Mrs. Hayne been a narrow enthusiast without visual range beyond the blinders of her own vocation; it was the consciousness that her aunt's perceptions included even such obvious inutility as hers which made her so tolerant of her aunt's usefulness. All this she had tried, on the way across the Atlantic, to put vividly before Corbett; but she was conscious of a vague inability on his part to adjust his conception of Mrs. Hayne to his wife's view of her; and Delia could only count on her aunt's abounding personality to correct the one-sidedness of his impression.

Mrs. Hayne lived in a wide brick house on Mount Vernon Street, which had belonged to her parents and grandparents, and from which she had never thought of moving. Thither, on the evening of their arrival in Boston, the Corbett's were driven from the Providence Station. Mrs. Hayne had written to her niece that Cyrus would meet them with a 'hack'; Cyrus was a sable factotum designated in Mrs. Hayne's vocabulary as a 'chore man.' When the train entered the station he was, in fact, conspicuous on the platform, his smile shining like an open piano, while he proclaimed with abundant gesture the proximity of 'de hack,' and Delia, descending from the train into his dusky embrace, found herself guiltily wishing that he could have been omitted from the function of their arrival. She could not help wondering what her husband's valet would think of him. The valet was to be lodged at a hotel: Corbett himself had suggested that his presence might disturb the routine of Mrs. Hayne's household, a view in which Delia had eagerly acquiesced. There was, however, no possibility of dissembling Cyrus, and under the valet's depreciatory eye the Corbetts suffered him to precede them to the livery stable landau, with blue shades and a confidentially disposed driver, which awaited them outside the station.

During the drive to Mount Vernon Street Delia was silent; but as they approached her aunt's swell-fronted domicile she said, hurriedly, 'You won't like the house.'

Corbett laughed. 'It's the inmate I've come to see,' he commented.

'Oh, I'm not afraid of her,' Delia almost too confidently rejoined.

The parlormaid who admitted them to the hall (a discouraging hall, with a large-patterned oilcloth and buff walls stenciled with a Greek border) informed them that Mrs. Hayne was above; and ascending to the next floor they found her genial figure, supported on crutches, awaiting them at the drawing room door. Mrs. Hayne was a tall, stoutish woman, whose bland expanse of feature was accentuated by a pair of gray eyes of such surpassing penetration that Delia often accused her of answering people's thoughts before they had finished thinking them. These eyes, through the close fold of Delia's embrace, pierced instantly to Corbett, and never had that accomplished gentleman been more conscious of being called upon to present his credentials. But there was no reservation in the uncritical warmth of Mrs. Hayne's welcome, and it was obvious that she was unaffectedly happy in their coming.

She led them into the drawing room, still clinging to Delia, and Corbett, as he followed, understood why his wife had said that he would not like the house. One saw at a glance that Mrs. Hayne had never had time to think of her house or her dress. Both were scrupulously neat, but her gown might have been an unaltered one of her mother's, and her drawing room wore the same appearance of contented archaism. There was a sufficient number of armchairs, and the tables (mostly marble-topped) were redeemed from monotony by their freight of books; but it had not occurred to Mrs. Hayne to substitute logs for hard coal in her fireplace, nor to replace by more personal works of art the smoky expanses of canvas 'after' Raphael and Murillo which lurched heavily forward from the walls. She had even preserved the knotty antimacassars on her high-backed armchairs, and Corbett, who was growing bald, resignedly reflected that during his stay in Mount Vernon Street he should not be able to indulge in any lounging.

• III •

DELIA held back for three days the question which burned her
lip; then, following her husband upstairs after an evening during
which Mrs. Hayne had proved herself especially comprehensive
(even questioning Corbett upon the tendencies of modern French
art), she let escape the imminent 'Well?'

'She's charming,' Corbett returned, with the fine smile which
always seemed like a delicate criticism.

'Really?'

'Really, Delia. Do you think me so narrow that I can't
value such a character as your aunt's simply because it's cast
in different lines from mine? I once told you that she must be
a bundle of pedantries, and you prophesied that my first sight
of her would correct that impression. You were right; she's a
bundle of extraordinary vitalities. I never saw a woman more
thoroughly alive; and that's the great secret of living – to be
thoroughly alive.'

'I knew it; I knew it!' his wife exclaimed. 'Two such people
couldn't help liking each other.'

'Oh, I should think she might very well help liking me.'

'She doesn't; she admires you immensely; but why?'

'Well, I don't precisely fit into any of her ideals, and the
worst part of having ideals is that the people who don't fit into
them have to be discarded.'

'Aunt Mary doesn't discard anybody,' Delia interpolated.

'Her heart may not, but I fancy her judgment does.'

'But she doesn't exactly fit into any of your ideals, and yet
you like her,' his wife persisted.

'I haven't any ideals,' Corbett lightly responded. '*Je prends mon
bien où je le trouve*; and I find a great deal in your Aunt Mary.'

Delia did not ask Mrs. Hayne what she thought of her
husband; she was sure that, in due time, her aunt would deliver
her verdict; it was impossible for her to leave anyone unclassified.
Perhaps, too, there was a latent cowardice in Delia's reticence;
an unacknowledged dread lest Mrs. Hayne should range Corbett
among the intermediate types.

After a day or two of mutual inspection and adjustment the
three lives under Mrs. Hayne's roof lapsed into their separate
routines. Mrs. Hayne once more set in motion the complicated

machinery of her own existence (rendered more intricate by the accident of her lameness), and Corbett and his wife began to dine out and return the visits of their friends. There were, however, some hours which Corbett devoted to the club or to the frequentation of the public libraries, and these Delia gave to her aunt, driving with Mrs. Hayne from one committee meeting to another, writing business letters at her dictation, or reading aloud to her the reports of the various philanthropic, educational, or political institutions in which she was interested. She had been conscious on her arrival of a certain aloofness from her aunt's militant activities; but within a week she was swept back into the strong current of Mrs. Hayne's existence. It was like stepping from a gondola to an ocean steamer; at first she was dazed by the throb of the screw and the rush of parting waters, but gradually she felt herself infected by the exhilaration of getting to a fixed place in the shortest possible time. She could make sufficient allowance for the versatility of her moods to know that, a few weeks after her return to Paris, all that seemed most strenuous in Mrs. Hayne's occupations would fade to unreality; but that did not defend her from the strong spell of the moment. In its light her own life seemed vacuous, her husband's aims trivial as the subtleties of Chinese ivory carving; and she wondered if he walked in the same revealing flash.

Some three weeks after the arrival of the Corbetts in Mount Vernon Street, it became manifest that Mrs. Hayne had overtaxed her strength and must return for an undetermined period to her lounge. The life of restricted activity to which this necessity condemned her left her an occasional hour of leisure when there seemed no more letters to be dictated, no more reports to be read; and Corbett, always sure to do the right thing, was at hand to speed such unoccupied moments with the ready charm of his talk.

One day when, after sitting with her for some time, he departed to the club, Mrs. Hayne, turning to Delia, who came in to replace him, said, emphatically, 'My dear, he's delightful.'

'Oh, Aunt Mary, so are you!' burst gratefully from Mrs. Corbett.

Mrs. Hayne smiled. 'Have you suspended your judgment of me until now?' she asked.

'No; but your liking each other seems to complete you both.'

'Really, Delia, your husband couldn't have put that more gracefully. But sit down and tell me about him.'

'Tell you about him?' repeated Delia, thinking of the voluminous letters in which she had enumerated to Mrs. Hayne the sum of her husband's merits.

'Yes,' Mrs. Hayne continued, cutting, as she talked, the pages of a report on state lunatic asylums; 'for instance, you've never told me why so charming an American has condemned America to the hard fate of being obliged to get on without him.'

'You and he will never agree on that point, Aunt Mary,' said Mrs. Corbett, coloring.

'Never mind; I rather like listening to reasons that I know beforehand I'm bound to disagree with; it saves so much mental effort. And besides, how can you tell? I'm very uncertain.'

'You are very broad-minded, but you'll never understand his just having drifted into it. Any definite reason would seem to you better than that.'

'Ah – he drifted into it?'

'Well, yes. You know his sister, who married the Comte de Vitrey and went to live in Paris, was very unhappy after her marriage; and when Laurence's mother died there was no one left to look after her; and so Laurence went abroad in order to be near her. After a few years Monsieur de Vitrey died too; but by that time Laurence didn't care to come back.'

'Well,' said Mrs. Hayne. 'I see nothing so shocking in that. Your husband can gratify his tastes much more easily in Europe than in America; and, after all, that is what we're all secretly striving to do. I'm sure if there were more lunatic asylums and poorhouses and hospitals in Europe that there are here I should be very much inclined to go and live there myself.'

Delia laughed. 'I knew you would like Laurence,' she said, with a wisdom bred of the event.

'Of course I like him; he's a liberal education. It's very interesting to study the determining motives in such a man's career. How old is your husband, Delia?'

'Laurence is fifty-two.'

'And when did he go abroad to look after his sister?'

'Let me see – when he was about twenty-eight; it was in 1867, I think.'

'And before that he had lived in America?'

'Yes, the greater part of the time.'

'Then of course he was in the war?' Mrs. Hayne continued, laying down her pamphlet. 'You've never told me about that. Did he see any active service?'

As she spoke Delia grew pale; for a moment she sat looking blankly at her aunt.

'I don't think he was in the war at all,' she said at length in a low tone.

Mrs. Hayne stared at her. 'Oh, you must be mistaken,' she said, decidedly. 'Why shouldn't he have been in the war? What else could he have been doing?'

Mrs. Corbett was silent. All the men of her family, all the men of her friends' families, had fought in the war; Mrs. Hayne's husband had been killed at Bull Run, and one of Delia's cousins at Gettysburg. Ever since she could remember it had been regarded as a matter of course by those about her that every man of her husband's generation who was neither lame, halt, nor blind should have fought in the war. Husbands had left their wives, fathers their children, young men their sweethearts, in answer to that summons; and those who had been deaf to it she had never heard designated by any name but one.

But all that had happened long ago; for years it had ceased to be a part of her consciousness. She had forgotten about the war; about her uncle who fell at Bull Run, and her cousin who was killed at Gettysburg. Now, of a sudden, it all came back to her, and she asked herself the question which her aunt had just put to her – why had her husband not been in the war? What else could he have been doing?

But the very word, as she repeated it, struck her as incongruous; Corbett was a man who never did anything. His elaborate intellectual processes bore no flower of result; he simply *was* – but had she not hitherto found that sufficient? She rose from her seat, turning away from Mrs. Hayne.

'I really don't know,' she said, coldly. 'I never asked him.'

• IV •

Two weeks later the Corbetts returned to Europe. Corbett had really been charmed with his visit, and had in fact shown a marked inclination to outstay the date originally fixed for their departure. But Delia was firm; she did not wish to remain in Boston. She acknowledged that she was sorry to leave her Aunt Mary; but she wanted to get home.

'You turncoat!' Corbett said, laughing. 'Two months ago you reserved that sacred designation for Boston.'

'One can't tell where it is until one tries,' she answered, vaguely.

'You mean that you don't want to come back and live in Boston?'

'Oh, no – no!'

'Very well. But pray take note of the fact that I'm very sorry to leave. Under your Aunt Mary's tutelage I'm becoming a passionate patriot.'

Delia turned away in silence. She was counting the moments which led to their departure. She longed with an unreasoning intensity to get away from it all; from the dreary house in Mount Vernon Street, with its stenciled hall and hideous drawing room, its monotonous food served in unappetizing profusion; from the rarefied atmosphere of philanthropy and reform which she had once found so invigorating; and most of all from the reproval of her aunt's altruistic activities. The recollection of her husband's delightful house in Paris, so framed for a noble leisure, seemed to mock the aesthetic barrenness of Mrs. Hayne's environment. Delia thought tenderly of the mellow bindings, the deep-piled rugs, the pictures, bronzes, and tapestries; of the 'first nights' at the Français, the eagerly discussed *conférences* on art or literature, the dreaming hours in galleries and museums, and all the delicate enjoyments of the life to which she was returning. It would be like passing from a hospital ward to a flower-filled drawing room; how could her husband linger on the threshold?

Corbett, who observed her attentively, noticed that a change had come over her during the last two weeks of their stay in Mount Vernon Street. He wondered uneasily if she were capricious; a man who has formed his own habits upon principles of the finest selection does not care to think that he has married a capricious woman. Then he reflected that the love of Paris is an insidious disease, breaking out when its victim least looks for it, and concluded that Delia was suffering from some such unexpected attack.

Delia certainly was suffering. Ever since Mrs. Hayne had asked her that innocent question – 'Why shouldn't your husband have been in the war?' – she had been repeating it to herself day and night with the monotonous iteration of a monomaniac. Whenever Corbett came into the room, with that air of giving the simplest act its due value which made episodes of his entrances, she was tempted to cry out to him – 'Why weren't you in the war?' When she heard him, at a dinner, point one of his polished epigrams, or smilingly demolish the syllogism of an antagonist, her pride in his achievement was chilled by the question – 'Why wasn't he in the war?' When she saw him in the street, give a coin to a crossing sweeper, or lift his hat ceremoniously to one of Mrs. Hayne's maidservants (he was always considerate of poor people and servants) her approval winced under the reminder – 'Why wasn't he in the war?' And when they were alone together, all through the spell of his talk and the exquisite pervasion of his presence ran the embittering undercurrent, 'Why wasn't he in the war?'

At times she hated herself for the thought; it seemed a disloyalty to life's best gift. After all, what did it matter now? The war was over and forgotten; it was what the newspapers call 'a dead issue.' And why should any act of her husband's youth affect their present happiness together? Whatever he might once have been, he was perfect now; admirable in every relation of life; kind, generous, upright; a loyal friend, an accomplished gentleman, and, above all, the man she loved. Yes – but why had he not been in the war? And so began again the reiterant torment of the question. It rose up and lay down with her; it watched with her through sleepless nights, and followed her into the street; it mocked her from the eyes of strangers, and she dreaded lest her husband should read it in her own. In her saner moments she told herself that she was under the influence of a passing mood, which would vanish at the contact of her wonted life in Paris. She had become overstrung in the high air of Mrs. Hayne's moral enthusiasms; all she needed was to descend again to regions of more temperate virtue. This thought increased her impatience to be gone; and the days seemed interminable which divided her from departure.

The return to Paris, however, did not yield the hoped-for alleviation. The question was still with her, clamoring for a reply, and reinforced, with separation, by the increasing fear of her aunt's unspoken verdict. That shrewd woman had never again alluded to the subject of her brief colloquy with Delia; up to the moment of his farewell she had been unreservedly cordial to Corbett; but she was not the woman to palter with her convictions.

Delia knew what she must think; she knew what name, in the old days, Corbett would have gone by in her aunt's uncompromising circle.

Then came a flash of resistance – the heart's instinct of self-preservation. After all, what did she herself know of her husband's reasons for not being in the war? What right had she to set down to cowardice a course which might have been enforced by necessity, or dictated by unimpeachable motives? Why should she not put to him the question which she was perpetually asking herself? And not having done so, how dared she condemn him unheard?

A month or more passed in that torturing indecision. Corbett had returned with fresh zest to his accustomed way of life, weaned, by his first glimpse of the Champs Élysées, from his factitious enthusiasm for Boston. He and his wife entertained their friends delightfully, and frequented all the 'first nights' and 'private views' of the season, and Corbett continued to bring back knowing 'bits' from the Hotel Drouot, and rare books from the quays; never had he appeared more cultivated, more decorative and enviable; people agreed that Delia Benson had been uncommonly clever to catch him.

One afternoon he returned later than usual from the club, and finding his wife alone in the drawing room, begged her for a cup of tea. Delia reflected, in complying, that she had never seen him look better; his fifty-two years sat upon him like a finish which made youth appear crude, and his voice, as he recounted his afternoon's doings, had the intimate inflections reserved for her ear.

'By the way,' he said presently, as he set down his teacup, 'I had almost forgotten that I've brought you a present – something I picked up in a little shop in the Rue Bonaparte. Oh, don't look too expectant; it's not a *chef-d'oeuvre*; on the contrary, it's about as bad as it can be. But you'll see presently why I bought it.'

As he spoke he drew a small, flat parcel from the breast pocket of his impeccable frock coat and handed it to his wife.

Delia, loosening the paper which wrapped it, discovered within an oval frame studded with pearls and containing the crudely executed miniature of an unknown young man in the uniform of a United States cavalry officer. She glanced inquiringly at Corbett.

'Turn it over,' he said.

She did so, and on the back, beneath two unfamiliar initials, read the brief inscription:

'Fell at Chancellorsville, May 3, 1863.'

The blood rushed to her face as she stood gazing at the words.

'You see now why I bought it?' Corbett continued. 'All the pieties of one's youth seemed to protest against leaving it in the clutches of a Jew pawnbroker in the Rue Bonaparte. It's awfully bad, isn't it? – but some poor soul might be glad to think that it had passed again into the possession of fellow countrymen.' He took it back from her, bending to examine it critically. 'What a daub!' he murmured. 'I wonder who he was? Do you suppose that by taking a little trouble one might find out and restore it to his people?'

'I don't know – I dare say,' she murmured, absently.

He looked up at the sound of her voice. 'What's the matter, Delia? Don't you feel well?' he asked.

'Oh, yes. I was only thinking' – she took the miniature from his hand. 'It was kind of you, Laurence, to buy this – it was like you.'

'Thanks for the latter clause,' he returned, smiling.

Delia stood staring at the vivid flesh tints of the young man who had fallen at Chancellorsville.

'You weren't very strong at his age, were you, Laurence? Weren't you often ill?' she asked.

Corbett gave her a surprised glance. 'Not that I'm aware of,' he said; 'I had the measles at twelve, but since then I've been unromantically robust.'

'And you – you were in America until you came abroad to be with your sister?'

'Yes – barring a trip of a few weeks in Europe.'

Delia looked again at the miniature; then she fixed her eyes upon her husband's.

'Then why weren't you in the war?' she said.

Corbett answered her gaze for a moment; then his lids dropped, and he shifted his position slightly.

'Really,' he said, with a smile, 'I don't think I know.'

They were the very words which she had used in answering her aunt.

'You don't know?' she repeated, the question leaping out like an electric shock. 'What do you mean when you say that you don't know?'

'Well – it all happened some time ago,' he answered, still smiling, 'and the truth is that I've completely forgotten the excellent reasons that I doubtless had at the time for remaining at home.'

'Reasons for remaining at home? But there were none; every man of your age went to the war; no one stayed at home who wasn't lame, or blind, or deaf, or ill, or – ' Her face blazed, her voice broke passionately.

Corbett looked at her with rising amazement.

'Or – ?' he said.

'Or a coward,' she flashed out. The miniature dropped from her hands, falling loudly on the polished floor.

The two confronted each other in silence; Corbett was very pale.

'I've told you,' he said, at length, 'That I was neither lame, deaf, blind, nor ill. Your classification is so simple that it will be easy for you to draw your own conclusion.'

And very quietly, with that admirable air which always put him in the right, he walked out of the room. Delia, left alone, bent down and picked up the miniature; its protecting crystal had been broken by the fall. She pressed it close to her and burst into tears.

An hour later, of course, she went to ask her husband's forgiveness. As a woman of sense she could do no less; and her conduct had been so absurd that it was the more obviously pardonable. Corbett, as he kissed her hand, assured her that he had known it was only nervousness; and after dinner, during which he made himself exceptionally agreeable, he proposed their ending the evening at the Palais Royal, where a new play was being given.

Delia had undoubtedly behaved like a fool, and was prepared to do meet penance for her folly by submitting to the gentle sarcasm of her husband's pardon; but when the episode was over, and she realized that she had asked her question and received her answer, she knew that she had passed a milestone in her existence. Corbett was perfectly charming; it was inevitable that he should go on being charming to the end of the chapter. It was equally inevitable that she should go on being in love with him; but her love had undergone a modification which the years were not to efface.

Formerly he had been to her like an unexplored country, full of bewitching surprises and recurrent revelations of wonder and beauty; now she had measured and mapped him, and knew beforehand the direction of every path she trod. His answer to her question had given her the clue to the labyrinth; knowing what he had once done, it seemed quite simple to forecast his future conduct. For that long-past action was still a part of his actual being; he had not outlived or disowned it; he had not even seen that it needed defending.

Her ideal of him was shivered like the crystal above the miniature of the warrior of Chancellorsville. She had the crystal replaced by a piece of clear glass which (as the jeweler pointed out to her) cost much less and looked equally well; and for the passionate worship which she had paid her husband she substituted a tolerant affection which possessed precisely the same advantages.

A Journey

As SHE LAY in her berth, staring at the shadows overhead, the rush of the wheels was in her brain, driving her deeper and deeper into circles of wakeful lucidity. The sleeping car had sunk into its night silence. Through the wet windowpane she watched the sudden lights, the long stretches of hurrying blackness. Now and then she turned her head and looked through the opening in the hangings at her husband's curtains across the aisle. . . .

She wondered restlessly if he wanted anything and if she could hear him if he called. His voice had grown very weak within the last months and it irritated him when she did not hear. This irritability, this increasing childish petulance seemed to give expression to their imperceptible estrangement. Like two faces looking at one another through a sheet of glass they were close together, almost touching, but they could not hear or feel each other: the conductivity between them was broken. She, at least, had this sense of separation, and she fancied sometimes that she saw it reflected in the look with which he supplemented his failing words. Doubtless the fault was hers. She was too impenetrably healthy to be touched by the irrelevancies of disease. Her self-reproachful tenderness was tinged with the sense of his irrationality: she had a vague feeling that there was a purpose in his helpless tyrannies. The suddenness of the change had found her so unprepared. A year ago their pulses had beat to one robust measure; both had the same prodigal confidence in an exhaustless future. Now their energies no longer kept step: hers still bounded ahead of life, pre-empting unclaimed regions of hope and activity, while his lagged behind, vainly struggling to overtake her.

330

When they married, she had such arrears of living to make up: her days had been as bare as the whitewashed schoolroom where she forced innutritious facts upon reluctant children. His coming had broken in on the slumber of circumstance, widening the present till it became the encloser of remotest chances. But imperceptibly the horizon narrowed. Life had a grudge against her: she was never to be allowed to spread her wings.

At first the doctors had said that six weeks of mild air would set him right; but when he came back this assurance was explained as having of course included a winter in a dry climate. They gave up their pretty house, storing the wedding presents and new furniture, and went to Colorado. She had hated it there from the first. Nobody knew her or cared about her; there was no one to wonder at the good match she had made, or to envy her the new dresses and the visiting cards which were still a surprise to her. And he kept growing worse. She felt herself beset with difficulties too evasive to be fought by so direct a temperament. She still loved him, of course; but he was gradually, undefinably ceasing to be himself. The man she had married had been strong, active, gently masterful: the male whose pleasure it is to clear a way through the material obstructions of life; but now it was she who was the protector, he who must be shielded from importunities and given his drops or his beef juice though the skies were falling. The routine of the sickroom bewildered her; this punctual administering of medicine seemed as idle as some uncomprehended religious mummery.

There were moments, indeed, when warm gushes of pity swept away her instinctive resentment of his condition, when she still found his old self in his eyes as they groped for each other through the dense medium of his weakness. But these moments had grown rare. Sometimes he frightened her: his sunken expressionless face seemed that of a stranger; his voice was weak and hoarse; his thin-lipped smile a mere muscular contraction. Her hand avoided his damp soft skin, which had lost the familiar roughness of health: she caught herself furtively watching him as she might have watched a strange animal. It frightened her to feel that this was the man she loved; there were hours when to tell him what she suffered seemed the one escape from her fears. But in general she judged herself more leniently, reflecting that she had perhaps been too long alone with him, and that she would feel differently when they were at home again, surrounded by her robust and buoyant family. How she had rejoiced when the doctors at last gave their consent to his going home! She knew, of course, what the decision meant; they both knew. It meant that he was to die; but they dressed the truth in hopeful euphemisms, and at times, in the joy of preparation, she really forgot the purpose of their journey, and slipped into an eager allusion to next year's plans.

At last the day of leaving came. She had a dreadful fear that they would never get away; that somehow at the last moment he would fail her; that the doctors held one of their accustomed treacheries in reserve; but nothing happened. They drove to the station, he was installed in a seat with a rug over his knees and a cushion at his back, and she hung out of the window waving unregretful farewells to the acquaintances she had really never liked till then.

The first twenty-four hours had passed off well. He revived a little and it amused him to look out of the window and to observe the humors of the car. The second day he began to grow weary and to chafe under the dispassionate stare of the freckled child with the lump of chewing gum. She had to explain to the child's mother that her husband was too ill to be disturbed: a statement received by that lady with a resentment visibly supported by the maternal sentiment of the whole car. . . .

That night he slept badly and the next morning his temperature frightened her: she was sure he was growing worse. The day passed slowly, punctuated by the small irritations of travel. Watching his tired face, she traced in its contractions every rattle and jolt of the train, till her own body vibrated with sympathetic fatigue. She felt the others observing him too, and hovered restlessly between him and the line of interrogative eyes. The freckled child hung about him like a fly; offers of candy and picture books failed to dislodge her: she twisted one leg around the other and watched him imperturbably. The porter, as he passed, lingered with vague proffers of help, probably inspired by philanthropic passengers swelling with the sense that 'something ought to be done'; and one nervous man in a skull cap was audibly concerned as to the possible effect on his wife's health.

The hours dragged on in a dreary inoccupation. Towards dusk she sat down beside him and he laid his hand on hers.

The touch startled her. He seemed to be calling her from far off. She looked at him helplessly and his smile went through her like a physical pang.

'Are you very tired?' she asked.

'No, not very.'

'We'll be there soon now.'

'Yes, very soon.'

'This time tomorrow – '

He nodded and they sat silent. When she had put him to bed and crawled into her own berth she tried to cheer herself with the thought that in less than twenty-four hours they would be in New York. Her people would all be at the station to meet her – she pictured their round unanxious faces pressing through the crowd. She only hoped they would not tell him too loudly that he was looking splendidly and would be all right in no time: the subtler sympathies developed by long contact with suffering were making her aware of a certain coarseness of texture in the family sensibilities.

Suddenly she thought she heard him call. She parted the curtains and listened. No, it was only a man snoring at the other end of the car. His snores had a greasy sound, as though they passed through tallow. She lay down and tried to sleep. . . . Had she not heard him move? She started up trembling. . . . The silence frightened her more than any sound. He might not be able to make her hear – he might be calling her now. . . . What made her think of such things? It was merely the familiar tendency of an overtired mind to fasten itself on the most intolerable chance within the range of its forebodings. . . . Putting her head out, she listened: but she could not distinguish his breathing from that of the other pairs of lungs about her. She longed to get up and look at him, but she knew the impulse was a mere vent for her restlessness, and the fear of disturbing him restrained her. . . . The regular movement of his curtain reassured her, she knew not why; she remembered that he had wished her a cheerful good night; and the sheer inability to endure her fears a moment longer made her put them from her with an effort of her whole sound-tired body. She turned on her side and slept.

She sat up stiffly, staring out at the dawn. The train was rushing through a region of bare hillocks huddled against a lifeless sky. It looked like the first day of creation. The air of the car was close, and she pushed up her window to let in the keen wind. Then she looked at her watch: it was seven o'clock, and soon the people about her would be stirring. She slipped into her clothes, smoothed her disheveled hair and crept to the dressing room. When she had washed her face and adjusted her dress she felt more hopeful. It was always a struggle for her not to be cheerful in the morning. Her cheeks burned deliciously under the coarse towel and the wet hair about her temples broke into strong upward tendrils. Every inch of her was full of life and elasticity. And in ten hours they would be at home!

She stepped to her husband's berth: it was time for him to take his early glass of milk. The window shade was down, and in the dusk of the curtained enclosure she could just see that he lay sideways, with his face away from her. She leaned over him and drew up the shade. As she did so she touched one of his hands. It felt cold. . . .

She bent closer, laying her hand on his arm and calling him by name. He did not move. She spoke again more loudly; she grasped his shoulder and gently shook it. He lay motionless. She caught hold of his hand again: it slipped from her limply, like a dead thing. A dead thing?

Her breath caught. She must see his face. She leaned forward, and hurriedly, shrinkingly, with a sickening reluctance of the flesh, laid her hands on his shoulders and turned him over. His head fell back; his face looked small and smooth; he gazed at her with steady eyes.

She remained motionless for a long time, holding him thus; and they looked at each other. Suddenly she shrank back: the longing to scream, to call out, to fly from him, had almost overpowered her. But a strong hand arrested her. Good God! If it were known that he was dead they would be put off the train at the next station —

In a terrifying flash of remembrance there arose before her a scene she had once witnessed in traveling, when a husband and wife, whose child had died in the train, had been thrust out at some chance station. She saw them standing on the platform with the child's body between them; she had never forgotten the dazed look with which they followed the receding train. And this was what would happen to her. Within the next hour she might find herself on the platform of some strange station, alone with her husband's body. . . . Anything but that! It was too horrible – She quivered like a creature at bay.

As she cowered there, she felt the train moving more slowly. It was coming then – they were approaching a station! She saw again the husband and wife standing on the lonely platform; and with a violent gesture she drew down the shade to hide her husband's face.

Feeling dizzy, she sank down on the edge of the berth, keeping away from his outstretched body, and pulling the curtains close, so that he and she were shut into a kind of sepulchral twilight. She tried to think. At all costs she must conceal the fact that he was dead. But how? Her mind refused to act: she could not plan, combine. She could think of no way but to sit there, clutching the curtains, all day long. . . .

She heard the porter making up her bed; people were beginning to move about the car; the dressing-room door was being opened and shut. She tried to rouse herself. At length with a supreme effort she rose to her feet, stepping into the aisle of the car and drawing the curtains tight behind her. She noticed that they still parted slightly with the motion of the car, and finding a pin in her dress she fastened them together. Now she was safe. She looked round and saw the porter. She fancied he was watching her.

'Ain't he awake yet?' he inquired.

'No,' she faltered.

'I got his milk all ready when he wants it. You know you told me to have it for him by seven.'

She nodded silently and crept into her seat.

At half-past eight the train reached Buffalo. By this time the other passengers were dressed and the berths had been folded back for the day. The porter, moving to and fro under his burden of sheets and pillows, glanced at her as he passed. At length he said: 'Ain't he going to get up? You know we're ordered to make up the berths as early as we can.'

She turned cold with fear. They were just entering the station.

'Oh, not yet,' she stammered. 'Not till he's had his milk. Won't you get it, please?'

'All right. Soon as we start again.'

When the train moved on he reappeared with the milk. She took it from him and sat vaguely looking at it: her brain moved slowly from one idea to another, as though they were steppingstones set far apart across a whirling flood. At length she became aware that the porter still hovered expectantly.

'Will I give it to him?' he suggested.

'Oh, no,' she cried, rising. 'He – he's asleep yet, I think – '

She waited till the porter had passed on; then she unpinned the curtains and slipped behind them. In the semiobscurity her husband's face stared up at her like a marble mask with agate eyes. The eyes were dreadful. She put out her hand and drew down the lids. Then she remembered the glass of milk in her other hand: what was she to do with it? She thought of raising the window and throwing it out; but to do so she would have to lean across his body and bring her face close to his. She decided to drink the milk.

She returned to her seat with the empty glass and after a while the porter came back to get it.

'When'll I fold up his bed?' he asked.

'Oh, not now – not yet; he's ill – he's very ill. Can't you let him stay as he is? The doctor wants him to lie down as much as possible.'

He scratched his head. 'Well, if he's *really* sick – '

He took the empty glass and walked away, explaining to the passengers that the party behind the curtains was too sick to get up just yet.

She found herself the center of sympathetic eyes. A motherly woman with an intimate smile sat down beside her.

'I'm real sorry to hear your husband's sick. I've had a remarkable amount of sickness in my family and maybe I could assist you. Can I take a look at him?'

'Oh, no – no please! He mustn't be disturbed.'

The lady accepted the rebuff indulgently.

'Well, it's just as you say, of course, but you don't look to me as if you'd had much experience in sickness and I'd have been glad to assist you. What do you generally do when your husband's taken this way?'

'I – I let him sleep.'

'Too much sleep ain't any too healthful either. Don't you give him any medicine?'

'Y – yes.'

'Don't you wake him to take it?'

'Yes.'

'When does he take the next dose?'

'Not for – two hours – '

The lady looked disappointed. 'Well, if I was you I'd try giving it oftener. That's what I do with my folks.'

After that many faces seemed to press upon her. The passengers were on their way to the dining car, and she was conscious that as they passed down the aisle they glanced curiously at the closed curtains. One lantern-jawed man with prominent eyes stood still and tried to shoot his projecting glance through the division between the folds. The freckled child, returning from breakfast, waylaid the passers with a buttery clutch, saying in a loud whisper, 'He's sick'; and once the conductor came by, asking for tickets. She shrank into her corner and looked out of the window at the flying trees and houses, meaningless hieroglyphs of an endlessly unrolled papyrus.

Now and then the train stopped, and the newcomers on entering the car stared in turn at the closed curtains. More and more people seemed to pass – their faces began to blend fantastically with the images surging in her brain. . . .

Later in the day a fat man detached himself from the mist of faces. He had a creased stomach and soft pale lips. As he pressed himself into the seat facing her she noticed that he was dressed in black broadcloth, with a soiled white tie.

'Husband's pretty bad this morning, is he?'

'Yes.'

'Dear, dear! Now that's terribly distressing, ain't it?' An apostolic smile revealed his gold-filled teeth. 'Of course you know there's no sech thing as sickness. Ain't that a lovely thought? Death itself is but a deloosion of our grosser senses. On'y lay yourself open to the influx of the sperrit, submit yourself passively to the action of the divine force, and disease and dissolution will cease to exist for you. If you could indooce your husband to read this little pamphlet – '

The faces about her again grew indistinct. She had a vague recollection of hearing the motherly lady and the parent of the freckled child ardently disputing the relative advantages of trying several medicines at once, or of taking each in turn; the motherly lady maintaining that the competitive system saved time; the other objecting that you couldn't tell which remedy had effected the cure; their voices went on and on, like bell buoys droning through a fog. . . . The porter came up now and then with questions that she did not understand, but somehow she must have answered since he went away again without repeating them; every two hours the motherly lady reminded her that her husband ought to have his drops; people left the car and others replaced them. . . .

Her head was spinning and she tried to steady herself by clutching at her thoughts as they swept by, but they slipped away from her like bushes on the side of a sheer precipice down which she seemed to be falling. Suddenly her mind grew clear again and she found herself vividly picturing what would happen when the train reached New York. She shuddered as it occurred to her that he would be quite cold and that someone might perceive he had been dead since morning.

She thought hurriedly: 'If they see I am not surprised they will suspect something. They will ask questions, and if I tell them the truth they won't believe me – no one would believe me! It will be terrible' – and she kept repeating to herself – 'I must pretend I don't know. I must pretend I don't know. When they open the curtains I must go up to him quite naturally – and then I must scream! She had an idea that the scream would be very hard to do.

Gradually new thoughts crowded upon her, vivid and urgent: she tried to separate and restrain them, but they beset her clamorously, like her school children at the end of a hot day, when she was too tired to silence them. Her head grew confused, and she felt a sick fear of forgetting her part, of betraying herself by some unguarded word or look.

'I must pretend I don't know,' she went on murmuring. The words had lost their significance, but she repeated them mechanically, as though they had been a magic formula, until suddenly she heard herself saying: 'I can't remember, I can't remember!'

Her voice sounded very loud, and she looked about her in terror; but no one seemed to notice that she had spoken.

As she glanced down the car her eye caught the curtains of her husband's berth, and she began to examine the monotonous arabesques woven through their heavy folds. The pattern was intricate and difficult to trace; she gazed fixedly at the curtains and as she did so the thick stuff grew transparent and through it she saw her husband's face – his dead face. She struggled to avert her look, but her eyes refused to move and her head seemed to be held in vice. At last, with an effort that left her weak and shaking, she turned away; but it was of no use; close in front of her, small and smooth, was her husband's face. It seemed to be suspended in the air between her and the false braids of the woman who sat in front of her. With an uncontrollable gesture she stretched out her hand to push the face away, and suddenly she felt the touch of his smooth skin. She repressed a cry and half started from her seat. The woman with the false braids looked around, and feeling that she must justify her movement in some way she rose and lifted her traveling bag from the opposite seat. She unlocked the bag and looked into it; but the first object her hand met was a small flask of her husband's, thrust there at the last moment, in the haste of departure. She locked the bag and closed her eyes . . . his face was there again, hanging between her eyeballs and lids like a waxen mask against a red curtain. . . .

She roused herself with a shiver. Had she fainted or slept? Hours seemed to have elapsed; but it was still broad day, and the people about her were sitting in the same attitudes as before.

A sudden sense of hunger made her aware that she had eaten nothing since morning. The thought of food filled her with disgust, but she dreaded a return of faintness, and remembering that she had some biscuits in her bag she took one out and ate it. The dry crumbs choked her, and she hastily swallowed a little brandy from her husband's flask. The burning sensation in her throat acted as a counterirritant, momentarily relieving the dull ache of her nerves. Then she felt a gently-stealing warmth, as though a soft air fanned her, and the swarming fears relaxed their clutch, receding through the stillness that enclosed her, a stillness soothing as the spacious quietude of a summer day. She slept.

Through her sleep she felt the impetuous rush of the train. It seemed to be life itself that was sweeping her on with headlong inexorable force – sweeping her into darkness and terror, and the awe of unknown days. – Now all at once everything was still – not a sound, not a pulsation. . . . She was dead in her turn, and lay beside him with smooth upstaring face. How quiet it was! – and yet she heard feet coming, the feet of the men who were to carry them away. . . . She could feel too – she felt a sudden prolonged vibration, a series of hard shocks, and then another plunge into darkness: the darkness of death this time – a black whirlwind on which they were both spinning like leaves, in wild uncoiling spirals, with millions and millions of the dead. . . .

She sprang up in terror. Her sleep must have lasted a long time, for the winter day had paled and the lights had been lit. The car was in confusion, and as she regained her self-possession she saw that the passengers were gathering up their wraps and bags. The woman with the false braids had brought from the dressing room a sickly ivy plant in a bottle, and the Christian Scientist was reversing his cuffs. The porter passed down the aisle with his impartial brush. An impersonal figure with a gold-banded cap asked for her husband's ticket. A voice shouted 'Baig-gage *ex*press!' and she heard the clicking of metal as the passengers handed over their checks.

Presently her window was blocked by an expanse of sooty wall, and the train passed into the Harlem tunnel. The journey was over; in a few minutes she would see her family pushing their joyous way through the throng at the station. Her heart dilated. The worst terror was past. . . .

'We'd better get him up now, hadn't we?' asked the porter, touching her arm.

He had her husband's hat in his hand and was meditatively revolving it under his brush.

She looked at the hat and tried to speak; but suddenly the car grew dark. She flung up her arms, struggling to catch at something, and fell face downward, striking her head against the dead man's berth.

The Line of Least Resistance

———————❧———————

MILLICENT WAS LATE – as usual. Mr. Mindon, returning unexpectedly from an interrupted yacht race, reached home with the legitimate hope of finding her at luncheon; but she was still out. 'Was she lunching out then?' he asked the butler, who replied, with the air of making an uncalled-for concession to his master's curiosity, that Mrs. Mindon had given no orders about the luncheon.

Mr. Mindon, on this negative information (it was the kind from which his knowledge of his wife's movements was mainly drawn), sat down to the grilled cutlet and glass of Vichy that represented his share in the fabulous daily total of the chef's book. Mr. Mindon's annual food consumption probably amounted to about half of one per cent on his cook's perquisites, and of the other luxuries of his complicated establishment he enjoyed considerably less than this fraction. Of course, it was nobody's fault but his own. As Millicent pointed out, she couldn't feed her friends on mutton chops and Vichy because of his digestive difficulty, nor could she return their hospitality by asking them to play croquet with the children because that happened to be Mr. Mindon's chosen pastime. If that was the kind of life he wanted to lead he should have married a dyspeptic governess, not a young confiding girl, who little dreamed what marriage meant when she passed from her father's roof into the clutches of a tyrant with imperfect gastric secretions.

It was his fault, of course, but then Millicent had faults too, as she had been known to concede when she perceived that the contemplation of her merits was beginning to pall; and it did seem unjust to Mr. Mindon that their life should be one long adaptation to Millicent's faults at the expense of

341

his own, Millicent was unpunctual – but that gave a sense of her importance to the people she kept waiting; she had nervous attacks – but they served to excuse her from dull dinners and family visits; she was bad-tempered – but that merely made the servants insolent to Mr. Mindon; she was extravagant – but that simply necessitated Mr. Mindon's curtailing his summer holiday and giving a closer attention to business. If ever a woman had the qualities of her faults, the woman was Millicent. Like the legendary goose, they laid golden eggs for her, and she nurtured them tenderly in return. If Millicent had been a perfect wife and mother, she and Mr. Mindon would probably have spent their summer in the depressing promiscuity of hotel piazzas. Mr. Mindon was shrewd enough to see that he reaped the advantages of his wife's imperfect domesticity, and that if her faults were the making of her, she was the making of him. It was therefore unreasonable to be angry with Millicent, even if she were late for luncheon, and Mr. Mindon, who prided himself on being a reasonable man, usually found some other outlet for his wrath.

On this occasion it was the unpunctuality of the little girls. They came in with their governess some minutes after he was seated: two small Millicents, with all her arts in miniature. They arranged their frocks carefully before seating themselves and turned up their little Greek noses at the food. Already they showed signs of finding fault with as much ease and discrimination as Millicent; and Mr. Mindon knew that this was an accomplishment not to be undervalued. He himself, for example, though Millicent charged him with being a discontented man, had never acquired her proficiency in deprecation; indeed, he sometimes betrayed a mortifying indifference to trifles that afforded opportunity for the display of his wife's fastidiousness. Mr. Mindon, though no biologist, was vaguely impressed by the way in which that accomplished woman had managed to transmit an acquired characteristic to her children: it struck him with wonder that traits of which he had marked the incipience in Millicent should have become intuitions in her offspring. To rebuke such costly replicas of their mother seemed dangerously like scolding Millicent – and Mr. Mindon's hovering resentment prudently settled on the governess.

He pointed out to her that the children were late for luncheon.

The governess was sorry, but Gladys was always unpunctual. Perhaps her papa would speak to her.

Mr. Mindon changed the subject. 'What's that at my feet? There's a dog in the room!'

He looked round furiously at the butler, who gazed impartially over his head. Mr. Mindon knew that it was proper for him to ignore his servants, but was not sure to what extent they ought to reciprocate his treatment.

The governess explained that it was Gwendolen's puppy.

'Gwendolen's puppy? Who gave Gwendolen a puppy?'

Fwank Antwin,' said Gwendolen through a mouthful of mushroom soufflé.

'Mr. Antrim,' the governess suggested, in a tone that confessed the futility of the correction.

'*We* don't call him Mr. Antrim; we call him Frank; he likes us to,' said Gladys icily.

'You'll do no such thing!' her father snapped.

A soft body came in contact with his toe. He kicked out viciously, and the room was full of yelping.

'Take the animal out instantly!' he stormed; dogs were animals to Mr. Mindon. The butler continued to gaze over his head, and the two footmen took their cue from the butler.

'I won't – I won't – I won't let my puppy go!' Gwendolen violently lamented.

But she should have another, her father assured her – a much handsomer and more expensive one; his darling should have a prize dog; he would telegraph to New York on the instant.

'I don't want a pwize dog; I want Fwank's puppy!'

Mr. Mindon laid down his fork and walked out of the room, while the governess, cutting up Gwendolen's nectarine, said, as though pointing out an error in syntax, 'You've vexed your papa again.'

'I don't mind vexing papa – nothing happens,' said Gwendolen, hugging her puppy; while Gladys, disdaining the subject of dispute, contemptuously nibbled caramels. Gladys was two years older than Gwendolen and had outlived the first freshness of her enthusiasm for Frank Antrim, who, with the notorious indiscrimination of the grownup, always gave the nicest presents to Gwendolen.

Mr. Mindon, crossing his marble hall between goddesses whose dishabille was still slightly disconcerting to his traditions, stepped out on the terrace above the cliffs. The lawn looked as expensive as a velvet carpet woven in one piece; the flower borders contained only exotics; and the stretch of blue-satin Atlantic had the air of being furrowed only by the keels of pleasure boats. The scene, to Mr. Mindon's imagination, never lost the keen edge of its costliness; he had yet to learn Millicent's trick of regarding a Newport villa as a mere *pied-à-terre*; but he could not help reflecting that, after all, it was to him she owed her fine sense of relativity. There are certain things one must possess in order not to be awed by them, and it was he who had enabled Millicent to take a Newport villa for granted. And still she was not satisfied! She had reached the point where taking the exceptional as a matter of course becomes in itself a matter of course; and Millicent could not live without novelty. That was the worst of it: she discarded her successes as rapidly as her gowns; Mr. Mindon felt a certain breathlessness in retracing her successive manifestations. And yet he had always made allowances: literally and figuratively, he had gone on making larger and larger allowances, till his whole income, as well as his whole point of view, was practically at Millicent's disposal. But after all, there was a principle of give and take – if only Millicent could have been brought to see it! One of Millicent's chief sources of strength lay in her magnificent obtuseness: there were certain obligations that simply didn't exist for her, because she couldn't be brought to see them, and the principle of give and take (a favorite principle of Mr. Mindon's) was one of them.

There was Frank Antrim, for instance. Mr. Mindon, who had a high sense of propriety, had schooled himself, not without difficulty, into thinking Antrim a charming fellow. No one was more alive than Mr. Mindon to the expediency of calling the Furies the Eumenides. He knew that as long as he chose to think Frank Antrim a charming fellow, everything was as it should be and his home a temple of the virtues. But why on earth did Millicent let the fellow give presents to the children? Mr. Mindon was dimly conscious that Millicent had been guilty of the kind of failure she would least have liked him to detect – a failure in taste – and a certain exultation tempered his resentment. To anyone who had suffered as Mr. Mindon had from Millicent's keenness in noting such lapses in others, it was not unpleasant to find she could be 'bad form.' A sense of unwonted astuteness fortified Mr. Mindon's wrath. He felt that he had every reason to be angry with Millicent, and decided to go and scold the governess; then he remembered that it was bad for him to lose his temper after eating, and, drawing a small phial from his pocket, he took a pepsin tablet instead.

Having vented his wrath in action, he felt calmer, but scarcely more happy. A marble nymph smiled at him from the terrace; but he knew how much nymphs cost, and was not sure that they were worth the price. Beyond the shrubberies he caught a glimpse of domed glass. His greenhouses were the finest in Newport; but since he neither ate fruit nor wore orchids, the yielded at best an indirect satisfaction. At length he decided to go and play with the little girls; but on entering the nursery he found them dressing for a party, with the rapt gaze and fevered cheeks with which Millicent would presently perform the same rite. They took no notice of him, and he crept downstairs again.

His study table was heaped with bills, and as it was bad for his digestion to look over them after luncheon, he wandered on into the other rooms. He did not stay long in the drawing room; it evoked too vividly the evening hours when he delved for platitudes under the inattentive gaze of listeners who obviously resented his not being somebody else. Much of Mr. Mindon's intercourse with ladies was clouded by the sense of this resentment, and he sometimes avenged himself by wondering if they supposed he would talk to them if he could help it. The sight of the dining-room increased his depression by recalling the long dinners where, with the pantry draft on his neck, he languished between the dullest women of the evening. He turned away; but the ballroom beyond roused even more disturbing association: an orchestra playing all night (Mr. Mindon crept to bed at eleven), carriages shouted for under his windows, and a morrow like the day after an earthquake.

In the library he felt less irritated but not more cheerful. Mr. Mindon had never quite known what the library was for; it was like one of those mysterious ruins over which archaeology endlessly disputes. It could not have been intended for reading, since no one in the house ever read, except an under-housemaid charged with having set fire to her bed in her surreptitious zeal for fiction; and smoking was forbidden there, because the hangings held the odor of tobacco. Mr. Mindon felt a natural pride in being rich enough to permit himself a perfectly useless room; but not liking to take the bloom from its inutility by sitting in it, he passed on to Millicent's boudoir.

Here at least was a room of manifold purposes, the center of Millicent's complex social system. Mr. Mindon entered with the awe of the modest investor treading the inner precincts of finance. He was proud of Millicent's social activities and liked to read over her daily list of engagements and the record of the invitations she received in a season. The number was perpetually swelling like a rising stock. Mr. Mindon had a vague sense that she would soon be declaring an extra dividend. After all, one must be lenient to a woman as hard-working as Millicent. All about him were the evidences of her toil: her writing table disappeared under an avalanche of notes and cards; the wastepaper basket overflowed with torn correspondence; and, glancing down, Mr. Mindon saw a crumpled letter at his feet. Being a man of neat habits, he was often tried by Millicent's genial disorder; and his customary rebuke was the act of restoring the strayed object to its place.

He stopped to gather the bit of paper from the floor. As he picked it up his eyes caught the words; he smoothed the page and read on. . . .

• II •

HE seemed to be cowering on the edge of a boiling flood, watching his small thinking faculty spin round out of reach on the tumult of his sensations. Then a fresh wave of emotion swept the tiny object – the quivering imperceptible ego – back to shore, and it began to reach out drowned tentacles in a faint effort after thought.

He sat up and glanced about him. The room looked back at him, coldly, unfamiliarly, as he had seen Millicent look when he asked her to be reasonable. And who are you? the walls seemed to say. Who am I? Mr. Mindon heard himself retorting. I'll tell you, by God! I'm the man that paid for you – paid for every scrap of you: silk hangings, china rubbish, glasses, chandeliers – every Frenchified rag of you. Why, if it weren't for me and my money you'd be nothing but a brick-and-plaster shell, naked as the day you were built – no better than a garret or a coal hole. Why, you wouldn't *be* at all if I chose to tear you down. I could tear the whole house down, if I chose.

He paused, suddenly aware that his eyes were on a photograph of Millicent, and that it was his wife he was apostrophizing. Her lips seemed to shape a 'hush'; when he said things she didn't like she always told him not to talk so loud. Had he been talking loud? Well, who was to prevent him? Wasn't the house his and everything in it? Who was Millicent, to bid him hush?

Mr. Mindon felt a sudden increase of stature. He strutted across the room. Why, of course, the room belonged to him, the house belonged to him, and he belonged to himself! That was the best of it! For years he had been the man that Millicent thought him, the mere projection of her disdain; and now he was himself.

It was odd how the expression of her photograph changed, melting, as her face did, from contempt to cajolery, in one of those transitions that hung him breathless on the skirts of her mood. She was looking at him gently now, sadly almost, with the little grieved smile that seemed always to anticipate and pardon his obtuseness. Ah, Millicent! The clock struck and Mr. Mindon stood still. Perhaps she was smiling so now – or the other way. He could have told the other fool where each of her smiles led. There was a fierce enjoyment in his sense of lucidity. He saw it all now. Millicent had kept him for years in bewildered subjection to exigencies as inscrutable as the decrees of Providence; but now his comprehension of her seemed a mere incident in his omniscience.

His sudden translation to the absolute gave him a curious sense of spectatorship; he seemed to be looking on at his own thoughts. His brain was like a brightly-lit factory, full of flying wheels and shuttles. All the machinery worked with the greatest rapidity and precision. He was planning, reasoning, arguing, with unimagined facility; words flew out like sparks from each revolving thought. But suddenly he felt himself caught in the wheels of his terrific logic, and swept round, red and shrieking, till he was flung off into space.

The acuter thrill of one sobbing nerve detached itself against his consciousness. What was it that hurt so? Someone was speaking; a voice probed to the central pain –

'Any orders for the stable, sir?'

And Mr. Mindon found himself the mere mouthpiece of a roving impulse that replied –

'No; but you may telephone for a cab for me – at once.'

• III •

He drove to one of the hotels. He was breathing more easily now, restored to the safe level of conventional sensation. His late ascent to the rarefied heights of the unexpected had left him weak and exhausted; but he gained reassurance from the way in which his thoughts were slipping back of themselves into the old grooves. He was feeling, he was sure, just as a gentleman ought to feel; all the consecrated phrases – 'outraged honor,' 'a father's heart,' 'the sanctity of home' – were flocking glibly at his call. He had the self-confidence that comes of knowing one has on the right clothes. He had certainly done the proper thing in leaving the house at once; but, too weak and tired to consider the next step, he yielded himself to one of those soothing intervals of abeyance when life seems to wait submissively at the door.

As his cab breasted the current of the afternoon drive he caught the greeting of the lady with whom he and Millicent were to have dined. He was troubled by the vision of that disrupted dinner. He had not yet reached the point of detachment at which offending Mrs. Targe might become immaterial, and again he felt himself jerked out of his grooves. What ought he to do? Millicent, now, could have told him – if only he might have consulted Millicent! He pulled himself together and tried to think of his wrongs.

At the hotel, the astonished clerk led him upstairs, unlocking the door of a room that smelt of cheap soap. The window had been so long shut that it opened with a jerk, sending a shower of dead flies to the carpet. Out along the sea front, at that hour, the south wind was hurrying the waters, but the hotel stood in one of the sheltered streets, where in midsummer there is little life in the air. Mr. Mindon sat down in the provisional attitude of a visitor who is kept waiting. Over the fireplace hung a print of the 'Landing of Columbus'; a fly-blown portrait of General Grant faced it from the opposite wall. The smell of soap was insufferable, and hot noises came up irritatingly from the street. He looked at his watch; it was just four o'clock.

He wondered if Millicent had come in yet, and if she had read his letter. The occupation of picturing how she would feel when she read it proved less exhilarating than he had expected, and he got up and wandered about the room. He opened a drawer in the dressing table, and seeing in it some burnt matches and a fuzz of hair, shut it with disgust; but just as he was ringing to rebuke the housemaid he remembered that he was not in his own house. He sat down again, wondering if the afternoon post were in, and what letters it had brought. It was annoying not to get his letters. What would be done about them? Would they be sent after him? Sent where? It suddenly occurred to him that he didn't in the least know where he was going. He must be going somewhere, of course; he hadn't left home to settle down in that stifling room. He supposed he should go to town, but with the heat at ninety the prospect was not alluring. He might decide on Lenox or Saratoga; but a doubt as to the propriety of such a course set him once more adrift on a chartless sea of perplexities. His head ached horribly and he threw himself on the bed.

When he sat up, worn out with his thoughts, the room was growing dark. Eight o'clock! Millicent must be dressing – but no; tonight at least, he grimly reflected, she was condemned to the hateful necessity of dining alone; unless, indeed, her audacity sent her to Mrs. Targe's in the always acceptable role of the pretty woman whose husband has been 'called away.' Perhaps Antrim would be asked to fill his place!

The thought flung him on his feet, but its impetus carried him no farther. He was borne down by the physical apathy of a traveler who has a week's journey in his bones. He sat down and thought of the little girls, who were just going to bed. They would have welcomed him at that hour: he was aware that they cherished him chiefly as a pretext, a sanctuary from bedtime and lessons. He had never in his life been more than an alternative to anyone.

A vague sense of physical apprehension resolved itself into hunger stripped of appetite, and he decided that he ought to urge himself to eat. He opened his door on a rising aroma of stale coffee and fry.

In the dining room, where a waiter offered him undefinable food in thick-lipped saucers, Mr. Mindon decided to go to New York. Retreating from the heavy assault of a wedge of pie, he pushed back his chair and went upstairs. He felt hot and grimy in the yachting clothes he had worn since morning, and the Fall River boat would at least be cool. Then he remembered the playful throngs that held the deck, the midnight hilarity of the waltz tunes, the horror of the morning coffee. His stomach was still tremulous from its late adventure into the unknown, and he shrank from further risks. He had never before realized how much he loved his home.

He grew soft at the vision of his vacant chair. What were they doing and saying without him? His little ones were fatherless – and Millicent? Hitherto he had evaded the thought of Millicent, but now he took a doleful pleasure in picturing her in ruins at his feet. Involuntarily he found himself stooping to her despair; but he straightened himself and said aloud, 'I'll take the night train, then.' The sound of his voice surprised him, and he started up. Was that a footstep outside? – a message, a note? Had they found out where he was, and was his wretched wife mad enough to sue for mercy? His ironical smile gave the measure of her madness; but the step passed on, and he sat down rather blankly. The impressiveness of his attitude was being gradually sapped by the sense that no one knew where he was. He had reached the point where he could not be sure of remaining inflexible unless someone asked him to relent.

• IV •

AT the sound of a knock he clutched his hat and bag.

'Mindon, I say!' a genial voice adjured him; and before he could take counsel with his newly-acquired dignity, which did not immediately respond to a first summons, the door opened on the reassuring presence of Laurence Meysy.

Mr. Mindon felt the relief of a sufferer at the approach of the eminent specialist. Laurence Meysy was the past tense of a dangerous man: though timeworn, still a favorite; a circulating library romance, dog-eared by many a lovely hand, and still perused with pleasure, though, alas! no longer on the sly. He was said to have wrought much havoc in his youth; and it being now his innocent pleasure to repair the damage done by others, he had become the consulting physician of injured husbands and imprudent wives.

Two gentlemen followed him: Mr. Mindon's uncle and senior partner, the eminent Ezra Brownrigg, and the Reverend Doctor Bonifant, rector of the New York church in which Mr. Mindon owned a pew that was almost as expensive as his opera box.

Mr. Brownrigg entered silently; to get at anything to say he had to sink an artesian well of meditation; but he always left people impressed by what he would have said if he had spoken. He greeted his nephew with the air of a distinquished mourner at a funeral – the mourner who consciously overshadows the corpse; and Doctor Bonifant did justice to the emotional side of the situation by fervently exclaiming, 'Thank heaven, we are not too late!'

Mr. Mindon looked about him with pardonable pride. This scene suggested something between a vestry meeting and a conference of railway directors; and the knowledge that he himself was its central figure, that even his uncle was an accessory, an incident, a mere bit of still life brushed in by the artist Circumstance to throw Mr. Mindon into fuller prominence, gave that gentleman his first sense of equality with his wife. Equality? In another moment he towered above her, picturing her in an attitude of vaguely imagined penance at Doctor Bonifant's feet. Mr. Mindon had always felt about the clergy much as he did about his library: he had never quite known what they were for; but, with the pleased surprise of the pious naturalist, he now saw that they had their uses, like every other object in the economy of nature.

'My dear fellow,' Meysy persuasively went on, 'we've come to have a little chat with you.'

Mr. Brownrigg and the Rector seated themselves. Mr. Mindon mechanically followed their example, and Meysy, asking the others if they minded his cigarette, cheerfully accommodated himself to the edge of the bed.

From the lifelong habit of taking the chair, Mr. Brownrigg coughed and looked at Doctor Bonifant. The Rector leaned forward, stroking his cheek with a hand on which a massive intaglio seemed to be rehearsing the part of the episcopal ring;

then his deprecating glance transferred the burden of action to Laurence Meysy. Meysy seemed to be surveying the case through the mitigating medium of cigarette smoke. His view was that of the professional setting to rights the blunders of two amateurs. It was his theory that the art of carrying on a love affair was very nearly extinct; and he had a far greater contempt for Antrim than for Mr. Mindon.

'My dear fellow,' he began, 'I've seen Mrs. Mindon – she sent for me.'

Mr. Brownrigg, peering between guarded lids, here interposed a 'Very proper.'

Of course Millicent had done the proper thing! Mr. Mindon could not repress a thrill of pride at her efficiency.

'Mrs. Mindon,' Meysy continued, 'showed me your letter.' He paused. 'She was perfectly frank – she throws herself on your mercy.'

'That should be remembered in her favor,' Doctor Bonifant murmured in a voice of absolution.

'It's a wretched business, Mindon – the poor woman's crushed – crushed. Your uncle here has seen her.'

Mr. Brownrigg glanced suspiciously at Meysy, as though not certain whether he cared to corroborate an unauthorized assertion; then he said, 'Mrs. Brownrigg has *not.*'

Doctor Bonifant sighed; Mrs. Brownrigg was one of his most cherished parishioners.

'And the long and short of it is,' Meysy summed up, 'that we're here as your friends – and as your wife's friends – to ask you what you mean to do.'

There was a pause. Mr. Mindon was disturbed by finding the initiative shifted to his shoulders. He had been talking to himself so volubly for the last six hours that he seemed to have nothing left to say.

'To do – to do?' he stammered. 'Why, I mean to go away – leave her –'

'Divorce her?'

'Why – y - yes – yes –'

Doctor Bonifant sighed again, and Mr. Brownrigg's lips stirred like a door being cautiously unbarred.

Meysy knocked the ashes off his cigarette. 'You've quite made up your mind, eh?'

Mr. Mindon faltered another assent. Then, annoyed at the uncertain sound of his voice, he repeated loudly, 'I mean to divorce her.'

The repetition fortified his resolve; and his declaration seemed to be sealed by the silence of his three listeners. He had no need to stiffen himself against entreaty; their mere presence was a pedestal for his wrongs. The words flocked of themselves, building up his conviction like a throng of masons buttressing a weak wall.

Mr. Brownrigg spoke upon his first pause. 'There's the publicity – it's the kind of thing that's prejudicial to a man's business interests.'

An hour earlier the words would have turned Mr. Mindon cold; now he brushed them aside. His business interests, forsooth! What good had his money ever done him? What chance had he ever had of enjoying it? All his toil hadn't made him a rich man – it had merely made Millicent a rich woman.

Doctor Bonifant murmured, 'The children must be considered.'

'They've never considered me!' Mr. Mindon retorted – and turned afresh upon his uncle. Mr. Brownrigg listened impassively. He was a very silent man, but his silence was not a receptacle for the speech of others – it was a hard convex surface on which argument found no footing. Mr. Mindon reverted to the Rector. Doctor Bonifant's attitude towards life was full of a benignant receptivity; as though, logically, a man who had accepted the Thirty-nine Articles was justified in accepting anything else that he chose. His attention had therefore an absorbent quality peculiarly encouraging to those who addressed him. He listened affirmatively, as it were.

Mr. Mindon's spirits rose. It was the first time that he had ever had an audience. He dragged his hearers over every stage of his wrongs, losing sight of the vital injury in the enumeration of incidental grievances. He had the excited sense that at last Millicent would know what he had always thought of her.

Mr. Brownrigg looked at his watch, and Doctor Bonifant bent his head as though under the weight of a pulpit peroration. Meysy, from the bed, watched the three men with the air of an expert who holds the solution of the problem.

He slipped to his feet as Mr. Mindon's speech flagged.

'I suppose you've considered, Mindon, that it rests with you to proclaim the fact that you're no longer – well, the chief object of your wife's affection?'

Mr. Mindon raised his head irritably; interrogation impeded the flow of his diatribe.

'That you – er – in short, created the situation by making it known?' Meysy glanced at the Rector. 'Am I right, Bonifant?'

The Rector took meditative counsel of his finger tips; then slowly, as though formulating a dogma, 'Under certain conditions,' he conceded, 'what is unknown may be said to be nonexistent.'

Mr. Mindon looked from one to the other.

'Damn it, man – before it's too late,' Meysy followed up, 'can't you see that *you're* the only person who can make you ridiculous?'

Mr. Brownrigg rose, and Mr. Mindon had the desperate sense that the situation was slipping out of his grasp.

'It rests with you,' Doctor Bonifant murmured, 'to save your children from even the shadow of obloquy.'

'You can't stay here, at any rate,' said Mr. Brownrigg heavily.

Mr. Mindon, who had risen, dropped weakly into his chair. His three counsellors were now all on their feet, taking up their hats with the air of men who have touched the limit of duty. In another moment they would be gone, and with them Mr. Mindon's audience, his support, his confidence in the immutability of his resolve. He felt himself no more than an evocation of their presence; and, in dread of losing the identity they had created, he groped for a dedaining word. 'I shan't leave for New York till tomorrow.'

'Tomorrow everything will be known,' said Mr. Brownrigg, with his hand on the door.

Meysy glanced at his watch with a faint smile. 'It's tomorrow now,' he added.

He fell back, letting the older men pass out; but, turning as though to follow, he felt a drowning clutch upon his arm.

'It's for the children,' Mr. Mindon stammered.

The Moving Finger

———— ❧ ————

THE NEWS of Mrs. Grancy's death came to me with the shock of an immense blunder – one of fate's most irretrievable acts of vandalism. It was as though all sorts of renovating forces had been checked by the clogging of that one wheel. Not that Mrs. Grancy contributed any perceptible momentum to the social machine: her unique distinction was that of filling to perfection her special place in the world. So many people are like badly-composed statues, overlapping their niches at one point and leaving them vacant at another. Mrs. Grancy's niche was her husband's life; and if it be argued that the space was not large enough for its vacancy to leave a very big gap, I can only say that, at the last resort, such dimensions must be determined by finer instruments than any ready-made standard of utility. Ralph Grancy's was in short a kind of disembodied usefulness: one of those constructive influences that, instead of crystallizing into definite forms, remain as it were a medium for the development of clear thinking and fine feeling. He faithfully irrigated his own dusty patch of life, and the fruitful moisture stole far beyond his boundaries. If, to carry on the metaphor, Grancy's life was a sedulously-cultivated enclosure, his wife was the flower he had planted in its midst – the embowering tree, rather, which gave him rest and shade at its foot and the wind of dreams in its upper branches.

We had all – his small but devoted band of followers – known a moment when it seemed likely that Grancy would fail us. We had watched him pitted against one stupid obstacle after another – ill-health, poverty, misunderstanding and, worst of all for a man of his texture, his first wife's soft insidious egotism. We had seen him sinking under the leaden embrace of her affection like a

355

swimmer in a drowning clutch; but just as we despaired he had always come to the surface again, blinded, panting, but striking out fiercely for the shore. When at last her death released him it became a question as to how much of the man she had carried with her. Left alone, he revealed numb withered patches, like a tree from which a parasite has been stripped. But gradually he began to put out new leaves; and when he met the lady who was to become his second wife – his one *real* wife, as his friends reckoned – the whole man burst into flower.

The second Mrs. Grancy was past thirty when he married her, and it was clear that she had harvested that crop of middle joy which is rooted in young despair. But if she had lost the surface of eighteen she had kept its inner light; if her cheek lacked the gloss of immaturity her eyes were young with the stored youth of half a lifetime. Grancy had first known her somewhere in the East – I believe she was the sister of one of our consuls out there – and when he brought her home to New York she came among us as a stranger. The idea of Grancy's remarriage had been a shock to us all. After one such calcining most men would have kept out of the fire; but we agreed that he was predestined to sentimental blunders, and we awaited with resignation the embodiment of his latest mistake. Then Mrs. Grancy came – and we understood. She was the most beautiful and the most complete of explanations. We shuffled our defeated omniscience out of sight and gave it hasty burial under a prodigality of welcome. For the first time in years we had Grancy off our minds. 'He'll do something great now!' the least sanguine of us prophesied; and our sentimentalist amended: 'He *has* done it – in marrying her!'

It was Claydon, the portrait painter, who risked this hyperbole; and who soon afterward, at the happy husband's request, prepared to defend it in a portrait of Mrs. Grancy. We were all – even Claydon – ready to concede that Mrs. Grancy's unwontedness was in some degree a matter of environment. Her graces were complementary and it needed the mate's call to reveal the flash of color beneath her neutral-tinted wings. But if she needed Grancy to interpret her, how much greater was the service she rendered him! Claydon professionally described her as the right frame for him; but if she defined she also enlarged, if she threw the whole into perspective she also cleared new ground, opened fresh vistas, reclaimed whole areas of activity that had run to waste under the harsh husbandry of privation. This interaction of sympathies was not without its visible expression. Claydon was not alone in maintaining that Grancy's presence – or indeed the mere mention of his name – had a perceptible effect on his wife's appearance. It was as though a light were shifted, a curtain drawn back, as though, to borrow another of Claydon's metaphors, Love the indefatigable artist were perpetually seeking a happier 'pose' for his model. In this interpretative light Mrs. Grancy acquired the charm which makes some women's faces like a book of which the last page is never turned. There was always something new to read in her eyes. What Claydon read there – or at least such scattered hints of the ritual as reached him through the sanctuary doors – his portrait in due course declared to us. When the picture was exhibited it was at once acclaimed as his masterpiece; but the people who knew Mrs. Grancy smiled and said it was flattered. Claydon, however, had not set out to paint *their* Mrs. Grancy – or ours even – but Ralph's; and Ralph knew his own at a glance. At the first confrontation he saw that Claydon had understood. As for Mrs. Grancy, when the finished picture was shown to her she turned to the painter and said simply: 'Ah, you've done me facing the east!'

The picture, then, for all its value, seemed a mere incident in the unfolding of their double destiny, a footnote to the illuminated text of their lives. It was not till afterward that it acquired the significance of last words spoken on a threshold never to be recrossed. Grancy, a year after his marriage, had given up his town house and carried his bliss an hour's journey away, to a little place among the hills. His various duties and interest brought him frequently to New York but we necessarily saw him less often than when his house had served as the rallying point of kindred enthusiasms. It seemed a pity that such an influence should be withdrawn, but we all felt that his long arrears of happiness should be paid in whatever coin he chose. The distance from which the fortunate couple radiated warmth on us was not too great for friendship to traverse; and our conception of glorified leisure took the form of Sundays spent in the Grancys' library, with its sedative rural outlook, and the portrait of Mrs. Grancy illuminating its studious walls. The picture was at its best in that setting; and we used to accuse Claydon of visiting Mrs. Grancy in order to see her portrait. He met this by declaring that the portrait *was* Mrs. Grancy; and there were moments when the statement seemed unanswerable. One of us, indeed – I think it must have been the novelist – said that Claydon had been saved from falling in love with Mrs. Grancy only by falling in love with his picture of her; and it was noticeable that he, to whom his finished work was no more than the shed husk of future effort, showed a perennial tenderness for this one achievement. We smiled afterward to think how often, when Mrs. Grancy was in the room, her presence reflecting itself in our talk like a gleam of sky in a hurrying current, Claydon, averted from the real woman, would sit as it were listening to the picture. His attitude, at the time, seemed only a part of the unusualness of those picturesque afternoons, when the most familiar combinations of life underwent a magical change. Some human happiness is a landlocked lake; but the Grancys' was an open sea, stretching a buoyant and illimitable surface to the voyaging interests of life. There was room and to spare on those waters for all our separate ventures; and always, beyond the sunset, a mirage of the fortunate isles toward which our prows were bent.

• II •

It was in Rome that, three years later, I heard of her death. The notice said 'suddenly'; I was glad of that. I was glad too – basely perhaps – to be away from Grancy at a time when silence must have seemed obtuse and speech derisive.

I was still in Rome when, a few months afterward, he suddenly arrived there. He had been appointed secretary of legation at Constantinople and was on the way to his post. He had taken the place, he said frankly, 'to get away.' Our relations with the Porte held out a prospect of hard work, and that, he explained, was what he needed. He could never be satisfied to sit down among the ruins. I saw that, like most of us in moments of extreme moral tension, he was playing a part, behaving as he thought it became a man to behave in the eye of disaster. The instinctive posture of grief is a shuffling compromise between defiance and prostration; and pride feels the need of striking a worthier attitude in face of such a foe. Grancy, by nature musing and retrospective, had chosen the role of the man of action, who answers blow for blow and opposes a mailed front to the thrusts of destiny; and the completeness of the equipment testified to his inner weakness. We talked only of what we were not thinking of, and parted, after a few days, with a sense of relief that proved the inadequacy of friendship to perform, in such cases, the office assigned to it by tradition.

Soon afterward my own work called me home, but Grancy remained several years in Europe. International diplomacy kept its promise of giving him work to do, and during the year in which he acted as *chargé d'affaires* he acquitted himself, under trying conditions, with conspicuous zeal and discretion. A political redistribution of matter removed him from office just as he had proved his usefulness to the government; and the following summer I heard that he had come home and was down at his place in the country.

On my return to town I wrote him and his reply came by the next post. He answered as it were in his natural voice, urging me to spend the following Sunday with him, and suggesting that I should bring down any of the old set who could be persuaded to join me. I thought this a good sign, and yet – shall I own it? – I was vaguely disappointed. Perhaps we are apt to feel that our friends' sorrows should be kept like those historic monuments from which the encroaching ivy is periodically removed.

That very evening at the club I ran across Claydon. I told him of Grancy's invitation and proposed that we should go down together; but he pleaded an engagement. I was sorry, for I had always felt that he and I stood nearer Ralph than the others, and if the old Sundays were to be renewed I should have preferred that we two should spend the first alone with him. I said as much to Claydon and offered to fit my time to his; but he met this by a general refusal.

'I don't want to go to Grancy's,' he said bluntly. I waited a moment, but he appended no qualifying clause.

'You've seen him since he came back?' I finally ventured.

Claydon nodded.

'And is he so awfully bad?'

'Bad? No, he's all right.'

'All right? How can he be, unless he's changed beyond all recognition?'

'Oh, you'll recognize *him*,' said Claydon, with a puzzling deflection of emphasis.

His ambiguity was beginning to exasperate me, and I felt myself shut out from some knowledge to which I had as good a right as he.

'You've been down there already, I suppose?'

'Yes; I've been down there.'

'And you've done with each other – the partnership is dissolved?'

'Done with each other? I wish to God we had!' He rose nervously and tossed aside the review from which my approach had diverted him. 'Look here,' he said, standing before me, 'Ralph's the best fellow going and there's nothing under heaven I wouldn't do for him – short of going down there again.' And with that he walked out of the room.

Claydon was incalculable enough for me to read a dozen different meanings into his words; but none of my interpretations satisfied me. I determined, at any rate, to seek no farther for a companion; and the next Sunday I traveled down to Grancy's alone. He met me at the station and I saw at once that he had changed since our last meeting. Then he had been in fighting array, but now if he and grief still housed together it was no longer as enemies. Physically the transformation was as marked but less reassuring. If the spirit triumphed the body showed its scars. At five-and-forty he was gray and stooping, with the tired gate of an old man. His serenity, however, was not the resignation of age. I saw that he did not mean to drop out of the game. Almost immediately he began to speak of our old interests; not with an effort, as at our former meeting, but simply and naturally, in the tone of a man whose life has flowed back into its normal channels. I remembered, with a touch of self-reproach, how I had distrusted his reconstructive powers; but my admiration for his reserved force was now tinged by the sense that, after all, such happiness as his ought to have been paid with his last coin. The feeling grew as we neared the house and I found how inextricably his wife was interwoven with my remembrance of the place: how the whole scene was but an extension of that vivid presence.

Within doors nothing was changed, and my hand would have dropped without surprise into her welcoming clasp. It was luncheon time, and Grancy led me at once to the dining room, where the walls, the furniture, the very plate and porcelain, seemed a mirror in which a moment since her face had been reflected. I wondered whether Grancy, under the recovered tranquillity of his smile, concealed the same sense of her nearness, saw perpetually between himself and the actual her bright unappeasable ghost. He spoke of her once or twice, in an easy incidental way, and her name seemed to hang in the air after he had uttered it, like a chord that continues to vibrate. If he felt her presence it was evidently as an enveloping medium, the moral atmosphere in which he breathed. I had never before known how completely the dead may survive.

After luncheon we went for a long walk through the autumnal fields and woods, and dusk was falling when we re-entered the house. Grancy led the way to the library, where, at this hour, his wife had always welcomed us back to a bright fire and a cup of tea. The room faced the west, and held a clear light of its own after the rest of the house had grown dark. I remembered how young she had looked in this pale gold light, which irradiated her eyes and hair, or silhouetted her girlish outline as she passed before the windows. Of all the rooms the library was most peculiarly hers; and here I felt that her nearness might take visible shape. Then, all in a moment, as Grancy opened the door, the feeling vanished and a kind of resistance met me on the threshold. I looked about me. Was the room changed? Had some desecrating hand effaced the traces of her presence? No; here too the setting was undisturbed. My feet sank into the same deep-piled Daghestan; the bookshelves took the firelight on the same rows of rich subdued bindings; her armchair stood in its old place near the tea table; and from the opposite wall her face confronted me.

Her face – but *was* it hers? I moved nearer and stood looking up at the portrait. Grancy's glance had followed mine and I heard him move to my side.

'You see a change in it?' he said.

'What does it mean?' I asked.

'It means – that five years have passed.'

'Over *her*?'

'Why not? – Look at me!' He pointed to his gray hair and furrowed temples. 'What do you think kept *her* so young? It was happiness! But now – ' he looked up at her with infinite tenderness. 'I like her better so,' he said. 'It's what she would have wished.'

'Have wished?'

'That we should grow old together. Do you think she would have wanted to be left behind?'

I stood speechless, my gaze traveling from his worn grief-beaten features to the painted face above. It was not furrowed like his; but a veil of years seemed to have descended on it. The bright hair had lost its elasticity, the cheek its clearness, the brow its light: the whole woman had waned.

Grancy laid his hand on my arm. 'You don't like it?' he said sadly.

'Like it? I – I've lost her!' I burst out.

'And I've found her,' he answered.

'In *that*?' I cried with a reproachful gesture.

'Yes, in that.' He swung round on me almost defiantly. 'The other had become a sham, a lie! This is the way she would have looked – does look, I mean. Claydon ought to know, oughtn't he?'

I turned suddenly. 'Did Claydon do this for you?'

Grancy nodded.

'Since your return?'

'Yes. I sent for him after I'd been back a week – ' He turned away and gave a thrust to the smoldering fire. I followed, glad to leave the picture behind me. Grancy threw himself into a chair near the hearth, so that the light fell on his sensitive variable face. He leaned his head back, shading his eyes with his hand, and began to speak.

• III •

'YOU fellows knew enough of my early history to guess what my second marriage meant to me. I say guess, because no one could understand – really. I've always had a feminine streak in me, I suppose: the need of a pair of eyes that should see with me, of a pulse that should keep time with mine. Life is a big thing, of course: a magnificent spectacle; but I got so tired of looking at it alone! Still, it's always good to live, and I had plenty of happiness – of the evolved kind. What I'd never had a taste of was the simple inconscient sort that one breathes in like the air.

'Well – I met her. It was like finding the climate in which I was meant to live. You know what she was – how indefinitely she multiplied one's point of contact with life, how she lit up the caverns and bridged the abysses! Well, I swear to you (though I suppose the sense of all that was latent in me) that what I used to think of on my way home at the end of the day, was simply that when I opened this door she'd be sitting over there, with the lamplight falling in a particular way on one little curl in her neck. When Claydon painted her he caught just the look she used to lift to mine when I came in – I've wondered, sometimes, at his knowing how she looked when she and I were alone. How I rejoiced in that picture! I used to say to her, 'You're my prisoner now – I shall never lose you. If you grew tired of me and left me you'd leave your real self there on the wall!' It was always one of our jokes that she was going to grow tired of me.

'Three years of it – and then she died. It was so sudden that there was no change, no diminution. It was as if she had suddenly become fixed, immovable, like her own portrait: as if Time had ceased at its happiest hour, just as Claydon had thrown down his brush one day and said, 'I can't do better than that.'

'I went away, as you know, and stayed over there five years. I worked as hard as I knew how, and after the first black months a little light stole in on me. From thinking that she would have been interested in what I was doing I came to feel that she *was* interested – that she was there and that she knew. I'm not talking any psychical jargon – I'm simply trying to express the sense I had that an influence so full, so abounding as hers couldn't pass like a spring shower. We had so lived into each other's hearts and minds that the consciousness of what she would have thought and felt illuminated all I did. At first she used to come back shyly; tentatively, as though not sure of finding me; then she stayed longer and longer, till at last she became again the very air I breathed. There was bad moments, of course, when her nearness mocked me with the loss of the real woman; but gradually the distinction between the two was effaced and the mere thought of her grew warm as flesh and blood.

'Then I came home. I landed in the morning and came straight down here. The thought of seeing her portrait possessed me and my heart beat like a lover's as I opened the library door. It was in the afternoon and the room was full of light. It fell on her picture – the picture of a young and radiant woman. She smiled at me coldly across the distance that divided us. I had the feeling that she didn't even recognize me. And then I caught sight of myself in the mirror over there – a gray-haired broken man whom she had never known!

'For a week we two lived together – the strange woman and the strange man. I used to sit night after night and question her smiling face; but no answer ever came. What did she know of me, after all? We were irrevocably separated by the five years of life that lay between us. At times, as I sat here, I almost grew to hate her; for her presence had driven away my gentle ghost, the real wife who had wept, aged, struggled with me during those awful years. It was the worst loneliness I've ever known. Then, gradually, I began to notice a look of sadness in the picture's eyes; a look that seemed to say: 'Don't you see that *I* am lonely too?' And all at once it came over me how she would have hated to be left behind! I remembered her comparing life to a heavy book that could not be read with ease unless two people held it together; and I thought how impatiently her hand would have turned the pages that divided us! So the idea came to me: 'It's the picture that stands between us; the picture that is dead, and not my wife. To sit in this room is to keep watch beside a corpse.' As this feeling grew on me the portrait became like a beautiful mausoleum in which she had been buried alive: I could hear her beating against the painted walls and crying to me faintly for help.

'One day I found I couldn't stand it any longer and I sent for Claydon. He came down and I told him what I'd been through and what I wanted him to do. At first he refused point-blank to touch the picture. The next morning I went off for a long tramp, and when I came home I found him sitting here alone. He looked at me sharply for a moment and then he said: "I've changed my mind; I'll do it." I arranged one of the north rooms as a studio and he shut himself up there for a day; then he sent for me. The picture stood there as you see it now – it was as though she'd met me on the threshold and taken me in her arms! I tried to thank him, to tell him what it meant to me, but he cut me short.

"There's an up train at five, isn't there?" he asked. "I'm booked for a dinner tonight. I shall just have time to make a bolt for the station and you can send my traps after me." I haven't seen him since.

'I can guess what it cost him to lay hands on his masterpiece; but, after all, to him it was only a picture lost, to me it was my wife regained!'

• IV •

AFTER that, for ten years or more, I watched the strange spectacle of a life of hopeful and productive effort based on the structure of a dream. There could be no doubt to those who saw Grancy during this period that he drew his strength and courage from the sense of his wife's mystic participation in his task. When I went back to see him a few months later I found the portrait had been removed from the library and placed in a small study upstairs, to which he had transferred his desk and a few books. He told me he always sat there when he was alone, keeping the library for his Sunday visitors. Those who missed the portrait of course made no comment on its absence, and the few who were in his secret respected it. Gradually all his old friends had gathered about him and our Sunday afternoons regained something of their former character; but Claydon never reappeared among us.

As I look back now I see that Grancy must have been failing from the time of his return home. His invincible spirit belied and disguised the signs of weakness that afterward asserted themselves in my remembrance of him. He seemed to have an inexhaustible fund of life to draw on, and more than one of us was a pensioner on his superfluity.

Nevertheless, when I came back one summer from my European holiday and heard that he had been at the point of death, I understood at once that we had believed him well only because he wished us to.

I hastened down to the country and found him midway in a slow convalescence. I felt then that he was lost to us and he read my thought at a glance.

'Ah,' he said, 'I'm an old man now and no mistake. I suppose we shall have to go half-speed after this; but we shan't need towing just yet!'

The plural pronoun struck me, and involuntarily I looked up at Mrs. Grancy's portrait. Line by line I saw my fear reflected in it. It was the face of a woman *who knows that her husband is dying*. My heart stood still at the thought of what Claydon had done.

Grancy had followed my glance. 'Yes, it's changed her,' he said quietly. 'For months, you know, it was touch and go with me – we had a long fight of it, and it was worse for her than for me.' After a pause he added: 'Claydon has been very kind; he's so busy nowadays that I seldom see him, but when I sent for him the other day he came down at once.'

I was silent and we spoke no more of Grancy's illness; but when I took leave it seemed like shutting him in alone with his death warrant.

The next time I went down to see him he looked much better. It was a Sunday and he received me in the library, so that I did not see the portrait again. He continued to improve and toward spring we began to feel that, as he had said, he might yet travel a long way without being towed.

One evening, on returning to town after a visit which had confirmed my sense of reassurance, I found Claydon dining alone at the club. He asked me to join him and over the coffee our talk turned to his work.

'If you're not too busy,' I said at length, 'you ought to make time to go down to Grancy's again.'

He looked up quickly. 'Why?' he asked.

'Because he's quite well again,' I returned with a touch of cruelty. 'His wife's prognostications were mistaken.'

Claydon stared at me a moment. 'Oh, *she* knows,' he affirmed with a smile that chilled me.

'You mean to leave the portrait as it is then?' I persisted.

He shrugged his shoulders. 'He hasn't sent for me yet!'

A waiter came up with the cigars and Claydon rose and joined another group.

It was just a fortnight later that Grancy's housekeeper telegraphed for me. She met me at the station with the news that he had been 'taken bad' and that the doctors were with him. I had to wait for some time in the deserted library before the medical men appeared. They had the baffled manner of empirics who have been superseded by the Great Healer; and I lingered only long enough to hear that Grancy was not suffering and that my presence could do him no harm.

I found him seated in his armchair in the little study. He held out his hand with a smile.

'You see she was right after all,' he said.

'She?' I repeated, perplexed for the moment.

'My wife.' He indicated the picture. 'Of course I knew she had no hope from the first. I saw that' – he lowered his voice – 'after Claydon had been here. But I wouldn't believe it at first!'

I caught his hands in mine. 'For God's sake don't believe it now!' I adjured him.

He shook his head gently. 'It's too late,' he said. 'I might have known that she knew.'

'But, Grancy, listen to me,' I began; and then I stopped. What could I say that would convince him? There was no common ground of argument on which we could meet; and after all it would be easier for him to die feeling that she *had* known. Strangely enough, I saw that Claydon had missed his mark.

• V •

GRANCY'S will named me as one of his executors; and my associate, having other duties on his hands, begged me to assume the task of carrying out our friend's wishes. This placed me under the necessity of informing Claydon that the portrait of Mrs. Grancy had been bequeathed to him; and he replied by the next post that he would send for the picture at once. I was staying in the deserted house when the portrait was taken away; and as the door closed on it I felt that Grancy's presence had vanished too. Was it his turn to follow her now, and could one ghost haunt another?

After that, for a year or two, I heard nothing more of the picture, and though I met Claydon from time to time we had little to say to each other. I had no definable grievance against the man and I tried to remember that he had done a fine thing in sacrificing his best picture to a friend; but my resentment had all the tenacity of unreason.

One day, however, a lady whose portrait he had just finished begged me to go with her to see it. To refuse was impossible, and I went with the less reluctance that I knew I was not the only friend she had invited. The others were all grouped around the easel when I entered, and after contributing my share to the chorus of approval I turned away and began to stroll about the studio. Claydon was something of a collector and his things were generally worth looking at. The studio was a long tapestried room with a curtained archway at one end. The curtains were looped back, showing a smaller apartment, with books and flowers and a few fine bits of bronze and porcelain. The tea table standing in this inner room proclaimed that it was open to inspection, and I wandered in. A *bleu poudré* vase first attracted me; then I turned to examine a slender bronze Ganymede, and in so doing found myself face to face with Mrs. Grancy's portrait. I stared up at her blankly and she smiled back at me in all the recovered radiance of youth. The artist had effaced every trace of his later touches and the original picture had reappeared. It throned alone on the paneled wall, asserting a brilliant supremacy over its carefully chosen surroundings. I felt in an instant that the whole room was tributary to it: that Claydon had heaped his treasures at the feet of the woman he loved. Yes – it was the woman he had loved and not the picture; and my instinctive resentment was explained.

Suddenly I felt a hand on my shoulder.

'Ah, how could you?' I cried, turning on him.

'How could I?' he retorted. 'How could I *not*? Doesn't she belong to me now?'

I moved away impatiently.

'Wait a moment,' he said with a detaining gesture. 'The others have gone and I want to say a word to you. Oh, I know what you've thought of me – I can guess! You think I killed Grancy, I suppose?'

I was startled by his sudden vehemence. 'I think you tried to do a cruel thing,' I said.

'Ah – what a little way you others see into life!' he murmured. 'Sit down a moment – here, where we can look at her – and I'll tell you.'

He threw himself on the ottoman beside me and sat gazing up at the picture, with his hands clasped about his knee.

'Pygmalion,' he began slowly, 'turned his statue into a real woman; *I* turned my real woman into a picture. Small compensation, you think – but you don't know how much of a woman belongs to you after you've painted her! Well, I made the best of it, at any rate – I gave her the best I had in me; and she gave me in return what such a woman gives by merely being. And after all she rewarded me enough by making me paint as I shall never paint again! There was one side of her, though, that was mine alone, and that was her beauty; for no one else understood it. To Grancy even it was the mere expression of herself – what language is to thought. Even when he saw the picture he didn't guess my secret – he was so sure she was all his! As though a man should think he owned the moon because it was reflected in the pool at his door.

'Well – when he came home and sent for me to change the picture it was like asking me to commit murder. He wanted me to make an old woman of her – of her who had been so divinely, unchangeably young! As if any man who really loved a woman would ask her to sacrifice her youth and beauty for his sake! At first I told him I couldn't do it – but afterward, when he left me alone with the picture, something queer happened. I suppose it was because I was always so confoundedly fond of Grancy that it went against me to refuse what he asked. Anyhow, as I sat looking up at her, she seemed to say, 'I'm not yours but his, and I want you to make me what he wishes.' And so I did it. I could have cut my hand off when the work was done – I dare say he told you I never would go back and look at it. He thought I was too busy – he never understood.

'Well – and then last year he sent for me again – you remember. It was after his illness, and he told me he'd grown twenty years older and that he wanted her to grow older too – he didn't want her to be left behind. The doctors all thought he was going to get well at that time, and he thought so too; and so did I when I first looked at him. But when I turned to the picture – ah, now I don't ask you to believe me; but I swear it was *her* face that told me he was dying, and that she wanted him to know it! She had a message for him and she made me deliver it.'

He rose abruptly and walked toward the portrait; then he sat down beside me again.

'Cruel! Yes, it seemed so to me at first; and this time, if I resisted, it was for *his* sake and not for mine. But all the while I felt her eyes drawing me, and gradually she made me understand. If she'd been there in the flesh (she seemed to say) wouldn't she have seen before any of us that he was dying? Wouldn't he have read the news first in her face? And wouldn't it be horrible if now he should discover it instead in strange eyes? – Well – that was what she wanted of me and I did it – I kept them together to the last!' He looked up at the picture again. 'But now she belongs to me,' he repeated. . . .

Expiation

———— ❧ ————

'I CAN NEVER,' said Mrs. Fetherel, 'hear the bell ring without a shudder.'

Her unruffled aspect – she was the kind of woman whose emotions never communicate themselves to her clothes – and the conventional background of the New York drawing room, with its pervading implication of an imminent tea tray and of an atmosphere in which the social functions have become purely reflex, lent to her declaration a relief not lost on her cousin Mrs. Clinch, who, from the other side of the fireplace, agreed, with a glance at the clock, that it *was* the hour for bores.

'Bores!' cried Mrs. Fetherel impatiently, 'If I shuddered at *them*, I should have a chronic ague!'

She leaned forward and laid a sparkling finger on her cousin's shabby black knee. 'I mean the newspaper clippings,' she whispered.

Mrs. Clinch returned a glance of intelligence. 'They've begun already?'

'Not yet; but they're sure to now, at any minute, my publisher tells me.'

Mrs. Fetherel's look of apprehension sat oddly on her small features, which had an air of neat symmetry somehow suggestive of being set in order every morning by the housemaid. Someone (there were rumours that it was her cousin) had once said that Paula Fetherel would have been very pretty if she hadn't looked so like a moral axiom in a copybook hand.

Mrs. Clinch received her confidence with a smile. 'Well,' she said, 'I suppose you were prepared for the consequences of authorship?'

370

Mrs. Fetherel blushed brightly. 'It isn't their coming,' she owned – 'it's their coming *now*.'

'Now?'

'The Bishop's in town.'

Mrs. Clinch leaned back and shaped her lips to a whistle which deflected in a laugh. 'Well!' she said.

'You see!' Mrs. Fetherel triumphed.

'Well – weren't you prepared for the Bishop?'

'Not now – at least, I hadn't thought of his seeing the clippings.'

'And why should he see them?'

'Bella – *won't* you understand? It's John.'

'John?'

'Who has taken the most unexpected tone – one might almost say out of perversity.'

'Oh, perversity – ' Mrs. Clinch murmured, observing her cousin between lids wrinkled by amusement. 'What tone has John taken?'

Mrs. Fetherel threw out her answer with the desperate gesture of a woman who lays bare the traces of a marital fist. 'The tone of being proud of my book.'

The measure of Mrs. Clinch's enjoyment overflowed in laughter.

'Oh, you may laugh,' Mrs. Fetherel insisted, 'but it's no joke to me. In the first place, John's liking the book is so – so – such a false note – it puts me in such a ridiculous position; and then it has set him watching for the reviews – who would ever have suspected John of knowing that books were *reviewed*? Why, he's actually found out about the clipping bureau, and whenever the postman rings I hear John rush out of the library to see if there are any yellow envelopes. Of course, when they *do* come he'll bring them into the drawing room and read them aloud to everybody who happens to be here – and the Bishop is sure to happen to be here!'

Mrs. Clinch repressed her amusement. 'The picture you draw is a lurid one,' she conceded, 'but your modesty strikes me as abnormal, especially in an author. The chances are that some of the clippings will be rather pleasant reading. The critics are not all union men.'

Mrs. Fetherel stared. 'Union men?'

'Well, I mean they don't all belong to the well-known Society-for-the-Persecution-of-Rising-Authors. Some of them have even been known to defy its regulations and say a good word for a new writer.'

'Oh, I dare say,' said Mrs. Fetherel, with the laugh her cousin's epigram exacted. 'But you don't quite see my point. I'm not at all nervous about the success of my book – my publisher tells me I have no need to be – but I *am* afraid of its being a *succès de scandale*.'

'Mercy!' said Mrs. Clinch, sitting up.

The butler and footman at this moment appeared with the tea tray and when they had withdrawn, Mrs. Fetherel, bending her brightly rippled head above the kettle, continued in a murmur of avowal, 'The title, even, is a kind of challenge.'

'*Fast and Loose,*' Mrs. Clinch mused. 'Yes, it ought to take.'

'I didn't choose it for that reason!' the author protested. 'I should have preferred something quieter – less pronounced; but I was determined not to shirk the responsibility of what I had written. I want people to know beforehand exactly what kind of book they are buying.'

'Well,' said Mrs. Clinch, 'that's a degree of conscientiousness that I've never met with before. So few books fulfill the promise of their titles that experienced readers never expect the fare to come up to the menu.'

'*Fast and Loose* will be no disappointment on that score,' her cousin significantly returned. 'I've handled the subject without gloves. I've called a spade a spade.'

'You simply make my mouth water! And to think I haven't been able to read it yet because every spare minute of my time has been given to correcting the proofs of "How the Birds Keep Christmas"! There's an instance of the hardships of an author's life!'

Mrs. Fetherel's eye clouded. 'Don't joke, Bella, please. I suppose to experienced authors there's always something absurd in the nervousness of a new writer, but in my case so much is at stake; I've put so much of myself into this book and I'm so afraid of being misunderstood . . . of being, as it were, in advance of my time . . . like poor Flaubert. . . . I *know* you'll think me ridiculous . . . and if only my own reputation were at stake, I should never give it a thought . . . but the idea of dragging John's name through the mire. . . .'

Mrs. Clinch, who had risen and gathered her cloak about her, stood surveying from her genial height her cousin's agitated countenance.

'Why did you use John's name, then?'

'That's another of my difficulties! I *had* to. There would have been no merit in publishing such a book under an assumed name; it would have been an act of moral cowardice. *Fast and Loose* is not an ordinary novel. A writer who dares to show up the hollowness of social conventions must have the courage of her convictions and be willing to accept the consequences of defying society. Can you imagine Ibsen or Tolstoi writing under a false name?' Mrs. Fetherel lifted a tragic eye to her cousin. 'You don't know, Bella, how often I've envied you since I began to write. I used to wonder sometimes – you won't mind my saying so? – why, with all your cleverness, you hadn't taken up some more exciting subject than natural history; but I see now how wise you were. Whatever happens, you will never be denounced by the press!'

'Is that what you're afraid of?' asked Mrs. Clinch, as she grasped the bulging umbrella which rested against her chair. 'My dear, if I had ever had the good luck to be denounced by the press, my brougham would be waiting at the door for me at this very moment, and I shouldn't have had to ruin this umbrella by using it in the rain. Why, you innocent, if I'd ever felt the slightest aptitude for showing up social conventions, do you suppose I should waste my time writing "Nests Ajar" and "How to Smell the Flowers"? There's a fairly steady demand for pseudo-science and colloquial ornithology, but it's nothing, simply nothing, to the ravenous call for attacks on social institutions – especially by those inside the institutions!'

There was often, to her cousin, a lack of taste in Mrs. Clinch's pleasantries, and on this occasion they seemed more than usually irrelevant.

'*Fast and Loose* was not written with the idea of a large sale.'

Mrs. Clinch was unperturbed. 'Perhaps that's just as well,' she returned, with a philosophic shrug. 'The surprise will be all the pleasanter, I mean. For of course it's going to sell tremendously; especially if you can get the press to denounce it.'

'Bella, how *can* you? I sometimes think you say such things expressly to tease me; and yet I should think you of all women would understand my purpose in writing such a book. It has always seemed to me that the message I had to deliver was not for myself alone, but for all the other women in the world who have felt the hollowness of our social shams, the ignominy of bowing down the idols of the market, but have lacked either the courage or the power to proclaim their independence; and I have fancied, Bella dear, that, however severely society might punish me for revealing its weaknesses, I could count on the sympathy of those who like you' – Mrs. Fetherel voice sank – 'have passed through the deep waters.'

Mrs. Clinch gave herself a kind of canine shake, as though to free her ample shoulders from any drop of the element she was supposed to have traversed.

'Oh, call them muddy rather than deep,' she returned; 'and you'll find, my dear, that women who've had any wading to do are rather shy of stirring up mud. It sticks – especially on white clothes.'

Mrs. Fetherel lifted an undaunted brow. 'I'm not afraid,' she proclaimed; and at the same instant she dropped her teaspoon with a clatter and shrank back into her seat. 'There's the bell,' she exclaimed, 'and I know it's the Bishop!'

It was in fact the Bishop of Ossining, who impressively announced by Mrs. Fetherel's butler, now made an entry that may best be described as not inadequate to the expectations the announcement raised. The Bishop always entered a room well; but, when unannounced, or preceded by a low church butler who gave him his surname, his appearance lacked the impressiveness conferred on it by the due specification of his diocesan dignity. The Bishop was very fond of his niece, Mrs. Fetherel, and one of the traits he most valued in her was the possession of a butler who knew how to announce a bishop.

Mrs. Clinch was also his niece; but, aside from the fact that she possessed no butler at all, she had laid herself open to her uncle's criticism by writing insignificant little books which had a way of going into five or ten editions, while the fruits of his own episcopal leisure – 'The Wail of Jonah' (twenty cantos in blank verse), and 'Through a Glass Brightly'; or, 'How to Raise Funds for a Memorial Window' – inexplicably languished on the back shelves of a publisher noted for his dexterity in pushing 'devotional goods.' Even this indiscretion the Bishop might, however, have condoned, had his niece thought fit to turn to him for support and advice at the painful juncture of her history when, in her own words, it became necessary for her to invite Mr. Clinch to look out for another situation. Mr. Clinch's misconduct was of the kind especially designed by Providence to test the fortitude of a Christian wife and mother, and the Bishop was absolutely distended with seasonable advice and edification; so that when Bella met his tentative exhortations with the curt remark that she preferred to do her own house cleaning unassisted, her uncle's grief at her ingratitude was not untempered with sympathy for Mr. Clinch.

It is not surprising, therefore, that the Bishop's warmest greetings were always reserved for Mrs. Fetherel; and on this occasion Mrs. Clinch thought she detected, in the salutation which fell to her share, a pronounced suggestion that her own presence was superfluous – a hint which she took with her usual imperturbable good humor.

• II •

LEFT alone with the Bishop, Mrs. Fetherel sought the nearest refuge from conversation by offering him a cup of tea. The Bishop accepted with the preoccupied air of a man to whom, for the moment, tea is but a subordinate incident. Mrs. Fetherel's nervousness increased; and knowing that the surest way of distracting attention from one's own affairs is to affect an interest in those of one's companion, she hastily asked if her uncle had come to town on business.

'On business – yes – ' said the Bishop in an impressive tone. 'I had to see my publisher, who has been behaving rather unsatisfactorily in regard to my last book.'

'Ah – your last book?' faltered Mrs. Fetherel, with a sickening sense of her inability to recall the name or nature of the work in question, and a mental vow never again to be caught in such ignorance of a colleague's productions.

' "Through a Glass Brightly," ' the Bishop explained, with an emphasis which revealed his detection of her predicament. 'You may remember that I sent you a copy last Christmas?'

'Of course I do!' Mrs. Fetherel brightened. 'It was that delightful story of the poor consumptive girl who had no money, and two little brothers to support – '

'Sisters – idiot sisters – ' the Bishop gloomily corrected.

'I mean sisters; and who managed to collect money enough to put up a beautiful memorial window to her – her grandfather, whom she had never seen – '

'But whose sermons had been her chief consolation and support during her long struggle with poverty and disease.' The Bishop gave the satisfied sigh of the workman who reviews his completed task. 'A touching subject, surely; and I believe I did it justice; at least so my friends assured me.'

'Why, yes – I remember there was a splendid review of it in the *Reredos*!' cried Mrs. Fetherel, moved by the incipient instinct of reciprocity.

'Yes – by my dear friend Mrs. Gollinger, whose husband, the late Dean Gollinger, was under very particular obligations to me. Mrs. Gollinger is a woman of rare literary acumen, and her praise of my book was unqualified; but the public wants more highly seasoned fare, and the approval of a thoughtful churchwoman carries less weight than the sensational comments of an illiterate journalist.' The Bishop bent a meditative eye on his spotless gaiters. 'At the risk of horrifying you, my dear,' he added, with a slight laugh, 'I will confide to you that my best chance of a popular success would be to have my book denounced by the press.'

Denounced?' gasped Mrs. Fetherel. 'On what ground?'

'On the ground of immorality.' The Bishop evaded her startled gaze, 'Such a thing is inconceivable to you, of course; but I am only repeating what my publisher tells me. If, for instance, a critic could be induced – I mean, if a critic were to be found, who called in question the morality of my heroine in sacrificing her own health and that of her idiot sisters in order to put up a memorial window to her grandfather, it would probably raise a general controversy in the newspapers, and I might count on a sale of ten or fifteen thousand within the next year. If he described her as morbid or decadent, it might even run to twenty thousand; but that is more than I permit myself to hope. In fact I should be satisfied with any general charge of immorality.' The Bishop sighed again. 'I need hardly tell you that I am actuated by no mere literary ambition. Those whose opinion I most value have assured me that the book is not without merit; but, though it does not become me to dispute their verdict, I can truly say that my vanity as an author is not at stake. I have, however, a special reason for wishing to increase the circulation of "Through a Glass Brightly"; it was written for a purpose – a purpose I have greatly at heart – '

'I know,' cried his niece sympathetically. 'The chantry window – ?'

'Is still empty, alas! and I had great hopes that, under Providence my little book might be the means of filling it. All our wealthy parishioners have given lavishly to the cathedral, and it was for this reason that in writing "Through a Glass," I addressed my appeal more especially to the less well-endowed, hoping by the example of my heroine to stimulate the collection of small sums throughout the entire diocese, and perhaps beyond it. I am sure,' the Bishop feelingly concluded, 'the book would have a widespread influence if people could only be induced to read it!'

His conclusion touched a fresh threat of association in Mrs. Fetherel's vibrating nerve centers. 'I never thought of that!' she cried.

The Bishop looked at her inquiringly.

'That one's books may not be read at all! How dreadful!' she exclaimed.

He smiled faintly. 'I had not forgotten that I was addressing an authoress,' he said. 'Indeed, I should not have dared to inflict my troubles on anyone not of the craft.'

Mrs. Fetherel was quivering with the consciousness of her involuntary self-betrayal. 'Oh, Uncle!' she murmured.

'In fact,' the Bishop continued, with a gesture which seemed to brush away her scruples, 'I came here partly to speak to you about your novel. "Fast and Loose," I think you call it?'

Mrs. Fetherel blushed assentingly.

'And is it out yet?' the Bishop continued.

'It came out about a week ago. But you haven't touched your tea and it must be quite cold. Let me give you another cup.'

'My reason for asking,' the Bishop went on, with the bland inexorableness with which, in his younger days, he had been known to continue a sermon after the senior warden had looked four times at his watch, '– my reason for asking it, that I hoped I might not be too late to induce you to change the title.'

Mrs. Fetherel set down the cup she had filled. 'The title?' she faltered.

The Bishop raised a reassuring hand. 'Don't misunderstand me, dear child; don't for a moment imagine that I take it to be in any way indicative of the contents of the book. I know you too well for that. My first idea was that it had probably been forced on you by an unscrupulous publisher. I know too well to what ignoble compromises one may be driven in such cases!' He paused, as though to give her the opportunity of confirming this conjecture, but she preserved an apprehensive silence, and he went on, as though taking up the second point in his sermon: 'Or, again, the name may have taken your fancy without your realizing all that implies to minds more alive than yours to offensive innuendoes. It is – ahem – excessively suggestive, and I hope I am not too late to warn you of the false impression it is likely to produce on the very readers whose approbation you would most value. My friend Mrs. Gollinger, for instance – '

Mrs. Fetherel, as the publication of her novel testified, was in theory a woman of independent views; and if in practice she sometimes failed to live up to her standard, it was rather from an irresistible tendency to adapt herself to her environment than from any conscious lack of moral courage. The Bishop's exordium had excited in her that sense of opposition which such admonitions are apt to provoke; but as he went on she felt herself gradually enclosed in an atmosphere in which her theories vainly gasped for breath. The Bishop had the immense dialectical advantage of invalidating any conclusions at variance with his own by always assuming that his premises were among the necessary laws of thought. This method, combined with the habit of ignoring any classifications but his own, created an element in which the first condition of existence was the immediate adoption of his standpoint; so that his niece, as she listened, seemed to feel Mrs. Gollinger's Mechlin cap spreading its conventual shadow over her rebellious brow and the *Revue de Paris* at her elbow turning into a copy of the *Reredos*. She had meant to assure her uncle that she was quite aware of the significance of the title she had chosen, that it had been deliberately selected as indicating the subject of her novel, and that the book itself had been written in direct defiance of the class of readers for whose susceptibilities he was alarmed. The words were almost on her lips when the irresistible suggestion conveyed by the Bishop's tone and language deflected them into the apologetic murmur, 'Oh, Uncle, you mustn't think – I never meant – ' How much farther this current of reaction might have carried her the historian is unable to compute, for at this point the door opened and her husband entered the room.

'The first review of your book!' he cried, flourishing a yellow envelope. 'My dear Bishop, how lucky you're here!'

Though the trials of married life have been classified and catalogued with exhaustive accuracy, there is one form of conjugal misery which had perhaps received inadequate attention; and that is the suffering of the versatile woman whose husband is not equally adapted to all her moods. Every woman feels for the sister who is compelled to wear a bonnet which does not 'go' with her gown; but how much sympathy is given to her whose husband refuses to harmonize with the pose of the moment? Scant justice has, for instance, been done to the misunderstood wife whose husband persists in understanding her; to the submissive helpmate whose taskmaster shuns every opportunity of browbeating her, and to the generous and impulsive being whose bills are paid with philosophic calm. Mrs. Fetherel, as wives go, had been fairly exempt from trials of this nature, for her husband, if undistinguished by pronounced brutality or indifference, had at least the negative merit of being her intellectual inferior. Landscape gardeners, who are aware of the usefulness of a valley in emphasizing the height of a hill, can form an idea of the account to which an accomplished woman may turn such deficiencies; and it need scarcely be said that Mrs. Fetherel had made the most of her opportunities. It was agreeably obvious to everyone, Fetherel included, that he was not the man to appreciate such a woman; but there are no limits to man's perversity, and he did his best to invalidate this advantage by admiring her without pretending to understand her. What she most suffered from was this fatuous approval: the maddening sense that, however she conducted herself, he would always admire her. Had he belonged to the class whose conversational supplies are drawn from the domestic circle, his wife's name would never have been off his lips; and to Mrs. Fetherel's sensitive perceptions his frequent silences were indicative of the fact that she was his one topic.

It was, in part, the attempt to escape this persistent approbation that had driven Mrs. Fetherel to authorship. She had fancied

that even the most infatuated husband might be counted on
to resent, at least negatively, an attack on the sanctity of the
hearth; and her anticipations were heightened by a sense of the
unpardonableness of her act. Mrs. Fetherel's relations with her
husband were in fact complicated by an irrepressible tendency
to be fond of him; and there was a certain pleasure in the
prospect of a situation that justified the most explicit expiation.

These hopes Fetherel's attitude had already defeated. He
read the book with enthusiasm, he pressed it on his friends,
he sent a copy to his mother; and his very soul now hung
on the verdict of the reviewers. It was perhaps this proof of
his general inaptitude that made his wife doubly alive to his
special defects; so that his inopportune entrance was aggravated
by the very sound of his voice and the hopeless aberration of
his smile. Nothing, to the observant, is more indicative of a
man's character and circumstances than his way of entering a
room. The Bishop of Ossining, for instance, brought with him
not only an atmosphere of episcopal authority, but an implied
opinion on the verbal inspiration of the Scriptures and on the
attitude of the Church toward divorce; while the appearance
of Mrs. Fetherel's husband produced an immediate impression
of domestic felicity. His mere aspect implied that there was a
well-filled nursery upstairs; that his wife, if she did not sew
on his buttons, at least superintended the performance of that
task; that they both went to church regularly, and that they
dined with his mother every Sunday evening punctually at
seven o'clock.

All this and more was expressed in the affectionate gesture
with which he now raised the yellow envelope above Mrs.
Fetherel's clutch; and knowing the uselessness of begging him
not to be silly, she said, with a dry despair, 'You're boring the
Bishop horribly.'

Fetherel turned a radiant eye on that dignitary. 'She bores us
all horribly, doesn't she, sir?' he exulted.

'Have you read it?' said his wife uncontrollably.

'Read it? Of course not – it's just this minute come. I say,
Bishop, you're not going – ?'

'Not till I've heard this,' said the Bishop, settling himself in
his chair with an indulgent smile.

His niece glanced at him despairingly 'Don't let John's nonsense detain you,' she entreated.

'Detain him? That's good,' guffawed Fetherel. 'It isn't as long as one of his sermons – won't take me five minutes to read. Here, listen to this, ladies and gentlemen: "In this age of festering pessimism and decadent depravity, it is no surprise to the nauseated reviewer to open one more volume saturated with the fetid emanations of the sewer – " '

Fetherel, who was not in the habit of reading aloud, paused with a gasp, and the Bishop glanced sharply at his niece, who kept her gaze fixed on the teacup she had not yet succeeded in transferring to his hand.

' "Of the sewer," ' her husband resumed; ' "but his wonder is proportionately great when he lights on a novel as sweetly inoffensive as Paula Fetherel's *Fast and Loose*. Mrs. Fetherel is, we believe, a new hand at fiction, and her work reveals frequent traces of inexperience; but these are more than atoned for by her pure fresh view of life and her altogether unfashionable regard for the reader's moral susceptibilities. Let no one be induced by its distinctly misleading title to forego the enjoyment of this pleasant picture of domestic life, which, in spite of a total lack of force in character drawing and of consecutiveness in incident, may be described as a distinctly pretty story." '

• III •

IT was several weeks later that Mrs. Clinch once more brought the plebeian aroma of heated tramcars and muddy street crossings into the violet-scented atmosphere of her cousin's drawing room.

'Well,' she said, tossing a damp bundle of proofs into the corner of a silk-cushioned bergère, 'I've read it at last and I'm not so awfully shocked!'

Mrs. Fetherel, who sat near the fire with her head propped on a languid hand, looked up without speaking.

'Mercy, Paula,' said her visitor, 'you're ill.'

Mrs. Fetherel shook her head. 'I was never better,' she said, mournfully.

'Then may I help myself to tea? Thanks.'

Mrs. Clinch carefully removed her mended glove before taking a buttered tea cake; then she glanced again at her cousin.

'It's not what I said just now – ?' she ventured.

'Just now?'

'About *Fast and Loose*? I came to talk it over.'

Mrs. Fetherel sprang to her feet. 'I never,' she cried dramatically, 'want to hear it mentioned again!'

'Paula!' exclaimed Mrs. Clinch, setting down her cup.

Mrs. Fetherel slowly turned on her an eye brimming with the incommunicable; then, dropping into her seat again, she added, with a tragic laugh: 'There's nothing left to say.'

'Nothing – ?' faltered Mrs. Clinch, longing for another tea cake, but feeling the inappropriateness of the impulse in an atmosphere so charged with the portentous. 'Do you mean that everything *has* been said?' She looked tentatively at her cousin. 'Haven't they been nice?'

'They've been odious – odious – ' Mrs. Fetherel burst out, with an ineffectual clutch at her handkerchief. 'It's been perfectly intolerable!'

Mrs. Clinch, philosophically resigning herself to the propriety of taking no more tea, crossed over to her cousin and laid a sympathizing hand on that lady's agitated shoulder.

'It *is* a bore at first,' she conceded; 'but you'll be surprised to see how soon one gets used to it.'

'I shall – never – get – used to it – ' Mrs. Fetherel brokenly declared.

'Have they been so very nasty – all of them?'

'Every one of them!' the novelist sobbed.

'I'm so sorry, dear; it *does* hurt, I know – but hadn't you rather expected it?'

'Expected it?' cried Mrs. Fetherel, sitting up.

Mrs. Clinch felt her way warily. 'I only mean, dear, that I fancied from what you said before the book came out that you rather expected – that you'd rather discounted – '

'Their recommending it to everybody as a perfectly harmless story?'

'Good gracious! Is *that* what they've done?'

Mrs. Fetherel speechlessly nodded.

'Every one of them?'

'Every one.'

'Phew!' said Mrs. Clinch, with an incipient whistle.

'Why, you've just said it yourself!' her cousin suddenly reproached her.

'Said what?'

'That you weren't so *awfully* shocked – '

'I? Oh, well – you see, you'd keyed me up to such a pitch that it wasn't quite as bad as I expected – '

Mrs. Fetherel lifted a smile steeled for the worst. 'Why not say at once,' she suggested, 'that it's a distinctly pretty story?'

'They haven't said *that*?'

'They've all said it.'

'My poor Paula!'

'Even the Bishop – '

'The Bishop called it a pretty story?'

'He wrote me – I've his letter somewhere. The title rather scared him – he wanted me to change it; but when he'd read the book he wrote that it was all right and that he'd sent several copies to his friends.'

'The old hypocrite!' cried Mrs. Clinch. 'That was nothing but professional jealousy.'

'Do you think so?' cried her cousin, brightening.

'Sure of it, my dear. His own books don't sell, and he knew the quickest way to kill yours was to distribute it through the diocese with his blessing.'

'Then you don't really think it's a pretty story?'

'Dear me, no! Not nearly as bad as that – '

'You're so good, Bella – but the reviewers?'

'Oh, the reviewers,' Mrs. Clinch jeered. She gazed meditatively at the cold remains of her tea cake. 'Let me see,' she said suddenly; 'do you happen to remember if the first review came out in an important paper?'

'Yes – the *Radiator*.'

'That's it! I thought so. Then the others simply followed suit: they often do if a big paper sets the pace. Saves a lot of trouble. Now if you could only have got the *Radiator* to denounce you – '

'That's what the Bishop said!' cried Mrs. Fetherel.

'He did?'

'He said his only chance of selling "Through a Glass Brightly" was to have it denounced on the ground of immorality.'

'H'm,' said Mrs. Clinch, 'I thought he knew a trick or two.' She turned an illuminated eye on her cousin. 'You ought to get *him* to denounce *Fast and Loose!*' she cried.

Mrs. Fetherel looked at her suspiciously. 'I suppose every book must stand or fall on its own merits,' she said in an unconvinced tone.

'Bosh! That view is as extinct as the post chaise and the packet ship – it belongs to the time when people read books. Nobody does that now; the reviewer was the first to set the example, and the public was only too thankful to follow it. At first people read the reviews; now they read only the publishers' extracts from them. Even these are rapidly being replaced by paragraphs borrowed from the vocabulary of commerce. I often have to look twice before I am sure if I am reading a department store advertisement or the announcement of a new batch of literature. The publishers will soon be having their "fall and spring openings" and their "special importations for Horse Show Week." But the Bishop is right, of course – nothing helps a book like a rousing attack on its morals; and as the publishers can't exactly proclaim the impropriety of their own wares, the task has to be left to the press or the pulpit.'

'The pulpit?' Mrs. Fetherel mused.

'Why, yes. Look at those two novels in England last year.'

Mrs. Fetherel shook her head hopelessly. 'There is so much more interest in literature in England than here.'

'Well, we've got to make the supply create the demand. The Bishop could run your novel up into the hundred thousands in no time.'

'But if he can't make his own sell – '

'My dear, a man can't very well preach against his own writings!'

Mrs. Clinch rose and picked up her proofs.

'I'm awfully sorry for you, Paula dear,' she concluded, 'but I can't help being thankful that there's no demand for pessimism in the field of natural history. Fancy having to write "The Fall of a Sparrow," or "How the Plants Misbehave"!'

• IV •

MRS. FETHEREL, driving up to the Grand Central Station one morning about five months later, caught sight of the distinguished novelist, Archer Hynes, hurrying into the waiting room ahead of her. Hynes, on his side, recognising her brougham, turned back to greet her as the footman opened the carriage door.

'My dear colleague! Is it possible that we are traveling together?'

Mrs. Fetherel blushed with pleasure. Hynes had given her two columns of praise in the *Sunday Meteor*, and she had not yet learned to disguise her gratitude.

'I am going to Ossining,' she said smilingly.

'So am I. Why, this is almost as good as an elopement.'

'And it will end where elopements ought to – in church.'

'In church? You're not going to Ossining to go to church?'

'Why not? There's a special ceremony in the cathedral – the chantry window is to be unveiled.'

'The chantry window? How picturesque! What *is* a chantry? And why do you want to see it unveiled? Are you after copy – doing something in the Huysmans manner? "La Cathédrale," eh?'

'Oh, no,' Mrs. Fetherel hesitated. 'I'm going simply to please my uncle,' she said at last.

'Your uncle?'

'The Bishop, you know.' She smiled.

'The Bishop – the Bishop of Ossining? Why, wasn't he the chap who made the ridiculous attack on your book? Is that prehistoric ass your uncle? Upon my soul, I think you're mighty forgiving to travel all the way to Ossining for one of his stained-glass sociables!'

Mrs. Fetherel's smiles flowed into a gentle laugh. 'Oh, I've never allowed that to interfere with our friendship. My uncle felt dreadfully about having to speak publicly against my book – it was a great deal harder for him than for me – but he thought it his duty to do so. He has the very highest sense of duty.'

'Well,' said Hynes, with a shrug, 'I don't know that he didn't do you a good turn. Look at that!'

They were standing near the bookstall and he pointed to a placard surmounting the counter and emblazoned with the conspicuous announcement: '*Fast and Loose*. New Edition with Author's Portrait. Hundred and Fiftieth Thousand.'

Mrs. Fetherel frowned impatiently. 'How absurd! They've no right to use my picture as a poster!'

'There's our train,' said Hynes; and they began to push their way through the crowd surging toward one of the inner doors.

As they stood wedged between circumferent shoulders, Mrs. Fetherel became conscious of the fixed stare of a pretty girl who whispered eagerly to her companion: 'Look, Myrtle! That's Paula Fetherel right behind us – I knew her in a minute!'

'Gracious – where?' cried the other girl, giving her head a twist which swept her Gainsborough plumes across Mrs. Fetherel's face.

The first speaker's words had carried beyond her companion's ear, and a lemon-colored woman in spectacles, who clutched a copy of the 'Journal of Psychology' in one drab cotton-gloved hand, stretched her disengaged hand across the intervening barrier of humanity.

'Have I the privilege of addressing the distinguished author of *Fast and Loose*? If so, let me thank you in the name of the Woman's Psychological League of Peoria for your magnificent courage in raising the standard of revolt against – '

'You can tell us the rest in the car,' said a fat man, pressing his good-humored bulk against the speaker's arm.

Mrs. Fetherel, blushing, embarrassed and happy, slipped into the space produced by this displacement, and a few moments later had taken her seat in the train.

She was a little late, and the other chairs were already filled by a company of elderly ladies and clergymen who seemed to belong to the same party, and were still busy exchanging greetings and settling themselves in their places.

One of the ladies, at Mrs. Fetherel's approach, uttered an exclamation of pleasure and advanced with outstretched hand. 'My dear Mrs. Fetherel! I am so delighted to see you here. May I hope you are going to the unveiling of the chantry window? The dear Bishop so hoped that you would do so! But perhaps I ought to introduce myself. I am Mrs. Gollinger' – she lowered her voice expressively – 'one of your uncle's oldest friends, one who has stood close to him through all this sad business, and who knows what he suffered when he felt obliged to sacrifice family affection to the call of duty.'

Mrs. Fetherel, who had smiled and colored slightly at the beginning of this speech, received its close with a depreciating gesture.

'Oh, pray don't mention it,' she murmured. 'I quite understood how my uncle was placed – I bore him no ill will for feeling obliged to preach against my book.'

'He understood that, and was so touched by it! He has often told me that it was the hardest task he was ever called upon to perform – and, do you know, he quite feels that this unexpected gift of the chantry window is in some way a return for his courage in preaching that sermon.'

Mrs. Fetherel smiled faintly. 'Does he feel that?'

'Yes; he really does. When the funds for the window were so mysteriously placed at his disposal, just as he had begun to despair of raising them, he assured me that he could not help connecting the fact with his denunciation of your book.'

'Dear Uncle!' sighed Mrs. Fetherel. 'Did he say that?'

'And now,' continued Mrs. Gollinger, with cumulative rapture – 'now that you are about to show, by appearing at the ceremony today, that there had been no break in your friendly relations, the dear Bishop's happiness will be complete. He was so longing to have you come to the unveiling!'

'He might have counted on me,' said Mrs. Fetherel, still smiling.

'Ah, that is so beautifully forgiving of you!' cried Mrs. Gollinger enthusiastically. 'But then, the Bishop has always assured me that your real nature was very different from that which – if you will pardon my saying so – seems to be revealed by your brilliant but – er – rather subversive book. "If you only knew my niece, dear Mrs. Gollinger," he always said, "you would see that her novel was written in all innocence of heart"; and to tell you the truth, when I first read the book I didn't think it so very, very, shocking. It wasn't till the dear Bishop had explained to me – but, dear me, I mustn't take up your time in this way when so many others are anxious to have a word with you.'

Mrs. Fetherel glanced at her in surprise, and Mrs. Gollinger continued with a playful smile: 'You forget that your face is familiar to thousands whom you have never seen. We all recognized you the moment you entered the train, and my friends here are so eager to make your acquaintance – even those' – her smile deepened – 'who thought the dear Bishop not *quite unjustified* in his attack on your remarkable novel.'

• V •

A RELIGIOUS light filled the chantry of Ossining Cathedral, filtering through the linen curtain which veiled the central window and mingling with the blaze of tapers on the richly adorned altar.

In this devout atmosphere, agreeably laden with the incense-like aroma of Easter lilies and forced lilacs, Mrs. Fetherel knelt with a sense of luxurious satisfaction. Beside her sat Archer Hynes, who had remembered that there was to be a church scene in his next novel and that his impressions of the devotional environment needed refreshing. Mrs. Fetherel was very happy. She was conscious that her entrance had sent a thrill through the female devotees who packed the chantry, and she had humor enough to enjoy the thought that, but for the good Bishop's denunciation of her book, the heads of his flock would not have been turned so eagerly in her direction. Moreover, as she entered she had caught sight of a society reporter, and she knew that her presence, and the fact that she was accompanied by Hynes, would be conspicuously proclaimed in the morning papers. All these evidences of the success of her handiwork might have turned a calmer head than Mrs. Fetherel's; and though she had now learned to dissemble her gratification, it still filled her inwardly with a delightful glow.

The Bishop was somewhat late in appearing, and she employed the interval in meditating on the plot of her next novel, which was already partly sketched out, but for which she had been unable to find a satisfactory dénouement. By a not uncommon process of ratiocination, Mrs. Fetherel's success had convinced her of her vocation. She was sure now that it was her duty to lay bare the secret plague spots of society, and she was resolved that there should be no doubt as to the purpose of her new book. Experience had shown her that where she had fancied she was calling a spade a spade she had in fact been alluding in guarded terms to the drawing-room shovel. She was determined not to repeat the same mistake, and she flattered herself that her coming novel would not need an episcopal denunciation to insure its sale, however likely it was to receive this crowning evidence of success.

She had reached this point in her meditations when the choir burst into song and the ceremony of the unveiling began. The Bishop, almost always felicitous in his addresses to the fair sex, was never more so than when he was celebrating the triumph of one of his cherished purposes. There was a peculiar mixture of Christian humility and episcopal exultation in the manner with which he called attention to the Creator's promptness in responding to his demand for funds, and he had never been more happily inspired than in eulogizing the mysterious gift of the chantry window.

Though no hint of the donor's identity had been allowed to escape him, it was generally understood that the Bishop knew who had given the window, and the congregation awaited in a flutter of suspense the possible announcement of a name. None came, however, though the Bishop deliciously titillated the curiosity of his flock by circling ever closer about the interesting secret. He would not disguise from them, he said, that the heart which had divined his inmost wish had been a woman's – is it not to woman's institutions that more than half the happiness of earth is owing? What man is obliged to learn by the laborious process of experience, woman's wondrous instinct tells her at a glance; and so it had been with this cherished scheme, this unhoped-for completion of their beautiful chantry. So much, at least, he was allowed to reveal; and indeed, had he not done so, the window itself would have spoken for him, since the first glance at its touching subject and exquisite design would show it to have originated in a woman's heart. This tribute to the sex was received with an audible sigh of contentment, and the Bishop, always stimulated by such evidence of his sway over his hearers, took up his theme with gathering eloquence.

Yes – a woman's heart had planned the gift, a woman's hand had executed it, and, might he add, without too far withdrawing the veil in which Christian beneficence ever loved to drape its acts – might he add that, under Providence, a book, a simple book, a mere tale, in fact, had had its share in the good work for which they were assembled to give thanks?

At this unexpected announcement, a ripple of excitement ran through the assemblage, and more than one head was abruptly turned in the direction of Mrs. Fetherel, who sat listening in an agony of wonder and confusion. It did not escape the observant novelist at her side that she drew down her veil to conceal an uncontrollable blush, and this evidence of dismay caused him to fix an attentive gaze on her, while from her seat across the aisle Mrs. Gollinger sent a smile of unctuous approval.

'A book – a simple book – ' the Bishop's voice went on above this flutter of mingled emotions. 'What is a book? Only a few pages and a little ink – and yet one of the mightiest instruments which Providence has devised for shaping the destinies of man . . . one of the most powerful influences for good or evil which the Creator has placed in the hands of his creatures. . . .'

The air seemed intolerably close to Mrs. Fetherel, and she drew out her scent bottle, and then thrust it hurriedly away, conscious that she was still the center of an unenviable attention. And all the while the Bishop's voice droned on. . . .

'And of all forms of literature, fiction is doubtless that which has exercised the greatest sway, for good or ill, over the passions and imagination of the masses. Yes, my friends, I am the first to acknowledge it – no sermon, however eloquent, no theological treatise, however learned and convincing, has ever inflamed the heart and imagination like a novel – a simple novel. Incalculable is the power exercised over humanity by the great magicians of the pen – a power ever enlarging its boundaries and increasing its responsibilities as popular education multiplies the number of readers. . . . Yes, it is the novelist's hand which can pour balm on countless human sufferings, or inoculate mankind with the festering poison of a corrupt imagination. . . .'

Mrs. Fetherel had turned white, and her eyes were fixed with a blind stare of anger on the large-sleeved figure in the center of the chancel.

'And too often alas, it is the poison and not the balm which the unscrupulous hand of genius proffers to its unsuspecting readers. But, my friends, why should I continue? None know better than an assemblage of Christian women, such as I am now addressing, the beneficent or baleful influences of modern fiction; and so, when I say that this beautiful chantry window of ours owes its existence in part to the romancer's pen' – the

Bishop paused, and bending forward, seemed to seek a certain face among the countenances eagerly addressed to his – 'when I say that this pen, which for personal reasons it does not become me to celebrate unduly – '

Mrs. Fetherel at this point half rose, pushing back her chair, which scraped loudly over the marble floor; but Hynes involuntarily laid a warning hand on her arm, and she sank down with a confused murmur about the heat.

'When I confess that this pen, which for once at least has proved itself so much mightier than the sword, is that which was inspired to trace the simple narrative of "Through a Glass Brightly" ' – Mrs. Fetherel looked up with a gasp of mingled relief and anger – 'when I tell you, my dear friends, that it was your Bishop's own work which first roused the mind of one of his flock to the crying need of a chantry window, I think you will admit that I am justified in celebrating the triumphs of the pen, even though it be the modest instrument which your own Bishop wields.'

The Bishop paused impressively, and a faint gasp of surprise and disappointment was audible throughout the chantry. Something very different from this conclusion had been expected, and even Mrs. Gollinger's lips curled with a slightly ironic smile. But Archer Hynes's attention was chiefly reserved for Mrs. Fetherel, whose face had changed with astonishing rapidity from surprise to annoyance, from annoyance to relief, and then back again to something very like indignation.

The address concluded, the actual ceremony of the unveiling was about to take place, and the attention of the congregation soon reverted to the chancel, where the choir had grouped themselves beneath the veiled window, prepared to burst into a chant of praise as the Bishop drew back the hanging. The moment was an impressive one, and every eye was fixed on the curtain. Even Hynes's gaze strayed to it for a moment, but soon returned to his neighbor's face; and then he perceived that Mrs. Fetherel, alone of all the persons present, was not looking at the window. Her eyes were fixed in an indignant stare on the Bishop; a flush of anger burned becomingly under her veil, and her hands nervously crumpled the beautifully printed program of the ceremony.

Hynes broke into a smile of comprehension. He glanced at the Bishop, and back at the Bishop's niece; then, as the episcopal hand was solemnly raised to draw back the curtain, he bent and whispered in Mrs. Fetherel's ear:

'Why, you gave it yourself! You wonderful woman, of course you gave it yourself!'

Mrs. Fetherel raised her eyes to his with a start. Her blush deepened and her lips shaped a hasty 'No'; but the denial was deflected into the indignant murmur – 'It wasn't *his* silly book that did it, anyhow!'

Les Metteurs en scène

------⌖------

IT WAS tea time at the Hotel Nouveau-Luxe.

For several moments now Jean Le Fanois had been standing in the doorway of one of the small Louis XV drawing rooms that opened onto the spacious lounge. Of medium height, lean and well-built in his impeccably tailored frock coat, he had the knowing and slightly impertinent air of the aristocratic Parisian too long caught up in the exotic, noisy world of first-class hotels and fashionable cabarets. From time to time, however, his pale, finely chiseled face was clouded by an anxious expression, which the carefree smile he bestowed on passing acquaintances did little to hide.

Several times he glanced impatiently at his watch; then his expression cleared, and he advanced rapidly to meet a young woman who had just appeared on the threshold of the lounge. Exquisite and slender in a street dress of understated elegance, she balanced on a long, slim neck the head of an ephebe. Her exceedingly pale pink lips and large limpid eyes complemented an intelligent forehead crowned with a soft haze of indecisively blond hair. Glancing about for the young man, she made her way across the room alone, with the confident air, the serenely audacious carriage, of the young American used to making her own way in life. A closer scrutiny, however, revealed that the slightly naïve air of independence characteristic of her compatriots was tempered in her by a nuance of Parisian refinement – as if a florid complexion had been softened by a film of tulle. Contact with another civilization had affected her in a totally different way than it had Le Fanois; she had gained, in this cosmopolitan exchange, as much as he seemed to have lost.

393

The young man approached her with a brotherly gesture of familiarity. 'You're alone! Did your friends leave you in the lurch?' he asked her, shaking her hand.

Miss Lambart smiled reassuringly as she scanned the room. 'No, I don't think so. I was supposed to find Mrs. Smithers and her daughter in one of the drawing rooms over there.' She pointed with her tortoise-shell lorgnette toward the series of rooms just off the lounge. 'If we look for them . . .,' she continued, but Le Fanois held her back.

'No, wait a moment,' he said, lowering his voice and propelling the young woman to one of the large glassed-in bays overlooking the hotel garden. 'Tell me what you told them about me and just what role I'm supposed to play.' He hesitated; then, with a vaguely ironic smile, 'In brief, what stage of social ambition have your friends reached?'

Miss Lambart smiled too. 'They still seem quite naïve to me,' she said; 'but one always has to be on one's guard. The most naïve are sometimes the most distrustful.' She threw him a teasing glance. 'Do you remember that pretty widow in Trouville – you know, from last year? If you'd been willing to present her to the Duchess of Sestre, what a marvelous trick you would have played!'

The young man shrugged slightly. 'She was simply asking too much,' he returned. 'And then – and then was she really a widow as we understand it here, or had she simply mislaid her last husband? Your country is so vast that such accidents must be common. Decidedly, her past was much too nebulous!'

The girl broke into a chuckle that revealed her even pearl-white teeth beneath pale pink lips that were a bit too thin. 'Well, as far as "nebulous pasts" go, I can't answer for Mrs. Smithers' because I've never raised the veil that surrounds it. But I *will* vouch for the fact that her daughter is charming and that you're terribly finicky if you don't agree.'

The young man shot her an indefinable glance which seemed to color his customary mockery with a nuance of affection.

'As charming as you are?' he asked banteringly.

Miss Lambart frowned and her eyes suddenly turned a cold metallic gray. 'Now then, my dear fellow, you're not speaking in character. Besides,' she went on, self-possessed and smiling once again, 'it's my job to point such things out to you. As

I was saying, I believe that for the moment Mrs. Smithers' ambitions are rather amorphous. Like many Americans who find themselves rich overnight, she wasn't able to establish the proper social connections in New York. So half out of spite and half out of sheer desire to spend her money, she jumped aboard the first available steamer with her daughter, no doubt hoping to acquire immediate social standing in a world where people are received in society without embarrassing inquiries into their past, provided they are wealthy and come from far enough away! As you know, it's only recently that I met Mrs. Smithers – on the liner that brought me back here – and she admitted to me with positively *noble* frankness that she wanted to establish ties with the French aristocracy, since her own aristocratic tastes made life in a plebeian society unbearable. Look, there she is,' she added with a subtly malicious smile.

Le Fanois turned around and saw a large woman with pale, puffy features and a complicated coiffure, on which was poised a hat laden with the remains of an entire aviary of exotic birds. She advanced toward them, her shoulders weighed down by a magnificent silver fox coat, her movements impeded by the folds of a lavishly embroidered dress, trailing in her wake a tall, rosy girl. Dressed with the same exaggerated elegance as her mother, the girl held in her hands a sable muff, a gold purse set with precious stones and a diamond-studded lorgnette, and her incredibly blond hair was crowned with a floral abundance as varied as the ornithological trimmings of the maternal bonnet. 'Here are Mrs. Smithers and her daughter Catherine,' Blanche Lambart repeated, and Le Fanois, following her toward the new arrivals, could not suppress a sigh; 'Oh, those poor people . . . those poor people!'

• II •

FOR almost ten years, Jean Le Fanois had led the tiresome and ambiguous life of a promoter of *nouveaux riches* in Parisian society. He had let himself be drawn into it little by little, as a result of accidental dealings with an extremely wealthy American at a time when he himself was down on his luck. How could this luxury-craving boy, accustomed from early youth to the easy-going and costly life of the Parisian club-man, have resisted the unhoped-for windfall such a relationship represented? His new friend, goodhearted and simple-minded, asked only to enjoy his millions in the company of a few choice friends. A dabbler in art collecting, like many of his compatriots, he was able to appreciate the artistic tastes of Le Fanois and commissioned him to furnish and decorate the elegant town house he had just bought from a bankrupt adventurer. Jean was delighted with the opportunity to distinguish himself in the role of enlightened amateur and, in acquiring handsome works of art for his friend, he experienced a little of the pleasure he would have had in buying them for himself. Then he learned that the stakes in this game included more durable rewards than mere altruistic pleasure. He received large sums of money from secondhand dealers highly pleased with the client he brought them; and although this arrangement embarrassed him slightly the first time it was proposed, he quickly grew accustomed to it, especially in view of the fact that sizeable gambling losses had seriously depreciated his modest fortune.

He enjoyed in more disinterested fashion the idle, luxurious life in which he found himself involved. The compatriots surrounding his friend led a completely empty existence, devoid of fixed occupations and stable relationships – but how artfully they hid its yawning emptiness under the appearances of frantic activity! Cruises on yachts, automobile trips, sumptuous dinners in fashionable restaurants, afternoons of elegant strolling at Bagatelle or Saint-James, trips to the race track and to art exhibits, evenings at those small theaters designed for tourists in the know: all of these expensive and monotonous diversions followed in succession time and time again without exhausting a need to be busy inherited from enterprising and tenacious ancestors, who had directed the same furious activity toward amassing fortunes that their descendants devoted to squandering them. Needless to say, Le Fanois was often bored in this childish and shifting milieu. Yet he found such sweet compensations in it! Not only did his transactions with antique dealers enable him to purchase at a fraction of their worth some of the exquisite objects with which he liked to surround himself, but his parasitic existence saved him a considerable sum of money, which finally allowed him to organize a life of his own.

One fine day his Maecenas died, leaving his entire fortune to American relatives – to the great disappointment of Le Fanois.

Happily, a successor soon appeared on the scene, and little by little the young man became accustomed to the role of 'metteur en scène' – his own definition – serving as advisor extraordinary to foreign pilgrims quickened by the pious desire to spend their millions for the benefit of idle Parisians.

His family ties and charming personality had enabled him to remain in contact with the exclusive social circles that keep their distance from the madding crowd; Le Fanois acted as intermediary between the renegades from this milieu, each of them tormented by a craving for luxury and movement, and the explorers from the New World who longed to penetrate their closed society.

His task had not assumed significant proportions, however – he had not really turned professional – until he met Miss Blanche Lambart at a gathering of the foreign colony. Her fine intelligence and open-mindedness had struck him immediately; he had frequented her compatriots too long not to realize promptly that she came from more refined stock than most Americans who try to storm Parisian society. Everything about her betrayed a careful education, an abundance of social graces, the habit of moving in elegant circles. He had soon guessed, however, that like himself, she lived at the expense of people she despised.

At the time of their meeting, Miss Lambart was the traveling companion of a wealthy widow from Chicago who had visions of an advantageous marriage. In no time at all, Le Fanois and Miss Lambart had joined forces to present her to society and look for a husband who met her specifications. But it seems that the widow was as ungrateful as Le Fanois' patron; for the moment she was married she dismissed Miss Lambart who was forced to search for another benefactress. Having found one without delay, she once again asked Le Fanois' assistance in introducing her protégée to society.

Their unspoken agreement was three or four years old now. Le Fanois still did not know what pressing circumstances had prompted her to choose such a life. Was it the taste for luxury or the need for perpetual motion that so often motivated her fellow-countrymen? Did she come from one of those small towns whose sad, monotonous atmosphere he had heard described, where the women die of boredom in idle solitude while their husbands pile up a fortune that neither of them can enjoy? Le Fanois thought he detected in her, rather, a casualty of New

York society, too poor to resist the luxury that surrounded her,
yet too proud and particular to tie herself down to a second-rate
marriage. But whatever her past, Le Fanois found her attractive
in a unique and undefinable way. He had never spoken to her of
love. In spite of her free manner and ultra-modern vocabulary,
he sensed in her an almost aggressive uprightness, that shielded
her from his advances even more effectively than her deliberately
ironic way of speaking.

So they simply remained the best of friends, enjoying their
meetings and at the same time protecting themselves from the
humiliation of their secret complicity by openly and cynically
making fun of it.

Blanche Lambart had guessed right; Mrs. Smithers and her
daughter were naïve souls.

Catherine in particular asked no more than to enjoy herself,
aspired to no more stable happiness. She wanted to go to the
races and the theater, to display her lovely outfits at the American
colony's dances and to meet the greatest possible number of
waltzers. Mrs. Smithers, however, already envisioned for her
daughter the inevitable 'marriage to a French count.' But she
realized only too well that she could not set her plan in motion
by herself. Won over immediately by Miss Lambart's charm,
she entrusted to her the creation of an existence consonant with
her social aspirations. The young woman secured the services of
Le Fanois, and before long the two of them had installed Mrs.
Smithers in the town house formerly owned by Le Fanois' first
patron and decorated by Le Fanois himself. Next they arranged
a splendid succession of dinners and balls, to which Le Fanois'
friends flocked with a pleasure they sometimes forgot to express
to the hostess. But they did take notice of Catherine. In spite of
her awkwardness, her twangy voice, her ear-splitting laugh, she
projected such freshness and youthful radiance that her lack of
savoir-faire was soon forgotten. She was a 'nice girl' and her
naïveté and joviality were much appreciated.

'After all the designing women you've sent us over here,
that child is a real relief,' Le Fanois remarked jestingly to
Blanche. 'I think her very faults will help us to marry her
off.'

They were sitting at the tea table in Miss Lambart's tiny
sitting room. Two years ago she had been able to move into

an unpretentious fifth-floor apartment, where she received callers
with the independence of a married woman.

('What else could I do?' she would say. 'I have no source
of income, no husband and no companion, so I have to be all
three to myself.')

She smiled at the young man's mild impertinence.

'I admit that the Americans we send you are not always models
of democratic pride,' she said. 'But are they any worse than the
husbands you unearth for them so effortlessly?'

He did not reply and she went on: 'I don't know if we'll find
it quite as easy to settle Catherine. I share your opinion of her
and I wouldn't want to see her unhappily married for anything
in the world.'

Le Fanois mused for a moment. Then he said:

'What would you say to Jean de Sestre?'

She started. 'You mean the young prince? He's the eldest son,
isn't he? That means he'll be the Duke of Sestre!'

'Exactly.'

'And you think . . .'

'I think he's sincerely smitten with our charming Catherine and
I don't foresee any difficulty in obtaining his parents' consent.'

She blinked at him as dumbfounded as ever.

'Now that's what's called a splendid match!' she said. 'And
he's a fine person, isn't he?'

'He's no genius, but I think he'll be an exemplary husband.
You'll be able to entrust your protégée to him without fear.'

Miss Lambart seemed lost in thought. Then she got up with a
sigh and took several steps across the tiny room.

'What's the matter?' the young man inquired, tilting his head
against the back of his chair to follow her graceful movements
more easily.

She came toward him and leaned against the mantelpiece.

'Well, I . . . it's just that I keep thinking about the awful
power of money. Quite an original thought, isn't it? But I can't
help it when I look at that sweet young thing, who is certainly
goodhearted enough, but who, when you come right down to
it, is neither beautiful, witty, imaginative nor charming. And yet
all she has to do is reach out her hand – oh! that pudgy red paw
– and pluck herself a name from the social register, security for
life and the heart of a respectable young man!'

Le Fanois was still gazing at her, with that indefinable gleam that sometimes came to his eyes when she was present.

'While you, poor dear, who have all that . . .'

'Oh, be quiet!' she interrupted.

A brick-red flush crept to her temples, and she returned abruptly to her place at the tea table.

Le Fanois shrugged.

'I thought we could be frank with one another.'

Her smile was full of bitterness.

'Very well, then. I'm worn out, I've had enough. But I've lived too long among the rich and the happy – the need for luxury is in my blood. And when I think that I'll have to start over again – put up another good fight . . .! Once Catherine is married, Mrs. Smithers will probably go back to America to conquer New York. If not, Catherine's position will make my services quite expendable.' An ironic laugh burst from her throat. 'Believe me, I've had enough!'

Le Fanois looked at her for a moment with a faintly sad expression; then he reassumed his bantering tone:

'Well, perhaps this time they'll give you a dowry, and I'll make a fine match for you.'

Their eyes met again; then she said smilingly:

'Oh! the dowry . . . the dowry I've dreamed of! How much do you think I would need to find a suitable husband?'

He seemed to reflect on it.

'A suitable husband? Why, for an income of sixty thousand francs, I solemnly promise to find you a man who adores you.'

She blushed a little, laughing incredulously.

'A man who adores me? Does such a person exist?'

'Trust me,' he said as he rose from his chair. 'And in the meantime, we're agreed, aren't we, that you'll feel out Mrs. Smithers while I take care of the de Sestres. I think our little affair is all but settled.

• III •

TEN days later, the two friends found themselves together again, this time in one of the gilded drawing rooms of the Smithers town house. Mrs. Smithers and her daughter had decided to go for a long drive, and Blanche had telephoned the young man to let him know she would wait for him alone at their house.

'My dear colleague,' he said, shaking her hand, 'it seems that your half of our venture has dragged on a bit! I had no difficulty at all with mine – I've just been waiting for a sign from you.'

Miss Lambart motioned him to an armchair opposite her own.

'And I couldn't give you a sign till this morning. It's been a fight to the finish.'

'A fight? What do you mean? They don't want my suitor?'

'Mrs. Smithers wants nothing more, as you might suspect.' She smiled wanly. 'But Catherine has other ideas.'

'What! That brainless girl?' Le Fanois frowned. 'What happened?'

Blanche hesitated, playing distractedly with the silk tassels that fringed the lapels of her dress. Finally she said, 'Well, in spite of myself, I sided with Catherine – I protected her from her mother.'

Le Fanois looked at her aghast.

'But what in the world does the child want? I'm completely lost.'

'On the contrary. You've *arrived,* my friend, because it's *you* she wants.'

The words, borne on her mocking laugh, struck him like a challenger's glove. He bolted from his chair, his face suddenly ashen, and began stroking his moustache nervously as if to hide his contorted lips.

'What? What do you mean by that?' he stammered.

'Just what I said. Catherine intends to marry the man she loves, and that man is you.'

He stood before her, bearing down with both hands on the bronze-laden table that separated them.

'Me? She loves *me?*' he repeated.

Blanche's laugh was tinged with a distinct note of mockery.

'Oh, come now! You can't be *that* surprised.'

'Surprised? I'm flabbergasted!' He glanced at her suddenly. 'Wait a minute. You don't think . . .'

'Oh, of course not! I'm well aware that you laid your cards on the table. Only, it's not the first time, is it, that someone has fallen in love with you without your assistance?'

He shrugged disdainfully; then he turned on his heel, paced the room once or twice, and came back to where Blanche was sitting.

'But the mother – the mother would never give her consent, would she?' he asked abruptly.

A sudden rush of color inflamed Blanche Lambart's cheeks. She stood up.

'Then it's all right with you?' she said, looking straight into his eyes.

He reddened too, and began to twist his gloves between his agitated fingers. 'All right with me? I have no idea. I was only asking . . .'

'In that case, the matter is settled. I have obtained Mrs. Smithers' permission.'

He looked at her, dumbfounded.

'You've obtained her permission? But how? It's unbelievable!'

'Not at all. She's a good woman at heart, and she adores Catherine. She wouldn't make her unhappy for anything in the world. The two of us broke down her resistance in no time. Catherine will marry for love – and Mrs. Smithers herself will make the brilliant match.'

Le Fanois gasped at this final surprise.

'Good Lord, you mean that *she* wants to marry Sestre?'

'Oh no! I don't think she intends to replace her daughter. But we should certainly be able to find someone her own age. You'll take care of it, won't you? She's really not too bad since she lost weight and began to wear dark colors.'

Blanche suddenly broke off. 'I hear the doorbell. They've come back.'

And, as Le Fanois looked around, searching for a way to escape without being seen, Blanche smiled and went on:

'No, don't go. You know we don't stand on ceremony in this household. Besides, I promised Catherine I would keep you here.'

She added softly as she left him. 'She's desperately in love with you. You'll be good to her, won't you?'

• IV •

SIX weeks later, Jean Le Fanois was again pacing Mrs. Smithers' gilded salon.

This time, he was alone; but, when he had crisscrossed the room several times and paced back and forth before the handsome bronze clock on the mantelpiece, he heard the soft rustle of a skirt behind him and turned to greet Miss Lambart.

It was the first time they had seen each other since the engagement.

The very day after her last conversation with him, she had left for London to visit some friends. In spite of Mrs. Smithers' supplications, she prolonged her stay far beyond the date set for her return. She wrote that she had caught a bad case of influenza, then alleged a slow convalescence which made her fear the strain of the trip home.

Her decision was finally triggered by a telegram stating that Catherine Smithers had become critically ill, and she had only been back for a few hours when Le Fanois arrived.

The moment she appeared, he was struck by the extreme pallor of her thin features, as drawn from anxiety over Catherine as from the traces of her own indisposition.

'It's really serious, then?' the young man asked after shaking hands with her.

'I'm afraid so. The poor child has double pneumonia, and her fever is raging.'

They continued to speak in hushed tones of Catherine's illness. Pneumonia had set in only the day before, complicating what had been a neglected cold. Mrs. Smithers, half out of her mind, never left her daughter's bedside. Four doctors and three nurses gave her the finest of care, and the mother, in despair, spoke of calling in a specialist from New York. For the time being, the symptoms were quite serious. However, the doctors would not be able to make their prognosis for twenty-four hours.

'The poor girl often asks for you, but they're afraid your visit might upset her. So Mrs. Smithers asked me to take her a message for you.'

Le Fanois had tears in his eyes.

'The poor child! Tell her, tell her that I . . .' He hesitated and suddenly seemed uncomfortable under Miss Lambart's serene gaze.

The hint of a sardonic smile crossed her pale lips.

'I'll know what to tell her,' she replied with a slightly bitter intonation.

Le Fanois looked at her; then he took her hand and kissed it.

'Would you?' he said. And she left him.

Two days later Catherine died. Her mother, having imagined till the very last minute that she could save her by sheer force of money, was profoundly shaken by the disaster, which seemed to show her for the time the impotence of her millions. She questioned Blanche and Le Fanois over and over again: 'What more could I have spent?' and blamed herself for not having sent for the specialist from New York, forgetting that Catherine had died before he could have arrived. Nevertheless, she was consoled a bit when she learned that Parisian high society, touched by the girl's tragic death, was bent on attending the funeral and she sent for a hundred copies of the *Paris Herald* to send to her friends in America.

Le Fanois and Miss Lambart did not see each other after the funeral. Greatly saddened by Catherine's death, Blanche had been forced to stay in bed by a recurrence of influenza; and the very next day Mrs. Smithers had asked Le Fanois to accompany her to Cannes, where she spoke of hiding her sorrow, in spite of the fact that the social season was at its height. The young man could hardly refuse the woman who was to have been his mother-in-law, so Miss Lambart remained alone in the luxurious hotel where she had stayed since her return from London.

Weeks slipped by. Mrs. Smithers did not write a word, so that Blanche, knowing that her patroness found spelling an insurmountable obstacle, finally wrote to Le Fanois to ask how she was. His answer was a week in arriving. Then he wrote from Barcelona, where he and Mrs. Smithers had gone by car in the hope that she would be diverted by a brief excursion in Spain.

Several days later, Blanche received from San Sebastian a card hastily scribbled by Mrs. Smithers, telling her that she would be home shortly and instructing her to order a selection of 'suitable' outfits from the couturiers of the rue de la Paix. In a postscript, she asked her to pick up at the jewelers her long strand of black pearls, 'the only ornament she would dream of wearing.' Miss Lambart carried out her orders and moved back into the town house on the eve of Mrs. Smithers return.

The next day at tea time Blanche was expecting a visit from Le Fanois, whom she had asked to stop by. When he appeared, paler and thinner than usual in his mourning clothes, she went to meet him with a sad smile somehow touched with tenderness. Le Fanois was struck by the soft luminosity of her wide gray eyes.

For the first time in her life, she seemed unafraid to take off the mask of irony that usually blurred her lovely features.

She put her hand in his and looked at him lingeringly.

'I've been so anxious to talk with you! I have so many things to tell you,' she said in a soft, affectionate tone of voice, motioning him to the armchair next to hers.

He sat down without saying a word and for a moment both were silent. Then, in a voice quavering with emotion, she began to speak of Catherine.

Le Fanois' face clouded and he made an almost irritated gesture.

'What's the matter?' asked Blanche astonished.

He stumbled over his words. 'It's . . . that that innocent child's love weighs me down. I . . . I'm ashamed I couldn't love her in return – the way I wanted to . . . the way she deserved. Please, let's not talk about it any more.'

Miss Lambart replied, smiling:

'She never suspected a thing. She thought you were sincerely in love.'

He reddened.

'Can't you see I'm ashamed of that too?'

She continued to gaze at him with a tender smile.

'Let's talk about Mrs. Smithers, then. I only saw her for a minute this morning. She was so busy with her dressmakers that I beat a hasty retreat.'

Le Fanois lowered his eyes.

'She seems better now. She's looking for activities to occupy her time,' he said casually.

'Yes, and I think she'll succeed. She spoke of an intimate luncheon she hopes to give next week for a grand duke passing through Paris. . . . Don't you think I'm right?' she went on, as Le Fanois remained silent. 'Don't you think Mrs. Smithers will find a good catch?'

'Really, this is hardly the moment to think about such things.'

'You don't think so? Well, I disagree. It seems to me that the poor woman needs to be diverted. She sincerely loved her daughter, but she doesn't know how to live with her sorrow. Besides, mourning suits her quite well. Her black dresses make her appear thinner, and she looks ten years younger since she stopped dyeing her hair. Was that your bright idea?'

Le Fanois frowned and uttered a short irritated burst of laughter.

'My dear girl, do you think I have nothing better to do than to supervise Mrs. Smithers' hairdresser?'

Miss Lambart smiled.

'If it bothers you to talk about Mrs. Smithers, why don't we talk about me for a while?'

Immediately he seemed more at ease.

'About you? That's a subject I never tire of.'

She was seated before him, slender and delicate in a dark dress which brought out the transparent pallor of her skin, making her lips seem even redder than they were. Golden highlights shimmered on her blond hair. Le Fanois decided she had never looked prettier, more captivating. When he felt her eyes softly meet his, however, he glanced away.

'Yes,' she continued, 'I want to talk to you about myself. I have some news – big news – to tell you.'

His head jerked up.

'You're getting married?'

'Perhaps. It's possible. I really don't know!'

She still enveloped him in her calm, sweet gaze, which seemed infused with an inner light.

'You asked me just a moment ago not to bring up the love of the poor child we're grieving over. However, I have to tell you that she was so ecstatic over your love for her that she wanted a little of her happiness to spill over onto others. The poor dear . . . She knew I was the one who had pleaded your cause with her mother – that I had fought for it loyally – and the very day she got sick she called me to her room to let me know how grateful she was.'

Le Fanois had pushed back his chair. He rose halfway, almost involuntarily, then changed his mind and sat down again.

'Go on,' he said in a low voice.

'She was so choked with emotion that she could hardly speak; but I knew instinctively what she wanted to tell me, and I hugged her and told her to be still for a moment and calm down. Then she answered that she couldn't enjoy her own happiness without doing her best to ensure my own. She knew I had almost no means of support and couldn't bear the idea of my continuing to live at others' expense. She had learned that a girl can't get married without a dowry in France, and she begged me to accept a gift that her feverish hand slipped into mine. I was already worried by the way she looked, so I accepted her present and kissed her without even glancing at the paper. The next day pneumonia set in, and three days later she was dead. I had put the paper away in my writing case, and I only looked at it the day after the burial.'

She stopped for a moment; then she slipped her hand under the lace of her bodice and withdrew a folded piece of paper that she gave to Le Fanois.

'Look,' she said, her voice trembling.

He unfolded the piece of paper automatically, and was astounded by what he saw.

'A million dollars, a million dollars . . .,' he stammered.

'Yes indeed! It's hard to believe how wealthy these people are. They give you a gift of a million dollars as if they were paying their butcher's bill.'

She said nothing, and their eyes met.

'It's like a fairy tale, isn't it?' she said with a short, high-pitched laugh.

Le Fanois had risen and given back the paper with a faintly trembling hand.

Again they fell silent. He had gone to lean against the mantelpiece, while Blanche, still seated, kept her hands crossed on her lap and her head slightly bowed. Le Fanois spoke first.

'I'm so happy for you! You don't doubt it, do you?' he said with obvious emotion, but without moving toward Blanche.

She raised her head slowly and looked at him, blushing.

'Have you forgotten your promise?' she asked with a smile.

'My promise?'

Le Fanois' cheeks flushed crimson.

She continued to gaze at him with her tender, fathomless eyes, as if to decipher what was going on inside him. But, as he still said nothing and stood propped against the fireplace with no apparent intention of coming toward her, she turned pale all of a sudden and stood up.

'I see that you *have* forgotten it – just my luck!' she said, struggling to maintain a lively tone of voice as her eyes filled with tears.

At the sound of her voice, Le Fanois wheeled around and came toward her, seizing her wrists with a violent movement.

'No, no! I haven't forgotten it, I haven't forgotten,' he cried, pulling her toward him.

She uttered a cry of joy and fright; then, just as she was about to yield to his embrace, she looked at him again and jerked backward, pushing him away with all the force of her stiffened arms.

'What is it? What's the matter?' she cried in a terror-stricken voice.

Le Fanois still clutched her wrists in a vise-like grip, and they stood stock-still for an instant, their eyes riveted on each other.

'Jean, what's the matter? Say something, I implore you!' she gasped.

Suddenly he let go of her hands and turned away from her with a hopeless gesture.

'The matter is . . . that I have engaged to marry the mother,' he said, with a bitter laugh.

Full Circle

———————⚭———————

GEOFFREY BETTON woke rather late – so late that the winter
sunlight sliding across his bedroom carpet struck his eyes as he
turned on the pillow.

Strett, the valet, had been in, drawn the bath in the adjoining
dressing room, placed the crystal and silver box at his side, put
a match to the fire, and thrown open the windows to the
bright morning air. It brought in, on the glitter of sun, all
the crisp morning noises – those piercing notes of the American
thoroughfare that seem to take a sharper vibration from the
clearness of the medium through which they pass.

Betton raised himself languidly. That was the voice of Fifth
Avenue below his windows. He remembered that, when he
moved into his rooms eighteen months before, the sound had
been like music to him: the complex orchestration to which the
tune of his new life was set. Now it filled him with disgust and
weariness, since it had become the symbol of the hurry and noise
of that new life. He had been far less hurried in the old days when
he had to be up at seven, and down at the office sharp at nine. Now
that he got up when he chose, and his life had no fixed framework
of duties, the hours hunted him like a pack of bloodhounds.

He dropped back on his pillow with a groan. Yes – not a
year ago there had been a positively sensuous joy in getting out of
bed, feeling under his barefeet the softness of the warm red carpet,
and entering the shining sanctuary where his great porcelain bath
proffered its renovating flood. But then a year ago he could still
call up the horror of the communal plunge at his earlier lodging:
the listening for other bathers, the dodging of shrouded ladies in
crimping pins, the cold wait on the landing, the descent into a

blotchy tin bath, and the effort to identify one's soap and
nailbrush among the promiscuous implements of ablution. That
memory had faded now, and Betton saw only the dark hours to
which his tiled temple of refreshment formed a kind of glittering
ante-chamber. For after his bath came his breakfast, and on the
breakfast tray his letters. His letters!

He remembered – and *that* memory had not not faded! – the
thrill with which, in the early days of his celebrity, he had opened
the first missive in a strange feminine hand: the letter beginning:
'I wonder if you'll mind an unknown reader's telling you all that
your book has been to her?'

Mind? Ye gods, he minded now! For more than a year
after the publication of *Diadems and Faggots* the letters, the
inane indiscriminate letters of commendation, of criticism, of
interrogation, had poured in on him by every post. Hundreds of
unknown readers had told him with unsparing detail all that his
book had been to them. And the wonder of it was, when all was
said and done, that it had really been so little – that when their
thick broth of praise was strained through the author's searching
vanity there remained to him so small a sediment of definite
specific understanding! No – it was always the same thing, over
and over and over again – the same vague gush of adjectives, the
same incorrigible tendency to estimate his effort according to each
writer's personal references, instead of regarding it as a work of
art, a thing to be measured by fixed standards!

He smiled to think how little, at first, he had felt the vanity
of it all. He had found a savour even in the grosser evidences of
popularity: the advertisements of his book, the daily shower
of 'clippings,' the sense that, when he entered a restaurant or a
theater, people nudged each other and said 'That's Betton.' Yes,
the publicity had been sweet to him – at first. He had been touched
by the sympathy of his fellow men: had thought indulgently of the
world, as a better place than the failures and the dyspeptics would
acknowledge. And then his success began to submerge him: he
gasped under the thickening shower of letters. His admirers were
really unappeasable. And they wanted him to do such ridiculous
things – to give lectures, to head movements, to be tendered
receptions, to speak at banquets, to address mothers, to plead for
orphans, to go up in balloons, to lead the struggle for sterilized
milk. They wanted his photograph for literary supplements, his

autograph for charity bazaars, his name on committees, literary, educational, and social; above all, they wanted his opinion on everything: on Christianity, Buddhism, tight lacing, the drug habit, democratic government, female suffrage and love. Perhaps the chief benefit of this demand was his incidentally learning from it how few opinions he really had: the only one that remained with him was a rooted horror of all forms of correspondence. He had been unspeakably thankful when the letters began to fall off.

Diadems and Faggots was now two years old, and the moment was at hand when its author might have counted on regaining the blessed shelter of oblivion – if only he had not written another book! For it was the worst part of his plight that the result of his first folly had goaded him to the perpetration of the next – that one of the incentives (hideous thought!) to his new work had been the desire to extend and perpetuate his popularity. And this very week the book was to come out, and the letters, the cursed letters, would begin again!

Wistfully, almost plaintively, he looked at the breakfast tray with which Strett presently appeared. It bore only two notes and the morning journals, but he knew that within the week it would groan under his epistolary burden. The very newspaper flung the fact at him as he opened them.

READY ON MONDAY.
GEOFFREY BETTON'S NEW NOVEL
ABUNDANCE.
BY THE AUTHOR OF 'DIADEMS AND FAGGOTS.'
FIRST EDITION OF ONE HUNDRED AND FIFTY THOUSAND
ALREADY SOLD OUT.
ORDER NOW.

A hundred and fifty thousand volumes! And an average of three readers to each! Half a million of people would be reading him within a week, and every one of them would write to him, and their friends and relations would write too. He laid down the paper with a shudder.

The two notes looked harmless enough, and the caligraphy of one was vaguely familiar. He opened the envelope and looked at the signature: *Duncan Vyse*. He had not seen the name in years – what on earth could Duncan Vyse have to say? He ran over the page and dropped it with a wondering exclamation, which the watchful, Strett, re-entering, met by a tentative 'Yes, sir?'

'Nothing. Yes – that is – ' Betton picked up the note. 'There's a gentleman, Mr. Vyse, coming at ten.'

Strett glanced at the clock. 'Yes, sir. You'll remember that ten was the hour you appointed for the secretaries to call, sir.'

Betton nodded. 'I'll see Mr. Vyse first. My clothes, please.'

As he got into them, in the state of nervous hurry that had become almost chronic with him, he continued to think about Duncan Vyse. They had seen a great deal of each other for the few years after both had left Harvard: the hard happy years when Betton had been grinding at his business and Vyse – poor devil! – trying to write. The novelist recalled his friend's attempts with a smile; then the memory of the one small volume came back to him. It was a novel: 'The Lifted Lamp.' There was stuff in that, certainly. He remembered Vyse's tossing it down on his table with a gesture of despair when it came back from the last publisher. Betton, taking it up indifferently, had sat riveted till daylight. When he ended, the impression was so strong that he said to himself: 'I'll tell Apthorn about it – I'll go and see him tomorrow.' His own secret literary yearnings increased his desire to champion Vyse, to see him triumph over the dullness and timidity of the publishers. Apthorn was the youngest of the guild, still capable of opinions and the courage of them, a personal friend of Betton's, and, as it happened, the man afterward to become known as the privilege publisher of *Diadems and Faggots*. Unluckily the next day something unexpected turned up, and Betton forgot about Vyse and his manuscript. He continued to forget for a month, and then came a note from Vyse, who was ill, and wrote to ask what his friend had done. Betton did not like to say 'I've done nothing,' so he left the note unanswered, and vowed again: 'I'll see Apthorn.'

The following day he was called to the West on business, and was away a month. When he came back, there was a third note from Vyse, who was still ill, and desperately hard up. 'I'll take anything for the book, if they'll advance me two hundred dollars.' Betton, full of compunction, would gladly have advanced the sum himself; but he was hard up too, and could only swear inwardly: 'I'll write to Apthorn.' Then glanced again at the manuscript, and reflected: 'No – there are things in it that need explaining. I'd better see him.'

Once he went so far as to telephone Apthorn, but the publisher was out. Then he finally and completely forgot.

One Sunday he went out of town, and on his return, rummaging among the papers on his desk, he missed 'The Lifted Lamp,' which had been gathering dust there for half a year. What the deuce could have become of it? Betton spent a feverish hour in vainly increasing the disorder of his documents, and then bethought himself of calling the maid-servant, who first indignantly denied having touched anything ('I can see that's true from the dust,' Betton scathingly remarked), and then mentioned with hauteur that a young lady had called in his absence and asked to be allowed to get a book.

'A lady? Did you let her come up?'

She said somebody'd sent her.'

Vyse, of course – Vyse had sent her for his manuscript! He was always mixed up with some woman, and it was just like him to send the girl of the moment to Betton's lodgings, with instructions to force the door in his absence. Vyse had never been remarkable for delicacy. Betton, furious, glanced over the table to see if any of his own effects were missing – one couldn't tell, with the company Vyse kept! – and then dismissed the matter from his mind, with a vague sense of magnanimity in doing so. He felt himself exonerated by Vyse's conduct.

The sense of magnanimity was still uppermost when the valet opened the door to announce 'Mr. Vyse,' and Betton, a moment later, crossed the threshold of his pleasant library.

His first thought was that the man facing him from the hearthrug was the very Duncan Vyse of old: small, starved, bleached-looking, with the same sidelong movements, the same air of anemic truculence. Only he had grown shabbier, and bald.

Betton held out a hospitable hand.

'This is a good surprise! Glad you looked me up, my dear fellow.'

Vyse's palm was damp and bony: he had always had a disagreeable hand.

'You got my note? You know what I've come for?'

'About the secretaryship? (Sit down). Is that really serious?'

Betton lowered himself luxuriously into one of his vast maple armchairs. He had grown stouter in the last year, and the cushion behind him fitted comfortably into the crease of his nape. As he leaned back he caught sight of his image in the mirror between the windows, and reflected uneasily that Vyse would not find *him* unchanged.

'Serious?' Vyse rejoined. 'Why not? Aren't *you*?'

'Oh, perfectly.' Betton laughed apologetically. 'Only – well, the fact is, you may not understand what rubbish a secretary of mine would have to deal with. In advertising for one I never imagined – I didn't aspire to anyone above the ordinary hack.'

'I'm the ordinary hack,' said Vyse drily.

Betton's affable gesture protested. 'My dear fellow – . You see it's not business – what I'm in now,' he continued with a laugh.

Vyse's thin lips seemed to form a noiseless '*Isn't* it?' which they instantly transposed into the audible reply: 'I judged from your advertisement that you want someone to relieve you in your literary work. Dictation, shorthand – that kind of thing?'

'Well, no: not that either. I type my own things. What I'm looking for is somebody who won't be above tackling my correspondence.'

Vyse looked slightly surprised. 'I should be glad of the job,' he then said.

Betton began to feel a vague embarrassment. He had supposed that such a proposal would be instantly rejected. 'It would be only for an hour or two a day – if you're doing any writing of your own?' he threw out interrogatively.

'No. I've given all that up. I'm in an office now – business. But it doesn't take all my time, or pay enough to keep me alive.'

'In that case, my dear fellow – if you could come every morning; but it's mostly awful bosh, you know,' Betton again broke off, with growing awkwardness.

Vyse glanced at him humorously. 'What you want me to write?'

'Well, that depends – ' Betton sketched the obligatory smile. 'But I was thinking of the letters you'll have to answer. Letters about my books, you know – I've another one appearing next week. And I want to be beforehand now – dam the flood before it swamps me. Have you any idea of the deluge of stuff that people write to a successful novelist?'

As Betton spoke, he saw a tinge of red on Vyse's thin cheek, and his own reflected it in a richer glow of shame. 'I mean – I mean – ' he stammered helplessly.

'No, I haven't,' said Vyse, 'but it will be awfully jolly finding out.'

There was a pause, groping and desperate on Betton's part, sardonically calm on his visitor's.

'You – you've given up writing altogether?' Betton continued.

'Yes; we've changed places, as it were.' Vyse paused. 'But about these letters – you dictate the answers?'

'Lord, no! That's the reason why I said I wanted somebody – er – well used to writing. I don't want to have anything to do with them – not a thing! You'll have to answer them as if they were written to *you* – ' Betton pulled himself up again, and rising in confusion jerked opened one of the drawers of his writing table.

'Here – this kind of rubbish,' he said, tossing a packet of letters onto Vyse's knee.

'Oh – you keep them, do you?' said Vyse simply.

'I – well – some of them; a few of the funniest only.'

Vyse slipped off the band and began to open the letters. While he was glancing over them Betton again caught his own reflection in the glass, and asked himself what impression he had made on his visitor. It occurred to him for the first time that his high-colored well-fed person presented the image of commercial rather than of intellectual achievement. He did not look like his own idea of the author of *Diadems and Faggots* – and he wondered why.

Vyse laid the letters aside. 'I think I can do it – if you'll give me a notion of the tone I'm to take.'

'The tone?'

'Yes – that is, if you expect me to sign your name.'

'Oh, of course you're to sign for me. As for the tone, say just what you'd – well, say all you can without encouraging them to answer.'

Vyse rose from his seat. 'I could submit a few specimens,' he suggested.

'Oh, as to that – you always wrote better than I do,' said Betton handsomely.

'I've never had this kind of thing to write. When do you wish me to begin?' Vyse inquired, ignoring the tribute.

'The book's out on Monday. The deluge will probably begin about three days after. Will you turn up on Thursday at this hour?' Betton held his hand out with real heartiness. 'It was great luck for me, your striking that advertisement. Don't be too harsh with my correspondents – I owe them something for having brought us together.'

• II •

THE deluge began punctually on the Thursday, and Vyse, arriving as punctually, had an impressive pile of letters to attack. Betton, on his way to the Park for a ride, came into the library, smoking the cigarette of indolence, to look over his secretary's shoulder.

'How many of 'em? Twenty? Good Lord! It's going to be worse than *Diadems*. I've just had my first quiet breakfast in two years – time to read the papers and loaf. How I used to dread the sight of my letter box! Now I shan't know that I have one.'

He leaned over Vyse's chair, and the secretary handed him a letter.

'Here's rather an exceptional one – lady, evidently. I thought you might want to answer it yourself – '

'Exceptional?' Betton ran over the mauve pages and tossed them down. 'Why, my dear man, I get hundreds like that. You'll have to be pretty short with her, or she'll send her photograph.'

He clapped Vyse on the shoulder and turned away, humming a tune. 'Stay to luncheon,' he called back gaily from the threshold.

After luncheon Vyse insisted on showing a few of his answers to the first batch of letters. 'If I've struck the note I won't bother you again,' he urged; and Betton groaningly consented.

'My dear fellow, they're beautiful – too beautiful. I'll be let in for a correspondence with every one of these people.'

Vyse, in reply, mused for a while above a blank sheet. 'All right – how's this?' he said, after another interval of rapid writing.

Betton glanced over the page. 'By George – by George! Won't she *see* it?' he exulted, between fear and rapture.

'It's wonderful how little people see,' said Vyse reassuringly.

The letters continued to pour in for several weeks after the appearance of *Abundance*. For five or six blissful days Betton did not even have his mail brought to him, trusting to Vyse to single out his personal correspondence, and to deal with the rest of the letters according to their agreement. During those days he luxuriated in a sense of wild and lawless freedom; then, gradually, he began to feel the need of fresh restraints to break, and learned that the zest of liberty lies in the escape from specific obligations. At first he was conscious only of a vague hunger, but in time the craving resolved itself into a shame-faced desire to see his letters.

'After all, I hated them only because I had to answer them'; and he told Vyse carelessly that he wished all his letters submitted to him before the secretary answered them.

The first morning he pushed aside those beginning: 'I have just laid down *Abundance* after a third reading,' or: 'Everyday for the last month I have been telephoning my bookseller to know when your novel would be out.' But little by little the freshness of his interest revived, and even this stereotyped homage began to arrest his eye. At last a day came when he read all the letters, from the first word to the last, as he had done when *Diadems and Faggots* appeared. It was really a pleasure to read them, now that he was relieved of the burden of replying: his new relation to his correspondents had the glow of a love affair unchilled by the contingency of marriage.

One day it struck him that the letters were coming in more slowly and in smaller numbers. Certainly there had been more of a rush when *Diadems and Faggots* came out. Betton began to wonder if Vyse were exercising an unauthorised discrimination, and keeping back the communications he deemed least important. This conjecture carried the novelist straight to his library, where he found Vyse bending over the writing table with his usual inscrutable pale smile. But once there, Betton hardly knew how to frame his question, and blundered into an inquiry for a missing invitation.

'There's a note – a personal note – I ought to have had this morning. Sure you haven't kept it back by mistake among the others?'

Vyse laid down his pen. 'The others? But I never keep back any.'

Betton had foreseen the answer. 'Not even the worst twaddle about my book?' he suggested lightly, pushing the papers about.

'Nothing. I understood you wanted to go over them all first.'

'Well, perhaps it's safer,' Betton conceded, as if the idea were new to him. With an embarrassed hand he continued to turn over the letters at Vyse's elbow.

'Those are yesterday's,' said the secretary; 'here are today's,' he added, pointing to a meager trio.

'H'm – only these?' Betton took them and looked them over lingeringly. 'I don't see what the deuce that chap means about the first part of *Abundance* "certainly justifying the title" – do you?'

Vyse was silent, and the novelist continued irritably: 'Damned cheek, his writing, if he doesn't like the book. Who cares what he thinks about it, anyhow?'

And his morning ride was embittered by the discovery that it was unexpectedly disagreeable to have Vyse read any letters which did not express unqualified praise of his books. He began to fancy that there was a latent rancor, a kind of baffled sneer, under Vyse's manner; and he decided to return to the practice of having his mail brought straight to his room. In that way he could edit the letters before his secretary saw them.

Vyse made no comment on the change, and Betton was reduced to wondering whether his imperturbable composure were the mask of complete indifference or of a watchful jealousy. The latter view being more agreeable to his employer's self-esteem, the next step was to conclude that Vyse had not forgotten the episode of 'The Lifted Lamp,' and would naturally take a vindictive joy in any unfavorable judgments passed on his rival's work. This did not simplify the situation, for there was no denying that unfavorable criticisms preponderated in Betton's correspondence. *Abundance* was neither meeting with the unrestricted welcome of *Diadems and Faggots*, nor enjoying the alternative of an animated controversy: it was simply found dull, and its readers said so in language not too tactfully tempered by comparisons with its predecessor. To withhold unfavourable comments from Vyse was, therefore, to make it appear that correspondence about the book had died out; and its author, mindful of his unguarded predictions, found this even more embarrassing. The simplest solution would be to get rid of Vyse; and to this end Betton began to address his energies.

One evening, finding himself unexpectedly disengaged, he asked Vyse to dine; it had occurred to him that, in the course of an after-dinner chat, he might hint his feeling that the work he had offered his friend was unworthy so accomplished a hand.

Vyse surprised him by a momentary hesitation. 'I may not have time to dress.'

Betton brushed the objection aside. 'What's the odds? We'll dine here – and as late as you like.'

Vyse thanked him, and appeared, punctually at eight, in all the shabbiness of his daily wear. He looked paler and more shyly truculent than usual, and Betton, from the height of his florid stature, said to himself, with the sudden professional instinct for 'type': 'He might be an agent of something – a chap who carries deadly secrets.'

Vyse, it was to appear, did carry a deadly secret; but one less perilous to society than to himself. He was simply poor-unpardonably, irremediably poor. Everything failed him, had always failed him: whatever he put his hand to went to bits.

This was the confession that, reluctantly, yet with a kind of white-lipped bravado, he flung at Betton in answer to the latter's tentative suggestion that, really the letter-answering job wasn't worth bothering him with – a thing that any typewriter could do.

'If you mean that you're paying me more than it's worth, I'll take less,' Vyse rushed out after a pause.

'Oh, my dear fellow – ' Betton protested, flushing.

'What *do* you mean, then? Don't I answer the letters as you want them answered?'

Betton anxiously stroked his silken ankle. 'You do it beautifully, too beautifully. I mean what I say: the work's not worthy of you. I'm ashamed to ask you – '

'Oh, hang shame,' Vyse interrupted. 'Do you know why I said I shouldn't have time to dress tonight? Because I haven't any evening clothes. As a matter of fact, I haven't much but the clothes I stand in. One thing after another's gone against me; all the infernal ingenuities of chance. It's been a slow Chinese torture, the kind where they keep you alive to have more fun killing you.' He straightened himself with a sudden blush. 'Oh, I'm all right now – getting on capitally. But I'm still walking rather a narrow plank; and if I do your work well enough – if I take your idea – '

Betton stared into the fire without answering. He knew next to nothing of Vyse's history, of the mischance or mismanagement that had brought him, with his brains and the training, to so unlikely a pass. But a pang of compunction shot through him as he remembered the manuscript of 'The Lifted Lamp' gathering dust on his table for half a year.

'Not that it would have made any earthly difference – since he's evidently never been able to get the thing published.' But this reflection did not wholly console Betton, and he found it impossible, at the moment, to tell Vyse that his services were not needed.

• III •

DURING the ensuing weeks the letters grew fewer and fewer, and Betton foresaw the approach of the fatal day when his secretary, in common decency, would have to say: 'I can't draw my pay for doing nothing.'

What a triumph for Vyse!

The thought was intolerable, and Betton cursed his weakness in not having dismissed the fellow before such a possibility arose.

'If I tell him I've no use for him now, he'll see straight through it, of course; and then, hang it, he looks so poor!'

This consideration came after the other, but Betton, in re-arranging them, put it first, because he thought it looked better there, and also because he immediately perceived its value in justifying a plan of action that was beginning to take shape in his mind.

'Poor devil, I'm damned if I don't do it for him!' said Betton, sitting down at his desk.

Three or four days later he sent word to Vyse that he didn't care to go over the letters any longer, and that they would once more be carried directly to the library.

The next time he lounged in, on his way to his morning ride, he found his secretary's pen in active motion.

'A lot today,' Vyse told him cheerfully.

His tone irritated Betton: it had the inane optimism of the physician reassuring a discouraged patient.

'Oh, Lord – I thought it was almost over,' groaned the novelist.

'No: they've just got their second wind. Here's one from a Chicago publisher – never heard the name – offering you thirty per cent on your next novel, with an advance royalty of twenty thousand. And here's a chap who wants to syndicate it for a bunch of Sunday papers: big offer, too. That's from Ann Arbor. And this – oh, *this* one's funny!'

He held up a small scented sheet to Betton, who made no movement to receive it.

'Funny? Why's it funny?' he growled.

'Well, it's from a girl – a lady – and she thinks she's the only person who understands *Abundance* – has the clue to it. Says she's never seen a book so misrepresented by the critics – '

'Ha, ha! That *is* good!' Betton agreed with too loud a laugh.

'This one's from a lady, too – married woman. Says she's misunderstood, and would like to correspond.'

'Oh, Lord,' said Betton. 'What are you looking at?' he added sharply, as Vyse continued to bend his blinking gaze on the letters.

'I was only thinking I'd never seen such short letters from women. Neither one fills the first page.'

'Well, what of that?' queried Betton.

Vyse reflected. 'I'd like to meet a woman like that,' he said wearily; and Betton laughed again.

The letters continued to pour in, and there could be no further question of dispensing with Vyse's services. But one morning, about three weeks later, the latter asked for a word with his employer, and Betton, on entering the library, found his secretary with half a dozen documents spread out before him.

'What's up?' queried Betton, with a touch of impatience.

Vyse was attentively scanning the outspread letters.

'I don't know: can't make out.' His voice had a faint note of embarrassment. 'Do you remember a note signed "Hester Macklin" that came three or four weeks ago? Married – misunderstood – Western army post – wanted to correspond?'

Betton seemed to grope among his memories; then he assented vaguely.

'A short note,' Vyse went on: 'The whole story in half a page. The shortness struck me so much – and the directness – that I wrote her: wrote in my own name, I mean.'

'In your own name?' Betton stood amazed; then he broke into a groan.

'Good Lord, Vyse – you're incorrigible!'

The secretary pulled his thin mustache with a nervous laugh. 'If you mean I'm an ass, you're right. Look here.' He held out an envelope stamped with the words: 'Dead Letter Office.' 'My effusion has come back to me marked "unknown." There's no such person at the address she gave you.'

Betton seemed for an instant to share his secretary's embarrassment; then he burst into an uproarious laugh.

'Hoax, was it? That's rough on you, old fellow!'

Vyse shrugged his shoulders. 'Yes; but the interesting question is – why on earth didn't *your* answer come back, too?'

'My answer?'

'The official one – the one I wrote in your name. If she's unknown, what's become of *that*?'

Betton's eyes were wrinkled by amusement. 'Perhaps she hadn't disappeared then.'

Vyse disregarded the conjecture. 'Look here – I believe *all* these letters are a hoax,' he broke out.

Betton stared at him with a face that turned slowly red and angry. 'What are you talking about? All what letters?'

'These I've got spread out here: I've been comparing them. And I believe they're all written by one man.'

Betton's redness turned to a purple that made his ruddy mustache seem pale. 'What the devil are you driving at?' he asked.

'Well, just look at it,' Vyse persisted, still bent above the letters. 'I've been studying them carefully – those that have come within the last two or three weeks – and there's a queer likeness in the writing of some of them. The *g*'s are all like corkscrews. And the same phrases keep recurring – the Ann Arbor news agent uses the same expressions as the President of the Girl's College at Euphorbia, Maine.'

Betton laughed. 'Aren't the critics always groaning over the shrinkage of the national vocabulary? Of course we all use the same expressions.'

'Yes,' said Vyse obstinately. 'But how about using the same *g*'s?'

Betton laughed again, but Vyse continued without heeding him: 'Look here, Betton – could Strett have written them?'

'Strett?' Betton roared. '*Strett*?' He threw himself into his armchair to shake out his mirth at greater ease.

'I'll tell you why. Strett always posts all my answers. He comes in for them everyday before I leave. He posted the letter to the misunderstood party – the letter from *you* that the Dead Letter Office didn't return. *I* posted my own letter to her; and that came back.'

A measurable silence followed the emission of this ingenious conjecture; then Betton observed with gentle irony: 'Extremely neat. And of course it's no business of yours to supply any valid motive for this remarkable attention of my valet's part.'

Vyse cast on him a slanting glance.

'If you've found that human conduct's generally based on valid motives – !'

'Well, outside of madhouses it's supposed to be not quite incalculable.'

Vyse had an odd smile under his thin mustache. 'Every house is a madhouse at some time or another.'

Betton rose with a careless shake of the shoulders. 'This one will be if I talk to you much longer,' he said, moving away with a laugh.

• IV •

BETTON did not for a moment believe that Vyse suspected the valet of having written the letters.

'Why the devil don't he say out what he thinks? He was always a tortuous chap,' he grumbled inwardly.

The sense of being held under the lens of Vyse's mute scrutiny became more and more exasperating. Betton, by this time, had squared his shoulders to the fact that *Abundance* was a failure with the public: a confessed and glaring failure. The press told him so openly, and his friends emphasized the fact by their circumlocutions and evasions. Betton minded it a good deal more than he had expected, but not nearly as much as he minded Vyse's knowing it. That remained the central twinge in his diffused discomfort. And the problem of getting rid of his secretary once more engaged him.

He had set aside all sentimental pretexts for retaining Vyse; but a practical argument replaced them. 'If I ship him now he'll think it's because I'm ashamed to have him see that I'm not getting any more letters.'

For the letters had ceased again, almost abruptly, since Vyse had hazarded the conjecture that they were the product of Strett's devoted pen. Betton had reverted only once to the subject – to ask ironically, a day or two later: 'Is Strett writing to me as much as ever?' – and, on Vyse's replying with a neutral headshake, had added, laughing: 'If you suspect *him* you'll be thinking next that I write the letters myself!'

'There are very few today,' said Vyse, with an irritating evasiveness; and Betton rejoined squarely: 'Oh, they'll stop soon. The book's a failure.'

A few mornings later he felt a rush of shame at his own tergiversations, and stalked into the library with Vyse's sentence on his tongue.

Vyse was sitting at the table making pencil sketches of a girl's profile. Apparently there was nothing else for him to do.

'Is that your idea of Hester Macklin?' asked Betton jovially, leaning over him.

Vyse started back with one of his anemic blushes. 'I was hoping you'd be in. I wanted to speak to you. There've been no letters the last day or two,' he explained.

Betton drew a quick breath of relief. The man had some sense of decency, then! He meant to dismiss himself.

'I told you so, my dear fellow; the book's a flat failure,' he said, almost gaily.

Vyse made a deprecating gesture. 'I don't know that I should regard the absence of letters as the final test. But I wanted to ask you if there isn't something else I can do on the days when there's no writing.' He turned his glance toward the book-lined walls. 'Don't you want your library catalogued?' he asked insidiously.

'Had it done last year, thanks.' Betton glanced away from Vyse's face. It was piteous how he needed the job!

'I see. . . . Of course this is just a temporary lull in the letters. They'll begin again – as they did before. The people who read carefully read slowly – you haven't heard yet what *they* think.'

Betton felt a rush of puerile joy at the suggestion. Actually, he hadn't thought of that!

'There *was* a big second crop after *Diadems and Faggots*,' he mused aloud.

'Of course. Wait and see,' said Vyse confidently.

The letters in fact began again – more gradually and in smaller numbers. But their quality was different, as Vyse had predicted. And in two cases Betton's correspondents, not content to compress into one rapid communication the thoughts inspired by his work, developed their views in a succession of really remarkable letters. One of the writers was a professor in Western college; the other was a girl in Florida. In their language, their point of view, their reasons for appreciating *Abundance*, they differed almost diametrically; but this only made the unanimity of their approval the more striking. The rush of correspondence evoked by Betton's earlier novel had produced nothing so personal, so exceptional as these communications. He had gulped the praise of *Diadems and Faggots* as undiscriminatingly as it was offered; now he knew for the first time the subtler pleasures of the palate. He tried to feign indifference, even to himself; and to Vyse he made no sign. But gradually he felt a desire to know what his secretary thought of the letters, and, above all, what he was saying in reply to them. And he resented acutely the possibility of Vyse's starting one of his clandestine correspondences with the girl in Florida. Vyse's notorious lack of delicacy had never been more vividly present to Betton's imagination; and he made up his mind to answer the letters himself.

He would keep Vyse on, of course: there were other communications that the secretary could attend to. And, if necessary, Betton would invent an occupation: he cursed his stupidity in having betrayed the fact that his books were already catalogued.

Vyse showed no surprise when Betton announced his intention of dealing personally with the two correspondents who showed so flattering a reluctance to take their leave. But Betton immediately read a criticism in his lack of comment, and put forth, on a note of challenge: 'After all, one must be decent!'

Vyse looked at him with an evanescent smile. 'You'll have to explain that you didn't write the first answers.'

Betton halted. 'Well – I – more or less dictated them, didn't I?'

'Oh, virtually, they're yours, of course.'

'You think I can put it that way?'

'Why not?' The secretary absently drew an arabesque on the blotting pad. 'Of course they'll keep it up longer if you write yourself,' he suggested.

Betton blushed, but faced the issue. 'Hang it all, I shan't be sorry. They interest me. They're remarkable letters.' And Vyse, without observation, returned to his writings.

The spring, that year, was delicious to Betton. His college professor continued to address him tersely but cogently at fixed intervals, and twice a week eight serried pages came from Florida. There were other letters, too; he had the solace of feeling that at last *Abundance* was making its way, was reaching the people who, as Vyse said, read slowly because they read intelligently. But welcome as were all these proofs of his restored authority they were but the background of his happiness. His life revolved for the moment about the personality of his two chief correspondents. The professor's letters satisfied his craving for intellectual recognition, and the satisfaction he felt in them proved how completely he had lost faith in himself. He blushed to think that his opinion of his work had been swayed by the shallow judgments of a public whose taste he despised. Was it possible that he had allowed himself to think less well of *Abundance* because it was not to the taste of the average novel reader? Such false humility was less excusable than the crudest appetite for praise: it was ridiculous to try to do conscientious work if one's self-esteem were at the mercy of popular judgments. All this the professor's letters delicately and indirectly conveyed to Betton, with the results that the authors of *Abundance* began to recognize in it the ripest flower of his genius.

But if the professor understood his book, the girl from Florida understood *him*; and Betton was fully alive to the superior qualities of discernment which this implied. For his lovely correspondent his novel was but the starting point, the pretext of her discourse: he himself was her real object, and he had the delicious sense, as their exchange of thoughts proceeded, that she was interested in *Abundance* because of its author, rather than in the author because of his book. Of course she laid stress on the fact that his ideas were the object of her contemplation; but Betton's agreeable person had permitted him some insight into the incorrigible subjectiveness of female judgments, and he was pleasantly aware, from the lady's tone, that she guessed him to be neither old nor ridiculous. And suddenly he wrote to ask if he might see her . . . .

The answer was long in coming. Betton fidgeted at the delay, watched, wondered, fumed; then he received the one word 'Impossible.'

He wrote back more urgently, and awaited the reply with increasing eagerness. A certain shyness had kept him from once more modifying the instructions regarding his mail, and Strett still carried the letters directly to Vyse. The hour when he knew they were passing under the latter's eyes was now becoming intolerable to Betton, and it was a relief when the secretary, suddenly advised of his father's illness, asked permission to absent himself for a fortnight.

Vyse departed just after Betton had dispatched to Florida his second missive of entreaty, and for ten days he tasted the joy of a first perusal of his letters. The answer from Florida was not among them; but Betton said to himself 'She's thinking it over,' and delay, in that light, seemed favorable. So charming, in fact, was this phase of sentimental suspense that he felt a start of resentment when a telegram apprised him one morning that Vyse would return to his post that day.

Betton had slept later than usual, and, springing out of bed with the telegram in his hand, he learned from the clock that his secretary was due in half an hour. He reflected that the morning's mail must long since be in; and, too impatient to wait for its appearance with his breakfast tray, he threw on a dressing gown and went to the library. There lay the letters, half a dozen of them: but his eyes flew to one envelope, and as he tore it open a warm wave rocked his heart.

The letter was dated a few days after its writer must have received his own; it had all the qualities of grace and insight to which his unknown friend had accustomed him, but it contained no allusion, however, indirect, to the special purport of his appeal. Even a vanity less ingenious than Betton's might have read in the lady's silence one of the most familiar motions of consent; but the smile provoked by this inference faded as he turned to his other letters. For the uppermost bore the superscription 'Dead Letter Office,' and the document that fell from it was his own last letter to Florida.

Betton studied the ironic 'Unknown' for an appreciable space of time; then he broke into a laugh. He had suddenly recalled Vyse's similar experience with Hester Macklin, and the light he was able to throw on that episode was searching enough to penetrate all the dark corners of his own adventure. He felt a rush of heat to the ears; catching sight of himself in the glass, he saw a ridiculous congested countenance, and dropped into a chair to hide it between his fists. He was roused by the opening of the door, and Vyse appeared.

'Oh, I beg pardon – you're ill?' said the secretary.

Betton's only answer was an inarticulate murmur of derision; then he pushed forward the letter with the imprint of the Dead Letter Office.

'Look at that,' he jeered.

Vyse peered at the envelope, and turned it over slowly in his hands. Betton's eyes, fixed on him, saw his face decompose like a substance touched by some powerful acid. He clung to the envelope as if to gain time.

'It's from the young lady you've been writing to at Swazee Springs?' he asked at length.

'It's from the young lady I've been writing to at Swazee Springs.'

'Well – I suppose she's gone away,' continued Vyse, rebuilding his countenance rapidly.

'Yes; and in a community numbering perhaps a hundred and fifty souls, including the dogs and chicken, the local post office is so ignorant of her movements that my letter has to be sent to the Dead Letter Office.'

Vyse meditated on this; then he laughed in turn. 'After all, the same thing happened to me – with Hester Macklin, I mean,' he suggested sheepishly.

'Just so,' said Betton, bringing down his clenched fist on the table. '*Just so*,' he repeated, in italics.

He caught his secretary's glance, and held it with his own for a moment. Then he dropped it as, in pity, one releases something scared and squirming.

'The very day my letter was returned from Swazee Springs she wrote me this from there,' he said, holding up the last Florida missive.

'Ha! That's funny,' said Vyse, with a damp forehead.

'Yes, it's funny,' said Betton. He leaned back, his hands in his pockets, staring up at the ceiling, and noticing a crack in the cornice. Vyse, at the corner of the writing table, waited.

'Shall I get to work?' he began, after a silence measurable by minutes. Betton's gaze descended from the cornice.

'I've got your seat, haven't I?' he said politely, rising and moving away from the table.

Vyse, with a quick gleam of relief, slipped into the vacant chair, and began to stir about among the papers.

'How's your father?' Betton asked from the hearth.

'Oh, better – better, thank you. He'll pull out of it.'

'But you had a sharp scare for a day or two?'

'Yes – it was touch and go when I got there.'

Another pause, while Vyse began to classify the letters.

'And I suppose,' Betton continued in a steady tone, 'your anxiety made you forget your usual precautions – whatever they were – about this Florida correspondence, and before you'd had time to prevent it the Swazee post office blundered?'

Vyse lifted his head with a quick movement. 'What do you mean?' he asked, pushing back his chair.

'I mean that you saw I couldn't live without flattery, and that you've been ladling it out to me to earn your keep.'

Vyse sat motionless and shrunken, digging the blotting pad with his pen. 'What on earth are you driving at?' he repeated.

'Though why the deuce,' Betton continued in the same steady tone, 'you should need to do this kind of work when you've got such faculties at your service – those letters were wonderful, my dear fellow! Why in the world don't you write novels, instead of writing to other people about them?'

Vyse straightened himself with an effort. 'What are you talking about, Betton? Why the devil do you think *I* wrote those letters?'

Betton held back his answer with a brooding face. 'Because I wrote Hester Macklin's – to myself!'

Vyse sat stock still, without the least outcry of wonder.

'Well – ?' he finally said, in a low tone.

'And because you found me out (you see, you can't even feign surprise!) – because you saw through it at a glance, knew at once that the letters were faked. And when you'd foolishly put me on my guard by pointing out to me that they were a clumsy forgery, and had then suddenly guessed that *I* was the forger, you drew the natural inference that I had to have popular approval, or at least had to make *you* think I had it. You saw that, to me, the worst thing about the failure of the book was having *you* know it was a failure. And so you applied your superior – your immeasurably superior – abilities to carrying on the humbug, and deceiving me as I'd tried to deceive you. And you did it so successfully that I don't see why the devil you haven't made your fortune writing novels!'

Vyse remained silent, his head slightly bent under the mounting tide of Betton's denunciation.

'The way you differentiated your people – characterized them – avoided my stupid mistake of making the women's letters too short and too logical, of letting my different correspondents use the same expressions: the amount of ingenuity and art you wasted on it! I swear, Vyse, I'm sorry that damned post office went back on you.' Betton went on, piling up the waves of his irony.

'But at this height they suddenly paused, drew back on themselves, and began to recede before the sight of Vyse's misery. Something warm and emotional in Betton's nature – a lurking kindliness, perhaps, for anyone who tried to soothe and smooth his writhing ego – softened his eye as it rested on the figure of his secretary.

'Look here, Vyse – I'm sorry – not altogether sorry this has happened!' He moved across the room, and laid his hand on Vyse's drooping shoulder. 'In a queer illogical way it evens up things, as it were. I did you a shabby turn once, years ago – oh, out of the sheer carelessness, of course – about the novel of yours I promised to give to Apthorn. If I *had* given it, it might not have made any difference – I'm not sure it wasn't too good for success – but anyhow, I dare say you thought my personal influence might have helped you, might at least have got you a quicker hearing. Perhaps you thought it was because the thing *was* so good that I kept it back, that I felt some nasty jealously of your superiority. I swear to you it wasn't that – I clean forgot it. And one day when I came home it was gone: you'd sent and taken it away. And I've always thought since that you might have owed me a grudge – and not unjustly; so this . . . this business of the letters . . . the sympathy you've shown . . . for I suppose it is sympathy . . . ?'

Vyse startled and checked him by a queer crackling laugh.

'It's *not* sympathy?' broke in Betton, the moisture drying out of his voice. He withdrew his hand from Vyse's shoulder. 'What is it, then? The joy of uncovering my nakedness? An eye for an eye? Is it *that*?'

Vyse rose from his seat, and with a mechanical gesture swept into a heap all the letters he had sorted.

I'm stone-broke, and wanted to keep my job – that's what it is,' he said wearily. . . .

The Daunt Diana

———————

'WHAT'S BECOME OF of the Daunt Diana? You mean to say you
never heard the sequel?'

Ringham Finney threw himself back into his chair with
the smile of the collector who has a good thing to show. He
knew he had a good listener, at any rate. I don't think much of
Ringham's snuffboxes, but his anecdotes are usually worth-while.
He's a psychologist astray among *bibelots*, and the best bits he
brings back from his raids on Christie's and the Hotel Drouot
are the fragments of human nature he picks up on those historic
battlefields. If his *flair* in enamel had been half as good we should
have heard of the Finney collection by this time.

He really has – queer fatuous investigator! – an unusually
sensitive touch for the human texture, and the specimens he
gathers into his museum of memories have almost always some
mark of the rare and chosen. I felt, therefore, that I was really to
be congratulated on the fact that I didn't know what had become
of the Daunt Diana, and on having before me a long evening in
which to learn. I had just led my friend back, after an excellent
dinner at Foyot's, to the shabby pleasant sitting room of my *Rive
Gauche* hotel; and I knew that, once I had settled him in a good
armchair, and put a box of cigars at his elbow, I could trust him
not to budge till I had the story.

· II ·

YOU remember old Neave, of course? Little Humphrey Neave,
I mean. We used to see him pottering about Rome years ago.

431

He lived in two rooms over a wine shop, on polenta and lentils, and prowled among the refuse of the Ripetta whenever he had a few coppers to spend. But you've been out of the collector's world for so long that you may not know what happened to him afterward. . . .

He was always a queer chap, Neave; years older than you and me, of course – and even when I first knew him, in my raw Roman days, he produced on me an unusual impression of age and experience. I don't think I've ever known anyone who was at once so intelligent and so simple. It's the precise combination that results in romance; and poor little Neave was romantic.

He told me once how he'd come to Rome. He was *originaire* of Mystic, Connecticut – and he wanted to get as far away from it as possible. Rome seemed as far as anything on the same planet could be; and after he'd worried his way through Harvard – with shifts and shavings that you and I can't imagine – he contrived to be sent to Switzerland as tutor to a chap who'd failed in his examinations. With only the Alps between, he wasn't likely to turn back; and he got another fellow to take his pupil home, and struck out on foot for the seven hills.

I'm telling you these early details merely to give you a notion of the man. There was a cool persistency and a headlong courage in his dash for Rome that one wouldn't have guessed in the pottering chap we used to know. Once on the spot, he got more tutoring, managed to make himself a name for coaxing balky youths to take their fences, and was finally able to take up the more congenial task of expounding 'the antiquities' to cultured travelers. I call it more congenial – but how it must have seared his soul! Fancy unveiling the sacred scars of Time to ladies who murmur: 'Was this *actually* the spot – ?' while they absently feel for their hatpins! He used to say that nothing kept him at it but the exquisite thought of accumulating the *lire* for his collection. For the Neave collection, my dear fellow, began early, began almost with his Roman life, began in a series of little nameless odds and ends, broken trinkets, torn embroideries, the amputated extremities of maimed marbles: things that even the rag-picker had pitched away when he sifted his haul. But they weren't nameless or meaningless to Neave; his strength lay in his instinct for identifying, putting together, seeing significant relations. He was a regular Cuvier of bric-a-brac. And during those early years, when he had time to brood over trifles and note imperceptible differences, he gradually sharpened his instinct, and made it into the delicate and redoubtable instrument it is. Before he had a thousand francs' worth of *anticaglie* to his name he began to be known as an expert, and the big dealers were glad to consult him. But we're getting no nearer the Daunt Diana. . . .

Well, some fifteen years ago, in London, I ran across Neave at Christie's. He was the same little man we'd known, effaced, bleached, indistinct, like a poor impression' – as unnoticeable as one of his own early finds, yet, like them, with *a quality*, if one had an eye for it. He told me he still lived in Rome, and had contrived, by persistent self-denial, to get a few bits together – 'piecemeal, little by little, with fasting and prayer; and I mean the fasting literally!' he said.

He had run over to London for his annual 'lookround' – I fancy one or another of the big collectors usually paid his journey – and when we met he was on his way to see the Daunt collection. You know old Daunt was a surly brute, and the things weren't easily seen; but he had heard Neave was in London, and had sent – yes, actually sent! – for him to come and give his opinion on a few bits, including the Diana. The little man bore himself discreetly, but you can imagine how proud he was! In his exultation he asked me to come with him – 'Oh, I've the *grandes et petites entrées*, my dear fellow: I've made my conditions – ' and so it happened that I saw the first meeting between Humphrey Neave and his fate.

For that collection *was* his fate: or, one may say, it was embodied in the Diana who was queen and goddess of the realm. Yes – I shall always be glad I was with Neave when he had his first look at the Diana. I see him now, blinking at her through his white lashes, and stroking his wisp of a mustache to hide a twitch of the muscles. It was all very quiet, but it was the *coup de foudre*. I could see that by the way his hands worked when he turned away and began to examine the other things. You remember Neave's hands – thin and dry, with long inquisitive fingers thrown out like antennae? Whatever they hold – bronze or lace, enamel or glass – they seem to acquire the very texture of the thing, and to draw out of it, by every fingertip, the essence it has secreted. Well, that day, as he moved about among Daunt's treasures, the Diana followed him everywhere. He didn't look back at her – he gave himself to the business he was there for – but whatever he touched, he felt her. And on the threshold he turned and gave her his first free look – the kind of look that says: '*You're mine.*'

It amused me at the time – the idea of little Neave making eyes at any of Daunt's belongings. He might as well have coquetted with the Kohinoor. And the same idea seemed to strike him; for as we turned away from the big house in Belgravia he glanced up at it and said, with a bitterness I'd never heard in him: 'Good Lord! To think of that lumpy fool having those things to handle! Did you notice his stupid stumps of fingers? I suppose he blunted them gouging nuggets out of gold fields. And in exchange for the nuggets he gets all that in a year – only has to hold out his callous palm to have that ripe sphere of beauty drop into it! That's my idea of heaven – to have a great collection drop into one's hand, as success, or love, or any of the big shining things, suddenly drop on some men. And I've had to worry along for nearly fifty years, saving and paring, and haggling and managing, to get here a bit and there a bit – and not one perfection in the lot! It's enough to poison a man's life.'

The outbreak was so unlike Neave that I remember every word of it; remember, too, saying in answer: 'But, look here, Neave, you wouldn't take Daunt's hands for yours, I imagine?'

He stared a moment and smiled. 'Have all that, and grope my way through it like a blind cave fish? What a question! But the sense that it's always the blind fish that live in that kind of aquarium is what makes anarchists, sir!' He looked back from the corner of the square, where we had paused while he delivered himself of this remarkable metaphor. 'God, I'd like to throw a bomb at that place, and be in at the looting!'

And with that, on the way home, he unpacked his grievance – pulled the bandage off the wound, and showed me the ugly mark it made on his little white soul.

It wasn't the struggling, screwing, stinting, self-denying that galled him – it was the smallness of the result. It was, in short, the old tragedy of the discrepancy between a man's wants and his power to gratify them. Neave's taste was too fine for his means – was like some strange, delicate, capricious animal, that he cherished and pampered and couldn't satisfy.

'Don't you know those little glittering lizards that die if they're not fed on some rare tropical fly? Well, my taste's like that, with one important difference – if it doesn't get its fly, it simply turns and feeds on *me*. Oh, it doesn't die, my taste – worse luck! It gets larger and stronger and more fastidious, and takes a bigger bite of me – that's all.'

That was all. Year by year, day by day, he had made himself into this delicate register of perceptions and sensations – as far above the ordinary human faculty of appreciation as some scientific registering instrument is beyond the rough human senses – only to find that the beauty which alone could satisfy him was unattainable, that he was never to know the last deep identification which only possession can give. He had trained himself, in short, to feel, in the rare great thing – such an utterance of beauty as the Daunt Diana, say – a hundred elements of perfection, a hundred *reasons why*, imperceptible, inexplicable even, to the average 'artistic' sense; he had reached this point by a long process of discrimination and rejection, the renewed great refusals of the intelligence which perpetually asks more, which will make no pact with its self of yesterday, and is never to be beguiled from its purpose by the wiles of the next best thing. Oh, it's a poignant case, but not a common one; for the next best thing usually wins. . . .

You see, the worst of Neave's state was the fact of his not being a mere collector, even the collector raised to his highest pitch. The whole thing was blended in him with poetry – his imagination had romanticized the acquisitive instinct, as the religious feeling of the Middle Ages turned passion into love. And yet his could never be the abstract enjoyment of the philosopher who says: 'This or that object is really mine because I'm capable of appreciating it.' Neave *wanted* what he appreciated – wanted it with his touch and his sight as well as with his brain.

It was hardly a year afterward that, coming back from a long tour in India, I picked up a London paper and read the amazing headline: 'Mr. Humphrey Neave buys the Daunt collection' I rubbed my eyes and read again. Yes, it could only be our old friend Humphrey. 'An American living in Rome . . . one of our most discerning collectors'; there was no mistaking the description. I bolted out to see the first dealer I could find, and there I had the incredible details. Neave had come into a fortune – two or three million dollars, amassed by an uncle who had a corset factory, and who had attained wealth as the creator of the Mystic Superstraight. (Corset factory sounds odd, by the way, doesn't it? One had fancied that the corset was a personal, a highly specialized garment, more or less shaped on the form it was to modify; but, after all, the Tanagras were all made from two or three molds – and so, I suppose, are the ladies who wear the Mystic Superstraight.)

The uncle had a son, and Neave had never dreamed of seeing a penny of the money; but the son died suddenly, and the father followed, leaving a codicil that gave everything to our friend. Humphrey had to go out to 'realize' on the corset factory; and his description of *that*! . . . Well, he came back with his money in his pocket, and the day he landed old Daunt went to smash. It all fitted in like a puzzle. I believe Neave drove straight from Euston to Daunt House: at any rate, within two months the collection was his, and at a price that made the trade sit up. Trust old Daunt for that!

I was in Rome the following spring, and you'd better believe I looked him up. A big porter glared at me from the door of the Palazzo Neave: I had almost to produce my passport to get in. But that wasn't Neave's fault – the poor fellow was so beset by people clamoring to see his collection that he had to barricade himself, literally. When I had mounted the state *Scalone,* and come on him, at the end of half a dozen echoing salons, in the farthest, smallest *réduit* of the suite, I received the same welcome that he used to give us in his den over the wine shop.

'Well – so you've got her?' I said. For I'd caught sight of the Diana in passing against the bluish blur of an old *verdure* – just the background for her hovering loveliness. Only I rather wondered why she wasn't in the room where he sat.

He smiled. 'Yes, I've got her,' he returned, more calmly than I had expected.

'And all the rest of the loot?'

'Yes. I had to buy the lump.'

'Had to? But you wanted to, didn't you? You used to say it was your idea of heaven – to stretch out your hand and have a great ripe sphere of beauty drop into it. I'm quoting your own words, by the way.'

Neave blinked and stroked his seedy mustache. 'Oh, yes. I remember the phrase. It's true – it *is* the last luxury.' He paused, as if seeking a pretext for his lack of warmth. 'The thing that bothered me was having to move. I couldn't cram all the stuff into my old quarters.'

'Well, I should say not! This is rather a better setting.'

He got up. 'Come and take a look round. I want to show you two or three things – new attributions I've made. I'm doing the catalogue over.'

The interest of showing me the things seemed to dispel the vague apathy I had felt in him. He grew keen again in detailing his redistribution of values, and above all in convicting old Daunt and his advisers of their repeated aberrations of judgment. 'The miracle is that he should have got such things, knowing as little as he did what he was getting. And the egregious asses who bought for him were not better, were worse in fact, since they had all sorts of humbugging wrong reasons for admiring what old Daunt simply coveted because it belonged to some other rich man.'

Never had Neave had so wondrous a field for the exercise of his perfected faculty; and I saw then how, in the real, the great collector's appreciations, the keenest scientific perception is suffused with imaginative sensibility, and how it is to the latter undefinable quality that, in the last resort, he trusts himself.

Nevertheless, I still felt the shadow of that hovering apathy, and he knew I felt it, and was always breaking off to give me reasons for it. For one thing, he wasn't used to his new quarters – hated their bigness and formality; then the requests to show his things drove him mad. 'The women – oh, the women!' he wailed, and interrupted himself to describe a heavy-footed German princess who had marched past his treasures as if she were viewing a cavalry regiment, applying an unmodulated *Mugneeficent* to everything from the engraved gems to the Hercules torso.

'Not that she was half as bad as the other kind,' he added, as if with a last effort at optimism. 'The kind who discriminate and say: "I'm not sure if it's Botticelli or Cellini I mean, but *one of that school*, at any rate." And the worst of all are the ones who know – up to a certain point: have the schools, and the dates and the jargon pat, and yet wouldn't recognize a Phidias if it stood where they hadn't expected it.'

He had all my sympathy, poor Neave; yet these were trials inseparable from the collector's lot, and not always without their secret compensations. Certainly they did not wholly explain my friend's state of mind; and for a moment I wondered if it were due to some strange disillusionment as to the quality of his treasures. But no! the Daunt collection was almost above criticism; and as we passed from one object to another I saw there was no mistaking the genuineness of Neave's pride in his possessions. The ripe sphere of beauty was his, and he had found no flaw in it as yet. . . .

A year later came the amazing announcement that the Daunt collection was for sale. At first we all supposed it was a case of weeding out (though how old Daunt would have raged at the thought of anybody's weeding *his* collection!). But no – the catalogue corrected that idea. Every stick and stone was to go under the hammer. The news ran like wildfire from Rome to Berlin, from Paris to London and New York. Was Neave ruined, then? Wrong again – the dealers nosed that out in no time. He was simply selling because he chose to sell; and in due time the things came up at Christie's.

But you may be sure the trade had found an answer to the riddle; and the answer was that, on close inspection, Neave had found the things less good than he had supposed. It was a preposterous answer – but then there was no other. Neave, by this time, was pretty generally acknowledged to have the sharpest *flair* of any collector in Europe, and if he didn't choose to keep the Daunt collection it could be only because he had reason to think he could do better.

In a flash this report had gone the rounds, and the buyers were on their guard. I had run over to London to see the thing through, and it was the queerest sale I ever was at. Some of the things held their own, but a lot – and a few of the best among them – went for half their value. You see, they'd been locked up in old Daunt's house for nearly twenty years and hardly shown to anyone, so that the whole younger generation of dealers and collectors knew of them only by hearsay. Then you know the effect of suggestion in such cases. The undefinable sense we were speaking of is a ticklish instrument, easily thrown out of gear by a sudden fall of temperature; and the sharpest experts grow shy and self-distrustful when the cold current of deprecation touches them. The sale was a slaughter – and when I saw the Daunt Diana fall at the wink of a little third-rate *brocanteur* from Vienna I turned sick at the folly of my kind.

For my part, I had never believed that Neave had sold the collection because he'd 'found it out'; and within a year my incredulity was justified. As soon as the things were put in circulation they were known for the marvels that they are. There was hardly a poor bit in the lot; and my wonder grew at Neave's madness. All over Europe, dealers began to fight for the spoils; and all kinds of stuff were palmed off on the unsuspecting as fragments of the Daunt collection!

Meantime, what was Neave doing? For a long time I didn't hear, and chance kept me from returning to Rome. But one day, in Paris, I ran across a dealer who had captured for a song one of the best Florentine bronzes in the Daunt collection – a marvelous *plaquette* of Donatello's. I asked him what had become of it, and he said with a grin: 'I sold it the other day,' naming a price that staggered me.

'Ye gods! Who paid you that for it?'

His grin broadened, and he answered: 'Neave.'

'*Neave*? Humphrey Neave?'

'Didn't you know he was buying back his things?'

'Nonsense!'

'He is, though. Not in his own name – but he's doing it.'

And he *was*, do you know – and at prices that would have made a sane man shudder! A few weeks later I ran across his tracks in London, where he was trying to get hold of a Penicaud enamel – another of his scattered treasures. Then I hunted him down at his hotel, and had it out with him.

'Look here, Neave, what are you up to?'

He wouldn't tell me at first: stared and laughed and denied. But I took him off to dine, and after dinner, while we smoked, I happened to mention casually that I had a pull over the man who had the Penicaud – and at that he broke down and confessed.

'Yes, I'm buying them back, Finney – it's true.' He laughed nervously, twitching his mustache. And then he let me have the story.

'You know how I'd hungered and thirsted for the *real thing* – you quoted my own phrase to me once, about the "ripe sphere of beauty." So when I got my money, and Daunt lost his, almost at the same moment, I saw the hand of Providence in it. I knew that, even if I'd been younger, and had had more time, I could never hope, nowadays, to form such a collection as *that*. There was the ripe sphere, within reach; and I took it. But when I got it, and began to live with it, I found out my mistake. The transaction was a *marriage de convenance* – there'd been no wooing, no winning. Each of my little old bits – the rubbish I chucked out to make room for Daunt's glories – had its own personal history, the drama of my relation to it, of the discovery, the struggle, the capture, the first divine moment of possession. There was a romantic secret between us. And then, I had absorbed its beauties one by one, they had become a part of my imagination, they held me by a hundred threads of far-reaching association. And suddenly I had expected to create this kind of personal tie between myself and a roomful of new cold alien presences – things staring at me vacantly from the depths of unknown pasts! Can you fancy a more preposterous hope? Why, my other things, my *own* things had wooed me as passionately as I wooed them: there was a certain little Italian bronze, a little Venus, who had drawn me, drawn me, drawn me, imploring me to rescue her from her unspeakable surroundings in a vulgar bric-a-brac shop at Biarritz, where she shrank out of sight among sham Sèvres and Dutch silver, as one has seen certain women – rare, shy, exquisite – made almost invisible by the vulgar splendors surrounding them. Well! that little Venus, who was just a specious seventeenth-century attempt at an "antique," but who had penetrated me with her pleading grace, touched me by the easily guessed story of her obscure anonymous origin, was more to me imaginatively – yes! more – than the cold bought beauty of the Daunt Diana. . . .'

'The Daunt Diana!' I broke in. 'Hold up, Neave – *the Daunt Diana?*'

He smiled contemptuously. 'A professional beauty, my dear fellow – expected every head to be turned when she came into a room.'

'Oh, Neave,' I groaned.

'Yes, I know. You're thinking of what we felt that day we first saw her in London. Many a poor devil has sold his soul as the result of such a first sight! Well, I sold *her* instead. Do you want the truth about her? *Elle était bête à pleurer.*'

He laughed and turned away with a shrug of disenchantment.

'And so you're impenitent?' I insisted. 'And yet you're buying some of the things back?'

Neave laughed again, ironically. 'I knew you'd find me out and call me to account. Well, yes: I'm buying back.' He stood before me, half sheepish, half defiant. 'I'm buying back because there's nothing else as good in the market. And because I've a queer feeling that, this time, they'll be *mine*. But I'm ruining myself at the game!' he confessed.

It was true. Neave was ruining himself. And he's gone on ruining himself ever since, till now the job's pretty nearly done. Bit by bit, year by year, he has gathered in his scattered treasures, at higher prices than the dealers ever dreamed of getting for them. There are fabulous details in the story of his quest. Now and then I ran across him, and was able to help him recover a fragment; and it was touching to see his delight in the moment of reunion. Finally, about two years ago, we met in Paris, and he told me he had got back all the important pieces except the Diana.

'The Diana? But you told me you didn't care for her.'

'Didn't care?' He leaned across the restaurant table that divided us. 'Well, no, in a sense I didn't. I wanted her to want me, you see; and she didn't then! Whereas now she's crying to me to come to her. You know where she is?' he broke off.

Yes, I knew: in the center of Mrs. Willy P. Goldmark's yellow and gold drawing room, under a thousand candle power chandelier, with reflectors aimed at her from every point of the compass. I had seen her, wincing and shivering there in her outraged nudity, at one of the Goldmark 'crushes.'

'But you can't get her, Neave,' I objected.

'No, I can't get her,' he said.

Well, last month I was in Rome, for the first time in six or seven years, and of course I looked about for Neave. The Palazzo Neave was let to some rich Russians, and the new porter didn't know where the proprietor lived. But I got on his trail easily enough, and it led me to a strange old place in the Trastevere, a crevassed black palace turned tenement house and fluttering with pauper linen. I found Neave under the leads, in two or three cold rooms that smelt of the *cuisine* of all his neighbors: a poor shrunken figure, smaller and shabbier than ever, yet more alive than when we had made the tour of his collection in the Palazzo Neave.

The collection was around him again, not displayed in tall cabinets and on marble tables, but huddled on shelves, perched on chairs, crammed in corners, putting the gleam of bronze, the luster of marble, the opalescence of old glass, into all the angles of his dim rooms. There they were, the presences that had stared at him down the vistas of Daunt House, and shone in cold transplanted beauty under his own cornices: there they were, gathered about him in humble promiscuity, like superb wild creatures tamed to become the familiars of some harmless wizard.

As we went from bit to bit, as he lifted one piece after another, and held it to the light, I saw in his hands the same tremor that I had noticed when he first handled the same objects at Daunt House. All his life was in his fingertips, and it seemed to communicate life to the things he touched. But you'll think me infected by his mysticism if I tell you they gained new beauty while he held them . . .

We went the rounds slowly and reverently; and then, when I supposed our inspection was over, and was turning to take my leave, he opened a door I had not noticed, and showed me into a room beyond. It was a mere monastic cell, scarcely large enough for his narrow bed and the chest which probably held his few clothes; but there, in a niche, at the foot of the bed – there stood the Daunt Diana.

I gasped at the sight and turned to him; and he looked back at me without speaking.

'In the name of magic, Neave, how did you do it?'

He smiled as if from the depths of some secret rapture. 'Call it magic, if you like; but I ruined myself doing it,' he said.

I stared at him in silence, breathless with the madness of it; and suddenly, red to the ears, he flung out his confession. 'I lied to you that day in London – the day I said I didn't care for her. I always cared – always worshiped – always wanted her. But she wasn't mine then, and I knew it, and she knew it . . . and now at last we understand each other.' He looked at me shyly, and then glanced about the bare room. 'The setting isn't worthy of her, I know; she was meant for glories I can't give her; but beautiful things, my dear Finney, like beautiful spirits, live in houses not made with hands. . . .'

His face shone with an extraordinary kind of light as he spoke; and I saw he'd got hold of the secret we're all after. No, the setting isn't worthy of her, if you like. The rooms are as shabby and mean as those we used to see him in years ago over the wine shop. I'm not sure they're not shabbier and meaner. But she rules there at last, she shines and hovers there above him, and there at night, I doubt not, comes down from her cloud to give him the Latmian kiss. . . .

Afterward

———————— ❦ ————————

'OH, THERE *is* one, of course, but you'll never know it.'

The assertion, laughingly flung out six months earlier in a bright June garden, came back to Mary Boyne with a new perception of its significance as she stood, in the December dusk, waiting for the lamps to be brought into the library.

The words had been spoken by their friend Alida Stair, as they sat at tea on her lawn at Pangbourne, in reference to the very house of which the library in question was the central, the pivotal 'feature.' Mary Boyne and her husband, in quest of a country place in one of the southern or southwestern counties, had, on their arrival in England, carried their problem straight to Alida Stair, who had successfully solved it in her own case; but it was not until they had rejected, almost capriciously, several practical and judicious suggestions that she threw out: 'Well, there's Lyng, in Dorsetshire. It belongs to Hugo's cousins, and you can get it for a song.'

The reason she gave for its being obtainable on these terms – its remoteness from a station, its lack of electric light, hot water pipes, and other vulgar necessities – were exactly those pleading in its favor with two romantic Americans perversely in search of the economic drawbacks which were associated, in their tradition, with unusual architectural felicities.

'I should never believe I was living in an old house unless I was thoroughly uncomfortable,' Ned Boyne, the more extravagant of the two, had jocosely insisted; 'the least hint of convenience would make me think it had been bought out of an exhibition, with the pieces numbered, and set up again.' And they had proceeded to enumerate, with humorous precision, their various

444

doubts and demands, refusing to believe that the house their cousin recommended was *really* Tudor till they learned it had no heating system, or that the village church was literally in the grounds till she assured them of the deplorable uncertainty of the water supply.

'It's too uncomfortable to be true!' Edward Boyne had continued to exult as the avowal of each disadvantage was successively wrung from her; but he had cut short his rhapsody to ask, with a relapse to distrust: 'And the ghost? You've been concealing from us the fact that there is no ghost!'

Mary, at the moment, had laughed with him, yet almost with her laugh, being possessed of several sets of independent perceptions, had been struck by a note of flatness in Alida's answering hilarity.

'Oh, Dorsetshire's full of ghosts, you know.'

'Yes, yes; but that won't do. I don't want to have to drive ten miles to see somebody else's ghost. I want one of my own on the premises. *Is* there a ghost at Lyng?'

His rejoinder had made Alida laugh again, and it was then that she had flung back tantalizingly: 'Oh, there *is* one, of course, but you'll never know it.'

'Never know it?' Boyne pulled her up. 'But what in the world constitutes a ghost except the fact of its being known for one?'

'I can't say. But that's the story.'

'That there's a ghost, but that nobody knows it's a ghost?'

'Well – not till afterward, at any rate.'

'Till afterward?'

'Not till long long afterward.'

'But if it's once been identified as an unearthly visitant, why hasn't it *signalement* been handed down in the family? How has it managed to preserve its incognito?'

Alida could only shake her head. 'Don't ask me. But it has.'

'And then suddenly' – Mary spoke up as if from cavernous depths of divination – 'suddenly, long afterward, one says to one's self "*That was it?*" '

She was startled at the sepulchral sound with which her question fell on the banter of the other two, and she saw the shadow of the same surprise flit across Alida's pupils. 'I suppose so. One just has to wait.'

'Oh, hang waiting!' Ned broke in. 'Life's too short for a ghost who can only be enjoyed in retrospect. Can't we do better than that, Mary?'

But it turned out that in the event they were not destined to, for within three months of their conversation with Mrs. Stair they were settled at Lyng, and the life they had yearned for, to the point of planning it in advance in all its daily details, had actually begun for them.

It was to sit, in the thick December dusk, by just such a wide-hooded fireplace, under just such black oak rafters, with the sense that beyond the mullioned panes the downs were darkened to a deeper solitude: it was for the ultimate indulgence of such sensations that Mary Boyne, abruptly exiled from New York by her husband's business, had endured for nearly fourteen years the soul-deadening ugliness of a Middle Western town, and that Boyne had ground on doggedly at his engineering till, with a suddenness that still made her blink, the prodigious windfall of the Blue Star Mine had put them at a stroke in possession of life and the leisure to taste it. They had never for a moment meant their new state to be one of idleness; but they meant to give themselves only to harmonious activities. She had her vision of painting and gardening (against a background of grey walls), he dreamed of the production of his long-planned book on the 'Economic Basic of Culture'; and with such absorbing work ahead no existence could be too sequestered: they could not get far enough from the world, or plunge deep enough into the past.

Dorsetshire had attracted them from the first by an air of remoteness out of all proportion to its geographical position. But to the Boynes it was one of the ever-recurring wonders of the whole incredibly compressed island – a nest of counties, as they put it – that for the production of its effects so little of a given quality went so far: that so few miles made a distance, and so short a distance a difference.

'It's that,' Ned had once enthusiastically explained, 'that gives such depth to their effects, such relief to their contrasts. They've been able to lay the butter so thick on every delicious mouthful.'

The butter had certainly been laid on thick at Lyng: the old house hidden under a shoulder of the downs had almost all the finer marks of commerce with a protracted past. The mere fact that it was neither large nor exceptional made it, to the Boynes, abound the more completely in its special charm – the charm of having been for centuries a deep dim reservoir of life. The life had probably not been of the most vivid order: for long periods, no doubt, it had fallen as noiselessly into the past as the quiet drizzle of autumn fell, hour after hour, into the fish pond between the yews; but these backwaters of existence sometimes breed, in their sluggish depths, strange acuities of emotion, and Mary Boyne had felt from the first the mysterious stir of intenser memories.

The feeling had never been stronger than on this particular afternoon when, waiting in the library for the lamps to come, she rose from her seat and stood among the shadows of the hearth. Her husband had gone off, after luncheon, for one of his long tramps on the downs. She had noticed of late that he preferred to go alone; and, in the tried security of their personal relations, had been driven to conclude that his book was bothering him, and that he needed the afternoons to turn over in solitude the problems left from the morning's work. Certainly the book was not going as smoothly as she had thought it would, and there were lines of perplexity between his eyes such as had never been there in his engineering days. He had often, then, looked fagged to the verge of illness, but the native demon of worry had never branded his brow. Yet the few pages he had so far read to her – the introduction, and a summary of the opening chapter – showed a firm hold on his subject, and an increasing confidence in his powers.

The fact threw her into deeper perplexity, since, now that he had done with business and its disturbing contingencies, the one other possible source of anxiety was eliminated. Unless it were his health, then? But physically he had gained since they had come to Dorsetshire, grown robuster, ruddier and fresher eyed. It was only within the last week that she had felt in him the undefinable change which made her restless in his absence, and as tongue-tied in his presence as though it were *she* who had a secret to keep from him!

The thought that there *was* a secret somewhere between them struck her with a sudden rap of wonder, and she looked about her down the long room.

'Can it be the house?' she mused.

The room itself might have been full of secrets. They seemed to be piling themselves up, as evening fell, like the layers and layers of velvet shadow dropping from the low ceiling, the rows of books, the smoke-blurred sculpture of the hearth.

'Why, of course – the house is haunted!' she reflected.

The ghost – Alida's imperceptible ghost – after figuring largely in the banter of their first month or two at Lyng, had been gradually left aside as too ineffectual for imaginative use. Mary had, indeed, as became the tenant of a haunted house, made the customary inquiries among her rural neighbors, but, beyond a vague 'They dü say so, Ma'am,' the villages had nothing to impart. The elusive specter had apparently never had sufficient identity for a legend to crystallize about it, and after a time the Boynes had set the matter down to their profit-and-loss account, agreeing that Lyng was one of the few houses good enough in itself to dispense with supernatural enhancements.

'And I suppose, poor ineffectual demon, that's why it beats its beautiful wings in vain in the void,' Mary had laughingly concluded.

'Or, rather,' Ned answered in the same strain, 'why, amid so much that's ghostly, it can never affirm its separate existence as *the* ghost.' And thereupon their invisible housemate had finally dropped out of their references, which were numerous enough to make them soon unaware of the loss.

Now, as she stood on the hearth, the subject of their earlier curiosity revived in her with a new sense of its meaning – a sense gradually acquired through daily contact with the scene of the lurking mystery. It was the house itself, of course, that possessed the ghost-seeing faculty, that communed visually but secretly with its own past; if one could only get into close enough communion with the house, one might surprise its secret, and acquire the ghost sight on one's own account. Perhaps, in his long hours in this very room, where she never trespassed till the afternoon, her husband *had* acquired it already, and was silently carrying about the weight of whatever it had revealed to him. Mary was too well versed in the code of the spectral world not to know that one could not talk about the ghosts one saw: to do so was almost as great a breach of taste as to name a lady in a club. But this explanation did not really satisfy her. 'What, after all, except for the fun of the shudder,' she reflected, 'would he really care for any of their old ghosts?' And thence she was thrown back once more on the fundamental dilemma: the fact that one's greater or less susceptibility to spectral influences had no particular bearing on the case, since, when one *did* see a ghost at Lyng, one did not know it.

'Not till long afterward,' Alida Stair had said. Well, supposing Ned *had* seen one when they first came, and had known only within the last week what had happened to him? More and more under the spell of the hour, she threw back her thoughts to the early days of their tenancy, but at first only to recall a lively confusion of unpacking, settling, arranging of books, and calling to each other from remote corners of the house as, treasure after treasure, it revealed itself to them. It was in this particular connection that she presently recalled a certain soft afternoon of the previous October, when, passing from the first rapturous flurry of exploration to a detailed inspection of the old house, she had pressed (like a novel heroine) a panel that opened on a flight of corkscrew stairs leading to a flat ledge of the roof – the roof which, from below, seemed to slope away on all sides too abruptly for any but practiced feet to scale.

The view from this hidden coign was enchanting, and she had flown down to snatch Ned from his papers and give him the freedom of her discovery. She remembered still how, standing at her side, he had passed his arm about her while their gaze flew to the long tossed horizon line of the downs, and then dropped contentedly back to trace the arabesque of yew hedges about the fish pond, and the shadow of the cedar on the lawn.

'And now the other way,' he had said, turning her about within his arm; and closely pressed to him, she had absorbed, like some long satisfying draught, the picture of the grey-walled court, the squat lions on the gates, and the lime avenue reaching up to the highroad under the downs.

It was just then, while they gazed and held each other, that she had felt his arm relax, and heard a sharp 'Hullo!' that made her turn to glance at him.

Distinctly, yes, she now recalled that she had seen, as she glanced, a shadow of anxiety, of perplexity, rather, fall across his face; and, following his eyes, had beheld the figure of a man – a man in loose greyish clothes, as it appeared to her – who was sauntering down the lime avenue to the court with the doubtful gait of a stranger who seeks his way. Her shortsighted eyes had given her but a blurred impression of slightness and greyishness, with something foreign, or at least unlocal, in the cut of the figure or its dress; but her husband had apparently seen more – seen enough to make him push past her with a hasty 'Wait!' and dash down the stairs without pausing to give her a hand.

A slight tendency to dizziness obliged her, after a provisional clutch at the chimney against which they had been leaning, to follow him first more cautiously; and when she had reached the landing she paused again, for a less definite reason, leaning over the banister to strain her eyes through the silence of the brown sun-flecked depths. She lingered there till, somewhere in those depths, she heard the closing of a door; then, mechanically impelled, she went down the shallow flights of steps till she reached the lower hall.

The front door stood open on the sunlight of the court, and hall and court were empty. The library door was open, too, and after listening in vain for any sound of voices within, she crossed the threshold, and found her husband alone, vaguely fingering the papers on his desk.

He looked up, as if surprised at her entrance, but the shadow of anxiety had passed from his face, leaving it even, as she fancied, a little brighter and clearer than usual.

'What was it? Who was it?' she asked.

'Who?' he repeated, with the surprise still all on his side.

'The man we saw coming toward the house.'

He seemed to reflect. 'The man? Why, I thought I saw Peters; I dashed after him to say a word about the stable drains, but he had disappeared before I could get down.'

'Disappeared? But he seemed to be walking so slowly when we saw him.'

Boyne shrugged his shoulders. 'So I thought; but he must have got up steam in the interval. What do you say to our trying a scramble up Meldon Steep before sunset?'

That was all. At the time the occurrence had been less than nothing, had, indeed, been immediately obliterated by the magic of their first vision from Meldon Steep, a height which they had dreamed of climbing ever since they had first seen its bare spine rising above the roof of Lyng. Doubtless it was the mere fact of the other incident's having occurred on the very day of their ascent to Meldon that had kept it stored away in the fold of memory from which it now emerged; for in itself it had no mark of the portentous. At the moment there could have been nothing more natural than that Ned should dash himself from the roof in the pursuit of dilatory tradesmen. It was the period when they were always on the watch for one or the other of the specialists employed about the place; always lying in wait for them, and rushing out at them with questions, reproaches or reminders. And certainly in the distance the grey figure had looked like Peters.

Yet now, as she reviewed the scene, she felt her husband's explanation of it to have been invalidated by the look of anxiety on his face. Why had the familiar appearance of Peters made him anxious? Why, above all, if it was of such prime necessity to confer with him on the subject of the stable drains, had the failure to find him produced such a look of relief? Mary could not say that any one of these questions had occurred to her at the time, yet, from the promptness with which they now marshalled themselves at her summons, she had a sense that they must all along have been there, waiting their hour.

• II •

WEARY with her thoughts, she moved to the window. The library was now quite dark, and she was surprised to see how much faint light the outer world still held.

As she peered out into it across the court, a figure shaped itself far down the perspective of bare limes: it looked a mere blot of deeper grey in the greyness, and for an instant, as it moved toward her, her heart thumped to the thought 'It's the ghost!'

She had time, in that long instant, to feel suddenly that the man of whom, two months earlier, she had had a distant vision from the roof, was now, at his predestined hour, about to reveal himself as *not* having been Peters; and her spirit sank under the impending fear of the disclosure. But almost with the next tick of the clock the figure, gaining substance and character, showed itself even to her weak sight as her husband's; and she turned to meet him, as he entered, with the confession of her folly.

'It's really too absurd,' she laughed out, 'but I never *can* remember!'

'Remember what?' Boyne questioned as they drew together.

'That when one sees the Lyng ghost one never knows it.'

Her hand was on his sleeve, and he kept it there, but with no response in his gesture or in the lines of his preoccupied face.

'Did you think you'd seen it?' he asked, after an appreciable interval.

'Why, I actually took *you* for it, my dear, in my mad determination to spot it!'

'Me – just now?' His arm dropped away, and he turned from her with a faint echo of her laugh. 'Really, dearest, you'd better give it up, if that's the best you can do.'

'Oh, yes, I give it up. Have *you*?' she asked, turning round on him abruptly.

The parlormaid had entered with letters and a lamp, and the light struck up into Boyne's face as he bent above the tray she presented.

'Have *you*?' Mary perversely insisted, when the servant had disappeared on her errand of illumination.

'Have I what?' he rejoined absently, the light bringing out the sharp stamp of worry between his brows as he turned over the letters.

'Given up trying to see the ghost.' Her heart beat a little at the experiment she was making.

Her husband, laying his letters aside, moved away into the shadow of the hearth.

'I never tried,' he said, tearing open the wrapper of a news-paper.

'Well, of course,' Mary persisted. 'the exasperating thing is that there's no use trying, since one can't be sure till so long afterward.'

He was unfolding the paper as if he had hardly heard her; but after a pause, during which the sheets rustled spasmodically between his hands, he looked up to ask, 'Have you any idea *how long*?'

Mary had sunk into a low chair beside the fireplace. From her seat she glanced over, startled, at her husband's profile, which was projected against the circle of lamplight.

'No; none. Have *you*?' she retorted, repeating her former phrase with an added stress of intention.

Boyne crumpled the paper into a bunch, and then, inconse-quently, turned back with it toward the lamp.

'Lord, no! I only meant,' he exclaimed, with a faint tinge of impatience, 'is there any legend, any tradition, as to that?'

'Not that I know of,' she answered; but the impulse to add 'What makes you ask?' was checked by the reappearance of the parlormaid, with tea and a second lamp.

With the dispersal of shadows, and the repetition of the daily domestic office, Mary Boyne felt herself less oppressed by that sense of something mutely imminent which had darkened her afternoon. For a few moments she gave herself to the details of her task, and when she looked up from it she was struck to the point of bewilderment by the change in her husband's face. He had seated himself near the farther lamp, and was absorbed in the perusal of his letters; but was it something he had found in them, or merely the shifting of her own point of view, that had restored his features to their normal aspect? The longer she looked the more definitely the change affirmed itself. The lines of tension had vanished, and such traces of fatigue as lingered were of the kind easily attributable to steady mental effort. He glanced up, as if drawn by her gaze, and met her eyes with a smile.

'I'm dying for my tea, you know; and here's a letter for you,' he said.

She took the letter he held out in exchange for the cup she proffered him, and, returning to her seat, broke the seal with the languid gesture of the reader whose interests are all enclosed in the circle of one cherished presence.

Her next conscious motion was that of starting to her feet, the letter falling to them as she rose, while she held out to her husband a newspaper clipping.

'Ned! What's this? What does it mean?'

He had risen at the same instant, almost as if hearing her cry before she uttered it; and for a perceptible space of time he and she studied each other, like adversaries watching for an advantage, across the space between her chair and his desk.

'What's what? You fairly made me jump!' Boyne said at length, moving toward her with a sudden half-exasperated laugh. The shadow of apprehension was on his face again, not now a look of fixed foreboding, but a shifting vigilance of lips and eyes that gave her the sense of his feeling himself invisibly surrounded.

Her hand shook so that she could hardly give him the clipping.

'This article – from the *Waukesha Sentinel* – that a man named Elwell has brought suit against you – that there was something wrong about the Blue Star Mine. I can't understand more than half.'

They continued to face each other as she spoke, and to her astonishment she saw that her words had the almost immediate effect of dissipating the strained watchfulness of his look.

'Oh, *that!*' He glanced down the printed slip, and then folded it with the gesture of one who handles something harmless and familiar. 'What's the matter with you this afternoon, Mary? I thought you'd got bad news.'

She stood before him with her undefinable terror subsiding slowly under the reassurance of his tone.

'You knew about this, then – it's all right?'

'Certainly I knew about it; and it's all right.'

'But what *is* it? I don't understand. What does this man accuse you of?'

'Pretty nearly every crime in the calendar.' Boyne had tossed the clipping down, and thrown himself into an armchair near the fire. 'Do you want to hear the story? It's not particularly interesting – just a squabble over interests in the Blue Star.'

'But who is this Elwell? I don't know the name.'

'Oh, he's a fellow I put into it – gave him a hand up. I told you all about him at the time.'

'I dare say. I must have forgotten.' Vainly she strained back among her memories. 'But if you helped him, why does he make this return?'

'Probably some shyster lawyer got hold of him and talked him over. It's all rather technical and complicated. I thought that kind of thing bored you.'

His wife felt a sting of compunction. Theoretically, she deprecated the American wife's detachment from her husband's professional interests, but in practice she had always found it difficult to fix her attention on Boyne's report of the transactions in which his varied interests involved him. Besides, she had felt during their years of exile, that, in a community where the amenities of living could be obtained only at the cost of efforts as arduous as her husband's professional labors, such brief leisure as he and she could command should be used as an escape from immediate preoccupations, a flight to the life they always dreamed of living. Once or twice, now that this new life had actually drawn its magic circle about them, she had asked herself if she had done right; but hitherto such conjectures had been no more than the retrospective excursions of an active fancy. Now, for the first time, it startled her a little to find how little she knew of the material foundation on which her happiness was built.

She glanced at her husband, and was again reassured by the composure of his face; yet she felt the need of more definite grounds for her reassurance.

'But doesn't this suit worry you? Why have you never spoken to me about it?'

He answered both questions at once. 'I didn't speak of it at first because it *did* worry me – annoyed me, rather. But it's all ancient history now. Your correspondent must have got hold of a back number of the *Sentinel*.'

She felt a quick thrill of relief. 'You mean it's over? He's lost his case?'

There was a just perceptible delay in Boyne's reply. 'This suit's been withdrawn – that's all.'

But she persisted, as if to exonerate herself from the inward charge of being too easily put off. 'Withdrawn it because he saw he had no chance?'

'Oh, he had no chance,' Boyne answered.

She was still struggling with a dimly felt perplexity at the back of her thoughts.

'How long ago was it withdrawn?'

He paused, as if with a slight return to his former uncertainty. 'I've just had the news now; but I've been expecting it.'

'Just now – in one of your letters?'

'Yes; in one of my letters.'

She made no answer, and was aware only, after a short interval of waiting, that he had risen, and, strolling across the room, had placed himself on the sofa at her side. She felt him, as he did so, pass an arm about her, she felt his hand seek hers and clasp it, and turning slowly, drawn by the warmth of his cheek, she met his smiling eyes.

'It's all right – it's all right?' she questioned, through the flood of her dissolving doubts; and 'I give you my word it was never righter!' he laughed back at her, holding her close.

• III •

ONE of the strangest things she was afterward to recall out of all the next day's strangeness was the sudden and complete recovery of her sense of security.

It was in the air when she woke in her low-ceiled, dusky room; it went with her downstairs to the breakfast table, flashed out at her from the fire, and reduplicated itself from the flanks of the urn and the sturdy flutings of the Georgian teapot. It was as if in some roundabout way, all her diffused fears of the previous day, with their moment of sharp concentration about the newspaper article – as if this dim questioning of the future, and startled return upon the past, had between them liquidated the arrears of some haunting moral obligation. If she had indeed been careless of her husband's affairs, it was, her new state seemed to prove, because her faith in him instinctively justified such carelessness; and his right to her faith had now affirmed itself in the very face of menace and suspicion. She had never seen him more untroubled, more naturally and unconsciously himself, than after the cross-examination to which she had subjected him: it was almost as if he had been aware of her doubts, and had wanted the air cleared as much as she did.

It was as clear, thank heaven, as the bright outer light that surprised her almost with a touch of summer when she issued from the house for her daily round of the gardens. She had left Boyne at his desk, indulging herself, as she passed the library door, by a last peep at his quiet face, where he bent, pipe in mouth, above his papers; and now she had her own morning's task to perform. The task involved, on such charmed winter days, almost as much happy loitering about the different quarters of her domain as if spring were already at work there. There were such endless possibilities still before her, such opportunities to bring out the latent graces of the old place, without a single irreverent touch of alteration, that the winter was all too short to plan what spring and autumn executed. And her recovered sense of safety gave, on this particular morning, a peculiar zest to her progress through the sweet still place. She went first to the kitchen garden, where the espaliered pear trees drew complicated patterns on the walls, and pigeons were fluttering and preening about the silvery-slated roof of their cot. There was something wrong about the piping of the hothouse, and she was expecting an authority from Dorchester, who was to drive out between trains and make a diagnosis of the boiler. But when she dipped into the damp heat of the greenhouses, among the spiced scents and waxy pinks and reds of old-fashioned exotics – even the flora of Lyng was in the note! – she learned that the great man had not arrived, and, the day being too rare to waste in an artificial atmosphere, she came out again and paced along the springy turf of the bowling green to the gardens behind the house. At their farther end rose a grass terrace, looking across the fish pond and yew hedges to the long house front with its twisted chimney stacks and blue roof angles all drenched in the pale gold moisture of the air.

Seen thus, across the level tracery of the gardens, it sent her, from open windows and hospitably smoking chimneys, the look of some warm human presence, of a mind slowly ripened on a sunny wall of experience. She had never before had such a sense of her intimacy with it, such a conviction that its secrets were all beneficent, kept, as they said to children, 'for one's good,' such a trust in its power to gather up her life and Ned's into the harmonious pattern of the long long story it sat there weaving in the sun.

She heard steps behind her, and turned, expecting to see the gardener accompanied by the engineer, from Dorchester. But only one figure was in sight, that of a youngish slightly built man, who, for reasons she could not on the spot have given, did not remotely resemble her notion of an authority on hothouse boilers. The newcomer, on seeing her, lifted his hat, and paused with the air of a gentleman – perhaps a traveler – who wishes to make it known that his intrusion is involuntary. Lyng occasionally attracted the more cultivated traveler, and Mary half expected to see the stranger dissemble a camera, or justify his presence by producing it. But he made no gesture of any sort, and after a moment she asked, in a tone responding to the courteous hesitation of his attitude: 'Is there anyone you wish to see?'

'I came to see Mr. Boyne,' he answered. His intonation, rather than his accent, was faintly American, and Mary, at the note, looked at him more closely. The brim of his soft felt hat cast a shade on his face, which, thus obscured, wore to her shortsighted gaze a look of seriousness, as of a person arriving on business, and civilly but firmly aware of his rights.

Past experience had made her equally sensible to such claims; but she was jealous of her husband's morning hours, and doubtful of his having given anyone the right to intrude on them.

'Have you an appointment with my husband?' she asked.

The visitor hesitated, as if unprepared for the question.

'I think he expects me,' he replied.

It was Mary's turn to hesitate. 'You see this is his time for work: he never sees anyone in the morning.'

He looked at her a moment without answering; then, as if accepting her decision, he began to move away. As he turned, Mary saw him pause and glance up at the peaceful house front. Something in his air suggested weariness and disappointment, the dejection of the traveler who has come from far off and whose hours are limited by the timetable. It occurred to her that if this were the case her refusal might have made his errand vain, and a sense of compunction caused her to hasten after him.

'May I ask if you have come a long way?'

He gave her the same grave look. 'Yes – I have come a long way.'

'Then, if you'll go to the house, no doubt my husband will see you now. You'll find him in the library.'

She did not know why she had added the last phrase, except from a vague impulse to atone for her previous inhospitality. The visitor seemed about to express his thanks, but her attention was distracted by the approach of the gardener with a companion who bore all the marks of being the expert from Dorchester.

'This way,' she said, waving the stranger to the house; and an instant later she had forgotten him in the absorption of her meeting with the boiler maker.

The encounter led to such far-reaching results that the engineer ended by finding it expedient to ignore his train, and Mary was beguiled into spending the remainder of the morning in absorbed confabulation among the flower pots. When the colloquy ended, she was surprised to find that it was nearly luncheon time, and she half expected, as she hurried back to the house, to see her husband coming out to meet her. But she found no one in the court but an undergardener raking the gravel, and the hall, when she entered it, was so silent that she guessed Boyne to be still at work.

Not wishing to disturb him, she turned into the drawing room, and there, at her writing table, lost herself in renewed calculations of the outlay to which the morning's conference had pledged her. The fact that she could permit herself such follies had not yet lost its novelty; and somehow, in contrast to the vague fears of the previous days, it now seemed an element of her recovered security, of the sense that, as Ned had said, things in general had never been 'righter.'

She was still luxuriating in a lavish play of figures when the parlormaid, from the threshold, roused her with an inquiry as to the expediency of serving luncheon. It was one of their jokes that Trimmle announced luncheon as if she were divulging a state secret, and Mary, intent upon her papers, merely murmured an absent-minded assent.

She felt Trimmle wavering doubtfully on the threshold, as if in rebuke of such unconsidered assent; then her retreating steps sounded down the passage, and Mary, pushing away her papers, crossed the hall and went to the library door. It was still closed, and she wavered in her turn, disliking to disturb her husband, yet anxious that he should not exceed his usual measure of work. As she stood there, balancing her impulses, Trimmle returned with the announcement of luncheon, and Mary, thus impelled, opened the library door.

Boyne was not at his desk, and she peered about her, expecting to discover him before the bookshelves, somewhere down the length of the room; but her call brought no response, and gradually it became clear to her that he was not there.

She turned back to the parlormaid.

'Mr. Boyne must be upstairs. Please tell him that luncheon is ready.'

Trimmle appeared to hesitate between the obvious duty of obedience and an equally obvious conviction of the foolishness of the injunction laid on her. The struggle resulted in her saying: 'If you please, Madam, Mr. Boyne's not upstairs.'

'Not in his room? Are you sure?'

'I'm sure, Madam.'

Mary consulted the clock. 'Where is he, then?'

'He's gone out,' Trimmle announced, with the superior air of one who has respectfully waited for the question that a well-ordered mind would have put first.

Mary's conjecture had been right, then. Boyne must have gone to the gardens to meet her, and since she had missed him, it was clear that he had taken the shorter way by the south door, instead of going round to the court. She crossed the hall to the French window opening directly on the yew garden, but the parlormaid, after another moment of inner conflict, decided to bring out: 'Please, Madam, Mr. Boyne didn't go that way.'

Mary turned back. 'Where *did* he go? And when?'

'He went out of the front door, up the drive, Madam.' It was a matter of principle with Trimmle never to answer more than one question at a time.

'Up the drive? At this hour?' Mary went to the door herself, and glanced across the court through the tunnel of bare limes. But its perspective was as empty as when she had scanned it on entering.

'Did Mr. Boyne leave no message?'

Trimmle seemed to surrender herself to a last struggle with the forces of chaos.

'No, Madam. He just went out with the gentleman.'

'The gentleman? What gentleman?' Mary wheeled about, as if to front this new factor.

'The gentleman who called, Madam,' said Trimmle resignedly.

'When did a gentleman call? Do explain yourself, Trimmle!'

Only the fact that Mary was very hungry, and that she wanted to consult her husband about the greenhouses, would have caused her to lay so unusual an injunction on her attendant; and even now she was detached enough to note in Trimmle's eye the dawning defiance of the respectful subordinate who has been pressed too hard.

'I couldn't exactly say the hour, Madam, because I didn't let the gentleman in,' she replied, with an air of discreetly ignoring the irregularity of her mistress's course.

'You didn't let him in?'

'No, Madam. When the bell rang I was dressing, and Agnes – '

'Go and ask Agnes, then,' said Mary.

Trimmle still wore her look of patient magnanimity. 'Agnes would not know, Madam, for she had unfortunately burnt her hand in trimming the wick of the new lamp from town' – Trimmle, as Mary was aware, had always been opposed to the new lamp – 'and so Mrs. Dockett sent the kitchenmaid instead.'

Mary looked again at the clock. 'It's after two! Go and ask the kitchenmaid if Mr. Boyne left any word.'

She went into luncheon without waiting, and Trimmle presently brought her there the kitchenmaid's statement that the gentleman had called about eleven o'clock, and that Mr. Boyne had gone out with him without leaving any message. The kitchenmaid did not even know the caller's name, for he had written it on a slip of paper, which he had folded and handed to her, with the injunction to deliver it at once to Mr. Boyne.

Mary finished her luncheon, still wondering, and when it was over, and Trimmle had brought the coffee to the drawing room, her wonder had deepened to a first faint tinge of disquietude. It was unlike Boyne to absent himself without explanation at so unwonted an hour, and the difficulty of identifying the visitor whose summons he had apparently obeyed made his disappearance the more unaccountable. Mary Boyne's experience as the wife of a busy engineer, subject to sudden calls and compelled to keep irregular hours, had trained her to the philosophic acceptance of surprises; but since Boyne's withdrawal from business he had adopted a Benedictine regularity of life. As if to make up for the dispersed and agitated years, with their 'stand-up' lunches, and dinners rattled down to the joltings of the dining cars, he cultivated the last refinements of punctuality and monotony, discouraging his wife's fancy for the unexpected, and declaring that to a delicate taste there were infinite gradations of pleasure in the recurrences of habit.

Still, since no life can completely defend itself from the unforeseen, it was evident that all Boyne's precautions would sooner or later prove unavailable, and Mary concluded that he had cut short a tiresome visit by walking with his caller to the station, or at least accompanying him for part of the way.

This conclusion relieved her from further preoccupation, and she went out herself to take up her conference with the gardener. Thence she walked to the village post office, a mile or so away; and when she turned toward home the early twilight was setting in.

She had taken a footpath across the downs, and as Boyne, meanwhile, had probably returned from the station by the highroad, there was little likelihood of their meeting. She felt sure, however, of his having reached the house before her; so sure that, when she entered it herself, without even pausing to inquire of Trimmle, she made directly for the library. But the library was still empty, and with an unwonted exactness of visual memory she observed that the papers on her husband's desk lay precisely as they had lain when she had gone in to call him to luncheon.

Then of a sudden she was seized by a vague dread of the unknown. She had closed the door behind her on entering, and as she stood alone in the long silent room, her dread seemed to take shape and sound, to be there breathing, and lurking among the shadows. Her shortsighted eyes strained through them, half-discerning an actual presence, something aloof, that watched and knew; and in the recoil from that intangible presence she threw herself on the bell rope and gave it a sharp pull.

The sharp summons brought Trimmle in precipitately with a lamp, and Mary breathed again at this sobering reappearance of the usual.

'You may bring tea if Mr. Boyne is in,' she said, to justify her ring.

'Very well, Madam. But Mr. Boyne is not in,' said Trimmle, putting down the lamp.

'Not in? You mean he's come back and gone out again?'

'No, Madam. He's never been back.'

The dread stirred again, and Mary knew that now it had her fast.

'Not since he went out with – the gentleman?'

'Not since he went out with the gentleman.'

'But who *was* the gentleman?' Mary insisted, with the shrill note of someone trying to be heard through a confusion of noises.

'That I couldn't say, Madam.' Trimmle, standing there by the lamp, seemed suddenly to grow less round and rosy, as though eclipsed by the same creeping shade of apprehension.

'But the kitchenmaid knows – wasn't it the kitchenmaid who let him in?'

'She doesn't know either, Madam, for he wrote his name on a folded paper.'

Mary, through her agitation, was aware that they were both designating the unknown visitor by a vague pronoun, instead of the conventional formula which, till then, had kept their allusions within the bounds of conformity. And at the same moment her mind caught at the suggestion of the folded paper.

'But he must have a name! Where's the paper?'

She moved to the desk, and began to turn over the documents that littered it. The first that caught her eye was an unfinished letter in her husband's hand, with his pen lying across it, as though dropped there at a sudden summons.

'My dear Parvis' – who was Parvis? – 'I have just received your letter announcing Elwell's death, and while I suppose there is now no further risk of trouble, it might be safer – '

She tossed the sheet aside, and continued her search; but no folded paper was discoverable among the letters and pages of manuscript which had been swept together in a heap, as if by a hurried or a startled gesture.

'But the kitchenmaid *saw* him. Send her here,' she commanded, wondering at her dullness in not thinking sooner of so simple a solution.

Trimmle vanished in a flash, as if thankful to be out of the room, and when she reappeared, conducting the agitated underling, Mary had regained her self-possession, and had her questions ready.

The gentleman was a stranger, yes – that she understood. But what had he said? And, above all, what had he looked like? The first question was easily enough answered, for the disconcerting reason that he had said so little – had merely asked for Mr. Boyne, and, scribbling something on a bit of paper, had requested that it should at once be carried in to him.

'Then you don't know what he wrote? You're not sure it *was* his name?'

The kitchenmaid was not sure, but supposed it was, since he had written it in answer to her inquiry as to whom she should announce.

'And when you carried the paper in to Mr. Boyne, what did he say?'

'The kitchenmaid did not think that Mr. Boyne had said anything, but she could not be sure, for just as she had handed him the paper and he was opening it, she had become aware that the visitor had followed her into the library, and she had slipped out, leaving the two gentlemen together.

'But then, if you left them in the library, how do you know that they went out of the house?'

This question plunged the witness into a momentary inarticulateness, from which she was rescued by Trimmle, who, by means of ingenious circumlocutions, elicited the statement that before she could cross the hall to the back passage she had heard the two gentlemen behind her, and had seen them go out of the front door together.

'Then, if you saw the strange gentleman twice, you must be able to tell me what he looked like.'

But with this final challenge to her powers of expression it became clear that the limit of the kitchenmaid's endurance had been reached. The obligation of going to the front door to 'show in' a visitor was in itself so subversive of the fundamental order of things that it had thrown her faculties into hopeless disarray, and she could only stammer out, after various panting efforts: 'His hat, mum, was different-like, as you might say – '

'Different? How different?' Mary flashed out, her own mind, in the same instant, leaping back to an image left on it that morning, and then lost under layers of subsequent impressions.

'His hat had a wide brim, you mean, and his face was pale – a youngish face?' Mary pressed her, with a white-lipped intensity of interrogation. But if the kitchenmaid found any adequate answer to this challenge, it was swept away for her listener down the rushing current of her own convictions. The stranger – the stranger in the garden! Why had Mary not thought of him before? She needed no one now to tell her that it was he who had called for her husband and gone away with him. But who was he, and why had Boyne obeyed him?

• IV •

IT leaped out at her suddenly, like a grin out of the dark, that they had often called England so little – 'such a confoundedly hard place to get lost in.'

A confoundedly hard place to get lost in! That had been her husband's phrase. And now, with the whole machinery of official investigation sweeping its flashlights from shore to shore, and across the dividing straits; now, with Boyne's name blazing from the walls of every town and village, his portrait (how that wrung her!) hawked up and down the country like the image of a hunted criminal; now the little compact populous island, so policed, surveyed and administered, revealed itself as a Sphinxlike guardian of abysmal mysteries, staring back into his wife's anguished eyes as if with the wicked joy of knowing something they would never know!

In the fortnight since Boyne's disappearance there had been no word of him, no trace of his movements. Even the usual misleading reports that raise expectancy in tortured bosoms had been few and fleeting. No one but the kitchenmaid had seen Boyne leave the house, and no one else had seen 'the gentleman' who accompanied him. All inquiries in the neighborhood failed to elicit the memory of a stranger's presence that day in the neighborhood of Lyng. And no one had met Edward Boyne, either alone or in company, in any of the neighboring villages, or on the road across the downs, or at either of the local railway stations. The sunny English noon had swallowed him as completely as if he had gone out into Cimmerian night.

Mary, while every official means of investigation was working as its highest pressure, had ransacked her husband's papers for any trace of antecedent complications, of entanglements or obligations unknown to her, that might throw a ray into the darkness. But if any such had existed in the background of Boyne's life, they had vanished like the slip of paper on which the visitor had written his name. There remained no possible thread of guidance except – if it were indeed an exception – the letter which Boyne had apparently been in the art of writing when he received his mysterious summons. That letter, read and reread by his wife, and submitted by her to the police, yielded little enough to feed conjecture.

'I have just heard of Elwell's death, and while I suppose there is now no further risk of trouble, it might be safer – ' That was all. The 'risk of trouble' was easily explained by the newspaper clipping which had apprised Mary of the suit brought against her husband by one of his associates in the Blue Star enterprise. The only new information conveyed by the letter was the fact of its showing Boyne, when he wrote it, to be still apprehensive of the results of the suit, though he had told his wife that it had been withdrawn, and though the letter itself proved that the plaintiff was dead. It took several days of cabling to fix the identity of the 'Parvis' to whom the fragment was addressed, but even after these inquiries had shown him to be a Waukesha lawyer, no new facts concerning the Elwell suit were elicited. He appeared to have had no direct concern in it, but to have been conversant with the facts merely as an acquaintance, and possible intermediary; and he declared himself unable to guess with what object Boyne intended to seek his assistance.

This negative information, sole fruit of the first fortnight's search, was not increased by a jot during the slow weeks that followed. Mary knew that the investigations were still being carried on, but she had a vague sense of their gradually slackening, as the actual march of time seemed to slacken. It was as though the days, flying horror-struck from the shrouded image of the one inscrutable day, gained assurance as the distance lengthened, till at last they fell back into their normal gait. And so with the human imaginations at work on the dark event. No doubt it occupied them still, but week by week and hour by hour it grew less absorbing, took up less space, was slowly but inevitably crowded out of the foreground of consciousness by the new problems perpetually bubbling up from the cloudy caldron of human experience.

Even Mary Boyne's consciousness gradually felt the same lowering of velocity. It still swayed with the incessant oscillations of conjecture; but they were slower, more rhythmical in their beat. There were even moments of weariness when, like the victim of some poison which leaves the brain clear, but holds the body motionless, she saw herself domesticated with the Horror, accepting its perpetual presence as one of the fixed conditions of life.

These moments lengthened into hours and days, till she passed into a phase of stolid acquiescence. She watched the routine of daily life with the incurious eye of a savage on whom the meaningless processes of civilization make but the faintest impression. She had come to regard herself as part of the routine, a spoke of the wheel, revolving with its motion; she felt almost like the furniture of the room in which she sat, an insensate object to be dusted and pushed about with the chairs and tables. And this deepening apathy held her fast at Lyng, in spite of the entreaties of friends and the usual medical recommendation of 'change.' Her friends supposed that her refusal to move was inspired by the belief that her husband would one day return to the spot from which he had vanished, and a beautiful legend grew up about this imaginary state of waiting. But in reality she had no such belief: the depths of anguish enclosing her were no longer lighted by flashes of hope.

She was sure that Boyne would never come back, that he had gone out of her sight as completely as if Death itself had waited that day on the threshold. She had even renounced, one by one, the various theories as to his disappearance which had been advanced by the press, the police, and her own agonized imagination. In sheer lassitude her mind turned from these alternatives of horror, and sank back into the blank fact that he was gone.

No, she would never know what had become of him – no one would ever know. But the house *knew*; the library in which she spent her long lonely evenings knew. For it was here that the last scene had been enacted, here that the stranger had come, and spoken the word which had caused Boyne to rise and follow him. The floor she trod had felt his tread; the books on the shelves had seen his face; and there were moments when the intense consciousness of the old dusky walls seemed about to break out into some audible revelation of their secret. But the revelation never came, and she knew it would never come. Lyng was not one of the garrulous old houses that betray the secrets entrusted to them. Its very legend proved that it had always been the mute accomplice, the incorruptible custodian, of the mysteries it had surprised. And Mary Boyne, sitting face to face with its silence, felt the futility of seeking to break it by any human means.

• V •

'I DON'T say it *wasn't* straight, and yet I don't say it *was* straight. It was business.'

Mary, at the words, lifted her head with a start, and looked intently at the speaker.

When, half an hour before, a card with 'Mr. Parvis' on it had been brought up to her, she had been immediately aware that the name had been a part of her consciousness ever since she had read it and at the head of Boyne's unfinished letter. In the library she had found awaiting her a small sallow man with a bald head and gold eyeglasses, and it sent a tremor through her to know that this was the person to whom her husband's last known thought had been directed.

Parvis, civilly, but without vain preamble – in the manner of a man who has his watch in his hand – had set forth the object of his visit. He had 'run over' to England on business, and finding himself in the neighborhood of Dorchester, had not wished to leave it without paying his respects to Mrs. Boyne; and without asking her, if the occasion offered, what she meant to do about Bob Elwell's family.

The words touched the spring of some obscure dread in Mary's bosom. Did her visitor, after all, know what Boyne had meant by his unfinished phrase? She asked for an elucidation of his question, and noticed at once that he seemed surprised at her continued ignorance of the subject. Was it possible that she really knew as little as she said?

'I know nothing – you must tell me,' she faltered out; and her visitor thereupon proceeded to unfold his story. It threw, even to her confused perceptions, and imperfectly initiated vision, a lurid glare on the whole hazy episode of the Blue Star Mine. Her husband had made his money in that brilliant speculation at the cost of 'getting ahead' of someone less alert to seize the chance; and the victim of his ingenuity was young Robert Elwell, who had 'put him on' to the Blue Star scheme.

Parvis, at Mary's first cry, had thrown her a sobering glance through his impartial glasses.

'Bob Elwell wasn't smart enough, that's all; if he had been, he might have turned round and served Boyne the same way. It's the kind of thing that happens everyday in business. I guess it's what the scientists call the survival of the fittest – see?' said Mr. Parvis, evidently pleased with the aptness of his analogy.

Mary felt a physical shrinking from the next question she tried to frame: it was as though the words on her lips had a taste that nauseated her.

'But then – you accuse my husband of doing something dishonorable?'

Mr. Parvis surveyed the question dispassionately. 'Oh, no, I don't. I don't even say it wasn't straight.' He glanced up and down the long lines of books, as if one of them might have supplied him with the definition he sought. 'I don't say it *wasn't* straight, and yet I don't say it *was* straight. It was business.' After all, no definition in his category could be more comprehensive than that.

Mary sat staring at him with a look of terror. He seemed to her like the indifferent emissary of some evil power.

'But Mr. Elwell's lawyers apparently did not take your view, since I suppose the suit was withdrawn by their advice.'

'Oh, yes; they knew he hadn't a leg to stand on, technically. It was when they advised him to withdraw the suit that he got desperate. You see, he'd borrowed most of the money he lost in the Blue Star, and he was up a tree. That's why he shot himself when they told him he had no show.'

The horror was sweeping over Mary in great deafening waves.

'He shot himself? He killed himself because of *that*?'

'Well, he didn't kill himself, exactly. He dragged on two months before he died.' Parvis emitted the statement as unemotionally as a gramophone grinding out its record.

'You mean that he tried to kill himself, and failed? And tried again?'

'Oh, he didn't have to *try* again,' said Parvis grimly.

They sat opposite each other in silence, he swinging his eyeglasses thoughtfully about his finger, she, motionless, her arms stretched along her knees in an attitude of rigid tension.

'But if you knew all this,' she began at length, hardly able to force her voice above a whisper, 'how is it that when I wrote you at the time of my husband's disappearance you said you didn't understand his letter?'

Parvis received this without perceptible embarrassment: 'Why, I didn't understand it – strictly speaking. And it wasn't the time to talk about it, if I had. The Elwell business was settled when the suit was withdrawn. Nothing I could have told you would have helped you to find your husband.'

Mary continued to scrutinize him. 'Then why are you telling me now?'

Still Parvis did not hesitate. 'Well, to begin with, I supposed you knew more than you appear to – I mean about the circumstances of Elwell's death. And then people are talking of it now; the whole matter's been raked up again. And I thought if you didn't know you ought to.'

She remained silent, and he continued: 'You see, it's only come out lately what a bad state Elwell's affairs were in. His wife's a proud woman, and she fought on as long as she could, going out to work, and taking sewing at home when she got too sick – something with the heart, I believe. But she had his mother to look after, and the children, and she broke down under it, and

159

finally had to ask for help. That called attention to the case, and the papers took it up, and a subscription was started. Everybody out there liked Bob Elwell, and most of the prominent names in the place are down on the list, and people began to wonder why – '

Parvis broke off to fumble in an inner pocket. 'Here,' he continued, 'here's an account of the whole thing from the *Sentinel* – a little sensational, of course. But I guess you'd better look it over.'

He held out a newspaper to Mary, who unfolded it slowly, remembering, as she did so, the evening when, in that same room, the perusal of a clipping from the *Sentinel* had first shaken the depths of her security.

As she opened the paper, her eyes, shrinking from the glaring headlines, 'Widow of Boyne's Victim Forced to Appeal for Aid,' ran down the column of text to two portraits inserted in it. The first was her husband's, taken from a photograph made the year they had come to England. It was the picture of him that she liked best, the one that stood on the writing table upstairs in her bedroom. As the eyes in the photograph met hers, she felt it would be impossible to read what was said of him, and closed her lids with the sharpness of the pain.

'I thought if you felt disposed to put your name down – ' she heard Parvis continue.

She opened her eyes with an effort, and they fell on the other portrait. It was that of a youngish man, slightly built, with features somewhat blurred by the shadow of a projecting hat brim. Where had she seen that outline before? She stared at it confusedly, her heart hammering in her ears. Then she gave a cry.

'This is the man – the man who came for my husband!'

She heard Parvis start to his feet, and was dimly aware that she had slipped backward into the corner of the sofa, and that he was bending above her in alarm. She straightened herself, and reached out for the paper, which she had dropped.

'It's the man! I should know him anywhere!' she persisted in a voice that sounded to her own ears like a scream.

Parvis's answer seemed to come to her from far off, down endless fog-muffled windings.

'Mrs. Boyne, you're not very well. Shall I call somebody? Shall I get a glass of water?'

'No, no, no!' She threw herself toward him, her hand frantically clutching the newspaper. 'I tell you, it's the man! I *know* him! He spoke to me in the garden!'

Parvis took the journal from her, directing his glasses to the portrait. 'It can't be, Mrs. Boyne. It's Robert Elwell.'

'Robert Elwell?' Her white stare seemed to travel into space. 'Then it was Robert Elwell who came for him.'

'Came for Boyne? The day he went away from here?' Parvis's voice dropped as hers rose. He bent over, laying a fraternal hand on her, as if to coax her gently back into her seat. 'Why, Elwell was dead! Don't you remember?'

Mary sat with her eyes fixed on the picture, unconscious of what he was saying.

'Don't you remember Boyne's unfinished letter to me – the one you found on his desk that day? It was written just after he'd heard of Elwell's death.' She noticed an odd shake in Parvis's unemotional voice. 'Surely you remember!' he urged her.

Yes, she remembered: that was the profoundest horror of it. Elwell had died the day before her husband's disappearance; and this was Elwell's portrait; and it was the portrait of the man who had spoken to her in the garden. She lifted her head and looked slowly about the library. The library could have borne witness that it was also the portrait of the man who had come in that day to call Boyne from his unfinished letter. Through the misty surgings of her brain she heard the faint boom of half-forgotten words – words spoken by Alida Stair on the lawn at Pangbourne before Boyne and his wife had ever seen the house at Lyng, or had imagined that they might one day live there.

'This was the man who spoke to me,' she repeated.

She looked again at Parvis. He was trying to conceal his disturbance under what he probably imagined to be an expression of indulgent commiseration; but the edges of his lips were blue. 'He thinks me mad; but I'm not mad,' she reflected; and suddenly there flashed upon her a way of justifying her strange affirmation.

She sat quiet, controlling the quiver of her lips, and waiting till she could trust her voice; then she said, looking straight at Parvis: 'Will you answer me one question, please? When was it that Robert Elwell tried to kill himself?'

'When – when?' Parvis stammered.

'Yes; the date. Please try to remember.'

She saw that he was growing still more afraid of her. 'I have a reason,' she insisted.

'Yes, yes. Only I can't remember. About two months before, I should say.'

'I want the date,' she repeated.

Parvis picked up the newspaper. 'We might see here,' he said, still humoring her. He ran his eyes down the page. 'Here it is. Last October – the – '

She caught the words from him. 'The 20th, wasn't it?' With a sharp look at her, he verified. 'Yes, the 20th. Then you *did* know?'

'I know now.' Her gaze continued to travel past him. 'Sunday, the 20th – that was the day he came first.'

Parvis's voice was almost inaudible. 'Came *here* first?'

'Yes.'

'You saw him twice, then?'

'Yes, twice.' She just breathed it at him. 'He came first on the 20th of October. I remember the date because it was the day we went up Meldon Steep for the first time.' She felt a faint gasp of inward laughter at the thought that but for that she might have forgotten.

Parvis continued to scrutinize her, as if trying to intercept her gaze.

'We saw him from the roof,' she went on. 'He came down the lime avenue toward the house. He was dressed just as he is in that picture. My husband saw him first. He was frightened, and ran down ahead of me; but there was no one there. He had vanished.'

'Elwell had vanished?' Parvis faltered.

'Yes.' Their two whispers seemed to grope for each other. 'I couldn't think what had happened. I see now. He *tried* to come then; but he wasn't dead enough – he couldn't reach us. He had to wait for two months to die; and then he came back again – and Ned went with him.'

She nodded at Parvis with the look of triumph of a child who has worked out a difficult puzzle. But suddenly she lifted her hands with a desperate gesture, pressing them to her temples.

'Oh, my God! I sent him to Ned – I told him where to go! I sent him to this room!' she screamed.

•

She felt the walls of books rush toward her, like inward falling ruins; and she heard Parvis, a long way off, through the ruins, crying to her, and struggling to get at her. But she was numb to his touch, she did not know what he was saying. Through the tumult she heard but one clear note, the voice of Alida Stair, speaking on the lawn at Pangbourne.

'You won't know till afterward,' it said. 'You won't know till long, long afterward.'

The Bolted Door

———————— ❧ ————————

HUBERT GRANICE, pacing the length of his pleasant lamplit library, paused to compare his watch with the clock on the chimney piece.

Three minutes to eight.

In exactly three minutes Mr. Peter Ascham, of the eminent legal firm of Ascham and Pettilow, would have his punctual hand on the doorbell of the flat. It was a comfort to reflect that Ascham was so punctual – the suspense was beginning to make his host nervous. And the sound of the doorbell would be the beginning of the end – after that there'd be no going back, by God – no going back!

Granice resumed his pacing. Each time he reached the end of the room opposite the door he caught his reflection in the Florentine mirror above the fine old *crédence* he had picked up at Dijon – saw himself spare, quick moving, carefully brushed and dressed, but furrowed, gray about the temples, with a stoop which he corrected by a spasmodic straightening of the shoulders whenever a glass confronted him: a tired middle-aged man, baffled, beaten, worn out.

As he summed himself up thus for the third or fourth time the door opened and he turned with a thrill of relief to greet his guest. But it was only the manservant who entered, advancing silently over the mossy surface of the old Turkey rug.

'Mr. Ascham telephones, sir, to say he's unexpectedly detained and can't be here till eight-thirty.'

Granice made a curt gesture of annoyance. It was becoming harder and harder for him to control these reflexes. He turned

474

on his heel, tossing to the servant over his shoulder: 'Very good. Put off dinner.'

Down his spine he felt the man's injured stare. Mr. Granice had always been so mild-spoken to his people – no doubt the odd change in his manner had already been noticed and discussed belowstairs. And very likely they suspected the cause. He stood drumming on the writing table till he heard the servant go out; then he threw himself into a chair, propping his elbows on the table and resting his chin on his locked hands.

Another half hour alone with it!

He wondered irritably what could have detained his guest. Some professional matter, no doubt – the punctilious lawyer would have allowed nothing less to interfere with a dinner engagement, more especially since Granice, in his note, had said: 'I shall want a little business chat afterward.'

But what professional matter could have come up at that unprofessional hour? Perhaps some other soul in misery had called on the lawyer; and, after all, Granice's note had given no hint of his own need! No doubt Ascham thought he merely wanted to make another change in his will. Since he had come into his little property, ten years earlier, Granice had been perpetually tinkering with his will.

Suddenly another thought pulled him up, sending a flush to his temples. He remembered a word he had tossed to the lawyer some six weeks earlier, at the Century Club. 'Yes – my play's as good as taken. I shall be calling on you soon to go over the contract. Those theatrical chaps are so slippery – I won't trust anybody but you to tie the knot for me!' That, of course, was what Ascham would think he was wanted for. Granice, at the idea, broke into an audible laugh – a queer stage laugh, like the cackle of a baffled villain in a melodrama. The absurdity, the unnaturalness of the sound abashed him, and he compressed his lips angrily. Would he take to soliloquy next?

He lowered his arms and pulled open the upper drawer of the writing table. In the right-hand corner lay a manuscript, bound in paper folders, and tied with a string beneath which a letter had been slipped. Next to the manuscript was a revolver. Granice stared a moment at these oddly associated objects; then he took the letter from under the string and slowly began to open it. He had known he should do so from the moment his hand touched the drawer. Whenever his eye fell on that letter some relentless force compelled him to reread it.

It was dated about four weeks back, under the letterhead of 'The Diversity Theater.'

My Dear Mr. Granice:

I have given the matter my best consideration for the last month, and it's no use – the play won't do. I have talked it over with Miss Melrose – and you know there isn't a gamer artist on our stage – and I regret to tell you she feels just as I do about it. It isn't the poetry that scares her – or me either. We both want to do all we can to help along the poetic drama – we believe the public's ready for it, and we're willing to take a big financial risk in order to be the first to give them what they want. *But we don't believe they could be made to want this.* The fact is, there isn't enough drama in your play to the allowance of poetry – the thing drags all through. You've got a big idea, but it's not out of swaddling clothes.

If this was your first play I'd say: *Try again.* But it has been just the same with all the others you've shown me. And you remember the result of *The Lee Shore* where you carried all the expenses of production yourself, and we couldn't fill the theater for a week. Yet *The Lee Shore* was a modern problem play – much easier to swing than blank verse. It isn't as if you hadn't tried all kinds – '

Granice folded the letter and put it carefully back into the envelope. Why on earth was he rereading it, when he knew every phrase in it by heart, when for a month past he had seen it, night after night, stand out in letters of flame against the darkness of his sleepless lids?

'It has been just the same with all the others you've shown me.'

That was the way they dismissed ten years of passionate unremitting work!

'You remember the result of "The Lee Shore."'

Good God – as if he were likely to forget it! He relived it all now in a drowning flash: the persistant rejection of the play, his resolve to put it on at his own cost, to spend ten thousand dollars of his inheritance on testing his chance of success – the fever of preparation, the dry-mouthed agony of the 'first night,' the flat fall, the stupid press, his secret rush to Europe to escape the condolence of his friends!

'It isn't as if you hadn't tried all kinds.'

No – he had tried all kinds: comedy, tragedy, prose and verse, the light curtain-raiser, the short sharp drama, the bourgeois-realistic and the lyrical-romantic – finally deciding that he would no longer 'prostitute his talent' to win popularity, but would impose on the public his own theory of art in the form of five acts of blank verse. Yes, he had offered them everything – and always with the same result.

Ten years of it – ten years of dogged work and unrelieved failure. The ten years from forty to fifty – the best ten years of his life! And if one counted the years before, the years of dreams, assimilation, preparation – then call it half a man's lifetime: half a man's lifetime thrown away!

And what was he to do with the remaining half? Well, he had settled that, thank God! He turned and glanced anxiously at the clock. Ten minutes past eight – only ten minutes had been consumed in that stormy rush through his past! And he must wait another twenty minutes for Ascham. It was one of the worst symptoms of his case that, in proportion as he had grown to shrink from human company, he dreaded more and more to be alone. . . . But why the devil was he waiting for Ascham? Why didn't he cut the knot himself? Since he was so unutterably sick of the whole business, why did he have to call in an outsider to rid him of this nightmare of living?

He opened the drawer again and laid his hand on the revolver. It was a slim ivory toy – just the instrument for a tired sufferer to give himself a 'hypodermic' with. Granice raised it in one hand, while with the other he felt under the thin hair at the back of his head, between the ear and the nape. He knew just where to place the muzzle: he had once got a surgeon to show him. And as he found the spot, and lifted the revolver to it, the inevitable phenomenon occurred. The hand that held the weapon began to shake, the tremor passed into his arm, his heart gave a leap which sent up a wave of deadly nausea to his throat, he smelt the powder, he sickened at the crash of the bullet through his skull, and a sweat broke out over his forehead and ran down his quivering face. . . .

He laid away the revolver and, pulling out his handkerchief, passed it tremulously over his brow and temples. It was of no use – he knew he could never do it in that way. His attempts at self-destruction were as futile as his snatches at fame! He couldn't make himself a real life, and he couldn't get rid of the life he had. And that was why he had sent for Ascham to help him. . . .

The lawyer, over the cheese and Burgundy, began to excuse himself for his delay.

'I didn't like to say anything while your man was about; but the fact is, I was sent for on a rather unusual matter – '

'Oh, it's all right,' said Granice cheerfully. He was beginning to feel the reaction that food and company always produced in him. It was not any recovered pleasure in life that he felt, but only a deeper withdrawal into himself. It was easier to go on automatically with the social gestures than to uncover to any human eye the abyss within him.

'My dear fellow, it's sacrilege to keep a dinner waiting – especially the production of an artist like yours.' Mr. Ascham sipped his Burgundy luxuriously. 'But the fact is, Mrs. Ashgrove sent for me.'

Granice raised his head with a movement of surprise. For a moment he was shaken out of his self-absorption.

'Mrs. Ashgrove?'

Ascham smiled. 'I thought you'd be interested; I know your passion for *causes célèbres*. And this promises to be one. Of course it's out of our line entirely – we never touch criminal cases. But she wanted to consult me as a friend. Ashgrove was a distant connection of my wife's. And, by Jove, it *is* a queer case!' The servant re-entered, and Ascham snapped his lips shut.

Would the gentlemen have their coffee in the dining room?

'No – serve it in the library,' said Granice, rising. He led the way back to the curtained confidential room. He was really curious to hear what Ascham had to tell him.

While the coffee and cigars were being served he fidgeted about, glancing at his letters – the usual meaningless notes and bills – and picking up the evening paper. As he unfolded it a headline caught his eye.

ROSE MELROSE WANTS TO PLAY POETRY.
THINKS SHE HAS FOUND HER POET.

He read on with a thumping heart – found the name of a young author he had barely heard of, saw the title of a play, a 'poetic drama,' dance before his eyes, and dropped the paper, sick, disgusted. It was true, then – she *was* 'game' – it was not the manner but the matter she mistrusted!

Granice turned to the servant, who seemed to be purposely lingering. 'I shan't need you this evening, Flint. I'll lock up myself.'

He fancied that the man's acquiescence implied surprise. What was going on, Flint seemed to wonder, that Mr. Granice should want him out of the way? Probably he would find a pretext for coming back to see. Granice suddenly felt himself enveloped in a network of espionage.

As the door closed he threw himself into an armchair and leaned forward to take a light from Ascham's cigar.

'Tell me about Mrs. Ashgrove,' he said, seeming to himself to speak stiffly, as if his lips were cracked.

'Mrs. Ashgrove? Well, there's not much to *tell*.'

'And you couldn't if there were?' Granice smiled.

'Probably not. As a matter of fact, she wanted my advice about her choice of counsel. There was nothing especially confidential in our talk.'

'And what's your impression, now you've seen her?'

'My impression is, very distinctly, *that nothing will ever be known.*'

'Ah – ?' Granice murmured, puffing at his cigar.

'I'm more and more convinced that whoever poisoned Ashgrove knew his business, and will consequently never be found out. That's a capital cigar you've given me.'

'You like it? I get them over from Cuba.' Granice examined his own reflectively. 'Then you believe in the theory that the clever criminals never *are* caught?'

'Of course I do. Look about you – look back for the last dozen years – none of the big murder problems are ever solved.' The lawyer ruminated behind his blue cloud. 'Why, take the instance in your own family: I'd forgotten I had an illustration at hand! Take old Joseph Lenman's murder – do you suppose that will ever be explained?'

As the words dropped from Ascham's lips his host looked about the library, and every object in it stared back at him with a stale unescapable familiarity. How sick he was of looking at that room! It was as dull as the face of a wife one has tired of. He cleared his throat slowly; then he turned his head to the lawyer and said: 'I could explain the Lenman murder myself.'

Ascham's eye kindled: he shared Granice's interest in criminal cases.

'By Jove! You've had a theory all this time? It's odd you never mentioned it. Go ahead and tell me. There are certain features in the Lenman case not unlike this Ashgrove affair, and your idea may be a help.'

Granice paused and his eye reverted instinctively to the table drawer in which the revolver and the manuscript lay side by side. What if he were to try another appeal to Rose Melrose? Then he looked at the notes and bills on the table, and the horror of taking up again the lifeless routine of life – of performing the same automatic gestures another day – dispelled his fleeting impulse.

'It's not an idea. I *know* who murdered Joseph Lenman.'

Ascham settled himself comfortable in his chair, prepared for enjoyment.

'You *know*? Well, who did?' he laughed.

'I did,' said Granice, rising to his feet.

He stood before Ascham, and the lawyer lay back, staring up at him. Then he broke into another laugh.

'Why, this is glorious! You murdered him, did you? To inherit his money, I suppose? Better and better! Go on, my boy! Unbosom yourself! Tell me all about it! confession is good for the soul.'

Granice waited till the lawyer had shaken the last peal of laughter from his throat; then he repeated doggedly: 'I murdered him.'

The two men looked at each other for a long moment, and this time Ascham did not laugh.

'Granice!'

'I murdered him – to get his money, as you say.'

There was another pause, and Granice, with a vague sense of amusement, saw his guest's look gradually change from pleasantry to apprehension.

'What's the joke, my dear fellow? I fail to see.'

'It's not a joke. It's the truth. I murdered him.' He had spoken painfully at first, as if there were a knot in his throat;

but each time he repeated the words he found they were easier to say.

Ascham laid down his cigar. 'What's the matter? Aren't you well? What on earth are you driving at?'

'I'm perfectly well. But I murdered my cousin, Joseph Lenman, and I want it known that I murdered him.'

'*You want it known?*'

'Yes. That's why I sent for you. I'm sick of living, and when I try to kill myself I funk it.' He spoke quite naturally now, as if the knot in his throat had been untied.

'Good Lord – good Lord,' the lawyer gasped.

'But I suppose,' Granice continued, 'there's no doubt this would be murder in the first degree? I'm sure of the chair if I own up?'

Ascham drew a long breath; then he said slowly: 'Sit down, Granice. Let's talk.'

• II •

GRANICE told his story simply, connectedly.

He began by a quick survey of his early years – the years of drudgery and privation. His father, a charming man who could never say 'no,' had so signally failed to say it on certain essential occasions that when he died he left an illegitimate family and a mortgaged estate. His lawful kin found themselves hanging over a gulf of debt, and young Granice, to support his mother and sister, had to leave Harvard and bury himself at eighteen in a broker's office. He loathed his work, and he was always poor, always worried and often ill. A few years later his mother died, but his sister, a helpless creature, remained on his hands. His own health gave out, and he had to go away for six months, and work harder than ever when he came back. He had no knack for business, no head for figures, not the dimmest insight into the mysteries of commerce. He wanted to travel and write – those were his inmost longings. And as the years dragged on, and he neared middle-age without making any more money, or acquiring any firmer health, a sick despair possessed him. He tried writing, but he always came home from the office so tired that his brain could not work. For half the year he did not reach his dim uptown flat till after dark, and could only 'brush up' for dinner, and afterward lie on the lounge with his pipe, while his sister droned through the evening paper. Sometimes he spent an evening at the theater; or he dined out or, more rarely, strayed off with an acquaintance or two in quest of what is known as 'pleasure.' And in summer, when he and Kate went to the sea side for a month, he dozed through the days in utter weariness. Once he fell in love with a charming girl – but what had he to offer her, in God's name? She seemed to like him, and in common decency he had to drop out of the running. Apparently no one replaced him, for she never married, but grew stoutish, grayish, philanthropic – yet how sweet she had been when he first kissed her! One more wasted life, he reflected. . . .

But the stage had always been his master passion. He would have sold his soul for the time and freedom to write plays! It was *in him* – he could not remember when it had not been his deepest-seated instinct. As the years passed it became a morbid, a relentless obsession – yet with every year the material conditions were more and more against it. He felt himself growing middle-aged, and he watched the reflection of the process in his sister's wasted face. At eighteen she had been pretty, and as full of enthusiasm as he. Now she was sour, trivial, insignificant – she had missed her chance of life. And she had no resources, poor creature, was fashioned simply for the primitive functions she had been denied the chance to fulfill! It exasperated him to think of it – and to reflect that even now a little travel, a little health, a little money, might transform her, make her young and desirable. . . . The chief fruit of his experience was that there is no such fixed state as age or youth – there is only health as against sickness, wealth as against poverty; and age or youth as the outcome of the lot one draws.

At this point in his narrative Granice stood up, and went to lean against the mantelpiece, looking down at Ascham, who had not moved from his seat, or changed his attitude of spellbound attention.

'Then came the summer when we went to Wrenfield to be near old Lenman – my mother's cousin, as you know. Some of the family always mounted guard over him – generally a niece or so. But that year they were all scattered, and one of the nieces offered to lend us her cottage if we'd relieve her of duty for two months. It was a nuisance for me, of course, for Wrenfield is two hours from town; but my mother, who was a slave to family observances, had always been good to the old man, so it was natural that we should be called on – and there was the saving of rent and the good air for Kate. So we went.

'You never knew Joseph Lenman? Well, picture to yourself an amoeba, or some primitive organism of that sort, under a Titan's microscope. He was large, undifferentiated, inert – since I could remember him he had done nothing but take his temperature and read the *Churchman*. Oh, and cultivate melons – that was his hobby. Not vulgar out-of-door melons – his were grown under glass. He had acres of it at Wrenfield – his big kitchen garden was surrounded by blinking battalions of greenhouses. And in nearly all of them melons were grown: early melons and late, French, English, Domestic – dwarf melons and monsters: every shape, color and variety. They were petted and nursed like children – a staff of trained attendants waited on them. I'm not sure they didn't have a doctor to take their temperature; at any rate the place was full of thermometers. And they didn't sprawl on the ground like ordinary melons; they were trained against the glass like nectarines, and each melon hung in a net which sustained its weight and left it free on all sides to the sun and air.

'It used to strike me sometimes that old Lenman was just like one of his own melons – the pale-fleshed English kind. His life, apathetic and motionless, hung in a net of gold, in an equable warm ventilated atmosphere, high above earthly worries. The cardinal rule of his existence was not to let himself be "worried." . . . I remember his advising me to try it myself, one day when I spoke to him about Kate's bad health, and her need of a change. "I always make it a rule not to let myself worry," he said complacently. "It's the worst thing for the liver – and you look to me as if you had a liver. Take my advice and be cheerful. You'll make yourself happier and others too." And all he had to do was to write a check, and send the poor girl off for a holiday!

'The hardest part of it was that the money half belonged to us already. The old skinflint only had it for life, in trust for us and the others. But his life was a good deal sounder than mine or Kate's – and one could picture him taking extra care of it for the joke of keeping us waiting. I always felt that the sight of our hungry eyes was a tonic to him.

'Well, I tried to see if I couldn't reach him through his vanity. I flattered him, feigned a passionate interest in his melons. And he was taken in, and used to discourse on them by the hour. On fine days he was driven to the greenhouses in his pony chair, and waddled through them, prodding and leering at the fruit, like a fat Turk in his seraglio. When he bragged to me of the expense of growing them I was reminded of a hideous old Lothario bragging of what his pleasures cost. And the resemblance was completed by the fact that he couldn't eat as much as a mouthful of his melons – had lived for years on butter milk and toast.

'But, after all, it's my only hobby – why shouldn't I indulge it?' he said sentimentally. As if I'd ever been able to indulge any of mine! On the keep of those melons Kate and I could have lived like gods. . . .

'One day toward the end of the summer, when Kate was too unwell to drag herself up to the big house, she asked me to go and spend the afternoon with cousin Joseph. It was a lovely soft September afternoon – a day to lie under a Roman stone pine, with one's eyes on the sky, and let the cosmic harmonies rush through one. Perhaps the vision was suggested by the fact that, as I entered cousin Joseph's hideous black walnut library, I passed one of the undergardeners, a handsome Italian, who dashed out in such a hurry that he nearly knocked me down. I remember thinking it queer that the fellow, whom I had often seen about the melon houses, did not bow to me or even seem to see me.

'Cousin Joseph sat in his usual seat, behind the darkened windows, his fat hands folded on his protuberant waistcoat, the last number of the *Churchman* at his elbow, and near it, on a huge dish, a melon – the fattest melon I'd ever seen. As I looked at it I pictured the ecstasy of contemplation from which I must have roused him, and congratulated myself on finding him in such a mood, since I had made up my mind to ask him a favor. Then I noticed that his face, instead of looking as calm as an eggshell, was distorted and whimpering – and without stopping to greet me he pointed passionately to the melon.

' "Look at it, look at it – did you ever see such a beauty? Such firmness – roundness – such delicious smoothness to the touch?" It was as if he had said "she" instead of "it," and when he put out his senile hand and touched the melon I positively had to look the other way.

'Then he told me what had happened. The Italian under-gardener, who had been specially recommended for the melon houses – though it was against my cousin's principles to employ a Papist – had been assigned to the care of the monster: for it had revealed itself, early in its existence, as destined to become a monster, to surpass its plumpest pulpiest sisters, carry off prizes at agricultural shows, and be photographed and celebrated in every gardening paper in the land. The Italian had done well – seemed to have a sense of responsibility. And that very morning he had been ordered to pick the melon, which was to be shown next day at the county fair, and to bring it in for Mr. Lenman to gaze on its blond virginity. But in picking it, what had the damned scoundrelly Jesuit done but drop it – drop it crash on the spout of a watering pot, so that it received a deep gash in its firm pale rotundity, and was henceforth but a bruised, ruined, fallen melon?

'The old man's rage was fearful in its impotence – he shook, spluttered and strangled with it. He had just had the Italian up and had sacked him on the spot, without wages or character – had threatened to have him arrested if he was ever caught prowling about Wrenfield. "By God, and I'll do it – I'll write to Washington – I'll have the pauper scoundrel deported! I'll show him what money can do!" As likely as not there was some murderous blackhand business under it – it would be found that the fellow was a member of a "gang". Those Italians would murder you for a quarter. He meant to have the police look into it. . . . And then he grew frightened at his own excitement. "But I must calm myself," he said. He took his temperature, rang for his drops, and turned to the *Churchman*. He had been reading an article on Nestorianism when the melon was brought in. He asked me to go on with it, and I read to him for an hour, in the dim close room, with a fat fly buzzing stealthily about the fallen melon.

'All the while one phrase of the old man's buzzed in my brain like the fly about the melon. "*I'll show him what money can do!*" Good heaven! If *I* could but show the old man! If I could make him see his power of giving happiness as a new outlet for his monstrous egotism! I tried to tell him something about my situation and Kate's – spoke of my ill-health, my unsuccessful drudgery, my longing to write, to make myself a name – I stammered out an entreaty for a loan. "I can guarantee to repay you, sir – I've a half-written play as security. . . ."

'I shall never forget his glassy stare. His face had grown as smooth as an eggshell again – his eyes peered over his fat cheeks like sentinels over a slippery rampart.

' "A half-written play – a play of *yours* as security?" He looked at me almost fearfully, as if detecting the first symptoms of insanity. "Do you understand anything of business?" he inquired. I laughed and answered: "No, not much."

'He leaned back with closed lids. "All this excitement has been too much for me," he said. "If you'll excuse me, I'll prepare for my nap." And I stumbled out of the room, blindly, like the Italian.'

Granice moved away from the mantelpiece, and walked across to the tray set out with decanters and soda water. He poured himself a tall glass of soda water, emptied it, and glanced at Ascham's dead cigar.

'Better light another,' he suggested.

The lawyer shook his head, and Granice went on with his tale. He told of his mounting obsession – how the murderous impulse had waked in him on the instant of his cousin's refusal, and he had muttered to himself: 'By God, if you won't, I'll make you.' He spoke more tranquilly as the narrative proceeded, as though his rage had died down once the resolve to act on it was taken. He applied his whole mind to the question of how the old man was to be 'disposed of.' Suddenly he remembered the outcry: 'Those Italians would murder you for a quarter!' But no definite project presented itself: he simply waited for an inspiration.

Granice and his sister moved to town a day or two afterward. But the cousins, who had returned, kept them informed of the old man's condition. One day, about three weeks later, Granice, on getting home, found Kate excited over a report from Wrenfield. The Italian had been there again – had somehow slipped into the house, made his way up to the library, and 'used threatening language.' The housekeeper found cousin Joseph gasping, the whites of his eyes showing 'something awful.' The doctor was sent for, and the attack warded off; and the police had ordered the Italian from the neighborhood.

But cousin Joseph, thereafter, languished, had 'nerves,' and lost his taste for toast and buttermilk. The doctor called in a colleague, and the consultation amused and excited the old man – he became once more an important figure. The medical men reassured the family – too completely! – and to the patient they recommended a more varied diet: advised him to take whatever 'tempted him.' And so one day, tremulously, prayer-fully, he decided on a tiny bit of melon. It was brought up with ceremony, and consumed in the presence of the housekeeper and a hovering cousin; and twenty minutes later he was dead. . . .

'But you remember the circumstances,' Granice went on; 'how suspicion turned at once on the Italian? In spite of the hint the police had given him he had been seen hanging about the house since "the scene." It was said that he had tender relations with the kitchenmaid, and the rest seemed easy to explain. But when they looked round to ask him for the explanation he was gone – gone clean out of sight. He had been "warned" to leave Wrenfield, and he had taken the warning so to heart that no one ever laid eyes on him again.'

Granice paused. He had dropped into a chair opposite the lawyer's and he sat for a moment, his head thrown back, looking about the familiar room. Everything in it had grown grimacing and alien, and each strange insistent object seemed craning forward from its place to hear him.

'It was I who put the stuff in the melon,' he said. 'And I don't want you to think I'm sorry for it. This isn't "remorse," understand. I'm glad the old skinflint is dead – I'm glad the others have their money. But mine's no use to me any more. My sister married miserably, and died. And I've never had what I wanted.'

Ascham continued to stare; then he said: 'What on earth was your object, then?'

'Why, to *get* what I wanted – what I fancied was in reach! I wanted change, rest, *life*, for both of us – wanted, above all, for myself, the chance to write! I traveled, got back my health, and came home to tie myself up to my work. And I've slaved at it steadily for ten years without reward – without the most distant hope of success! Nobody will look at my stuff. And now I'm fifty, and I'm beaten, and I know it.' His chin dropped forward on his breast. 'I want to chuck the whole business,' he ended.

• III •

IT was after midnight when Ascham left.

His hand on Granice's shoulder, as he turned to go – 'District Attorney be hanged; see a doctor, see a doctor!' he had cried; and so, with an exaggerated laugh, had pulled on his coat and departed.

Granice turned back into the library. It had never occurred to him that Ascham would not believe his story. For three hours he had explained, elucidated, patiently and painfully gone over every detail – but without once breaking down the iron incredulity of the lawyer's eye.

At first Ascham had feigned to be convinced – but that, as Granice now perceived, was simply to get him to expose himself, to entrap him into contradictions. And when the attempt failed, when Granice triumphantly met and refuted each disconcerting question, the lawyer dropped the mask, and broke out with a good-humored laugh: 'By Jove, Granice, you'll write a successful play yet. The way you've worked this all out is a marvel.'

'Granice swung about furiously – that last sneer about the play inflamed him. Was all the world in a conspiracy to deride his failure?

'I did it, I did it,' he muttered, his rage spending itself against the impenetrable surface of the other's mockery; and Ascham answered with a quieting smile: 'Ever read any of those books on hallucinations? I've got a fairly good medico-legal library. I could send you one or two if you like. . . .'

Left alone, Granice cowered down in the chair before his writing table. He understood that Ascham thought him off his head.

'Good God – what if they all think me crazy?'

The horror of it broke out over him in a cold sweat – he sat there and shook, his eyes hidden in his hands. But gradually, as he began to rehearse his story for the thousandth time, he saw again how incontrovertible it was, and felt sure that any criminal lawyer would believe him.

'That's the trouble – Ascham's not a criminal lawyer. And then he's a friend. What a fool I was to talk to a friend! Even if he did believe me, he'd never let me see it – his instinct would be to cover the whole thing up . . . But in that case – if he *did* believe me – he might think it a kindness to get me shut up in an asylum. . . .' Granice began to tremble again. 'Good heaven! If he should bring in an expert – one of those damned alienists! Ascham and Pettilow can do anything – their word always goes. If Ascham drops a hint that I'd better be shut up, I'll be in a strait-jacket by tomorrow! And he'd do it from the kindest motives – be quite right to do it if he thinks I'm a murderer!'

The vision froze him to his chair. He pressed his fists to his bursting temples and tried to think. For the first time he hoped that Ascham had not believed his story.

'But he did – he did! I can see it now – I noticed what a queer eye he cocked at me. Good God, what shall I do – what shall I do?'

He started up and looked at the clock. Half-past one. What if Ascham should think the case urgent, rout out an alienist, and come back with him? Granice jumped to his feet, and his gesture brushed the morning paper from the table. As he stooped to pick it up the movement started a new train of association.

He sat down again, and reached for the telephone book in the rack by his chair.

'Give me three-o-ten . . . yes.'

The new idea in his mind had revived his energy. He would act – act at once. It was only by thus planning ahead, committing himself to some unavoidable line of conduct, that he could pull himself through the meaningless days. Each time he reached a fresh decision it was like coming out of a foggy weltering sea into a calm harbor with lights. One of the queerest phases of his long agony was the relief produced by these momentary lulls.

'That the office of the *Investigator*? Yes? Give me Mr. Denver, please . . . Hallo, Denver . . . Yes, Hubert Granice . . . Just caught you? Going straight home? Can I come and see you . . . yes, now . . . have a talk? It's rather urgent . . . Yes, might give you some first-rate "copy". . . . All right!' He hung up the receiver with a laugh. It had been a happy thought to call up the editor of the *Investigator* – Robert Denver was the very man he needed. . . .

Granice put out the lights in the library – it was odd how the automatic gestures persisted! – went into the hall, put on his hat and overcoat, and let himself out of the flat. In the hall, a sleepy elevator boy blinked at him and then dropped his head on his arms. Granice passed out into the street. At the corner of Fifth Avenue he hailed a cab, and called out an

uptown address. The long thoroughfare stretched before him, dim
and deserted, like an ancient avenue of tombs. But from Denver's
house a friendly beam fell on the pavement; and as Granice
sprang from his cab the editor's electric turned the corner.

The two men grasped hands, and Denver, feeling for his
latchkey, ushered Granice into the hall.

'Disturb me? Not a bit. You might have, at ten tomorrow
morning . . . but this is my liveliest hour . . . you know my
habits of old.'

Granice had known Robert Denver for fifteen years – watched
his rise through all the stages of journalism to the Olympian
pinnacle of the *Investigator's* editorial office. In the thick-set man
with grizzling hair there were few traces left of the hungry-eyed
young reporter who, on his way home in the small hours, used
to 'bob in' on Granice, while the latter sat grinding at his plays.
Denver had to pass Granice's flat on the way to his own,
and it became a habit, if he saw a light in the window, and
Granice's shadow against the blind, to go in, smoke a pipe, and
discuss the universe.

'Well – this is like old times – a good old habit reversed.' The
editor smote his visitor genially on the shoulder. 'Reminds me of
the nights when I used to rout you out. How's the play, by the
way? There *is* a play, I suppose? It's as safe to ask you that as to
say to some men: 'How's the baby?'

Denver laughed good-naturedly, and Granice thought how
thick and heavy he had grown. It was evident, even to Granice's
tortured nerves, that the words had not been uttered in malice –
and the fact gave him a new measure of his insignificance. Denver
did not even know that he had been a failure! The fact hurt more
than Ascham's irony.

'Come in – come in.' The editor led the way into a small
cheerful room, where there were cigars and decanters. He pushed
an armchair toward his visitor, and dropped into another with a
comfortable groan.

'Now, then – help yourself. And let's hear all about it.'

He beamed at Granice over his pipe bowl, and the latter,
lighting his cigar, said to himself: 'Success makes men comfortable, but it makes them stupid.'

Then he turned, and began: 'Denver, I want to tell you – '

*

The clock ticked rhythmically on the mantelpiece. The room was gradually filled with drifting blue layers of smoke, and through them the editor's face came and went like the moon through a moving sky. Once the hour struck – then the rhythmical ticking began again. The atmosphere grew denser and heavier, and beads of perspiration began to roll from Granice's forehead.

'Do you mind if I open the window?'

'No. It *is* stuffy in here. Wait – I'll do it myself.' Denver pushed down the upper sash, and returned to his chair. 'Well – go on,' he said, filling another pipe. His composure exasperated Granice.

'There's no use in my going on if you don't believe me.'

The editor remained unmoved. 'Who says I don't believe you? And how can I tell till you've finished?'

Granice went on, ashamed of his outburst. 'It was simple enough, as you'll see. From the day the old man said to me "Those Italians would murder you for a quarter" I dropped everything and just worked at my scheme. It struck me at once that I must find a way of getting to Wrenfield and back in a night – and that led to the idea of a motor. A motor – that never occurred to you? You wonder where I got the money, I suppose. Well, I had a thousand or so put by, and I nosed around till I found what I wanted – a secondhand racer. I knew how to drive a car, and I tried the thing and found it was all right. Times were bad, and I bought it for my price, and stored it away. Where? Why, in one of those no-questions-asked garages where they keep motors that are not for family use. I had a lively cousin who had put me up to that dodge, and I looked about till I found a queer hole where they took in my car like a baby in a foundling asylum. . . . Then I practiced running to Wrenfield and back in a night. I knew the way pretty well, for I'd done it often with the same lively cousin – and in the small hours, too. The distance is over ninety miles, and on the third trial I did it under two hours. But my arms were so lame that I could hardly get dressed the next morning.

'Well, then came the report about the Italian's threats, and I saw I must act. . . . I meant to break into the old man's room, shoot him, and get away again. It was a big risk, but I thought I could manage it. Then we heard that he was ill – that there'd been a consultation. Perhaps the fates were going to do it for me! Good Lord, if that could only be! . . .'

Granice stopped and wiped his forehead: the open window did not seem to have cooled the room.

'Then came word that he was better; and the day after, when I came up from my office, I found Kate laughing over the news that he was to try a bit of melon. The housekeeper had just telephoned her – all Wrenfield was in a flutter. The doctor himself had picked out the melon, one of the little French ones that are hardly bigger than a large tomato – and the patient was to eat it at his breakfast the next morning.

'In a flash I saw my chance. It was a bare chance, no more. But I knew the ways of the house – I was sure the melon would be brought in overnight and put in the pantry icebox. If there were only one melon in the icebox I could be fairly sure it was the one I wanted. Melons didn't lie around loose in that house – every one was known, numbered, catalogued. The old man was beset by the dread that the servants would eat them, and he took all sorts of mean precautions to prevent it. Yes, I felt pretty sure of my melon . . . and poisoning was much safer than shooting. It would have been the devil and all to get into his bedroom without his rousing the house; but I ought to be able to break into the pantry without much trouble.

'It was a cloudy night, too – everything served me. I dined quietly, and sat down at my desk. Kate had one of her usual headaches, and went to bed early. As soon as she was gone I slipped out. I had got together a sort of disguise – red beard and queer-looking ulster. I shoved them into a bag, and went round to the garage. There was no one there but a half-drunken machinist whom I'd never seen before. That served me, too. They were always changing machinists, and this new fellow didn't even bother to ask if the car belonged to me. It was a very easy-going place. . . .

'Well, I jumped in, ran up Broadway, and let the car go as soon as I was out of Harlem. Dark as it was, I could trust myself to strike a sharp pace. In the shadow of a wood I stopped a second and got into the beard and ulster. Then away again – it was just eleven-thirty when I got to Wrenfield.

'I left the car in a lane behind the Lenman place, and slipped through the kitchen garden. The melon houses winked at me through the dark – I remember thinking that they knew what I wanted to know. . . . By the stable a dog came out growling –

but he nosed me out, jumped on me, and went back. . . . The house was as dark as the grave. I knew everybody went to bed by ten. But there might be a prowling servant – the kitchenmaid might have come down to let in her Italian. I had to risk that, of course. I crept around by the back door and hid in the shrubbery. Then I listened. It was all as silent as death. I crossed over to the house, pried open the pantry window, and climbed in. I had a little electric lamp in my pocket, and shielding it with my cap I groped my way to the icebox, opened it – and there was the little French melon . . . only one.

'I stopped to listen – I was quite cool. Then I pulled out my bottle of stuff and my syringe, and gave each section of the melon a hypodermic. It was all done inside of three minutes – at ten minutes to twelve I was back in the car. I got out of the lane as quietly as I could, struck a back road, and let the car out as soon as I was beyond the last houses. I only stopped once on the way in, to drop the beard and ulster into a pond. I had a big stone ready to weight them with and they went down plump, like a dead body – and at two I was back at my desk.'

Granice stopped speaking and looked across the smoke fumes at his listener; but Denver's face remained inscrutable.

At length he said: 'Why did you want to tell me this?'

The question startled Granice. He was about to explain, as he had explained to Ascham; but suddenly it occurred to him that if his motive had not seemed convincing to the lawyer it would carry much less weight with Denver. Both were successful men, and success does not understand the subtle agony of failure. Granice cast about for another reason.

'Why, I – the thing haunts me . . . remorse, I suppose you'd call it. . . .'

Denver struck the ashes from his empty pipe.

'Remorse? Bosh!' he said energetically.

Granice's heart sank. 'You don't believe in – *remorse*?'

'Not an atom: in the man of action. The mere fact of your talking of remorse proves to me that you're not the man to have planned and put through such a job.'

Granice groaned. 'Well – I lied to you about remorse. I've never felt any.'

Denver's lips tightened sceptically about his freshly-filled pipe. 'What *was* your motive, then? You must have had one.'

'I'll tell you' – And Granice began once more to rehearse the story of his failure, of his loathing for life. 'Don't say you don't believe me this time . . . that this isn't a real reason!' he stammered out as he ended.

Denver meditated. 'No, I won't say that. I've seen too many queer things. There's always a reason for wanting to get out of life – the wonder is that we find so many for staying in!'

Granice's heart grew light. 'Then you *do* believe me?'

'Believe that you're sick of the job? Yes. And that you haven't the nerve to pull the trigger? Oh, yes – that's easy enough, too. But all that doesn't make you a murderer – though I don't say it proves you could never have been one.'

'I *have* been one, Denver – I swear to you.'

'Perhaps.' Again the journalist mused. 'Just tell me one or two things.'

'Oh, go ahead. You won't stump me!' Granice heard himself say with a laugh.

'Well – how did you make all those trial trips without exciting your sister's curiosity? I knew your night habits pretty well at that time, remember. You were seldom out late. Didn't the change in your ways surprise her?'

'No; because she was away at the time. She went to pay several visits in the country after we came back from Wrenfield, and had only been in town a night or two before – before I did the job.'

'And that night she went to bed with a headache?

'Yes – blinding. She didn't know anything when she had that kind. And her room was at the back of the flat.'

There was another pause in Denver's interrogatory. 'And when you got back – she didn't hear you? You got in without her knowing it?'

'Yes. I went straight to my work – took it up at the word where I'd left off – *why, Denver, don't you remember?*' Granice passionately interjected.

'Remember – ?'

'Yes; how you found me – when you looked in that morning, between two and three . . . your usual hour . . . ?'

'Yes,' the editor nodded.

Granice gave a short laugh. 'In my old coat – with my pipe: looked as if I'd been working all night, didn't I? Well, I hadn't been in my chair ten minutes!'

Denver uncrossed his legs and then crossed them again. 'I didn't know whether *you* remembered that.'

'What?'

'My coming in that particular night – or morning.'

Granice swung round in his chair. 'Why, man alive! that's why I'm here now. Because it was you who spoke for me at the inquest, when they looked round to see what all the old man's heirs had been doing that night – you who testified to having dropped in and found me at my desk as usual. . . . I thought *that* would appeal to your journalistic sense if nothing else would!'

Denver smiled. 'Oh, my journalistic sense is still susceptible enough – and the idea's picturesque, I grant you: asking the man who proved your alibi to establish your guilt.'

'That's it – that's it!' Granice's laugh had a ring of triumph.

'Well, but how about the other chap's testimony – I mean that young doctor: what was his name? Ned Ranney. Don't you remember my testifying that I'd met him at the elevated station, and told him I was on my way to smoke a pipe with you, and his saying: 'All right; you'll find him in. I passed the house two hours ago, and saw his shadow against the blind, as usual.' And the lady with the toothache in the flat across the way: she corroborated his statement, you remember.'

'Yes; I remember.'

'Well, then?'

'Simple enough. Before starting I rigged up a kind of manne-quin with old coats and a cushion – something to cast a shadow on the blind. All you fellows were used to seeing my shadow there in the small hours – I counted on that, and knew you'd take any vague outline as mine.'

'Simple enough, as you say. But the woman with the tooth-ache saw the shadow move – you remember she said she saw you sink forward, as if you'd fallen asleep.'

'Yes; and she was right. It *did* move. I suppose some extra-heavy dray must have jolted by the flimsy building – at any rate, something gave my mannequin a jar, and when I came back he had sunk forward, half over the table.'

There was a long silence between the two men. Granice, with a throbbing heart, watched Denver refill his pipe. The editor, at any rate, did not sneer and flout him. After all, journalism gave a deeper insight than the law into the fantastic possibilities of life, prepared one better to allow for the incalculableness of human impulses.

'Well?' Granice faltered out.

Denver stood up with a shrug. 'Look here, man – what's wrong with you? Make a clean breast of it! Nerves gone to smash? I'd like to take you to see a chap I know – an ex-prizefighter – who's a wonder at pulling fellows in your state out of their hole – '

'Oh, oh – ' Granice broke in. He stood up also, and the two men eyed each other. 'You don't believe me, then?'

'This yarn – how can I? There wasn't a flaw in your alibi.'

'But haven't I filled it full of them now?'

Denver shook his head. 'I might think so if I hadn't happened to know that you *wanted* to. There's the hitch, don't you see?'

Granice groaned. 'No, I didn't. You mean my wanting to be found guilty – ?'

'Of course! If somebody else had accused you, the story might have been worth looking into. As it is, a child could have invented it. It doesn't do much credit to your ingenuity.'

Granice turned sullenly toward the door. What was the use of arguing? But on the threshold a sudden impulse drew him back. 'Look here, Denver – I dare say you're right. But will you do just one thing to prove it? Put my statement in the *Investigator*, just as I've made it. Ridicule it as much you like. Only give the other fellows a chance at it – men who don't know anything about me. Set them talking and looking about. I don't care a damn whether *you* believe me – what I want is to convince the Grand Jury! I ought'nt to have come to a man who knows me – your cursed incredulity is infectious. I don't put my case well, because I know in advance it's discredited, and I almost end by not believing it myself. That's why I can't convince *you*. It's a vicious circle.' He laid a hand on Denver's arm. Send a stenographer, and put my statement in the paper.'

But Denver did not warm to the idea. 'My dear fellow, you seem to forget that all the evidence was pretty thoroughly sifted at the time, every possible clue followed up. The public would have been ready enough then to believe that you murdered old Lenman – you or anybody else. All they wanted was a murderer – the most improbable would have served. But your alibi was too confoundedly complete. And nothing you've told me has shaken it.' Denver laid his cool hand over the other's burning fingers.

'Look here, old fellow, go home and work up a better case – then come in and submit it to the *Investigator*.'

• IV •

THE perspiration was rolling off Granice's forehead. Every few minutes he had to draw out his handkerchief and wipe the moisture from his face.

For an hour and a half he had been talking steadily, putting his case to the District Attorney. Luckily he had a speaking acquaintance with Allonby, and had obtained, without much difficulty, a private audience on the very day after his talk with Robert Denver. In the interval between he had hurried home, got out of his evening clothes, and gone forth again at once into the dreary dawn. His fear of Ascham and the alienist made it impossible for him to remain in his rooms. And it seemed to him that the only way of averting that hideous peril was to establish, in some sane impartial mind, the proof of his guilt. Even if he had not been so incurably sick of life, the electric chair seemed now the only alternative to the strait-jacket.

As he paused to wipe his forehead he saw the District Attorney glance at his watch. The gesture was significant, and Granice lifted an appealing hand. 'I don't expect you to believe me now – but can't you put me under arrest, and have the thing looked into?'

Allonby smiled faintly under his heavy grayish mustache. He had a ruddy face, full and jovial, in which his keen professional eyes seemed to keep watch over impulses not strictly professional.

'Well, I don't know that we need lock you up just yet. But of course I'm bound to look into your statement – '

Granice rose with an exquisite sense of relief. Surely Allonby wouldn't have said that if he hadn't believed him!

'That's all right. Then I needn't detain you. I can be found at any time at my apartment.' He gave the address.

The District Attorney smiled again, more openly. 'What do you say to leaving it for an hour or two this evening? I'm giving a little supper at Rector's – quiet little affair: just Miss Melrose – I think you know her – and a friend or two; and if you'll join us. . . .'

Granice stumbled out of the office without knowing what reply he had made.

He waited for four days – four days of concentrated horror. During the first twenty-four hours the fear of Ascham's alienist dogged him; and as that subsided, it was replaced by the growing conviction that his avowal had made no impression on the District Attorney. Evidently, if he had been going to look into the case, Allonby would have been heard from before now. . . . And that mocking invitation to supper showed clearly enough how little the story had impressed him!

Granice was overcome by the futility of any further attempt to inculpate himself. He was chained to life – a 'prisoner of consciousness.' Where was it he had read the phrase? Well, he was learning what it meant. In the long night hours, when his brain seemed ablaze, he was visited by a sense of his fixed identity, of his irreducible, inexpugnable *selfness*, keener, more insidious, more unescapable, than any sensation he had ever known. He had not guessed that the mind was capable of such intricacies of self-realization, of penetrating so deep into its own dark windings. Often he woke from his brief snatches of sleep with the feeling that something material was clinging to him, was on his hands and face, and in his throat – and as his brain cleared he understood that it was the sense of his own personality that stuck to him like some thick viscous substance.

Then, in the first morning hours, he would rise and look out of his window at the awakening activities of the street – at the street cleaners, the ash cart drivers, and the other dingy workers flitting by through the sallow winter light. Oh, to be one of them – any of them – to take his chance in any of their skins! they were the toilers – the men whose lot was pitied – the victims wept over and ranted about by altruists and economists; and how thankfully he would have taken up the load of any one of them, if only he might have shaken off his own! But, no – the iron circle of consciousness held them too: each one was handcuffed to his own detested ego. Why wish to be any one man rather than another? The only absolute good was not to be. . . . And Flint, coming in to draw his bath, would ask if he preferred his eggs scrambled or poached that morning?

On the fifth day he wrote a long letter to Allonby; and for the succeeding two days he had the occupation of waiting for an answer. He hardly stirred from his rooms in his fear of missing the letter by a moment; but would the District Attorney write, or send a representative: a policeman, a 'secret agent,' or some other mysterious emissary of the law?

On the third morning Flint, stepping softly – as if, confound it! his master were ill – entered the library where Granice sat behind an unread newspaper, and proffered a card on a tray.

Granice read the name – J. B. Hewson – and underneath, in pencil, 'From the District Attorney's office.' He started up with a thumping heart, and signed an assent to the servant.

Mr. Hewson was a sallow nondescript man of about fifty – the kind of man of whom one is sure to see a specimen in any crowd. 'Just the type of the successful detective,' Granice reflected as he shook hands with his visitor.

It was in that character that Mr. Hewson briefly introduced himself. He had been sent by the District Attorney to have 'a quiet talk' with Mr. Granice – to ask him to repeat the statement he had made about the Lenman murder.

His manner was so quiet, so reasonable and receptive, that Granice's self-confidence returned. Here was a sensible man – a man who knew his business – it would be easy enough to make *him* see through that ridiculous alibi! Granice offered Mr. Hewson a cigar, and lighting one himself – to prove his coolness – began again to tell his story.

He was conscious, as he proceeded, of telling it better than ever before. Practice helped, no doubt; and his listener's detached, impartial attitude helped still more. He could see that Hewson, at least, had not decided in advance to disbelieve him, and the sense of being trusted made him more lucid and more consecutive. Yes, this time his words would certainly convince. . . .

• V •

DESPAIRINGLY, Granice gazed up and down the street. Beside him stood a young man with bright prominent eyes, a smooth but not too smoothly-shaven face, and an Irish smile. The young man's nimble glance followed Granice's.

'Sure of the number, are you?' he asked briskly.

'Oh, yes – it was 104.'

'Well, then, the new building has swallowed it up – that's certain.'

He tilted his head back and surveyed the half-finished front of a brick and limestone flat house that reared its flimsy elegance above the adjacent row of tottering tenements and stables.

'Dead sure?' he repeated.

'Yes,' said Granice, discouraged. 'And even if I hadn't been, I know the garage was just opposite Leffler's over there.' He pointed across the street to a tumble-down building with a blotched sign on which the words 'Livery and Boarding' were still faintly discernible.

The young man glanced at the stable. 'Well, that's something – may get a clue there. Leffler's – same name there, anyhow. You remember that name?'

'Yes – distinctly.'

Granice had felt a return of confidence since he had enlisted the interest of the *Explorer's* 'smartest' reporter. If there were moments when he hardly believed his own story, there were others when it seemed impossible that everyone should not believe it; and young Peter McCarren, peering, listening, questioning, jotting down notes, inspired him with new hope. McCarren had fastened on the case at once, 'like a leech,' as he phrased it – jumped at it, thrilled to it, and settled down to 'draw the last drop of fact from it, and not let go till he had.' No one else had treated Granice in that way – even Allonby's detective had not taken a single note. And though a week had elapsed since the visit of that authorized official, nothing had been heard from the District Attorney's office: Allonby had apparently dropped the matter again. But McCarren wasn't going to drop it – not he! He hung on Granice's footsteps. They had spent the greater part of the previous day together, and now they were off again, running down fresh clues.

But at Leffler's they got none, after all. Leffler's was no longer a stable. It was condemned to demolition, and in the respite between sentence and execution it had become a vague place of storage, a hospital for broken-down carriages and carts, presided over by a bleary-eyed old woman who knew nothing of Flood's garage across the way – did not even remember what had stood there before the new flat house began to rise.

'Well – we may run Leffler down somewhere; I've seen harder jobs done,' said McCarren, cheerfully noting down the name.

As they walked back toward Sixth Avenue he added, in a less sanguine tone: 'I'd undertake now to put the thing through if you could only put me on the track of that cyanide.'

Granice's heart sank. Yes – there was the weak spot; he had felt it from the first! But he still hoped to convince McCarren that his case was strong enough without it; and he urged the reporter to come back to his rooms and sum up the facts with him again.

'Sorry, Mr. Granice, but I'm due at the office now. Besides, it'd be no use till I get some fresh stuff to work on. Suppose I call you up tomorrow or next day?'

He plunged into a trolley and left Granice gazing desolately after him.

Two days later he reappeared at the apartment, a shade less jaunty in demeanor.

'Well, Mr. Granice, the stars in their courses are against you, as the bard says. Can't get a trace of Flood, or of Leffler either. And you say you bought the motor through Flood, and sold it through him, too?'

'Yes,' said Granice wearily.

'Who bought it, do you know?'

Granice wrinkled his brows. 'Why, Flood – yes, Flood himself. I sold it back to him three months later.'

'Flood? The devil! And I've ransacked the town for Flood. That kind of business disappears as if the earth had swallowed it.'

Granice, discouraged, kept silence.

'That brings us back to the poison,' McCarren continued, his notebook out. 'Just go over that again, will you?'

And Granice went over it again. It had all been so simple at the time – and he had been so clever in covering up his traces! As soon as he decided on poison he looked about for an acquaintance who manufactured chemicals; and there was Jim Dawes, a Harvard classmate, in the dyeing business – just the man. But at the last moment it occurred to him that suspicion might turn toward so obvious an opportunity, and he decided on a more tortuous course. Another friend, Carrick Venn, a student of medicine whose own ill-health had kept him from the practice of his profession, amused his leisure with experiments in physics, for the execution of which he had set up a simple laboratory. Granice had the habit of dropping in to smoke a cigar with him on Sunday afternoons, and the friends generally sat in Venn's workshop, at the back of the old family house in Stuyvesant Square. Off this workshop was the cupboard of supplies, with its row of deadly bottles. Carrick Venn was an original, a man of restless curious tastes, and his place, on a Sunday, was often full of visitors: a cheerful crowd of journalists, scribblers, painters, experimenters in diverse forms of expression. Coming and going among so many, it was easy enough to pass unperceived; and one afternoon Granice, arriving before Venn had returned home, found himself alone in the workshop, and quickly slipping into the cupboard, transferred the drug to this pocket.

But that had happened ten years ago; and Venn, poor fellow, was long since dead of his dragging ailment. His old father was dead, too, the house in Stuyvesant Square had been turned into a boardinghouse, and the shifting life of New York had passed its sponge over every trace of their history. Even the optimistic McCarren seemed to acknowledge the hopelessness of seeking for proof in that direction.

'And there's the third door slammed in our faces.' He shut his notebook, and throwing back his head, rested his bright inquisitive eyes on Granice's anxious face.

'Look here, Mr. Granice – you see the weak spot, don't you?'

The other made a despairing motion. 'I see so many!'

'Yes: but the one that weakens all the others. Why the deuce do you want this thing known? Why do you want to put your head into the noose?'

Granice looked at him hopelessly, trying to take the measure of his quick light irreverent mind. No one so full of cheerful animal life would believe in the craving for death as a sufficient motive; and Granice racked his brain for one more convincing. But suddenly he saw the reporter's face soften, and melt to an artless sentimentalism.

Mr. Granice – has the memory of this thing always haunted you?'

Granice stared a moment, and then leapt at the opening. 'That's it – the memory of it . . . always. . . .'

McCarren nodded vehemently. 'Dogged your steps, eh? Wouldn't let you sleep? The time came when you *had* to make a clean breast of it?'

'I had to. Can't you understand?'

The reporter struck his fist on the table. 'God, sir! I don't suppose there's a human being with a drop of warm blood in him that can't picture the deadly horrors of remorse – '

The Celtic imagination was aflame, and Granice mutely thanked him for the word. What neither Ascham nor Denver would accept as a conceivable motive the Irish reporter seized on as the most adequate; and, as he said, once one could find a convincing motive, the difficulties of the case became so many incentives to effort.

'Remorse – *remorse*,' he repeated, rolling the word under his tongue with an accent that was a clue to the psychology of the popular drama; and Granice, perversely, said to himself: 'If I could only have struck that note I should have been running in six theaters at once.'

He saw that from that moment McCarren's professional zeal would be fanned by emotional curiosity; and he profited by the fact to propose that they should dine together, and go on afterward to some music hall or theater. It was becoming necessary to Granice to feel himself an object of preoccupation, to find himself in another mind. He took a kind of gray penumbral pleasure in riveting McCarren's attention on his case; and to feign the grimaces of moral anguish became an engrossing game. He had not entered a theater for months; but he sat out the meaningless performances, sustained by the sense of the reporter's observation.

Between the acts McCarren amused him with anecdotes about the audience: he knew everyone by sight, and could lift the curtain from each physiognomy. Granice listened indulgently. He had lost all interest in his kind, but he knew that he was himself the real center of McCarren's attention, and that every word the latter spoke had an indirect bearing on his own problem.

See that fellow over there – the little dried-up man in the third row, pulling his mustache? *His* memoirs would be worth publishing,' McCarren said suddenly in the last *entr'acte*.

Granice, following his glance, recognized the detective from Allonby's office. For a moment he had the thrilling sense that he was being shadowed.

'Caesar, if *he* could talk – !' McCarren continued. 'Know who he is, of course? Dr. John B. Stell, the biggest alienist in the country – '

Granice, with a start, bent again between the heads in front of him. '*That* man – the fourth from the aisle? You're mistaken. That's not Dr. Stell.'

McCarren laughed. 'Well, I guess I've been in court often enough to know Stell when I see him. He testifies in nearly all the big cases where they plead insanity.'

A shiver ran down Granice's spine, but he repeated obstinately: 'that's not Dr. Stell.'

'Not Stell? Why, man, I *know* him. Look – here he comes. If it isn't Stell, he won't speak to me.'

The little dried-up man was moving slowly up the aisle. As he neared McCarren he made a gesture of recognition.

'How'do, Doctor Stell? Pretty slim show, ain't it?' the reporter cheerfully flung out at him. And Mr. J. B. Hewson, with a nod of assent, passed on.

Granice sat benumbed. He knew that he had not been mistaken – the man who had just passed was the same man whom Allonby had sent to see him: a physician disguised as a detective. Allonby, then, had thought him insane, like the other, had regarded his confession as the maundering of a maniac. The discovery froze Granice with horror – he saw the madhouse gaping for him.

'Isn't there a man a good deal like him – a detective named J. B. Hewson?'

But he knew in advance what McCarren's answer would be. 'Hewson? J. B. Hewson? Never heard of him. But that was J. B. Stell fast enough – I guess he can be trusted to know himself, and you saw he answered to his name.'

• VI •

SOME days passed before Granice could obtain a word with the District Attorney: he began to think that Allonby avoided him.

But when they were face to face Allonby's jovial countenance showed no sign of embarrassment. He waved his visitor to a chair, and leaned across his desk with the encouraging smile of a consulting physician.

Granice broke out at once: 'That detective you sent me the other day – '

Allonby raised a deprecating hand.

'– I know: it was Stell the alienist. Why did you do that, Allonby?'

The other's face did not lose its composure. 'Because I looked up your story first – and there's nothing in it.'

'Nothing in it?' Granice furiously interposed.

'Absolutely nothing. If there is, why the deuce don't you bring me proof? I know you've been talking to Peter Ascham, and to Denver, and to that little ferret McCarren of the *Explorer*. Have any of them been able to make out a case for you? No. Well, what am I to do?'

Granice's lips began to tremble. 'Why did you play me that trick?'

'About Stell? I had to, my dear fellow: it's part of my business, Stell *is* a detective, if you come to that – every doctor is.'

The trembling of Granice's lips increased, communicating itself in a long quiver to his facial muscles. He forced a laugh through his dry throat. 'Well – and what did he detect?'

'In you? Oh, he thinks it's overwork – overwork and too much smoking. If you look in on him someday at his office he'll show you the record of hundreds of cases like yours, and tell you what treatment he recommends. It's one of the commonest forms of hallucination. Have a cigar, all the same.'

'But, Allonby I killed that man!'

The District Attorney's large hand, outstretched on his desk, had an almost imperceptible gesture, and a moment later, as if in answer to the call of an electric bell, a clerk looked in from the outer office.

'Sorry, my dear fellow – lot of people waiting. Drop in on Stell some morning,' Allonby said, shaking hands.

McCarren had to own himself beaten: there was absolutely no flaw in the alibi. And since his duty to his journal obviously forbade his wasting time on insoluble mysteries, he ceased to frequent Granice, who dropped back into a deeper isolation. For a day or two after his visit to Allonby he continued to live in dread of Dr. Stell. Why might not Allonby have deceived him as to the alienist's diagnosis? What if he were really being shadowed, not by a police agent but by a mad doctor? To have the truth out, he determined to call on Dr. Stell.

The physician received him kindly, and reverted without embarrassment to their previous meeting. 'We have to do that occasionally, Mr. Granice; it's one of our methods. And you had given Allonby a fright.'

Granice was silent. He would have liked to reaffirm his guilt, to produce the fresh arguments which had occurred to him since his last talk with the physician; but he feared his eagerness might be taken for a symptom of derangement, and he affected to smile away Dr. Stell's allusion.

'You think, then, it's a case of brain fag – nothing more?'

'Nothing more. I should advise you to knock off tobacco you smoke a good deal, don't you?'

He developed his treatment, recommending massage, gymnastics, travel, or any form of diversion that did not – that in short –

Granice interrupted him impatiently. 'Oh, I loathe all that – and I'm sick of traveling.'

'H'm. Then some larger interest – politics, reform, philanthropy? Something to take you out of yourself.'

'Yes. I understand,' said Granice wearily.

'Above all, don't lose heart. I see hundreds of cases like yours,' the doctor added cheerfully from the threshold.

On the doorstep Granice stood still and laughed. Hundreds of cases like his – the case of a man who had committed a murder, who confessed his guilt, and whom no one would believe! Why, there had never been a case like it in the world. What a good figure Stell would have made in a play: the great alienist who couldn't read a man's mind any better than that!

Granice saw huge comic opportunities in the type.

But as he walked away, his fears dispelled, the sense of listlessness returned on him. For the first time since his avowal to Peter Ascham he found himself without an occupation, and understood that he had been carried through the past weeks only by the necessity of constant action. Now his life had once more become a stagnant backwater, and as he stood on the street corner watching the tides of traffic sweep by, he asked himself desparingly how much longer he could endure to float about in the sluggish circle of his consciousness.

The thought of self-destruction came back to him; but again his flesh recoiled. He yearned for death from other hands, but he could never take it from his own. And, aside from his insuperable physical fear, another motive restrained him. He was possessed by the dogged desire to establish the truth of his story. He refused to be swept aside as an irresponsible dreamer – even if he had to kill himself in the end, he would not do so before proving to society that he had deserved death from it.

He began to write long letters to the papers; but after the first had been published and commented on, public curiosity was quelled by a brief statement from the District Attorney's office, and the rest of his communications remained unprinted. Ascham came to see him, and begged him to travel. Robert Denver dropped in, and tried to joke him, out of his delusion; till Granice, mistrustful of their motives, began to dread the reappearance of Dr. Stell, and set a guard on his lips. But the words he kept back engendered others and still others in his brain. His inner self became a humming factory of arguments, and he spent long hours reciting and writing down elaborate statements, which he constantly retouched and developed. Then his activity began to languish under the lack of an audience, the sense of being buried beneath deepening drifts of indifference. In a passion of resentment he swore that he would prove himself a murderer, even if he had to commit another crime to do it; and for a night or two the thought flamed red on his sleeplessness. But daylight dispelled it. The determining impulse was lacking and he hated to choose his victim promiscuously. . . . So he was thrown back on the struggle to impose the truth of his story. As fast as one channel closed on him he tried to pierce another through the sliding sands of incredulity. But every issue seemed blocked, and the whole human race leagued together to cheat one man of the right to die.

Thus viewed, the situation became so monstrous that he lost his last shred of self-restraint in contemplating it. What if he were really the victim of some mocking experiment, the center of a ring of holiday-makers jeering at a poor creature in its blind dashes against the solid walls of consiousness? But, no – men were not so uniformly cruel: there were flaws in the close surface of their indifference, cracks of weakness and pity here and there. . . .

Granice began to think that his mistake lay in having appealed to persons more or less familiar with his past, and to whom the

visible conformities of his life seemed a complete disproof of its
one fierce secret deviation. The general tendency was to take for
the whole of life the slit seen between the blinders of habit:
and in his walk down that narrow vista Granice cut a correct
enough figure. To a vision free to follow his whole orbit his
story would be more intelligible: it would be easier to convince
a chance idler in the street than the trained intelligence hampered
by a sense of his antecedents. This idea shot up in him with the
tropic luxuriance of each new seed of thought, and he began to
walk the streets, and to frequent out-of-the-way chophouses and
bars in his search for the impartial stranger to whom he should
disclose himself.

At first every face looked encouragement; but at the crucial
moment he always held back. So much was at stake, and it was
so essential that his first choice be decisive. He dreaded stupidity,
timidity, intolerance. The imaginative eye, the furrowed brow,
were what he sought. He must reveal himself only to a heart
versed in the tortuous motions of the human will; and he
began to hate the dull benevolence of the average face. Once
or twice, obscurely, allusively, he made a beginning – once
sitting down by a man in a basement chophouse, another day
approaching a lounger on an east side wharf. But in both cases
the premonition of failure checked him on the brink of avowal.
His dread of being taken for a man in the clutch of a fixed idea
gave him an abnormal keenness in reading the expression of his
listeners, and he had provided himself in advance with a series
of verbal alternatives, trap doors of evasion from the first dart of
ridicule or suspicion.

He passed the greater part of the day in the streets, coming
home at irregular hours, dreading the silence and orderliness
of his apartment, and the mute scrutiny of Flint. His real life
was spent in a world so remote from this familiar setting
that he sometimes had the sense of a living metempsychosis,
a furtive passage from one identity to another – yet the other as
unescapably himself!

One humiliation he was spared: the desire to live never
revived in him. Not for a moment was he tempted to a shabby
pact with existing conditions. He wanted to die, wanted it with
the fixed unwavering desire which alone attains its end. And still
the end eluded him! It would not always, of course – he had full

faith in the dark star of his destiny. And he could prove it best by repeating his story, persistently and indefatigably, pouring it into indifferent ears, hammering it into dull brains, till at last it kindled a spark, and some one of the careless millions paused, listened, believed. . . .

It was a mild March day, and he had been loitering on the west side docks, looking at faces. He was becoming an expert in physiognomies: his eagerness no longer made rash darts and awkward recoils. He knew now the face he needed, as clearly as if it had come to him in a vision; and not till he found it would he speak. As he walked eastward through the shabby streets he had a premonition that he should find it that morning. Perhaps it was the promise of spring in the air – certainly he felt calmer than for days. . . .

He turned into Washington Square, struck across it obliquely, and walked up University Place. Its heterogeneous passers always attracted him – they were less hurried than in Broadway, less enclosed and classified than in Fifth Avenue. He walked slowly, watching for his face.

At Union Square he had a relapse into discouragement, like a votary who has watched too long for a sign from the altar. Perhaps, after all, he should never find his face. . . . The air was languid, and he felt tired. He walked between the bald grass plots and the twisted trees, making for a seat. Presently he passed a bench on which a girl sat alone, and something as definite as the twitch of a cord caused him to stop before her. He had never dreamed of telling his story to a girl, had hardly looked at the women's faces as they passed. His case was man's work: how could a woman help him? But this girl's face was extraordinary – quiet and wide as an evening sky. It suggested a hundred images of space, distance, mystery, like ships he had seen, as a boy, berthed by a familiar wharf, but with the breath of far seas and strange harbors in their shrouds. . . . Certainly this girl would understand. He went up to her, lifting his hat, observing the forms – wishing her to see at once that he was 'a gentleman.'

'I am a stranger to you,' he began sitting down beside her, 'but your face is so extremely intelligent that I feel . . . I feel it is the face I've waited for . . . looked for everywhere; and I want to tell you – '

The girl's eyes widened: she rose to her feet. She was escaping him!

In his dismay he ran a few steps after her, and caught her by the arm.

'Here – wait – listen! Oh, don't scream, you fool!' he shouted out.

He felt a hand on his own arm; turned and confronted a policeman. Instantly he understood that he was being arrested, and something hard within him was loosened and ran to tears.

'Ah, you know – you *know* I'm guilty?'

He was conscious that a crowd was forming, and that the girl had disappeared. But what did he care about the girl? It was the policeman who had understood him. He turned and followed, the crowd at his heels. . . .

• VII •

IN the charming place in which he found himself there were so many sympathetic faces that he felt more than ever convinced of the certainty of making himself heard.

It was a bad blow, at first, to find that he had not been arrested for murder; but Ascham, who had come at once, convinced him that he needed rest, and the time to 'review' his statements; it appeared that reiteration had made them a little confused and contradictory. To this end he had readily acquiesced in his removal to a large quiet establishment, with an open space and trees about it, where he had found a number of intelligent companions, some, like himself, engaged in preparing or reviewing statements of their cases, and others ready to lend an attentive ear to his own recital.

For a time he was content to let himself go on the current of this new existence; but although his auditors gave him for the most part an encouraging attention, which, in some, went the length of really brilliant and helpful suggestion, he gradually felt a recurrence of his doubts. Either his hearers were not sincere, or else they had less power to help him than they boasted. His endless conferences resulted in nothing, and the long rest produced an increased mental lucidity which made inaction more and more unbearable. At length he discovered that on certain days visitors from the outer world were admitted to his retreat; and he wrote out long and logically constructed relations of his crime, and furtively slipped them into the hands of these messengers of hope.

This gave him a fresh lease of patience, and he now lived only to watch for the visitors' days, and scan the faces that swept by him like stars seen and lost in the rifts of a hurrying sky.

Mostly, these faces were strange and less intelligent than those of his companions. But they represented his last means of access to the world, a kind of subterranean channel on which he could set his 'statements' afloat, like paper boats which a mysterious current might sweep out into the open seas of life.

One day, however, his attention was arrested by a familiar contour, a pair of bright prominent eyes, and a chin insufficiently shaved. He sprang up and stood in the path of Peter McCarren.

The journalist looked at him doubtfully, then held out his hand with a startled '*Why* – ?'

'You didn't know me? I'm so changed?' Granice faltered, feeling the rebound of the other's wonder.

'Why, no; but you're looking quieter – smoothed out,' McCarren smiled.

'Yes: that's what I'm here for – to rest. And I've taken the opportunity to write out a clearer statement – '

Granice's hand shook so that he could hardly draw the paper from his pocket. As he did so he noticed that the reporter was accompanied by a tall man with compassionate eyes. It came to Granice in a wild thrill of conviction that this was the face he had waited for. . . .

'Perhaps your friend – he *is* your friend? – would glance over it – or I could put the case in a few words if you have time?' Granice's voice shook like his hand. If this chance escaped him he felt that his last hope was gone. McCarren and the stranger looked at each other, and the reporter glanced at his watch.

'I'm sorry we can't stay and talk it over now, Mr. Granice; but my friend has an engagement, and we're rather pressed – '

Granice continued to proffer the paper. 'I'm sorry – I think I could have explained. But you'll take this, at any rate?'

The stranger looked at him gently. 'Certainly – I'll take it.' He had his hand out. 'Good-bye.'

'Good-bye,' Granice echoed.

He stood watching the two men move away from him through the long hall; and as he watched them a tear ran down his face. But as soon as they were out of sight he turned and walked toward his room, beginning to hope again, already planning a new statement. . . .

Outside the building the two men stood still, and the journalist's companion looked up curiously at the long rows of barred windows.

'So that was Granice?'

'Yes – that was Granice, poor devil,' said McCarren.

'Strange case! I suppose there's never been one just like it? He's still absolutely convinced that he committed that murder?'

'Absolutely. Yes.'

The stranger reflected. 'And there was no conceivable ground for the idea? No one could make out how it started? A quiet conventional sort of fellow like that – where do you suppose he got such a delusion? Did you ever get the least clue to it?'

McCarren stood still, his hands in his pockets, his head cocked up in contemplation of the windows. Then he turned his bright hard gaze on his companion.

'That was the queer part of it. I've never spoken of it – but I *did* get a clue.'

'By Jove! That's interesting. What was it?'

McCarren formed his red lips into a whistle. 'Why – that it wasn't a delusion.'

'He produced his effect – the other turned a startled glance on him.

'He murdered the man all right. I tumbled on the truth by the merest accident, when I'd pretty nearly chucked the whole job.'

'He murdered him – murdered his cousin?'

'Sure as you live. Only don't split on me. It's about the queerest business I ever ran into. . . . *Do about it*? Why, what was I to do? I couldn't hang the poor devil, could I? Lord, but I was glad when they collared him, and had him stowed away safe in there!'

The tall man listened with a grave face, grasping Granice's statement in his hand.

'Here – take this; it makes me sick,' he said abruptly, thrusting the paper at the reporter; and the two men turned and walked in silence to the gates.

The Temperate Zone

'TRAVELING, SIR,' a curt parlormaid announced from Mrs. Donald Paul's threshold in Kensington; adding, as young Willis French's glance slipped over her shoulder down a narrow and somewhat conventional perspective of white paneling and black prints: 'If there's any message you'd like to write – '

He did not know if there were or not; but he instantly saw that his hesitation would hold the house door open a minute longer, and thus give him more time to stamp on his memory the details of the cramped London hall, beyond which there seemed no present hope of penetrating.

'Could you tell me where?' he asked, in a tone implying that the question of his having something to write might be determined by the nature of the answer.

The parlormaid scrutinized him more carefully. 'Not exactly, sir: Mr. and Mrs. Paul are away motoring, and I believe they're to cross over to the continent in a day or two.' She seemed to have gathered confidence from another look at him, and he was glad he had waited to unpack his town clothes, instead of rushing, as he had first thought of doing, straight from the steamer train to the house. 'If it's for something important, I could give you the address,' she finally condescended, apparently reassured by her inspection.

'It *is* important,' said the young man almost solemnly; and she handed him a sheet of gold-monogrammed note paper across which was tumbled, in large loose characters: 'Hotel Nouveau Luxe, Paris.'

The unexpectedness of the address left Willis French staring. There was nothing to excite surprise in the fact of the Donald

513

Pauls having gone to Paris; or even in their having gone there in their motor; but that they should be lodged at the Nouveau Luxe seemed to sap the very base of probability.

'Are you *sure* they're staying there?'

To the parlormaid, at this point, it evidently began to look as if, in spite of his reassuring clothes, the caller might have designs on the umbrellas.

'I couldn't say, sir. It's the address, sir,' she returned, adroitly taking her precautions about the door.

These were not lost on the visitor, who, both to tranquilize her and to gain time, turned back toward the quiet Kensington street and stood gazing doubtfully up and down its uneventful length.

All things considered, he had no cause to regret the turn the affair had taken; the only regret he allowed himself was that of not being able instantly to cross the threshold hallowed by his young enthusiasm. But even that privilege might soon be his; and meanwhile he was to have the unforeseen good luck of following Mrs. Donald Paul to Paris. His business in coming to Europe had been simply and solely to see the Donald Pauls; and had they been in London he would have been obliged, their conference over, to return at once to New York, whence he had been sent, at his publisher's expense, to obtain from Mrs. Paul certain details necessary for the completion of his book: 'The Art of Horace Fingall.' And now, by a turn of what he fondly called his luck – as if no one else's had ever been quite as rare – he found his vacation prolonged, and his prospect of enjoyment increased, by the failure to meet the lady in London.

Willis French had more than once had occasion to remark that he owed some of his luckiest moments to his failures. He had tried his hand at several of the arts, only to find, in each case, the same impassable gulf between vision and execution; but his ill success, which he always promptly recognized, had left him leisure to note and enjoy all the incidental compensations of the attempt. And how great some of these compensations were, he had never more keenly felt than on the day when two of the greatest came back to him merged in one glorious opportunity.

It was probable, for example, that if he had drawn a directer profit from his months of study in a certain famous Parisian *atelier*, his labors would have left him less time in which to observe and study Horace Fingall, on the days when the great painter

made his round among the students; just as, if he had written
better poetry, Mrs. Morland, with whom his old friend Lady
Brankhurst had once contrived to have him spend a Sunday in
the country, might have given him, during their long confidential
talk, less of her sweet compassion and her bracing wisdom. Both
Horace Fingall and Emily Morland had, professionally speaking,
discouraged their young disciple, the one had said 'don't write'
as decidedly as the other had said 'don't paint'; but both had let
him feel that interesting failures may be worth more in the end
than dull successes, and that there is range enough for the artistic
sensibilities outside the region of production. The fact of the
young man's taking their criticism without flinching (as he himself
had been thankfully aware of doing) no doubt increased their
liking, and thus let him farther into their intimacy. The insight
into two such natures seemed, even at the moment, to outweigh
any personal success within his reach; and as time removed him
from the experience he had less and less occasion to question the
completeness of the compensation.

Since then, as it happened, his two great initiators had died
within a few months of each other, Emily Morland prematurely,
and at the moment when her exquisite art was gaining new
warmth from the personal happiness at last opening to her,
and Horace Fingall in his late golden prime, when his genius
also seemed to be winged for new flights. Except for the
nearness of the two death dates, there was nothing to bring
together in the public mind the figures of the painter and the
poet, and Willis French's two experiences remained associated in
his thoughts only because they had been the greatest revelations
of temperament he had ever known. No one but Emily Morland
had ever renewed in him that sense of being in the presence of
greatness that he had first felt on meeting Horace Fingall. He
had often wondered if the only two beings to whom he owed
this emotion had ever known each other, and he had concluded
that, even in this day of universal meetings, it was unlikely.
Fingall, after leaving the United States for Paris toward his
fortieth year, had never absented himself from France except on
short occasional visits to his native country; and Mrs. Morland,
when she at last broke away from her depressing isolation in a
Staffordhire parsonage, and set up her own house in London,
had been drawn from there only by one or two holiday journeys

in Italy. Nothing, moreover, could have been more unlike than the mental quality and the general attitude of the two artists. The only point of resemblance between them lay in the effect they produced of the divine emanation of genius. Willis French's speculations as to the result of a meeting between them had always resulted in the belief that they would not have got on. The two emanations would have neutralized each other, and he suspected that both natures lacked the complementary qualities which might have bridged the gulf between them. And now chance had after all linked their names before posterity, through the fact that the widow of the one had married the man who had been betrothed to the other! . . .

French's brief glimpses of Fingall and Mrs. Morland had left in him an intense curiosity to know something more of their personal history, and when his publisher had suggested his writing a book on the painter his first thought had been that here was an occasion to obtain the desired light, and to obtain it, at one stroke, through the woman who had been the preponderating influence in Fingall's art, and the man for whom Emily Morland had written her greatest poems.

That Donald Paul should have met and married the widow of Horace Fingall was one of the facts on which young French's imagination had always most appreciatively dwelt. It was strange indeed that these two custodians of great memories, for both of whom any other marriage would have been a derogation, should have found the one way of remaining on the heights; and it was almost equally strange that their inspiration should turn out to be Willis French's opportunity!

At the very outset, the wonder of it was brought home to him by his having to ask for Mrs. Paul at what had once been Mrs. Morland's house. Mrs. Morland had of course bequeathed the house to Donald Paul; and equally of course it was there that, on his marriage to Mrs. Fingall, Donald Paul had taken his wife. If that wife had been any other, the thought would have been one to shrink from; but to French's mind no threshold was too sacred for the feet of Horace Fingall's widow.

Musing on these things as he glanced up and down the quiet street, the young man, with his sharp professional instinct for missing no chance that delay might cancel, wondered how, before turning from the door, he might get a glimpse of the house which was still – which, in spite of everything, would always be – Emily Morland's.

'You were not thinking of looking at the house, sir?'

French turned back with a start of joy. 'Why, yes – I was!' he said instantly.

The parlormaid opened the door a little wider. 'Of course, properly speaking, you should have a card from the agent; but Mrs. Paul *did* say, if anyone was *very* anxious – May I ask, sir, if you know Mrs. Paul?'

The young man lowered his voice reverently to answer: 'No; but I knew Mrs. Morland.'

The parlormaid looked as if he had misunderstood her question. After a moment's thought she replied: 'I don't think I recall the name.'

They gazed at each other across incalculable distances, and Willis French found no reply. 'What on earth can she suppose I want to see the house for?' he could only wonder.

Her next question told him. 'If it's very urgent, sir – ' another glance at the cut of his coat seemed to strengthen her, and she moved back far enough to let him get a foot across the threshold. 'Would it be to hire or to buy?'

Again they stared at each other till French saw his own wonder reflected in the servant's doubtful face; then the truth came to him in a rush. The house was not being shown to him because it had once been Emily Morland's and he had been recognized as a pilgrim to the shrine of genius, but because it was Mrs. Donald Paul's and he had been taken for a possible purchaser!

All his disenchantment rose to his lips; but it was checked there by the leap of prudence. He saw that if he showed his wonder he might lose his chance.

'Oh, it would be to buy!' he said; for, though the mere thought of hiring was desecration, few things would have seemed more possible to him, had his fortune been on the scale of his enthusiasm, than to become the permanent custodian of the house.

The feeling threw such conviction into his words that the parlormaid yielded another step.

'The drawing room in this way,' she said as he bared his head.

• II •

IT was odd how, as he paced up and down the Embankment late that evening, musing over the vision vouchsafed him, one detail continued to detach itself with discordant sharpness from the harmonious blur.

The parlormaid who had never heard of Mrs. Morland, and who consequently could not know that the house had ever been hers, had naturally enough explained it to him in terms of its new owners' habits. French's imagination had so promptly anticipated this that he had, almost without a shock, heard Mrs. Morland's library described as 'the gentlemans' study,' and marked how an upstairs sitting room with faded Venetian furniture and rows of old books in golden-brown calf had been turned, by the intrusion of a large pink toilet table, into 'the lady's dressing room, sir.' It did not offend him that the dwelling should be used as suited the convenience of the persons who lived in it; he was never for expecting life to stop, and the Historic House which has been turned into a show had always seemed to him as dead as a blown egg. He had small patience with the kind of reverence which treats fine things as if their fineness made them useless. Nothing, he thought, was too fine for natural uses, nothing in life too good for life, he liked the absent and unknown Donald Pauls the better for living naturally in this house which had come to them naturally, and not shrinking into the mere keepers of a shrine. But he had winced at just one thing: at seeing there, on the writing table which had once been Emily Morland's, and must still, he quickly noted, be much as she had left it – at seeing there, among pens and pencils and ink-stained paper cutters, halfway between a lacquer cup full of elastic bands and a blotting book with her initials on it, one solitary object of irrelevant newness: an immense expensively framed photograph of Fingall's picture of his wife.

The portrait – the famous first one, now in the Luxembourg – was so beautiful, and so expressive of what lovers of Fingall's art most loved in it, that Willis French was grieved to see it so indelicately and almost insolently out of place. If ever a thing of beauty can give offence, Mrs. Fingall's portrait on Emily Morland's writing table gave offence. Its presence there shook down all manner of French's faiths. There was something shockingly crude in the way it made the woman in possession triumph over the woman who was gone.

It would have been different, he felt at once, if Mrs. Morland had lived long enough to marry the man she loved; then the dead and the living woman would have faced each other on an equality. But Mrs. Morland, to secure her two brief years of happiness, had had to defy conventions and endure affronts. When, breaking away from the unhappy conditions of her married life, she had at last won London and freedom, it was only to learn that the Reverend Ambrose Morland, informed of her desire to remarry, and of his indisputable right to divorce her, found himself, on religious grounds, unable to set her free. From this situation she sought no sensational escape. Perhaps because the man she loved was younger than herself, she chose to make no open claim on him, to place no lien on his future; she simply let it be known to their few nearest friends that he and she belonged to each other as completely as a man and woman of active minds and complex interests can ever belong to each other when such life as they live together must be lived in secret. To a woman like Mrs. Morland the situation could not be other than difficult and unsatisfying. If her personal distinction saved her from social slights it could not save her from social subserviences. Never once, in the short course of her love history, had she been able to declare her happiness openly, or to let it reveal itself in her conduct; and it seemed, as one considered her case, small solace to remember that some of her most moving verse was the expression of that very privation.

At last her husband's death had freed her, and her coming marriage to Donald Paul been announced; but her own health had already failed, and a few weeks later she too was dead, and Donald Paul lost in the crowd about her grave, behind the Morland relations who, rather generously as people thought, came up from Staffordshire for the funeral of the woman who had brought scandal and glory to their name.

So, tragically and inarticulately, Emily Morland's life had gone out; and now, in the house where she and her lover had spent their short secret hours, on the very table at which she had sat and imperishably written down her love, he had put the portrait of the other woman, her successor; the woman to whom had been given the one great thing she had lacked. . . .

Well, that was life too, French supposed: the ceaseless ruthless turning of the wheel! If only – yes, here was where the real pang lay – if only the supplanting face had not been so different from the face supplanted! Standing there before Mrs. Fingall's image, how could he not recall his first sight of Emily Morland, how not feel again the sudden drop of all his expectations when the one woman he had not noticed on entering Lady Brankhurst's drawing room, the sallow woman with dull hair and a dowdy dress, had turned out to be his immortal? Afterward, of course, when she began to talk, and he was let into the deep world of her eyes, her face became as satisfying as some grave early sculpture which, the imagination once touched by it, makes more finished graces trivial. But there remained the fact that she was what it called plain, and that her successor was beautiful; and it hurt him to see that perfect face, so all-expressive and all-satisfying, in the very spot where Emily Morland, to make her beauty visible, had had to clothe it in poetry. What would she not have given, French wondered, just once to let her face speak for her instead?

The sense of injustice was so strong in him that when he returned to his hotel he went at once to his portmanteau and, pulling out Mrs. Morland's last volume, sat down to reread the famous love sonnets. It was as if he wanted to make up to her for the slight of which he had been the unwilling witness. . . .

The next day, when he set out for France, his mood had changed. After all, Mrs. Morland had had her compensations. She had been inspired, which, on the whole, is more worth-while than to inspire. And then his own adventure was almost in his grasp; and he was at the age when each moment seems to stretch out to the horizon.

The day was fine, and as he sat on the deck of the steamer watching the white cliffs fade, the thought of Mrs. Morland was displaced by the vision of her successor. He recalled the day when Mrs. Fingall had first looked out at him from her husband's famous portrait of her, so frail, so pale under the gloom and glory of her hair, and he had been told how the sight of her had suddenly drawn the painter's genius from its long eclipse. Fingall had found her among the art students of one of the Parisian studios which he fitfully inspected, had rescued her from financial difficulties and married her within a few weeks of their meeting: French had

had the tale from Lady Brankhurst, who was an encyclopedia of illustrious biographies.

'Poor little Bessy Reck – a little American waif sent out from some prairie burrow to "learn art" – that was literally how she expressed it! She hadn't a relation of her own, I believe: the people of the place she came from had taken pity on her and scraped together enough money for her passage and for two years of the Latin Quarter. After that she was to live on the sale of her pictures! And suddenly she met Fingall, and found out what she was really made for.'

So far Lady Brankhurst had been satisfying, as she always was when she trod on solid fact. But she never knew anything about her friends except what had happened to them, and when questioned as to what Mrs. Fingall was really like she became vague and slightly irritable.

'Oh, well, he transformed her, of course: for one thing he made her do her hair differently. Imagine; she used to puff it out over her forehead! And when we went to the studio she was always dressed in the most marvellous Eastern things. Fingall drank cups and cups of Turkish coffee, and she learned to make it herself – it *is* better, of course, but so messy to make! The studio was full of Siamese cats. It was somewhere over near the Luxembourg – very picturesque, but one *did* smell the drains. I used always to take my salts with me; and the stairs were pitch black.' That was all.

But from her very omissions French had constructed the vision of something too fine and imponderable not to escape Lady Brankhurst, and had rejoiced in the thought that, of what must have been the most complete of blisses, hardly anything was exposed to crude comment but the stairs which led to it.

Of Donald Paul he had been able to learn even less, though Lady Brankhurst had so many more facts to give. Donald Paul's life lay open for everybody in London to read. He had been first a 'dear boy,' with a large and eminently respectable family connection, and then a not especially rising young barrister, who occupied his briefless leisure by occasionally writing things for the reviews. He had written an article about Mrs. Morland, and when, soon afterward, he happened to meet her, he had suddenly realized that he hadn't understood her poetry in the least, and had told her so and written another article – under her guidance, the malicious whispered, and boundlessly enthusiastic, of course;

people said it was that which had made her fall in love with him. But Lady Brankhurst thought it was more likely to have been his looks – with which French, on general principles, was inclined to agree. 'What sort of looks?' he asked. 'Oh, like an old picture, you know'; and at that shadowy stage of development the image of Donald Paul had hung. French, in spite of an extensive search, had not even been able to find out where the fateful articles on Mrs. Morland's verse had been published; and light on that point was one of the many lesser results he now hoped for.

Meanwhile, settled in his chair on deck, he was so busy elaborating his own picture of the couple he was hastening to that he hardly noticed the slim figure of traveler with a sallow keen face and small dark beard who hovered near, as if for recognition.

'André Jolyesse – you don't remember me?' the gentleman at length reminded him in beautifully correct English; and French woke to the fact that it was of course Jolyesse, the eminent international portrait painter, whose expensively gloved hand he was shaking.

'We crossed together on the "Gothic" the last time I went to the States,' Monsieur Jolyesse reminded him, 'and you were so amiable as to introduce me to several charming persons, who added greatly to the enjoyment of my visit.'

'Of course, of course,' French assented; and seeing that the painter was in need of a listener, the young man reluctantly lifted his rugs from the next chair.

It was because Jolyesse, on the steamer, had been so shamelessly in quest of an article that French, to escape his importunities, had passed him on to the charming persons referred to; and if he again hung about in this way, and recalled himself, it was doubtless for a similarly shameless purpose. But French was more than ever steeled against the celebrating of such art as that of Jolyesse; and, to cut off a possible renewal of the request, he managed – in answer to a question as to what he was doing with himself – to mention casually that he had abandoned art criticism for the writing of books.

The portrait painter was far too polite to let his attention visibly drop at this announcement; too polite, even, not to ask with a show of interest if he might know the subject of the work. Mr. French was at the moment engaged on.

'Horace Fingall – *bigre*!' he murmured, as if the aridity of the task impressed him while it provoked his pity. 'Fingall – Fingall –'

he repeated, his incredulous face smilingly turned to French, while he drew a cigarette from a gold case as flat as an envelope.

French gave back the smile. It delighted him, it gave him a new sense of the importance of his task, to know that Jolyesse, in spite of Fingall's posthumous leap to fame, still took that view of him. And then, with a start of wonder, the young man remembered that the two men must have known each other, that they must have had at least casual encounters in the crowded promiscuous life of the painters' Paris. The possibility was so rich in humor that he was moved to question his companion.

'You must have come across Fingall now and then, I suppose?'

Monsieur Jolyesse shrugged his shoulders. 'Not for years. He was a savage – he had no sense of solidarity. And envious – !' The artist waved the ringed hand that held his cigarette. 'Could one help it if one sold more pictures than he did? But it was gall and wormwood to him, poor devil. Of course he sells *now* – tremendously high, I believe. But that's what happens: when an unsuccessful man dies, the dealers seize on him and make him a factitious reputation. Only it doesn't last. You'd better make haste to finish your book; that sort of celebrity collapses like a soap bubble. Forgive me,' he added, with a touch of studied compunction, 'for speaking in this way of your compatriot. Fingall had aptitudes – immense, no doubt – but no technique, and no sense of beauty; none whatever.'

French, rejoicing, let the commentary flow on; he even felt the need to stimulate its flow.

'But how about his portrait of his wife – you must know it?'

Jolyesse flung away his cigarette to lift his hands in protest. 'That consumptive witch in the Luxembourg? *Ah, mais non!* She looks like a vegetarian vampire. *Voyez vous, si l'on a beaucoup aimé les femmes –* ' the painter's smile was evidently intended to justify his championship of female loveliness. He puffed away the subject with his cigarette smoke, and turned to glance down the deck. 'There – by Jove, that's what I call a handsome woman! Over there, with the sable cloak and the brand new traveling bags. A honeymoon outfit, *hein?* If your poor Fingall had had the luck to do *that* kind – ! I'd like the chance myself.'

French, following his glance, saw that it rested on a tall and extremely elegant young woman who was just settling herself in a deck chair with the assistance of an attentive maid and a hovering steward. A young man, of equal height and almost superior elegance, strolled up to tuck a rug over her shining boot tips before seating himself at her side; and French had to own that, at least as a moment's ornament, the lady was worth all the trouble spent on her. She seemed, in truth, framed by nature to bloom from one of Monsieur Jolyesse's canvases, so completely did she embody the kind of beauty it was his mission to immortalize. It was annoying that eyes like forest pools and a mouth like a tropical flower should so fit into that particular type; but then the object of Monsieur Jolyesse's admiration had the air of wearing her features, like her clothes, simply because they were the latest fashion, and not because they were a part of her being. Her inner state was probably a much less complicated affair than her lovely exterior: it was a state, French guessed, of easy apathetic good humor, galvanised by the occasional need of a cigarette, and by a gentle enjoyment of her companion's conversation. French had wondered, since his childhood, what the Olympian lovers in fashion plates found to say to each other. Now he knew. They said (he strolled nearer to the couple to catch it): 'Did you wire about reserving a compartment?' and 'I haven't seen my golf clubs since we came on board' and 'I do hope Marshall's brought enough of that new stuff for my face' – and lastly, after a dreamy pause: 'I *know* Gwen gave me a book to read when we started, but I can't think where on earth I've put it.'

It was odd too that, handsome and young as they still were (both well on the warm side of forty), this striking couple were curiously undefinably old-fashioned – in just the same way as Jolyesse's art. They belonged, for all their up-to-date attire, to a period before the triumph of the slack and the slouching: it was as if their elegance had pined too long in the bud, and its related flowering had a tinge of staleness.

French mused on these things while he listened to Jolyesse's guesses as to the class and nationality of the couple, and finally, in answer to the insistent question: 'But where do you think they come from?' replied a little impatiently: 'Oh, from the rue de la Paix, of course!' He was tired of the subject, and of his companion, and wanted to get back to his thoughts of Horace Fingall.

'Ah, I hope so – then I may run across them yet!' Jolyesse, as he gathered up his bags, shot a last glance at the beauty. 'I'll haunt the dressmakers till I find her – she looks as if she spent most of her time with them. And the young man evidently refuses her nothing. You'll see, I'll have her in the next Salon!' He turned back to add: 'She might be a compatriot of yours. Women who look as if they came out of the depths of history usually turn out to be from your newest Territory. If you run across her, do say a good word for me. My full-lengths are fifty thousand francs now – to Americans.'

• III •

ALL that first evening in Paris the vision of his book grew and grew in French's mind. Much as he loved the great city, nothing it could give him was comparable, at that particular hour, to the rapture of his complete withdrawal from it into the sanctuary of his own thoughts. The very next day he was to see Horace Fingall's widow, and perhaps to put his finger on the clue to the labyrinth: that mysterious tormenting question of the relation between the creative artist's personal experience and its ideal expression. He was to try to guess how much of Mrs. Fingall, beside her features, had passed into her husband's painting; and merely to ponder on that opportunity was to plunge himself into the heart of his subject. Fingall's art had at last received recognition, genuine from the few, but mainly, no doubt, inspired by the motives to which Jolyesse had sneeringly alluded; and, intolerable as it was to French to think that snobbishness and cupidity were the chief elements in the general acclamation of his idol, he could not forget that he owed to these baser ingredients the chance to utter his own panegyric. It was because the vulgar herd at last wanted to know what to say, when it heard Fingall mentioned, that Willis French was to be allowed to tell them; such was the base rubble the Temple of Fame was built of! Yes, but future generations would enrich its face with lasting marbles; and it was to be French's privilege to put the first slab in place.

The young man, thus brooding, lost himself in the alluring and perplexing alternatives of his plan. The particular way of dealing with a man's art depended, of course, so much on its relation to his private life, and on the chance of a real insight into that. Fingall's life had been obdurately closed and aloof; would it be his widow's wish that it should remain so? Or would she understand that any

serious attempt to analyze so complex and individual an art must
be preceded by a reverent scrutiny of the artist's personality?
Would she, above all, understand how reverent French's scrutiny
would be, and consent, for the sake of her husband's glory, to
guide and enlighten it? Her attitude, of course, as he was nervously
aware, would greatly depend on his: on his finding the right
words and the convincing tone. He could almost have prayed
for guidance, for some supernatural light on what to say to her!
It was late that night when, turning from his open window above
the throbbing city, he murmured to himself: 'I wonder what on
earth we shall begin by saying to each other?'

Her sitting room at the Nouveau Luxe was empty when he was
shown into it the next day, though a friendly note had assured
him that she would be in by five. But he was not sorry she was
late, for the room had its secrets to reveal. The most conspicuous
of these was a large photograph of a handsome young man, in a
frame which French instantly recognized as the mate of the one
he had noticed on Mrs. Morland's writing table. Well – it was
natural, and rather charming, that the happy couple should choose
the same frame for each other's portraits, and there was nothing
offensive to Fingall's memory in the fact of Donald Paul's picture
being the most prominent object in his wife's drawing room.

Only – if this were indeed Donald Paul, where had French
seen him already? He was still questioning the lines of the pleasant
oft-repeated face when his answer entered the room in the shape
of a splendidly draped and feathered lady.

'I'm sorry! The dressmakers are *such* beasts – they've been
sticking pins in me ever since two o'clock.' She held out her
hand with a click of bracelets slipping down to the slim wrist.
'Donald! Do come – it's Mr. French,' she called back over
her shoulder; and the gentleman of the photograph came in
after her.

The three stood looking at each other for an interval deeply
momentous to French, obviously less stirring to his hosts; then
Donald Paul said, in a fresh voice a good deal younger than
his ingenuous middle-aged face: 'We've met somewhere before,
surely. Wasn't it the other day at Brighton – at the Metropole?'

His wife looked at him and smiled, wrinkling her perfect
brows a little in the effort to help his memory. 'We go to so many

hotels! *I* think it was at the Regina at Harrogate.' She appealed to their visitor for corroboration.

'Wasn't it simply yesterday, on the Channel?' French suggested, the words buzzing a little in his own ears; and Mrs. Paul instantly remembered.

'Of course! How stupid of me!' Her random sweetness grew more concentrated. 'You were talking to a dark man with a beard – André Jolyesse, wasn't it? I *told* my husband it was Jolyesse. How awfully interesting that you should know him! Do sit down and let me give you some tea while you tell us all about him.'

French, as he took the cup from her hand, remembered that, a few hours earlier, he had been wondering what he and she would first say to each other.

It was dark when he walked away from the blazing front of the Nouveau Luxe. Mrs. Donald Paul had given him two generous hours, and had filled them with talk of her first husband; yet as French turned from the hotel he had the feeling that what he brought away with him had hardly added a grain to his previous knowledge of Horace Fingall. It was perhaps because he was still too blankly bewildered – or because he had not yet found the link between what had been and what was – that he had been able to sift only so infinitesimal a residue out of Mrs. Paul's abundance. And his first duty, plainly, if he were ever to thread a way through the tangle, was to readjust himself and try to see things from a different point of view.

His one definite impression was that Mrs. Paul was very much pleased that he should have come to Paris to see her, and acutely, though artlessly, aware of the importance of his mission. Artlessness, in fact, seemed her salient quality: there looked out of her great Sphinx eyes a consciousness as cloudless as a child's. But one thing he speedily discovered: she was keenly alive to her first husband's greatness. On that point French saw that she needed no enlightenment. He was even surprised, sitting opposite to her in all the blatancy of hotel mirrors and gilding, to catch on her lips the echoes of so different a setting. But he gradually perceived that the words she used had no meaning for her save, as it were, a symbolic one: they were like the mysterious price marks with which dealers label their treasures. She knew that her husband had been proud and isolated, that he had 'painted only for himself' and had 'simply despised popularity'; but she rejoiced that he was now at last receiving 'the kind of recognition even *he* would have cared for'; and when French, at this point, interposed, with an impulse of self-vindication: 'I didn't know that, as yet, much had been written about him that he would have liked,' she opened her fathomless eyes a little wider, and answered: 'Oh, but the dealers are simply fighting for his things.'

The shock was severe; but presently French rallied enough to understand that she was not moved by a spirit of cupidity, but was simply applying the only measure of greatness she knew. In Fingall's lifetime she had learned her lesson, and no doubt repeated it correctly – her conscientious desire for correctness was disarming – but now that he was gone his teaching had got mixed with other formulas, and she was serenely persuaded that, in any art, the proof and corollary of greatness was to become a best seller. 'Of course he was his own worst enemy,' she sighed. 'Even when people *came* to buy he managed to send them away discouraged. Whereas now – !'

In the first chill of his disillusionment French thought for a moment of flight. Mrs. Paul had promised him all the documentation he required: she had met him more than halfway in her lavish fixing of hours and offering of material. But everything in him shrank from repeating the experience he had just been subjected to. What was the use of seeing her again, even though her plans included a visit to Fingall's former studio? She had told him nothing whatever about Fingall, and she had told him only too much about herself. To do that, she had not even had to open her beautiful lips. On his way to her hotel he had stopped in at the Luxembourg, and filled his eyes again with her famous image. Everything she was said to have done for Fingall's genius seemed to burn in the depths of that quiet face. It was like an inexhaustible reservoir of beauty, a still pool into which the imagination could perpetually dip and draw up new treasure. And now, side by side with the painter's vision of her, hung French's own: the vision of the too-smiling beauty set in glasses and glitter, preoccupied with dressmakers and theater stalls, and affirming her husband's genius in terms of the auction room and the stock exchange!

'Oh, hang it – what can she give me? I'll go straight back to New York,' the young man suddenly resolved. The resolve even carried him precipitately back to his hotel; but on its threshold another thought arrested him. Horace Fingall had not been the only object of his pilgrimage: he had come to Paris to learn what he could of Emily Morland too. That purpose he had naturally not avowed at the Nouveau Luxe: it was hardly the moment to confess his double quest. But the manifest friendliness of Donald Paul convinced him that there would be no difficulty in obtaining whatever enlightenment it was in the young man's power to give. Donald Paul, at first sight, seemed hardly more expressive than his wife; but though his last avatar was one so remote from literature, at least he had once touched its borders and even worn its livery. His great romance had originated in the accident of his having written an article about its heroine; and transient and unproductive as that phase of his experience had probably been, it must have given him a sense of values more applicable than Mrs. Paul's to French's purpose.

Luck continued to favor him; for the next morning, as he went down the stairs of his hotel, he met Donald Paul coming up.

His visitor, fresh and handsome as his photograph, and dressed in exactly the right clothes for the hour and the occasion, held out an eager hand.

'I'm so glad – I hoped I'd catch you,' he smiled at the descending French; and then, as if to tone down what might seem an excess of warmth, or at least make it appear the mere overflow of his natural spirits, he added: 'My wife rushed me off to say how sorry she is that she can't take you to the studio this morning. She'd quite forgotten an appointment with her dressmaker – *one* of her dressmakers!' Donald Paul stressed it with a frank laugh; his desire, evidently, was to forestall French's surprise. 'You see,' he explained, perhaps guessing that a sense of values was expected of him, 'it's rather more of a business for her than for – well, the average woman. These people – the big ones – are really artists themselves nowadays, aren't they? And they all regard her as a sort of Inspiration; she really tries out the coming fashions for them – lots of things succeed or fail as they happen to look on *her*.' Here he seemed to think another laugh necessary. 'She's always been an inspiration; it's come to be a sort of obligation to her. You see, I'm sure?'

French protested that he saw – and that any other day was as convenient –

'Ah, but that's the deuce of it! The fact is, we're off for Biarritz
the day after tomorrow; and St. Moritz later. We shan't be back
here, I suppose, till the early spring. And of course *you* have your
plans; ah, going back to America next week? Jove, that is bad.' He
frowned over it with an artless boyish anxiety. 'And tomorrow
– well, you know what a woman's last day in Paris is likely to
be, when she's had only three of them! Should you mind most
awfully – think it hopelessly inadequate, I mean – if I offered to
take you to the studio instead?' He reddened a little, evidently not
so much at the intrusion of his own person into the setting of his
predecessor's life, as at his conscious inability to talk about Horace
Fingall in any way that could possibly interest Willis French.

'Of course,' he went on, 'I shall be a wretched substitute
. . . I know so little . . . so little in any sense . . . I never met
him,' he avowed, as if excusing an unaccountable negligence.
'You know how savagely he kept to himself. . . . Poor Bessy –
she could tell you something about that!' But he pulled up sharp
at this involuntary lapse into the personal, and let his smile of
interrogation and readiness say the rest for him.

'Go with you? But of course – I shall be delighted,' French
responded; and a light of relief shone in Mr. Paul's transparent
eyes.

'That's very kind of you; and of course she can tell you all
about it later – add the details. She told me to say that if you
didn't mind turning up again this afternoon late, she'll be ready
to answer any questions. Naturally, she's used to that too!'

This sent a slight shiver through French, with its hint of glib
replies insensibly shaped by repeated questionings. He knew, of
course, that after Fingall's death there had been an outpouring
of articles on him in the journals and the art reviews of every
country: to correct their mistakes and fill up their omissions
was the particular purpose of his book. But it took the bloom –
another layer of bloom – from his enthusiasm to feel that Mrs.
Paul's information, meagre as it was, had already been robbed
of its spontaneity, that she had only been reciting to him what
previous interrogators had been capable of suggesting, and had
themselves expected to hear.

Perhaps Mr. Paul read the disappointment in his looks, and
misinterpreted it, for he added: 'You can't think how I feel the
absurdity of trying to talk to *you* about Fingall!'

His modesty was disarming. French answered with sincerity: 'I assure you I shall like nothing better than going there with you,' and Donald Paul, who was evidently used to assuming that the sentiments of others were as genuine as his own, at once brightened into recovered boyishness.

'That's jolly. Taxi!' he cried, and they were off.

• IV •

ALMOST as soon as they entered the flat, French had again to hail the reappearance of his 'luck.' Better, a thousand times better, to stand in this place with Donald Paul than with Horace Fingall's widow!

Donald Paul, slipping the key into the rusty lock, had opened the door and drawn back to let the visitor pass. The studio was cold and empty – how empty and how cold! No one had lived in the flat since Fingall's death: during the first months following it the widow had used the studio to store his pictures, and only now that the last were sold, or distributed for sale among the dealers, had the place been put in the hands of the agents – like Mrs. Morland's house in Kensington.

In the wintry overhead light the dust showed thick on the rough paint-stained floor, on the few canvases leaning against the walls, and the painter's inconceivably meager 'properties.' French had known that Fingall's studio would not be the upholstered setting for afternoon teas of Lady Brankhurst's vision, but he had not dared to expect such a scornful bareness. He looked about him reverently.

Donald Paul remained silent; then he gave one of his shy laughs. 'Not much in the way of cozy corners, eh? Looks rather as if it had been cleared for a prize fight.'

French turned to him. 'Well, it *was*. When he wrestled with the Angel until dawn.

Mr. Paul's open gaze was shadowed by a faint perplexity, and for half a second French wondered if his metaphor had been taken as referring to the former Mrs. Fingall. But in another moment his companion's eyes cleared. 'Of course – I see! Like What's-in-his name: in the Bible, wasn't he?' He stopped, and began again impulsively: 'I like that idea, you know; he *did* wrestle with his work! Bessy says he used to paint a thing over twenty times – or thirty, if necessary. It drove his sitters nearly mad. That's why he had to wait so long for success, I suppose.' His glance seemed to appeal to French to corroborate this rather adventurous view.

'One of the reasons,' French assented.

His eyes were traveling slowly and greedily about the vast cold room. He had instantly noted that, in Lady Brankhurst's description of the place, nothing was exact but the blackness of the stairs that led there. The rest she must have got up from muddled memories of other studios – that of Jolyesse, no doubt, among the number. French could see Jolyesse, in a setting of bibelots, dispensing Turkish coffee to fashionable sitters. But the nakedness of Fingall's studio had assuredly never been draped: as they beheld it now, so it must have been when the great man painted there – save, indeed, for the pictures once so closely covering the walls (as French saw from the number of empty nails) that to enter it must have been like walking into the heart of a sunset.

None were left. Paul had moved away and stood looking out of the window, and timidly, tentatively, French turned around, one after another, the canvases against the wall. All were as bare as the room, though already prepared for future splendors by the hand from which the brush had dropped so abruptly. On one only a few charcoal strokes hinted at a head – unless indeed it were a landscape? The more French looked the less intelligible it became – the mere first stammer of an unuttered message. The young man put it back with a sigh. He would have liked, beyond almost everything, here under Fingall's roof to discover just one of his pictures.

'If you'd care to see the other rooms? You know he and Bessy lived here,' he heard his companion suggest.

'Oh, immensely!'

Donald Paul opened a door, struck a match in a dark passage, and preceded him.

'Nothing's changed.'

The rooms, which were few and small, were still furnished; and this gave French the measure of their humbleness – for they were almost as devoid of comfort as the studio. Fingall must have lived so intensely and constantly in his own inner vision that nothing external mattered. He must have been almost as detached from the visible world as a great musician or a great ascetic; at least till one sat him down before a face or a landscape – and then what he looked at became the whole of the visible world to him.

'Rather doleful diggings for a young woman,' Donald Paul commented with a half-apologetic smile, as if to say: 'Can you wonder that she likes the Nouveau Luxe?'

French acquiesced. 'I suppose, like all the very greatest of them, he was indifferent to lots of things we think important.'

'Yes – and then . . .' Paul hesitated, 'then they were so frightfully poor. He didn't know how to manage – how to get on with people, either sitters or dealers. For years he sold nothing, literally nothing. It *was* hard on her. She saw so well what he ought to have done; but he wouldn't listen to her!'

'Oh – ' French stammered; and saw the other faintly redden.

'I don't mean, of course, that an artist, a great creative artist, isn't always different . . . on the contrary . . .' Paul hesitated again. 'I understand all that . . . I've experienced it. . . .' His handsome face softened, and French, mollified, murmured to himself: 'He was awfully kind to Emily Morland – I'm sure he was.'

'Only,' Mrs. Paul's husband continued with a deepening earnestness, as if he were trying to explain to French something not quite clear to himself, 'only, if you're not a great creative artist yourself, it is hard sometimes, sitting by and looking on and feeling that if your were just allowed to say a word – Of course,' he added abruptly, 'he was very good to her in other ways; very grateful. She was his inspiration.'

'It's something to have been that,' French said; and at the words his companion's color deepened to a flush which took in his neck and ears, and spread up to his white forehead.

'It's everything,' he agreed, almost solemnly.

French had wandered up to a bookshelf in what had apparently been Fingall's dressing room. He had seen no other books about, and was curious to learn what these had to tell him. They were chiefly old Tauchnitz novels – mild mid-Victorian fiction rubbing elbows with a few odd volumes of Dumas, Maupassant and Zola. But under a loose pile the critic, with beating heart, had detected a shabby sketchbook. His hand shook as he opened it; but its pages were blank, and he reflected ironically that had they not been the dealers would never have left it there.

'They've been over the place with a fine toothcomb,' he muttered to himself.

'What have you got hold of?' Donald Paul asked, coming up.

French continued mechanically to flutter the blank pages; then his hand paused at one which was scribbled over with dots and diagrams, and marginal notes in Fingall's small cramped writing.

'Tea party,' it was cryptically entitled, with a date beneath; and on the next page, under the heading 'For tea party,' a single figure stood out – the figure of a dowdily-dressed woman seated in a low chair, a cup in her hand, and looking up as if to speak to someone who was not yet sketched in. The drawing, in three chalks on a gray ground, was rapidly but carefully executed: one of those light and perfect things which used to fall from Fingall like stray petals from a great tree in bloom. The woman's attitude was full of an ardent interest; from the forward thrust of her clumsily-shod foot to the tilt of her head and the highlight on her eyeglasses, everything about her seemed electrified by some eager shock of ideas. 'Who was talking to her – and what could he have been saying?' was the first thought the little drawing suggested. But it merely flashed through French's mind, for he had almost instantly recognized the portrait – just touched with caricature, yet living, human, even tender – of the woman he least expected to see there.

'Then she *did* know him!' he triumphed out aloud, forgetting who was at his elbow. He flushed up at his blunder and put the book in his companion's hand.

Donald Paul stared at the page.

'She – who?'

French stood confounded. There she sat – Emily Morland – acquiver in every line with life and sound and color: French could hear her very voice running up and down its happy scales! And beside him stood her lover, and did not recognize her. . . .

'Oh – ' Paul stammered at length. 'It's – you mean?' He looked again. 'You think he meant it for Mrs. Morland?' Without waiting for an answer he fixed French with his large boyish gaze, and exclaimed abruptly: 'Then you knew her?'

'Oh, I saw her only once – just once.' French couldn't resist laying a little stress on the *once*.

But Donald Paul took the answer unresentfully. 'And yet you recognized her. I suppose you're more used than I am to Fingall's way of drawing. Do you think he was ever very good at likenesses? I *do* see now, of course . . . but, come, I call it a caricature, don't you?'

'Oh, what does that matter?'

'You mean, you think it's so clever?'

'I think it's magnificent!' said French with emotion.

The other still looked at him ingeniously, but with a dawning light of eagerness. It recalled to French the suppressed, the exaggerated warmth of his greeting on the hotel stairs. 'What is it he wants of me? For he wants something.'

'I never knew, either,' Paul continued, 'that she and Fingall had met. Some one must have brought her here, I suppose. It's curious.' He pondered, still holding the book. 'And I didn't know *you* knew her,' he concluded.

'Oh, how should you? She was probably unconscious of the fact herself. I spent a day with her once in the country, years ago. Naturally, I've never forgotten it.'

Donald Paul's eyes continued obscurely to entreat him. 'That's wonderful!'

'What – that one should never forget having once met Emily Morland?' French rejoined, with a smile he could not repress.

'No,' said Emily Morland's lover with simplicity. 'But the coincidence. You see, I'd made up my mind to ask you – ' He broke off, and looked down at the sketch, as if seeking guidance where doubtless he had so often found it. 'The fact is,' he began again, 'I'm going to write her 'Life.' She left me all her papers – I dare say you know about all that. It's a trust – a sacred trust; but it's also a most tremendous undertaking! And yesterday, after hearing something of what you're planning about Fingall, I realized how little I'd really thought the book out, how unprepared I was – what a lot more there was in that sort of thing than I'd at first imagined. I used to write – a little; just short reviews, and that kind of thing. But my hand's out nowadays; and besides, this is so different. And then, my time's not quite my own any longer. . . . So I made up my mind that I'd consult you, ask you if you'd help me . . . oh, as much as ever you're willing. . . .' His smile was irresistible. 'I asked Bessy. And she thought you'd understand.'

'Understand?' gasped French. 'Understand?'

'You see,' Paul hurried on, 'there are heaps and heaps of letters – her beautiful letters! I don't mean' – his voice trembled slightly – 'only the ones to me; though some of those . . . well,

I'll leave it to you to judge. . . . But lots of others too, that all sorts of people have sent me. Apparently everybody kept her letters. And I'm simply swamped in them,' he ended helplessly, 'unless you will. . . .'

French's voice was as unsteady as his. 'Unless I will? There's nothing on earth I'd have asked . . . if I could have imagined it. . . .'

'Oh, really?' Paul's voice dropped back with relief to its everyday tone. He was clearly unprepared for exaltation. 'It's amazingly kind of you – so kind that I don't in the least know how to thank you.'

He paused, his hand still between the pages of the sketchbook. Suddenly he opened it and glanced down again at the drawing, and then at French.

'Meanwhile – if you really like this thing; you *do*?' He smiled a little incredulously and bent his handsome head to give the leaf a closer look. 'Yes, there are his initials; well, that makes it all the more. . . .' He tore out the page and handed it to French. 'Do take it,' he said. 'I wish I had something better of her to give you – but there's literally nothing else; nothing except the beautiful enlarged photograph she had done for me the year we met; and that, of course – '

• V •

MRS. PAUL, as French had foreseen she would be, was late at their second appointment; later even than at the first. But what did French care? He could have waited contentedly for a week in that blatant drawing room, with such hopes in his bosom and such a treasure already locked up in his portmanteau. And when at last she came she was just as cordial, as voluble and as unhelpful as ever.

The great difficulty, of course, was that she and her husband were leaving Paris so soon, and that French, for his part, was under orders to return at once to America. 'The things I could tell you if we only had the time!' she sighed regretfully. But this left French unmoved, for he knew by now how little she really had to tell. Still, he had a good many more questions to ask, a good many more dates and facts to get at, than could be crowded into their confused hour over a laden tea table, with belated parcels perpetually arriving, the telephone ringing, and the maid putting in her head to ask if the orange-and-silver brocade was to go to Biarritz, or to be sent straight on with the furs and the sports clothes to St. Moritz.

Finally, in the hurried parenthesis between these weightier matters, he extracted from her the promise to meet him in Paris in March – March at the latest – and give him a week, a whole week. 'It will be so much easier, then, of course,' she agreed. 'It's the deadest season of the year in Paris. There'll be nobody to bother us, and we can really settle down to work' – her lovely eyes kindled at the thought – 'and I can give you all the papers you need, and tell you everything you want to know.'

With that he had to be content, and he could afford to be – now. He rose to take leave; but suddenly she rose also, a new eagerness in her eyes. She moved toward the door with him, and there her look detained him.

'And Donald's book too; you can get to work with Donald at the same time, can't you?' She smiled on him confidentially. 'He's told me that you've promised to help him out – it's so angelically good of you! I do assure you he appreciates it immensely. Perhaps he's a little too modest about his own ability; but it *is* a terrible burden to have had imposed on him, isn't it, just as he and I were having our first real holiday! It's been a nightmare to him all these months. Reading all those letters and manuscripts, and deciding – Why don't authors do those things for themselves?' She appealed to French, half indignantly. 'But after all,' she concluded, her smile deepening, 'I understand that you should be willing to take the trouble, in return for the precious thing he's given you.'

French's heart gave a frightened thump: her smile had suddenly become too significant.

'The precious thing?'

She laughed. 'Do you mean to say you've forgotten it already? Well, if you have, I don't think you deserve it. The portrait of Mrs. Morland – the *only* one, apparently! A signed drawing of Horace's; it's something of a prize, you'll admit. Donald tells me that you and he made the discovery of the sketchbook together. I can't for the life of me imagine how it ever escaped those harpies of dealers. You can fancy how they went through everything . . . like detectives after fingerprints, I used to say! Poor me – they used to have me out of bed everyday at daylight! How furious they'd be if they knew what they've missed!' She paused and laughed again, leaning in the doorway in one of her long Artemis attitudes.

French felt his head spinning. He dared not meet her eyes, for fear of discovering in them the unmasked cupidity he fancied he had once before detected there. He felt too sick for any thought but flight; but every nerve in him cried out: 'Whatever she says or does, she shall never have that drawing back!'

She said and did nothing; which made it even more difficult for him. It gave him the feeling that if he moved she would move too – with a spring, as if she herself were a detective, and suspected him of having the treasure in his pocket ('Thank God I haven't!' he thought). And she had him so entirely at her mercy, with all the Fingall dates and documents still in her hold; there was nothing he could do but go – pick up the portmanteau with the drawing in it, and fly by the next train, if need be!

The idea traversed him in a flash, and then gave way again to the desolating sense of who she was, and what it was that they were maneuvering and watching each other about. That was the worst of all – worse even than giving up the drawing, or renouncing the book on Fingall. He felt that he must get away at any cost, rather than prolong their silent duel; and, sick at heart, he reached out for the doorknob.

'Oh, no!' she exclaimed, her hand coming down on his wrist.

He forced an answering smile. 'No?'

She shook her head, her eyes still on his. 'You're not going like that.' Though she held him playfully her long fine fingers seemed as strong as steel. 'After all, business is business, isn't it? We ordinary mortals, who don't live in the clouds among the gods, can't afford to give nothing for nothing. . . . *You* don't – so why should I?'

He had never seen her so close before, and as her face hovered over him, so warm, persuasive, confident, he noted in it, with a kind of savage satisfaction, the first faint lines of age.

'So why should I?' she repeated gaily. He stood silent, imprisoned; and she went on, throwing her head back a little, and letting her gaze filter down on him through her rich lowered lashes: 'But I know you'll agree with me that it's only fair. After all, Donald has set you the example. He's given you something awfully valuable in return for the favor you're going to do him – the immense favor. Poor darling – there never was anybody as generous as Donald! Don't be alarmed; I'm not going to ask you to give me a present on *that* scale.' She drew herself up and threw back her lids, as if challenging him. 'You'd have difficulty in finding one – anybody would!'

French was still speechless, bewildered, not daring to think ahead, and all the while confusedly aware that his misery was feeding some obscure springs of amusement in her.

'In return for the equally immense favor I'm going to do you – coming back to Paris in March, and giving you a whole week – what are you going to give *me*? Have you ever thought about *that*?' she flung out at him; and then, before he could answer: 'Oh, don't look so miserable – don't rack your brains over it! I told you I wasn't grasping – I'm not going to ask for anything unattainable. Only, you see' – she paused, her face grown suddenly tender and young again – 'you see, Donald wants so dreadfully to have a portrait of me, one for his very own, by a painter he really admires; a *likeness*, simply, you see, not one of those wild things poor Horace used to do of me – and what I want is to beg and implore you to ask Jolyesse if he'll do me. I can't ask him myself: Horace despised his things, and was always ridiculing him, and Jolyesse knew it. It's all very well – but, as I used to tell Horace, success does mean something after all, doesn't it? And no one has been more of a success than Jolyesse – I hear his prices have doubled again. Well, that's a proof, in a way . . . what's the use of denying it? Only it makes it more difficult for poor me, who can't afford him, even if I dared to ask!' She wrinkled her perfect brows in mock distress. 'But if *you* would – an old friend like you – if you'd ask it as a personal favor, and make him see that for the widow of a colleague he ought to make a reduction in his price – really a *big* reduction! – I'm sure he'd do it. After all, it's not my fault if my husband didn't like his pictures. And I should be so grateful to you, and so would Donald.'

She dropped French's arm and held out both her shining hands to him. 'You *will* – you really will? Oh, you dear good man, you!' He had slipped his hands out of hers, but

she caught him again, this time not menacingly but exuber-
antly.

'If you could arrange it for when I'm here in March, that
would be simply perfect, wouldn't it? You can, you think? Oh,
bless you! And mind, he's got to make it a full-length!' she called
after him joyfully across the threshold.

Diagnosis

———————

N<small>OTHING</small> <small>TO</small> <small>WORRY</small> <small>ABOUT</small> – absolutely nothing. Of course not . . . just what they all say!' Paul Dorrance walked away from his writing table to the window of his high-perched flat. The window looked south, over the crowded towering New York below Wall Street which was the visible center and symbol of his life's work. He drew a great breath of relief – for under his surface incredulity a secret reassurance was slowly beginning to unfold. The two eminent physicians he had just seen had told him he would be all right again in a few months; that his dark fears were delusions; that all he needed was to get away from work till he had recovered his balance of body and brain. Dorrance had smiled acquiescence and muttered inwardly: 'Infernal humbugs; as if I didn't know how I felt!'; yet hardly a quarter of an hour later their words had woven magic passes about him, and with a timid avidity he had surrendered to the sense of returning life. 'By George, I *do* feel better,' he muttered, and swung about to his desk, remembering he had not breakfasted. The first time in months that he had remembered that! He touched the bell at his elbow, and with a half-apologetic smile told his servant that . . . well, yes . . . the doctors said he ought to eat more. . . . Perhaps he'd have an egg or two with his coffee . . . yes, with bacon. . . . He chafed with impatience till the tray was brought.

Breakfast over, he glanced through the papers with the leisurely eye of a man before whom the human comedy is likely to go on unrolling itself for many years. 'Nothing to be in a hurry about, after all,' was his half-conscious thought. That line which had so haunted him lately, about 'Time's wingèd chariot,' relapsed into the region of pure aesthetics, now that in his case the

541

wings were apparently to be refurled. 'No reason whatever why you shouldn't live to be an old man.' That was pleasant hearing, at forty-nine. What did they call an old man, nowadays? He had always imagined that he shouldn't care to live to be an old man; now he began by asking himself what he understood by the term 'old.' Nothing that applied to himself, certainly; even if he were to be mysteriously metamorphosed into an old man at some far distant day – what then? It was too far off to visualize, it did not affect his imagination. Why, old age no longer began short of seventy; almost every day the papers told of hearty old folk celebrating their hundredth birthdays – sometimes by re-marriage. Dorrance lost himself in pleasant musings over the increased longevity of the race, evoking visions of contemporaries of his grandparents, infirm and toothless at an age which found their descendants still carnivorous and alert.

The papers read, his mind drifted agreeably among the rich possibilities of travel. A busy man ordered to interrupt his work could not possibly stay in New York. Names suggestive of idleness and summer clothes floated before him: the West Indies, the Canaries, Morocco – why not Morocco, where he had never been? And from there he could work his way up through Spain. He rose to reach for a volume from the shelves where his travel books were ranged – but as he stood fluttering its pages, in a state of almost thoughtless beatitude, something twitched him out of his dream. 'I suppose I ought to tell her – ' he said aloud.

Certainly he ought to tell her; but the mere thought let loose a landslide of complications, obligations, explanations . . . their suffocating descent made him gasp for breadth. He leaned against the desk, closing his eyes.

But of course she would understand. The doctors said he was going to be all right – that would be enough for her. She would see the necessity of his going away for some months; a year perhaps. She couldn't go with him; that was certain! So what was there to make a fuss about? Gradually, insidiously, there stole into his mind the thought – at first a mere thread of a suggestion – that this might be the moment to let her see, oh, ever so gently, that things couldn't go on forever – nothing did – and that, at his age, and with this new prospect of restored health, a man might reasonably be supposed to have his own views, his own plans; might think of marriage; marriage with a young girl; children; a

place in the country . . . his mind wandered into that dream as it
had into the dream of travel. . . .

Well, meanwhile he must let her know what the diagnosis was.
She had been awfully worried about him, he knew, though all
along she had kept up so bravely. (Should he, in the independence
of his recovered health, confess under his breath that he celebrated
'braveness' sometimes got a little on his nerves?) Yes, it had been
hard for her; harder than for anyone; he owed it to her to tell her
at once that everything was all right; all right as far as *he* was
concerned. And in her beautiful unselfishness nothing else would
matter to her – at first. Poor child! He could hear her happy voice!
'Really – really and truly? They both said so? You're *sure*? Oh, of
course, I've always known . . . haven't I always told you?' Bless
her, yes; but he'd known all along what she was thinking. . . .
He turned to the desk, and took up the telephone.

As he did so, his glance lit on a sheet of paper on the rug at
his feet. He had keen eyes: he saw at once that the letterhead bore
the name of the eminent consultant whom his own physician had
brought in that morning. Perhaps the paper was one of the three
or four prescriptions they had left with him; a chance gust from
door or window might have snatched it from the table where the
others lay. He stooped and picked it up –

That was the truth, then. That paper on the floor held his fate.
The two doctors had written out their diagnosis, and forgotten
to pocket it when they left. There were their two signatures; and
the date. There was no mistake. . . . Paul Dorrance sat for a long
time with the paper on the desk before him. He propped his chin
on his locked hands, shut his eyes, and tried to grope his way
through the illimitable darkness. . . .

Anything, anything but the sights and sounds of the world
outside! If he had had the energy to move he would have jumped
up, drawn the curtains shut, and cowered in his armchair in
absolute blackness till he could come to some sort of terms
with this new reality – for him henceforth the sole reality.
For what did anything matter now except that he was doomed
– was dying? That these two scoundrels had known it, and had
lied to him? And that, having lied to him, in their callous
professional haste, they had tossed his death sentence down
before him, forgotten to carry it away, left it there staring up at
him from the floor?

Yes; it would be easier to bear in a pitch-black room, a room from which all sights and sounds, all suggestions of life, were excluded. But the effort of getting up to draw the curtains was too great. It was easier to go on sitting there, in the darkness created by pressing his fists against his lids. 'Now, then, my good fellow – this is what it'll be like in the grave. . . .'

Yes; but if he had known the grave was *there*, so close, so all-including, so infinitely more important and real than any of the trash one had tossed the years away for; if somebody had told him . . . he might have done a good many things differently, put matters in a truer perspective, discriminated, selected, weighed. . . . Or, no! A thousand times no! Be beaten like that? Go slinking off to his grave before it was dug for him? His folly had been that he had not packed enough into life; that he had always been sorting, discriminating, trying for a perspective, choosing, weighing – God! When there was barely time to seize life before the cup that held it was cracked, and gulp it down while you had a throat that could swallow!

Ah, well – no use in retrospection. What was done was done: what undone must remain so to all eternity. Eternity – what did the word mean? How could the least fringe of its meaning be grasped by ephemeral creatures groping blindly through a few short years to the grave? Ah, the pity of it – pity, pity! That was the feeling that rose to the surface of his thoughts. Pity for all the millions of blind gropers like himself, the millions and millions who thought themselves alive, as he had, and suddenly found themselves dead; as he had! Poor mortals all, with that seed of annihilation that made them brothers – how he longed to help them, how he winced at the thought that he must so often have hurt them, brushing by in his fatuous vitality! How many other lives had he used up in his short span of living? Not consciously, of course – that was the worst of it! The old nurse who had slaved for him when he was a child, and then vanished from his life, to be found again, years after, poor, neglected, dying – well, for her he had done what he could. And that thin young man in his office, with the irritating cough, who might perhaps have been saved if he had been got away sooner? Stuck on to the end because there was a family to support – of course! And the old bookkeeper whom Dorrance had inherited from his father, who was deaf and half blind, and wouldn't go either till he had to be gently told – ?

All that had been been, as it were, the stuff out of which he, Paul
Dorrance, had built up his easy, affluent, successful life. But, no,
what nonsense! He had been fair enough, kind enough, whenever
he found out what was wrong; only he hadn't really pitied them,
had considered his debt discharged when he had drawn a cheque
or rung up a Home for Incurables. Whereas pity, he now saw –
oh, curse it, he was talking like a Russian novel! Nonsense . . .
nonsense . . . everybody's turn came sooner or later. The only
way to reform the world was to reform Death out of it. And
instead of that, Death was always there, was there now, at the
door, in the room, at his elbow . . . *his* Death, his own private
and particular end-of-everything. *Now!* He snatched his hands
away from his face. They were wet.

A bell rang hesitatingly and the door opened behind him. He
heard the servant say: 'Mrs. Welwood.' He stood up, blinking at
the harsh impact of light and life. 'Mrs. Welwood.' Everything
was going on again, going on again . . . people were behaving
exactly as if he were not doomed . . . the door shut.
'Eleanor!'
She came up to him quickly. How close, alive, oppressive
everyone seemed! She seldom came to his flat – he wondered
dully why she had come today.
She stammered: 'What has happened? You promised to telephone at ten. I've been ringing and ringing. They said nobody
answered. . . .'
Ah, yes: he remembered now. He looked at the receiver. It lay
on the desk, where he had dropped it when his eye had lit on that
paper. All that had happened in his other life – before. . . . Well,
here she was. How pale she looked, her eyelids a little swollen.
And yet how strong, how healthy – how obviously undiseased.
Queer! She'd been crying too! Instinctively he turned, and put
himself between her and the light.
'What's all the fuss about, dear?' he began jauntily.
She colored a little, hesitating as if he had caught her at fault.
'Why, it's nearly one o'clock; and you told me the consultation
was to be at nine. And you promised. . . .'
Oh, yes; of course. He had promised. . . . With the hard
morning light on her pale face and thin lips, she looked twenty
years older. Older than what? After all, she was well over forty,

and had never been beautiful. Had he ever thought her beautiful? Poor Eleanor – oh, poor Eleanor!

'Well, yes; it's my fault,' he conceded. 'I suppose I telephoned to somebody' (this fib to gain time) 'and forgot to hang up the receiver. There it lies; I'm convicted!' He took both her hands – how they trembled! – and drew her to him.

This was Eleanor Welwood, for fifteen years past the heaviest burden on his conscience. As he stood there, holding her hands, he tried to recover a glimpse of the beginnings, and of his own state of mind at the time. He had been captivated; but never to the point of wishing she were free to marry him. Her husband was a pleasant enough fellow; they all belonged to the same little social group; it was a delightful relation, just as it was. And Dorrance had the pretext of his old mother, alone and infirm, who lived with him and whom he could not leave. It was tacitly understood that old Mrs. Dorrance's habits must not be disturbed by any change in the household. So love, on his part, imperceptibly cooled (or should he say ripened?) into friendship; and when his mother's death left him free, there still remained the convenient obstacle of Horace Welwood. Horace Welwood did not die; but one day, as the phrase is, he 'allowed' his wife to divorce him. The news had cost Dorrance a sleepless night or two. The divorce was obtained by Mrs. Welwood, discreetly, in a distant and accommodating state; but it was really Welwood who had repudiated his wife, and because of Paul Dorrance. Dorrance knew this, and was aware that Mrs. Welwood knew he knew it. But he had kept his head, she had silenced her heart; and life went on as before, except that since the divorce it was easier to see her, and he could telephone to her house whenever he chose. And they continued to be the dearest of friends.

He had often gone over all this in his mind, with an increasing satisfaction in his own shrewdness. He had kept his freedom, kept his old love's devotion – or as much of it as he wanted – and proved to himself that life was not half bad if you knew how to manage it. That was what he used to think – and then, suddenly, two or three hours ago, he had begun to think differently about everything, and what had seemed shrewdness now unmasked itself as a pitiless egotism.

He continued to look at Mrs. Welwood, as if searching her face for something it was essential he should find there. He saw her lips begin to tremble, the tears still on her lashes, her features gradually dissolving in a blur of apprehension and incredulity. 'Ah – this is beyond her! She won't be "brave" now,' he thought with an uncontrollable satisfaction. It seemed necessary, at the moment, that someone should feel the shock of his doom as he was feeling it – should *die with him*, at least morally, since he had to die. And the strange insight which had come to him – this queer 'behind-the-veil' penetration he was suddenly conscious of – had already told him that most of the people he knew, however sorry they might think they were, would really not be in the least affected by his fate, would remain as inwardly unmoved as he had been when, in the plenitude of his vigour, someone had said before him: 'Ah, poor so-and-so – didn't you know? The doctors say it's all up to him.'

With Eleanor it was different. As he held her there under his eyes he could almost trace the course of his own agony in her paling dissolving face, could almost see her as she might one day look if she were his widow – *his widow*! Poor thing. At least if she were that she could proclaim her love and her anguish, could abandon herself to open mourning on his grave. Perhaps that was the only comfort it was still in his power to give her . . . or in hers to give him. For the grave might be less cold if watered by her warm tears. The thought made his own well up, and he pressed her closer. At that moment his first wish was to see how she would look if she were really happy. His friend – his only friend! How he would make up to her now for his past callousness!

'Eleanor – '

'Oh, won't you tell me?' she entreated.

'Yes. Of course. Only I want you to promise me something first – '

'Yes. . . .'

'To do what I want you – whatever I want you to.'

She could not still the trembling of her hands, though he pressed them so close. She could scarcely articulate: 'Haven't I, always – ?'

Slowly he pronounced: 'I want you to marry me.'

Her trembling grew more violent, and then subsided. The shadow of her terrible fear seemed to fall from her, as the shadow of living falls from the face of the newly dead. Her face looked young and transparent; he watched the blood rise to her lips and cheeks.

'Oh, Paul, Paul – then the news is *good*?'

He felt a slight shrinking at her obtuseness. After all, she was alive (it wasn't her fault), she was merely alive, like all the rest. . . . Magnanimously he rejoined: 'Never mind about the news now.' But to himself he muttered: '*Sancta Simplicitas!*'

She had thought he had asked her to marry him because the news was good!

• II •

THEY were married almost immediately, and with as little circumstance as possible. Dorrance's ill-health, already vaguely known of in his immediate group of friends, was a sufficient pretext for hastening and simplifying the ceremony; and the next day the couple sailed for France.

Dorrance had not seen again the two doctors who had pronounced his doom. He had forbidden Mrs. Welwood to speak of the diagnosis, to him or to anyone else. 'For God's sake, don't let's dramatize the thing,' he commanded her; and she acquiesced.

He had shown her the paper as soon as she had promised to marry him; and had hastened, as she read it, to inform her that of course he had no intention of holding her to her promise. 'I only wanted to hear you say "yes,"' he explained, on a note of emotion so genuine that it deceived himself as completely as it did her. He was sure he would not accept his offer to release her; if he had not been sure he might not have dared to make it. For he understood now that he must marry her; he simply could not live out these last months alone. For a moment his thoughts had played sentimentally with the idea that he was marrying her to acquit an old debt, to make her happy before it was to late; but that delusion had been swept away like a straw on the torrent of his secret fears. A new form of egotism, fiercer and more impatient than the other, was dictating his words and gestures – and he knew it. He was marrying simply to put a sentinel between himself and the presence lurking on his threshold – with the same blind instinct of self-preservation which had made men, in old days, propitiate death by the lavish sacrifice of life. And, confident as he was, he had felt an obscure dread of her failing him till his ring was actually on her finger; and a great ecstasy of reassurance and gratitude as he walked out into the street with that captive hand on his arm. Could it be that together they would be able to cheat death after all?

They landed at Genoa, and traveled by slow stages toward the Austrian Alps. The journey seemed to do Dorrance good; he was bearing the fatigue better than he had expected; and he was conscious that his attentive companion noted the improvement, though she forbore to emphasize it. 'Above all, don't be too cheerful,' he had warned her, half smilingly, on the day when he had told her of his doom. 'Marry me if you think you can stand it; but don't try to make me think I'm going to get well.'

She had obeyed him to the letter, watching over his comfort, sparing him all needless fatigue and agitation, carefully serving up to him, on the bright surface of her vigilance, the flowers of travel stripped of their thorns. The very qualities which had made her a perfect mistress – self-effacement, opportuneness, the art of being present and visible only when he required her to be – made her (he had to own it) a perfect wife for a man cut off from everything but the contemplation of his own end.

They were bound for Vienna, where a celebrated specialist was said to have found new ways of relieving the suffering caused by such cases as Dorrance's – sometimes even (though Dorrance and his wife took care not to mention this to each other) of checking the disease, even holding it for years in abeyance. 'I owe it to the poor child to give the thing a trial,' the invalid speciously argued, disguising his own passionate impatience to put himself in the great man's hands. 'If she *wants* to drag out her life with a half-dead man, why should I prevent her?' he thought, trying to sum up all the hopeful possibilities on which the new diagnostician might base his verdict. . . . 'Certainly,' Dorrance thought, 'I have had less pain lately. . . .'

It had been agreed that he should go to the specialist's alone; his wife was to wait for him at their hotel. 'But you'll come straight back afterward? You'll take a taxi – you won't walk?' she had pleaded, for the first time betraying her impatience. 'She knows the hours are numbered, and she can't bear to lose one,' he thought, a choking in his throat; and as he bent to kiss her he had a vision of what it would have been, after the interview that lay ahead of him, the verdict he had already discounted, to walk back to an hotel in which no one awaited him, climb to an empty room and sit down alone with his doom. 'Bless you, child, of course I'll take a taxi. . . .'

Now the consultation was over, and he had descended from the specialist's door, and stood alone in the summer twilight, watching the trees darken against the illumination of the street lamps. What a divine thing a summer evening was, even in a crowded city street! He wondered that he had never before felt its peculiar loveliness. Through the trees the sky was deepening from pearl gray to blue as the stars came out. He stood there, unconscious of the hour, gazing at the people hurrying to and fro on the pavement, the traffic flowing by in an unbroken stream, all the ceaseless tides of the city's life which had seemed to him, half an hour ago, forever suspended. . . .

'No, it's too lovely; I'll walk,' he said, rousing himself, and took a direction opposite to that in which his hotel lay. 'After all,' he thought 'there's no hurry. . . . What a charming town Vienna is – I think I should like to live here,' he mused as he wandered on under the trees. . . .

When at last he reached his hotel he stopped short on the threshold and asked himself: 'How am I going to tell her?' He realized that during his two hours' perambulations since he had left the doctor's office he had thought out nothing, planned nothing, not even let his imagination glance at the future, but simply allowed himself to be absorbed into the softly palpitating life about him, like a tired traveller sinking, at his journey's end, into a warm bath. Only now, at the foot of the stairs, did he see the future facing him, and understand that he knew no more how to prepare for the return to life than he had for the leaving it. . . . 'If only she takes it quietly – without too much fuss,' he thought, shrinking in advance from any disturbance of those still waters into which it was so beatific to subside.

'That New York diagnosis was a mistake – an utter mistake,' he began vehemently, and then paused, arrested, silenced, by something in his wife's face which seemed to oppose an invisible resistance to what he was in the act of saying. He had hoped she would not be too emotional – and now: what was it? Did he really resent the mask of composure she had no doubt struggled to adjust during her long hours of waiting? He stood and stared at her. 'I suppose you don't believe it? he broke off, with an aimless irritated laugh.

She came to him eagerly. 'But of course I do, of course!' She seemed to hesitate for a second. 'What I never did believe,' she said abruptly, 'was the other – the New York diagnosis.'

He continued to stare, vaguely resentful of this new attitude, and of the hint of secret criticism it conveyed. He felt himself suddenly diminished in her eyes, as though she were retrospectively stripping him of some prerogative. If she had not believed in the New York diagnosis, what must her secret view of him have been all the while? 'Oh, you never believed in it? And may I ask why?' He heard the edge of sarcasm in his voice.

She gave a little laugh that sounded almost as aimless as his. 'I – I don't know. I suppose I couldn't *bear* to, simply; I couldn't believe fate could be so cruel.'

Still with a tinge of sarcasm he rejoined: 'I'm glad you had your incredulity to sustain you.' Inwardly he was saying: 'Not a tear . . . not an outbreak of emotion . . .' and his heart, dilated by the immense inrush of returning life, now contracted as if an invisible plug had been removed from it, and its fullness were slowly ebbing. 'It's a queer business, anyhow,' he mumbled.

'What is, dear?'

'This being alive again. I'm not sure I know yet what it consists in.'

She came up and put her arms about him, almost shyly. 'We'll try to find out, love – together.'

· III ·

THIS magnificent gift of life, which the Viennese doctor had restored to him as lightly as his New York colleagues had withdrawn it, lay before Paul Dorrance like something external, outside of himself, an honour, an official rank, unexpectedly thrust on him: he did not discover till then how completely he had dissociated himself from the whole business of living. It was as if life were a growth which the surgeon's knife had already extirpated, leaving him, disembodied, on the pale verge of nonentity. All the while that he had kept saying to himself: 'In a few weeks more I shall be dead,' had he not really known that he was dead already?

'But what are we to do, then, dearest?' he heard his wife asking. 'What do you want? Would you like to go home at once? Do you want me to cable to have the flat got ready?'

He looked at her in astonishment, wounded by such unperceivingness. Go home – to New York? To his old life there? Did she really think of it as something possible, even simple and natural? Why, the small space he had occupied there had closed up already; he felt himself as completely excluded from that other life as if his absence had lasted for years. And what did she mean by 'going home'? The old Paul Dorrance who had made his will, wound up his affairs, resigned from his clubs and directorships, pensioned off his old servants and married his old mistress – that Dorrance was as dead as if he had taken that final step for which all those others were but the hasty preparation. He *was* dead; this new man, to whom the doctor had said: 'Cancer? Nothing of the sort – not a trace of it. Go home and tell your wife that in a few months you'll be as sound as any man of fifty I ever met – ' this new Dorrance, with his new health, his new leisure and his new wife, was an intruder for whom a whole new existence would have to be planned out. And how could anything be decided until one got to know the new Paul Dorrance a little better?

Conscious that his wife was waiting for his answer, he said: 'Oh, this fellow here may be all wrong. Anyhow, he wants me to take a cure somewhere first – I've got the name written down. After that we'll see. . . . But wouldn't you rather travel for a year or so? How about South Africa or India next winter?' he ventured at random, after trying to think of some point of the globe even more remote from New York.

• IV •

THE cure was successful, the Viennese specialist's diagnosis proved to be correct; and the Paul Dorrances celebrated the event by two years of foreign travel. But Dorrance never felt again the unconditioned ecstasy he had tasted as he walked out from the doctor's door into the lamplit summer streets. After that, at the very moment of re-entering his hotel, the effort of readjustment had begun; and ever since it had gone on.

For a few months the wanderers, weary of change, had settled in Florence, captivated by an arcaded villa on a cypress-walled hill, and the new Paul Dorrance, whom it was now the other's incessant task to study and placate, had toyed with the idea of a middle life of cultivated leisure. But he soon grew tired of his opportunities, and found it necessary to move on, and forget in strenuous travel his incapacity for assimilation and reflection. And before the two years were over the old Paul Dorrance, who had constituted himself the other's courier and prime minister, discovered that the old and the new were one, and that the original Paul Dorrance was there, unchanged, unchangeable, and impatient to get back to his old niche because it was too late to adapt himself to any other. So the flat was reopened and the Dorrances returned to New York.

The completeness of his identity with the old Paul Dorrance was indelibly impressed on the new one on the first evening of his return home. There he was, the same man in the same setting as when, two years earlier, he had glanced down from the same armchair and seen the diagnosis of the consulting physicians at his feet. The hour was late, the room profoundly still; no touch of outward reality intervened between him and that hallucinating vision. He almost saw the paper on the floor, and with the same gesture as before he covered his eyes to shut it out. Two years ago – and nothing was changed, after so many changes, except that he should not hear the hesitating ring at the door, should not again see Eleanor Welwood, pale and questioning, on the threshold. Eleanor Welwood did not ring his doorbell now; she had her own latchkey; she was no longer Eleanor Welwood but Eleanor Dorrance, and asleep at this moment in the bedroom which had been Dorrance's, and was now encumbered with feminine properties, while his own were uncomfortably wedged into the cramped guest room of the flat.

Yes – that was the only change in his life; and how aptly the change in the rooms symbolized it! During their travels, even after Dorrance's return to health, his wife's presence had been like a soft accompaniment of music, a painted background to the idle episodes of convalescence; now that he was about to fit himself into the familiar furrow of old habits and relations he felt as if she were already expanding and crowding him into a corner. He did not mind about the room – so he assured himself, though with a twinge of regret for the slant of winter sun which never reached the guest room; what he minded was that he now recognized as the huge practical joke that fate had played on him. He had never meant, he the healthy, vigorous, middle-aged Paul Dorrance, to marry this faded woman for whom he had so long ceased to feel anything but a friendly tenderness. It was the bogey of death, starting out from the warm folds of his closely-curtained life, that had tricked him into the marriage, and then left him to expiate his folly.

Poor Eleanor! It was not her fault if he had imagined, in a moment of morbid retrospection, that happiness would transform and enlarge her. Under the surface changes she was still the same: a perfect companion while he was ill and lonely, an unwitting encumbrance now that (unchanged also) he was restored to the life from which his instinct of self-preservation had so long excluded her. Why had he not trusted to that instinct, which had warned him she was the woman for a sentimental parenthesis, not for the pitiless continuity of marriage? Why, even her face declared it. A lovely profile, yes; but somehow the full face was inadequate. . .

Dorrance suddenly remembered another face; that of a girl they had met in Cairo the previous winter. He felt the shock of her young fairness, saw the fruity bloom of her cheeks, the light animal vigor of every movement, he heard her rich beckoning laugh, and met the eyes questioning his under the queer slant of her lids. Someone had said: 'She's had an offer from a man who can give her everything a woman wants; but she's refused, and no one can make out why. . . .' Dorrance knew. . . . She had written to him since, and he had not answered her letters. And now here he was, installed once more in the old routine he could not live without, yet from which all the old savor was gone. 'I wonder why I was so scared of dying,' he thought; then the truth flashed on him. 'Why, you fool, you've been dead all the time. That first diagnosis was the true one. Only they put it on the physical plane by mistake. . . .' The next day he began to insert himself painfully into his furrow.

• V •

ONE evening some two years later, as Paul Dorrance put his latchkey into his door, he said to himself reluctantly: 'Perhaps I really ought to take her away for a change.'

There was nothing nowadays that he dreaded as much as change. He had had his fill of the unexpected, and it had not agreed with him. Now that he had fitted himself once more into his furrow all he asked was to stay there. It had even become an effort, when summer came, to put off his New York habits and go with his wife to their little place in the country. And the idea that he might have to go away with her in mid-February was positively disturbing.

For the past ten years she had been fighting a bad bronchitis, following on influenza. But 'fighting' was hardly the right word. She, usually so elastic, so indomitable, had not shown her usual resiliency, and Dorrance, from the vantage ground of his recovered health, wondered a little at her lack of spirit. She mustn't not let herself go, he warned her gently. 'I was in a good deal tighter place myself not so many years ago – and look at me now. Don't you let the doctors scare you.' She had promised him again that morning that she wouldn't, and he had gone off to his office without waiting for the physician's visit. But during the day he began in an odd way to feel his wife's nearness. It was as though she needed him, as though there were something she wanted to say; and he concluded that she probably knew she ought to go south, and had been afraid to tell him so. 'Poor child – of course I'll take her if the doctor says it's really necessary.' Hadn't he always done everything he could for her? It seemed to him that they had been married for years and years, and that as a husband he had behind him a long and irreproachable record. Why, he hadn't even answered that girl's letters. . . .

As he opened the door of the flat a strange woman in a nurse's dress crossed the hall. Instantly Dorrance felt the alien atmosphere of the place, the sense of something absorbing and exclusive which ignores and averts itself from the common doings of men. He had felt that same atmosphere, in all its somber implications, the day he had picked up the cancer diagnosis from the floor.

The nurse stopped to say 'Pneumonia,' and hurried down the passage to his wife's room. The doctor was coming back at nine o'clock; he had left a note in the library, the butler said. Dorrance knew what was in the note before he opened it. Precipitately, with the vertical drop of a bird of prey, death was descending on his house again. And this time there was no mistake in the diagnosis.

The nurse said he could come in for a minute; but he wasn't to stay long, for she didn't like the way the temperature was rising . . . and there, between the chalk-white pillows, in the green-shaded light, he saw his wife's face. What struck him first was the way it had shrunk and narrowed after a few hours of fever; then, that though it wore a just-perceptible smile of welcome, there was no sign of the tremor of illumination which usually greeted his appearance. He remembered how once, encountering that light, he had grumbled inwardly: 'I wish to God she wouldn't always unroll a red carpet when I come in – ' and then been ashamed of his thought. She never embarrassed him by any public show of feeling; that subtle play of light remained invisible to others, and his irritation was caused simply by knowing it was there. 'I don't want to be anybody's sun and moon,' he concluded. But now she was looking at him with a new, an almost critical equality of expression. His first thought was: 'Is it possible she doesn't know me?' But her eyes met his with a glance of recognition, and he understood that the change was simply due to her being enclosed in a world of her own, complete, and independent of his.

'Please, now – ' the nurse reminded him; and obediently he stole out of the room.

The next day there was a slight improvement; the doctors were encouraged; the day nurse said: 'If only it goes on like this – '; and as Dorrance opened the door of his wife's room he thought: 'If only she looks more like her own self – !'

But she did not. She was still in that new and self-contained world which he had immediately identified as the one he had lived in during the months when he had thought he was to die. 'After all, I didn't die,' he reminded himself; but the reminder brought no solace, for he knew exactly what his wife was feeling, he had tested the impenetrability of the barrier which shut her off from the living. 'The truth is, one doesn't only die once,' he mused, aware that he had died already; and the memory of the process, now being re-enacted before him, laid a chill on his heart. If only he could have helped her, made her understand! But the barrier was there, the transparent barrier through which everything on the hither side looked so different. And today it was he who was on the hither side.

Then he remembered how, in his loneliness, he had yearned for the beings already so remote, and the beings on the living side; and he felt for his wife the same rush of pity as when he had thought himself dying, and known what agony his death would cost her.

That day he was allowed to stay for five minutes; the next day ten; she continued to improve, and the doctors would have been perfectly satisfied if her heart had not shown signs of weakness. Hearts, however, medically speaking, are relatively easy to deal with; and to Dorrance she seemed much stronger.

Soon the improvement became so marked that the doctor made no objection to his sitting with her for an hour or two; the nurse was sent for a walk, and Dorrance was allowed to read the morning paper to the invalid. But when he took it up his wife stretched out her hand. 'No – I want to talk to you.'

He smiled, and met her smile. It was as if she had found a slit in the barrier and were reaching out to him. 'Dear – but won't talking tire you?'

'I don't know. Perhaps.' She waited. 'You see, I'm talking to you all the time, while I lie here. . . .'

He knew – he knew! How her pangs went through him! 'But you see, dear, raising your voice. . . .'

She smiled incredulously, that remote behind-the-barrier smile he had felt so often on his own lips. Though she could reach through to him the dividing line was still there, and her eyes met his with a look of weary omniscience.

'But there's no hurry,' he argued. 'Why not wait a day or two? Try to lie there and not even think.'

'Not think!' She raised herself on a weak elbow. 'I want to think every minute – every second. I want to relive everything, day by day, to the last atom of time. . . .'

'Time? But there'll be plenty of time!'

She continued to lean on her elbow, fixing her illumined eyes on him. She did not seem to hear what he said; her attention was concentrated on some secret vision of which he felt himself the mere transparent mask.

'Well,' she exclaimed, with a sudden passionate energy, 'it was worth it! I always knew – '

Dorrance bent toward her. 'What was worth – ?' But she had sunk back with closed eyes, and lay there reabsorbed into the cleft of the pillows, merged in the inanimate, a mere part of the furniture of the sick-room. Dorrance waited for a moment, hardly understanding the change; then he started up, rang, called, and in a few minutes the professionals were in possession, the air was full of ether and camphor, the telephone ringing, the disarray of death in the room. Dorrance knew that he would never know what she had found worth it. . . .

• VI •

HE sat in his library, waiting. Waiting for what? Life was over for him now that she was dead. Until after the funeral a sort of factitious excitement had kept him on his feet. Now there was nothing left but to go over and over those last days. Every detail of them stood out before him in unbearable relief; and one of the most salient had been the unexpected appearance in the sick room of Dorrance's former doctor – the very doctor who, with the cancer specialist, had signed the diagnosis of Dorrance's case. Dorrance, since that day, had naturally never consulted him professionally; and it chanced that they had never met. But Eleanor's physician, summoned at the moment of her last heart attack, without even stopping to notify Dorrance, had called in his colleague. The latter had a high standing as a consultant (the idea made Dorrance smile); and besides, what did it matter? By that time they all knew – nurses, doctors and most of all Dorrance himself – that nothing was possible but to ease the pangs of Eleanor's last hours. And Dorrance had met his former doctor without resentment; hardly even with surprise.

But the doctor had not forgotten that he and his former patient had been old friends; and the day after the funeral, late in the evening, had thought it proper to ring the widower's doorbell and present his condolences. Dorrance, at his entrance, looked up in surprise, at first resenting the intrusion, then secretly relieved at the momentary release from the fiery wheel of his own thoughts. 'The man is a fool – but perhaps,' Dorrance reflected, 'he'll give me something that will make me sleep. . . .'

The two men sat down, and the doctor began to talk gently of Eleanor. He had known her for many years, though not professionally. He spoke of her goodness, her charity, the many instances he had come across his poor patients of her discreet and untiring ministrations. Dorrance, who had dreaded hearing her spoken of, and by this man above all others, found himself listening with a curious avidity to these reminiscences. He needed no one to tell him of Eleanor's kindness, her devotion – yet at the moment such praise was sweet to him. And he took up the theme; but not without a secret stir of vindictiveness, a vague desire to make the doctor suffer for the results of his now-distant blunder. 'She always gave too much of herself – that was the trouble. No one knows that better than I do. She was never really the same after those months of incessant anxiety about me that you doctors made her undergo.' He had not intended to say anything of the sort; but as he spoke the resentment he had thought extinct was fanned into flame by his words. He had forgiven the two doctors for himself, but he suddenly found he could not forgive them for Eleanor, and he had an angry wish to let them know it. 'That diagnosis of yours nearly killed her, though it didn't kill *me*,' he concluded sardonically.

The doctor had followed this outburst with a look of visible perplexity. In the crowded life of a fashionable physician, what room was there to remember a mistaken diagnosis? The sight of his forgetfulness made Dorrance continue with rising irritation: 'The shock of it *did* kill her – I see that now.'

'Diagnosis – what diagnosis?' echoed the doctor blankly.

'I see you don't remember,' said Dorrance.

'Well, no; I don't, for the moment.'

'I'll remind you, then. When you came to see me with that cancer specialist four or five years ago, one of you dropped your diagnosis by mistake in going out. . . .'

'Oh, *that*?' The doctor's face lit up with sudden recollection. 'Of course! The diagnosis of the other poor fellow we'd been to see before coming to you. I remember it all now. Your wife – Mrs. Welwood then, wasn't she? – brought the paper back to me a few hours later – before I'd even missed it. I think she said you'd picked it up after we left, and thought it was meant for *you*.' The doctor gave an easy retrospective laugh. 'Luckily I was able to reassure her at once.' He leaned back comfortably in his armchair and shifted his voice to the pitch of condolence. 'A beautiful life, your wife's was. I only wish it had been in our power to prolong it. But these cases of heart failure . . . you must tell yourself that at least you had a few happy years; and so many of us haven't even that.' The doctor stood up and held out his hand.

'Wait a moment, please,' Dorrance said hurriedly. 'There's something I want to ask you.' His brain was whirling so that he could not remember what he had started to say. 'I can't sleep. . . .' he began.

'Yes?' said the doctor, assuming a professional look, but with a furtive glance at his wrist watch.

Dorrance's throat felt dry and his head empty. He struggled with the difficulty of ordering his thoughts, and fitting rational words of them.

'Yes – but no matter about my sleeping. What I meant was: do I understand you to say that the diagnosis you dropped in leaving was not intended for me?'

The doctor stared. 'Good Lord, no – of course it wasn't. You never had a symptom. Didn't we both tell you so at the time?'

'Yes,' Dorrance slowly acquiesced.

'Well, if you didn't believe us, your scare was a short one, anyhow,' the doctor continued with a mild jocularity; and he put his hand out again.

'Oh, wait,' Dorrance repeated. 'What I really wanted to ask was what day you said my wife returned the diagnosis to you? But I suppose you don't remember.'

The doctor reflected. 'Yes, I do; it all comes back to me now. It was the very same day. We called on you in the morning, didn't we?'

'Yes; at nine o'clock,' said Dorrance, the dryness returning to his throat.

'Well, Mrs. Welwood brought the diagnosis back to me directly afterward.'

'You think it was the very same day?' (Dorrance wondered to himself why he continued to insist on this particular point.)

The doctor took another stolen glance at his watch. 'I'm sure it was. I remember now that it was my consultation day, and that she caught me at two o'clock, before I saw my first patient. We had a good laugh over the scare you'd had.'

'I see,' said Dorrance.

'Your wife had one of the sweetest laughs I ever heard,' continued the doctor, with an expression of melancholy reminiscence.

There was a silence, and Dorrance was conscious that his visitor was looking at him with growing perplexity. He too gave a slight laugh. 'I thought perhaps it was the day after,' he mumbled vaguely. 'Anyhow, you did give me a good scare.'

'Yes,' said the doctor. 'But it didn't last long, did it? I asked your wife to make my peace with you. You know such things will happen to hurried doctors. I hope she persuaded you to forgive me?'

'Oh, yes,' said Dorrance, as he followed the doctor to the door to let him out.

'Well, now about that sleeping – ' the doctor checked himself on the threshold to ask.

'Sleeping?' Dorrance stared. 'Oh, I shall sleep all right tonight,' he said with sudden decision, as he closed the door on his visitor.

The Day of the Funeral

———————

His wife had said: 'If you don't give her up I'll throw myself from the roof.' He had not given her up, and his wife had thrown herself from the roof.

Nothing of this had of course come out in the inquest. Luckily Mrs. Trenham had left no letters or diary – no papers of any sort, in fact; not even a little mound of ashes on the hearth. She was the kind of woman who never seemed to have many material appurtenances or encumbrances. And Dr. Lanscomb, who had attended her ever since her husband had been called to his professorship at Kingsborough, testified that she had always been excessively emotional and high-strung, and never 'quite right' since her only child had died. The doctor's evidence closed the inquiry; the whole business had not lasted more than ten minutes.

Then, after another endless interval of forty-eight hours, came the funeral. Ambrose Trenham could never afterward recall what he did during those forty-eight hours. His wife's relations lived at the other end of the continent, in California; he himself had no immediate family; and the house – suddenly became strange and unfamiliar, a house that seemed never to have been his – had been given over to benevolent neighbors, soft-stepping motherly women, and to glib, subservient men who looked like a cross between book agents and revivalists. These men took measures, discussed technical questions in undertones with the motherly women, and presently came back with a coffin with plated handles. Someone asked Trenham what was to be engraved on the plate on the lid, and he said: 'Nothing.' He understood afterward that the answer had not been what was expected; but at the time everyone evidently ascribed it to his being incapacitated by grief.

Before the funeral one horrible moment stood out from the others, though all were horrible. It was when Mrs. Cossett, the wife of the professor of English Literature, came to him and said: 'Do you want to see her?'

'See her – ?' Trenham gasped, not understanding.

Mrs. Cossett looked surprised, and a little shocked. 'The time has come – they must close the coffin. . . .'

'Oh, let them close it,' was on the tip of the widower's tongue; but he saw from Mrs. Cossett's expression that something very different was expected of him. He got up and followed her out of the room and up the stairs. . . . He looked at his wife. Her face had been spared. . . .

That too was over now, and the funeral as well. Somehow, after all, the time had worn on. At the funeral, Trenham had discovered in himself – he, the absent-minded, the unobservant – an uncanny faculty for singling out every one whom he knew in the crowded church. It was incredible; sitting in the front pew, his head bowed forward on his hands, he seemed suddenly gifted with the power of knowing who was behind him and on either side. And when the service was over, and to the sound of 'O Paradise' he turned to walk down the nave behind the coffin, though his head was still bowed, and he was not conscious of looking to the right or the left, face after face thrust itself forward into his field of vision – and among them, yes: of a sudden, Barbara Wake's!

The shock was terrible; Trenham had been so sure she would not come. Afterward he understood that she had had to – for the sake of appearances. 'Appearances' still ruled at Kingsborough – where didn't they, in the university world, and more especially in New England? But at the moment, and for a long time, Trenham had felt horrified, and outraged in what now seemed his holiest feelings. What right had she? How dare she? It was indecent. . . . In the reaction produced by the shock of seeing her, his remorse for what had happened hardened into icy hate of the woman who had been the cause of the tragedy. The sole cause – for in a flash Trenham had thrown off his own share in the disaster. 'The woman tempted me – ' Yes, she had! It was what his poor wronged Milly had always said: 'You're so weak: and she's always tempting you – '

He used to laugh at the idea of Barbara Wake as a temptress; one of poor Milly's delusions! It seemed to him, then, that he was always pursuing, the girl evading; but now he saw her as his wife had seen her, and despised her accordingly. The indecency of her coming to the funeral! To have another look at him, he supposed . . . she was insatiable . . . it was as if she could never fill her eyes with him. But, if he could help it, they should never be laid on him again. . . .

• II •

His indignation grew; it filled the remaining hours of the endless day, the empty hours after the funeral was over; it occupied and sustained him. The President of the University, an old friend, had driven him back to his lonely house, had wanted to get out and come in with him. But Trenham had refused, had shaken hands at the gate, and walked alone up the path to his front door. A cold lunch was waiting on the dining-room table. He left it untouched, poured out some whiskey and water, carried the glass into his study, lit his pipe and sat down in his armchair to think, not of his wife, with whom the inquest seemed somehow to have settled his account, but of Barbara Wake. With her he must settle his account himself. And he had known at once how he would do it; simply by tying up all her letters, and the little photograph he always carried in his notecase (the only likeness he had of her), and sending them back without a word.

A word! What word indeed could equal the emphasis of that silence? Barbara Wake had all the feminine passion for going over and over things; talking them inside out; in that respect she was as bad as poor Milly had been, and nothing would humiliate and exasperate her as much as an uncommented gesture of dismissal. It was so fortifying to visualize that scene – the scene of her opening the packet alone in her room – that Trenham's sense of weariness disappeared, his pulses begun to drum excitedly, and he was torn by a pang of hunger, the first he had felt in days. Was the cold meat still on the table, he wondered? Shamefacedly he stole back to the dining room. But the table had been cleared, of course – just today! On ordinary days the maid would leave the empty dishes for hours unremoved; it was one of poor Milly's household grievances. How often he had said to her, impatiently: 'Good Lord, what does it matter?' and she had answered: 'But,

Ambrose, the flies!' . . . And now, of all days, the fool of a maid
had cleared away everything. He went back to his study, sat down
again, and suddenly felt too hungry to think of anything but his
hunger. Even his vengeance no longer nourished him; he felt as if
nothing would replace that slice of pressed beef, with potato salad
and pickles, of which his eyes had rejected the disgusted glimpse
an hour or two earlier.

He fought his hunger for a while longer; then he got up and
rang. Promptly, attentively, Jane, the middle-aged disapproving
maid, appeared – usually one had to rip out the bell before she
disturbed herself. Trenham felt sheepish at having to confess his
hunger to her, as if it made him appear unfeeling, unheroic; but
he could not help himself. He stammered out that he supposed
he ought to eat something . . . and Jane, at once, was all tearful
sympathy. 'That's right, sir; you must *try* . . . you must force
yourself. . . .' Yes, he said; he realized that. He would force
himself. 'We were saying in the kitchen, Katy and me, that you
couldn't go on any longer this way. . . .' He could hardly wait
till she had used up her phrases and got back to the pantry. . . .
Through the half-open dining-room door he listened avidly to
her steps coming and going, to the clatter of china, the rattle of
the knife basket. He met her at the door when she returned to tell
him that his lunch was ready . . . and that Katy had scrambled
some eggs for him the way he liked them.

At the dining-room table, when the door had closed on her, he
squared his elbows, bent his head over his plate, and emptied every
dish. Had he ever before known the complex exquisiteness of a
slice of pressed beef? He filled his glass again, leaned luxuriously,
waited without hurry for the cheese and biscuits, the black coffee,
and a slice of apple pie apologetically added from the maids' dinner
– and then – oh, resurrection! – felt for his cigar case, and calmly,
carelessly almost, under Jane's moist and thankful eyes, cut his
Corona and lit it.

'Now he's saved,' her devout look seemed to say.

• III •

THE letters must be returned at once. But to whom could he
entrust them? Certainly not to either one of the maidservants. And

there was no one else but the slow-witted man who looked after
the garden and the furnace, and who would have been too much
dazed by such a commission to execute it without first receiving
the most elaborate and reiterated explanations, and then would
probably have delivered the packet to Professor Wake, or posted it
– the latter a possibility to be at all costs avoided, since Trenham's
writing might have been recognized by someone at the post
office, one of the chief centers of gossip at Kingsborough. How
it complicated everything to live in a small, prying community!
He had no reason to suppose that any one divined the cause of his
wife's death, yet he was aware that people had seen him more than
once in out-of-the-way places, and at queer hours, with Barbara
Wake; and if his wife knew, why should not others suspect? For
a while, at any rate, it behooved him to avoid all appearance
of wishing to communicate with the girl. Returning a packet
to her on the very day of the funeral would seem particularly
suspicious. . . .

Thus, after coffee and cigar, and a nip of old Cognac, argued
the normal sensible man that Trenham had become again. But if
his nerves had been steadied by food his will had been strengthened
by it, and instead of a weak, vacillating wish to let Barbara Wake
feel the weight of his scorn he was now animated by the furious
resolution to crush her with it, and at once. That packet should
be returned to her before night.

He shut the study door, drew out his keys, and unlocked the
cabinet in which he kept the letters. He had no need now to listen
for his wife's step, or to place himself between the cabinet and the
door of the study, as he used to when he thought he heard her
coming. Now, had he chosen, he could have spread the letters
out all over the table. Jane and Katy were busy in the kitchen,
and the rest of the house was his to do what he liked in. He could
have sat down and read the serried pages one by one, lingeringly,
gloatingly, as he had so often longed to do when the risk was too
great – and now they were but so much noisome rubbish to him,
to be crammed into a big envelope, and sealed up out of sight. He
began to hunt for an envelope. . . .

God! What dozens and dozens of letters there were! And
all written within eighteen months. No wonder poor Milly
. . . but what a blind reckless fool he had been! The reason of
their abundance was, of course, the difficulty of meeting. . . .

So often he and Barbara had had to write because they couldn't contrive to see each other . . . but still, this bombardment of letters was monstrous, inexcusable. . . . He hunted for a long time for an envelope big enough to contain them; finally found one, a huge linen-lined envelope meant for college documents, and jammed the letters into it with averted head. But what, he thought suddenly, if she mistook his silence, imagined he had sent her the letters simply as a measure of prudence? No – that was hardly likely, now that all need of prudence was over; but she might affect to think so, use the idea as a pretext to write and ask what he meant, what she was to understand by his returning her letters without a word. It might give her an opening, which was probably what she was hoping for, and certainly what he was most determined she should not have.

He found a sheet of note paper, shook his fountain pen, wrote a few words (hardly looking at the page as he did so), and thrust the note in among the letters. His hands turned clammy as he touched them; he felt cold and sick . . . and the cursed flap of the envelope wouldn't stick – those linen envelopes were always so stiff. And where the devil was the sealing wax? He rummaged frantically among the odds and ends on his desk. A provision of sealing wax used always to be kept in the lower left-hand drawer. He groped about in it and found only some yellowing newspaper clippings. Milly used to be so careful about seeing that his writing table was properly supplied; but lately – ah, his poor poor Milly! If she could only know how he was suffering and atoning already. . . . Some string, then. . . . He fished some string out of another drawer. He would have to make it do instead of sealing wax; he would have to try to tie a double knot. But his fingers, always clumsy, were twitching like a drug fiend's; the letters seemed to burn them through the envelope. With a shaking hand he addressed the packet, and sat there, his eyes turned from it, while he tried again to think out some safe means of having it delivered. . . .

• IV •

HE dined hungrily, as he had lunched; and after dinner he took his hat from its peg in the hall, and said to Jane: 'I think I'll smoke my cigar in the campus.'

That was a good idea; he saw at once that she thought it a
hopeful sign, his wanting to take the air after being mewed up
in the house for so long. The night was cold and moonless, and
the college grounds, at that hour, would be a desert . . . after all,
delivering the letters himself was the safest way: openly, at the
girl's own door, without any mystery. . . . If Malvina, the Wakes'
old maid, should chance to open the door, he'd pull the packet
out and say at once: 'Oh, Malvina, I've found some books that
Miss Barbara lent me last year, and as I'm going away – ' He had
gradually learned that there was nothing as safe as simplicity.

He was reassured by the fact that the night was so dark. It
felt queer, unnatural somehow, to be walking abroad again like
the Ambrose Trenham he used to be; he was glad there were so
few people about, and that the Kingsborough suburbs were so
scantily lit. He walked on, his elbow hitting now and then against
the bundle, which bulged out of his pocket. Every time he felt it a
sort of nausea rose in him. Professor Wake's house stood halfway
down one of the quietest of Kingsborough's outlying streets. It
was withdrawn from the road under the hanging boughs of old
elms; he could just catch a glint of light from one or two windows.
And suddenly, as he was almost abreast of the gate, Barbara Wake
came out of it.

For a moment she stood glancing about her; then she turned
in the direction of the narrow lane bounding the farther side of
the property. What took her there, Trenham wondered? His first
impulse had been to draw back, and let her go her way; then he saw
how providential the encounter was. The lane was dark, deserted –
a mere passage between widely scattered houses, all asleep in their
gardens. The chilly night had sent people home early; there was
not a soul in sight. In another moment the packet would be in her
hands, and he would have left her, just silently raising his hat.

He remembered now where she was going. The garage,
built in the far corner of the garden, opened into the lane. The
Wakes had no chauffeur, and Barbara, who drove the car, was
sole mistress of the garage and of its keys. Trenham and she had
met there sometimes; a desolate trysting place! But what could
they do, in a town like Kingsborough? At one time she had
talked of setting up a studio – she dabbled in painting; but the
suggestion had alarmed him (he knew the talk it would create),
and he had discouraged her. Most often they took the train and

went to Ditson, a manufacturing town an hour away, where no one knew them . . . but what could she be going to the garage for at this hour?

The thought of his wife rushed into Trenham's mind. The discovery that she had lived there beside him, knowing all, and that suddenly, when she found she could not regain his affection, life had seemed worthless, and without a moment's hesitation she had left it. . . . Why, if he had known the quiet woman at his side had such springs of passion in her, how differently he would have regarded her, how little this girl's insipid endearments would have mattered to him! He was a man who could not live without tenderness, without demonstrative tenderness; his own shyness and reticence had to be perpetually broken down, laughingly scattered to the winds. His wife, he now saw, had been too much like him, had secretly suffered from the same inhibitions. She had always seemed ashamed, and frightened by her feeling for him, and half repelled, half fascinated by his response. At times he imagined that she found him physically distasteful, and wondered how, that being the case, she could be so fiercely jealous of him. Now he understood that her cold reluctant surrender concealed a passion so violent that it humiliated her, and so incomprehensible that she had never mastered its language. She reminded him of a clumsy little girl he had once known at a dancing class he had been sent to as a boy – a little girl who had a feverish passion for dancing, but could never learn the steps. And because he too had felt the irresistible need to join in the immemorial love dance he had ended by choosing a partner more skilled in its intricacies. . . .

These thoughts wandered through his mind as he stood watching Barbara Wake. Slowly he took a few steps down the lane; then he halted again. He had not yet made up his mind what to do. If she were going to the garage to get something she had forgotten (as was most probable, at that hour) she would no doubt be coming back in a few moments, and he could meet her and hand her the letters. Above all, he wanted to avoid going into the garage. To do so at that moment would have been a profanation of Milly's memory. He would have liked to efface from his own all recollection of the furtive hours spent there; but the vision returned with intolerable acuity as the girl's slim figure, receding from him, reached the door. How often he had stood at that corner, under those heavy trees, watching for her to appear and slip in ahead of him – so that they should not be seen entering together. The elaborate precautions with which their meetings had been surrounded – how pitiably futile they now seemed! They had not even achieved their purpose, but had only belittled his love and robbed it of its spontaneity. Real passion ought to be free, reckless, audacious, unhampered by the fear of a wife's feelings, of the university's regulations, the president's friendship, the deadly risk of losing one's job and wrecking one's career. It seemed to him now that the love he had given to Barbara Wake was almost as niggardly as that which he had doled out to his wife. . . .

He walked down the lane and saw that Barbara was going into the garage. It was so dark that he could hardly make out her movements; but as he reached the door she drew out her electric lamp (that recalled memories too), and by its flash he saw her slim gloveless hand put the key into the lock. The key turned, the door creaked, and all was darkness. . . .

The glimpse of her hand reminded him of the first time he had dared to hold it in his and press a kiss on the palm. They had met accidentally in the train, both of them on their way home from Boston, and he had proposed that they should get off at the last station before Kingsborough, and walk back by a short cut he knew, through the woods and along the King river. It was a shining summer day, and the girl had been amused at the idea and had accepted. . . . He could see now every line, every curve of her hand, a quick strong young hand, with long fingers, slightly blunt at the tips, and a sensuous elastic palm. It would be queer to have to carry on life without ever again knowing the feel of that hand. . . .

Of course he would go away; he would have to. If possible he would leave the following week. Perhaps the faculty would let him advance his sabbatical year. If not, they would probably let him off for the winter term, and perhaps after that he might make up his mind to resign, and look for a professorship elsewhere – in the South, or in California – as far away from that girl as possible. Meanwhile what he wanted was to get away to some hot climate, steamy, tropical, where one could lie out all night on a white beach and hear the palms chatter to the waves, and the trade winds blow from God knew where . . . one of those fiery flowery islands where marriage and love were not regarded so solemnly, and a man could follow his instinct without calling down a catastrophe, or feeling himself morally degraded. . . . Above all, he never wanted to see again a woman who argued and worried and reproached, and dramatized things that ought to be as simple as eating and drinking. . . .

Barbara, he had to admit, had never been frightened or worried, had never reproached him. The girl had the true sporting instinct; he never remembered her being afraid of risks, or nervous about 'appearances.' Once or twice, at moments when detection seemed imminent, she had half frightened him by her cool resourcefulness. He sneered at the remembrance. 'An old hand, no doubt!' But the sneer did not help him. Whose fault was it if the girl had had to master the arts of dissimulation? Whose but his? He alone (he saw in sudden terror) was responsible for what he supposed would be called her downfall. Poor child – poor Barbara! Was it possible that he, the seducer, the corrupter, had presumed to judge her? The thought was monstrous. . . . His resentment had already vanished like a puff of mist. The feeling of his responsibility, which had seemed so abhorrent, was now almost sweet to him. He was responsible – he owed her something! Thank heaven for that! For now he could raise his passion into a duty, and thus disguised and moralized, could once more – oh, could he, dared he? – admit it openly into his life. The mere possibility made him suddenly feel less cold and desolate. That the something – not – himself that made for righteousness should take on the tender lineaments, the human warmth of love, should come to sit by his hearth in the shape of Barbara – how warm, how happy and reassured it made him! He had a swift vision of her, actually sitting there in the shabby old leather chair (he would have it re-covered), her slim feet on the faded Turkey rug (he would have it replaced). It was almost a pity – he thought madly – that they would probably not be able to stay on at Kingsborough, there, in that very house where for so long he had not even dared to look at her letters. . . . Of course, if they did decide to, he would have it all done over for her.

• V •

THE garage door creaked and again he saw the flash of the
electric lamp on her bare hand as she turned the key; then she
moved toward him in the darkness.

'Barbara!'

She stopped short at his whisper. They drew closer to each
other. 'You wanted to see me?' she whispered back. Her voice
flowed over him like summer air.

'Can we go in there – ?' he gestured.

'Into the garage? Yes – I suppose so.'

They turned and walked in silence through the obscurity. The
comfort of her nearness was indescribable.

She unlocked the door again, and he followed her in. 'Take
care; I left the wheel jack somewhere,' she warned him. Automatically he produced a match, and she lit the candle in an old
broken-paned lantern that hung on a nail against the wall. How
familiar it all was – how often he had brought out his matchbox
and she had lit that candle! In the little pool of yellowish light they
stood and looked at each other.

'You didn't expect me?' he stammered.

'I'm not sure I didn't,' she returned softly, and he just caught
her smile in the half-light. The divineness of it!

'I didn't suppose I should see you. I just wandered out. . . .'
He suddenly felt the difficulty of accounting for himself.

'My poor Ambrose!' She laid her hand on his arm. 'How I've
ached for you – '

Yes; that was right; the tender sympathizing friend . . .
anything else, at that moment, would have been unthinkable. He
drew a breath of relief and self-satisfaction. Her pity made him
feel almost heroic – had he not lost sight of his own sufferings in
the thought of hers? 'It's been awful – ' he muttered.

'Yes; I know.'

She sat down on the step of the old Packard, and he found a
wooden stool and dragged it into the candle ray.

'I'm glad you came,' she began, still in the same soft healing
voice, 'because I'm going away tomorrow early, and – '

He started to his feet, upsetting the stool with a crash. 'Going
away? Early tomorrow?' Why hadn't he known of this? He felt
weak and injured. Where could she be going in this sudden way?

If they hadn't happened to meet, would he have known nothing of it till she was gone? His heart grew small and cold.

She was saying quietly: 'You must see – it's better. I'm going out to the Jim Southwicks, in California. They're always asking me. Mother and father think it's on account of my colds . . . the winter climate here . . . they think I'm right.' She paused, but he could find nothing to say. The future had become a featureless desert. 'I wanted to see you before going,' she continued, 'and I didn't exactly know . . . I hoped you'd come – '

'When are you coming back?' he interrupted desperately.

'Oh, I don't know; they want me for the winter, of course. There's a crazy plan about Hawaii and Samoa . . . sounds lovely, doesn't it? And from there on. . . . But I don't know. . . .'

He felt a suffocation in his throat. If he didn't cry out, do something at once to stop her, he would choke. 'You can't go – you can't leave me like this!' It seemed to him that his voice had risen to a shout.

'Ambrose – ' she murmured, subdued, half warning.

'You can't. How can you? It's madness. You don't understand. You say you ought to go – it's better you should go. What do you mean – why better? Are you afraid of what people might say? Is that it? How can they say anything when they know we're going to be married? Don't you know we're going to be married?' he burst out weakly, his words stumbling over each other in the effort to make her understand.

She hesitated a moment, and he stood waiting in an agony of suspense. How women loved to make men suffer! At last she said in a constrained voice: 'I don't think we ought to talk of all this yet – '

Rebuking him – she was actually rebuking him for his magnanimity! But couldn't she see – couldn't she understand? Or was it that she really enjoyed torturing him? 'How can I help talking of it, when you tell me you're going away tomorrow morning? Did you really mean to go without even telling me?'

'If I hadn't seen you I should have written,' she faltered.

'Well, now I'm here you needn't write. All you've got to do is to answer me,' he retorted almost angrily. The calm way in which she dealt with the situation was enough to madden a man – actually as if she hadn't made up her mind, good God! 'What are you afraid of?' he burst out harshly.

'I'm not afraid – only I didn't expect . . . I thought we'd talk of all this later . . . if you feel the same when I come back – if we both do.'

'If we both do!' Ah, there was the sting – the devil's claw! What was it? Was she being superhumanly magnanimous – or proud, over-sensitive, afraid that he might be making the proposal out of pity? Poor girl – poor child! That must be it. He loved her all the more for it, bless her! Or was it (ah, now again the claw tightened), was it that she really didn't want to commit herself, wanted to reserve her freedom for this crazy expedition, to see whether she couldn't do better by looking about out there – she, so young, so fresh and radiant – than by binding herself in advance to an elderly professor at Kingsborough? Hawaii – Samoa – swarming with rich idle yachtsmen and young naval officers (he had an excruciating vision of a throng of *Madame Butterfly* tenors in immaculate white duck and gold braid) – cocktails, fox-trot, moonlight in the tropics . . . he felt suddenly middle-aged, round shouldered, shabby, with thinning graying hair. . . . Of course what she wanted was to look round and see what her chances were! He retrieved the fallen stool, set it up again, and sat down on it.

'I suppose you're not sure you'll feel the same when you get back? Is that it?' he suggested bitterly.

Again she hesitated. 'I don't think we ought to decide now – tonight. . . .'

His anger blazed. 'Why oughtn't we? Tell me that! I've decided. Why shouldn't you?'

'You haven't really decided either,' she returned gently.

'I haven't – haven't I? Now what do you mean by that?' He forced a laugh that was meant to be playful but sounded defiant. He was aware that his voice and words were getting out of hand – but what business had she to keep him on the stretch like this?

'I mean, after what you've been through. . . .'

'After what I've been through? But don't you see that's the very reason? I'm at the breaking point – I can't bear any more.'

'I know; I know.' She got up and came close, laying a quiet hand on his shoulder. 'I've suffered for you too. The shock it must have been. That's the reason why I don't want to say anything now that you might – '

He shook off her hand, and sprang up. 'What hypocrisy!' He heard himself beginning to shout again. 'I suppose what you mean is that you want to be free to marry out there if you see anybody you like better. Then why not admit it at once?'

'Because it's not what I mean. I don't want to marry anyone else, Ambrose.'

Oh, the melting music of it! He lifted his hands and hid his burning eyes in them. The sound of her voice wove magic passes above his forehead. Was it possible that such bliss could come out of such anguish? He forgot the place – forgot the day – and abruptly, blindly, caught her by the arm, and flung his own about her.

'Oh, Ambrose – ' he heard her, reproachful, panting. He struggled with her, feverish for her lips.

In the semiobscurity there was the sound of something crashing to the floor between them. They drew apart, and she looked at him, bewildered. 'What was that?'

What was it? He knew well enough; a shiver of cold ran over him. The letters, of course – her letters! The bulging clumsily-tied envelope had dropped out of his pocket onto the floor of the garage; in the fall the string had come undone, and the mass of papers had tumbled out, scattering themselves like a pack of cards at Barbara's feet. She picked up her electric lamp, and bending over shot its sharp ray on them.

'Why, they're letters! Ambrose – are they my letters?' She waited; but silence lay on him like lead. 'Was that what you came for?' she exclaimed.

If there was an answer to that he couldn't find it, and stupidly, without knowing what he was doing, he bent down and began to gather up the letters.

For a while he was aware of her standing there motionless, watching him; then she too bent over, and took up the gaping linen envelope. 'Miss Barbara Wake,' she read out; and suddenly she began to laugh. 'Why,' she said, 'there's something left in it! A letter for *me*? Is that it?'

He put his hand out. 'Barbara – don't! Barbara – I implore you!'

She turned the electric ray on the sheet of paper, which detached itself from the shadows with the solidity of a graven tablet. Slowly she read out, in a cool measured voice, almost as though she were parodying his poor phrases: ' "November tenth. . . . You will probably feel as I do" (no – don't snatch! Ambrose, I forbid you!) "You will probably feel, as I do, that after what has happened you and I can never" – ' She broke off and raised her eyes to Trenham's. ' "After what has happened"? I don't understand. What do you mean? What *has* happened, Ambrose – between you and me?'

He had retreated a few steps, and stood leaning against the side of the motor. 'I didn't say "between you and me."'

'What did you say?' She turned the light once more on the fatal page. ' "You and I can never wish to meet again."' Her hand sank, and she stood facing him in silence.

Feeling her gaze fixed on him, he muttered miserably: 'I asked you not to read the thing.'

'But if it was meant for me why do you want me not to read it?'

'Can't you see? It doesn't mean anything. I was raving mad when I wrote it. . . .'

'But you wrote it only a few hours ago. It's dated today. How can you have changed so in a few hours? And you say: "After what has happened." That must mean something. What does it mean? What *has* happened?'

He thought he would go mad indeed if she repeated the word again. 'Oh, don't – !' he exclaimed.

'Don't what?'

'Say it over and over – "what has happened?" Can't you understand that just at first – '

He broke off, and she prompted him: 'Just at first – ?'

'I couldn't bear the horror alone. Like a miserable coward I let myself think you were partly responsible – I wanted to think so, you understand. . . .'

Her face seemed to grow white and wavering in the shadows. 'What do you mean? Responsible for what?'

He straightened his shoulders and said slowly: 'Responsible for her death. I was too weak to carry it alone.'

'Her death?' There was a silence that seemed to make the shadowy place darker. He could hardly see her face now, she was so far off. 'How could I be responsible?' she broke off, and then began again: 'Are you – trying to tell me – that it wasn't an accident?'

'No – it wasn't an accident.'

'She – '

'Well, can't you guess?' he stammered, panting.

'You mean – she killed herself?'

'Yes.'

'Because of us?'

He could not speak, and after a moment she hurried on: 'But what makes you think so? What proof have you? Did she tell anyone? Did she leave a message – a letter?'

He summoned his voice to his dry throat. 'No; nothing.'

'Well, then – ?'

'She'd told me beforehand; she'd warned me – '

'Warned you?'

'That if I went on seeing you . . . and I did go on seeing you . . . she warned me again and again. Do you understand now?' he exclaimed, twisting round on her fiercely, like an animal turning on its torturer.

There was an interval of silence – endless it seemed to him. She did not speak or move; but suddenly he heard a low sobbing sound. She was weeping, weeping like a frightened child. . . . well, of all the unexpected turns of fate! A moment ago he had seemed to feel her strength flowing into his cold veins, had thought to himself: 'I shall never again be alone with my horror – ' and now the horror had spread from him to her, and he felt her inwardly recoiling as though she shuddered away from the contagion.

'Oh, how dreadful, how dreadful – ' She began to cry again, like a child swept by a fresh gust of misery as the last subsides.

'Why dreadful?' he burst out, unnerved by the continuance of her soft unremitting sobs. 'You must have known she didn't like it – didn't you?'

Through her lament a whisper issued: 'I never dreamed she knew.'

'You mean to say you thought we'd deceived her? All those months? In a one-horse place where everybody is on the watch to see what everybody else is doing? Likely, isn't it? My God – '

'I never dreamed . . . I never dreamed. . . .' she reiterated.

'His exasperation broke out again. 'Well, now you begin to see what I've suffered – '

'Suffered? *You* suffered?' She uttered a low sound of derision. 'I see what she must have suffered – what we both of us must have made her suffer.'

'Ah, at least you say "both of us"!'

She made no answer, and through her silence he felt again that she was inwardly shrinking, averting herself from him. What! His accomplice deserting him? She acknowledged that she was his accomplice – she said 'both of us' – and yet she was drawing back from him, flying from him, leaving him alone! Ah, no – she shouldn't escape as easily as that, she shouldn't leave him; he couldn't face that sense of being alone again. 'Barbara!' he cried out, as if the actual distance between them had already doubled.

She still remained silent, and he hurried on, almost cringingly: 'Don't think I blame you, child – don't think. . . .'

'Oh, what does it matter, when I blame myself?' she wailed out, her face in her hands.

'Blame yourself? What folly! When you say you didn't know – '

'Of course I didn't know! How can you imagine – ? But this dreadful thing has happened; and *you* knew it might happen . . . you knew it all along . . . all the while it was in the back of your mind . . . the days when we used to meet here . . . and the days when we went to Ditson . . . oh, that horrible room at Ditson! All that time she was sitting at home alone, knowing everything, and hating me as if I'd been her murderess. . . .'

'Good God, Barbara! Don't you suppose I blame myself?'

'But if you blamed yourself how could you go on, how could you let me think she didn't care?'

'I didn't suppose she did,' he muttered sullenly.

'But you say she told you – she warned you! Over and over again she warned you.'

'Well, I didn't want to believe her – and so I didn't. When a man's infatuated. . . . Don't you see it's hard enough to bear without all this? Haven't you any pity for me, Barbara?'

'Pity?' she repeated slowly. 'The only pity I feel is for *her* – for what she must have gone through, day after day, week after week, sitting there all alone and knowing . . . imagining exactly what you were saying to me . . . the way you kissed me . . . and watching the clock, and counting the hours . . . and then having you come back, and explained, and pretend – I suppose you *did* pretend? . . . and all the while secretly knowing you were lying, and yet longing to believe you . . . and having warned you, and seeing that her warnings made no difference . . . that you didn't care if she died or not . . . that you were doing all you could to kill her . . . that you were probably counting the days till she was dead!' Her passionate apostrophe broke down in a sob, and again she stood weeping like an inconsolable child.

Trenham was struck silent. It was true. He had never been really able to enter into poor Milly's imaginings, the matter of her lonely musings; and here was this girl to whom, in a flash, that solitary mind lay bare. Yes; that must have been the way Milly felt – he knew it now – and the way poor Barbara herself would feel if he ever betrayed her. Ah, but he was never going to betray her – the thought was monstrous! Never for a moment would he cease to love her. This catastrophe had bound them together as a happy wooing could never have done. It was her love for him, her fear for their future, that was shaking her to the soul, giving her this unnatural power to enter into Milly's mind. If only he could find words to reassure her, now, at once. But he could not think of any.

'Barbara – Barbara,' he kept on repeating, as if her name were a sort of incantation.

'Oh, think of it – those lonely endless hours! I wonder if you ever did think of them before? When you used to go home after one of our meetings, did you remember each time what she'd told you, and begin to wonder, as you got near the house, if she'd done it *that day*?'

'Barbara – '

'Perhaps you did – perhaps you were even vexed with her for being so slow about it. Were you?'

'Oh, Barbara – Barbara. . . .'

'And when the day came at last, were you surprised? Had you got so impatient waiting that you'd begun to believe she'd never do it? Were these days when you went almost mad at having to wait so long for your freedom? It was the way I used to feel when I was rushing for the train to Ditson, and father would call me at the last minute to write letters for him, or mother to replace her on some charity committee; there were days when I could have *killed* them, almost, for interfering with me, making me miss one of our precious hours together. *Killed them*, I say! Don't you suppose I know how murderers feel? How *you* feel – for you're a murderer, you know! And now you come here, when the earth's hardly covered her, and try to kiss me, and ask me to marry you – and think, I suppose, that by doing so you're covering up her memory more securely, you're pounding down the earth on her a little harder. . . .'

She broke off, as if her own words terrified her, and hid her eyes from the vision they called up.

Trenham stood without moving. He had gathered up the letters, and they lay in a neat pile on the floor between himself and her, because there seemed no other place to put them. He said to himself (reflecting how many million men must have said the same thing at such moments): 'After this she'll calm down, and by tomorrow she'll be telling me how sorry she is. . . .' But the reflection did not seem to help him. She might forget – but he would not. He had forgotten too easily before; he had an idea that his future would be burdened with long arrears of remembrance. Just as the girl described Milly, so he would see her in the years to come. He would have to pay the interest on his oblivion; and it would not help much to have Barbara pay it with him. The job was probably one that would have to be accomplished alone. At last words shaped themselves without his knowing it. 'I'd better go,' he said.

Unconsciously he had expected an answer, an appeal; a protest, perhaps. But none came. He moved away a few steps in the direction of the door. As he did so he heard Barbara break into a laugh, and the sound, so unnatural in that place, and at that moment, brought him abruptly to a halt.

'Yes – ?' he said, half turning, as though she had called him.

'And I sent a wreath – I sent her a wreath! It's on her grave now – it hasn't even had time to fade!'

'Oh – ' he gasped, as if she had struck him across the face. They stood forlornly confronting each other. Her last words seemed to have created an icy void between them. Within himself a voice whispered: 'She can't find anything worse than that.' But he saw by the faint twitch of her lips that she was groping, groping –

'And the worst of it is,' she broke out, 'that if I didn't go away, and we were to drag on here together, after a time I might even drift into forgiving you.'

Yes; she was right; that was certainly the worst of it. Human imagination could not go beyond that, he thought. He moved away again stiffly.

'Well, you *are* going away, aren't you?' he said.

'Yes; I'm going.'

He walked back slowly through the dark deserted streets. His brain, reeling with the shock of the encounter, gradually cleared, and looked about on the new world within itself. At first the inside of his head was like a deserted house out of which all the furniture had been moved, down to the last familiar encumbrances. It was empty, absolutely empty. But gradually a small speck of consciousness appeared in the dreary void, like a mouse scurrying across bare floors. He stopped on a street corner to say to himself: 'But after all nothing is changed – absolutely nothing. I went there to tell her that we should probably never want to see each other again; and she agreed with me. She agreed with me – that's all.'

It was a relief, almost, to have even that little thought stirring about in the resonant of his brain. He walked on more quickly, reflecting, as he reached his own corner: 'In a minute it's going to rain.' He smiled a little at his unconscious precaution in hurrying home to escape the rain. 'Jane will begin to fret – she'll be sure to notice that I didn't take my umbrella.' And his cold heart felt a faint warmth at the thought that someone in the huge hostile world would really care whether he had taken his umbrella or not. 'But probably she's in bed and asleep,' he mused, despondently.

On his doorstep he paused and began to grope for his latchkey. He felt impatiently in one pocket after another – but the key was not to be found. He had an idea that he had left it lying on his study table when he came in after – after what? Why, that very morning, after the funeral! He had flung the key down among his papers – and Jane would never notice that it was there. She would never think of looking; she had been bidden often enough on no account to meddle with the things on his desk. And besides she would take for granted that he had the key in his pocket. And here he stood, in the middle of the night, locked out of his own house –

A sudden exasperation possessed him. He was aware that he must have lost all sense of proportion, all perspective, for he felt as baffled and as angry as when Barbara's furious words had beaten down on him. Yes; it made him just as unhappy to find himself locked out of his house – he could have sat down on the doorstep and cried. And here was the rain beginning. . . .

He put his hand to the bell; but did the front doorbell ring in the far-off attic where the maids were lodged? And was there the least chance of the faint tinkle from the pantry mounting two flights, and penetrating to their sleep-muffled ears? Utterly improbable, he knew. And if he couldn't make them hear he would have to spend the night at a hotel – the night of his wife's funeral! And the next morning all Kingsborough would know of it, from the President of the University to the boy who delivered the milk. . . .

But his hand had hardly touched the bell when he felt a vibration of life in the house. First there was a faint flash of light through the transom above the front door; then, scarcely distinguishable from the noises of the night, a step sounded far off; it grew louder on the hall floor, and after an interval that seemed endless the door was flung open by a Jane still irreproachably capped and aproned.

'Why, Jane – I didn't think you'd be awake! I forgot my key. . . .'

'I know, sir. I found it. I was waiting.' She took his wet coat from him. Dear, dear! And you hadn't your umbrella.'

He stepped into his own hall, and heard her close and bar the door behind him. He liked to listen to that familiar slipping of the bolts and clink of the chain. He liked to think that she minded about his not having his umbrella. It was his own house, after all – and this friendly hand was shutting him safely into it. The dreadful sense of loneliness melted a little at the old reassuring touch of habit.

'Thank you, Jane; sorry I kept you up,' he muttered, nodding to her as he went upstairs.

Confession

---◆---

THIS IS THE WAY it began; stupidly, trivially, out of nothing as fatal things do.

I was sitting at the corner table in the hotel restaurant; I mean the left-hand corner as you enter from the hall . . . as if that mattered! A table in that angle, with a view over the mountains, was too good for an unaccompanied traveler, and I had it only because the headwaiter was a good-natured fellow who . . . as if that mattered, either! Why can't I come to the point?

The point is that, entering the restaurant that day with the doubtful step of the newly-arrived, she was given the table next to me. Colossal Event – eh? But if you've ever known what it is, after a winter of semi-invalidism on the Nile, to be told that, before you're fit to go back and take up your job in New York – before that little leak in your lung is patched up tight – you've got to undergo another three or four months of convalescence on top of an Alp; if you've dragged through all those stages of recovery, first among one pack of hotel idlers, then among another, you'll know what small incidents can become Colossal Events against the empty horizon of your idleness.

Not that a New York banker's office (even before the depression) commanded a very wide horizon, as I understand horizons; but before arguing that point with me, wait and see what it's like to look out day after day on a dead-level of inoccupation, and you'll know what a towering affair it may become to have your temperature go up a point, or a woman you haven't seen before stroll into the dining room, and sit down at the table next to yours.

But what magnified this very ordinary incident for me was the immediate sense of something out of the ordinary in the woman

583

herself. Beauty? No; not even. (I say 'even' because there are far deadlier weapons, as we all know.) No, she was not beautiful; she was not particularly young; and though she carried herself well, and was well-dressed (though overexpensively, I thought), there was nothing in that to single her out in a fashionable crowd.

What then? Well, what struck me first in her was a shy but intense curiosity about everything in that assemblage of common-place and shopworn people. Here was a woman, evidently well-bred and well-off, to whom a fashionable hotel restaurant in the Engadine during the summer was apparently a sight so unusual, and composed of elements so novel and inexplicable, that she could hardly remember to eat in the subdued excitement of watching all that was going on about her.

As to her own appearance, it obviously did not preoccupy her – or figured only as an element of her general and rather graceful timidity. She was so busy observing all the dull commonplace people about her that it had presumably never occurred to her that she, who was neither dull nor commonplace, might be herself the subject of observation. (Already I found myself resenting any too protracted stare from the other tables.)

Well, to come down to particulars: she was middling tall, slight, almost thin; pale, with a long somewhat narrow face and dark hair; and her wide blue-gray eyes were so light and clear that her hair and complexion seemed dusky in contrast. A melancholy mouth, which lit up suddenly when she smiled – but her smiles were rare. Dress, sober, costly, severely 'ladylike'; her whole appearance, shall I say a trifle old-fashioned – or perhaps merely provincial? But certainly it was not only her dress which singled her out from the standardized beauties at the other tables. Perhaps it was the fact that her air of social inexperience was combined with a look, about the mouth and eyes, of having had more experience, of some other sort, than any woman in the room.

But of what sort? That was what baffled me. I could only sum it up by saying to myself that she was different; which, of course, is what every man feels about the woman he is about to fall in love with, no matter how painfully usual she may appear to others. But I had no idea that I was going to fall in love with the lady at the next table, and when I defined her as 'different' I did not mean it subjectively, did not mean different to *me*, but in herself, mysteriously, and independently of the particular impression she made on me. In short, she appeared, in spite of her dress and bearing, to be a little uncertain and ill at ease in the ordinary social scene, but at home and sure of herself elsewhere. Where?

I was still asking myself this when she was joined by a companion. One of the things one learns in traveling is to find out about people by studying their associates; and I wished that the lady who interested me had not furnished me with this particular kind of clue. The woman who joined her was probably of about her own age; but that seemed to be the only point of resemblance between them. The newcomer was stout, with mahogany-dyed hair, and small eyes set too close to a coarse nose. Her complexion, through a careless powdering, was flushed, and netted with little red veins, and her chin sloped back under a vulgar mouth to a heavy white throat. I had hoped she was only a chance acquaintance of the dark lady's; but she took her seat without speaking, and began to study the menu without as much as a glance at her companion. They were fellow travelers, then; and though the newcomer was as richly dressed as the other, and I judged more fashionably, I detected at once that she was a subordinate, probably a paid one, and that she sought to conceal it by an exaggerated assumption of equality. But how could the one woman have chosen the other as a companion? It disturbed my mental picture of the dark lady to have to fit into it what was evidently no chance association.

'Have you ordered my beer?' the last comer asked, drawing off her long gloves from thick red fingers crammed with rings (the dark lady wore none, I had noticed.)

'No, I haven't,' said the other.

Her tone somehow suggested: 'Why should I? Can't you ask for what you want yourself?' But a moment later she had signed to the headwaiter, and said, in a low tone: 'Miss Wilpert's Pilsener, please – as usual.'

'Yes; *as usual*. Only nobody ever remembers it! I used to be a lot better served when I had to wait on myself.'

The dark lady gave a faint laugh of protest.

Miss Wilpert, after a critical glance at the dish presented to her, transferred a copious portion to her plate, and squared herself before it. I could almost imagine a napkin tucked into the neck of her dress, below the crease in her heavy white throat.

'There were three women ahead of me at the hairdresser's,' she grumbled.

The dark lady glanced at her absently. 'It doesn't matter.'

'What doesn't matter?' snapped her companion. 'That I should be kept there two hours, and have to wait till two o'clock for my lunch?'

'I meant that your being late didn't matter to me.'

'I dare say not,' retorted Miss Wilpert. She poured down a draft of Pilsener, and set the empty glass beside her plate. 'So you're in the "nothing matters" mood again, are you?' she said, looking critically at her companion.

The latter smiled faintly. 'Yes.'

'Well, then – what are we staying here for? You needn't sacrifice yourself for me, you know.'

A lady, finishing her lunch, crossed the room, and in passing out stopped to speak to my neighbor. 'Oh, Mrs. Ingram' (so her name was Ingram), 'can't we persuade you to join us at bridge when you've had your coffee?'

Mrs. Ingram smiled, but shook her head. 'Thank you so much. But you know I don't play cards.'

'Principles!' jerked out Miss Wilpert, wiping her rouged lips after a second glass of Pilsener. She waved her fat hand toward the retreating lady. 'I'll join up with you in half an hour,' she cried in a penetrating tone.

'Oh, do,' said the lady with an indifferent nod.

I had finished my lunch, drunk my coffee, and smoked more than my strict ration of cigarettes. There was no other excuse for lingering, and I got up and walked out of the restaurant. My friend Antoine, the headwaiter, was standing near the door, and in passing I let my lips shape the inaudible question: 'The lady at the next table?'

Antoine knew everyone, and also everyone's history. I wondered why he hesitated for a moment before replying: 'Ah – Mrs. Ingram? Yes. From California.'

'Er – regular visitor?'

'No. I think on her first trip to Europe.'

'Ah. Then the other lady's showing her about?'

Antoine gave a shrug. 'I think not. She seems also new.'

'I like the table you've given me, Antoine,' I remarked; and he nodded compliantly.

I was surprised, therefore, that when I came down to dinner that evening I had been assigned to another seat, on the farther side of the restaurant. I asked for Antoine, but it was his evening off, and the understudy who replaced him could only say that I had been moved by Antoine's express orders. 'Perhaps it was on account of the draft, sir.'

'Draft be blowed! Can't I be given back my table?'

He was very sorry, but, as I could see, the table had been allotted to an infirm old lady, whom it would be difficult, and indeed impossible, to disturb.

'Very well, then. At lunch tomorrow I shall expect to have it back,' I said severely.

In looking back over the convalescent life, it is hard to recall the exaggerated importance every trifle assumes when there are only trifles to occupy one. I was furious at having had my place changed; and still more so when, the next day at lunch, Antoine, as a matter of course, conducted me to the table I had indignantly rejected the night before.

'What does this mean? I told you I wanted to go back to that corner table – '

Not a muscle moved in his noncommittal yet all-communicating face. 'So sorry, sir.'

'Sorry? Why, you promised me – '

'What can I do? Those ladies have our most expensive suite; and they're here for the season.'

'Well, what's the matter with the ladies? I've no objection to them. They're my compatriots.'

Antoine gave me a spectral smile. 'That appears to be the reason, sir.'

'The reason? They've given you a reason for asking to have me moved?'

'The big red one did. The other, Mrs. Ingram, as you can see, is quite different – though both are a little odd,' he added thoughtfully.

'Well – the big red one?'

'The *dame de compagnie*. You must excuse me, sir; but she says she doesn't like Americans. And as the management is anxious to oblige Mrs. Ingram – '

I gave a haughty laugh. 'I see. Whereas a humble lodger like myself – But there are other hotels at Mont Soleil, you may remind the management from me.'

'Oh, Monsieur, Monsieur – you can't be so severe on a lady's whim,' Antoine murmured reprovingly.

Of course I couldn't. Antoine's advice was always educational. I shrugged, and accepting my banishment, looked about for another interesting neighbor to watch instead of Mrs. Ingram. But I found that no one else interested me. . . .

• II •

'DON'T you think you might tell me now,' I said to Mrs. Ingram a few days later, 'why your friend insisted on banishing me to the farther end of the restaurant?'

I need hardly say that, in spite of Miss Wilpert's prejudice against her compatriots, she had not been able to prevent my making the acquaintance of Mrs. Ingram. I forgot how it came about – the pretext of a dropped letter, a deck chair to be moved out of the sun, or one of the hundred devices which bring two people together when they are living idle lives under the same roof. I had not gained my end without difficulty, however, for the ill-assorted pair were almost always together. But luckily Miss Wilpert played bridge, and Mrs. Ingram did not, and before long I had learned to profit by this opportunity, and in the course of time to make the fullest use of it.

Yet after a fortnight I had to own that I did not know much more about Mrs. Ingram than when I had first seen her. She was younger than I had thought, probably not over thirty-two or three; she was wealthy; she was shy; she came from California, or at any rate had lived there. For the last two years or more she appeared to have traveled, encircling the globe, and making long stays in places as far apart as Ceylon, Tenerife, Rio and Cairo. She seemed, on the whole, to have enjoyed these wanderings. She asked me many questions about the countries she had visited, and I saw that she belonged to the class of intelligent but untaught travelers who can learn more by verbal explanations than from books. Unprepared as she was for the sights awaiting her, she had necessarily observed little, and understood less; but she had been

struck by the more conspicuous features of the journey, and the
Taj, the Parthenon and the Pyramids had not escaped her. On
the subject of her travels she was at least superficially com-
municative; and as she never alluded to husband or child, or
to any other friend or relative, I was driven to conclude that
Miss Wilpert had been her only companion. This deepened the
mystery, and made me feel that I knew no more of her real self
than on the day when I had first seen her; but, perhaps partly
for that reason, I found her increasingly interesting. It was clear
that she shrank from strangers, but I could not help seeing that
with me she was happy and at ease, and as ready as I was to profit
by our opportunities of being together. It was only when Miss
Wilpert appeared that her old shyness returned, and I suspected
that she was reluctant to let her companion see what good friends
we had become.

I had put my indiscreet question about Miss Wilpert somewhat
abruptly, in the hope of startling Mrs. Ingram out of her usual
reserve; and I saw by the quick rise of color under her pale skin
that I had nearly succeeded. But after a moment she replied, with
a smile: 'I can't believe Cassie ever said anything so silly.'

'You can't? Then I wish you'd ask her; and if it was just
an invention of that headwaiter's I'll make him give me back my
table before he's a day older.'

Mrs. Ingram still smiled. 'I hope you won't make a fuss about
such a trifle. Perhaps Cassie did say something foolish. She's not
used to traveling, and sometimes takes odd notions.'

The ambiguity of the answer was obviously meant to warn
me off; but having risked one question I was determined to risk
another. 'Miss Wilpert's a very old friend, I suppose?'

'Yes; very,' said Mrs. Ingram noncommittally.

'And was she always with you when you were at home?'

My question seemed to find her unprepared. 'At home – ?'

'I mean, where you lived. California, wasn't it?'

She looked relieved. 'Oh, yes; Cassie Wilpert was with me
in California.'

'But there she must have had to associate with her compatriots?'

'Yes; that's one reason why she was so glad when I decided
to travel,' said Mrs. Ingram with a faint touch of irony, and
then added: 'Poor Cassie was very unhappy at one time; there

were people who were unkind to her. That accounts for her prejudices, I suppose.'

'I'm sorry I'm one of them. What can I do to make up to her?'

I fancied I saw a slight look of alarm in Mrs. Ingram's eyes. 'Oh, you'd much better leave her alone.'

'But she's always with you; and I don't want to leave you alone.'

Mrs. Ingram smiled, and then sighed. 'We shall be going soon now.'

'And then Miss Wilpert will be rid of me?'

Mrs. Ingram looked at me quickly; her eyes were plaintive, almost entreating. 'I shall never leave her; she's been like a – a sister to me,' she murmured, answering a question I had not put.

The word startled me; and I noticed that Mrs. Ingram had hesitated a moment before pronouncing it. A sister to her – that coarse red-handed woman? The words sounded as if they had been spoken by rote. I saw at once that they did not express the speaker's real feeling, and that, whatever that was, she did not mean to let me find it out.

Some of the bridge players with whom Miss Wilpert consorted were coming toward us, and I stood up to leave. 'Don't let Miss Wilpert carry you off on my account. I promise you I'll keep out of her way,' I said laughing.

Mrs. Ingram straightened herself almost imperiously. 'I'm not at Miss Wilpert's orders; she can't take me away from any place I choose to stay in,' she said; but a moment later, lowering her voice, she breathed to me quickly: 'Go now; I see her coming.'

• III •

I DON'T mind telling you that I was not altogether happy about my attitude toward Mrs. Ingram. I'm not given to prying into other people's secrets; yet I had not scrupled to try to trap her into revealing hers. For that there was a secret I was now convinced; and I excused myself for trying to get to the bottom of it by the fact that I was sure I should find

Miss Wilpert there, and that the idea was abhorrent to me. The relation between the two women, I had by now discovered, was one of mutual animosity; not the kind of animosity which may be the disguise of more complicated sentiments, but the simple incompatibility that was bound to exist between two women so different in class and character. Miss Wilpert was a coarse, uneducated woman, with, as far as I could see, no redeeming qualities, moral or mental, to bridge the distance between herself and her companion; and the mystery was that any past tie or obligation, however strong, should have made Mrs. Ingram tolerate her.

I knew how easily rich and idle women may become dependent on some vulgar tyrannical housekeeper or companion who renders them services and saves them trouble; but I saw at once that this theory did not explain the situation. On the contrary, it was Miss Wilpert who was dependent on Mrs. Ingram, who looked to her as guide, interpreter, and manager of their strange association. Miss Wilpert possessed no language but her own, and of that only a local vernacular which made it difficult to explain her wants (and they were many) even to the polyglot servants of a Swiss hotel. Mrs. Ingram spoke a carefully acquired if laborious French, and was conscientiously preparing for a winter in Naples by taking a daily lesson in Italian; and I noticed that whenever an order was to be given, an excursion planned, or any slight change effected in the day's arrangement, Miss Wilpert, suddenly embarrassed and helpless, always waited for Mrs. Ingram to interpret for her. It was obvious, therefore, that she was a burden and not a help to her employer, and that I must look deeper to discover the nature of their bond.

Mrs. Ingram, guidebook in hand, appealed to me one day about their autumn plans. 'I think we shall be leaving next week; and they say here we ought not to miss the Italian lakes.'

'Leaving next week? But why? The lakes are not at their best till after the middle of September. You'll find them very stuffy after this high air.'

Mrs. Ingram sighed. 'Cassie's tired of it here. She says she doesn't like the people.'

I looked at her, and then ventured with a smile: 'Don't you mean that she doesn't like me?'

'I don't see why you think that – '

'Well, I dare say it sounds rather fatuous. But you *do* know why I think it; and you think it yourself.' I hesitated a moment, and then went on, lowering my voice: 'Since you attach such importance to Miss Wilpert's opinions, it's natural I should want to know why she dislikes seeing me with you.'

Mrs. Ingram looked at me helplessly. 'Well, if she doesn't like you – '

'Yes; but in reality I don't think it's me she dislikes, but the fact of my being with you.'

She looked disturbed at this. 'But if she dislikes you, it's natural she shouldn't want you to be with me.'

'And do her likes and dislikes regulate all your friendships?'

'Friendships? I've so few; I know hardly anyone,' said Mrs. Ingram, looking away.

'You'd have as many as you chose if she'd let you,' I broke out angrily.

She drew herself up with the air of dignity she could assume on occasion. 'I don't know why you find so much pleasure in saying disagreeable things to me about my – my friend.'

The answer rushed to my lips: 'Why did she begin by saying disagreeable things about me?' – but just in time I saw that I was on the brink of a futile wrangle with the woman whom, at that moment, I was the most anxious not to displease. How anxious, indeed, I now saw for the first time, in the light of my own anger. For what on earth did I care for the disapproval of a creature like Miss Wilpert, except as it interfered with my growing wish to stand well with Kate Ingram? The answer I did make sprang to my lips before I could repress it. 'Because – you must know by this time. Because I can't bear that anything or any one should come between us.'

'Between us – ?'

I pressed on, hardly knowing what I was saying. 'Because nothing matters to me as much as what you feel about me. In fact, nothing else matters at all.'

The words had rushed out, lighting up the depths of my feeling as much to myself as to Mrs. Ingram. Only then did I remember how little I knew of the woman to whom they were addressed – not even her maiden name, nor as much as one fact of her past history. I did not even know if she were married, widowed or divorced. All I did know was that I had fallen in love with her – and had told her so.

She sat motionless, without a word. But suddenly her eyes filled, and I saw that her lips were trembling too much for her to speak.

'Kate – ' I entreated; but she drew back, shaking her head. 'No – '

'Why "no"? Because I've made you angry – ?'

She shook her head again. 'I feel that you're a true friend – '

'I want you to feel much more than that.'

'It's all I can ever feel – for anyone. I shall never – never . . .' She broke down, and sat struggling with her tears.

'Do you say that because you're not free?'

'Oh, no – oh, no – '

'Then is it because you don't like me? Tell me that, and I won't trouble you again.'

We were sitting alone in a deserted corner of the lounge. The diners had scattered to the wide verandahs, the card room or the bar. Miss Wilpert was safely engaged with a party of bridge players in the farthest room of the suite, and I had imagined that at last I should be able to have my talk out with Mrs. Ingram. I had hardly meant it to take so grave a turn; but now that I had spoken I knew my choice was made.

'If you tell me you don't like me, I won't trouble you any more,' I repeated, trying to keep her eyes on mine. Her lids quivered, and she looked down at her uneasy hands. I had often noticed that her hands were the only unquiet things about her, and now she sat clasping and unclasping them without ceasing.

'I can't tell you that I don't like you,' she said, very low. I leaned over to capture those restless fingers, and quiet them in mine; but at the same moment she gave a start, and I saw that she was not looking at me, but over my shoulder at someone who must have crossed the lounge behind me. I turned and saw a man I had not noticed before in the hotel, but whose short square-shouldered figure struck me as vaguely familiar.

'Is that someone you know?' I asked, surprised by the look in her face.

'N-no. I thought it was . . . I must have been mistaken. . . .' I saw that she was struggling to recover her self-control, and I looked again at the newcomer, who had stopped on his way to the bar to speak to one of the hall porters.

'Why, I believe it's Jimmy Shreve – Shreve of the New York *Evening Star*,' I said. 'It looks like him. Do you know him?'

'No.'

'Then, please – won't you answer the question I was just asking you?'

She had grown very pale, and was twisting her long fingers distressfully. 'Oh, not now; not now. . . .'

'Why not now? After what you've told me, do you suppose I'm going to be put off without a reason?'

'There's my reason!' she exclaimed with a nervous laugh. I looked around, and saw Miss Wilpert approaching. She looked unusually large and flushed, and her elaborate evening dress showed a displeasing expanse of too-white skin.

'Ah, that's your reason? I thought so!' I broke out bitterly.

One of Mrs. Ingram's quick blushes overswept her. 'I didn't mean that – you've no right to say so. I only meant that I'd promised to go with her. . . .'

Miss Wilpert was already towering over us, loud-breathing and crimson. I suspected that in the intervals of bridge she had more than once sought refreshment at the bar. 'Well, so this is where you've hidden yourself away, is it? I've hunted for you all over the place; but I didn't suppose you'd choose a dark corner under the stairs. I presume you've forgotten that you asked them to reserve seats for us for those Javanese dances. They won't keep our places much longer; the ballroom's packed already.'

I sat still, almost holding my breath, and watched the two women. I guessed that a crucial point in the struggle between them had been reached, and that a word from me might wreck my chances. Mrs. Ingram's color faded quickly, as it always did, but she forced a nervous smile. 'I'd no idea it was so late.'

'Well, if your watch has stopped, there's the hall clock right in front of you,' said Miss Wilpert, with quick panting breaths between the words. She waited a moment. 'Are you coming?'

Mrs. Ingram leaned back in her deep armchair. 'Well, no – I don't believe I am.'

'You're *not*?'

'No. I think I like it better here.'

'But you must be crazy! You asked that Italian Countess to keep us two seats next to hers – '

'Well, you can go and ask her to excuse me – say I'm tired. The ballroom's always so hot.'

'Land's sake! How'm I going to tell her all that in Italian? You know she don't speak a word of English. She'll think it's pretty funny if you don't come; and so will the others. You always say you hate to have people talk about you; and yet here you sit, stowed away in this dark corner, like a schoolgirl with her boy friend at a Commencement dance – '

Mrs. Ingram stood up quickly. 'Cassie, I'm afraid you must have been losing at bridge. I never heard you talk so foolishly. But of course I'll come if you think the Countess expects us.' She turned to me with a little smile, and suddenly, shyly, held out her hand. 'You'll tell me the rest tomorrow morning,' she said, looking straight at me for an instant; then she turned and followed Cassie Wilpert.

I stood watching them with a thumping heart. I didn't know what held these women together, but I felt that in the last few minutes a link of the chain between them had been loosened, and I could hardly wait to see it snap.

I was still standing there when the man who had attracted Mrs. Ingram's notice came out of the bar, and walked toward me; and I saw that it was in fact my old acquaintance Jimmy Shreve, the bright particular ornament of the *Evening Star*. We had not met for a year or more, and his surprise at the encounter was as great as mine. 'Funny, coming across you in this jazz crowd. I'm here to get away from my newspaper; but what has brought you?'

I explained that I had been ill the previous year, and, by the doctor's orders, was working out in the Alps the last months of my convalescence; and he listened with the absent-minded sympathy which one's friends give to one's ailments, particularly when they are on the mend.

'Well – well – too bad you've had such a mean time. Glad you're out of it now, anyway,' he muttered, snapping a reluctant cigarette lighter, and finally having recourse to mine. As he bent over it he said suddenly: 'Well, what about Kate Spain?'

I looked at him in bewilderment. For a moment the question was so unintelligible that I wondered if he too were a sufferer, and had been sent to the heights for medical reasons; but his sharp little professional eyes, burned with a steady spark of curiosity as he took a close-up of me across the lighter. And then I understood; at least I understood the allusion, though its relevance escaped me.

'Kate Spain? Oh, you mean that murder trial at Cayuga? You got me a card for it, didn't you? But I wasn't able to go.'

'I remember. But you've made up for it since, I see.' He continued to twinkle at me meaningly; but I was still groping. 'What do you think of her?' he repeated.

'Think of her? Why on earth should I think of her at all?'

He drew back and squared his sturdy shoulders in evident enjoyment. 'Why, because you've been talking to her as hard as you could for the last two hours,' he chuckled.

I stood looking at him blankly. Again it occurred to me that under his tight journalistic mask something had loosened and gone adrift. But I looked at the steadiness of the stumpy fingers which held his cigarette. The man had himself under perfect control.

'Kate Spain?' I said, collecting myself. 'Does that lady I was talking to really look to you like a murderess?'

Shreve made a dubious gesture. 'I'm not so sure what murderesses look like. But, as it happens, Kate Spain was acquitted.'

'So she was. Still, I don't think I'll tell Mrs. Ingram that she looks like her.'

Shreve smiled incredulously. 'Mrs. Ingram? Is that what you call her?'

'It's her name. I was with Mrs. Ingram, of California.'

'No, you weren't. You were with Kate Spain. She knows me well enough – ask her. I met her face to face just now, going into the ballroom. She was with a red-headed Jezebel that I don't know.'

'Ah, you don't know the red-headed lady? Well, that shows you're mistaken. For Miss Cassie Wilpert has lived with Mrs. Ingram as her companion for several years. They're inseparable.'

Shreve tossed away his cigarette and stood staring at me. 'Cassie Wilpert? Is that what that great dressed-up prize fighter with all the jewelry calls herself? Why, see here, Severance, Cassie was the servant girl's name, sure enough: Cassie – don't you remember? It was her evidence that got Kate Spain off. But at the trial she was a thin haggard Irish girl in dirty calico. To be sure, I suppose old Ezra Spain starved his servant as thoroughly as he starved his daughter. You remember Cassie's description of the daily fare: Sunday, boiled mutton; Monday, cold mutton; Tuesday, mutton hash; Wednesday, mutton stew – and I forget what day the dog got the mutton bone. Why, it was Cassie who knocked the prosecution all to pieces. At first it was doubtful how the case would go; but she testified that she and Kate Spain were out shopping together when the old man was murdered; and the prosecution was never able to shake her evidence.'

Remember it? Of course I remembered every detail of it, with a precision which startled me, considering I had never, to my knowledge, given the Kate Spain trial a thought since the talk about it had died out with the woman's acquittal. Now it all came back to me, every scrap of evidence, all the sordid and sinister gossip let loose by the trial: the tale of Ezra Spain, the wealthy miser and tyrant, of whom no one in his native town had a good word to say, who was reported to have let his wife die of neglect because he would not sent for a doctor till it was too late, and who had been too mean to supply her with food and medicines, or to provide a trained nurse for her. After his wife's death his daughter had continued to live with him, browbeaten and starved in her turn, and apparently lacking the courage to cast herself penniless and inexperienced upon the world. It had been almost with a sense of relief that Cayuga had learned of the old man's murder by a wandering tramp who had found him alone in the house, and had killed him in his sleep, and got away with what little money there was. Now at last, people said, that poor persecuted daughter with the wistful eyes and the frightened smile would be free, would be rich, would be able to come out of her prison, and marry and enjoy her life, instead of wasting and dying as her mother had died. And then came the incredible rumor that, instead of coming out of prison – the prison of her father's house – she was to go into another, the kind one entered in handcuffs, between two jailers: was to go there accused of her father's murder.

'I've got it now! Cassie Donovan – that was the servant's name,' Shreve suddenly exclaimed. 'Don't you remember?'

'No, I don't. But this woman's name, as I've told you, isn't Donovan – it's Wilpert, Miss Wilpert.'

'Her new name, you mean? Yes. And Kate Spain's new name, you say, is Mrs. Ingram. Can't you see that the first thing they'd do, when they left Cayuga, would be to change their names?'

'Why should they, when nothing was proved against them? And you say yourself you didn't recognize Miss Wilpert,' I insisted, struggling to maintain my incredulity.

'No; I didn't remember that she might have got fat and dyed her hair. I guess they do themselves like fighting cocks now, to make up for past privations. They say the old man cut up even fatter than people expected. But prosperity hasn't changed Kate Spain. I knew her at once; I'd have known her anywhere. And she knew me.'

'She didn't know you,' I broke out; 'she said she was mistaken.'

Shreve pounced on this in a flash. 'Ah – so at first she thought she did?' He laughed. 'I don't wonder she said afterward she was mistaken. I don't dye my hair yet, but I'm afraid I've put on nearly as much weight as Cassie Donovan.' He paused again, and then added: 'All the same, Severance, she did know me.'

I looked at the little journalist and laughed back at him.

'What are you laughing at?'

'At you. At such a perfect case of professional deformation. Wherever you go you're bound to spot a criminal; but I should have thought even Mont Soleil could have produced a likelier specimen than my friend Mrs. Ingram.'

He looked a little startled at my tone. 'Oh, see here, if she's such a friend I'm sorry I said anything.'

I rose to heights of tolerance. 'Nothing you can say can harm her, my dear fellow.'

'Harm her? Why on earth should it? I don't want to harm her.'

'Then don't go about spreading such ridiculous gossip. I don't suppose anyone cares to be mistaken for a woman who's been tried for her life; and if I were a relation of Mrs. Ingram's I'm bound to tell you I should feel obliged to put a stop to your talk.'

He stared in surprise, and I thought he was going to retort in the same tone; but he was a fair-minded little fellow, and after a moment I could see he'd understood. 'All right, Severance; of course I don't want to do anything that'll bother her. . . .'

'Then don't go on talking as if you still thought she was Kate Spain.'

He gave a hopeless shrug. 'All right. I won't. Only she *is*, you know; what'll you bet on it, old man?'

'Good night,' I said with a nod, and turned away. It was obviously a fixed idea with him; and what harm could such a crank do to me, much less to a woman like Mrs. Ingram?

As I left him he called after me: 'If she ain't, who is she? Tell me that, and I'll believe you.'

I walked away without answering.

• IV •

I WENT up to bed laughing inwardly at poor Jimmy Shreve. His craving for the sensational had certainly deformed his critical faculty. How it would amuse Mrs. Ingram to hear that he had identified her with the wretched Kate Spain! Well, she should hear it; we'd laugh over it together the next day. For she had said, in bidding me good night: 'You'll tell me the rest in the morning.' And that meant – could only mean – that she was going to listen to me, and if she were going to listen, she must be going to answer as I wished her to. . . .

Those were my thoughts as I went up to my room. They were scarcely less confident while I was undressing. I had the hope, the promise almost, of what, at the moment, I most wished for – the only thing I wished for, in fact. I was amazed at the intensity with which I wished it. From the first I had tried to explain away my passion by regarding it as the idle man's tendency to fall into sentimental traps; but I had always known that what I felt was not of that nature. This quiet woman with the wide pale eyes and melancholy mouth had taken possession of me; she seemed always to have inhabited my mind and heart; and as I lay down to sleep I tried to analyze what it was in her that made her seem already a part of me.

But as soon as my light was out I knew I was going to lie awake all night; and all sorts of unsought problems instantly crowded out my sentimental musings. I had laughed at Shreve's inept question: 'If she ain't Kate Spain, who is she?' But now an insistent voice within me echoed: Who is she? What, in short, did I know of her? Not one single fact which would have permitted me to disprove his preposterous assertion. Who was she? Was she married, unmarried, divorced, a widow? Had she children, parents, relations distant or near? Where had she lived before

going to California, and when had she gone there? I knew neither
her birthplace, nor her maiden name, or indeed any fact about her
except the all-dominating fact of herself.

In rehearsing our many talks with the pitiless lucidity of
sleeplessness I saw that she had the rare gift of being a perfect
listener; the kind whose silence supplies the inaudible questions
and answers most qualified to draw one on. And I had been drawn
on; ridiculously, fatuously, drawn on. She was in possession of all
the chief facts of my modest history. She knew who I was, where
I came from, who were my friends, my family, my antecedents;
she was fully informed as to my plans, my hopes, my preferences,
my tastes and hobbies. I had even confided to her my passion
for Brahms and for book collecting, and my dislike for the
wireless, and for one of my brothers-in-law. And in return for
these confidences she had given me – what? An understanding
smile, and the occasional murmur: 'Oh, do you feel that too?
I've always felt it.'

Such was the actual extent of my acquaintance with Mrs.
Ingram; and I perceived that, though I had laughed at Jimmy
Shreve's inept assertion, I should have been utterly unable to
disprove it. I did not know who Mrs. Ingram was, or even one
single fact about her.

From that point to supposing that she could be Kate Spain
was obviously a long way. She might be – well, let's say almost
anything; but not a woman accused of murder, and acquitted only
because the circumstantial evidence was insufficient to hang her.
I dismissed the grotesque supposition at once; there were problems
enough to keep me awake without that.

When I said that I knew nothing of Mrs. Ingram I was
mistaken. I knew one fact about her; that she could put up
with Cassie Wilpert. It was only a clue, but I had felt from
the first that it was a vital one. What conceivable interest or
obligation could make a woman like Mrs. Ingram endure such
an intimacy? If I knew that, I should know all I cared to
know about her; not only about her outward circumstances but
her inmost self.

Hitherto, in indulging my feeling for her, I had been disposed
to slip past the awkward obstacle of Cassie Wilpert; but now I
was resolved to face it. I meant to ask Kate Ingram to marry me.
If she refused, her private affairs were obviously no business of

mine; but if she accepted I meant to have the Wilpert question out with her at once.

It seemed a long time before daylight came; and then there were more hours to be passed before I could reasonably present myself to Mrs. Ingram. But at nine I sent a line to ask when she would see me; and a few minutes later my note was returned to me by the floor waiter.

'But this isn't an answer; it's my own note,' I exclaimed.

Yes; it was my own note. He had brought it back because the lady had already left the hotel.

'Left? Gone out, you mean?'

'No; left with all her luggage. The two ladies went an hour ago.'

In a few minutes I was dressed and had hurried down to the concierge. It was a mistake, I was sure; of course Mrs. Ingram had not left. The floor waiter, whom I had long since classed as an idiot, had simply gone to the wrong door. But no; the concierge shook his head. It was not a mistake. Mrs. Ingram and Miss Wilpert had gone away suddenly that morning by motor. The chauffeur's orders were to take them to Italy; to Baveno or Stresa, he thought; but he wasn't sure, and the ladies had left no address. The hotel servants said they had been up all night packing. The heavy luggage was to be sent to Milan; the concierge had orders to direct it to the station. That was all the information he could give – and I thought he looked at me queerly as he gave it.

• V •

I DID not see Jimmy Shreve again before leaving Mont Soleil that day; indeed I exercised all my ingenuity in keeping out of his way. If I were to ask any further explanations, it was of Mrs. Ingram that I meant to ask them. Either she was Kate Spain, or she was not; and either way, she was the woman to whom I had declared my love. I should have thought nothing of Shreve's insinuations if I had not recalled Mrs. Ingram's start when she first saw him. She herself had owned that she had taken him for someone she knew; but even this would not have meant much if she and her companion had not disappeared from the hotel a few hours later, without leaving a message for me, or an address with the hall porter.

I did not for a moment suppose that this disappearance was connected with my talk of the previous evening with Mrs. Ingram. She herself had expressed the wish to prolong that talk when Miss Wilpert interrupted it; and failing that, she had spontaneously suggested that we should meet again the next morning. It would have been less painful to think that she had fled before the ardor of my wooing than before the dread of what Shreve might reveal about her; but I knew the latter reason was the more likely.

The discovery stunned me. It took me some hours to get beyond the incredible idea that this woman, whose ways were so gentle, with whose whole nature I felt myself in such delightful harmony, had stood her trial as a murderess – and the murderess of her own father. But the more I revolved this possibility the less I believed in it. There might have been other – and perhaps not very creditable – reasons for her abrupt flight; but that she should be flying because she knew that Shreve had recognized her seemed, on further thought, impossible.

Then I began to look at the question from another angle. Supposing she *were* Kate Spain? Well, her father had been assassinated by a passing tramp; so the jury had decided. Probably suspicion would never have rested on her if it had not been notorious in Cayuga that the old man was a selfish miser, who for years had made his daughter's life intolerable. To those who knew the circumstances it had seemed conceivable, seemed almost natural, that the poor creature should finally turn against him. Yet she had had no difficulty in proving her innocence; it was clearly established that she was out of the house when the crime was committed. Her having been suspected, and tried, was simply one of those horrible blunders of which innocent persons have so often been the victims. Do what she would to live it down, her name would always remain associated with that sordid tragedy; and wasn't it natural that she should flee from any reminder of it, any suspicion that she had been recognized, and her identity proclaimed by a scandal-mongering journalist? If she were Kate Spain, the dread of having the fact made known to everyone in that crowded hotel was enough to drive her out of it. But if her departure had another cause, in no way connected with Shreve's arrival, might it not have been inspired by a sudden whim of Cassie Wilpert's? Mrs. Ingram had told me that Cassie was bored and wanted to get away; and it was all too clear that, however loudly she proclaimed her independence, she always ended by obeying Miss Wilpert.

It was a melancholy alternative. Poor woman – poor woman either way, I thought. And by the time I had reached this conclusion, I was in the train which was hurrying me to Milan. Whatever happened I must see her, and hear from her own lips what she was flying from.

I hadn't much hope of running down the fugitives at Stresa or Baveno. It was not likely that they would go to either of the places they had mentioned to the concierge; but I went to both the next morning, and carried out a minute inspection of all the hotel lists. As I had foreseen, the travelers were not to be found, and I was at a loss to know where to turn next. I knew, however, that the luggage the ladies had sent to Milan was not likely to arrive till the next day, and concluded that they would probably wait for it in the neighborhood; and suddenly I remembered that I had once advised Mrs. Ingram – who was complaining that she was growing tired of fashionable hotels – to try a little *pension* on the lake of Orta, where she would be miles away from 'palaces', and from the kind of people who frequent them. It was not likely that she would have remembered this place; but I had put a pencil stroke beside the name in her guidebook, and that might recall it to her. Orta, at any rate, was not far off; and I decided to hire a car at Stresa, and go there before carrying on my journey.

• VI •

I DON'T suppose I shall ever get out of my eyes the memory of the public sitting room in the *pension* at Orta. It was there that I waited for Mrs. Ingram to come down, wondering if she would, and what we should say to each other when she did.

There were three windows in a row, with clean heavily starched Nottingham lace curtains carefully draped to exclude the best part of the matchless view over lake and mountains. To make up for this privation the opposite wall was adorned with a huge oil painting of a Swiss waterfall. In the middle of the room was a table of sham ebony, with ivory inlays, most of which had long since worked out of their grooves, and on the table the usual dusty collection of tourist magazines, fashion papers, and tattered copies of *Zion's Weekly* and the *Christian Science Monitor*.

What is the human mind made of, that mine, at such a moment, should have minutely and indelibly registered these depressing details? I even remember smiling at the thought of the impression my favorite *pension* must have made on travelers who had just moved out of the most expensive suite in the Mont Soleil Palace.

And then Mrs. Ingram came in.

My first impression was that something about her dress or the arrangement of her hair had changed her. Then I saw that two dabs of rouge had been unskilfully applied to her pale cheeks, and a cloud of powder dashed over the dark semicircles under her eyes. She must have undergone some terrible moral strain since our parting to feel the need of such a disguise.

'I thought I should find you here,' I said.

She let me take her two hands, but at first she could not speak. Then she said, in an altered voice: 'You must have wondered – '

'Yes; I wondered.'

'It was Cassie who suddenly decided – '

'I supposed so.'

She looked at me beseechingly. 'But she was right, you know.'

'Right – about what?'

Her rouged lips began to tremble, and she drew her hands out of mine.

'Before you say anything else,' I interrupted, 'there's one thing you must let me say. I want you to marry me.'

I had not meant to bring it out so abruptly; but something in her pitiful attempt to conceal her distress had drawn me closer to her, drawn me past all doubts and distrusts, all thought of evasion or delay.

She looked at me, still without speaking, and two tears ran over her lids, and streaked the untidy powder on her cheeks.

'No - no - no!' she exclaimed, lifting her thin hand and pressing it against my lips. I drew it down and held it fast.

'Why not? You knew I was going to ask you, the day before yesterday, and when we were interrupted you promised to hear me the next morning. You yourself said: "tomorrow morning."'

'Yes; but I didn't know then – '

'You didn't know – ?'

I was still holding her, and my eyes were fixed on hers. She gave me back my look, deeply and desperately. Then she freed herself.

'Let me go. I'm Kate Spain,' she said.

We stood facing each other without speaking. Then I gave a laugh, and answered, in a voice that sounded to me as though I were shouting: 'Well, I want to marry you, Kate Spain.'

She shrank back, her hands clasped across her breast. 'You knew already? That man told you?'

'Who – Jimmy Shreve? What does it matter if he did? Was that the reason you ran away from me?' She nodded.

'And you thought I wouldn't find you?'

'I thought you wouldn't try.'

'You thought that, having told you one day that I loved you, I'd let you go out of my life the next?'

She gave me another long look. 'You – you're generous. I'm grateful. But you can't marry Kate Spain,' she said, with a little smile like the grimace on a dying face.

I had no doubt in my own mind that I could; the first sight of her had carried that conviction home, and I answered: 'Can't I, though? That's what we'll see.'

'You don't know what my life is. How would you like, wherever you went, to have some one suddenly whisper behind you: "Look. That's Kate Spain"?'

I looked at her, and for a moment found no answer. My first impulse of passionate pity had swept me past the shock of her confession; as long as she was herself, I seemed to feel, it mattered nothing to me that she was also Kate Spain. But her last words called up a sudden vision of the life she must have led since her acquittal; the life I was asking to share with her. I recalled my helpless wrath when Shreve had told me who she was; and now I seemed to hear the ugly whisper – 'Kate Spain, Kate Spain' – following us from place to place, from house to house; following my wife and me.

She took my hesitation for an answer. 'You hadn't thought of that, had you? But I think of nothing else, day and night. For three years now I've been running away from the sound of my name. I tried California first; it was at the other end of the country, and some of my mother's relations lived there. They were kind to me, everybody was kind; but wherever I went I heard my name: Kate

Spain – Kate Spain! I couldn't go to church, or to the theater, or into a shop to buy a spool of thread, without hearing it. What was the use of calling myself Mrs. Ingram, when, wherever I went, I heard Kate Spain? The very school children knew who I was, and rushed out to see me when I passed. I used to get letters from people who collected autographs, and wanted my signature: "Kate Spain, you know." And when I tried shutting myself up, people said: "What's she afraid of? Has she got something to hide, after all?" and I saw that it made my cousins uncomfortable, and shy with me, because I couldn't lead a normal life like theirs. . . . After a year I couldn't stand it, and so we came away, and went round the world. . . . But wherever we go it begins again: and I know now I can never get away from it.' She broke down, and hid her face for a moment. Then she looked up at me and said: 'And so you must go away, you see.'

I continued to look at her without speaking: I wanted the full strength of my will to go out to her in my answer. 'I see, on the contrary, that I must stay.'

She gave me a startled glance. 'No – no.'

'Yes, yes. Because all you say is a nervous dream; natural enough, after what you've been through, but quite unrelated to reality. You say you've thought of nothing else, day and night; but why think of it at all – in that way? Your real name is Kate Spain. Well – what of it? Why try to disguise it? You've never done anything to disgrace it. You've suffered through it, but never been abased. If you want to get rid of it there's a much simpler way; and that is to take mine instead. But meanwhile, if people ask you if you're Kate Spain, try saying yes, you are, instead of running away from them.'

She listened with bent head and interlocked hands, and I saw a softness creep about her lips. But after I had ceased she looked up at me sadly. 'You've never been tried for your life,' she said.

The words struck to the roots of my optimism. I remembered in a flash that when I had first seen her I had thought there was a look about her mouth and eyes unlike that of any other woman I had known; as if she had had a different experience from theirs. Now I knew what that experience was: the black shadow of the criminal court, and the long lonely fight to save her neck. And I'd been trying to talk reason to a woman who'd been through that!

'My poor girl – my poor child!' I held out my arms, and she fell into them and wept out her agony. There were no more words to be said; no words could help her. Only the sense of human nearness, human pity, of a man's arms about her, and his heart against hers, could draw her out of her icy hell into the common warmth of day.

Perhaps it was the thought of that healing warmth which made me suddenly want to take her away from the Nottingham lace curtains and the Swiss waterfall. For a while we sat silent, and I held her close; then I said: 'Come out for a walk with me. There are beautiful walks close by, up through the beechwoods.'

She looked at me with a timid smile. I knew now that she would do all I told her to; but before we started out I must rid my mind of another load. 'I want to have you all to myself for the rest of the day. Where's Miss Wilpert?' I asked.

Miss Wilpert was away in Milan, she said, and would not be back till late. She had gone to see about passport visas and passages on a cruising liner which was sailing from Genoa to the Aegean in a few days. The ladies thought of taking the cruise. I made no answer, and we walked out through the *pension* garden, and mounted the path to the beechwoods.

We wandered on for a long time, saying hardly anything to each other; then we sat down on the mossy steps of one of the little pilgrimage chapels among the trees. It is a place full of sweet solitude, and gradually it laid its quieting touch on the tormented creature at my side.

As we sat there the day slipped down the sky, and we watched, through the great branches, the lake turning golden and then fading, and the moon rising above the mountains. I put my hand on hers. 'And now let's make some plans,' I said.

I saw the apprehensive look come back to her eyes. 'Plans – oh, why, today?'

'Isn't it natural that two people who've decided to live together should want to talk over their future? When are we going to be married – to begin with?'

She hesitated for a long time, clasping and unclasping her unhappy hands. She had passed the stage of resistance, and I was almost sure she would not turn to it again. I waited, and at length she said, looking away from me: 'But you don't like Cassie.'

The words were a shock, though I suppose I must have expected them. On the whole, I was glad they had been spoken; I had not known how to bring the subject up, and it was better she should do it for me.

'Let's say, dear, that Cassie and I don't like each other. Isn't that nearer the truth?'

'Well, perhaps; but – '

'Well, that being so, Cassie will certainly be quite as anxious to strike out for herself as I shall be to – '

She interrupted me with a sudden exclamation. 'No, no! She'll never leave me – never.'

'Never leave you? Not when you're my wife?'

She hung her head, and began her miserable finger-weaving again. 'No; not even if she lets me – '

'Lets you – ?'

'Marry you,' she said in a whisper.

I mastered her hands, and forced her to turn around to me. 'Kate – look at me; straight at me. Shall I tell you something? Your worst enemy's not Kate Spain; it's Cassie Wilpert.'

She freed herself from my hold and drew back. 'My worst enemy? Cassie – she's been my only friend!'

'At the time of the trial, yes. I understand that; I understand your boundless gratitude for the help she gave you. I think I feel about that as you'd want me to. But there are other ways of showing your gratitude than by sharing the rest of your life with her.'

She listened, drooping again. 'I've tried every other way,' she said at length, below her breath.

'What other ways?'

'Oh, everything. I'm rich you know, now,' she interrupted herself, her color rising. 'I offered her the house at Cayuga – it's a good house; they say it's very valuable. She could have sold it if she didn't want to live there. And of course I would have continued the allowance I'm giving her – I would have doubled it. But what she wanted was to stay with me; the new life she was leading amused her. She was a poor servant girl, you know; and she had a dreadful time when – when my father was alive. She was our only help. . . . I suppose you read about it all . . . and even then she was good to me. . . . She dared to speak to him as I didn't. . . . And then, at the trial . . . the trial lasted a whole month; and

it was a month with thirty-one days. . . . Oh, don't make me go
back to it – for God's sake don't!' she burst out, sobbing.

It was impossible to carry on the discussion. All I thought of
was to comfort her. I helped her to her feet, whispering to her as
if she had been a frightened child, and putting my arm about her
to guide her down the path. She leaned on me, pressing her arm
against mine. At length she said: 'You see it can't be; I always
told you it could never be.'

'I see more and more that it must be; but we won't talk about
that now,' I answered.

We dined quietly in a corner of the *pension* dining room, which
was filled by a colony of British old maids and retired army
officers and civil servants – all so remote from the world of the
'Ezra Spain case' that, if Shreve had been there to proclaim Mrs.
Ingram's identity, the hated syllables would have waked no echo.
I pointed this out to Mrs. Ingram, and reminded her that in a few
years all memory of the trial would have died out, even in her own
country, and she would be able to come and go unobserved and
undisturbed. She shook her head and murmured: 'Cassie doesn't
think so', but when I suggested that Miss Wilpert might have her
own reasons for cultivating this illusion, she did not take up the
remark, and let me turn to pleasanter topics.

After dinner it was warm enough to wander down to the shore
in the moonlight, and there, sitting in the little square along the
lakeside, she seemed at last to cast off her haunting torment, and
abandon herself to the strange new sense of happiness and safety.
But presently the church bell rang the hour, and she started up,
insisting that we must get back to the *pension* before Miss Wilpert's
arrival. She would be there soon now, and Mrs. Ingram did not
wish her to know of my presence till the next day.

I agreed to this, but stipulated that the next morning the news
of our approaching marriage should be broken to Miss Wilpert,
and that as soon as possible afterward I should be told of the
result. I wanted to make sure of seeing Kate the moment her talk
with Miss Wilpert was over, so that I could explain away – and
above all, laugh away – the inevitable threats and menaces before
they grew to giants in her tormented imagination. She promised
to meet me between eleven and twelve in the deserted writing
room, which we were fairly sure of having to ourselves at that

hour; and from there I could take her up the hillside to have our talk out undisturbed.

• VII •

I DID not get much sleep that night, and the next morning before the *pension* was up I went out for a short row on the lake. The exercise braced my nerves, and when I got back I was prepared to face with composure whatever further disturbances were in store. I did not think they would be as bad as they appeared to my poor friend's distracted mind, and was convinced that if I could keep a firm hold on her will the worst would soon be over. It was not much past nine, and I was just finishing the *café au lait* I had ordered on returning from my row, when there was a knock at my door. It was not the casual knock of a tired servant coming to remove a tray, but a sharp nervous rap immediately followed by a second; and, before I could answer, the door opened and Miss Wilpert appeared. She came directly in, shut the door behind her, and stood looking at me with a flushed and lowering stare. But it was a look I was fairly used to seeing when her face was turned to mine, and my first thought was one of relief. If there was a scene ahead, it was best that I should bear the brunt of it; I was not half so much afraid of Miss Wilpert as of the Miss Wilpert of Kate's imagination.

I stood up and pushed forward my only armchair. 'Do you want to see me, Miss Wilpert? Do sit down.'

My visitor ignored the suggestion. 'Want to see you? God knows I don't . . . I wish we'd never laid eyes on you either of us,' she retorted in a thick passionate voice. If the hour had not been so early I should have suspected her of having already fortified herself for the encounter.

'Then, if you won't sit down, and don't want to see me – ' I began affably; but she interrupted me.

'I don't *want* to see you; but I've got to. You don't suppose I'd be here if I didn't have something to say to you?'

'Then you'd better sit down, after all.'

She shook her head, and remained leaning in the window jamb, one elbow propped on the sill. 'What I want to know is: what business has a dandified gentleman like you to go round worming women's secrets out of them?'

Now we were coming to the point. 'If I've laid myself open to the charge,' I said quietly, 'at least it's not because I've tried to worm out yours.'

The retort took her by surprise. Her flush darkened, and she fixed her small suspicious eyes on mine.

'*My* secrets?' she flamed out. 'What do you know about my secrets?' she pulled herself together with a nervous laugh. 'What an old fool I am! You're only trying to get out of answering my question. What I want to know is what call you have to pry into my friend's private affairs?'

I hesitated, struggling again with my anger. 'If I've pried into them, as you call it, I did so, as you probably know, only after I'd asked Mrs. Ingram to be my wife.'

Miss Wilpert's laugh became an angry whinny. 'Exactly! If indeed you didn't ask her to be your wife to get her secret out of her. She's so unsuspicious that the idea never crossed her mind till I told her what I thought of the trick you'd played on her.'

'Ah, you suggested it was a trick? And how did she take the suggestion?'

Miss Wilpert stood for a moment without speaking; then she came up to the table and brought her red fist down on it with a bang. 'I tell you she'll never marry you!' she shouted.

I was on the verge of shouting back at her; but I controlled myself, conscious that we had reached the danger point in our struggle. I said nothing, and waited.

'Don't you hear what I say?' she challenged me.

'Yes; but I refuse to take what you say from anyone but Mrs. Ingram.' My composure seemed to steady Miss Wilpert. She looked at me dubiously, and then dropped into the chair I had pushed forward. 'You mean you want her to tell you herself?'

'Yes.' I sat down also, and again waited.

Miss Wilpert drew a crumpled handkerchief across her lips. 'Well, I can get her to tell you – easy enough. She'll do anything I tell her. Only I thought you'd want to act like a gentleman, and spare her another painful scene – '

'Not if she's unwilling to spare me one.'

Miss Wilpert considered this with a puzzled stare. 'She'll tell you just what I'm telling you – you can take my word for that.'

'I don't want anybody's word but hers.'

'If you think such a lot of her I'd have thought you'd rather have gone away quietly, instead of tormenting her any more.' Still I was silent, and she pulled her chair up to the table, and stretched her thick arms across it. 'See here, Mr. Severance – now you listen to me.'

'I'm listening.'

'You know I love Kate so that I wouldn't harm a hair of her head,' she whimpered. I made no comment, and she went on, in a voice grown oddly and unsteady: 'But I don't want to quarrel with you. What's the use?'

'None whatever. I'm glad you realize it.'

'Well, then let's you and me talk it over like old friends. Kate can't marry you, Mr. Severance. Is that plain? She can't marry you, and she can't marry anybody else. All I want is to spare her more scenes. Won't you take my word for it, and just slip off quietly if I promise you I'll make it all right, so she'll bear you no ill will?'

I listened to this extraordinary proposal as composedly as I could; but it was impossible to repress a slight laugh. Miss Wilpert took my laugh for an answer, and her discolored face crimsoned furiously. 'Well?'

'Nonsense, Miss Wilpert. Of course I won't take your orders to go away.'

She rested her elbows on the table, and her chin on her crossed hands. I saw she was making an immense effort to control herself. 'See here, young man, now you listen. . . .'

Still I sat silent, and she sat looking at me, her thick lower lip groping queerly, as if it were feeling for words she could not find.

'I tell you – ' she stammered.

I stood up. 'If vague threats are all you have to tell me, perhaps we'd better bring our talk to an end.'

She rose also. 'To an end? Any minute, if you'll agree to go away.'

'Can't you see that such arguments are wasted on me?'

'You mean to see her?'

'Of course I do – at once, if you'll excuse me.'

She drew back unsteadily, and put herself between me and the door. 'You're going to her now? But I tell you you can't! You'll half kill her. Is that what you're after?'

'What I'm after, first of all, is to put an end to this useless talk,' I said, moving toward the door. She flung herself heavily backward, and stood against it, stretching out her two arms to block my way. 'She can't marry – she can't marry you!' she screamed.

I stood silent, my hands in my pockets. 'You – you don't believe me?' she repeated.

'I've nothing more to say to you, Miss Wilpert.'

'Ah, you've nothing more to say to me? Is that the tune? Then I'll tell you that I've something more to say to you; and you're not going out of this room till you've heard it. And you'll wish you were dead when you have.'

'If it's anything about Mrs. Ingram, I refuse to hear it; and if you force me to, it will be exactly as if you were speaking to a man who's stone deaf. So you'd better ask yourself if it's worth-while.'

She leaned against the door, her heavy head dropped queerly forward. 'Worth-while – worth-while? It'll be worth your while not to hear it – I'll give you a last chance,' she said.

'I should be much obliged if you'd leave my room, Miss Wilpert.'

' "Much obliged?" ' she simpered, mimicking me. 'You'd be much obliged, would you? Hear him, girls – ain't he stylish? Well, I'm going to leave your room in a minute, young gentleman; but not till you've heard your death sentence.'

I smiled. 'I shan't hear it, you know. I shall be stone deaf.'

She gave a little screaming laugh, and her arms dropped to her sides. 'Stone deaf, he says. And to the day of his death he'll never get out of his ears what I'm going to tell him. . . .' She moved forward again, lurching a little; she seemed to be trying to take the few steps back to the table, and I noticed that she had left her handbag on it. I took it up. 'You want your bag?'

'My bag?' Her jaw fell slightly, and began to tremble again. 'Yes, yes . . . my bag . . . give it to me. Then you'll know all about Kate Spain. . . .' She got as far as the armchair, dropped into it sideways and sat with hanging head, and arms lolling at her sides. She seemed to have forgotten about the bag, though I had put it beside her.

I stared at her, horrified. Was she as drunk as all that – or was she ill, and desperately ill? I felt cold about the heart, and went up, and took hold of her. 'Miss Wilpert – won't you get up? Aren't you well?'

Her swollen lips formed a thin laugh, and I saw a thread of foam in their corners. 'Kate Spain . . . I'll tell you. . . .' Her head sank down onto her creased white throat. Her arms hung lifeless; she neither spoke nor moved.

• VIII •

AFTER the first moment of distress and bewilderment, and the two or three agitated hours spent in consultations, telephonings, engaging of nurses, and inquiring about nursing homes, I was at last able to have a few words with Mrs. Ingram.

Miss Wilpert's case was clear enough; a stroke induced by sudden excitement, which would certainly – as the doctors summoned from Milan advised us – result in softening of the brain, probably followed by death in a few weeks. The direct cause had been the poor woman's fit of rage against me; but the doctors told me privately that in her deteriorated condition any shock might have brought about the same result. Continual overindulgence in food and drink – in drink especially – had made her, physiologically, an old woman before her time; all her organs were worn out, and the best that could be hoped was the bodily resistance which sometimes develops when the mind fails would not keep her too long from dying.

I had to break this as gently as I could do Mrs. Ingram, and the same time to defend myself against the painful inferences she might draw from the way in which the attack had happened. She knew – as the whole horrified *pension* knew – that Miss Wilpert had been taken suddenly ill in my room; and anyone living on the same floor must have been aware that an angry discussion had preceded the attack. But Kate Ingram knew more; she, and she alone, knew Cassie Wilpert had gone to my room, and when I found myself alone with her instantly read that knowledge in her face. This being so, I thought it better to make no pretense.

'You saw Miss Wilpert, I suppose, before she came to me?' I asked.

She made a faint assenting motion; I saw that she was too shaken to speak.

'And she told you, probably, that she was going to tell me I must not marry you.'

'Yes – she told me.'

I sat down beside her and took her hand. 'I don't know what she meant,' I went on, 'or how she intended to prevent it; for before she could say anything more – '

Kate Ingram turned to me quickly. I could see the life rushing back to her striken face. 'You mean – she didn't say anything more?'

'She had no time to.'

'Not a word more?'

'Nothing – '

Mrs. Ingram gave me one long look; then her head sank between her hands. I sat beside her in silence, and at last she dropped her hands and looked up again. 'You've been very good to me,' she said.

'Then, my dear, you must be good too. I want you to go to your room at once and take a long rest. Everything is arranged; the nurse has come. Early tomorrow morning the ambulance will be here. You can trust me to see that things are looked after.'

Her eyes rested on me, as if she were trying to grope for the thoughts beyond this screen of words. 'You're sure she said nothing more?' she repeated.

'On my honor, nothing.'

She got up and went obediently to her room.

It was perfectly clear to me that Mrs. Ingram's docility during those first grim days was due chiefly to the fact of her own helplessness. Little of the practical experience of everyday life had come into her melancholy existence, and I was not surprised that, in a strange country and among unfamiliar faces, she should turn to me for support. The shock of what had occurred, and God knows what secret dread behind it, had prostrated the poor creature, and the painful details still to be dealt with made my nearness a necessity. But, as far as our personal relations were concerned, I knew that sooner or later an emotional reaction would come.

For the moment it was kept off by other cares. Mrs. Ingram turned to me as to an old friend, and I was careful to make no other claim on her. She was installed at the nursing home in Milan to which her companion had been transported; and I saw her there two or three times daily. Happily for the sick woman, the end was near; she never regained consciousness, and before the month was out she was dead. Her life ended without a struggle, and Mrs. Ingram was spared the sight of protracted suffering; but the shock of the separation was inevitable. I knew she did not love Cassie Wilpert, and I measured her profound isolation when I saw that the death of this woman left her virtually alone.

When we returned from the funeral I drove her back to the hotel where she had engaged rooms, and she asked me to come to see her there the next afternoon.

At Orta, after Cassie Wilpert's sudden seizure, and before the arrival of the doctors, I had handed her bag over to Mrs. Ingram, and had said: 'You'd better lock it up. If she gets worse the police might ask for it.'

She turned ashy pale. 'The police – ?'

'Oh, you know there are endless formalities of that kind in all Latin countries. I should advise you to look through the bag yourself, and see if there's anything in it she might prefer not to have you keep. If there is, you'd better destroy it.'

I knew at the time that she had guessed I was referring to some particular paper; but she took the bag from me without speaking. And now, when I came to the hotel at her summons, I wondered whether she would allude to the matter, whether in the interval it has passed out of her mind, or whether she had decided to say nothing. There was no doubt that the bag had contained something which Miss Wilpert was determined that I should see; but, after all, it might have been only a newspaper report of the Spain trial. The unhappy creature's brain was already so confused that she might have attached importance to some document that had no real significance. I hoped it was so, for my one desire was to put out of my mind the memory of Cassie Wilpert, and of what her association with Mrs. Ingram had meant.

At the hotel I was asked to come up to Mrs. Ingram's private sitting room. She kept me waiting for a little while, and when she appeared she looked so frail and ill in her black dress that I feared she might be on the verge of a nervous breakdown.

'You look too tired to see anyone today. You ought to go straight to bed and let me send for the doctor,' I said.

'No – no.' She shook her head, and signed to me to sit down. 'It's only . . . the strangeness of everything. I'm not used to being alone. I think I'd better go away from here tomorrow,' she began excitedly.

'I think you had, dear. I'll make any arrangements you like, if you'll tell me where you want to go. And I'll come and join you, and arrange as soon as possible about our marriage. Such matters can be managed fairly quickly in France.'

'In France?' she echoed absently, with a little smile.

'Or wherever else you like. We might go to Rome.'

She continued to smile; a strained mournful smile, which began to frighten me. Then she spoke. 'I shall never forget what you've been to me. But we must say good-bye now. I can't marry you. Cassie did what was right – she only wanted to spare me the pain of telling you.'

I looked at her steadily. 'When you say you can't marry me,' I asked, 'do you mean that you're already married, and can't free yourself?'

She seemed surprised. 'Oh, no. I'm not married – I was never married.'

'Then, my dear – '

She raised one hand to silence me; with the other she opened her little black handbag and drew out a sealed envelope. 'This is the reason. It's what she meant to show you – '

I broke in at once: 'I don't want to see anything she meant to show me. I told her so then, and I tell you so now. Whatever is in that envelope, I refuse to look at it.'

Mrs. Ingram gave me a startled glance. 'No, no. You must read it. Don't force me to tell you – that would be worse. . . .'

I jumped up and stood looking down into her anguished face. Even if I hadn't loved her, I should have pitied her then beyond all mortal pity.

'Kate,' I said, bending over her, and putting my hand on her icy-cold one, 'when I asked you to marry me I buried all such questions, and I'm not going to dig them up again today – or any other day. The past's the past. It's at an end for us both, and tomorrow I mean to marry you, and begin our future.'

She smiled again, strangely, I thought, and then suddenly began to cry. Then she flung her arms about my neck, and pressed herself against me. 'Say good-bye to me now – say good-bye to Kate Spain,' she whispered.

'Good-bye to Kate Spain, yes; but not to Kate Severance.'

'There'll never be a Kate Severance. There never can be. Oh, won't you understand – won't you spare me? Cassie was right; she tried to do her duty when she saw I couldn't do it. . . .'

She broke into terrible sobs, and I pressed my lips against hers to silence her. She let me hold her for a while, and when she drew back from me I saw that the battle was half-won. But she stretched out her hand toward the envelope. 'You must read it – '

I shook my head. 'I won't read it. But I'll take it and keep it. Will that satisfy you, Kate Severance?' I asked. For it had suddenly occurred to me that, if I tore the paper up before her, I should only force her, in her present mood, to the more cruel alternative of telling me what it contained.

I saw at once that my suggestion quieted her. 'You will take it, then? You'll read it tonight? You'll promise me?'

'No, my dear. All I promise you is to take it with me, and not to destroy it.'

She took a long sobbing breath, and drew me to her again. 'It's as if you'd read it already, isn't it?' she said below her breath.

'It's as if it had never existed – because it never will exist for me.' I held her fast, and kissed her again. And when I left her I carried the sealed envelope away with me.

• IX •

ALL that happened seven years ago; and the envelope lies before me now, still sealed. Why should I have opened it?

As I carried it home that night at Milan, as I drew it out of my pocket and locked it away among my papers, it was as transparent as glass to me. I had no need to open it. Already it had given me the measure of the woman who, deliberately, determinedly, had thrust it into my hands. Even as she was in the act of doing so, I had understood that with Cassie Wilpert's death the one danger she had to fear had been removed; and that, knowing herself at last free, at last safe, she had voluntarily placed her fate in my keeping.'

'Greater love hath no man – certainly no woman,' I thought. Cassie Wilpert, and Cassie Wilpert alone, held Kate Spain's secret – the secret which would doubtless have destroyed her in the eyes of the world, as it was meant to destroy her in mine. And that secret, when it had been safely buried with Cassie Wilpert, Kate Spain had deliberately dug up again, and put into my hands.

It took her some time to understand the use I meant to make of it. She did not dream, at first, that it had given me a complete insight into her character, and that that was all I wanted of it. Weeks of patient waiting, of quiet reasoning, of obstinate insistence, were required to persuade her that I was determined to judge her, not by her past, whatever it might have been, but by what she had unconsciously revealed of herself since I had known her and loved her.

'You can't marry me – you know why you can't marry me,' she had gone on endlessly repeating; till one day I had turned on her, and declared abruptly: 'Whatever happens, this is to be our last talk on the subject. I will never return to it again, or let you return to it. But I swear one thing to you now; if you know how your father died, and have kept silence to shield someone – to shield I don't care who' – I looked straight into her eyes as I said this – 'if this is your reason for thinking you ought not to marry me, then I tell you now that it weighs nothing with me, and never will.'

She gave me back my look, long and deeply; then she bent and kissed my hands. That was all.

I had hazarded a great deal in saying what I did; and I knew the risk I was taking. It was easy to answer for the present; but how could I tell what the future, our strange incalculable future together, might bring? It was that which she dreaded, I knew; not for myself, but for me. But I was ready to risk it, and a few weeks after that final talk – for final I insisted on its being – I gained my point, and we were married.

We were married; and for five years we lived our strange perilous dream of happiness. That fresh unfading happiness which now and then mocks the lot of poor mortals; but not often – and never for long.

At the end of five years my wife died; and since then I have lived alone among memories so made of light and darkness that sometimes I am blind with remembered joy, and sometimes numb under present sorrow. I don't know yet which will end by winning the day with me; but in my uncertainty I am putting old things in order – and there on my desk lies the paper I have never read, and beside it the candle with which I shall presently burn it.

Afterword

———————

IT WAS as a short story writer that Edith Wharton made her literary debut in the 1890s. She continued to write short stories throughout her life: her last collection – *The World Over* – came out one year before her death in 1937. There is a remarkable consistency in her work, with puzzlingly few hints as to how or why she started to write these consummately professional pieces, or how she departed from this restrained format to write her finest novel, the brilliant and worldly-wise *House of Mirth*. If one charts a graph of her progress one sees a reassuring regularity in her biannual, sometimes annual, production, starting in 1895 and ending in 1936, with the years of greatest maturity between 1905 and 1920, the years that saw the publication of her major novels, *The House of Mirth* (1905), *Ethan Frome* (1911), *The Reef* (1912), *The Custom of the Country* (1913), and *The Age of Innocence* (1920). Few short stories were written in these years, which also saw Edith Wharton established in Paris, and in love, for the first time in her life, with the evasive Morton Fullerton. No great lady ever stooped more whole-heartedly to folly, yet whatever her grief on a human level the experience mysteriously benefited her powers of invention. The novels written in this period have a depth and a brilliance that are, on the whole, denied to the short stories, which remain harnessed to a possibly restrictive formula: situation, said the author, is what makes a short story, whereas the study of character is the preserve of the novel.

The situations which she appropriates – and which are all firmly set before the reader in her first paragraph – have to do with matters that might have been discussed among New York hostesses or New York clubmen: the laughable attempts of the New Rich

621

to get on in society, the stratagems that ladies and gentlemen, reduced to the status of companions or secretaries, must employ in order to satisfy their desire for luxury, the gullibility of the fashionable many and the shrewdness of the unfashionable few, the power of art and the dubious impulses of the collector, and the abiding fascination for the comfortably established of haunted houses and revenants, wives or husbands betrayed, or dead too soon. 'Do New York!', Henry James instructed her, thinking thus to distance her from himself, and reserving for himself the great theme of innocence abroad, native Americans coming to grips with the lures and deceptions and ironies of old Europe. But Edith Wharton lived in Europe (far more comfortably, it must be said, than Henry James ever did) and what she retains of New York is a sense of amusement at its pretention. She is, in fact, more of a New Yorker than James, who found in Europe a complexity that answered to the complexity of his own mind. Where James is profuse Edith Wharton is sharp, sunny, alert; where James is frequently terror-stricken Edith Wharton remains very much on the safe side of the line dividing sanity from madness.

Yet in her own life there were episodes that drove her off her balance. Between 1894 and 1895 she suffered a protracted nervous breakdown, characterized by exhaustion, nausea, and profound melancholia. This may have been – probably was – occasioned by the disappointments of her marriage to the unstable Teddy Wharton. She managed to find the cure for herself: she simply wrote her way out of her disarray and enjoyed outstandingly good health for the rest of her life. Thus one is justified in making the claim that for Edith Wharton writing and good health were synonymous.

Her other stratagem was to remove herself from the restrictions of her well-bred background and suitable marriage to live as a free woman and a grand hostess in Paris, at 53 rue de Grenelle. In this beautiful house she entertained lavishly and received scores of visitors and guests, departing regularly for a 'motor-tour' of Italy, France, Germany, Austria, Spain, Morocco – trips that would take the cautious modern writer a year to prepare and unimaginable wealth to pursue. Edith Wharton was, of course, a rich woman, but she also had a sense of magnificence: nothing was allowed to hold her back, and the sense of liberty which she gained in exile empowered her, so that she was able to combine a life of fêtes, travels, and visits with the simple routine of a working day, with the morning reserved for writing and the afternoon for company. Her enormously wide range of reading was reserved for the small hours, when her guests had gone to bed.

The other strange episode in her life was her love for Morton Fullerton, a handsome and probably bisexual journalist with whom she conducted an affair between 1907 and 1909. The recent publication of 400 of her estimated 4000 letters provided an unexpected sidelight onto Edith Wharton the queenly novelist (photographs show her firm-jawed, with bird's nest hair and pearl choker) and her abrupt descent into Edith Wharton the powerless mistress. To her enormous credit she emerged from the experience, perhaps the most bitter she was ever to know, to urge friendship on the unworthy and possibly embarrassed recipient of her passion. Yet however noble her overtures the wretched Fullerton seems to have been unable to respond in kind. It may be that her friendship was a little overwhelming. Henry James is known to have groaned before succumbing to her invitations. Yet her conception of friendship was an elevated one, which managed to forgive or overlook an inadequate return. The friendship of Henry James she described as 'the pride and honour of my life'. An equally strong sentiment bound her to the lawyer Walter Berry, with whom she enjoyed an *amitié amoureuse* that was terminated only by Berry's death.

James could not quite overlook the fact that Edith Wharton sold tremendously and made a great deal of money from her writing. It has been calculated that between 1920 and 1924 she earned the modern equivalent of three million dollars before tax. She needed this money to sustain a particularly lavish and by all accounts beautiful way of life, yet she never ceased to consider herself a professional writer, and one whose position she had established at the very outset of her career. Her literary taste was simple and straightforward: she disliked anything effortful, obscure, tricky or subjective, and it is true that her work is distinguished by a directness and a certain bright clarity. She had tremendous reservations about James's late style (although there is more than a hint of his influence in the story called *The Moving Finger*) and one is not surprised to learn that her favourite among the Master's novels was *The Portrait of a Lady*. James Joyce, Eliot, and Scott Fitzgerald were condemned without the slightest hesitation, although the latter made her feel her age. She was in fact found to be old-fashioned when a reviewer in a London paper scrutinized Virginia Woolf's *Mrs. Dalloway* together with Edith Wharton's *The Mother's Recompense* in the same article, to the detriment of the latter. 'My heroine belongs to the day when scruples existed,' retorted Mrs. Wharton.

Indeed, scruples exist in everything she writes, and are particularly in evidence in the short stories. In making this second selection I have concentrated on less familiar work, and have included examples from every stage of Edith Wharton's career. The connecting link is the writer's own firmness of purpose and her refusal to sacrifice abundant good sense to tricks of the trade. If 'good sense' sounds rather too reductive a term of praise the reader should reflect how much he is being spared in the way of mystification. Good sense in this instance goes hand in hand with great style: there is not a clumsy sentence in the whole of her 86 short stories. Indeed, the reader might, for his own benefit and delight, measure the length of one of Mrs. Wharton's sentences and see how lightly it falls into place.

She was not unaware that her reputation was a little too popular to be taken seriously. She wrote to a cousin, 'As my work reaches its close I feel so sure that it is either nothing, or far more than they know. And I wonder, a little desolately, which?' As her fame increases – and there are signs that it continues to do so – her question is answered by an ever larger and more discriminating public. She is, in every sense, 'far more than they know'.

ANITA BROOKNER

List of Sources

'The Pelican' was first collected in *The Greater Inclination*, 1899; 'The Other Two,' 'The Mission of Jane' and 'The Reckoning' in *The Descent of Man*, 1904; 'The Last Asset' in *The Hermit and the Wild Woman*, 1908; 'The Letters' in *Tales of Men and Ghosts*, 1910; 'Autres Temps…' and 'The Long Run' in *Xingu*, 1916; 'After Holbein' and 'Atrophy' in *Certain People*, 1930; 'Pomegranate Seed' and 'Charm Incorporated' in *The World Over*, 1936; 'Her Son' in *Human Nature*, 1933; 'All Souls' in *Ghosts*, 1937; 'The Lamp of Psyche' in *Early Uncollected Stories*, 1895; 'A Journey' in *The Greater Inclination*, 1899; 'The Line of Least Resistance' in *Early Uncollected Stories*, 1900; 'The Moving Finger' in *Crucial Instances*, 1901; 'Expiation' in *The Descent of Man*, 1904; '*Les Metteurs en Scène*' (originally published in French) in *Uncollected Stories*, 1908; 'Full Circle,' 'The Daunt Diana,' 'Afterward,' and 'The Bolted Door' in *Tales of Men and Ghosts*, 1909; 'The Temperate Zone' in *Here and Beyond*, 1924; 'Diagnosis' and 'The Day of the Funeral' in *Human Nature*, 1933; and 'Confession' in *The World Over*, 1936.